5 ✗ 6-14
3-15
7 ✗ 9/15 - 5/16
9 ✗ (12/16) ✓ 9/17
10 ✗ 10/17 - 7/18

COME AND TAKE THEM

COME AND TAKE THEM

TOM KRATMAN

COME AND TAKE THEM

Copyright © 2013 by Tom Kratman

A Baen Books Original

Baen Publishing Enterprises
P.O. Box 1403
Riverdale, NY 10471
www.baen.com

ISBN: 978-1-4516-3936-0

Cover art by Kurt Miller

First printing, November 2013

Distributed by Simon & Schuster
1230 Avenue of the Americas
New York, NY 10020

Library of Congress Cataloging-in-Publication Data

Kratman, Tom.
     Come and take them / Tom Kratman.
          pages cm.
     Summary: "On the colony planet of Terra Nova, soldier turned political leader Carrera has achieved his revenge, destroying those who killed his wife and children in a terrorist strike, and helping establish a free country. But Carrera's fight isn't over. War with the Tauran Union is inevitable. Carrera has been preparing his new country for this conflict for years. He doesn't care that he's outnumbered one hundred to one. He doesn't care the Taurans are one thousand times wealthier. But then his own government calls a halt. Any other government, giving similar orders, Carrera would overthrow without hesitation. But this is his own creation; he must follow orders. However, he knows that sooner or later, he must fight and Carrera will do whatever it takes to win" — Provided by publisher.
     ISBN 978-1-4516-3936-0 (hardback)
1. Space colonies—Fiction. I. Title.
     PS3611.R375C66 2013
     813'.6—dc23

                                                    2013033603

10 9 8 7 6 5 4 3 2 1

Pages by Joy Freeman (www.pagesbyjoy.com)
Printed in the United States of America

For the very brave teacher, Victoria Soto, who should have had a gun to balance her big brass balls, as she placed her body between death and her little ones.

And for her principal, Dawn Hochsprung, who charged bare-handed to the rescue, when she ought to have been armed with more than fighting spirit.

As long as our country has such women,
hope is not lost.

And for Juliana, Patrick, and Cossima, may they never need a woman like Victoria or Dawn to protect them.

Contents

viii   Maps

1   *Come and Take Them*

565   Appendix A: Glossary

571   Appendix B: Legionary Rank Equivalents

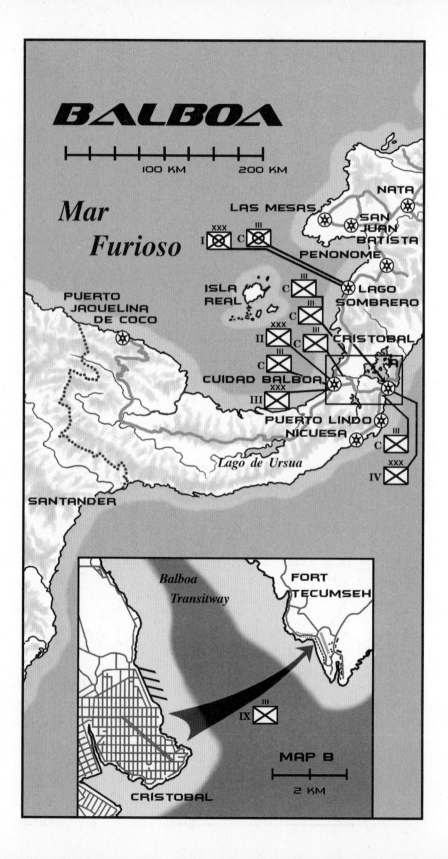

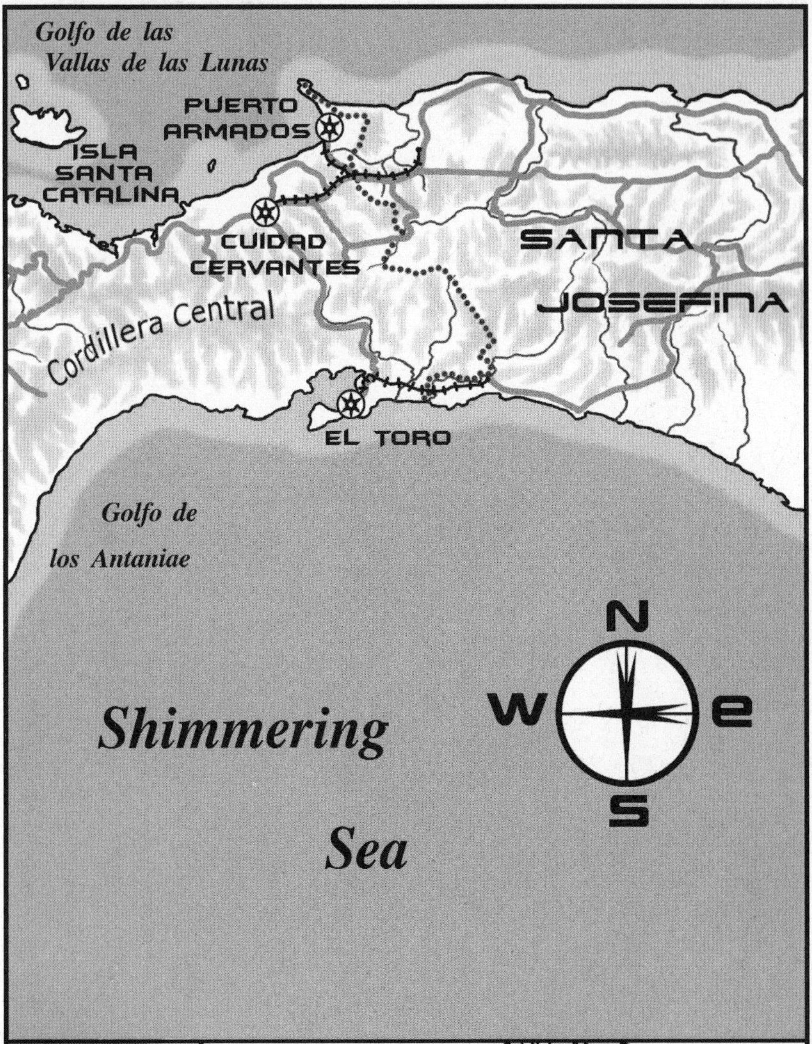
Golfo de las
Vallas de las Lunas
PUERTO
ARMADOS
ISLA
SANTA
CATALINA
CUIDAD
CERVANTES
Cordillera Central
SANTA
JOSEFINA
EL TORO
Golfo de
los Antaniae
Shimmering
Sea
N
W
E
S

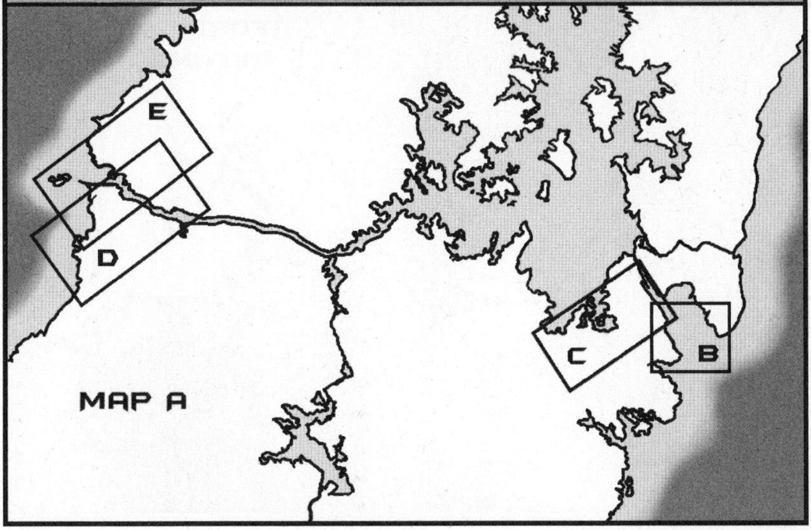
E
D
C
B
MAP A

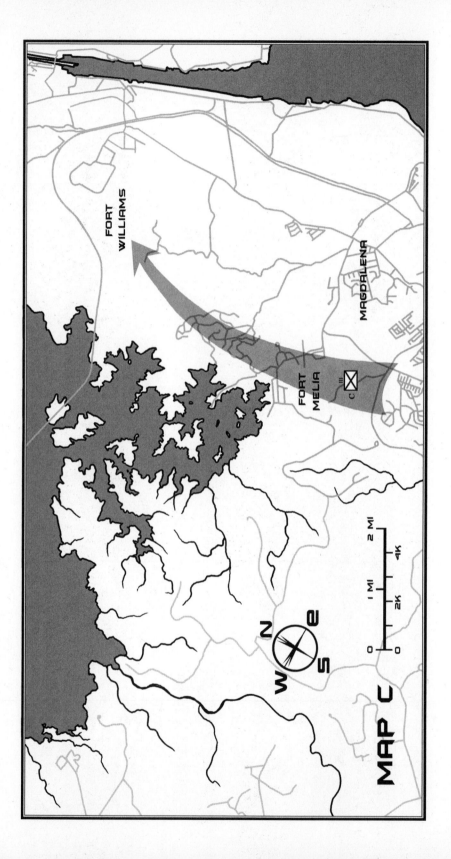

MAP C

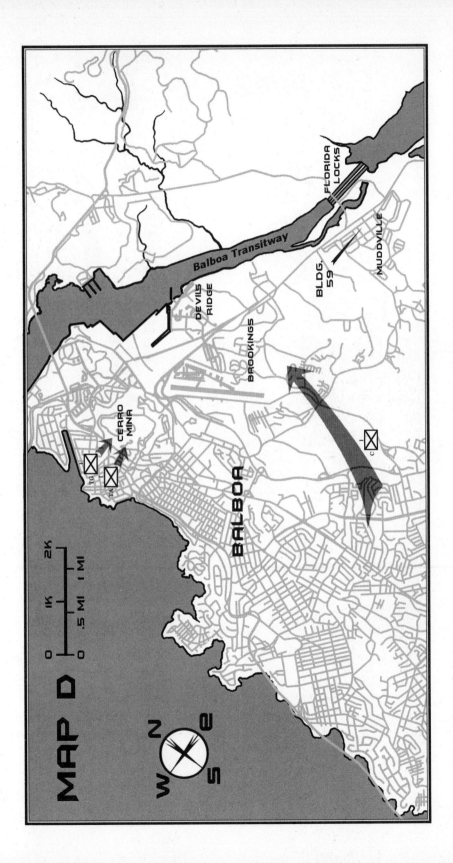

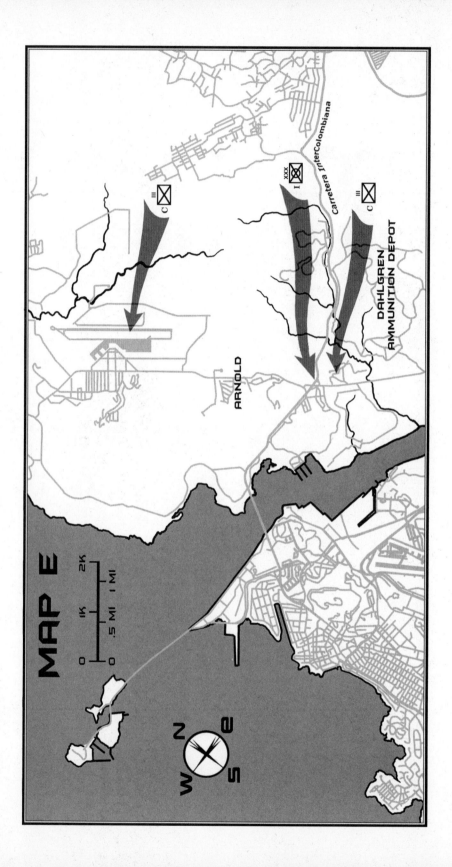

MOLON LABE:

"Come—and if you succeed in that—
then you can take them."

—Leonidas I, Agiad King of Sparta

WHAT HAS GONE BEFORE

5,000,000 BC through Anno Condita (AC) 472

Long ago, long before the appearance of man, came to Earth the aliens known by man only as the "Noahs." About them, as a species, nothing is known. Their very existence can only be surmised by the project they left behind. Somewhat like the biblical Noah, these aliens transported from Earth to another planet samples of virtually every species existing in the time period approximately five hundred thousand to five million years ago. Having transported these species, and having left behind various other, genengineered species, apparently to inhibit the development of intelligent life on the new world, the Noahs disappeared, leaving no other trace beyond a few incomprehensible and inert artifacts, and possibly the rift through which they moved from the Earth to the new world.

In the year 2037 AD a robotic interstellar probe, the *Cristobal Colon*, driven by lightsail, disappeared en route to Alpha Centauri. Three years later it returned, under automated guidance, through the same rift in space into which it had disappeared. The *Colon* brought with it wonderful news of another Earthlike planet, orbiting another star. (Note, here, that not only is the other star *not* Alpha Centauri, it's not so far been proved that it is even in the same galaxy, or universe for that matter, as ours.) Moreover, implicit in its disappearance and return was the news that here, finally, was a relatively cheap means to colonize another planet.

The first colonization effort was an utter disaster, with the ship, the *Cheng Ho*, breaking down into ethnic and religious strife that annihilated almost every crewman and colonist aboard her. Thereafter, rather than risk further bloodshed by mixing colonies, the colonization effort would be run by regional supranationals such as NAFTA, the European Union, the Organization of African Unity, MERCOSUR, the Russian Empire and the Chinese Hegemony. Each of these groups was given colonization rights to specific

1

areas on the new world, which was named—with a stunning lack of originality—"Terra Nova" or something in another tongue that meant the same thing. Most groups elected to establish national colonies within their respective mandates, some of them under United Nations' "guidance."

With the removal from Earth of substantial numbers of the most difficult portions of the populations of Earth's various nations, the power and influence of transnational organizations such as the UN and EU increased dramatically. With the increase of transnational power, often enough expressed in corruption, even more of Earth's more difficult, ethnocentric, and tradition-alist population volunteered to leave. Still others were deported forcibly. Within not much more than a century and a quarter, and much less in many cases, nations had ceased to have much meaning or importance on Earth. On the other hand, and over about the same time scale, nations had become preeminent on Terra Nova. Moreover, because of the way the surface of the new world had been divided, these nations tended to reflect—if only generally—the nations of Old Earth.

Warfare was endemic, beginning with the wars of liberation by many of the weaker colonies to throw off the yoke of Earth's United Nations.

In this environment Patrick Hennessey was born, grew to man-hood, and was a soldier for many years. Some years after leav-ing service, Hennessey's wife, Linda, a native of the Republic of Balboa, along with their three children were killed in a massive terrorist attack on Hennessey's native land, the Federated States of Columbia. The same attack likewise killed Hennessey's uncle, the head of his extended and rather wealthy family. As his dying testament, Uncle Bob changed his will to leave Hennessey with control over the entire corpus of his estate.

Half mad with grief, Hennessey, living in Balboa, ruthlessly provoked and then mercilessly gunned down six local supporters of the terrorists. In retaliation, and with that same astonishing bad judgment that had made their movement and culture remarkable across two worlds, the terrorist organization, the Salafi *Ikhwan*, attacked Balboa, killing hundreds of innocent civilians, including many children.

With Balboa now enraged, and money from his uncle's rather impressive estate, Hennessey began to build a small army within the Republic. This army, the *Legion del Cid,* was initially about the size of a reinforced brigade, though differently organized. For reasons of internal politics, Hennessey began to use his late wife's maiden name, Carrera. It was as Carrera that he became well known to the world of Terra Nova.

The legion was hired out to assist the Federated States of Columbia in a war against the Republic of Sumer, a nominally Islamic but politically secular—indeed fascist—state that had been known to have supported terrorism in the past, to have used chemical weapons in the past, and to have had a significant biological warfare program. It was widely believed to have been developing nuclear weapons, as well.

Against some expectations, the *Legion del Cid* performed quite well. Equally against expectations, its greatest battle in the campaign was against a Sumeri infantry brigade led by a first rate officer, Adnan Sada, who not only fought well but stayed within the customs, rules, and laws of war.

Impressed with the legion's performance (even while loathing the openly brutal ways it had of enforcing the laws of war), and needing foreign troops badly, the War Department of the Federated States offered Carrera a long-term employment contract. Impressed with Sada, and with some of the profits from the contract with the Federated States, Carrera likewise offered to not only hire, but substantially increase, Sada's military force. Accepting the offer, and loyal to his salt, Sada revealed seven nuclear weapons to Carrera, three of which were functional and the rest restorable. These Carrera quietly removed, telling no one except a very few, *very* close subordinates.

The former government of Sumer had a cadre and arms for an insurgency in place before the Federated States and its allies invaded. In Carrera's area of responsibility, this insurgency, while bloody, was contained through the help of Sada's men and Carrera's ruthlessness. In the rest of the country, however, the unwise demobilization of the former armed forces of the Republic of Sumer left so many young men unemployed that the insurgency grew to nearly unmanageable levels. Eventually, Carrera's area of responsibility was changed and he was forced to undertake a difficult campaign against a city, Pumbadeta, held by the rebels. He surrounded and starved the city, forcing women and children to remain within it until he was certain that every dog, cat and rat had been eaten. Only then did he permit the women and children to leave. His clear intention was to kill every male in Pumbadeta capable of sprouting a beard.

After the departure of the noncombatants, Carrera's legion continued the blockade until the civilians within the town rebelled against the rebels. Having a rare change of heart, Carrera aided the rebels against rebellion to take the town. Thereafter nearly every insurgent found within Pumbadeta was executed, along with several members of the press sympathetic to the rebels. The few insurgents he—temporarily—spared were sent to a surface ship for *rigorous* interrogation.

With the war in Sumer winding down, the Federated States, now under Progressive rather than Federalist leadership, unwisely fired Carrera and his legion. And, as should have been predicted, the terrorist money and recruits that had formerly been sent to Sumer, where the Salafi cause was lost, were instead redirected to Pashtia, where it still had a chance. The campaign in Pashtia then began to flow against the Federated States and its unwilling allies of the Tauran Union.

More than a little bitter at having his contract violated and being let go on short notice, Carrera exacted an exorbitant price from the Federated States before he would commit his forces to the war in Pashtia. That price being paid, however, and in gold, he didn't stint but waged a major—and typically ruthless—campaign to restore the situation in Pashtia, which had deteriorated badly under Tauran interference and faint support.

Ultimately, Carrera got wind of a major meeting taking place across the nearby border with Kashmir between the chief of the United Earth Peace Fleet and the emir of the terrorists, the Salafi *Ikhwan*. He attacked and in the attack and its aftermath killed thousands, captured hundreds, and seized a dozen more nuclear weapons, gifts of the UEPF to their terrorist allies. One of these weapons Carrera delivered to the capital of the major terrorist supporting state of Yithrab. When detonated, this weapon not only killed the entire clan of the chief of the Salafi *Ikhwan*, but also at *least* a million citizens of that city. In the process, he framed the Salafis for the detonation.

That destruction, seemingly at the hand of an Allah grown weary of terrorism, along with the death or capture and execution of the core of the Salafi movement in the attack across the

Pashtian-Kashmiri border, effectively ended the terrorist war on Terra Nova.

The price to Carrera had also been heavy. With the end of the war with the terrorists, and having had more revenge against the murderers of his family than any man ought desire, he collapsed, physically, mentally, and emotionally. Recovery was slow and guarded by his second wife, Lourdes.

Unfortunately, he was still needed by his adopted home of Balboa. Having arranged for Carrera's wife to be disarmed, Legate Jimenez and Sergeant Major McNamara ultimately persuaded him back to active duty. There followed a vicious no-holds-barred-and-little-quarter-given war with the quasi sovereign drug cartels of Santander, along with an attempted *coup d'état*, by the treacherous Legate Pigna. This was ultimately foiled by Lourdes, with the help of the Volgans of the Twenty-Second Tercio. In the same coup, the rump of the old, oligarchic Balboan state was reabsorbed into the rest of the country, the oligarchs and their lackeys being driven from the country or killed. Very nearly the last remaining scion of the oligarchs, and the man who had set up Carrera for assassination, Belisario Endara-Rocaberti, had fled to Hamilton, in the Federated States, where he'd done everything up to and including giving the use of his wife to the president of the Federated States to get the Parilla regime overthrown. But, while the president of the FSC was more than willing to make extensive use of Mrs. Rocaberti or, indeed, pretty much anything in a skirt, he really had no interest in getting the FSC into a war.

It remains now to remove the Tauran Union from its death grip around Balboa's mid-section. To this end, no resource will be left unmobilized.

PART I

CHAPTER ONE

Walled towns, stored arsenals and armories, goodly races of horses, chariots of war, elephants, ordnance, artillery, and the like; all this is but a sheep in a lion's skin except that the breed and disposition of the people be stout and warlike.

—Francis Bacon, *Essays*, XXIX

Headquarters, Tauran Union Security Force-Balboa, Building 59, Fort Muddville, Balboa, Terra Nova

Pummeled by waves of sound, a roughly one-by-two-meter piece of plywood rattled against one wall. Glued to its surface was a white plasticized sheet, upon which was scrawled the intel section's best estimate of the size and composition of the enemy forces. It was a fearsome thing to contemplate, perhaps made more fearsome still by the holes in it.

What caused the plastic estimate to rattle, the source of those waves of sound, was a recoilless rifle range on the other side of the Florida Locks to the Balboa Transitway. The crash of those not-too-very distant blasts also caused dust to spring up from the seams of the office window. Still more dust began to filter down from the ceiling.

A short but shapely blond captain stood and stared out of the window of a door. The dust raised a cough, then caused her to dab fingers at huge blue eyes beginning to tear up. These were framed by a heart-shaped face.

The door led to a long balcony that ran from just off the center of the building all the way to the end. There was a mate to that on the other side, and still more to the rear, facing the parade field.

"May yer lums reek lang and weil," muttered Captain Jan Campbell, "ye mingin' radge." To the noninitiate, this sounded worse than it was: *May your chimneys produce a profusion of smoke, you filthy madman.* Normally, Campbell's English was just a shade gingerwise from received pronunciation. Under stress, though, she tended to revert to either gutter Saint Mungan or, if particularly annoyed, to the accent of the hardscrabble fishing village in which she's spent a still harder childhood.

The chimneys whereof she spoke were, in fact, two dozen of the recoilless rifles the Balboan legion seemed to have in profusion. They were smoking a plenty—and kicking up no little dust, too—quite without her curses. The smoke she could have lived with. But the bloody recoilless range was only about twelve hundred meters away, across the major channel and the Florida Locks with their swing bridge. The counterrecoilling gas literally shook the headquarters with every shot fired in the opposite direction.

Conscious of having fallen into her native dialect, she forced herself into something closer to Received Pronunciation. "How fucking long can this go on?" she asked her associate, Sergeant Major Kris Hendryksen, Army of Cimbria, seconded to TUSF-B.

Hendryksen grimaced. "Last time His Gribbitzness"—Gallic General Janier, the head of the TUSF-B—"annoyed the Balboans they released enough recoilless ammunition from war stocks to training to keep this up for three days. This? This, I think, is just their annual training for one of their regiments, with all the antitank platoons of each of the line battalions consolidated to take advantage of a hard to get range. Should be over by about ten or eleven this evening. Until the next regiment is called up, that is."

"Until the next regiment..." Campbell muttered. She was new to the command and not nearly as expert yet on Balboan forces as she intended to become. Still she had a pretty good idea at least of what G-2 knew of the enemy's combat forces. "Twenty-six big bloody, fuckin' regiments. That we know about. On the ground. Of ground-gaining maneuver arms. Not countin' the fuckin' artillery. Or the sappers. Or the aviation. Or the naval. Or God-knows what."

"They want us gone," Hendryksen observed. "They don't seem to have any sense of limitations on what they're willing to do to get rid of us, either. And I don't believe that number twenty-six for a minute. In every other particular they're set up for a lot more than that, thirty-seven or thirty-eight ground regiments."

As if on cue—though it was a frequent enough event that no cues were really needed—two Volgan-built, Balboan-owned Artem-Mikhail 82s, also known as "Mosaic Ds," streaked almost straight up over the Florida Locks before veering to come in low over the headquarters. Another brace immediately followed, even before the windows had stopped rattling from the first pair. The shock sent Campbell's innards vibrating in time with the glass. From where she stood, she could see the whites of the lead pilot's eyes as he just barely missed the building.

"And how many of those do the bastards have?" she asked Hendryksen.

Hendryksen shook his head. "We don't actually *know*," he said. "We think maybe four hundred." There was a trace of unofficial skepticism in his voice.

"We?" Campbell queried, with an eyebrow raised.

"'We,' as defined by the Frogs running the local show," Hendryksen conceded. "And sure, there are about four hundred in country. But me? I think twice that, and the missing four hundred are probably still sitting in Volga, or Jagelonia." Hendryksen's face grew contemplative for a moment. "I also think that maybe they don't have enough pilots for all of those. Or at least not enough replacement pilots. Or not enough good replacement pilots.

"Or maybe they think they don't need two or two and a half pilots per plane."

"Undeveloped world bullshit?" Campbell asked. "All show, no go?"

"You might suspect that," Hendryksen answered. "But it would be so totally out of line with everything else we know about the legion that it just strikes me as a terrible bet. And since our lives are the ante..." The Cimbrian shrugged eloquently.

"Fucking Frogs," Campbell muttered.

"It's not really them anymore," Hendryksen corrected. "Or at least not mostly them. Janier seems a broken reed since the failure of the coup. Instead..." To explain, he pointed the index finger of his right hand straight up.

Campbell's gaze followed Hendryksen's upturned finger. "Them, too," she scowled.

Range 18, Imperial Range Complex, Balboa, Terra Nova

Beneath the jinking Mosaic jets, a ship heading to the *Mar Furioso* slowly descended as the water in the Florida Locks was let run out toward the sea. A man and a boy stood on an historic overlook above the locks. They had no eyes for the ship but concentrated entirely on the enemy headquarters on the opposite side of the Transitway.

Carrera and his oldest living son, Hamilcar, aged twelve in local years, watched the building intently despite the backblast from the recoilless rifles. It pounded them, if anything, worse than the Taurans in Building 59. But Carrera could leave anytime he wanted. The Taurans couldn't. Man and boy watched the building through a couple of pairs of the best binoculars made anywhere on Terra Nova.

"You are a *cruel* bastard, Dad," the boy observed, loudly enough to be heard over the thumping of the "reckless rifles."

"Son, you have no idea," Carrera mostly agreed. *But you'll find out in a little while.*

The boy had only been home about a month. In that short period of time, any number of problems had arisen which, so far, had proved impossible to correct easily. Drastic measures were in the offing, though the boy didn't know about those.

A glint in one of the windows caught Carrera's eye. It came from one of the windows off to the left of the portal in the center of the building and two floors above ground level.

Ham noticed his father's movement. "You looking for the flash, Dad?"

"Yeah." *Is the little bastard trying to remind me I'm getting old and my eyes aren't what they were?*

"It's a woman," the boy said. "Her hair's done up but she's short and you can just make out the tits..."

"Where'd you learn to talk like that?"

Ham didn't bother answering, instead just rolling his eyes. *From you, among others, old man.*

Headquarters, Tauran Union Security Force-Balboa, Building 59, Fort Muddville, Balboa, Terra Nova

"Kris, come here, please," Campbell asked. When he stood beside her she handed him her own binoculars and asked, "Is that who I think it is, behind those field glasses?"

Hendryksen took the field glasses and, adjusting them to his eyes, focused on a couple of Balboan soldiers, one taller, one shorter, half-exposed amidst the jungle of the hill opposite.

"Your lucky day," he confirmed. "It's Carrera and, if I'm not mistaken, his son."

"What's he doing with a boy out amongst all this dangerous crap?" she asked.

Hendryksen shrugged. "There's almost no telling. He doesn't seem to think like normal people."

Campbell contemplated the implications of the boy's existence. "Oh, I'll bet he does." With that she twisted the knob to the door, opened it, and stepped out onto the balcony. As she did she made sure to turn right to present a side profile to the man and boy standing on the other side of the Transitway, perhaps a half a mile away.

"That's right, boys," she whispered, needlessly, "get a *good* look." Then she turned slowly toward the hill on the other side and waved.

Range 18, Imperial Range Complex, Balboa, Terra Nova

"I did mention tits, Dad." said the boy, keeping his glasses firmly fixed on the heavily front-loaded hourglass shape across the water.

"Yeah…yeah, you did. And you didn't lie, either. They're… impressive. I wonder what the purpose of the show is?"

"Find out who she is and you'll probably find the purpose," the boy said. "Legate Fernandez will know. Or can find out."

"Yeah," Carrera agreed. He lowered his binoculars and then, on a whim, raised his hand and waved back.

"She's very pretty," Ham said. One didn't see too many blondes in Balboa, which made flaxen hair rather exotic and desirable.

"Tell you what," answered Carrera, "if you don't tell your mother I waved, I won't tell your wives you were looking at another woman."

"That seems very fair." True, the boy's wives were in name only, so far. Soon that would be changing, at least with the older ones, if nothing interfered. And it was also true that they would never think to criticize their god, Iskandr, less still to nag. But they could make him feel like dirt with the mildest sniffle or flash of hurt eyes. *So, yes, very fair indeed.*

Headquarters, Tauran Union Security Force-Balboa, Building 59, Fort Muddville, Balboa, Terra Nova

"Why the show, Jan?" Hendryksen asked, once Campbell had reentered the office. Closing the door didn't do a lot to reduce the sound of shock of the counterrecoiling gas from Range 18. "You're usually content to let them flaunt themselves."

"I want him to ask his intel folks—what was his intel chief's name?"

"Fernandez," the Cimbrian replied. "Legate Fernandez."

"Right, Fernandez. I want him to ask Fernandez who the new blonde with the big tatas is. That will get this Fernandez looking at me, too. And when he tries to look at me, I'll get, or at least I may get, a chance to look right back. And maybe I'll even get a close look back."

Hendryksen *tsk*ed, quoting, "'And when you gaze long into an abyss, the abyss also gazes into you.'"

"Precisely," Campbell agreed, with a happy smile, stretching slightly and letting her chest flaunt itself. The smile dissolved into a frown when she looked once again out of the door's vibrating window only to see that her ultimate quarry had disappeared.

"Now that's hardly fair," she said.

InterColombiana Highway, east of the Puente de las Colombias, Balboa, Terra Nova

With one armored car ahead and two trailing, Carrera's big black armored Phaeton, with Warrant Officer Soult at the wheel, whizzed past jungle and small town and smaller still roadside stand. The armored cars were driven by Carrera's own troops. Following, however, were another two trucks with forty-eight of Hamilcar's in-laws, armed to the teeth, seated on center-running benches, and glaring out.

"My wives are not going to think that's very fair, Dad," said the boy. "They've been very good girls, not doing proskynesis where anyone can see, waiting until I was old enough to do a proper... umm, what's that word?"

"Deflowering."

"Right. They've been waiting two years—*over* two years—for a proper deflowering. And they're expecting me to start within the next month or two."

Carrera shook his head firmly. "Not gonna happen. You're not legally married in the Republic. They're all under age, even if all but one is older than you." The father frowned. "They're . . . What are you smiling at?"

"Close-in-age exception, Dad. Forget it. I can fuck 'em all perfectly legally. Even if I wasn't married to them. But I am. Alena the witch checked and the Republic recognizes foreign marriages and has no express bar to polygamy. And I learned to talk like that from you, so forget bitching about that, too."

Alena, sometimes called, "the witch," was probably less of a witch than just a supremely intelligent and observant woman. She'd been the first among her people to recognize Ham's striking resemblance to the image on an ancient gold platter, smuggled from Old Earth when her people had been exiled. Thereafter she'd become Ham's caretaker, guardian, surrogate mother, chief acolyte, and matchmaker. All the boy's twelve wives had been selected by her.

Carrera sat back heavily in the well-upholstered seat of the limousine. "Yeah, well consider this: They're all too young to bear a child without unnecessary risk. None of them had any real choice before they were married to you. Their families told them, 'go,' and they went. And they've all been told you're the avatar of God, so they aren't even fully people in their own eyes. You want to talk about fair and unfair, boy?"

Hamilcar sighed heavily. "I know. So you want me to go off to military school so the girls can grow a little?"

"Least of my concerns," the father answered. "I'm not that nice a man. No . . . it's more about you than them."

"Ham, you've got all kinds of attributes to make you an effective commander already . . . among people who think you're a god and can't be convinced otherwise. You try relying on that crap with the legion and they'll kick your ass. And the girls only make it worse. Maybe you haven't seen it, but they've even been teaching your sister to do proskynesis where they think no one can see them. That's not good for you. And they sleep on the floor around your bed, confident that no guards could possibly protect you as well as they can. Son . . . that *can't* be good for you. And it's perverse, besides, a male hiding behind females."

"I admit," said the boy, "that that part troubles me. On the other hand, who'll take care of them when I'm gone?"

"Your mother's volunteered. And their Spanish is coming along very nicely, you may have noticed."

Casa Linda, Balboa, Terra Nova

Weeping and banging of pretty little heads on hard wooden floors was interspersed with pleas for mercy. "*Por favor, señor! Por favor, no llevar a nuestra esposo Iskandr.*"

Carrera looked down at the—*So much for orders, even from "God." Hmmm . . . lemme count. Yep, thirteen of them. They've got one of his sisters begging, too*—little lake of exotically clad, barely post-pubescent feminine humanity clustered around his feet. Some were beating their heads on the floor. Still others looked up with huge brown, green, or blue tear-filled eyes, hands clasped in supplication. He looked more closely for his own daughter, Julia, then bent over and picked her up by one arm. Setting her to her feet he spun her in the direction of the stairs, applied a swat to her fundament, and ordered, "Go to your room!" The child ran off with a shriek.

"For the rest of you, shut up and get on your feet."

Silence descended like a falling axe, suddenly and decisively. Hamilcar was their god, but who was it who could tell God what to do? Most of the girls really weren't up to the theological depths of that question. Rather than test the thought, they simply shut up and arose to their feet. Sniffling, at reduced volume, continued.

"Into the living room . . . MARCH."

Carrera judged his success in explaining matters to his daughters-in-law by the level of sniffling and the flow or tears. When he had those down to a tolerable degree he was pretty sure he'd won. There was, however, an exception. This was the youngest and, pretty much everyone agreed, the second prettiest, Pililak. In her language the name meant, "Ant." Twelve years old only, strawberry blonde, with enormous green eyes, the girl was the hardest working and possibly the brightest among a hard-working and bright lot. Her Spanish was the best, as well.

No Christian martyr was ever firmer in the faith. "You are trying to separate me from my husband and lord," she told Carrera, chin lifting fearlessly. "It will not happen."

✧   ✧   ✧

No adult guards would be permitted to Ham while he was away, any more than wives were allowed at any of the academies. Even so, the world being the way it was, he being who he was, and the Tauran Union being something like the wicked and hypocritical organization his father thought it was, Ham would need some kind of extra security. To this end Carrera had had Alena select five boys of the right age from among the families of Hamilcar's Pashtun guards. These he had briefed personally, extracting promises that there would be no special treatment of his son, other than to watch out for his physical safety from external threats. Alena had administered the oaths in her own language, with Cano, her husband, present to verify that the oath was what Carrera wanted, rather than what Alena thought was proper for a god. He'd extracted an oath from Alena, even so, in advance.

Places had been made for each of the boys in the Sergeant Juan Malvegui Military Academy, two in Ham's company, but not his platoon or section, and three in the next company over. Their bags—one overnighter, each—were stored in the trunks of the armored Phaeton and another sedan. Everything else would be issued at school.

The girls, Carrera could see, lined both sides of the long driveway that led down from the house to the InterColombiana. Also lined up, in addition to those twelve, were Alena and both of Ham's sisters. He shot a dirty look at Lourdes who shrugged in return. *What can one do against religious faith?* Even so, she strode over to first the little one, Linda, then Julia, picking each up by her waistband and carrying them, luggagelike, kicking and weeping, to the house.

The boys, too, stood in a short line, in front of the open space left between the cars. Solemnly, Carrera walked the line, shaking each boy's hand and giving a few words of encouragement. Most of them answered to the effect of, "I won't let you down, father of our lord."

Ham just said, "I'm ready, Dad." He gave a quick look to the door through which his mother had carted off his sisters. "And if you had any doubts about whether this is the right thing, forget it. It is."

At a word the boys split up, three to each vehicle. The engines started smoothly and the drivers began easing them down the driveway. Alena shouted a command, in her own language. All thirteen of the females still lining the driveway dropped to their knees, then to all fours, and then placed their faces into the dirt as the car bearing Hamilcar passed. The Moslems among whom Alena's people lived would have been appalled. She and her people, however, were anything but monotheistic Muslims.

After the first sedan passed they began to rise, all except Ant, aka Pililak, who, still on her knees, shot Carrera a look: *This tyranny will not stand.*

He wondered, *I wonder what makes Ant so pigheaded about this? More of a monotheist than the ones who are afraid of me?*

Past that, Carrera ignored the girl, the more so as his digital personal data assistant beeped with a message that, upon checking, he saw was from one of Fernandez's drops.

CHAPTER TWO

The secret of all victory lies in the
organization of the non-obvious.

—Marcus Aurelius

High Admiral's Conference Room, UEPF *Spirit of Peace*, in orbit over Terra Nova

One of the earlier high admirals, perhaps a hundred years prior, had ordered the conference room paneled in rare Terra Novan silverwood. This material shone iridescently from the walls, reflecting the light of a fixed chandelier mounted above a long conference table of the same material as those walls.

Around the conference table sat United Earth Peace Force High Admiral Marguerite Wallenstein's seven subordinate squadron commanders, her own staff, and the frightfully young captain of the flagship, Richard, earl of Care. Richard's mistress and Marguerite's lovely, olive-skinned cabin girl, Esmeralda, a freed former slave from Old Earth, stood in the back, pitcher in hand, ready to refill a water glass or, later on, provide more potent comestibles.

Though a former slave and now just a cabin girl, the sixteen-year-old Esmeralda had grown close to Marguerite on the long journey from Old Earth, through the Rift, to Terra Nova. Esmeralda knew the high admiral cared for her, and probably deeply. The best proof of that, to her mind, was the fact that, though the high admiral liked girls at least as much as boys, and though Esmeralda would have gone to her bed—joylessly, true, but she'd have gone—if asked or ordered, the request never came; the order was never given. That, alone, was so unlike the normal attitude of a Class One...

She loves me, thought Esmeralda, *but like a daughter. Or maybe a favored pet.* The thought of being a pet sent a shiver through the girl. Even so, she thought, *Beats becoming a bowl of chili for the neo-Azteca. Which I almost became.* She sent an encouraging smile over the table to her admiral.

Marguerite Wallenstein, High Admiral of the United Earth Peace Fleet, acknowledged the smile, but only with her eyes. About a century and a half old, she was a leggy, slender—even svelte—Scandinavian-descended Old Earther, with blue eyes that were a bit too small and a nose that was just a trifle too large to qualify her as a true beauty. Even so, she was still a woman who rated a second look; one just wouldn't be enough.

Over the rest of her face she maintained a screen, stonelike and detached. It was the best she could do as her fleet maintenance officer went down the list of major deficiencies in her command. She knew them all by heart anyway. Until quite recently nothing had changed with the fleet, except for the worse, in decades. Now, finally, with the old mothballed colonization fleet substantially looted for the parts now being disgorged from the repurposed colonization ship, *Jean Monnet,* some improvements were being made. With the significant push on the part of the secretary general of the Consensus, United Earth's governing body, to support the distant Peace Fleet, more should be possible soon.

Still, with ships that were centuries old, there was a great deal of room for improvement. Even her own flagship, *Spirit of Peace,* was a century and a quarter old, as were her sisters of the *Spirit* class.

Marguerite turned her attention from the fleet maintenance officer to the captain, pro tem, of the *Monnet,* McFarland. His face was as blank as her own, something she knew that came hard to her former chief engineer. Indeed, it came so hard that if the maintenance wallah had been bullshitting McFarland wouldn't have been able to hide it.

Good. It's going about as well as reported, then.

Back in Old Earth orbit she'd intended to put someone else in as skipper as soon as she had a replacement trained to take over from McFarland. Instead, time being short and the success-ful transition of *Monnet* from the Solar System to Terra Nova so critical, she'd pulled Buthelezi in to serve as *Peace's* chief engineer. He was doing well enough in the job for her to wonder if she shouldn't make it permanent, leaving McFarland in command of *Monnet* for at least several more supply runs back home.

Something that requires serious thought, Marguerite reminded herself. *Buthelezi is on top of things on a ship that McFarland tuned to a T before transferring completely to* Monnet. *That doesn't mean he can handle it as things begin to wear again.*

And if there's anything that better refutes the core philosophy behind the system on Old Earth, that man's just malleable clay in the hands of the elites, then I can't imagine what or who it could be than McFarland. After all, if it were true, that core belief, how is it that the system didn't ruin him? Or convince him, being only a Class Three, after all, that he just wasn't up to the job.

That thought, "Class Three," scared her suddenly. She spared McFarland another glance, looking over the bald pate fringed with gray, the sagging skin under his chin, and the wrinkles framing eyes and ears. *Elder gods, what if he dies on me? He's only a Three; no really good anti-agathics for him. Note to self: if it takes blowing the SecGen of the Consensus to get Mac raised then I can do that.*

Well, she silently corrected herself, *I could if I could go back home before I've settled the Terra Novan question. Hmmm ... maybe I should ship Khan the wife back with McFarland on his next supply run to make an ... ummm ... an oral ... request.*

At that Marguerite did permit herself a small smile. Small as it was it caught the maintenance officer's attention. "Ma'am?" he asked worriedly.

"Nothing, Chief," she answered with a shake of her head. "Keep going."

"Yes, High Admiral."

The invisible speaker mounted behind Wallenstein beeped, then squawked. A very natural sounding computer-generated voice announced, "Admiral's barge ready for transport to the surface."

Marguerite pointed at McFarland. "Captain, take over the briefing," she said. "Esma, assuming you've finished packing us?"

"Yes, ma'am," the Earth-girl replied. "Your bags should already be at the shuttle."

"Excellent. Let's go."

✧   ✧   ✧

For a number of reasons, not least that the major power on
the planet below, the Federated States of Columbia, utterly feared,
hated, and despised the United Earth Peace Fleet, and was both
capable and prepared to destroy it on fairly minimal provocation,
Wallenstein found it wise to go first to the UEPF base on Atlantis
Island, in the *Mar Furioso*, before boarding a more conventional
aircraft for the mainland. From there she would fly to the Tauran
Union, then to Balboa. The second and third legs of that journey
would be in aircraft registered on the planet, and not marked as
owned by the Peace Fleet. It might not fool anyone who was looking, but would at least keep casual comment to a minimum. Her
final segment, Tauran Union to Balboa, would be on a Gallic Air
Force dirigible with several high functionaries of the TU aboard
as well. The dirigible would be carrying necessary supplies, too,
for partial cover, along with a few hundred replacements.

Still, the journey of a thousand miles or, in this case, about
forty thousand, began with a single . . .

*I hope to hell Buthelezi's right about this elder gods-damned
thing,* Marguerite thought as she climbed the three steps from the
hangar deck to her shuttle. The steps formed the lower third or
so of the shuttle's main hatch. Behind her the hatch whined shut
as she settled herself into her—it had to be admitted—luxurious
seat. On the other side, Esmeralda, already seated and strapped
in, fidgeted nervously.

She had reason to worry; they both did. A different shuttle
had once nearly killed Marguerite's immediate predecessor, High
Admiral Robinson. She spared a quick glance out her porthole to
the pressure indicator. The balloon system some prole had come
up with was still in place but, comfortingly, the digital display
was working again.

She felt a metallic vibration through the shuttle's body, as the
clamps were let go, then sensed more than felt a slight rise as it
was magnetically pulled upward. Again glancing out the porthole,
she saw the hangar deck sliding by as the shuttle was magnetically moved out of the bay. She realized it was just as well that
she couldn't see forward, as the hangar deck spun with the ship
and the sight of spinning moons, stars, or planets was an almost
guaranteed nausea inducer.

And then the hangar's rectangular portal slid past. The pilot
waited perhaps half a minute before firing a brace of attitude

rockets to aim himself, then another to stop. Marguerite braced herself.

Whoomf!

Personally, I prefer a more sedate flight, Marguerite thought. *But if I'm going to turn this gaggle of inbred mules into stallions... well, a little discomfort is probably required.*

The plane to the mainland was waiting when Marguerite's shuttle set down. She was quickly hustled out and into a locally produced limousine, Esmeralda trailing behind, watching but not carrying the baggage. The limo then raced to the plane. No sooner were the admiral and her cabin girl strapped in than the thing started its takeoff run. In seconds, it seemed, she was airborne and heading toward Valdivia, in the shadow of the Atacama mountain range, in Colombia del Norte. The UEPF wasn't precisely popular in Valdivia, which retained a fairly strong alliance with the Federated States, and very friendly relations with the Republic of Balboa, but as long as war wasn't actually in the offing and there was a *peseta* to be made, a limited trade—mostly limited by the UEPF's emphasis on security and secrecy—was kept up. For the most part the trade was by air, but three or four times a local year a ship was allowed in Atlantean waters with heavier and bulkier goods. This was always presented as a case of mere efficiency over shipping goods from Old Earth.

In truth, though, thought Wallenstein, as her plane lifted wheels up, *the fleet couldn't survive six months without the planet, even with the* latifundia *on Atlantis Island. Speaking of which, if the locals ever discover how we do our farming even the bloody Gauls will be up in arms over it. But what the hell am I going to do with the slaves and serfs? I can't free them, not really. Oh, sure, I have the power to, but if I do, they'll start to leave. No food would be bad enough. But when they start leaving and the locals, especially the Federated States, discover what bad shape we're still in they'll nuke us on general principle.*

Fuck, I hate my own system. But I have to tolerate some evil— and I know it's an evil—for a longer-term good. I have to.

The plane was supersonic. This didn't completely eliminate engine noise—it travelled through the material of the hull—but at least reduced it to a tolerable level.

"Do they have slavery here on Terra Nova, High Admiral?" Esmeralda asked.

Reluctantly, Wallenstein nodded, adding, "Commonly, in some places and some cultures. The more civilized local states try to stop it, but...well...even there there's slavery. Mostly for girls. Mostly for sex."

Esmeralda shivered. "You know what happened to me before you freed me at Razona Market? You never asked, but you know?"

"I know," admitted the high admiral. "I wish I'd gotten to you sooner. Before..."

The olive skinned cabin girl had no trouble believing that. *But would you also have saved my sister whose heart was cut out by the Neo-Azteca on your* Ara Pacis? she wondered silently. She had to admit, in fairness, *Yes, you likely would have.*

Esmeralda could read, but what had been a more or less vestigial ability was now, under the instruction of her lover, the earl of Care and captain of the *Peace*, quite polished. And she had read, too. She'd read enough to know that her admiral's ultimate destination was in the middle of a place settled by her own distant relatives. She knew, too, that the physical layout was very similar. None of the books she had read on screen seemed to explain why, but to her it was obvious. The people—the "Noahs," they were called—who built or created the transit point, the people with that kind of power, who had also moved populations of Earth animals to the new world, had also simply used their immense power to modify the new Earth to closely match the old. Precisely why they did this she didn't know.

The books from which Esmeralda was allowed to read were strictly limited by a system even the high admiral would have found a chore to override. And none of their authors had really cared all that much about the new world. On Terra Nova, on the other hand, where many people were deeply concerned with the planet of their birth, there was, in fact, a cogent theory as to why their world physically matched Old Earth so closely. It had to do with weather or, more properly, with weather and the animals the Noahs had brought, from sabertooth to megalodon to phorohacos.

Plainly, the Noahs had wanted those animals to live. *That* required a proper climate, proper seasons, proper winds and rain. And, since weather was largely a function of the layout of a planet's surface, that had necessitated raising up continents and islands here, moving others there, and perhaps sinking others, still.

At least, that was the prevailing theory among those who cared.

Gaul Field, Balboa Transitway Zone, Balboa, Terra Nova

Both the admiral and the cabin girl had changed out of UEPF blacks into mufti during the second leg of their flight. That way they raised no comment as they made their way from one airport portal to the next in Valdivia, or in Taurus, or here.

It smells exactly *like home,* Esmeralda thought, as she and the high admiral walked the short distance from the Tauran dirigible's hatchway to a waiting helicopter a quarter of a mile away. *Well, underneath that funny oily stink it does. Sea salt. Flowers. The jungle.*

The TU's political and diplomatic crew lagged respectfully behind Wallenstein, who outranked them any way they cared to look at it. Her cabin girl, conversely, stayed by her side. About two hundred meters from the waiting TH-527 helicopter the wind shifted. Esmeralda sniffed again. *Even the food . . . it's all the same.*

Suddenly the girl was overwhelmed by a sense of homesickness and loss. It was all she could do not to break down in tears at the thought, *I'll never see home again.*

Wallenstein hadn't gotten to be as old as she had without learning to read people. That she and the cabin girl had spent about the last two years in close company helped, too. Gently, she patted Esmeralda. "Yes, child, you will someday go home. Moreover, you'll go home free and rich and famous all over. With a nice jump in caste to see you through a long and happy life."

And when I hang the last of the Castro-Nyeres—foul brood—you'll be there to set the ropes. I promise.

Esmeralda wasn't as good at reading her admiral as her admiral was at reading her.

Headquarters, Tauran Union Security Force-Balboa, Building 59, Fort Muddville, Balboa, Terra Nova

Marguerite had it on very good authority that the TU's headquarters was an intelligence sieve, that the domestic staff and some of the secretarial staff spied for the other side, that the phones were tapped, and even that some areas were subject to sound amplification via parabolic mirror. She thought that last was paranoia but... *Never hurts to be a little bit paranoid.*

Indeed, she'd been paranoid enough to force a third of the more senior TU personnel to precede her out of the helicopter, having ordered the Gaul, Janier, to greet them. While all of that folderol was going on, she and Esmeralda escaped into the building via a less obvious door, held open by a short, well-stacked, very damned pretty blonde with very large blue eyes.

Who, unfortunately, Wallenstein realized in an instant, *isn't remotely interested in girls. Oh, well.*

The blonde's nametag read "Campbell," while the rank on her epaulets indicated captain of ground forces.

"This way, ma'am," Campbell said, leading Marguerite and Esmeralda down a narrow, brown-painted corridor, up an even narrower flight of steps, then around two corners and into a thick-walled conference room of perhaps four by six meters. The door to the conference room was doubled, with a small chamber between doors, very much like the air lock of a star ship.

Almost, Wallenstein ordered Esmeralda to go with the captain. In the end, though, she not only recognized the captain as straight but as an intel type. No way she was letting an intel type get anywhere near her cabin girl.

"His Gribbitzness will be along shortly," the captain said, before leaving through the double door.

I wonder what the hell "Gribbitzness" means, Wallenstein wondered. *The tone she used said it was not a compliment. I suppose I'd better not ask. Yet.*

Whatever Marguerite had come to expect from reports about Gallic General Janier, the broken reed seated opposite her didn't quite fit it. He hadn't even donned the reproduction uniform of a marshal of Napoleonic France, and she'd been certain he would. Why, he wasn't even carrying the marshal's baton that was supposed to be his constant companion.

"I could have taken them four years ago," the Gaul said, shaking his head regretfully. "Maybe even three years ago, I could have. We had a good plan for doing it. We'd go after their leadership, before they could mobilize, using forces here and others brought in from Taurus. Then we could have turned on and destroyed the leaderless rabble one small unit at a time.

"Back then they were in the throes of reorganization. They had people in high places we could have gotten to. Eventually we did get to some of them, too. And there was—thanks to Federated States meddling—an existing opposed government to step in and give legitimacy to the entire operation."

There was a touch of frenzy on the Gaul's voice as, leaning forward excitedly, he insisted, "It's all gone now. We can't win anymore, not with any likely level of force the TU will give me. There are too many of them—not even counting the parts we don't know about but which I am sure exist." Janier collapsed back into his chair.

"Like what?" Wallenstein asked, ignoring the outburst.

Janier sat up a little straighter. It was pleasant, after all, to have someone his political masters would happily grovel to, and who also possibly understood some military realities.

He replied, "Like, for example, what do you call a three- or four-thousand-man construction company that has no official formation or barracks or anything else, but where every man is a veteran of the legion and where the CEO is never referred to by anything but his legionary rank?"

Marguerite agreed, "I'd call it a brigade of engineers."

"Precisely," the Gaul said. "And that, I think, is just the tip of the iceberg. Worse, still, my own political superiors are willing neither to retreat from this place nor to put in an effort to win here. They are, for all practical purposes frozen, like a megaloceros caught in headlights."

"What if I could unfreeze them, General?" the high admiral asked.

"They're cowards," he replied.

Marguerite smiled wickedly. "Oh, I'd count on that. What if I could unfreeze them by offering them a limited rejuvenation, about twenty or twenty-five years' worth?"

"You could do this?" Seeing she could, Janier grinned for the first time since the meeting began. "They'd be on it like a child molester on a six-year-old." *Which, come to think of it, and though the controlled press avoids the subject, some of them are.*

"All right then," the Gaul said, "I could do something with the kind of political support that would drum up."

"What would you do?" Wallenstein asked.

"I'd build us up to eighteen light and heavy—mostly light— infantry battalions here," he answered, without any noticeable hesitation. "With all the usual support. This would require some civil construction, to be sure. I'd beg, borrow, or bribe transit rights through Santander to the west and Santa Josefina to the east. I would begin stockpiling in those places as well as here and in Cienfuegos to support a moderately lengthy campaign. I would get substantial sections of both our fleet and the Anglians to control the coasts. I would . . ."

Marguerite held up a hand, palm forward. "At least you know what you would do, General. That's more than most can say. It's also more than I need to know, in any detail. I'll get you the political support. You use it to good effect."

Again, as if one cue and even though no cue was needed, the entire headquarters building shook as a couple of Balboan fighters skimmed low over the roof.

"And I'm going to fuck with them mercilessly," the Gaul finished.

Marguerite reached into a pocket, pulling out a thin communications device. "We'll need to talk from time to time. Use this."

Cerro Mina Road, Balboa Transitway Area, Balboa, Terra Nova

Esmeralda was a country girl, basically. The nearest she'd ever seen of a city was the Razona Market on Old Earth where, caged, she'd been put on display as goods to be sold. The twisting road carved into the side of the hill in the course of quarrying for stone for the Florida Locks was mostly framed by jungle. But every now and again the soil had been too thin to support much in the way of plant life and a vista opened up of the sprawling cosmopolitan city below the hill. She wasn't at all sure she liked the city; it was just too different from what she'd known.

The people she'd seen along the streets, though, between the gate under Building 59 at Fort Muddville and the MP shack at the base of this winding road were not different from what she'd grown up with: generally brown, stocky, and calm of countenance. She felt an immediate affinity for them, as if she could step out of Janier's staff limousine and just blend in among them.

Except for one thing, thought the girl, *my "Spanish" is so contaminated by English, the language of Old Earth, and limited by the experience of the last five hundred years while theirs, supposedly, is pretty pure. I don't know if we could even talk.*

Janier and the high admiral rode in back, with the glass barrier rolled up between them and the peasantry. What they talked about Esmeralda didn't know, though she was sure the high admiral would tell her anything she needed to know. She did know, though, that Janier had said he'd had a set of quarters set aside on this sleepy post for the use of the high admiral.

He intends to bed her, Esmeralda was certain. *Which is good. Then I won't have to feel guilty for not crawling into her bed on my own, after all she's done for me.*

CHAPTER THREE

Disciplined in the school of hard campaigning,
Let the young Roman study how to bear
Rigorous difficulties without complaining,
And camp with danger in the open air.

—Horace, *Odes, III, 2*

Estado Mayor, Balboa City, Balboa, Terra Nova

A weasel-faced man, wheelchair-bound, eased his powered chair out from behind his desk and around to face his commander, seated in one of the overstuffed chairs in one corner of the office.

"She's here right now, Patricio," said Omar Fernandez, "the high admiral of the United Earth Peace Fleet, herself. I'd have known a lot sooner except that Yamatan Imperial Intelligence didn't rush the information from their special source to me, and it took a while to track down the aerial routes through my own sources in the Federated States, once I knew to start looking.

"I don't know if there's anything you want to do about that or even anything you *can* do about it. Still, I thought you should know as soon as I could tell you without compromising anything."

Carrera ran a dozen possible responses through his mind, very, very quickly, dismissing each as either impractical or undesirable.

"And," Fernandez continued, "although it isn't proof, I consider it evidence that none of my people actually in the enemy head-quarters saw anything beyond a flock of Tauran Union bureaucrats, while one did see that their super secure conference room was used, but with none of the visiting bureaucrats in it. And then she and a young aide—or maybe lover; you never really know with the Kosmos—were seen being escorted by the Frog general to *Cerro Mina*. I should have a report of where they're staying by midnight. But I already suspect where it will be, and I don't have that building infiltrated." The intel chief shrugged apologetically. "I never thought I'd need it, since the building was never used for the last ten or fifteen years."

"I'd like to know whatever you can come up with, Omar," Carrera agreed. "But I think I wouldn't do anything if I could. Former High Admiral Robinson is still healthy?" At Fernandez's nod, he continued, "Then I have a hold over the bitch to use at my convenience. Speaking of which, how's the shuttle program coming along?"

"We have five acceptably trained pilots for it," Fernandez said. "But we ran into a glitch that we really should have anticipated."

Carrera raised a quizzical eyebrow.

"Assuming we can bluff or force our way into a hangar, there's no frigging air unless the ship we try to board closes the hangar doors and fills the compartment. That, or we find space suits from *somebody* and outfit a boarding party with them . . . or develop some ourselves. Even there . . ."

"Even there," Carrera finished, "it doesn't really give us control of a fleet . . . or maybe even control of that one ship, since we won't have a crew to fly or fight it. Okay, let me mull it some. But, for God's sake, keep Robinson healthy."

Training Area C, *Academia Militar Sergento* Juan Malvegui, west of *Puerto Lindo,* Balboa, Terra Nova

In the rest of Balboa it was the dry season. On the Shimmering Sea side of the isthmus, there was never really a dry season. Rather, there was a wet season, a wetter season, and "forty days and forty nights," which, interestingly enough, usually lasted about forty days and forty nights. Currently, it was the wet season, which meant there would be the occasional dry day.

Keeping healthy's not a huge problem, Ham mused, *but keeping happy sure as hell is. I never realized before how utterly essential women and girls are to keeping happy.*

The boy sat alone underneath a stretched out rubber poncho. Rain drummed the sheet like a distant barrage before gathering and rolling off the sides. Most of that water splashed up a bit of mud but then rolled downhill and away. From uphill, however, which was behind him, a neat little stream formed and ran under the frame of the rucksack he'd been issued, between his feet, and then off.

The stream wasn't a problem, yet, but...

Serious doubts that I can divert it with a narrow run-off trench. Serious lack of desire to sleep in the middle of a stream. Serious desire to *sleep, as soon as they let us.*

Ham's family was, of course, not poor. Indeed, they were so not poor that his father had given away about seventy-five *billion* drachma and still could fund whole regiments and schools out of his own remaining wealth. But many of the students at the military academies, of which there were six, were from poor families. Since, unlike the rest of the country's educational system, the military schools were totally free—in fact, they paid a small stipend—there were more applicants than there were slots. Thus, Ham and several hundred new boys were out in the jungle—the real, deep, dark, wet, stinky, snake-crawling, *antaniae*-crying, black palm-sticking triple canopy jungle—to drive as many boys who lacked motivation as possible out before wasting a precious school slot on them.

So far it had all been very efficient and, compared to what Ham had expected, surprisingly gentle. There hadn't been a lot of screaming—some shouting, yes, but a man had to be heard—and no real brutality, as the boys had been hustled through medical exams, shots, dental checks, the field uniform and equipment issue line, the small-caliber rifle issue line, and any of half a hundred other things to prepare them for what came next.

What came next had been a walk. A long walk. A hot long walk...with blisters. It was all made a great deal worse by the fact that none of the boys, Ham included, knew how to keep up. Thus, it had been mile after mile of stop, march in place, run, run faster, stop, bump into the boy in front of you, stop, run, run, dammit...

Where they'd ended up even Ham didn't know, and it was probably his family's property. What it looked like though: banana plants and palm trees at the edges of the few open areas. For the rest, bare dirt at ground level and some other, a lot of other, stouter trees growing up from that, with their branches intertwined overhead, blocking out direct sunlight.

Apparently Carrera or his chief for cadet training, the Volgan, Sitnikov, had been very firm that the boys were not to be hit, starved, or kept from sleeping more than two days in a row. But the food... Ham looked down at the unappetizing mess slopped on the metal plate resting on his knees and wondered, *Is this food?* He sniffed, carefully. *Doesn't smell rotten, anyway. Doesn't actually smell like anything at all. My mother or my sister or my wives or, least of all, Alena the Witch, would never have given me something like this to eat.*

I miss my womenfolk. But I am Hamilcar Carrera, son of Patricio, and I will not *cry.*

He sniffed again at his evening meal. *Unappetizing or not, nothing better is going to be forthcoming. I suppose I'd better eat it.*

Casa Linda, Balboa, Terra Nova

Meals at the *casa* had always had an odd, military aspect to them. Purchased as a run-down and abandoned old pile, it had entered modern life as a staff headquarters and barracks. It had served in that capacity while Carrera and his men had been planning and putting together the first increment of the legion, the one that fought the initial campaign in Sumer. It had since gone through various other renditions. Currently, it was mostly civilian, but with two hundred of Hamilcar's in-laws as guard, in barracks outside, it still had a strong military aspect to it, at least out on the grounds and at the doors.

Even inside, though, with the presence of Tribune Cano, his wife, Alena the Witch, and Ham's dozen wives, Artemisia McNamara and her brood, plus the domestic staff, the sheer numbers demanded a more than ordinary degree of organization, one highly reminiscent of a military organization. Thus, one might say there was an officers' mess, where Carrera, Lourdes, and Artemisia, the widow of Sergeant Major McNamara, took their meals, along with, usually, Lourdes' major domo. Then there was a staff mess, for the maids and cooks and groundskeepers, along with any of the guards on duty inside the house, as a few invariably were. Then there was the children's dining room, which had originally been the sole dining room, but had been specialized once Ham came back accompanied by his wives.

Alena and her husband supervised that mess, and Ham's sisters, naturally enough, gravitated to the other girls who were not, in any case, all that much older. And besides, Ham's wives spoiled Julia and Linda rotten, something always appreciated.

They *all* spoiled Alena's child, Dido, as the only real baby on the premises. That last was currently engaged in her own feed, courtesy of Alena's abundant breasts. Cano, seated at the opposite end of the table, was reminded, *And how can man die better...?*

Ant looked up from an empty plate as Alena was switching her baby off. "May I be excused?" she asked.

"Surely, child, run along."

Neither Cano nor his wife, both quite intent on Dido, noticed that Ant left with several packages of crackers concealed in the folds of her native costume. On the other hand, if she *had* noticed, Alena would likely have guessed the reason and thoroughly approved.

Ant didn't know quite how far her husband's father's powers stretched, only that they were immense, far above any of the chieftains of any of the clans of her own people. And she watched enough of the television and read enough over the GlobalNet—from the extensive house library, as well, for that matter—to know that power here meant a lot more than it did in her homeland, too.

Looking over the map of Balboa she'd found over the GlobalNet, she fumed, *If I knew how to drive I could be there at my lord's school within a few hours, half a day at the most. But I haven't the first clue. And if I try to get someone to pick me up on the road—"hitch-hiking," they call it—the police will have me in irons in a matter of half an hour after I am reported missing. And there will be no second chance; the father of my lord gives me the impression that he never gives anyone a second chance.*

So it is on foot, and not on the roads, either. And not even on foot all the way; there are rivers I must swim and even a lake I must cross. Hmmm... maybe before I set out I had better learn to swim better than I do. Fortunately, the ocean—strange and frightful thing!—is only down the steep walkway to the north.

And when I am ready, and make my way to my lord, I will be blessed among women, for—youngest or not—I will be the first to take my lord into her body, and the first to bear him a semidivine child!

Training Area C, *Academia Militar Sergento* Juan Malvegui, west of *Puerto Lindo*, Balboa, Terra Nova

For guard duty, they'd told Ham to sling his small-caliber rifle and given him a 20-gauge pump shotgun. He'd pass it on to the relief; they'd all done familiarization firing a few days past. In any case, the dangers against which he guarded his young comrades at night just weren't the kind a .22 could help with. The shotgun had a strong flashlight mounted in parallel with the muzzle, the light being activated by a button near his thumb.

Hamilcar walked gingerly. Despite the ministrations of the school medicos, his feet were still blistered from the march out here.

From off in the distance, well past the perimeter, he heard the cries of hungry *antaniae: mnnbt, mnnbt, mnnbt.*

The problems with the antaniae, thought Ham as, shotgun in hand, he patrolled the perimeter of the encampment, *are triple. One is that they go after the small and young, which includes me. Another is that they come in mass if they think they can get away with it. The third is that they hate the light and like to attack when it's darkest.* He spared a glace upward at the light-blocking interwoven jungle above. *I don't even know if the fucking moons are up.*

The *antaniae* themselves were winged beasts, and more or less reptilian. It was widely believed they were genengineered life forms, as the equally dangerous bolshiberries, tranzitrees, and progressivines were engineered life forms. The difference was that the three forms of genengineered flora were dangerous only to intelligent life, while the *antaniae* specialized in devouring the eyes and brains of the young, the weak, the defective, and the feebleminded.

Worse, not unlike some of the monitor lizards found on various parts of the planet, the *antaniae* had vilely septic mouths that caused infections that only the most heroic medical treatment could cure, and not always then.

Fortunately, the little bastards are cowards. Even so, I wish we had a small flock of trixies to pull guard. They can see the anta-niae without the night vision equipment the cadre didn't give me.

Well... of course they didn't give me any, though they have some for themselves. They didn't give any of the other cadets any either. And I'm pretty sure the old man wasn't lying when he told me what he'd told them: "You coddle the boy half a gram; you give him a goddamn thing more than any other cadets gets, and your balls go up on the fireplace mantle."

'Course, I hope he was more tactful than that. You would think so, after the Pigna coup. But he has his flaws still, so maybe not.

Some of those flaws, I suppose, I've inherited. Though if my mother and sisters and wives and Alena have anything to say about it, I'll never have a clue.

'Course, not everything the old man had in mind is working out. The other cadets know who I am and who he is. They don't kowtow, but they grew up in Balboa. Here people just assume family connections matter a lot more than they do to Dad. So they sometimes defer to me a little more than Dad would approve of and sometimes detest me more than I approve of. And there's more of the latter.

'Course, I ate better all my life than most of them did, so I'm taller than most. And I'm taller still because Mom's oversized and Dad's bigger than most of our people. Height gets you a little deference, too, on average. Maybe it isn't all who I am or who I'm related to or who I know.

I hope. I...

Suddenly, the boy had the distinct sense of being watched, from close by, by something or things that didn't necessarily bear him good will. He froze, instantly, then began corkscrewing his eyes to keep from wearing out the night vision in any given sector of his visual rods.

He couldn't quite make out what it was, though his indistinct night vision was telling his brain that *something* was out there. Slowly, very slowly, he raised the shotgun to his shoulder, pointing it generally at the indistinct shapes his eyes couldn't quite grasp.

They'll so *be on my ass if I use the light and don't need to. And worse if I open fire and don't need to. But there's* something *there ... something ... ahhhh, fuckit.*

Ham's thumb came down on the light button. The light flashed on three little horrors, red-eyed, green and gray splotched, about two feet long, with their frills spread and wings folded in, hissing and drooling.

"Shiiitttt!" *Kaboom, kaclick*—"shit"—*kaboom, kaclick*—"shit"—*Kaboom!*

The encampment behind Ham began springing to life, even as

the jungle outside cracked with the flap of reptilian wings. A *lot* of reptilian wings.

Ham looked closely in the area lit by the narrow beam. One of the little beasts had apparently escaped, maybe wounded, maybe not. One was so much strawberry jam spread unevenly across the bare jungle floor. The last was crying out piteously, writhing and crawling in a circle, with one wing and two legs on one side gone, and the pus that passed for blood leaking out. They'd only given him the three rounds and he'd sort of forgotten about the .22 slung across his back. Instead, he walked up to the wounded *antania*, reversed the shotgun, and brought the butt down on the nasty creature's head with a satisfying crunch.

Casa Linda beach, Balboa, Terra Nova

Though the air and water were both warm, the girl trembled. She had her reasons.

Depending on whose book one read, swimming in Terra Nova's oceans was either quite safe or an obvious attempt at suicide. After all, the Noahs had brought, among other hungry things, a healthy, albeit now declining, population of carcharodon megalodons, for whom one small girl would have been barely an appetizer.

In practice it wasn't as simple as that. A meg was so big that it really couldn't come close to shore, usually. This tended to drive lesser predators shoreward for protection. One the other hand, a meg ate so much, not least lesser predators, that there weren't as many dangerous sharks and other forms of marine life as there might otherwise have been, partly through being eaten and partly through there not being enough for them to eat after a meg had eaten its fill.

Conversely, from the meg's point of view, they themselves ate so much and required such a large range that the species had never really learned cooperation. So they were vulnerable, at least when young, to smaller but more intelligent predators with a sense of teamwork, like orca.

In an interesting oversight, while the three forms of genengineered flora left by the Noahs kept down the natural rise of intelligent life ashore, nothing anyone had yet found had done the same at sea. Orcas, as it turned out, were very bright indeed.

None of that was really all that comforting to Pililak as she nervously waded to about waist deep in the sea. For the underwater slope of the *casa*'s private beach, that worked out to perhaps fifteen feet from shore. The girl didn't have a bathing suit. Instead she wore one of Ham's left behind t-shirts and that was all. Her clothes were back on the sand.

Facing out to sea, scanning for sharks and who knew what, she saw the family yacht gently and slowly bobbing at the private wharf to her left. This was the same boat that had carried Lourdes to find help to defeat the Pigna coup, though repaired and repainted from the damage taken in crashing into the dock at *Punta Gorgona* Naval Station.

For a moment Ant thought about practicing her swimming over by the yacht. The water was deeper there. Then she thought, *No. Here I have a better chance of seeing something coming for me. Over there something could come right under the boat with no warning.*

This might not have been entirely rational, but it was most sincerely felt.

Ant had no one she could trust to teach her to swim. And, since water in her homeland and her village either came from a well or flowed fast about half a meter deep over sharp rocks, she'd never learned. Instead, she dug from the 'net how to do it and practiced that in her mind until she felt ready to try.

Putting her palms together, the girl—with a bravery that no one would have understood who didn't know her background and how absolutely scared to death she was of being eaten—bent forward at the waist, thrust her arms ahead of her, and dove in.

Stream Crossing Site Two, *Rio Cuango,* Training Area C, *Academia Militar Sergento* Juan Malvegui, west of *Puerto Lindo,* Balboa, Terra Nova

Victor Chapayev's day-to-day and permanent rank was Tribune III, roughly equivalent to a major in most of the armies of Terra Nova, though in the legion carrying more responsibility and prestige, both. His full mobilization rank, on the other hand, was Legate II, roughly the equivalent of a colonel, which was a significant rank even in the most overofficered armies on the planet.

Today, the Volgan wore his permanent rank. Indeed, the true reason why he had a higher rank was highly secret, although the fact that most legionary officers and centurions held higher rank was not. Few knew the reasons for the special exception for Chapayev and a couple of hundred others. They themselves didn't, though it was generally assumed it was just to give retirement pay parity to those who were not assigned to a mobilizable tercio. That was the official story, in any case.

Chapayev didn't buy the official *pravda,* though he kept his doubts and opinions on the matter to himself. He'd learned, as a young officer in the army of the now deposed (and very, very dead) Red Tsar (whose large extended family was also very, very dead), that this was a sound policy (as was making sure that the families of one's deposed tyrants joined them in death).

I'm not sure, though, thought Chapayev, *that Carrera tossing his son in amongst a bunch or regular kids—okay, better than regular kids but still not in the same class or league as Hamilcar Carrera—is such a good idea. The boy might learn to lead them or he might learn just to manipulate them. He might learn to love them but he might just as easily learn contempt for them. He might get the common touch or it might end up being nothing but* noblesse oblige *masquerading as the common touch. And it strikes me all as needlessly risking the worst possibilities without sufficient probability of achieving the best.*

Victor leaned against a tree at the moment, arms folded, watching the new class of boys trying to set up a two-rope bridge under the leadership, for the exercise, of one of them. That one was not Hamilcar and was not doing spectacularly well, either. And, so Victor could plainly see, Ham was practically bursting at the seams to tell the other boy, Cadet Oscar Arrias, how to do it, how to command it. He also saw that First Centurion Ricardo Cruz, temporarily detached from his maniple for a month of cadet support, supervising the exercise up close and personally, was practically bursting at the seams to tell the boy to jump in and take over.

And there's no good answer I could give you, Ham, ran Chapayev's thoughts. *Tell him how to do it and maybe you make a friend for life . . . but it's just about as likely you make an enemy. Don't do a thing but follow along and everyone in your section who knows anything about you assumes you're a selfish slacker. Hell, I wouldn't know what to do myself, boy.*

And peer reports will be coming in a few weeks. I wonder if your old man thought of that, or that all this might just ruin you.

CHAPTER FOUR

There never was a good war or a bad peace.

—Benjamin Franklin

Everyone's a pacifist between wars. It's like being a vegetarian between meals.

—Colman McCarthy

Palacio de las Trixies, *Ciudad* Balboa, Republic of Balboa

Since the defeat of Pigna's coup and the extinction of the rival regime, *Presidente*, and former *Duque*, Raul Parilla had moved into the official and traditional executive mansion, an open-courted *"Palazzo"* in the Venetian style. It even had, per the name, a dozen or so trixies, colorful archaeopteryxes brought to Terra Nova by the Noahs. Under recent administrations, the trixies had been effective captives. Now the wire over the courtyard was mechanized, to roll back during the day. That was Carrera's doing, as part of his trixie breeding and *antaniae* reduction programs.

Most trixies did, in fact, leave while the sun was up. Usually they returned by nightfall—when the wire rolled back over the open top—for their free meal.

The style of the palace, a carryover from early days of colonization, was extremely appropriate. No less than one once could have in Old Earth's Venice—now sadly landlocked as a result of falling seas from global cooling—from his bedroom balcony Parilla could hit the waves of the sea with a hand-tossed rock.

Antaniae lived in the neighborhood, of course, that was the original point of keeping trixies there. Even now, the area was very old, very built up, with hidden spots, nooks, and crannies sufficient to shelter the *antaniae* from the day's harsh sunlight. No extermination program had ever proven quite thorough enough.

Though the exterior of the palace was Venetian, the interior courtyard was very Arabesque, with sparkling columns in the Moorish style, a simple but elegant central fountain, sixteen symmetric but nonuniform arches, and a long staircase that arose in the back to lead to the second floor. Someone had probably had coup prevention in mind when that staircase had been designed; it was the only way up that led to the presidential quarters.

Parilla—short, stocky, swarthy, and with steel gray hair—was waiting at the top of the stairs, hand on a railing, as Carrera walked through the courtyard, skirting the central fountain. A gray, emerald green, and red trixie, bent over and drinking at the fountain, ignored him entirely.

He looks so old now, Carrera thought, looking up the staircase. *And, well . . . I suppose he is.*

"It's not the years," said Parilla, as if reading his chief soldier's mind, "it's the mileage."

Carrera nodded, answering, "A year ago, Raul, you didn't need a railing to hold yourself up."

"Cascading failure," Parilla said. "When things start to go wrong they all go wrong together . . . and fast. Come on, let's go chat in my office."

I don't like the sound of that word, "chat," Carrera thought. *Maybe he was always more politician than soldier, but the old man was a pretty fair soldier too. A "chat" could be unpleasant.*

The silverwood paneling in the presidential office was considerably older than that on the walls of *Spirit of Peace*'s conference room. It was also reflective enough that the light spilling in from the window was more than sufficient.

"Fernandez's boys and girls swept the place two days ago," Parilla said, as Carrera took a leather seat. "We can speak freely here." Then the president went to a liquor cabinet and pulled out two glasses. These he filled with ice, then took a bottle of ancient rum and poured several generous fingers in each.

Carrera stood up, took one glass and set it down, then took

the other, which he placed on Parilla's desk. Only then did he retrieve his own glass and resume his seat.

"I have a sense of the Senate," Parilla said.

I like the sound of that even less.

"There is a sufficient consensus that we should avert a war with the Tauran Union if at all possible. If I asked for a declaration of war today, I would not get it."

"Even though they're sitting in the Transitway like a rope around the country's neck?" Carrera asked.

"Even though," the president confirmed.

"They don't have faith I can win it?"

Parilla shook his head. "No, they believe you can win it. They don't believe you or anyone alive or anyone who has ever lived could win it without getting ten or fifteen percent of the country killed."

And I could not gainsay that with a straight face or clear conscience. It just might cost that much.

"So what do they want... what do *you* want, Mr. President?"

Parilla frowned. "Don't you get formal with me, Patricio. I'm still Raul. And don't get your back up over the Senate, either. They're *your* creation, not your creature, and *you* set them up that way.

"As to what I want... I want us to back off from provoking the Taurans. I want us to... let's say... give peace a chance."

"I think that's a mistake," said Carrera.

Parilla shook his head. "It's not a mistake; it's a gamble. It's gambling a somewhat less advantageous position should war come against the chance of avoiding war altogether. Are you trying to tell me that that is always a losing bet?"

"I'm... no." Patricio likewise shook his head. "No; Machiavellianism notwithstanding, human history is replete with instances where a little restraint might have avoided endless grief. It's just that in this case, in our circumstances, I don't think that's going to happen."

"You knew the new high admiral of the Peace Fleet visited the Taurans, here, recently?" Carrera asked.

"Yes," the president agreed, "my aide de camp got the briefing from Fernandez and briefed me."

"You don't agree it's a bad sign?"

"Could be," Parilla conceded. "Equally, it could be a good sign. We just don't know."

"I can contact her, you know," Carrera said. "I haven't because I don't trust the bitch as far as I could throw one of her starships."

"Yes, I knew. Maybe you should."

Carrera shrugged his shoulders. He really didn't know if he should or shouldn't.

"So what say you?" the president asked.

"I don't want to stop preparations for a war I consider inevitable."

"Can you break those preparations into nice to have and necessary?" asked Parilla. "Into those that you can keep hidden from those you can't? From the innocuous to the provocational?"

"Maybe, maybe, and maybe."

"Try. Try. Try."

Carrera smirked at the retort. "And when they sense weakness and start to provoke us?"

"Restraint. Restraint. Restraint."

It was Parilla's turn then to smirk at Carrera's scowl. "You've recently put your son into one of the military schools, haven't you?"

"It's common knowledge," Carrera answered.

"When you're weighing this gamble I want you to take, don't forget to weigh the life of your son if we go to war with someone a hundred times bigger and a thousand times wealthier."

"I suppose there is that . . . Okay, Raul, I'll try; I'll lay off harassing the Taurans. But I'm still going to keep preparing in everything that's key."

And the only reason I'm not throwing a shit fit is because I can ignore most of what you've ordered—as you fully expect me to.

Batteria McNamara (former Battery Ranald, FS Army), Cristobal Province, Balboa, Terra Nova

There was information that was open. Then there were secrets, deeper secrets, and deepest, top secrets. It was, for example, no secret that the legion had bought an impressive number of 180mm guns from the Volgans. The exact number, though, was secret. It was no secret that some dozens of these had been mounted in old Federated States-built coastal artillery batteries along both the Shimmering Sea and *Mar Furioso* coasts. That an additional fifty-four had been hidden out on the *Isla Real* was very secret. It was not a secret that the legion had laser-homing shells for many of their heavier artillery pieces and mortars; they'd used some of those during the campaigns in both Sumer and Pashtia. That they had developed lengthened, subcaliber, laser-guided shells for the 180mm guns, which shells could range over eighty kilometers, was almost the deepest secret in Balboa.

The battery—then named "*Iglesias* Point Battery"—had once housed two twelve-inch rifles on barbette carriages, which is to say carriages that allowed a gun to be fired over a parapet. Other batteries, up and down the coast, had housed twelve-inch mortars, fourteen- and sixteen-inch rifles, and an assortment of lesser pieces. None of those were required anymore, since ships no longer mounted the armor such beasts were designed and built to punch through. The gun about to be fired, at just over seven inches, was more, much more, than required to punch through the thin metal of a modern warship, if punching though armor at longish range had been the objective.

Near this two-gun, open but parapeted firing pad, itself sitting atop a deep bunker for both ready ammunition and fire control, Carrera watched as the crew of one 180mm gun went through the drill of loading and laying. Trap doors opened to the rear of the position, as a reconditioned ammunition elevator pushed up one of the long shells. Longer than the previous twelve-inch shells, this one came up on a frame that held it at an angle. The projectile in its sabot was, to say the least, oddly shaped for an artillery round. The lengthy fuse with the high-strength golden glass nose made it appear odder still.

The propellant popped up from a different elevator, fed by a different compartment.

The crew was not the gun's normal complement. Oh, no, the regular crew were reservists and militia and weren't even mobilized. Instead, for now, the gun was manned by a special test crew, specially vetted for reliable closed-mouthedness, from *Obras Zorilleras*, or OZ, the legion's research and development division. Their chief had drilled them numb over the preceding week on a sister gun, though that one was held underground in a different battery, about twenty-four hundred meters to the southwest.

They were only going to get one chance at the test, though the test would involve twelve shots. These were five of the special shells, that being the number on hand at Battery McNamara, and seven normal high explosive shells to mask the specials. The special shells were inert, the normal explosive filler replaced by a mostly plastic mix of the same density. Four other gun positions, three to the west and one to the east, were manned by reservists and militia mobilized for training. These were also along the Shimmering Sea coast and on both sides of the Transitway's mouth. They would also be firing for this exercise, mostly to divert attention from the test firing of the special shells. Their ammunition was limited to standard 180mm High Explosive. Five forward observer stations, as heavily fortified as the gun positions, held FO teams with laser range finders indistinguishable from the laser that would be used to mark the target for the special shells.

Carrera turned away from the gun crew, walking into a dark, open rectangle in the concrete wall. Once past the edges of the entrance, red lights in metal cages set high on the walls marked his way to the fire direction center. Before anyone could notice his presence, he ordered, "As you were," code for, "keep doing what you were doing."

There were a half-dozen closed-circuit television sets to one side of the bunker. One of these was large. It gave Carrera the same view as the forward observation and lasing team for Battery McNamara had. That team sat inside a concrete position high atop a cliff facing the sea. The image, enhanced both for light and magnification showed him a radio controlled ship—more of a barge, really—twenty miles out to sea. This was nothing like the shells' maximum range.

It had been a matter of considerable discussion. The short, balding, Volgan-descended Kuralski, also there for the test, had wanted to fire at near maximum range. Carrera had overridden that—he didn't want anyone to know how far the guns could shoot the new ammunition. There were other barges out to sea as targets, as many as there were batteries firing for the day.

The job was not without its risks, but risks or not, a screen of patrol boats insured no other ships came close to the barge targets to see what was happening. The crews of those boats wore laser protective goggles.

Carrera was reasonably certain that the UEPF was taking considerable interest in goings on in the Republic of Balboa. He didn't know the precise capabilities of their remote sensing, but assumed it was at least on a par with that of the planet's premier power, the Federated States. Thus, he didn't hope to hide that he was firing a certain kind of gun at a certain range. All he could do—and he hoped it was enough—was misdirect the Peace Fleet as to the real nature of the firing.

The other five televisions, all smaller, showed the barge itself, from a camera housed near the stern, as well as its nearby waters. Those cameras were mounted in an armored casing, sternward. Those televisions' signals were encrypted to prevent anyone else from receiving them. Again, though, Carrera doubted that the UEPF couldn't break the encryption. He had to assume they could.

There was a seventh camera in operation, though it wasn't transmitting. Instead, that one took video showing a remote and distant view of the test firing. The camera was carried in a Cricket light aircraft.

The data from the fire direction center was on the sight, the gun loaded and laid. The special fuse that made the shell special was keyed to the laser frequency of the forward observer team that would lase its target. With his left hand, the gun chief stretched the firing lanyard taut. On command from the FDC, he struck the stretched lanyard with his right fist.

Kaboommm! Ahead, muzzle blast ripped leaves from jungle trees as concussion caused the crew's inner organs to ripple and pulse in a sickening manner. Shortly after reaching the muzzle, the twelve sections of sabot that had held the shell steady in its travel down the tube split away. Much lighter than the shell, and of deliberately nonaerodynamic cross-section, the pieces of the sabot lost velocity rapidly, careening off into the jungle in a random pattern.

"Reload!" shouted the gun chief, as another long and oddly shaped shell arose through the elevator doors. A split second later another three bags of propellant arose from the other elevator.

The entire crew of the FDC groaned as a single man. The incredibly expensive and supremely secret shell had missed. It missed despite laser guidance. It missed despite the select crew and forward observer team. Admittedly, it didn't miss by much, no more than a dozen feet. But still . . .

The TV showed the barge twisting in the water, just as would a ship that knew it was under fire. A second great splash, the mark of a missed shell, flew up about five meters off the port side. Kuralski exclaimed, "Damn it!"

The third shell came in, causing a splash even farther away, at perhaps nine meters, or about thirty feet. The fourth? No one in the FDC had a clue where that had gone. The fifth landed about as far away as the first had.

"It's *perfect*," Carrera said, and started to laugh. "Fucking *perfect*!"

In a pure fluke, the barge was actually struck by the third normal shell which, since it contained high explosive and a normal fuse, duly detonated, shredding the barge like tissue.

Kuralski's chin hung on his chest. "Every one of them, every goddamned one of them..."

"Yeah, so?"

"Twelve thousand drachma a shot! Useless."

"Oh, bullshit," Carrera said.

"Huh?"

"Oh, c'mon, Dan! How wide is a fucking warship?"

"Oh. Well...yeah...I guess so."

"Order more shells, Dan," Carrera said. "Order at least fourteen hundred of them. We've got or will soon have fifty-four guns just like these on this island, plus several dozen more at other spots. Not counting the ones in the Tenth Artillery Legion. I want each, barring the Tenth's, to have at least twenty shells. If there's a significantly reduced unit price in ordering more, you can go up to twenty-five million drachma, total."

Kuralski nodded. "There's something else, Pat. We've used Volgan laser-guided heavy mortar shells since Sumer. They've got a new one—well, a completely new system, actually—called 'Trapeze.' No, I have no clue why they chose that name. Anyway, it's a 240mm mortar, special laser designator, special shell with—"

"Nah."

"But...I thought, with these twelve-inch mortar positions on both sides, all four sides, rather, of the Transitway..."

"They won't last days if it comes to war. No, the 122/180s make sense, because we can protect and hide them and their guns. But 240mm mortars in open pits? With us conceding to the enemy air supremacy ninety-nine and forty-four one-hundredths percent of the time? I don't think so."

With a shrug, Kuralski said, "Just a thought."

UEPF *Spirit of Peace*, High Orbit over Atlantis Island, Terra Nova

"So what was that all about?" asked the fleet watch officer, a few moments after the last of sixty shells splashed into the water or blew up. The images had been forwarded by the *Spirit of Harmony*, in orbit over Balboa.

The fleet's surface reconnaissance officer shook her short-cropped, blond head. "We don't have access to any of their internal communications, since that was apparently all done by land line. It will be a few hours before we can break the encryption on their television signals. But, just on the face of it, it looked to me like they were exercising their coastal artillery's capabilities on landing craft and that the exercise failed."

"One hit out of sixty rounds?" mused the watch officer. "Yes, I'd call that a failure. Even so, run it by the Analysis Office before passing it on to the high admiral as a briefing. She can decide if she wants to let our allies down below know about it."

Intel Office, Tauran Union Security Force-Balboa, Building 59, Fort Muddville, Balboa Transitway Area, Terra Nova

To the relief of everyone who worked there in Building 59, and every man, woman, child, dog, cat, trixie, *antaniae*, snake and coatimundi who lived on Fort Muddville, the recoilless range, Range 18, was silent. No Chinese water torture of *boom...boom... boomboomboom...boom* was ongoing. Several people, in gratitude, were currently on their knees at the post chapel, thanking God that the Balboans had let off for a while.

For that matter, some noticed, the almost daily sonic booms from the Mosaic-Ds hadn't been heard for a week or so now.

In the office fronted by the balcony that lay toward the Florida Locks and the range beyond that, Sergeant Major Hendryksen and Captain Campbell puzzled over the short and seemingly unimportant piece of intelligence passed on by the fleet orbiting overhead.

"No film," Hendryksen said, "just a synopsis. And that says bad things about Balboan cannon gunnery. Or, at least, whoever wrote it thinks it does."

Jan Campbell asked, "Does it make sense, the synopsis?"

"No," said the Cimbrian, "not entirely. Maybe not at all. It's..."

what you would expect from someone who doesn't really under-stand warfare on the ground—or maybe any warfare—and is unaware of the failing.

"For example, the Balboans fired sixty rounds of what we're taking to be 180mm. About ten percent of those didn't explode. Bad fuses? Incompetent gunners? Maybe some of both. The table says the first five rounds fired from one battery—or one gun; they're not too clear on the difference—failed to detonate, but then the next seven did.

"Now what would cause that?"

"Ma guess," said Campbell, in a softer version of her native accent, "is that somebody who was supposed to pull a safety pin from a super quick fuse got nervous and didna. Then his sergeant beat him about the ears and he didna make the same mistake agin."

"Which could speak well of his sergeant," said Hendryksen.

"Aye."

"And it's as likely a guess as any."

"Aye tae that, too," the blond captain agreed.

"Which doesn't explain to me," said Hendryksen, "why they bothered at all. The ammunition's not that cheap."

"Ohhh. Weel, I think I found the answer to that," she said, "and to a lot of what else makes no sense to us. I dug through one of their manuals. They do damned near everything they do for one or more of five reasons. In this case, it was probably reason five: test the doctrine and equipment. And they'd do that, from what I can tell, just for its own sake."

Hendryksen nodded. "All right, I could buy that. The short version is that, so far as anyone can tell, the firing meant noth-ing and proved nothing."

"Correct," Jan said.

"Any—you should pardon the expression—nibbles on the bait you provided?"

Campbell looked down at her chest and said, "No, and as magnificent as these girls are, I canna hardly understand it."

CHAPTER FIVE

The persistence with which social scientists have
confused war with the tools of war would be no less
astounding did their writing not reveal . . . complete
ignorance of the simpler aspects of military history. It
would be hard to find a noncommissioned officer in the
professional armies of the second rate powers who has
been as confused as most analysts of human society.

—Harry Turney-High,
Primitive War

Estado Mayor, **Balboa City, Balboa, Terra Nova**

It had taken Fernandez about two days to find out who the new
Anglian Army captain was, the one who had put on a minor
show for Carrera and his boy. He'd just now found the time to
think on it, what with having to find a way to get an operative
into *Cerro Mina*'s Quarters 16.

"But the question," he said to an empty office, "is *why* she
bothered. And the possible reasons for that range from the sordid
to the sublime."

It was actually frustrating that, while both armed forces had the
other infiltrated, the retrieval of personal information was uneven.
Fernandez had a senior clerk in the Tauran Union Security Force
on his payroll but, since the genuine records were maintained by
any of the twenty-seven-odd departments of defense and defence
in the TU, and since the local force had little power over the
personnel of those armed forces, only synopses of personnel

records were available. Fernandez could get a synopsis quickly, but it remained just a broad brush, with none of the details that normally made his job so fascinating.

Conversely, so far as he could tell, the one private and one corporal on the Tauran Union's payroll, one of whom had been turned and the other of whom was already slated to be shot on the outbreak of hostilities, could produce for the enemy a complete record on most people in the legion in a matter of a few days or weeks. But those two were overwhelmed with personnel information requests and, as suggested, fifty percent of what they sent the TU intel office had serious disinformation contained therein.

Fernandez looked down once again at the almost bare file, the synopsis, on Anglian Army Captain Jan Campbell and cursed.

Still, I can tell some things. What can I infer from the fact that she was a late entry officer, taking a commission after a long career as an enlisted woman?

Hmmm; I've met a fair number of Anglian officers. Some are fine. Others are the kind of human material that has one clicking one's knitting needles and muttering, "Aha, guillotine!" She surely saw enough of both types, but probably put up with all too many of the guillotine bait.

Or maybe she was one of those women attracted by power. In many ways that would be ideal.

"Ah," Fernandez mused, "what a coup it would be to turn an officer in their intel office! What a solid coup!"

Ah, well, for now we'll leave the ball in the blonde's court. If she really wants to turn, she'll find a way. That much, at least, I can glean from the synopsis.

Still, might be useful to offer her some way to get in contact with us. Hmmm... I think maybe I'll buck this one up to Carrera.

Reluctantly, Fernandez folded the thin copy of Campbell's file and turned to more pressing matters. *So, Patricio's being forced to back off from the Taurans. Already, he's cancelled overflights and explosions. How very dull that will be. So what can I do to openly support what he's been ordered to do, while still setting us up the better to prosecute a war...?*

Training Area C, *Academia Militar Sergento* Juan Malvegui, west of *Puerto Lindo*, Balboa, Terra Nova

More so than in the Federated States or Secordia, somewhat more so than in the Tauran Union, fast going amorally familistic, life in Balboa tended to run informally and as much by connections as by rules. Thus, for example, Lourdes Nuñez-Cordoba de Carrera and Caridad Morales-Herrera de Cruz were good friends and had been since the day both their men had boarded aircraft for the war with Sumer. When Caridad, with a troublesome pregnancy about five years back, had needed an arrogant doctor browbeaten, Lourdes had made a call and had a long chat with a very humbled doctor. Now, when Lourdes had a son in a military school where Ricardo Cruz was temporarily instructing, Cara had made a call. Following that, Cruz had had a long chat with Lourdes' son.

His father tended to treat all legionaries as moral equals, but centurions as social equals, as well. This made them minor gods to damned near everybody. Even Ham, who had grown up around them, tended to treat the centurions with vast respect and no little deference.

"Relax," said First Centurion Ricardo Cruz to the boy standing at attention in front of his desk. Seeing that "relax" had only gotten the boy to parade rest, he pointed at a camp chair and ordered, "Sit."

"Yes, Centurion." The boy more or less jumped into the camp chair and sat. At attention.

Cruz was tempted to pick up his badge of office, his stick, and wave it in the boy's face until he, in *fact,* relaxed. *Ah . . . no, that won't work. Hmm . . . what will? Ah.*

Leaning back in his chair, Cruz plopped his booted feet on the desk. "I said, 'relax,' cadet, and I meant, 'relax.' So relax."

"Yes, Centurion," Ham answered. He managed, at least, to slouch a little in the chair.

"The first peer reviews have been tabulated," Cruz announced formally. It was a silly statement and he knew it was a silly statement. *Everyone* knew the peers were done.

At the words, though, Ham went from slouching in his chair to sinking into it. He seemed nearly to melt.

"I'm at the bottom of my section, right?"

Cruz nodded.

"So, father or not, I'm going to get the boot, right."

"Wrong," the centurion answered. "Peers are for the information of the leadership cadre and are nonbinding on them. Or didn't you know that?"

Shaking his head, Ham said, "No...I...all of us thought they were binding."

"Puhleeze!" said the centurion. "Like we're going to let thirteen-year-olds decide the futures of honest-to-God, actual human beings? Your father and I may look stupid, boy, but only when we drink and even that takes a while."

"Oh."

"But we do use them, and not always in ways that are obvious." He decided to leave that last as a mystery.

"For example, without attribution, let me read you a few comments from your fellow cadets: 'When I needed help, where was he?' 'Pushy; tries to do too much.' 'Too good to talk to the rest of us.' 'Talks down to us.' Worst of all, this one: 'I can't believe this snob is the child of our *Dux Bellorum*.'"

With each sentence, Ham sank a little deeper into the chair. "But...but..."

Cruz sighed. "But they're all bullshit, son. I've watched you for the last couple of weeks closely. The *only* one of those that has any relationship to reality was the 'too good to talk to the rest of us' one. And that wasn't because you think you're too good, was it?"

The boy's voice was breaking as he answered, "No. It's because I don't know what to say. I never had to talk to regular kids before...not as one of them. That's why the old man sent me here."

"That's one of the reasons, yes," Cruz concurred. "There are others. Tell me, Ham, do you like the other kids in your section?"

"Some yes, some no. Mostly I don't really know them."

"They don't know you, either."

"I suppose not. They only know about me."

"No," Cruz countered. "They don't know a damned thing about you past your name. They know what they *imagine* about you: rich boy, powerful family, never had to do anything for himself, spoiled, soft..."

And that last was about all Ham could take. His eyes flashed. "Soft? Soft?! Jesus Christ, Centurion, I was in my first firefight when I was nine years old! And I *won*, too. I was living in a camp at the war, getting mortared about every third day, when I was three! And you think it's easy growing up under a father who's never happy, never content, who always expects more?"

"Yes," Cruz said, "I knew all that. I was in the same camp, son. Or camps. But *they* don't, and you can't just tell them."

Again, the boy deflated, anger spent. "What am I going to do, Centurion?"

"Mostly," Cruz replied, "you're going to have to figure it out for yourself, with a different approach for everyone or, at least, everyone that matters. But for the group and in the main, I want you to try three things. Number one, don't talk about yourself, ask them about themselves. Number two, help them when they need help. Once. Don't worry about offending them. If they don't object, you can keep helping. If they do, fuck 'em; don't help anymore. And number three, if you need to, pick one and beat his ass.

"You would be surprised how often getting along depends on the willingness to beat someone's ass."

Prey Nokor, Cochin, Terra Nova

Cochin was important to Balboan defense. It had a place in research and development. It was involved in a certain amount of arms funneling, manufacture of sundry odd items of military utility, and provision of training. That latter included both advisors to the legion and in training for the legion—pilots and sappers, especially—within Cochin. It was also creating a few important systems from plans drawn up by *Obras Zorilleras*. Since the legion had money while Cochin aspired to rise *to* poverty someday, they'd have been willing to do still more. The limit was in how much could be done there without attracting unwanted attention.

On the surface, the ship looked like just another Ro-Ro. It was only when one went inside and looked that one became impressed with the power hidden within. And, after that, when one thought about how that power had gotten inside, without it being obvious, one became very impressed.

"It was a labor of love," said Terry's Cochinese guide, Commander Nguyen. "We hate the fucking Gauls and figure you'll use this against them."

Terrence Johnson had met Nguyen on his arrival in Cochin two weeks prior. Since that time, besides dealing with some bureaucratic intricacies peculiar to paranoid and quasi-communist states, he had inspected the ship known so far only as the ALTA (*Armada Legionario, Transporte de Assalto*). He had acquired some under-standing of ship-to-shore attacks during the counter–drug war in La Palma Province. Since that time he had studied more on the subject.

Johnson was extremely impressed by the amount of thought that had gone into modifying the ships, and said so.

"Labor of love," Nguyen had repeated, lifting his breathing mask to speak. The mask was necessary as the entire deck was flooded with nitrogen gas to preserve both the launchers and their rockets.

Walking Terry through the missile deck of the modified Ro-Ro, Nguyen pointed out blast shields, controls, and back-up controls. On that missile deck seventy-three thirty-centimeter multibarreled rocket launchers, minus the heavy trucks that normally carried them, had been mounted with their tops flush with the top deck. In this form, though the rockets were pricey, the elevating and traversing mechanisms were not all that expensive while the launch tubes were almost frightfully cheap.

Nguyen's finger traced the tell-tale lines above each launcher. "We've got shipping containers above to hide the marks in the deck that show where the launchers will rise to fire. They're empty and will rise up with the launcher covers, then fold down onto them."

The mechanisms that would raise the launchers and move them through their limited traverse were protected behind armor plating. Also at the missile deck level the starboard side of the ship had been cut away and replaced with blow-out panels to vent away the explosive power of the rockets that drove the missiles to a range of over ninety kilometers. Likewise the decks above and below had been reinforced. Johnson noted that the ship could only fire to the port, or left.

Nguyen then led Johnson to the deck just below the missile deck. There he removed his mask and said Terry could do the same.

Johnson saw twenty-eight helicopters, three-quarters troop carriers and one-quarter gunships. Those were all contained in plastic sheeting. He suspected, even before Nguyen confirmed it, that the helicopters had had their air replaced with nitrogen under their plastic covers.

A long ramp led up from the hangar deck to the top deck, which was covered by hydraulically moved decking. There were vehicles on the hangar deck to pull the helicopters up the ramp. Along both sides were elevators for moving ordnance from the magazine to the hangar deck.

The next two decks down had living quarters for a small tercio of infantry and their supporting troops, some space being taken up by containers. Nguyen had some Cochinese open several of the containers, chosen by Terry at random, to insure they held what their labeling said.

In the rear of the ship was a closed ramp, not too different from the bow of an Old Earth style LST, except for being in the rear where it would not be subject to the full force of an angry sea.

Behind the ramp sat six Volgan-built hovercraft, each capable of carrying upwards of fifty men with their supplies and equipment. These, too, were protected from the salt and water by sheeting and nitrogen gas. They would be able to leave their deck and make for the sea along the ramp once it was lowered to the water.

Impressed as he was, Terry still had his doubts. "How the hell did you manage to do this without anyone the wiser?" Johnson was, in fact, sure that no one outside the legion and Cochin knew about the ALTA, if only because the assembly of such awesome raiding power would have meant an international, if not indeed interplanetary, shit storm. And that hadn't happened.

Nguyen smiled wickedly. "Trade secret. But consider how good we were at hiding things from your native country's best efforts during your war here."

Terry nodded soberly. It was true enough, the Cochinese had driven the Federated States armed forces batshit insane for better than a decade. "How about the other three?" he asked.

"Those are easier, so they are a lower priority," Nguyen replied. "They're almost ready, even so."

Turonensis, Republic of Gaul, Tauran Union, Terra Nova

Reconnaissance wasn't really Khalid's main line of work. Oh, sure, he'd had all the courses Fernandez's department had to offer, plus a few from the line elements of the legion. But . . . really . . . *anybody can do recon. My specialty is assassination, and not just anybody can do that. Still, I suppose the chief has his reasons. Actually, I think I know what they are: Do triple duty, find targets, set up a few cells of terrorists who think I am one of them, and get to*

*know my way around in the areas I am going to operate in if...
when...war breaks out.*

A Druze from Sumer, Khalid had entered the legion in a
roundabout way. Having lost family to terror, he'd been recruited
for counter-terror. In this, he'd proven skilled enough—remarkably
skilled, really, and ruthlessly imaginative, to boot—that his contract
had been transferred from Carrera's ally, Sada, to Fernandez. With
that employment had come new training, a new face—several new
faces, actually, over the years; right now he had blue eyes and
red hair—and for the most part the most difficult assignments.
Want a grotesquely fat cinematic moral gangster to suffocate on
film under a neck-wrapped plastic bag? Khalid was your man.
Want a sewer cover explosively driven more or less up the ass
of a family member of the enemy? Oh, Khalid? Need a corrupt
female journalist terrorized into toeing the legion's line? *I would
have been hurt if you had assigned anyone else to the bitch.*

Khalid had worked for Fernandez, the legion, and Balboa for
many years now. In that time he'd had close comrades from the
legion. The sister of one of those was now Khalid's wife and the
mother of his children. He'd grown used to Balboa's green, at
least twenty percent as sacred to his own faith as it was to the
Islam from which important elements of that faith had sprung.

Like nearly all Druze, Khalid was fiercely loyal to his countries, first Sumer and now Balboa, so long as said country did
not oppress the Druze. In Zion, for example, formed by Israelis
enticed away or deported from Old Earth, the most Zionist group
in the country were the Druze. Also in Zion, Druze who were
citizens of bordering countries occupied by Zion gave up not a
bit of their loyalty to the countries of their birth. A small people
the Druze may have been, but they were mighty of heart, courageous, and trustworthy, for all that. Better, they were, in a famous
poet's famous words, "Few, but apt in the field."

Khalid was of that ilk. He had never yet voted in a Balboan
senatorial or presidential election, and would not until released from
service by Legate Fernandez. But it was still...it had become...
his country. And, on his country's behalf, he was a *fine* assassin.

Or saboteur, Khalid thought, *if that's what Fernandez wants.
Though it's funny that they have me reconning, and getting twelve-
digit grids for, power stations, airplane factories, windows in same,
key cranes at shipyards, bridges...everything...except nuke plants*

and nuclear weapons sites. I guess Fernandez or his boss figures nukes are just that step too far.

Actually, though, Khalid's purview was restricted to certain provinces in Gaul, Castile, and Sachsen. Other people—he knew no names and knew better than to rely on alterable faces—had other areas, in those countries and in other countries. Still others checked behind the primary operatives, so Khalid surmised.

Aiming a small laser range finder from his rental car toward a window in a four-story office building that housed the management for a trucking firm, Khalid took down the range in his notepad, then consulted his military-grade Global Locating System receiver for the grid. *2197 meters . . . 004121482337 . . . up 4.5 meters.*

Lastly, he took a final series of digital pictures of the nearest wall before starting his engine and driving off. Tomorrow he'd come back for an appointment with the human resources people of the trucking firm, so he could make an assessment of interior vulnerability.

Sound Studio, *Canal Siete, Ciudad* Balboa, Terra Nova

The studio had been pretty thoroughly trashed during the fighting in and around the Pigna coup. Carrera and Parilla could have just let the channel go off the air. Still, it hadn't been the owners' faults that an unwittingly renegade unit of the legion had taken it over. So repairs had been made at government expense.

Still, if Parilla was generous hearted, Carrera very rarely gave anything without strings. Sometimes the strings were in plain sight, at other times hidden. In the case of Channel Seven, those strings—mostly hidden—included it becoming a de facto arm of the legion, of *Television Legionario*, hence heavily into propaganda.

In one little, really fine, really hard to see string, the studio was making audio recordings in several languages, all of women, all of whom had very sweet and sexy voices.

Lourdes, for example, spoke excellent French and English, while Artemisia McNamara had both her native Spanish and fair Italian from her modeling days. Two girls who might be useful if the legion ever formed a *Tercio Amazona* would be doing the honors in German and Portuguese. Currently—rank, even hidden rank, having its privileges—it was Lourdes doing the recording.

The sound chief shook his head, slightly. "Given the message, *Señora* Carrera, and what your husband seems to want to accomplish within it, I think we need to get the excitement completely out of it, to make your message initially no different in tone from 'Please wash your hands before leaving the lavatory.' And then turn *imperative* right at the end. Does that make sense?"

Lourdes giggled over the chief's little joke, then answered, "I think that's probably right. Shall we try again?"

"Please."

Sitting upright to relax her diaphragm and get maximum clarity thereby, Lourdes spoke into the microphones in front of her, "*Votre attention s'il-vous-plaît, je suis une bombe à retardement de cinq minutes. Votre attention s'il-vous-plaît, je suis une bombe à retardement de cinq minutes. Veuillez évacuer la zone. Je suis une bombe à retardement de cinq minutes. Veuillez évacuer la zone. Je suis une grande bombe à retardement de cinq minutes. Mon délai de détonation a été fixé au maximum à cinq minutes mais pourrait bien y être inférieur. Sortez d'ici sur-le-champ. Quatre minutes cinquante-cinq . . . quatre minutes cinquante . . . une minute . . . cinquante-neuf . . . cinquante-huit . . . cinq . . . quatre . . . trois . . . deux . . . adieu.*"

"And that's a wrap. Mrs. McNamara? Your turn."

CHAPTER SIX

Evil and madness are not synonyms. Societies that cannot distinguish between the two are destined to get more of both.

—Jonah Goldberg

Estado Mayor, Balboa City, Balboa, Terra Nova

Terry Johnson had brought back with him from Cochin a video disc prepared by Siegel, now on his third research and development tour in Cochin. Interestingly, Sig's now freed former slave, Han, was still with him.

Carrera, Parilla, and Fernandez sat in a completely secure and shielded conference room watching the grainy video on a wide screen television. The grains disappeared to be replaced by a clear image of Siegel, centered on screen. Behind him a diminutive Cochinese—male, so not Han—was tethering a goat to a stake in the ground.

"Hello, sir," Siegel's picture said. "I know you can't come here and we sure as hell can't test fire one of these things in Balboa, so I'm sending you this video by courier to let you see what it's capable of... or not."

Siegel began walking as he spoke. He wavered across the screen. Plainly his cameraman was inexpert. "It isn't as good as we hoped. Let me tell you that right up front. 'Why not' I hear you ask. Just this, it isn't a straight line progression in power from a five-hundred-pound Fuel Air Explosive bomb to a fifty-thousand-pound FAE. This big boy uses up all the oxygen in the immediate area and then stops exploding because there isn't any more oxygen for the misted fuel to react with. We've solved that problem partly by making it multichambered, with some chambers containing pure liquid oxygen to continue to feed the explosion after the air is gone and partly by addition of some enhanced high explosive the Cochinese got from the Volgans, along with ethylene oxide and powdered aluminum. That helps but we're still not getting a one-hundredfold straight increase in power from the five-hundred-pounder.

"There are other problems. Because the thing explodes into half a sphere a lot of the explosion is wasted up where there are no people. In any event, for all that bang you get an area on the ground with about a four times bigger radius than you would get with just a five-hundred-pound bomb. That's not much bang for the buck, is it?

"On the plus side, the visual impact, especially from someone standing a good distance away, is as near to a nuke as I ever want to be. Well, I'll show you."

The cameraman had obviously stopped filming, because the image cut out and then changed to a completely different scene. Siegel began to speak again. "We've put about fifty animals, pigs, goats, monkeys...one water buffalo, at different ranges from the bomb. Some of those are in bunkers, some in armored vehicles. The Cochinese wanted to give me a condemned man in place of the water buffalo. It would have been a lot cheaper but I said 'No' anyway. I hope you don't mind but I bought the condemned prisoner from them. He might be useful...a thief, they say; name of Nguyen." Sig gave off a small laugh. "If you didn't know, boss, everybody here is named Nguyen, just about.

"Anyway, the bomb is about three kilometers from here. That will give you a pretty good visual shot of its detonation..." Siegel consulted his watch "...in about two minutes." Pointing at a tripod, Sig ordered, "Tranh, lock down the camera."

Again the scene changed, this time to a small hill off in the distance. A large cylinder dominated the hill.

Suddenly the hill was shaken with an explosion. A dozen or so sparklerlike things traced up and out across the image. Within a fraction of a second the first explosion was swept away by one altogether of an order of magnitude, or perhaps several, greater than the first. The fuel had reached the sparklers.

The second explosion grew and grew. Trees were blown down

or uprooted near it and tossed outward. The camera shook in its mount. Then the explosion receded, sucking back everything it had thrown out and more. A mushroom cloud began to form, rising past the upper field of view of the camera.

Siegel came back onto the screen, the cloud still rising behind him. "As I said, it's a lot like a nuke.

"We've also tested the seismic detonators you want, using an equivalent charge to the high explosive in a normal 180mm shell at the normal range probable error. There are also delays that can be set by retreating troops so that the detonators aren't set off prematurely by either our fire or an enemy's." The screen went briefly black.

The next scene was of an armored vehicle. Carrera, but not Parilla, recognized it as an old Federated States M14. The hatches were partly open. Siegel climbed on top and completely opened the commander's hatch. The camera stopped and shifted again to point down the hatch. Inside lay three dead pigs.

"I don't know what killed these. It's maybe twenty minutes since we set off the mine. There isn't a mark on them, so it's possible they suffocated. But it was more likely the concussion. I won't know for sure until I look at the video made by a camera I've got inside the tank, assuming it survived, that is." The scene shifted again.

"Now here," said Siegel, pointing his finger into the firing port of a bunker, "is almost certainly a concussion kill." The camera showed a dead goat on the floor on the fighting position. "This is about five hundred and fifty meters from where we set off the bomb.

"I won't bother showing you any more dead animals. Take it from me, everything within about five hundred meters of the mine is dead as shit.

"One other thing, though. I remembered an old project the FS Army had going for a while before they killed it. You probably couldn't see it but I put several mines, some antitank, some antipersonnel, at various distances up to five hundred meters from the explosion. It set off *almost* every one. Might be useful for clearing paths through friendly minefields, if you're ruthless enough for it.

"Anyway, the Cochinese can make these for us at a reasonable cost, considering that the mines have gotten more complex since we had to add the liquid oxygen. How you're going to fix it so we can emplace these and then fill them up I leave to you. I don't have enough details of the plans.

"Oh, yeah. The barrage balloons are in production now, though you still need to find a good source of helium. Would hydrogen work? I know its flammable but, what the hell, you told me these are throwaways.

"The balloons work pretty well. We tested the cable against an old wing from an FSAF fighter. At seven hundred knots the wing was royally screwed up before the cable broke. If it had been the plane moving rather than the cable, the plane would have come down.

"I've done everything you sent me here to do, boss."

"So can I come home now?"

The tape ended.

Carrera wrote down in his notebook, since he trusted electronic devices not at all, "Cut orders returning Warrant Officer Siegel to the Republic of Balboa...effective in one month...at his discretion, six weeks."

Parilla looked shocked by the test. Normally quite dark, his face had gone pale. It wasn't that the president was a stranger to violence. That, he most certainly was not. And he was also one of a *very* few people in Balboa who knew the country was a nuclear power. But it seemed to him just too risky to threaten the Taurans—some of whom also had nukes—with anything that even looked like one.

He began, "Patricio..."

"Mr. President," answered Carrera, "with all due respect, can it. Those things are not to threaten anybody with. They're to use when we'll be in a position to reveal that we're a lot more dangerous than they think. And I've backed off from provoking them. I will *not* back off from preparing what I expect to result from that."

"On that note," said Fernandez, "I've got some unpleasant news. Firstly, the Taurans *have* taken our restraint as a sign of weakness. They are going to begin to fuck with us in eight days. 'Operation Carbuncle,' they're calling it."

"Define fuck with us," the president ordered.

"Just what you would expect, Mr. President; midnight alerts, troops massing in assault positions, overflights of armed aircraft... pretty much anything that will cause us to get troops out of bed, anything that will cause those troops to get out of hand and do something stupid, so that they can justify an attack."

Parilla shook his head. "I don't get it. We had them cowed. What's changed?"

Though his baser nature might have tried to pin the blame on Parilla's newly found sense of restraint, Carrera had to answer, honestly, that that wasn't it. "They haven't had time yet to even realize how far we've backed off so that they could be emboldened by it. No, I think it's that bitch of a high admiral."

Parilla shot a glance at Fernandez.

"That's his guess," the latter said, "not mine. I frankly don't understand it at all. We know she's been down here, though, so the *Duque* might be right. I've been trying to get someone in the house they assigned her but, so far, all I've been able to do is get a groundskeeper on the next street over.

"There is something I want to try, though, gentlemen, and it's something that might serve my purposes as well as your own, to the extent those differ tactically."

As Fernandez's weasel face split in a grin, Carrera asked, "What?"

"You recall the large breasted Tauran who put on a display for you and your son, Patricio?"

"Hard to forget."

"It wasn't hard to find out who she is, a Captain Jan Campbell, an Intel type, seconded here from the Anglian Army. I want to invite her and a male escort of her own choosing to spend a full annual training period with one of our fully mobilized infantry tercios. We'll let her see everything to do with that tercio, just as it is. If there's anything I can think of that would incline the Taurans to peace, it's full realization of just how much blood we'll draw, even if they come against us with everything they have.

"Then, too . . . it's just possible we might be able to turn her if we got close contact with her."

Parilla, who was by no means a starry-eyed, pacifist fool, asked Carrera, "What will that do to your plans, if it still comes to war?"

Carrera shrugged, "Nothing really. We're pretty good—better than Helvetians or Zionis, anyway—and the proof that we are is there for anyone with eyes to see. If they don't see it, it will be because they don't want to. If they do see it, it might, as Omar says, lead to fear which might lead to peace.

"In short, while I am not enthusiastic, if you order it, Raul, I won't object or interfere."

Parilla thought in silence for a few minutes, then announced, "I think it's an acceptable risk for peace. But Patricio? Make it a really frightful regiment that we show off."

Isla Real, Balboa, Terra Nova

For most things that most armies on the planet would have used a helicopter for, the legion usually used Crickets. These were very short takeoff and landing propeller-driven, fixed-wing aircraft that could do ninety or ninety-five percent of what a small helicopter could at a still smaller fraction of the cost. The things could actually hover if facing into a stiff breeze. They had to be staked down in high winds—that, or have their wings folded back—to prevent them from taking off on their own.

Carrera's Cricket landed on the main parade field at what had once been the entire legion's island home. The pilot taxied in under trees to where a small and unobtrusive vehicle waited. As Carrera was boarding the vehicle, the Cricket pilot was already folding and locking the wings.

Carrera gave the driver, a corporal provided by Eighth Legion (Training), the building number he wanted to go to. It was a small research facility that mostly served to mask the entrance to one of the island's major underground forts.

When the legion had purchased five Suvarov Class cruisers for eleven million FSD—Federated States Drachma—from the Volgan Republic, it had insisted on them retaining all arms and equipment. The Volgans had at first balked, being too weak and poor at the time to lightly risk the wrath of the Federated States or even the gentler Tauran Union. But when one cruiser was delivered and promptly cut up for scrap, they had decided they could plausibly deny they were selling major warships to Balboa.

The sixteen turrets of the four scrapped cruisers, each mounting three 152mm guns, had not been cut up. After delivery of the last ship the legion had had the turrets mounted in concrete positions. Some of these were mounted inside of, or on, old Federated States coastal artillery positions.

Left undecided was the fate of each Suvarov's laser range finders. These were powerful—much more so than tank laser range finders—and *extremely* dangerous to human eyes. The lasers sat in a warehouse for some years, gathering dust, until at length the section of *Obras Zorilleras* responsible for developing air defense doctrine and equipment had decided that there was much merit in attacking the pilot if one couldn't attack his plane with impunity or effectiveness.

Then someone remembered the old Suvarov lasers. It was known, in some circles, that the former Volgan Empire had been far ahead of the west in directed energy weapons—lasers, charged particle beams, and possibly masers.

Tests were carried out on otherwise condemned prisoners, before they were hanged. At six thousand meters the men were blinded, instantly and irreparably, even if they were looking to the side. If the victims were directed, under duress, to look directly in the direction of the unseen lasers, they were blinded at a much greater distance. Mercy killings followed each test, killings far more merciful than the now harsh Balboan law typically dished out.

The next steps had been to mount the lasers on carriers, install electrical generating systems capable of serving them in action, and determine an acceptable means of target acquisition . . . without any of that becoming known to the world at large.

The Project was called "Self-Propelled Laser Air Defense," or SPLAD, for short. They'd had the lasers, stripped out of the Suvarovs, for quite a while. They'd been towed systems, though, obvious as to what they were, incapable of firing on the move, indeed, requiring a fair amount of time to set up, and highly vulnerable, once an enemy knew what to look for.

The holdup in mechanizing them had been power. There was only so much cube inside an armored vehicle, and only so much power generation or storage capability that could be installed therein.

Carrera's escort was Balboan, one of a small but growing number of homegrown engineers.

The first stop on the briefing tour was an armored vehicle, indistinguishable at first glance from any of the three hundred or so self-propelled, multibarreled air defense systems the legion had bought from Volga.

The engineer said, "We gave a lot of thought to what should be the chassis of the system. We finally decided that this was our best choice. This was not because it was the most common system in the legion. Of course, it isn't. But we don't see the need for a great deal of armor for these, and the air defense units that will use it already have expertise in supplying and maintaining them.

"I've got to tell you up front, *Duque*," said the escort, as he waved a hand at the squarish fighting vehicle, "that we haven't beaten the power problem so much as accepted some serious limits."

"But where's the laser?" Carrera asked.

The engineer climbed on top, reaching a hand—which Carrera scorned—down to help his chief climb aboard.

"It's inside," the engineer said, once his chief was in position to look down into the turret. "The guns are only the barrels. We cut out the receivers and mounted the main laser centered between where they were, with the acquisition laser offset from that. That round plate opens up to fire.

"By doing that, we were able to dump the ammunition and free up a lot of space for power generation and storage. Enough that we can fire the main laser half a dozen times at full power before having to recharge the capacitors to fire again."

"Do we need to fire at full power?" Carrera asked. "All the time?"

"Probably not," the engineer admitted.

With Carrera peering down into the dark interior, the escort pointed at a small box mounted above the main laser and offset to the right.

"That's the low powered acquisition laser, *Duque*. In use, the gunner will aim that at his target, either visually or via the radar. It, when it gets a bounceback signal that says 'not clouds, birds, or balloons,' actually fires the main...gun.

"Sir, if you would climb inside with me?"

The engineer and Carrera crawled down separate hatches, into the interior of the vehicle. Carrera took the rearward-stationed commander's seat, allowing the gunner's seat to the engineer.

"Like I said, *Duque*, we have removed all the ammunition storage except for the top-mounted machine guns. In their place are two generators and a whole shitpot of supercapacitors."

The engineer turned away from the generator and batteries. He indicated two boxes, one with a control panel, one with a small television screen. "These are a fairly cheap thermal imager and a computer. We bought the imager from the Volgans. They're just beginning to turn them out in mass...and they're not all that good. They are rather cheap, however, and good enough to spot an aircraft with no background but sky and space.

"There are three ways to make the system work. One is manual. This way the gunner picks up an aerial target on the thermals. He then manipulates the turret to bring the less powerful laser on line with the target. Of course, the lesser laser must be borescoped to the sight. It is also projected continuously if the gunner so selects. When the gunner has moved the cross hairs approximately onto the target, the lesser laser will get some energy bounced back from its own beam. It will then automatically fire the more powerful laser. And the pilot's eyeballs will be ... well, fried, more or less.

"The second way is more automatic. And we still haven't perfected it. That's what this computer is for. We hope to make it so that, when the thermal sight picks up a target, it will notify the computer. Then the computer will direct the main laser onto the target without need of the gunner."

For the first time, Carrera interrupted. "Can that. It's a silly idea."

Undeterred, the engineer answered, "It's true, we don't need that feature for now; the manual method works well enough. But what we hope to do someday is to mount the thermal on top, where the old radar dish is, then have it sweep three hundred sixty degrees until it finds a target with enough heat to be a possible target. Then the computer will automatically bring the main projector around, the ranging laser will fire to get a reflection that indicates the target is acquired. At that point the main laser will fire to blind the crew. Sir, this would be a much better weapon."

"Does the thing work as is?"

"Yes, sir, and we have a third way, which is also automatic. It works, but it *is* risky. That's to let the radar do the tracking and control the turret and lasers."

Carrera thought about that and decided, *It's actually a fairly minor mod—gunnery-wise—so it probably does work.*

"What about if the pilot is wearing some kind of night vision goggles or extremely thick and dark sun glasses?" he asked.

"We'd burn out the image intensifier tube in the goggles and any set of sunglasses capable of stopping all the possible frequencies we can use wouldn't just be dark. They would be black."

"Then produce it. Skip the fancy frills on this model. Produce it and I may cut you enough research and development money to continue trying the other, the second, way. But first, show me how this one works in action."

CHAPTER SEVEN

"Will you walk into my parlour?" said the Spider to the Fly,
"'Tis the prettiest little parlour that ever you did spy;
The way into my parlour is up a winding stair,
And I've a many curious things to shew when you are there."

"Oh no, no," said the little Fly, "to ask me is in vain,
For who goes up your winding stair
—can ne'er come down again."

—Mary Howitt, "The Spider and the Fly"

**Building 59, Tauran Union Security Force-Balboa,
Fort Muddville, Balboa Transitway Area, Terra Nova**

"Bullshit," said Hendryksen to Campbell, as she waved—Fernandez didn't lack for a sense of drama—a gilt-engraved invitation, in good English, for her and a male escort of her choosing to spend a full month with Second Infantry Tercio, during the annual training. "Let me see that."

She handed over the invitation, then arched her back ever so slightly. Looking down she said, "Aye, lassies, ye did it."

"I doubt it was them," said Hendryksen, rolling his eyes eloquently.

"You leave me ma own delusions and I'll leave you yours," Campbell retorted.

"Sure," he said, with bad grace. "You realize you're going to need de Villepin's approval, right?"

De Villepin was the Gallic chief of intelligence for the Tauran

Union Security Force-Balboa, and their local superior. In fact, he had little direct power over anybody not in the Gallic Army, and had to really work at it, as did General Janier, to *influence* the army for which they really did work.

"Oh, teach yer mither to suck eggs, Kris; I *know* how a military bureaucracy works, yes. You want to be ma escort?"

"I'd love to," he said, "but the Frogs are going to want a Frog."

"Fock!" was all she could say to that prospect.

"It will be all right provided they give you an enlisted man or noncom," Hendryksen assured her. "Tell you what, though; I will give you a list of questions I'd like answers to. Hmmm...what date did they give you?"

Campbell rechecked the invitation, then did a little figuring in her head. "Thirty-seven days from today."

"Don't count on doing it then. His Gribbitzness will be starting Operation Carbuncle before that. About ten minutes after the Balboans realize the rules have changed, and that their current degree of restraint is going unappreciated, they're going to become rather less open and friendly."

"So I'd better accept soon, hadn't I, so that their gentlemanly instincts will kick in and they'll refuse to disappoint a lady."

Hendryksen sighed. "There are many words I would use to describe you, Jan, all of them complimentary, but until this moment 'lady' probably would not have been among them."

"Heathen," she answered, with a sniff of pseudo-hurt.

Casa Linda, Balboa, Terra Nova

It had been easy for Ant to find the direction to Hamilcar's new school. She'd simply asked one of the compound's Pashtun Scout guards for the use of a compass so that she could pay proper obeisance to their joint lord daily. That had sounded good enough for the guard that he'd gone to supply and gotten her one to keep, then trained her in how to use it. Thereafter, every evening, she, her co-wives, Hamilcar's sisters (when they could sneak away), and Alena had all gathered in his bedroom at the *casa*, then prostrated themselves in the direction of *Puerto Lindo* and the Sergeant Juan Malvegui Military Academy, praying fervently to be reunited with their god.

Meanwhile, Ant's swimming lessons, her minor thefts of relatively nonperishable food, and her acquisitions of necessary equipment and information continued apace.

But I'm not ready yet, she sighed to herself in the dark. *Not yet. My feet aren't tough enough yet. I don't know the dangerous plants and animals well enough yet. I can't swim well enough yet. And, though I've been practicing, I can't use a map and compass well enough yet.*

But soon.

Training Area C, *Academia Militar Sergento* Juan Malvegui, west of *Puerto Lindo*, Balboa, Terra Nova

It's about time to take some of Centurion Cruz's advice, thought Ham.

It was also dinner time. Better still, dinner was combat rations, rather than the deliberately tasteless crap they usually dished out. Rather, it was combat rations, minus, since the boys were not going to get the rum ration until they were much, much older. The rations had been prepared by the camp cooks, themselves almost all discharged veterans, reservists, or militia. The boys had formed in line to pass through a field kitchen where the cooks had splashed the chow more or less randomly into the trays of their mess kits. Most of the alcohol would probably go into the cooks over the next couple of weeks.

The boys sat on the ground or on fallen logs and upright stumps, wolfing their rations down before the setting sun released a horde of homicidal mosquitoes, some of whom would surely end up stuck in the gravy.

There were eleven other boys in his section. They'd started with fourteen, total, but two were gone already, having left fairly early. The remainder, besides Ham, were Augustino, Belisario—named for Belisario Carrera—Francisco, Jorge, Jose, Oscar, Ramon, Raul—named for the president, though he hadn't been president back then—Roger, Virgil, and Vladimiro.

Ham knew that was the wrong order to alphabetize them into, but, *Screw it. I'm twelve and I think in terms of first names. And it's a little funny that none of them are named for my father. I would have thought . . . but maybe he knows what he's doing by staying out of politics. He's not the most charming guy on the planet, no matter what Mom may think.*

And, speaking of politics...

"Pick one and beat his ass," the centurion said. *Sadly, Centurion Cruz has forgotten the code of honor of boys. I'm bigger than any of them. So it's inherently unfair. But I'm not so big that I can handle two of them. At least, not for sure.*

So it's number one, which is way harder than beating someone's ass.

So who can I get to talk about himself, and how do I start? I should know this, but I never had to learn, because everybody always treated me as special and different or, with my Pashtun, divine. I wonder what they'd say if they knew how much they fucked me over.

Probably something like, "It's for your own good, Lord."

Ah, well, I know they mean well. No ... actually they mean the best.

And now, which one to break the ice with ... ah, Jorge's always seemed fairly reasonable. Jorge, last name Rodrigues, sat alone with his back resting against a tree.

Sitting down on the ground on the next quarter over from Jorge, Ham said, "I was actually in on the testing of this crap."

The boys talked between half chewed gulps.

"Doesn't seem like crap to me," Jorge said.

"Right now, it doesn't to me, either," Ham admitted. "At least it has a taste to it. But when the old man made us all, himself and my mom and sisters included, eat ration *sancocho* for a week straight to see how much we'd learn to hate it, I sure thought it was crap."

"He does that?"

"Every time something in the menu changes," Ham confirmed.

"Must be nice." Jorge said, wistfully. "Nice to always have enough to eat, I mean. That's what's so great about this place; if I get hungry it doesn't last for long before they feed me."

Great? This place? What kind of suckiness do you come from? But ... best to let that go for now. Besides, I knew there were poor people and poor areas, still.

"Where are you from?" Ham asked.

"Little town you never heard of by the sea. No road to it and the trails aren't much. And, yes, before you ask, dirt poor. Not just my family, the whole town. We didn't even have a full-time teacher until the legion put one in about ten years ago. Not much electricity, still, except for some solar power the legion put in so a cell phone—just one in town, and that only for emergencies—a refrigerator, and a single small TV, in the school, could be powered."

Wow. That is *poor. Doesn't sound bitter though.*

"How did you...?"

"End up here?" Jorge finished. "The teacher's a medically retired corporal—missing one foot—who seems to do some recruiting on the side. We had one opening in a military academy allocated to the village, but it wasn't going to go to me. I asked the teacher to help and he pulled a couple of strings and got us another one, here, though it's not close to home. So, also yes, before you ask, I *really* wanted to be here."

"I don't know if I wanted to be here or not," Ham said. "The old man ordered me here and so I went."

"Now *that* sounds rough. Being here when you don't want to be here."

"Didn't say I didn't want to be here," Ham corrected. "Said I didn't know. On the other hand, I *do* know I don't want to piss the old man off, so here I'm going to stay.

"You planning on enlisting when your time here's up?" Ham asked. "You don't have to, you know."

"No," Jorge said, "I know you don't. But I probably will. It's the best way I can think of to never have to go back to my village. You?"

"I don't think I've had a choice about anything once I was potty trained," Hamilcar replied. "So I doubt I'll get a choice about that."

"Bet you didn't get any choice about the potty training, either," Jorge said, with a smile.

That raised a chuckle from Ham. "I can't really remember too much about that but, no, I suspect not. Though I seem to remember my mother with this flexible switch..."

It was the chuckle that did it. *Hmmm...poor little rich boy seems human after all,* thought Jorge.

The latter then stood up and looked down. Yes, Ham had cleaned off his plate as thoroughly as he had, himself. "Seems like eating that for a week didn't make it too nasty."

Ham looked up and answered, "Well, about halfway through I realized this couldn't possibly be the same stuff, since I was sick of that but haven't had hardly enough of this."

"C'mon," said Jorge, reaching a hand down to help Ham to his feet. "Let's go get our mess kits and cutlery cleaned. You *know* what they do to people they catch with dirty kits."

One down, ten to go, thought Ham, as the two young cadets walked to the wash line.

Headquarters, IVth Corps, Cristobal, Balboa, Terra Nova

About forty miles east of where Ham was making his first friend and convert at the Academy, Patricio Carrera walked the lines of one of Jimenez's units, an infantry tercio, conducting a fairly rare in ranks inspection. It was rare because Carrera hated to waste what could have been training time conducting inspections of the troops in garrison. Jimenez had, however, for some reason of his own, requested it. Since Carrera had a strong faith that Jimenez had trained his corps exceptionally well and would not ask without a good reason, he had agreed.

As such things went, the inspection had gone fairly well. Carrera noted few faults, none of them serious. Afterwards, in Jimenez's office, facing the ocean and with a refreshing breeze coming through the open, screened windows, Jimenez had asked if Carrera was willing to entertain an idea, even if it came from a junior enlisted man.

Carrera's eyes narrowed at the tall, whippet thin, coal black senior legate. "Xavier," he asked, "when the fuck have I ever given you the impression that I wouldn't listen to a junior trooper who had something to say?"

"Never," Jimenez admitted. "But you're a lot busier than you used to be and spread a lot thinner on the ground. Things could have changed. God knows, we never see much of you over on this side." Fourth Corps was on the opposite side of the isthmus from the capital and legion headquarters.

"That's half the reason I wanted you to come over here, so the troops could see they're not just a 'lost command.'"

"What's the other half?" Carrera asked.

For answer, Jimenez cast head and eyes toward the door to his office and shouted, "Centurion Candidate Ruiz; *report!*"

The door was flung open by an orderly. Through it, stiffer than his starched uniform, marched a young corporal, shorter than either Carrera or Jimenez, as black as the latter, and broader through the shoulders than either. Carrera noted the miniature insignia on the boy's sleeve marking him as a centurion candidate.

The boy—he couldn't have been more than nineteen—stamped to a halt, then snapped a salute. "Sir, Corporal Ruiz-Jones reports as ordered!"

Carrera returned the salute, more or less casually, then ordered,

"At ease." With that he shot an inquisitive look at Jimenez: *What's this bullshit about?*

"Corporal Ruiz is a sapper, Patricio," Jimenez said. "He has a very interesting idea, one I think you ought to consider carefully and then act on. Corporal Ruiz, show the *Duque*."

The young sapper reached into a pocket and pulled out two or three dozen small magnets. Holding them out in the palm of one hand, to demonstrate, he told Carrera, "Sir, I was reading a couple of months ago about a big push by the Taurans and Secordians to get our world to adopt that Old Earth treaty, the one that bans antipersonnel landmines. One proposal I read—I think it came from the Federated States—was to make all mines detectable, no more plastic jobbies."

The corporal shivered. "Sir, I really love mines, especially the neat little plastic ones—the toe poppers. It bothered me, you know. I mean, sir, what's a sapper without mines?

"So one day I was playing with some of those magnets they use around the orderly room to hold papers to metal desks. And it hit me. Go ahead and make mines detectable from magnetism. But if we issue every mine with a couple of hundred of these little motherfuckers and scatter them about, whoever is looking for the mines will still have to stop and probe and dig for millions of these little suckers before he can be sure there are no mines in the area. After all, a magnetically detectable mine in a magnetized field is still invisible.

"Of course, we'll have to either push these into the ground with some kind of probe or scatter them early enough to sink into the earth on their own. I figured we could call them 'Dianas,' in tribute to the Old Earth princess who they say started the movement back there, but that might give the game away."

Carrera reached out and gently plucked up one of the little magnets from Ruiz's hand. "Won't work," he said. "They've got new mine detectors, ground penetrating radar based, that will see the difference between a magnet and a mine."

"Yes, sir," Ruiz agreed. "I know about those." The corporal then reached into a trouser pocket and pulled out half a dozen flat, metallic can tops. These he spread with his fingers like playing cards. "The new mine detectors won't know the difference between these and a mine, sir.

"And, sir? I really doubt it would be too expensive, and it sure wouldn't take up much space in a crate of mines, if we manufactured thin metal discs like these, but with a magnet in the middle."

Carrera looked at the young man with a touch of wonder. "All really good ideas are simple," he said warmly. He took note of the sapper's name, intending to have an aide enquire into the boy's status for Cazador School and accelerate his course date. Squeezing the sapper's shoulder, he said "This is a *really* good idea, son. We're going to do it. But we're not going to call them 'Dianas.' No, they'll be called 'Ruizes.'"

"Sir, it would be so much funnier if you call them 'Dianas.' Really."

Later, over drinks in Jimenez's officer, Carrera observed, "You would not call me over here just for a morale-building exercise. And you would not call me over here just for an informal briefing from a—need I say really, really, *really* smart—corporal, nor even both of those together. So just what the hell did you have in mind?"

Jimenez smiled, wickedly. "I intended to get to it, but not until you were on your second drink.

"Has the Legionary II shop ever briefed you on personnel issues in Fourth Corps? When you were actually paying attention, I mean?"

"Probably," Carrera answered, "though...I think it's been a while."

"Okay. Well I'll give you the short version," said Jimenez. "I have—it is widely recognized and acknowledged—probably the best Centurionate in the country. I am also roughly twenty-nine percent under even our low allowable strength for officers. Do those two bits of data suggest anything to you, Patricio?"

Carrera waved dismissive fingers. "I hate guessing games. Just tell me the meat of the thing."

"You don't get off that easily, friend.

"Have you also noticed that our world is being run by people who do very well on standardized intelligence tests and then go to the very best schools?"

"Hard not to notice," said Carrera. "Hard not to notice they're running the whole planet into the ground, too."

"You do well on those tests, I am sure," said Jimenez. "I do well on them. And, surely, both of us are at least reasonably bright. But I've got to ask you, Patricio, do we do well on those tests because we are bright, or despite the fact that we're bright? Because most of the people who do well on standardized intelligence tests are, as near as I can figure, incompetent, arrogant morons who are ruining our world. Whatever those tests measure, it is not intelligence, and whatever the schools are delivering that those tests get people into, it is not competence."

Carrera shrugged. "I don't have any necessary argument with that," he said. "But would you *please* get to the point?"

"Sure. Corporal Ruiz-Jones, an obviously hugely bright young man, is on the centurion track rather than the officer track because his IQ test score was only a hundred and fourteen. That's from the legion's own standardized test.

"That may be in part because Cristobal Province was the ass end of the country's educational system until well after the good corporal entered school." Jimenez looked down at the back of his own hand and said, "It could be because us black folk are just stupid. But, in my personal opinion, the evidence for that proposition is somewhat weak. Though it might well be true that, for whatever reason, we do not usually do as well on the tests.

"But I think what we really have going on is a set of bad presumptions and assumptions going into how we measure intelligence. And that's why I have a tremendously bright corporal, who someday ought to be a legate of engineers, about to go to school to become a centurion."

"So," asked Carrera, "you want me to grant him an exemption to go to OCS after Cazador School rather than CCS?"

"That? Well, sure. And—though it's going to sound like some Kosmo-Progressive racial preference, quota system bullshit—I need to start shunting higher IQ centurion candidates to OCS, because they're smarter than their test scores say they are. But I really think we need to move Heaven and Terra Nova to come up with a better way to measure intelligence."

"Let me mull it some," Carrera said.

Carrera's armored Phaeton was framed by armored cars, front and rear. He wasn't a fool; he knew that the Taurans—and probably United Earth, too—would like him dead. And the Pigna coup had been better than any counseling session to demonstrate that he'd been taking his own security too lightly. But it grated on him even so, having to hide behind others.

Oh, well; I didn't make the world, I just have to live in it. That was just a comforting fiction, of course. He intended to remake the world, two of them, if possible.

Jamey Soult asked, as Carrera strapped himself into the Phaeton, "Where to, boss?"

"*Puerto Lindo*, Jamey," Carrera said.

"Going to see to the boy, sir?"

Carrera shook his head. "No, I'll check on him with someone, but I don't want Ham to know I did. Mostly I want to see Chapayev and then swing by and talk to Centurion Cruz.

"And, Jamey, tell me; what in your opinion is intelligence and how do we identify it?"

CHAPTER EIGHT

Any sane person should be instinctively skeptical when all the smart people agree.

—Mark Steyn

Academia Militar Sergento Juan Malvegui, *Puerto Lindo*, Balboa, Terra Nova

Victor Chapayev, slender, middling tall, blond, blue-eyed, and Volgan, was probably the third- or fourth-youngest legate in the legion.

I suppose the adjutant could tell me exactly where he stands, age-wise, thought Carrera, *but who really cares about things like that? It's not like the knowledge would change anything. Besides, I trust both him and his abilities, and that's knowledge enough.*

Carrera had good reason for the trust. After all, he and Chapayev had fought side by side in Santander. More importantly, during the Pigna coup Chapayev's intervention had been instrumental in saving the pro-Balboan Castilian colonel, Muñoz-Infantes. Better still, the Gauls' attempt to get rid of him had prompted the latter to defect, along with his entire regiment—really a reinforced battalion—to Balboa. The defection wasn't entirely open, of course. Muñoz-Infantes' men were still paid and fed by Castile, which pretended that its contribution to the Tauran Union Security Force-Balboa was still under TU command. Personnel replacements, too, were still provided by Castile, but only if vetted and approved of by their colonel on the ground. And he selected only from Castilian soldiers who *detested* the Tauran Union.

Muñoz-Infantes was also Chapayev's father-in-law, which helped mutual trust all around. Moreover, Victor always got the Castilian battalion a generous allocation of tickets to the cadets' game, as well as rides on the buses to those games. The Castilian never mentioned it to anyone, but he had a sneaking suspicion that the massive use of buses bringing the kids to one sporting event or another was a cover—a "*maskirovka*," his son-in-law would have called it—for something else entirely.

Perhaps the best marker of Carrera's trust in Chapayev was that, of six military schools run by the legion, he'd picked Chapayev's to send his boy to.

"Which is an honor, *Duque*," the Volgan said in the school's conference room. "And the boy . . ."

"We'll discuss the kid later," Carrera said. Thunder rolled above, a long rumbling barrage. He held out a hand and felt the first drops of a seasonal deluge begin. "For now I want you to show me the . . . mmm . . . more sheltered aspects of your school."

Chapayev jingled a ring of keys that he never allowed more than arm's reach from his person. "Sure thing, sir."

All of the academy's buildings—offices, mess halls, academics, the auditorium, post exchange, clinic, the twelve cadet barracks, etc.—were connected by tunnels, put in when the school was first built. In addition, a few of the officer and senior NCO quarters were likewise connected to narrow feeder tunnels. Lastly, when the main sewer line had been put in, deep down, above it had been laid yet another tunnel that branched off from the trace of the sewer to emerge in several places in the jungle to the north.

Satisfied with the general layout, Carrera asked, "Class I?" Food. "Class III?" Petroleum, oil, and lubricants. "Class V?" Ammunition. "Class VIII?" Medical supplies.

"Green, green, green, and green," Chapayev answered. "Except for tank ammunition."

"No matter. It's not like you're going to use tanks," Carrera said. "They're really still here only for the cadet tank club."

"Fair enough, *Duque*. And we do have enough for the few Ocelots." The Ocelot was the legion's infantry fighting vehicle, though often pressed into duty as assault guns. It was fitting that the cadet tank club should have some and equally fitting, if they were to be allowed to shoot the cannon, that it be cheaper 100mm shells than expensive 125mm penetrators.

Carrera looked up, suddenly aware that, "I can still hear the rain. Why?"

"We're more than three meters deep," Chapayev replied. "And you saw that I closed the vault doors behind us. But what happens is that the sound gets in the buildings and is transmitted right through the concrete."

"Okay," Carrera said. "I just didn't want the boys buried alive by a Tauran bomb if I can help it."

"They're hypocrites and ruthless, to boot," Chapayev said, then asked, "but do you really think they'd bomb children?"

"Yes," Carrera answered. "Now tell me how you would move the boys out if you had to. Without being noticed, I mean. Just in case the Taurans decided to attack a group of fleeing children, of course."

"Of course, *Duque*," agreed Chapayev, with a knowing smile.

Training Area C, *Academia Militar Sergento* Juan Malvegui, west of *Puerto Lindo*, Balboa, Terra Nova

"*Cabo* Escobar?" shouted Ricardo Cruz, as he closed his folding cell phone. He'd intended to go along with the cadets but sometimes one ran into a higher calling, so to speak.

"*Si, Centurio!*" answered the former narco-guerilla, since recruited, and now assisting his centurion in the training of the young cadets.

"Move the boys out!"

"Yes, Centurion... Cadets... riiighttt... FACE. Fowarrrd... MARCH."

Escobar counted off, "One, two, three, four, left, right, left right," then began a song: "In the morning we rise early—"

The cadets picked the tune up immediately, a few of their immature voices breaking:

> "...Long before the break of dawn,
> Trixies screeching in the jungle,
> Moonbats scurrying from the sun.
>
> Now assemble, *mis compadres*.
> Gather, boys, and muster, men,
> Hand to hand with butt and bayonet,
> Let their blood across the homeland run."

Cruz stood where he was, smiling, watching the cadets' receding backs, until they rounded a turn in the jungle trail. With their disappearance into the jungle's perpetual twilight, he turned around himself and walked past the parking area, itself halfway between camp and the main road to *Puerto Lindo,* then continued on to a little indentation in the jungle.

Cruz saw him there, leaning against a big, black Phaeton, arms folded and a couple of armored cars on guard. *He must have got my number from his wife who got it from mine.*

Cruz reported with a snappy salute, duly and formally returned by Carrera who stood to attention away from the Phaeton for the brief ceremony.

"Anything you absolutely need to be present for, Centurion?" Carrera asked.

Cruz shook his head in negation. "Nothing the corporal I brought with me can't handle, *Duque.*"

"Great. There's a cantina about three miles down the road. Let's go chat."

"Oh, a little chat with the boss, eh?"

Carrera chuckled. "Not like that, Ricardo. But I do want to know about the boy. I do want to know if there's anything— beyond staying out of the way which, you will note, I've been doing—that I can do to help."

The cantina's name was "Miramar" and one could, in fact, see the Shimmering Sea from it. At an unusually high tide one could possibly wash one's feet in the Shimmering Sea from the *bohio* facing the water. A regular tide and it would be a walk of perhaps fifty meters.

For the moment, though, the tide was out. Near the lapping waves—above them too—hopped or flew several species of seagull cognates or cousins. They looked a lot like Old Earth gulls, being rather solid and quite feathery, but retained teeth as well as clawed fingers on each wing. They also sounded a lot like gulls.

With the tide out, the smell of the sea, which was actually the smell of the land—salty and slightly rotten—competed with the flowers and vegetable and animal decay of the nearby jungle. Over all of that was the aroma, by no means unpleasant, of a simmering stew—or possibly a *sopa seca,* a dry soup—hidden from sight by a woven reed wall.

Carrera called for a couple of beers.

As the proprietress was cracking those, Cruz laid his "stick," his badge of office as a centurion, on the table, setting it against the salt shaker to keep it from rolling off. Then he whispered, "Try the *paella de marisco* but stay away from the *empanadas*. Seriously." He made a closed fist thumping the chest gesture: *heartburn.*

"You've been here before?" Carrera asked. He waved the answer off. "Wait; stupid question; of course you have."

Two bottles of cold *Cervesa Legionaria* appeared on the table. No glasses, it was not a glasses kind of place. Carrera and Cruz each ordered *paella de marisco.*

"Found it a couple of weeks ago," Cruz confirmed, "not long after starting cadet training."

"There's no way in Hell for me to keep up with all the transfers, even though we don't do that many, but no one's cut orders permanently moving you to the academy, have they?"

"No, sir," Cruz answered. "I'm still just temporary help. Go back to the Second Tercio in three weeks or so."

"Okay. We'll get back to that. For now though..." And from there silence descended and hung for a bit.

I never would have thought, thought the centurion, *that* el Duque *would ever be at a loss for words.*

"I'm not sure you didn't make a mistake," Cruz said. "Sir."

Carrera sighed. "Neither am I. The boy is...well...he could go either way. He could be my replacement, an asset for the legion and for Balboa or..."

"Or he could be a monster," finished Cruz, then added, "The problem is, though, that this might turn him into a monster. I shudder to think"—and the centurion did, in fact, shudder—"just what it might mean if all he learns here is to manipulate people, without ever learning to care for them, as people."

"That's a possibility, isn't it?" Carrera put his elbows on the table then lowered his head to massage his temples.

"Yes, sir," Cruz nodded, "it's a real possibility. I've seen him do it once, already. At least I *think* I have. He's clever so it's hard to be sure."

"Yeah," Carrera said, "he's clever. So do I pull him out of here or leave him?"

Cruz hesitated. This was not normally one of his failings.

Finally, he said, "Leave him here. If you pull him out now, while he's still teetering between success and failure, he'll assume you've judged him a failure. You'll never get an honest day's use of the boy after that.

"And—since he *is* clever—he's been picking off the low hanging fruit in his section. But it's about to get much tougher from him. The boys he hasn't yet swung over to his side are the middle or upper middle class ones, the self-confident ones, the athletes, and the ones who already have strong military connections."

Cruz took a long pull from his beer, the condensation on the bottle gathering and then running down to drip from his chin. "It's going to be interesting to see anyway."

Carrera agreed, reluctantly, "Okay, I'll leave him here for a while, at least. There's something else, though. You're moving up, aren't you?"

"Yes, sir," Cruz said. "Giving up my maniple and taking over cohort sergeant major for Second of the Second."

"Okay, honest opinion; if you had to judge the best cohorts on the *Mar Furioso* side, which would they be? And then which ones on this side?"

"Including the heavy cohorts by *Lago Sombrero*?" Cruz asked.

"No, just the regular infantry near the terminal cities on each end of the Transitway."

"I can't say I've seen enough to judge," Cruz admitted. "I *can* tell you some that are good. For example, Eighth Tercio, from hereabouts, relieved mine, Second, down in *La Palma* during the drug war. Lotsa snap, lotsa drive, to the Eighth Infantry.

"On my side I'm too self-interested to call a fair judge."

Carrera glared.

"Buuut...Second of the Second or First of the Third. We work with Third Tercio a lot and their first cohort is the one that's most impressed me.

"But, sir, if I may ask, why?"

"Two reasons, only one of which I'll tell you. Parilla wants peace, if at all possible. One of the ways we get peace is to convince the Taurans we're too tough a prospect to attack. So Fernandez has invited them...well, he invited one of them who caught our collective eye...to come and see just how tough a prospect we might be. I'm not going to tell her—"

"Her?"

"Yes, 'her.' Extravagantly 'her.' I'm not going to tell her which units she can see. But I'm not above manipulating the annual training schedule a little so that her choices are limited."

"Ohhh...well, in that case, don't let the Taurans see anybody from the Seventh or the Tenth. The Seventh is still shamefaced and, I think, a little unreliable over their involvement in the Pigna coup. Yeah, you and I both know, *Duque,* that that wasn't their fault. They still feel guilty. And the Tenth Tercio is just frigging weird. In my personal opinion. Sir."

Carrera let that one go. The Tenth Tercio, it was well known, pushed the Roman-ness of the legion to an unusual degree, Caesar's Tenth and all.

"Okay," he agreed, "during the window we have given Captain Campbell, Anglian Army, the Second of the Second, First of the Third, and Third of the Eighth will be training at Imperial Range. That work?"

"Think so, sir," Cruz affirmed. "Best we can do, anyway."

The pair went silent as the *paella* arrived. Cruz, the more religious of the two, crossed himself before picking up a fork. He speared a healthy looking whole shrimp, then held it in front of his face, contemplatively. He rotated the fork in his fingers, examining the shrimp from every angle.

"*Duque,*" Cruz asked, "what if the Taurans don't understand or won't let themselves understand that our cadre is better than theirs and our rank and file, if maybe not as well trained as theirs, technically, is more than willing?"

"I suppose, eventually, we fight. Hmmm...on a related subject, and based only on your own observations, Centurion, what would you say about the relative intelligence between the officers and centurions of your own tercio, or any of those on the *Furioso* side, and the ones here?"

Cruz replied, after a moment's reflection, "Never gave it any thought before. On average, I'd say 'no difference.' But I haven't seen all that many, really."

"How about the ones you were with in Cazador School or Centurion Candidate School?" Carrera asked.

"Not there, either," Cruz shook his head. "Then again, we'll never again see the quality of manpower we had for that first call up for the war in Sumer. In other words, hard to tell the difference between twenty-four-karat gold and twenty-three point nine."

"Fair point," Carrera said, then added, "Here's my problem: I am becoming convinced that the standardized tests we're using are not doing all that good a job on this side. But if, as you say, there's no difference between officers and centurions on this side and those on the other, then maybe they *are* accurate and, for whatever reasons, the folks on this side just don't do as well."

"You mean aren't as bright, don't you, *Duque?*"

Carrera answered softly, "Yes."

"So you're thinking about maybe pushing a little over here, to balance things out? A little thumb on the scales?"

Still softly, "Yes."

"I see," Cruz said. He ate a few forkfuls of *paella*, thinking hard. "*Duque*, there's something I've always wondered. Your wife and mine are best buddies. Given the way our society is—yes, mostly still is, despite your best efforts—there's a lot of who you know being as important as, or more important than, what you know. So...when I take over as sergeant major of Second of the Second, is that because your wife's been nagging you to help me along, behind the scenes?"

"I wouldn't do that to you, Centurion. I wouldn't rob you of... Oh, I see."

Cruz gave a shallow smile. "Yes, sir. If you start plussing up the men on the Shimmering Sea side you'll rob them of the self-confidence they deserve, inside themselves, and of the respect that they deserve from others. Besides, it's just a shitty precedent to set. And worse for us since we *are* still a who you know and who you're related to culture."

"Smart son of a bitch, aren't you? So what do I do then? I spent a good part of the morning talking to a centurion candidate who is just fucking brilliant."

"You could try two...no, come to think of it, three things," Cruz said, after a moment's reflection. "I don't know if anyone but me has ever noticed—yeah, yeah, sir; I know somebody must have—but the Spanish they speak over here is different from what we speak on the *Mar Furioso* side. I wonder if that, and having to take the time to translate in their heads from what we speak to what they speak, and back again, doesn't cost them a few points. Then there's the education issue. You could maybe fix that with a special course for new recruits over here. Don't know what it would cost but were I you I would think about it, *Duque*.

"Lastly, how hard to deemphasize the standardized test scores a little and weight more heavily hands-on problem solving ability, especially in basic training?"

"Might work, I suppose," Carrera said.

"There's a fourth way, too," said Cruz. "Don't know if it's a good idea though."

"What's that?" Carrera asked.

"Put your personal prestige on the line and select a dozen or two centurion candidates for officer candidate school, just as a matter of being the big cheese."

"I've already put a lot of my personal prestige on the line just sending my son here," Carrera said.

"No shit. Sir."

Palacio de las Trixies, *Ciudad* Balboa, Republic of Balboa, Terra Nova

Stomping up the stairs, though at a dignified brisk walk rather than a run, Carrera ignored the squawking of the bright red, green, and gray trixie rushing to get out of his way. He hooked one hand around the finial gracing the top of the bannister, propelling himself toward Parilla's home office.

The door to Parilla's office was open, as were the ocean-facing windows. This allowed a cool breeze to pass through and had the effect, with other windows and doors, of cooling the entire presidential palace without the need for air conditioning.

Stopping at the door, Carrera announced, "Raul, I want us to get on the 'Ban Plastic Landmines' bandwagon in a big way."

Looking up from his desk in dual surprise, Parilla said, "Huh? I've heard you curse yourself silly over that one."

"True. That was before. Now we can have the only undetectable metallic mines in the world. For a while, at least." Carrera briefly explained Corporal Ruiz-Jones's insight. "And just think of all those old metallic mines we can buy for dirt."

"Okay," the president agreed, "I'll put the diplomats to it. But, if you don't mind, I'll want to wring some concessions out of somebody for our signature."

"Money?" Carrera asked. "We can always use money, I suppose. But, if you really want peace, why not use it as leverage with the Taurans to reduce their forces here?"

"It's a thought," Parilla said. "Let me mull it over. By the way"—Parilla lifted a folder and waved it—"are you going to the executions?"

"Which ones?" Carrera asked.

"The senior tribune and the junior corporal."

"Oh," Carrera said, "the fraternization case. Yes, I'll be going. Least I can do. The tribune's been with us since the beginning."

Parade Field, Eleventh Tercio Cuartel, *Ciudad* Balboa, Balboa, Terra Nova

The not quite risen morning was damp and chill, with a thick fog arising from the drainage ditches and hovering above the erstwhile parade field, now a place of execution. The fog stuck at about knee level, thick enough that a standing man could see neither his feet nor the ground.

There was a sloped berm along the long end of the oblong cuartel's parade field, facing inward. Normally, families who came to witness the full tercio on parade, usually before or after its annual period of training, would take seats on the grass of the slope. No family members were present today.

On the side of the berm facing away from the parade field there was no real slope, but an almost vertical wall. About six feet in front of that wall, two stakes, each about eight inches thick, had been erected. One was set directly into a concrete frame, sunk into the earth. Fresh dirt around the base of one or the other suggested that the Eleventh had never really expected to have to shoot two men at once. Two lines of six men, at ease and each with a rifle at "order arms," stood parallel to the earthen wall and the two stout stakes. Off to their left stood two junior tribunes, one with a holstered pistol hanging from his belt and the other with a clipboard under his arm.

On the right side of the firing squads Carrera stood with the regimental commander, Herrera, the legion commander, Chin, and the corps commander, Suarez. Carrera always found it amusing that Chin looked more pure Castilian than any of them.

A trio of sergeants major stood in a separate group, nearer the wall. About thirty witnesses, mostly enlisted men and junior noncoms, but including a couple or three each centurions and junior officers, gaggled behind those more august groupings.

There was a little nervous talk among the groupings, though all of that was subdued and further muffled by the fog. All such talk ceased, though, as a green-painted step van emerged from the fog and pulled up in front of the stakes. The van's rear doors burst open. Two legionaries emerged, then turned to help another keep his balance as he stepped out. That one had his hands bound behind his back, hence the need for help. He looked at the upright stakes and, lifting his chin, marched directly for the further one. His escorts had trouble keeping up. Indeed, one nearly fell from a misstep caused by some unseen irregularity in the ground.

Carrera recognized the tribune he'd once decorated for courage under fire. *Damn,* he thought, as the escort used straps to bind him to the stake, *you were a fine soldier, González. Why the hell couldn't you keep your trousers zipped?*

A second bound man was pulled from the van. That one, Corporal Juarez, took one look at the second stake, then gave an inarticulate cry as his knees collapsed under him. His two escorts just barely managed to grab him by his pinioned arms before he fell completely to the ground. They carried him to the stake by those arms then likewise strapped him to it. He wept as the straps were tightened.

"Die like a man," the bound and condemned tribune shouted. If that did any good it was only to reduce the volume of weeping.

Once the strapping up was complete, the escorts offered blindfolds to each. The tribune refused his, while the other wasn't really capable of articulating a refusal. His eyes were covered. One escort for each bent a head to find the heartbeat for each man, then pinned a white marker, about two inches on a side, over it. Then the escorts hurried off, one of them slapping the side of the van to tell the driver to get out of the way. The van, too, rolled off.

The tribune with the clipboard stepped forward, then read off the charges in a breaking voice. He stepped back. It was now the turn of the officer with the holstered pistol.

"Detachment...attention...ready...aim...*fuego!*"

A long explosion rang out in the misty morning, like a single shot but drawn out to fill nearly a full second. The weeping man was spun half about his stake, but went completely silent instantly. The tribune was slapped back to his stake, then sagged limp against the straps.

The commander of the firing squad ordered the men to order arms, then marched forward briskly to ensure that the condemned were, in fact, dead. He didn't, he was relieved to see, have to use his pistol to blow the brains of the condemned out onto the dirt, a meal for ants.

What a fucking waste, thought a grim and saddened Carrera, as he walked to his Phaeton. *But what can one do?*

CHAPTER NINE

> *Naturam expellas furca, tamen usque recurret,*
> *et mala perrumpet furtim fastidia victrix.* [You
> may drive out Nature with a pitchfork, but she
> will ever hurry back, to triumph in stealth over
> your foolish contempt.]
>
> —Horace, *Epistles Book I, X, 24*

Estado Mayor, Ciudad Balboa, Balboa, Terra Nova

Tribune III Roberto Silva reported to Carrera's office precisely on time. To Carrera the tribune seemed exaggeratedly masculine and, therefore, a little creepy. The tribune's not unimpressive official file sat folded on Carrera's desk, along with another file prepared by Fernandez's department.

Funny, Carrera thought, *we don't usually freak out about what gays or lesbians do, because we just won't think about it, any more than we dwell on Mom blowing Dad. It's when the signals are crossed though, when a man borders on pretty or a woman on manly, or when they're extreme, like this guy is, that we get uncomfortable.*

"Sir, Tribune Silva reports," said the man, rendering a smart salute while standing at rigid attention in front of Carrera's desk.

Carrera returned the salute, casually, then said, "Have a seat, Tribune." Carrera indicated a chair. "Some coffee, perhaps."

"Yes, sir, thank you, sir." Carrera buzzed the secretary to bring in two cups of coffee.

And it gets hard to talk about when we get uncomfortable.

"Silva... I don't want you to get the wrong idea of this. And I

91

won't say precisely why I thought you were the man to consult. But you *have* heard of the executions in Eleventh Tercio at their cuartel last week, haven't you?"

Silva immediately tensed. He did not give an immediate answer.

Carrera quickly interjected, "Relax, Tribune. I don't know or care what your sexual orientation is. Fernandez told me that despite his suspicions, you don't seem to *do* anything one way or the other. Or, if you do, you're very careful. I don't, for the time being, *want* to know, for that matter. But let's imagine that you are someone who might, just possibly, have some insights into the problem."

"The problem with homosexuals in the force, you mean, sir?"

"Yes."

Silva relaxed only slightly, but answered, "It's the same problem as with the straight men and women. It isn't entirely sex, so much as it's *love.* And the favoritism, the de facto prostitution, and the demoralization of everybody else that go with them. González and Juarez were sloppy, true. They got caught. But for every pair you catch and shoot, sir, I'll guarantee you that there are a thousand you won't catch. Or at least won't catch until they've had a chance to damage the discipline and morale of the force."

"That's about what I think, too. Any suggestions?"

"I can suggest what you can't do. You can't legalize it without legalizing the same conduct between men and women of different ranks. And that will make your problem ten times worse, a hundred times worse. If you try to limit the proscription to those in the same unit you'll just make it a somewhat subtler problem: people of different ranks who fall in love will arrange to be put in different units, but they'll still use their ranks to influence the other unit for the betterment of their beloved.

"You see, sir, the problem isn't that all the homosexuals are *bad* soldiers. Oh, no, that would be easy to fix. No, sir, the problem is that some of them are very *good* soldiers. They rise in rank." Silva's eyes glanced briefly in the direction of his own collar.

Carrera took the hint. *Good man. He wants it known, so he can speak with authority, but wants the knowledge unofficial so I don't feel compelled to act. To keep this one in service and protected, all on its own, would be good enough reason for what I'm thinking of.*

Message delivered, Silva continued, "But, good legionaries or not, they remain just people, as likely to fall in love . . . or lust, as anyone else. As likely to use their rank to favor the object of that love—or lust—as anyone else."

Carrera thought briefly, then asked, "What if we put all the homosexuals in the same unit?"

"Sir, whatever their sexual orientation most men are about as promiscuous as rabbits. You may cut down the problem in the rest of the army by reducing the number of potential causes of problems that are spread around. But that unit will be an undisciplined rabble, everybody fucking everybody and no guard duty or fatigue detail for whoever gives the best blow job."

Carrera grimaced slightly. "Pardon me, Tribune, but I find the idea—no pun intended—distasteful."

Silva shrugged. He continued, "Actually, a lesbian unit might work better. They tend to be fairly faithful to their partners and lovers. Although the favoritism problem would remain in any case. Another thing, too. If you tried to keep people from showing favoritism with—oh, say—a sleeping roster, some of them would still fall into more or less permanent couples. Sex is, after all, pretty common and unimportant stuff compared to love."

"What," asked Carrera, "if we had a sort of married regiment?"

"You're thinking of the Sacred Band on Old Earth?" At Carrera's confirming nod, Silva sighed. "In battle, there would be absolutely no telling what would happen, how one member of such a pair might react if his partner were in danger. He might fight harder; he might stop in place or run away to protect his partner. Just no telling."

"What about a sleeping roster, then? What if sex were a unit thing? Would that make for a bonded unit, Tribune?"

Silva snorted. "No way, sir. No fucking way. There's still the love issue. A sex roster won't stop people from falling in love. Though it's likely to lead to any number of murders once they do. They'll find a way around it and no threat of death will stop them. That's the one thing more powerful than the fear of death or death itself, you know: love."

Carrera considered the question of permanent couples silently for a few moments. Of Silva he asked, "How many homosexuals do you suppose are in the force?"

Again Silva shrugged. "I think...somewhere between five and seven thousand. Could be a few more."

"How many of those are already in permanent pairings?"

"That I really don't know. I'd guess...maybe five hundred or so. That's total, not five hundred pairs."

Carrera then sighed. "Let there be no bullshit between us, Tribune. Do you have a partner? Of about the same rank, or a civilian? Nothing will pass these walls if you do."

Silva looked pained for a moment. Carrera knew what he was thinking. *How far can I trust this straight dude?* Finally, after a period of obvious pain, Silva answered, "Yes, another tribune... slightly junior, a II...in the Fourteenth Cazador Tercio."

"Excellent!" Carrera, to Silva's intense shock, smiled broadly and sincerely. Then he stood and perused one of his bookcases briefly. He selected a volume of ancient biographies. He opened the book, dog-eared a section, then handed it to Silva. "Tribune Silva, read the pages I have marked. Then I have a mission for you. A recruiting mission of sorts. And congratulations. You're going to become a daddy. And your partner a mommy."

Silva, who had never expected to be a father, snorted. He then added, "He's not at all the maternal type."

Carrera likewise snorted, then said, "Tough shit. He'll have to learn. Now this is going to take a while to set up, so just keep it subtle until I give the word. But look around for other stable pairs, why don't you?"

"Don't know how many I'll find," said the tribune. "Don't know how many will be interested."

Leader Assessment Course, Training Area D, *Academia Militar Sergento* Juan Malvegui, west of *Puerto Lindo*, Balboa, Terra Nova

Quite probably no one on the planet really knew where the idea for a Leader Assessment Course or Leader Reaction Course originated. Centurion Cruz, himself, couldn't have said, not for certain. Above the planet, neither Marguerite Wallenstein nor any of her officers could have said. They'd never gone through anything like it, of course, with officer selection on Old Earth being a matter more of caste and connections than capability.

In fact, the earliest known version had been developed in pre-Nazi Germany, on Old Earth, during the 1920s, by psychologists working for the German Army. The idea had been to identify officer candidates with the requisite imagination, learning ability,

ability to adjust, emotional stability, and sheer force of character to lead peers through tasks that were, on their face, impossible. (Though every task actually could be accomplished, they were set up to *appear* impossible, at least, and were always very difficult.)

From Germany the idea had been picked up by the British Army and Royal Air Force. From the old United Kingdom it had moved, in one form or another, to the "cousins" of the United States and likely also Canada, Australia, and New Zealand. It had rarely, if ever, taken hold in other states of the old Commonwealth.

In a sense, of course, the Federated States Army's Ranger School—which, it was known, *had* been consciously carried from Old Earth to New—was just an elaborate and exquisitely miserable version of it, as was Balboa's *Escuela de Cazadores*, itself a version of the FSA's Ranger School. Sending twelve- and thirteen-year-olds to something as grueling and wearing as Cazador School seemed a bit much, even to Carrera. Thus, for its limited purposes, the Leader Assessment Course would serve.

(Besides, no one was commissioned out of the military academies, anyway. Those, at most, gave someone a leg up if they later decided, as most did, to enlist in the legion and buck for a commission or centurion's stick.)

For a while, in the Federated States, the course had become something of a corporate team-building fad. Like other fads, of course, it didn't last.

But had it been carried from Old Earth to Terra Nova? History Ph.D. candidates on Terra Nova had looked. There was no paper or digital record indicating it had been brought over from Old Earth. Whether someone had carried it in his head to the new world could never be known. Even that seemed unlikely, too, since the first recorded use of it on Terra Nova had been in Atzlan, of all places, and that not until seventy-five years after the last big load of transportees from old Earth to Atzlan had been landed, also long after Old Earth had effectively demilitarized and depoliticized, placing all power in the hands of unelected hereditary bureaucrats.

The odds were that, like other good ideas, it had simply been invented at different places and different times.

The Sergeant Juan Malvegui Academy's Leader Assessment Course stretched along about nineteen hundred meters of a narrow,

winding stream diverted from the main one, the *Rio Cuango*. There
were twenty-two stations, separated from each other by eighty or
ninety meters, with the view blocked by thick secondary jungle
growth, or berms, or, in a couple of cases, walls. The problems
were set up over the stream to prevent broken bones, especially
broken necks, by softening the inevitable falls.

Generally speaking, a cadet training company of about a hundred and forty at this point would leave about half the stations
unused at any given time, thus giving some scheduling cushion
while preventing subsequent groups from learning anything about
their next problem from the shouting of those who preceded them.
The problems were, for the most part, *engineering* problems, at
some level, though using engineering to accomplish the missions
required leadership, the more so as every problem seemed, at first
glance, impossible to most.

The current problem, for example, the one that Hamilcar Carrera's section was about to try to negotiate, was concerned with
getting a barrel of "fuel," about a hundred pounds' worth, across
a destroyed bridge using materials to supplement the bridge that
were, on their face, wholly inadequate for the task. In fact, those
materials, a ten-foot piece of rope, two wooden planks, each
consisting of two lesser planks, nailed together and running just
under seven feet, in one case, and precisely ten, in the other,
were adequate to the task. The fuel drum that the boys had to get
across the stream diverted from the main run of the *Rio Cuango*
had no fuel in it—no sense in polluting the water, after all—but
did have a filling of concrete, hollowed out by a smaller drum,
to make up the weight.

Historically, rather less than a third of the groups succeeded
in getting their "fuel" drum to the other side of the stream. Of
those who did, about sixty percent really succeeded by planning
and understanding, while about forty percent either instinctively
caught the core of the problem or just blundered through.

The problem didn't seem impossible to Ham, acting as assistant
section leader. He'd figured it out instantly.

As well I should have, Ham thought, *since the old man's been
grilling me and drilling me on the Twelfth Principle of War, Shape,
since I was a toddler.*

Explaining it to the section leader for the exercise, Vladimiro
Adame, was tougher. The latter, olive-toned scion of the yearning

middle class, really didn't have a lot of use for the all-too-white upper class of which Hamilcar seemed to him the epitome. Getting through that was a much greater challenge than solving the bloody problem.

"The problem, Miro," Ham said, "is that somebody has to go out on the end on one of the nailed-together planks, pass the other plank to the far side, then tie them together. To do that, someone else—more likely four or five someone elses—are going to have to stand on the end of the plank while he ties them together. Once that's done, he can cross and then we can move people to the far side. Then he and they can stand on the end of the plank to balance the weight of one of us and the drum. Think: Leverage."

Vladimiro looked at Ham suspiciously, obviously wondering, *How far can I trust this well-connected bastard?*

"And I'm not technically a bastard," Ham said, "since my mother and father managed to get to the altar first. Now what's your excuse?"

That got Carrera's boy a laugh and a question. "So how do we keep enough weight on the near plank?"

"You lead from in front," Ham replied. "Get on your belly and crawl out. As you clear space on the rear of the plank, moving forward, I'll get others to stand on it in the rear. Go slow because getting them stable might take a little effort.

"Once you're at the end, we'll pass you the second plank across your back, then you feed it all the way over. It *has* to be the short plank or you'll lose control of it. Then you tie them together and cross over yourself. I'll feed three more cadets over to you to stand on the far end." Ham fluttered his fingers. "Three...maybe even four. Then we use somebody small and strong..."

"Jorge Rodrigues," Miro decided. "He's not the smallest but he's strong for his weight."

"Yes," Ham agreed, instantly, knowing he'd won the point and also that the glory of the thing would accrue to Jorge, whom he counted a friend.

"Don't fuck this up on me," Miro warned.

"Don't *you*."

"Time is wasting, gentlemen," announced Cruz, looking down at the broad and thick nylon band holding his watch to his right wrist. He pulled the protective tab over the watch's face and glared out at the boys, struggling to get their little one plank bridge assembled. The centurion's right boot tapped theatrically on the ground.

Hamilcar, the biggest boy in the section, stood at the very end of the longer plank, holding it down with his body weight. In front of him he had the next largest boy, likewise applying weight to balance out Miro, slithering down toward the free end. At a certain point, Miro was out too far and the leverage was not quite enough.

"Get your feet on the plank, Roger!" Ham ordered. Then, feeling the plank start to rise, he amended, "Screw that. Sit on it. Belisario, sit on his lap. Raul, crawl up on my back and hang on."

With the weight of five boys on the friendly side, that end of the plank settled back down to the dirt. Still, Ham found it pure hell to try to balance with Raul on his back, the more so as Miro set the plank to vibrating.

Worse than learning to ride a bicycle, he thought.

"I'm as far as I can go," Miro said, over his left shoulder. Lying flat on his belly, he had the rope draped loosely around his neck. "Send me the other plank."

That was more trouble than anyone, including Ham, had expected. In the first place, the plank caught on Miro's fatigue shirt. He found he had to use both hands to hold the shirt tight to his back to let the plank pass it. Since the plank was actually two, nailed together, the ridge where they were nailed likewise caught. The boy feeding the plank had to pull it back then, flip it, and start over. In that action he nearly lost the plank over the side.

Almost Ham lost control of himself and lunged for the plank. Whether he stopped from presence of mind or because the other boy managed to get control of it he wasn't quite sure. Still, the other boy did get control of it and began once again feeding it across to Miro.

And there arose another problem. The angle was just all wrong. Miro *couldn't* hold the plank with his hands behind his head feeding it forward.

"Flip over on your back," Ham shouted. That seemed like good advice, so Miro tried it. It worked but the motion set the longer rearward plank to vibrating again. The boys clustered at that end began to sway...

"Shit!" Ham exclaimed.

"Two demerits, Cadet," Centurion Cruz announced.

"Shit," Ham whispered, then, "Jorge! Get over here and balance us!"

That helped.

Miro, flat on his back and feeding the plank forward—or up, depending on how one wanted to look at it—couldn't see the far end. "Guide me, Hamilcar," he ordered. "I can't see shit."

"Two demerits, Cadet."

"Shit," Miro likewise whispered.

Cruz, who could still hear him perfectly well, permitted himself a thin smile. *Damn, I wish we'd had these schools when I was a boy. This shit—two demerits, Centurion—is too much fun.*

"About two feet from the far bank," Ham advised. "But you've got to lift the far end or you'll put it in the water."

As Miro struggled against the reverse leverage of the plank, Ham guided, "Up . . . up . . . little more . . . set it!"

Miro jammed the far end of the plank into the dirt on the far side, then slithered like a snake, but backwards, before easing the friendly end down to the plank on which he lay. Flipping over to his belly—which movement very nearly cost him the rope—he slithered forward again and began to tie the planks together. In the excitement, he tied them with the wrong knot, and perhaps a bit too close to the lower and longer plank, but you'll get that on those big jobs.

"TIME IS WASTING, CADETS!"

Shit, thought Ham and Miro and just about every one of the others, all at the same time.

"Far side, Miro," Ham reminded.

Exhausted from his struggle with the plank, Miro just nodded and began belly crawling across the shorter plank. For a moment the other plank began to teeter, but then he was past that danger point and the thing settled back down. In less than half a minute, he was standing at the edge of the far plank, saying, "Send one man over."

"Francisco, go," Ham ordered. "Augustino, get ready. You're next."

Centurion Ricardo Cruz was mildly impressed. The boys had the bridge up. They were using the weight of their bodies to keep the planks up. And they had one small but strong boy carefully rolling the "fuel drum" across.

I think they're going to make...uh, oh...

What followed wasn't really the fault of Jorge Rodrigues, the boy rolling the drum. Rather, it was a combination of things. In the first place, even with five boys on one plank and four on the other, the weight of drum and boy combined introduced a certain amount of vibration. That stretched the rope. Then there was the rise where one plank lay atop the other. Getting the drum over that induced more vibration to the planks, drove the short plank a little farther away, and further loosened the rope. Then the drum hit the rope, nudging it just a bit, and bouncing back.

All of that would have been survivable. But the rope was already very near the edge of the lower plank...

"Oh...SHIT!" cried a dozen cadets as the two spanning planks were disconnected, and all the weight of both boy and drum rested on the near one, which had just a little bit too little weight holding its near side down.

"MORE DEMERITS THAN YOU PEOPLE CAN COUNT TO!"

Ham felt himself and the other four boys with him lift up. Two boys fell off almost immediately. Ham and the other two picked up speed...upward.

Meanwhile, Jorge fell forward, smashing his belly on the drum and his face on the far plank. Blood burst from the boy's mouth as hard teeth penetrated soft lip. Stunned, he rolled off to one side with the heavy drum following him.

Ham, standing at the very edge of the longer plank, had more velocity than the others. He was thrown, arms and legs splayed, forward into the stream. It was a belly flop, stunning and painful, both. Arms wrapping around his midsection, Ham began to sink. He came to his senses when his face brushed the cold, painted metal of the drum.

Jorge, he thought, then began frantically feeling around for his friend. He thought the back of his hand brushed clothing once, but before he could twist it to make a grab it had passed.

Downstream...downstream...he must be floating downstream. I can't see shit in this crap. He began paddling furiously in the direction he thought Jorge must have been swept. Then, suddenly, Ham felt something grab the back of his shirt. He was hauled back and upward faster than he could even form the thought to break away. Just as suddenly, he was out of the water and into the light and air. Blinking the muddy water from his eyes, he saw

Centurion Cruz holding Jorge above the water by the scruff of his collar. Jorge seemed disoriented, but otherwise fine. Miro was wading in, too, to take control of Jorge away from the centurion.

He must be fine, was Ham's thought, *else Cruz wouldn't be laughing.*

A soaking and muddy Ham sat with his back to a tree and his arms wrapped around his knees. *Failure. Miserable failure. Everyone's gonna hate me. Why? Why? Why? With each "why" he slammed his head back against the tree.*

Unaccountably, when Miro came walking by from his after action review with the centurion, he was smiling broadly. Miro sat down beside Ham and said, "Your turn."

"Fuck, what's the point?" Ham asked. "We failed. My plan and I caused you to fail."

"Oh, shut up, you snot," Miro said, still smiling. "The centurion said the objective isn't really getting the drum over. It's all about planning and execution, leadership and what he called 'troop leading procedures.' He said I passed and that we 'done pretty good for a bunch of runny-nosed kids.'"

"No shit?" Ham asked, looking up at last from his blue funk.

"No shit," Miro said. "Now go take your beating because, pass or not, we must have our daily beating."

Ham reported, then took a seat as directed. He didn't wait for Cruz to say a word, but said immediately, "You planned it that way, Centurion."

"Not exactly," Cruz corrected. "I—silly me—really thought your plan was going to work. Not sure why it didn't."

"That's not what I mean," Ham said. "You planned for me to make a friend by assisting someone to pass."

The centurion smiled, slyly. "Just figuring that out, are you? And there I thought you were a bright boy. I guess . . ."

"Oh, come on, Centurion."

"Okay, son. Here's the deal. You're going to be the assistant for a plurality of the problems your section will face. Not a majority, just a plurality. Not only will it teach you some valuable humility, but it will make your squad mates very dependent on you.

"And no, before you ask, I will *not* be passing anyone just to make you look good. I expect you to make them look good.

"Speaking of which, since a) I need an excuse to make you assistant so often and b) your section did, after all, fail to get the drum over the creek, you are a failure for this task, Cadet Carrera. Sucks, doesn't it?"

As a visibly shrunken Hamilcar slunk away from Cruz's field office, the centurion thought, *I didn't tell your old man I had a trick to help you along. He needed the moral space. That, and to let someone else decide, anyway. He's always been too close to the problem. And that's my trick. 'Course, after that, it's up to you, boy. They'll need you, each in his turn, but only if you prove that you can help them.*

CHAPTER TEN

Nothing in the world is more flexible and yielding
than water. Yet when it attacks the firm and the
strong, none can withstand it, because they have
no way to change it. So the flexible overcome the
adamant, the yielding overcome the forceful.

—Lao Tzu, *Tao Teh Ching*

Nyen, Volgan Republic

Kuralski, sometime chief of staff for the combined legions, but
more often more valuable as arms purchaser in Volga, walked
around some dozens of heavy-duty shipping containers and crates,
checking off items on an old-fashioned clipboard. The weather
was typical Volgan winter, bitter, miserable, and more miserable
still for Nyen's proximity to a cold sea. Had it just been snow,
Kuralski might have enjoyed the weather. But no, it was a winter
mix of snow, rain, and sleet.

Open the dictionary, thought Carrera's legate, *to the word "shitty"
and there will be a two-by-three color glossy of Nyen in the winter.*

In this fortress town by the Ancylus Sea, site of the first colonization party—monarchistic dissidents all—sent out from Old
Russia, a major arms shipment sat in unwalled sheds near the
docks awaiting their transportation. These included, crated up
for shipment, twenty-four one-seat and seven two-seat Artem-
Mikhail-23-465 Gaur jet fighters, heavily modernized but still
cheap since they were such old basic designs, plus fifty-two cargo
helicopters, IM-71s or some variant thereto, likewise crated. The

103

helicopter would be going straight to Balboa, but the fighters had a lengthy stop off scheduled in Zion for further upgrades.

Obsolete by Columbian, Tauran, and Volgan standards, the Gaur were still perfectly adequate to serve as training aids. Moreover, by Northern Colombian standards, they were almost top of the line aircraft. The Volgans had originally asked for over four million drachma, each, for them, on the theory that this was still cheaper than anything from the TU or Federated States. By showing the arms dealer a copy of a civilian publication dedicated to the sale of small arms, in which Gaur were being offered for sale to private individuals at just over two million Federated States Drachma, each, Kuralski had gotten the price, with shipping, reduced to just over two million each, with avionics.

The outsides of each of twenty-six shipping containers were marked FMTG, Inc., the wholly legion-owned, but largely Southern Columbian–manned, corporation that provided a certain amount of training support for Balboa, especially in areas, air and naval, where the foreigners had greater expertise.

The helicopters were similarly marked. Some months earlier, though, a totally unmarked set of twenty-two cargo choppers and eight gunships had gone by rail to Cochin. Further, eight hovercraft had gone by sea to Cochin, sailing from a different port. From there, the criminal organization that had sold them to Kuralski had no clue and less interest.

Expecting that United Earth Peace Fleet's satellite reconnaissance would see the crates containing the aircraft sitting at the dock, Carrera had had FMTG try to defuse the matter by bringing it up first. Since the aircraft were alleged to be essentially unarmed—which was true; the armaments were to be shipped separately—and were the theoretical property of a foreign defense contractor, there was no Federated States reaction to the shipments. For their own purposes, though, the FSC confirmed their existence through satellite photography.

The UEPF and Tauran Union were another story. Their reaction was to demand that the crates not be shipped anywhere. So far, the problem was being kept low key. That might change as the shipments got closer to Balboan hands.

It is possible that Carrera had another purpose is having FMTG bring the aircraft up first. After all, when someone is concentrating their remote sensing capability at one port, they're more likely to miss another, and quite likely to miss movement by rail.

The crates of the other twenty-six helicopters were instead marked *Servicio Helicoptores Balboenses, S.A.*, SHEBSA for short. These were newer than the other group, configured as civilian choppers, and distinguishable by their more comfortable seats and large rectangular, rather than small and round, windows. Also, they had their tail rotors on the left, rather than the right, side of the tail boom. SHEBSA, Kuralski knew, was a part of the "hidden" reserve, much like the five merchant shipping corporations and the two construction companies. Though how hidden they actually were was a matter of some speculation.

Having made his last minute check of the shipment, Kuralski left the dock area for a meeting with a retired Volgan pilot who needed a job.

UEPF *Spirit of Peace,* in orbit over Taurus, Terra Nova

There were two Khans on the high admiral's staff, husband and wife, to the extent those terms had meaning within Old Earth's ruling classes. They did, of course, though the meaning was not necessarily one that would have been accepted on most of Terra Nova.

Both Khans were concerned with intelligence. The wife, Iris, who despite being quite blond and blue-eyed had had a much darker ancestress among the hereditary bureaucrats who had eventually risen to rule of mankind's home planet, was concerned with political and social intelligence gathering and analysis. Her husband, conversely, was more involved in operational and strategic intelligence, to include such aspects of technological intelligence as might impact on those.

They both sat with High Admiral Marguerite Wallenstein in her private office, just abutting her own quarters. The office sat in the mid-gravity area, halfway between the ship's central spine and the spinning outer hull. Rather than the ostentatious locally harvested silverwood of the conference room, Wallenstein's private office was more subdued, without wood on the walls—beyond picture frames—and with only the built-in carbon fiber desk.

Iris Khan was speaking.

"I just don't detect a lot of disunity within Balboa, and I don't sense a lot of unity in the Tauran Union. The TU certainly doesn't show the will to engage in major war."

She's really quite pretty, thought Marguerite, wistfully, as Khan the wife briefed her on developments below. *If only she were not a submissive, I wouldn't be half so lonely and not at all frustrated. It's funny how in matters sexual and romantic most of us need whatever real life can't provide. I have to be the bull dyke bitch of the fleet in my public persona but in my private life I want the exact opposite. And can't have it. Dammit.*

She sighed, raising an inquisitive cough from Khan the wife.

"Nothing, Commander," Marguerite said. "Continue."

"There's not much else, High Admiral," she said. "Janier was supposed to start provoking the Balboans over a week ago. He hasn't because he can't get the political authorization, which we were supposed to deliver. We simply haven't been able to."

"Even though we've offered their ruling classes another quarter-century of life, youth, and health?" Wallenstein asked.

"Not that simple, High Admiral. Some are willing, sure. Many of them are. But some are idealistic, transcendentally motivated; they really believe in whatever their pet philosophy is—from pacifism to cosmopolitanism to Tsarist Marxism—and won't trade away their political faiths for mere personal gain.

"Fortunately, there are few of those. Unfortunately, they carry weight over and above their numbers."

"The personal gain isn't so very 'mere,' you know," said Marguerite. "An extra twenty-five years of youth and health? They should be begging us."

"Most of them would," agreed Iris. "But those others? The fanatics? They are dangerous to the more reasonable types. Well... except for the pacifists, of course. They're only dangerous to themselves and their own."

"You wouldn't have brought this to me if you didn't have a solution," the high admiral said.

"Not me," replied Iris, "but my husband may have one."

Wallenstein turned her attention, perhaps a little reluctantly, away from the pretty wife and toward the—*let's be honest, not bad himself*—husband.

"The key word there is 'may,' High Admiral," began Commander Khan, husband. "That is to say, *maybe* the Balboans have given us something to work with. I confess, I am not precisely full of confidence. And, for that matter, I've had the glimmering of an idea. My lovely wife is the one who figured out—"

"But it was you—" began Iris, before Wallenstein cut her off with, "Shut up. I don't care whose idea it is, if it has a chance of working."

"It revolves around two things," said Khan the husband. "One is the Balboan military threat to Colombia Latina as a whole, though more specifically the threat to their eastern neighbor, Santa Josefina."

"Santa Josefina got rid of its army decades ago," said Iris. "The cosmopolitans love that, while the pacifists approve enough that their resistance to knocking out a threat to Santa Josefina will be muted."

"Yes," agreed her husband, "while the second item is that the Balboans have played into our hands by engaging in an arms buildup the likes of which Colombia Latina has *never* seen.

"Mind you, High Admiral, they don't have the logistical where-withal to support more than a small fraction of their army at any distance from home...well, except if they can support it by sea. But the common ruck and muck of the Tauran Union see tanks and guns and aren't bright enough to realize that those go nowhere without sufficient trucks and rail."

Marguerite considered all that. "You think, you really think, Balboa is a threat to Santa Josefina?"

Khan the husband shrugged. "I think they could be if they wanted to be. They don't want to because they get everything they want from Santa Josefina—namely volunteers to be cannon fodder—already, without having to worry about the costs of administering the country."

"It might help," said Iris, "if we used the longevity treatments to bribe the Santa Josefinan politicos to ask for Tauran Union protection. Might even throw the Federated States off guard, come to think of it."

"Tangled web-wise," said Marguerite, "I kind of like that."

Classroom Shed 47, *Isla Real*, Balboa, Terra Nova

Carrera had a lot more things to hide than just some aircraft, some hovercraft, or some ships. Some were hidden on the island, the *Isla Real,* that served as the legion's primary training base and was already most of the way there to becoming the strongest fortress in the history of two worlds.

On the northwest quarter of the island, not too far from the solar chimney that provided power to the place, a slender, aesthetic and intelligent looking warrant named Saenz taught a portion of a course under a metal shed, without walls but screened against insects. Outside the shed four three-ton trucks waited, their engines shut off. Saenz was seconded from Fernandez's department to teach a portion of the course for a few months a year.

The course was top secret, forbidden even to discuss. Of course the techniques taught there were to be passed on to the units that sent men to the course. It was the existence of the course, itself, that was top secret. Indeed, although it was largely about deceiving and defeating the most high tech means of reconnaissance, the course was billed as, "Advanced Field Fortifications."

Some of it actually took place around fortified areas. Other portions, like this one, were under cover. Some, the deepest secrets, were passed on underground.

Exactly on time the instructor, Warrant Officer Saenz, began to speak from a rostrum sitting centered on a low podium.

"Gentlemen," said the instructor, "today we will continue with the discussion of tactical deception on the battlefield. I remind you that this is key, because deception is the handmaiden of surprise. Further, it is also simply a great way to reduce the effectiveness of extremely high technology weapons and sensors."

Saenz looked over the students for the one who had likely failed to study. Not finding one, at least from a facial expression, he asked, "Now who has studied for today's lesson? Yes . . . you over there in the third row. Tell me? How many types of remote sensing are there? Name one of them and state briefly how it works."

The corporal chosen stood up from his desk and answered, "That we know of, there are several. The simplest, but not the easiest to defeat, is aerial photography. Aerial photography, whether from satellites or from aircraft, can take extremely detailed pictures. In days past the preferred technique for defeating aerial photography was by camouflage, natural or artificial . . . or both. Special films, however, can tell whether camouflage, say vegetation or something that looks like vegetation, is alive . . . or even real. Computer programs and spectral analysis do the same things, only quicker.

So it is possible to make yourself more obvious with camouflage than without it."

"Very good," the warrant complimented. "Take a seat, please. The man next to you . . . yes, you, Rudolfo. Give the group another, please."

"Sir," the legionary answered. "Heat is another method of detecting even carefully hidden targets. Our weapons are mostly steel; they cool at different rates than the air or soil around and under them . . . even over them. And vehicles' engines put out enough heat that they will show up like a spotlight even through many feet of dirt or concrete."

"Good. Who's next? Ah, good. Another, son?"

"Sir. Radar can be used to find out where we are if we are above the surface of the planet. Then, too, there's ground penetrating radar. It is like other radars but on a different wavelength; one that will see right through the earth . . . or water. The limitation is how far down it will see; and with what detail. Also trees tend to absorb the radar energy."

"Do we know how far down those radars will see, son?"

"Not precisely, sir," the soldier answered. "Depending on the type of system and its computer power—computers to make sense out of the jumbled image—anywhere from three to fifteen meters. Possibly more, we just don't know."

"Possibly," Saenz agreed. "And we may never know. And if we ever find out, we may not like the reason why or the manner how for beans."

Pointing to the other side of the classroom, Saenz said, "Next man."

"They can smell us . . ."

The class broke into laughter. A couple of students muttered, none too softly, "They can smell *you*."

"No, really," the soldier continued. "They can drop sensors that pick up the smell of shit or urine, probably even our body odor. They can also pick up the smell of explosives, diesel fumes and smoke. I don't know about food cooking, though."

"Neither do I," Saenz said. "But it *is* possible. Next."

"Magnetic. Like Rudolfo said, our weapons are steel, also much of the ammunition. It is possible to pick up the magnetism from those and, based on intensity, figure out what is hidden from view; or at least if it is worth it to bomb the source."

"Good." Saenz's finger moved. "Another."

"They can drop seismic detectors that will pick up on the vibrations in the earth from passing vehicles, or even feet."

"Yes," Saenz agreed, then added, "and *anything* we do actively, show ourselves, use lights, use the radio, *turn on a fucking truck or car engine* ... even some kinds of field telephones; that can all be picked up and analyzed by folks that are smart and well trained to do so.

"But we're not helpless, boys."

Saenz raised a hand to indicate he had no more questions. "Follow me out to the trucks," he ordered.

The class stood and shuffled through the twin screen doors at the rear of the classroom shed. Outside, they loaded the three-ton trucks, men being boosted from below and pulled up by those already mounted. Once loaded, they were driven out into the interior of the island, to a spot north of the main impact area. It was a bone wrenching journey that took almost an hour. When the trucks came to a stop, Saenz, who had driven himself, was already on the ground waiting for the students.

The instructor motioned for the troops to take seats on the ground in a semicircle around him. He raised a finger to his lips. "Boys, you can never ... and I mean never, divulge what I am about to show you or tell you. It is simply this. Any remote sensing system can be defeated on its own, any of them. The trouble is that they are never used singly. Put camouflage overhead, they will pick up your heat signature. Hide your heat signature by digging deep, the ground penetrating radar will find your holes or tunnels. Put up a radar defeating screen and they'll bomb the screen out of existence and then bomb you.

"And better than half the effort you use has to be to make the enemy think there is a better target elsewhere. Put out a dummy tank. When the engine doesn't get hot every day they'll know it's a fake. Even if you light a reasonable fire under the dummy it won't have the magnetic signature of a real tank, so it will be ignored. And there is only so far down you can dig a tank in and still be able to get it up again quickly."

"Now, single file. Follow me." The centurion led the troops through the jungle and into a tunnel. The boys stumbled along into the ever increasing gloom. After several minutes they passed through a double cloth barrier and came to an opening. The centurion flicked on a light switch when the barrier finally closed behind the last of the troops. They saw an Ocelot, an infantry fighting vehicle that the legion typically used as a light tank, in the opening. The roof was concrete, the walls dirt, except for one that was thick steel, with hinges on the sides and a part in the middle. Several other tunnels led off in different directions.

"This," said a solemn Saenz, "is how we defeat remote sensing. And it isn't easy or cheap. Although it is cheaper than the sensing systems themselves. This tank, with a combat load, weighs about seventeen tons. If you follow those tunnels you will come to six other bunkers just like this one. In each bunker is a large pile of metal, steel and iron, of roughly seventeen tons weight, cost about two thousand, one hundred drachma. The magnetism detectors *can't* tell the difference between the piles of scrap and the real tank. So much for magnetism. We are also working on the practicalities of using magnetized scrap to cut down on the cost."

Saenz pointed overhead. "The roof of this bunker is made of concrete. So much you can see for yourselves. What you can't see is that chicken wire was put in with the concrete when it was poured. Also for all the other *dummy* bunkers. Ground penetrating radar only operates well at certain frequencies. The chicken wire's gauge is set to disrupt those frequencies. Thus the radar can't tell what's real and what isn't. So much for GPR."

"What about GPR when we're in the open or under the jungle's canopy?" asked one of the students.

"Good question," Saenz said. "It's not due to be covered yet but, what the hell. We've got some hundreds of tons of metallic strips cut to the right lengths—actually, twice the right lengths, and varying for different possible frequencies—we'll drop from helicopters onto the jungle roof over *wide* stretches. We hired a foreign oil exploration team to test it with aerially mounted GPR. They couldn't see through the shit."

Picking up a length of flexible hose, Saenz fitted it to the tank's exhaust. He pointed to six plastic pipes near the wall and sticking up from the bunker's dirt floor. "This hose connects to those pipes. The pipes connect to one of the dummy bunkers, each one to a different bunker. You can switch from one to the other by moving the hose's connection. So much for sniffing diesel. It also tends to send the heat elsewhere.

"Of course, when you run the engine for very long it tends to get *very* hot. The flyboys will pick up on that in a heartbeat. So you avoid running it for long if you can, and if you can't you do this." The instructor walked over and pulled aside a canvas curtain. Behind the curtain was an alcove. In the alcove were sheets of four-inch-thick polyurethane. He directed the students to take the sheets of polyurethane. He then showed them how to place them along the concrete ceiling. "That's about the best heat insulator in the world, boys. Before you run the engine you cover the tank with this stuff and no heat escapes . . . or so little, anyway, that you won't be picked up."

Saenz pointed to another hose. "That hose leads to a water tank that is filled off the island drainage system. After you run the tank a while you can cool it off with water. So much for infrared. Now come with me." He led the way through one of the smaller tunnels. More gloom. At length they broke into another bunker just like the first except that there was no tank and the polyurethane panels were already in place on the ceiling. In the tank's place was a roughly rectangular pile of scrap steel, most of it in small pieces. There was also a fifty-five-gallon fuel drum and what looked like an explosive charge.

The instructor flicked another light switch. "Let's not deny the enemy his fun. We want him to feel he's doing well. He might bomb the whole complex, all seven bunkers, at a cost of some millions of drachmas in guided bombs. More likely, he'll go after them one at a time until he strikes pay dirt. How will he know? Why he'll know by the secondary explosions from cans and charges like that one over there," Saenz pointed at the fuel drum.

Turning away, the warrant pushed open the wide doors at one end of the bunker. "Of course he can still sniff you. But that's not hard to fool either. C'mon."

The students walked out into the jungle smothered light. "What can they smell?" asked the instructor rhetorically. "They smell *you*, you nasty buggers." He pointed at various metal buckets and gourds on the ground and hanging from the trees. "So you save your piss and shit in buckets or gourds and you hang the buckets from the trees . . . those in your area and those some distance away. Likewise your filthy socks and sweaty uniforms. There are still two more things we must defeat." The instructor led the way down from the bunker to its base. There he lifted a small tarp. The boys all laughed.

Beneath the tarp, standing on a metal pole stuck into the earth was a little wooden man with a little wooden hammer. Saenz spun a tiny windmill and the hammer rose and fell, rose and fell.

"That's one technique. We have others that run from rainfall. Some solar powered, some battery. Some are on the main power grid for the island. So much for seismic detection.

"Can anyone tell me what's left?"

"Aerial photographs, sir?"

"Right." Saenz pointed straight up again at the jungle canopy overhead. "But not through that shit. And we can play a shell game, too. Say the enemy hits a bunker. We can...maybe...it *is* risky... move the tank to the bunker that was hit, then move the scrap metal by hand to take the tank's place. Remember...sensors are probably not looking at you all the time. You will never have every kind of sensor looking at you all the time. And the more sensors you have looking at you, the better the odds that the enemy won't have the trained people on hand to interpret what they're looking at.

"One caveat...the signature you *don't* have tells the enemy a lot about you, too. If they see something one way, and if we've defeated all the other ways they could have seen that something with, they may well blast it, just in case. Same if there are unique types of targets. So you must, must, *must* make things look as similar as possible, and have as many of them as possible.

"Ten-minute break. Next we look at a heavy mortar position."

Before the boys separated for their break, one asked, "Mr. Saenz? Ah, how much does this cost?"

The centurion rubbed his chin as he pretended to think. "Let's see...about twenty-five hundred drachma for seven concrete roofs, maybe fourteen thousand for the scrap metal. For nine hundred meters of narrow tunnel...about twelve hundred...nine hundred meters flexible hose...about four hundred drachma. Polyurethane...maybe another four hundred. Labor is a couple thousand more. It would be worse but we use convict labor for a lot of it. Steel doors cost a bit over a thousand as well. Call it about nineteen to twenty-two thousand, depending on where we build. For a bigger tank, a Jaguar, say, it can be about twice that."

The warrant smiled wickedly. "Although, since it can cost anywhere from ten thousand to a half-million drachma to make and deliver a bomb good enough to have a fifty percent chance of taking out whatever is in *one* of these bunkers, it's a small price to pay. I'll give you an example: If someone used...oh say, *fire and*

forget missiles to attack this complex, and say they had to use...
mmm...nine or so of 'em to make sure, the missiles themselves
would cost about six hundred thousand drachma. Wear and tear
on the aircraft might be almost as high, depending on what kind
of fight we put up from the ground. And they still would probably not know if they got one tank...or seven tanks...or if they
really got anything at all. Now go take your break."

The boy hesitated with a final question. "Oh, go ahead, son."

"Sir...can't they forget about guided bombs and just flatten
the island?"

Saenz's wicked smile grew broader still. "Not, really, son, no.
Contemplate this: how many sorties did the coalition assembled
by the Federated States fly every day in the war in Sumer?"

The boy frowned, trying to remember. Perhaps a little doubtfully he said, "About two thousand seven hundred, I think I read."

"About. No one's saying for sure but that is a close figure. And
they flew for about fifty days, right? So call it a hundred and
forty or fifty thousand sorties. How many thousands of tons of
bombs was that?"

The student did some figuring. *At about six or seven tons per
sortie...call it...* "Nine hundred thousand tons, sir?"

"Decent kitchen math," Saenz said, "but you're off by a factor
of ten. The coalition dropped maybe ninety thousand tons, call
it three hundred thousand bombs...or a bit more. Most of even
the combat sorties carried nothing like their theoretical load of
bombs. And a huge percent were for refueling other aircraft. Then,
too, command and control took up a bunch. Ninety thousand tons
of unguided bombs *might* inflict ten or perhaps twenty percent
casualties on this island, though probably not so many. Guided
bombs would improve that. Although, for reasons you don't need
to know about, it wouldn't improve it by all that much. But even
if it did it would surely not be enough to make *us* quit. If that
were all that had to be bombed, if even the *Federated States* could
send that many sorties today. Which I doubt. And even if they
could and did...what do you think that kind of bombing would
do to the island? It would chew up the surface so bad that offensive movement would become as hard as it was in Sachsen and
Gaul during the early years of the Great Global War. It would
be nothing but mud interspersed with muddy water. Oh, and
disease-carrying bugs, too, of course."

PART II

CHAPTER ELEVEN

Peace is *not* our profession.

—Sign over the door of Number Two
Maniple (Second Cohort, full mobi-
lization), Second Infantry Tercio,
Second Legion, *Legion del Cid*

**Intel Office, Tauran Union Security Force-Balboa, Building 59,
Fort Muddville, Balboa Transitway Area, Terra Nova**

Jan Campbell counted herself doubly blessed. Not only had the
planned round of provocations of the Balboans not begun yet, but
for some unaccountable reason none of the Gauls had wanted to
escort her. Thus, she had her old friend and comrade, Sergeant
Major Hendryksen for driver and escort. Of course, driving a
captain around was pretty much beneath a sergeant major. Spying, however, was not.

Her invitation had had a number to call. Somehow, she hadn't
been surprised when it rang in the *Estado Mayor*, and in Carrera's
office, no less. Not that the enemy commander had answered
himself, of course, but a couple of questions had made it clear
enough that one of his aides de camp *had*. She called on a speaker
phone so Hendryksen could listen in.

"Tribune Santillana," the answerer had announced. "*Officina
del Duque.*"

It was an odd rank, to Campbell's ear. Worse, she didn't speak
much Spanish. Still… "Tribune, this is Captain Campbell, Army
of Anglia seconded to the Tauran Union Security Force…"

The tribune switched to not badly accented English without missing a beat. Indeed, his English would probably have been more easily understandable to someone not from Campbell's own country than her English was.

"Yes, Captain," the tribune said, "Legate Fernandez advised me you would probably be calling and *Duque* Carrera approved. How can I help you? I know you've been invited to observe training."

Jan breathed a minor sigh of relief. She *hated* speaking or trying to speak in a language she wasn't totally fluent in.

"What do I do from here?" she asked. "The instructions gave... well... not a lot of detail."

"I haven't seen them," Santillana said. "We're not that great administratively, frankly. All I had was nothing more than the bare word that you were invited, that you had a choice of units, and that you were to be shown every courtesy consistent with not letting a no doubt clever girl like yourself see too much."

That last was said with half a laugh and got a full one in return from Campbell.

"So what would you like to see?"

Infantry, Hendryksen mouthed. "Infantry," Campbell repeated.

"Okay," said Santillana, "Second Maniple, Second Tercio, Second Legion is about to do a full mobilization as Second Cohort, Second Tercio. They're pretty representative. Honestly, personal opinion, they're a little better than most, but still nobody too special or elite. Will that do?"

At Hendryksen's exaggerated nod, Campbell said, "Splendidly."

"Very good," said the tribune. "If you will be so kind as to meet me at the main gate of Fort Guerrero at, let's say, nine tomorrow morning?"

"Done," said Campbell. "And thank you, Tribune."

After she'd broken the connection, she asked Hendryksen, "Why infantry?"

"Because if all else fails," the sergeant major answered, "the quality of the infantry they can field will tell us a lot about how much they're going to make us bleed."

Fuerte Guerrero, Balboa, Terra Nova

With the sun rising blood red in the east, Legate Suarez, Commander of the 2nd Legion, walked briskly into the Legion conference room accompanied by the CO of the Second Tercio, Legate Chin. Nobody was quite sure where Chin's name had come from; anybody would have taken him for a pure Castilian.

The first centurion of Number Two Maniple, Ricardo Cruz, back from his temporary duty with the cadets, called the room to attention. Suarez walked up to the rostrum standing in front of the chairs and ordered the assembled officers, centurions, and NCOs to take their seats.

"Gentlemen. This has become something of a tradition over the years. It is a tradition I can live with. Although, perhaps much like you, I will not mourn the day when this will not be necessary...when we will be able to assume our full ranks for a bit over three weeks, once a year."

Suarez turned to his adjutant. "Are you prepared to post the orders?"

"Sir!"

"Gentlemen...if you will stand...Adjutant, read the orders."

"Attention to orders." All the men present stiffened slightly. "Number Two Maniple, Second Infantry Tercio, Second Legion, *Legion del Cid*, is raised to Second Cohort, Second Infantry Tercio, Second Legion, *Legion del Cid*, by order of *Duque* Patricio Carrera, Commander, *Legion del Cid*. Further, it is ordered by the same authority that the officers, warrant officers, centurions, noncommissioned officers, and enlisted men of Second Cohort are to are to assume their Mobilization Level Three ranks and titles; such ranks and titles to be in effect until completion of the cohort's annual training.

"The purpose of said elevation is to conduct annual training for Second Cohort (MobLev 3).

"Signed: P. Carrera, *Duque*."

Suarez called, "At ease...assume your ranks."

The men of Second Cohort relaxed and, with much joking and laughing, began to help each other to change insignia. The centurions and reserve centurions needed no help. They simply unscrewed the baser metal end pieces from their sticks and replaced them with a metal of higher standing. Ricardo Cruz changed his silver end pieces for gold. Next to him young Julio Porras tried putting on the pips for tribune I in place of his small signifer's pips. Porras seemed nervous, fumbling with the insignia, until Cruz offered to help.

"Thanks, Centur... Sergeant Major."

"No sweat, sir."

Two and a half hours later, after the obligatory series of toasts to the success of the fully mobilized Second Cohort at their upcoming training, along with some related pleasantries, the command and staff of the cohort met in the conference room outside the commander's office. These included the cohort exec, the sergeant major, the operations officer, also called by the Roman numeral I—Ia, Ib, and Ic, operations, quartermaster, and intelligence, respectively—the II, also called the adjutant, the assistant for each, plus five company commanders, their executive officers, plus the combat support company's platoon leaders, Scouts, Heavy Mortars, Sappers, and Light Armor, and the medical platoon leader and supply and transport platoon leader.

Before the commander, a legate I, entered the room, there was a knock on the door. Sergeant Major Cruz opened it, to see someone he recognized as Carrera's aide de camp, Tribune Santillana. Behind the tribune was an extravagantly well-built blonde, with skin so white she'd have stood out among even the blondest and whitest of the locals.

Almost Cruz whistled. *Carrera didn't tell me back at that beach joint that he was going to send us a movie star. I am impressed. I am also going to act surprised.*

"What *is* this, Tribune?" the sergeant major asked.

Santillana produced Campbell's invitation, then explained it in as few words as possible.

"We're going to be living rough, hard, and fast," said Cruz, feigning ignorance. "I don't know if a woman..."

"I'll keep up," said Jan Campbell, in Spanish.

"She will, too," piped in a goateed and uniformed foreigner, from behind Campbell, and in better Spanish. "She's Captain Jan Campbell, Army of Anglia. I'm Sergeant Major Hendryksen, Army of Cimbria."

Cruz looked again at Santillana. "What are they allowed to...?"

"Everything but the secret things. The boss told me that he wants them to see the unvarnished reality of the legion, what we're good at, what we're not so good at or even bad at."

"All right," said Cruz. "I'll explain it to the legate. In the interim, welcome to you both. You're just about in time for our first staff meeting as a mobilized cohort, this year. Come on in and find seats, while I go inform the legate."

"I'm to stick around for a couple of days," said Santillana, "until they have their feet on the ground and are comfortable."

"That's very decent of you, Tribune," said Hendryksen.

"Just part of the job."

On ordinary days, in ordinary months, the "Old Man" of the maniple was a tribune II, Velasquez by name. Velasquez would plus up to a tribune III when the reservists were mobilized, to include for weekend training assemblies. But when the entire body of the cohort, regulars, reservists, and militia were called up, as now, he pinned on the silver eagle of a junior legate. He wasn't really comfortable with the system but, like most, put up with it.

He and his new sergeant major had known each other since a few days before the now-legate had worked out a short-term cease fire in the middle of a vicious fight for Ninewa, Sumer. Cruz had acquired his estimate of the legate back then: *Decency and balls, and you can't ask for a lot more than those.*

"Why us?" Velasquez asked. "What the hell did we do to deserve this?"

"I . . . ummm . . . I volunteered us, sir," Cruz admitted.

"Why the fuck would you do that?" Velasquez asked, bewildered.

"I was asked to make a recommendation, sir. By the *Duque*. You would have preferred I told him, 'Oh, anybody but us, *Duque*. Second of the Second sucks aurochs cock; it's well known.'"

"Phrased that way," Velasquez admitted, "maybe not. But, Jesus, this is going to be a pain in the ass."

Cruz shook his head. "I don't think so, sir. Both the Taurans seem pretty reasonable. And sir? When you see the tits on the Anglian woman, you will think it's all worth it."

"Really?" Velasquez asked doubtfully.

"Sir, the very platonic essence of feminine boobage. Magnificent."

"All right. At least I'll put a good face on it. Go out to the conference room. I'll be there about thirty seconds after you."

"II," Velasquez said, addressing the adjutant, "status of the cohort?"

The adjutant stood up and consulted his clipboard. "Sir, the cohort has an assigned strength of seven hundred and seventy-six, not including attachments. This is twenty-nine less than full strength, but certainly combat capable. The men, again not including attachments, include forty-seven regulars, one hundred and forty reservists, and five hundred and eighty-nine militia. Of these, seven hundred and fifty-five have reported for duty. That puts us at approximately ninety-three and a bit percent of war-time strength, still counting attached teams and sections. Of the missing twenty-one, one—Corporal Peña—has called to announce that his wife is having a baby. After checking with the doctor I took it upon myself to authorize him a forty-eight-hour unpaid leave. The Tercio sergeant major, Sergeant Major Arredondo, will foot march Peña out to join us on Sunday."

Everyone but the two Taurans winced in sympathy. Getting foot marched out to the field by "Scarface" Arredondo was *not* something anyone would look forward to.

"Three men are in jail," the adjutant continued. "I have notified the authorities and they will be released to us this afternoon, their sentences to be served after annual training. A further eleven are at various technical and leadership courses, including two at the advanced field fortification course out on the island and three at Cazador School.

"A further two are in advanced civil schooling. The cohort staff judge advocate has a civil trial coming up he says he can't delay any more. He'll join us the end of next week. Two are sick and in hospital; I sent my assistant around to check and they *are* sick."

"That's twenty," Velasquez said.

"Private Carillo," the adjutant muttered. Cruz and two other centurions, along with two officers, rolled their eyes.

"I'm afraid he's given no word, sir," said the adjutant. "The police force has been informed of his failure to report. His... Private Carillo's... apprehension is expected within the hour..."

Velasquez told the adjutant, "Send flowers... my tab... to Mrs. Peña." He then asked of Cruz, "What do you recommend be done with Carillo, Top?"

"Sir. Frankly, Carillo is a piece of shit. Or, rather, his wife is and he dotes on the bitch. We've tried to accommodate him—or her—before, without success. I suggest that, this time, the full rigor of the law be applied. I also suggest that the police be informed to watch the wife in his absence. We owe him that much, anyway." Cruz looked at Carillo's centurion as if defying a contrary answer.

Velasquez observed the visual exchange and assumed that the platoon leader, Centurion Ramos, agreed with Cruz. "Very well, Top. Seventeen days at hard labor in the civil prison system... unpaid... followed by another thirty in the tercio disciplinary platoon... half-pay, but only upon condition of adequate performance. If that doesn't work then we'll court-martial him, kick him out, and he'll never become a citizen."

Velasquez's gaze shifted to his Ib. "Quartermaster, speak to me of more material matters."

"Sir. Broadly speaking, we're at a little better than ninety percent. All the mortars are up... well, one was in for borescoping but I borrowed a tube from Third Cohort, so they're up. Of the six Ocelots tercio attached to us, only five are working. The other needs a new engine and the maintenance platoon doesn't have one on hand. Trucks... we've got nineteen of twenty-three up. The other four should be up within a day or two. All the lighter vehicles are in fair form and the mules are recently shod, though the farmers that had to give them to us are not happy campers."

"They never are," Velasquez said. "Even so, let's make damned sure they get their mules back in at least as good a shape as they gave them to us. The vet's inspected them?"

"Yes, sir," the quartermaster said, "just before we signed.

"Night vision and radios are good, but we're having a minor battery shortage, so we're going to have to conserve a bit."

"Ration schedule?" asked Velasquez.

"Well... sir... we're going to have to talk about that one..."

The cohort, including vehicles and the mobilized mule train, stretched back for five kilometers, the foot troops marching—weighed down like pack animals—in the blistering Balboan sun. Though, of course, Velasquez had an assigned vehicle, he marched up front, laden like his men. At the rear marched Sergeant Major Cruz's, likewise bowed under a near killing load. Signifer Porras marched by Cruz's side, more heavily laden because much less experienced. Laden or not, though, between the two they managed to keep control of the inevitable stragglers; inevitable because two thirds of the men were militia, trained for only twenty-five or so days a year. And it had been a year.

An older militiaman gritted his teeth and tried to smile as he forced worn legs to the limit to keep ahead of Cruz and Porras.

Cruz took a couple of deep breaths then churned out, "Just right, Private San Sebastio. One foot in front of the other and knowing the pain won't last forever." Cruz felt a bit of a hypocrite; San Sebastio had a good dozen years on him and had made it this far only on sheer mule-headedness.

"No sweat, Sergeant Major," said the elderly private. "I'll make it."

"I have no doubt of that," encouraged Cruz. "You *will* make it."

Porras asked Cruz in a whisper why the "Old Man," the commander, was setting such a difficult pace considering how old and out of shape some of the militia were.

"It's a judgment call," answered Cruz, equally softly. "In this case, I think he's right. We've got the militia with us. They haven't trained officially, other than weapons qualification, in a year. Hurting the ones who didn't make the effort to keep in shape on their own is probably the only way to get them to keep themselves in some kind of shape throughout the year. Sure, it's hard on the old salts like San Sebastio. But if we didn't make this first march a hard, painful memory, even the younger militiamen would get sloppy."

"Okay, I guess," Porras said. The younger man was in some awe of the *Cruz de Coraje* in gold—the medal was actually the field version, dull black with a little dull brushed gold showing—that glittered at Cruz's neck. He was equally in awe of the sergeant major's complete self-confidence, and the way the men all looked up to him.

It was whispered that on one occasion Cruz had pulverized three half-drunk privates and a corporal who had dared to speak back to the company commander. Porras hadn't seen that—it had been before his time—but he believed it completely.

It was also whispered that that had been the last incident of that kind of indiscipline that old unit had ever experienced.

Maybe Velasquez is the brains of the outfit, thought Porras, *but the sergeant major is its heart and soul.*

Porras knew that he himself was, at best, a brain under training, adjudged too bright to be a heart. He knew he was not needed, although all hoped he might someday become useful.

Cruz reached out with his badge of office, his stick, the metal ornamented baton that was a centurion or sergeant major's sole badge of rank, and tapped a militiaman—not San Sebastio—who had begun to fall behind.

"Back up with your platoon, son," said the sergeant major. "I mean ... RUN!" Cruz's stick slapped again ... and rather more stingingly. The militiaman began to run to catch up, panting and dripping sweat.

Porras noted the absolute certainty with which Cruz had acted and hoped ... hoped ... that someday he might be able to command so effortlessly.

The radio Porras carried on his back, in addition to the rest of his load, crackled to life. Porras answered immediately. It was the commander.

"Top, the old man wants you at the front of the column, now."

"Right, sir," said Cruz, as he quickly changed pace to a slow trot. "You keep up the rear."

Cruz had just about made the front of the column when it began to turn into its bivouac area for the night.

Hendryksen had offered to let Jan drive and walk himself, *bu' nooo, she wouldna lis'en.* Thus, he arrived at the cohort's bivouac site in fine form, with no more sweat than might be expected of a Cimbrian in a tropical rain forest. She, on the other hand ...

"Oh, God, Kris," she moaned, stripped down to trousers and a sweat soaked t-shirt, back against a tree, and bare and blistered feet elevated and resting on her rucksack, "these people are fuckin' maniacs."

"It's possible," he concurred. "But speaking of maniacs ..."

"Ah, fuck off, ye bloody Viking."

"Do you want me to find a medic to look at your feet?" he asked.

"Nah, I can do it meself," she replied. "Mostly, I already have. But if you could dig through me rucksack and find a sheet o' moleskin ..."

"And some disinfectant?" he suggested.

"Oh, by all means the disinfectant. And some clean, dry socks."

While Hendryksen was rifling the captain's pack, the short and mean looking sergeant major came up. He squatted down near Jan's feet, craning his neck slightly to look at them from both sides.

"Be careful to disinfect completely," Cruz said to Hendryksen. "There are kinds of fungus in this country that I think the Noahs put here specifically to destroy anybody stupid enough to do a march under a heavy pack."

"Sure," Kris agreed.

"And, if you want to attend, you're welcome to; the commander's giving initial orders to the maniples in half an hour."

CHAPTER TWELVE

All diplomacy is a continuation of war by other means.

—Chou En-Lai, *Saturday Evening Post*
(27 March 1954)

Aserri, Santa Josefina, Terra Nova

Being driven through the streets of the city, unfamiliar in its details but totally familiar in it sounds, smells, and overarching culture, Esmeralda was absolutely thrilled to be ashore and unsupervised. She had a job to do, of course, but that the high admiral had entrusted it to *her*...that was just *too* delicious. Of course the high admiral entrusted her with myriad things in the course of a month, but this was different. This was trust beyond sight.

The reason that High Admiral Wallenstein had sent someone else, rather than going herself, had to do with *not* making the whole thing—Santa Josefina's president calling for disarming the Balboans—seem like an Old Earth trick. It made sense, too. The only known possible match for the Peace Fleet was the Federated States of Columbia. Let the FSC know that the Peace Fleet wanted X and they would automatically push for whatever was the opposite of X. After all, the United Earth Peace Fleet had once destroyed two cities of the Federated States. The FSC simply *hated* the UEPF with a passion. Even the progressives in the FSC shared in that hate.

For the same reason that Marguerite couldn't go below to Santa Josefina—or couldn't go conveniently, anyway—Esmeralda couldn't wear her uniform. That would be as much of a warning to the FSC as if Wallenstein had been caught going herself.

But not wearing a uniform had presented problems, as well. First and foremost had been the fact that not a single female garment in the entire fleet had been suitable for wear in Santa Josefina. Old Earth had been going through a Minoan fashion fad for some time now, which fashion trend extended to both the Peace Fleet and Atlantis Base. Liberal, Santa Josefina might have been. They weren't liberal enough to have women in open-front bodices parading down *Calle Central* to the presidential palace.

Not even if I'd committed the fashion faux pas of not rouging my nipples, thought Esmeralda.

In desperation, the girl had turned to Commander Khan, female, for help and guidance. It was the commander's responsibility to prepare her for the mission, generally, so why not some fashion advice?

Khan's initial thought had been to dress her in something like the national costume of Santa Josefina. A little checking though, and, "Uh, uh, honey. Those are for debutante balls and national patriotic festivals. They don't appear ever—or hardly ever—to be seen on the streets."

Ultimately, Khan had settled on *South* Columbian dress, a lightweight business suit of a dark cashmere-silk blend, over an embroidered beige silk top.

"No accounting for taste," the commander had said, "but no matter, either. There are so many FSCers in Santa Josefina that you'll blend right in."

"I guess so. Commander?"

"Yes, honey?"

"Why me? I'm nobody. Not so long ago I was a slave. I didn't even really learn to read and write well until I came here. So why *me*?"

Khan smiled knowingly. She had her flaws, but inability to judge people was not among them. "Because the high admiral trusts you. There are a few other people she trusts—the earl of Care, for one— but none of them are available. And in our system there are never enough people you can actually trust. She doesn't, for example, trust me or my husband. Oh, sure, she trusts our judgment. But she does *not* trust our loyalty. You? She trusts your *loyalty*.

"Hmmm...that reminds me."

"Yes?" Esmeralda asked.

"The Josefinans can be a formal and stuck up crew, I understand. I think I'd better advise the high admiral to brevet you to . . . mmm . . . you're young so . . . lieutenant, junior grade, I think. Yes, that's a good rank for a naval emissary. That should at least keep them from sneering."

"But I *am*," Esmeralda objected.

"Yes, aren't you just. And, since you're going down there to sell the fountain of youth, what better advertisement than you could there be?"

"You mean tell them I'm older than I am?"

"See? The high admiral had more reasons than one for picking you."

"Why not use our ambassador to Santa Josefina?"

"Again," said Khan, holding up a single finger for emphasis, "*trust*. Now run along to my husband's office. He has something to give you and show you how to operate."

Dressed, packed, and with a secure visual recorder *cum* communicator obtained from Commander Khan, husband, in her purse, along with the equivalent of several thousand drachma, Esmeralda had gone to the hangar deck for her flight down to Atlantis Base. Her lover, Richard, earl of Care, was there to see her off. He was also visibly unhappy to see her go.

It would be better, she thought, *if I could believe he was only distressed for the lack of sex. But be serious, Esma, sex is the cheapest thing in the universe. As captain of the* Spirit of Peace *he could have any woman aboard except for the high admiral. Maybe even her, too, if she were in the mood. No, he really loves me and is going to miss me. And maybe he's a little worried for me, too.*

And how do I feel? I care for him, yes. But love? I love my family back on Old Earth. I loved my sister, murdered by those psychopathic Orthodox Druid bastards. No one else.

Though hate, now . . . that I have lots of.

The girl's journey began following the same track as she and the high admiral had taken before: Ship to Atlantis, Atlantis to *Colombia del Norte*, and from there to Taurus. Instead of picking up a Gallic Air Force dirigible in Taurus, however, she'd taken one from the Federated States, to the Federated States, and from there yet another to Aserri.

She didn't know how the Josefinan government had been informed to have a car meet her at the capital airport. That they had was enough. From that airport she was whisked to the presidential palace, through busy streets, not always all that well kept.

Still, thought Esmeralda, thinking back to her little home village, *a street, even with trash and potholes, is better than no street.*

The limousine carrying Esmeralda wasn't marked with anything that would indicate an official capacity. That didn't mean it wasn't official, of course; she learned a great deal from Commander Khan, female, during the latter's extensive briefings concerning euphemism, deceit, sleight of hand, and hypocrisy, especially among the political classes of both worlds.

Suddenly, the limo swung right, through a guarded open gate framed by a high dressed stone wall. Unseen behind the limo, uniformed and armed guards swung closed a stout iron-banded gate, then brought down a thick cross bar to lock it shut.

The limousine pulled into a stone and tile *porte cochere,* where another uniformed guard opened the rear door for Esmeralda, then stepped smartly out of the way. Another man, this one not uniformed but wearing an appallingly heavy looking tuxedo, asked—with a obsequious deference she found quite disgusting—that she follow him. The limo, with her overnight bag still in the trunk, pulled away gently but stopped, she saw, only a few hundred feet down the driveway, under a spreading tree. She had her purse in hand, still, and that was the important thing.

Esmeralda had noticed the uniformed guards and not thought much of it. In theory, Santa Josefina didn't have an army, nor even a national guard or gendarmerie. In fact, they had all those things, but not much of them, what they had being not particularly well led, trained, or equipped, and none of it going by those names. In effect, they had abandoned any notion of self-defense and left themselves to the mercies of the international community of the very, very caring and sensitive—who could not really be relied on for much—and the Federated States, which could. That this was a form of moral welfare that seemed to bother the average citizen of Santa Josefina not a bit.

"Remember, child," Khan had said, "sleight of hand and hypocrisy. They are the grease that makes civilization possible."

✧　　✧　　✧

The tuxedo clad "major domo"—that was how he had introduced himself—led Esmeralda through long corridors, up and down winding stairs, through doorways, and outside again. Once back in the open air, he led her through a walled garden, across a bright green lawn via a line of flagstones, over a possibly artificial stream by a narrow wooden bridge, and then to a small, stuccoed garden building surrounded by dense hedges.

If I had to guess, Esmeralda, in fact, guessed, *this would be where the presidential weasel deflowers twelve-year-olds.*

She was wrong. The president of Santa Josefina kept a mistress, of course, virtually all men of his class in his country did. But he thought it vile to have sex with a girl under thirteen and didn't think it was much better to sleep with girls anywhere near the age of consent, which was fifteen. Eighteen or nineteen? Well... maybe.

"*Señor Presidente*?" asked the major domo, with a light knock on the small building's door.

"Come in," President Calderón said. Esmeralda found it odd that his accent essentially matched her own. She also found it odd that he was actually good looking; thin but not too thin, hair a distinguished gray at the temples, green eyes.

Old enough to be my father, of course, but even so...

The major domo didn't enter, but stepped aside holding the door for her. She walked in, with a confidence she didn't really feel, and took a seat at the president's invitation, opposite him across a small, round table. She noted the telephone on the desk—it looked enough like one of the shipboard back-up communicators—and made a note of the number.

"Lieutenant Esmeralda Miranda, Mr. President," she announced. She saw no reason to append "Junior Grade" to that, since none of the real shipboard officers would have.

"United Earth's ambassador to my country said your high admiral had an offer for me. She would not say what it was."

"She *could* not say what it was, Mr. President. She didn't know." Esmeralda took from her purse the recorder-communicator, set it on the table and pushed one button. Nothing happened immediately and absolutely nothing happened that was obvious, but the recorder-communicator had the special ability of scrambling any other electronic devices within a radius of forty or fifty feet. *That* was why Khan the husband had given it to her, from intelligence stores.

At the push of a second button a miniature hologram of High

Admiral Wallenstein, decked out in dress blacks, with her hands clasped behind her, appeared to float a few inches above the table.

"Mr. President," said the hologram, "this is merely a recording. It cannot respond to your questions. Neither can it negotiate with you, not that there's much to negotiate. Lieutenant Miranda is my plenipotentiary and could sign on my behalf... if we were going to sign anything, which we are not."

Esmeralda studied the president's face carefully while Wallenstein's hologram spoke. She knew from watching the sailors aboard the *Spirit of Peace* play poker that there was such a thing as a poker face. If ever she had seen anyone with such a face, it was the president of Santa Josefina.

The high admiral's recording continued, "President Calderón, the basic problem is this: I see a threat to the entire planet growing in the country next door to yours. Some in the Tauran Union see it as well. Almost no one in the Federated States does, and the Federated States stymies me from doing anything about it, on general principle reinforced by immeasurable hatred. The Zhong aren't telling anyone their opinions on the matter, but the fact they've said nothing means, at least, that they don't care.

"Surely you, too, see that the military colossus arising next to you could squash your country like an insect. Worse, it has at least twenty thousand of your citizens in its army; it could use them to squash you.

"You *must* raise the world's awareness of this threat."

Esmeralda reached out and pressed a button again, causing the hologram to freeze in place. Still poker faced, the president asked, "What's in it for me and mine?"

"For you alone," Esmeralda corrected. "Twenty years' worth of rejuvenation once the Balboan threat is eliminated. It will be a UEPF special contribution to the World League Peace Prize, which the fleet will arrange for you to receive. There are a couple of million drachma involved, and you can do what you want with those."

"It's not so easy," said Calderón. "The Balboans, they're popular here. Sure, it's not like we didn't fight a war or five over the last four centuries, but it was always a family dispute, no really hard feelings. There's not enough real difference between us to drive a needle through.

"And then there are those twenty thousand—really closer to twenty-five thousand—Josefinans in Balboan service. We let them go because we don't have our own army for domestic political reasons that seem good to us, while there's still a certain kind of young man who is nothing but trouble for a few years unless you give him an army to join. Before the Balboans began raising their legion we had young men fighting over half of the world, I think. Every guerilla movement from a place that spoke Spanish used to set up recruiting booths right at the university and in the shopping malls.

"Now they're all, or almost all, with Balboa. And those twenty-five thousand Balboan soldiers not only send money home, they represent at least twenty thousand Josefinan families who will be pretty damned annoyed if their kids get killed."

"And what if the Balboans get vindictive?"

Esmeralda shrugged, not with indifference but to cover the fact that she didn't have a clue what then.

"You haven't met their president or *duque*, have you, Lieutenant? President Parilla is not an unreasonable man. But their military commander, Carrera, sends shivers up my spine."

This much Wallenstein *had* briefed her on. Again she hit the button.

The hologram paced a few inches back and forth across the table. "I know you're concerned about a possible Balboan over-reaction. The Tauran Union's commander in the Transitway area has committed to me to fly in an initial two battalions with support, as soon as you a) denounce the Balboan arms buildup, b) ask for protection, and c) demand they be disarmed. Larger forces will follow on then.

"We are talking mere hours here for that first screening force, much less time than the Balboans can mobilize a force to punish you."

Again Esmeralda tapped the button to freeze the hologram once more. *Damn, she's* good.

"Can I think about this for a couple of days?" Calderón asked.

Esmeralda didn't need the recorder-communicator to answer that one. "You may, Mr. President."

United Earth Embassy, Aserri, Santa Josefina, Terra Nova

High Admiral Wallenstein had cautioned Esmeralda against telling the ambassador a damned thing when she went to overnight at the embassy. This wasn't easy; the ambassador was a Class One in Old Earth's hierarchy.

And I'm nothing but a freed slave girl who came within inches of becoming a big bowl of chili, with a thermos full sent back home for the discerning palate of Count Castro-Nyere. I can't even converse with the woman; she'd find me out in minutes. Minutes? Hah! Seconds.

She thought long and hard on the problem on the drive from the *Casa Presidencial.* Finally, she decided she could put on a good enough show of being one of the arrogant, near-psychopathic rulers of her home planet and her home province to fool someone who didn't get a chance to engage her in conversation.

Thus, instead of conversing, or even giving the ambassador a chance to invite her to dinner, Esmeralda put her head down, forced her shoulders forward, and barged from the Santa Josefinan-provided limousine, through the embassy doors, demanding, "My room, you pigs! Show me to my room this instant. Heads will roll if it's not ready for me! If you're lucky. And bring me food, you filthy peasants. And a bottle of wine. You crawling excrement should have anticipated my needs. Heads will roll!"

And who says I learned nothing of use from the Castro-Nyeres?

Casa Presidencial, Aserri, Santa Josefina, Terra Nova

Despite Esmeralda's initial thoughts on the matter, President Calderón was about as decent a man as Northern Colombian politics permitted to rise. Corrupt? Sure, a little. Take care of his family first? If you can't count on them, which also means take care of them, who *can* you count on? Even so, and even though family came first, he was unusual in that country was not all that distant a second.

And it is the fate of my country I need to be concerned with. Provoking the Balboan eagles, as I told that charming young— hmm . . . is she young?—girl, is not something to undertake lightly. They have a lot more of our people in their ranks than we do of our people in our supposed ranks. The best case I could hope for, if they decided to turn those soldiers loose on me, is that some portion would side with country over military organization. And how "good" would that be if it just plunged us into civil war? Not much. Maybe better to just lose quickly.

And yet . . . and yet . . . whatever her real reasons, the Old Earth admiral is right. I have read the political underpinnings of the

Balboan system and it is the end of everything I have ever believed in. Social democracy would die wherever they spread their system. Progress as I think of progress would be a joke in poor taste. They are dangerous, deadly dangerous. If even half of what I've heard of their conduct in the war is true ... even a quarter ... well, there's no place for that kind of barbarism on my continent, in my culture, or on my planet.

But why now? Why raise a stink now? It's not for rejuvenation, though there may be advantages in letting the Old Earther think it is. But no, that's not it. What it is, is that until she raised the subject I thought I was completely alone.

Not that I intend to turn down the rejuvenation, of course.

As she was going to sleep that night, it occurred to Esmeralda that, if the high admiral were going to use her as a regular go between, and that seemed the way to bet it, then she really had to get some more clothing than the two business suits the ship's tailor had ginned up for her. That meant going shopping. The problem there was:

I know what the word means. I've even seen it done, when the brothel keepers and under priests and low ranking orthodox druids were looking for fresh meat to pimp out or sacrifice. But I've never actually done it myself. All our needs at home Mama or Papa made or traded for with the locals, or bought off of the occasional traveling salesman. How the hell does one "shop"?

In the end, she'd gone to the embassy's chief of housekeeping, a local, and demanded, in her snottiest tone, a driver and a guide to the city. The guide, as it turned out, was the ambassador's own secretary, Estefani Melendez-Rios.

A spy, in other words. Be careful, Esma.

The secretary, who wouldn't have been released from the ambassador's immediate service except for this service, was altogether kind and friendly, so much so that Esmeralda almost decided to trust her.

But I've been around the fleet enough to know not to trust anybody lightly, and most people not at all.

"I'm going to be coming back regularly, I suspect," Esmeralda told Estefani. "I need to blend in better when I do. Take me to the best woman's shop in the city and get me properly outfitted."

CHAPTER THIRTEEN

The soldiers like training provided it is carried out sensibly.
—Alexander Suvarov

Imperial Base Camp, Balboa, Terra Nova

In theory, both Imperial Range Complex and Imperial Base Camp were jointly administered by the legion and the Tauran Union Security Force. In theory, and with much good will, that could even have worked. In practice, however, since the reservoir of good will at both ends of the tank was pretty much bone dry, it didn't work at all.

The cohorts of the *Legion del Cid* made it a point never to coordinate with the Taurans concerning the ranges and the base camp. They simply had occupied the latter by force, years prior, and made sure that none of the former were ever free.

The camp was a collection of about thirty "buildings," just barely adequate to house a battalion or cohort. The nineteen barracks buildings had roofs, waist-high walls, bare concrete floors, and were otherwise screened against bugs. They were small, so to stuff in the maximum forty or forty-five legionaries of a typical Balboan platoon, bunk beds were required. For many good reasons, high among them vector control (insect infestation prevention) there were no mattresses to the bunks, nor springs, but only plywood bolted to the frames. The troops were expected to blow up their air mattresses and place those above the plywood. From a vector control point of view, this was entirely satisfactory. In the tropic heat of lowland Balboa, however, rubberized air mattresses were some depth below the summit of comfort.

Short version: They sucked so badly that some legionaries dispensed with the air mattresses and made do with the plywood alone.

There were also quarters, differing only in size and the number of sleepers they were required to hold, for the company and field grade officers, as well as the centurions. Cruz and Velasquez got their own individual buildings, each of perhaps a hundred square feet, or a bit less.

A largish mess hall occupied one corner of the camp, and a series of latrines with showers (cold water only) the other. More or less centered in the camp was the headquarters building, different because it was squared and about thirty-five feet on a side. On the southern side, two troopers in mess whites sold cold drinks from a large ice chest. A line for the drinks stretched from the chest, down to the asphalt highway that paralleled the nearby Transitway, and along the highway for some distance.

On one wall on a large blackboard—no high tech out here—was written a week's worth of events for each company and platoon. Standing and staring at it, doing her best to ignore the hustle and bustle of the headquarters, as well as the friendly banter from the sales operation outside, Jan shook her head.

"I just dinna' understan' it. Weeel, barring the dates and places and such."

Cruz, standing next to her, had *serious* issues with the Anglian Army captain's accent. She might as well have been speaking Volgan for all he understood.

On the other side, Hendryksen, who had his own issues with the accent she sometimes fell into, was still able to explain it to Cruz in Spanish. Santillana might have helped, but he'd been called away a bit early, though not until he'd seen to the Tauran visitors' billeting.

"You've got nobody doing the same things, on any given day, from the same units," the Cimbrian said. "It is very confusing."

"In a way," Cruz answered, "it's supposed to be. Or, at least, it's not supposed to be predictable. We call it 'vertical slice evaluation,' and it's one of the core features of our training system and philosophy.

"Basically, any cohort in the legion has ten things it has to be able to do. Why ten? Because that's usually a close approximation of the number of collective missions that may be important, yes, but also because it's a useful number of different kinds of missions for the purpose of developing problem-solving ability in problems involving the use of force to overcome force. Also, since we're a species with ten digits . . . without taking off our boots or unbuttoning our flies, anyway . . . it's an easy number for the troops to understand and relate to. 'Ah, my maniple can do nine of ten missions well. We're ninety percent effective, which isn't bad.' You see?"

"Maybe," Hendryksen answered, noncommitally.

"Okay . . ." Cruz thought about how to explain it. "Let's try this. For my cohort and pretty much any infantry cohort—cohorts in the mountain, marine, and cazador tercios have slightly different ones—the missions are move to contact, hasty attack, deliberate attack, raid, recon, ambush, defend, conduct hasty defense, and delay, plus the mission to suppress civil disturbances. Trust me, in this country, traditionally, that last one is the closest you can get to combat without actually being there."

Listening to the conversation, Jan suddenly found she understood a little more of the board. "MTC" equaled movement to contact. "Amb" was probably ambush. "HDef" was likely hasty defense.

"Now some of those missions translate down directly. Others do not. For mission: Move to Contact, for example, it's really a platoon or maniple mission, and we mostly train it at that level, because if they can do it, the cohort can tag pretty much along in a column of twos. On the other hand, mission: Deliberate Attack *might* be a platoon or maniple mission, but probably not, and there's a whole lot of shit battalion has to be doing for any serious deliberate attack. So we train the platoons and maniples, plus the staff, plus the heavy weapons and specialty people, and we only say 'we can do this,' when everybody in cohort can do their part."

"And that . . . ummm . . . what did you call it—'vertical slice,' was it?—part?" Hendryksen asked.

"We've only got twenty-five days with the militia. Two of those will be taken up with road marches. Four more are slated for weapons qualification. Of the remaining nineteen, we follow the three-to-one rule, approximately."

At Hendryksen's quizzically raised eyebrow, Cruz explained, "Okay, in troop leading procedures higher is supposed to take no more than one-third of the time, right?"

Hendryksen just snorted. *Like* that *ever happens.*

"Well...yeah, we're not perfect about it either. But the principle stands. Our equivalent principle for training is the one quarter rule: Higher headquarters can take no more than one quarter of available time for training it runs or evaluation it insists upon or projects or details. So the maniples get fourteen days to train on the core missions, and we take five to test how well they trained." Cruz sighed with unaimed exasperation. "Yeah, yeah, it's not perfect. Every time the *Duque* has a sit down with the officers or centurions, somebody always asks for a longer annual training period for the militia. At least once that was me. He always tells us to fuck off because the civil economy can't take much more.

"Anyway, because we have so many missions, to be done under so many possible sets of conditions, at so many echelons, squad through cohorts, and only five days to evaluate them, we select a 'vertical slice.' Some squads from each company will get evaluated on a recon patrol or night ambush. Some platoons will do a live-fire trench clearing exercise to allow for their part of a deliberate attack. A couple will do a live fire exercise in building clearing, with grenades. One will be picked to do a deliberate defense. And so on. We test just enough to ensure that the maniples train as hard and well as possible on what's important."

Range 5, Imperial Range Complex, Balboa, Terra Nova

Jan lay beside Cruz about fifteen meters from a straight path cut in the surrounding jungle. She could *feel* the insects feasting on her. Not much she could do about it, either, since the legionaries were forbidden from using insect repellent on a night patrol. As a sort of guest, Captain Campbell felt obliged to follow the custom. The mosquitoes, therefore, feasted.

Ah, well, she thought. *While they're eating at least I don't have to listen to their goddammned buzzing.*

The First Platoon, Third Maniple after a nearly sleepless night on Friday, and a grueling march on Saturday morning, had spent most of the rest of Saturday preparing for ambushes. The veteran senior centurion leading the platoon had set up a sleep plan that had given everyone, except for himself and his optio, at least a couple of hours sleep.

And, mused a more than slightly annoyed Sergeant Major Cruz, *that centurion and I are going to have a little prayer meeting on the subject of whether he and his assistant need sleep sometime tomorrow morning.*

Well after sunset, the men of First Platoon, Cruz accompanying to observe, had marched by road to a release point, then navigated through the jungle to their designated ambush position. There were three such, with Cruz observing one, the maniple commander another, and the maniple's first centurion the third. Weapons platoon was supporting from a firing point a few kilometers away, with the maniple exec hovering over it.

They'd arrived near the position and halted while the platoon leader went forward with five men to recon the ambush position. Carrera's legion made a positive fetish out of never allowing its units to train on the same tactical problem in the same place; so a leader's recon was very important to avoid walking in blind.

By the time the platoon leader had returned to the platoon— after leaving four of the men as flank security for the position—it was well after eleven at night. The position was occupied within half an hour. Then came a long...a very long, buzzing, biting, sucking and draining wait. Some of the blood came from a short blonde with a funny accent.

When Cruz determined that a sufficient amount of time had passed to allow the bone-weary soldiers to fall asleep if they didn't strain to stay alert he spoke a word, softly, into the radio he carried.

At hearing the word, a group of fifteen men walked by the leftmost flank security and then cut into the jungle to be behind the field of fire. The senior man of the left flank security team squeezed a field telephone twice. At the other end bare wire entwined one of the platoon leader's fingers. The shock startled him to full alertness. The outposted troops squeezed once more for every soldier/target that crossed their line of sight.

Ah, fifteen targets, thought the platoon leader.

The men who had presented themselves as fifteen targets took off at a brisk walk for the next ambush position, where a guide would meet them and lead them into position, lest they blunder into a live ambush.

Perhaps two minutes later, and two hundred meters to the

northeast, thus well out of the ambushing platoon's field of fire, two soldiers from the company headquarters had heard the same word as Cruz and began to walk, pulling a rope behind them. The rope ran to a series of targets, connected to each other and hanging from a cable strung overhead. Only balloons, in sandbags and held in place by coat hanger wire, kept the targets fixed to the cable. When the balloons were hit the sandbags would collapse, letting the targets fall to the ground.

As a courtesy, Cruz tapped Jan's shoulder to let her know the action was about to begin. She nodded in the jungle's blackness. Looking intently forward, she thought he could make out the shape of something moving along the trail to his front.

Two directional antipersonnel mines exploded when the platoon leader squeezed the detonators—"clackers" in militarese—he'd held in each hand. *KABOOM! KABOOM!* The mines weren't daisy-chained so there was a small but noticeable lag between blasts.

Jan had never before been so close to such large explosions without being behind cover. A few fragments of plastic casing careened backwards but most of the backblast was absorbed by filled sandbags placed behind the mines. Immediately the night was lit by the muzzle flashes of rifle and machine gun fire . . . and the long bright sparks of tracers. Even the rifles fired on full automatic. Jan was astonished at the cloth-ripping rate of fire of the legionary rifles and light machine guns.

Facing those, she thought, *would be a very scary proposition.*

A rifleman dropped his rifle and sat up. "I'm hit!" he cried. A piece of plastic from a mine had scored the man's arm.

Before Cruz could walk close enough to strike the man with his baton the trooper's fire team leader pulled the—slightly—bleeding soldier to the ground and slapped him into passivity. Cruz breathed more easily. He didn't like to strike a fellow soldier down.

At the first sound of the explosions the men pulling the rope broke into a run. The targets, and most had not been hit by the pellets from the mines, picked up speed. Trip flares lit up the scene for the riflemen and machine gunners. Fire closed on those still remaining targets until, their balloons pierced, they fell to the ground along the line of flight.

Seeing the last target drop, the platoon leader blew his whistle. Almost immediately, the firing ceased. Another whistle, this time a double blast, and certain members got up from the ground, screaming, and assaulted across the killing zone. As they did, each man in the assault team shot a target or two in the "head" as he passed through the kill zone. On the far side, they took up the best positions they could find to secure the rest of their platoon.

Cruz, looked on through one of the cohort's not exactly rare but still precious Volgan-made night vision goggles. He noted with satisfaction that each target was shot at least once more at close range by the assault team. His view swept across the line of men remaining in the ambush position. Again he observed and approved of noncoms, ordinarily privates and corporals of the reserve, checking each man's rifle by touch to determine that they had been placed on "safe." Best of all was when he saw a young corporal—Cruz recognized the striker as PFC Faraudo—slap one soldier's helmet, apparently hard, because the man had failed to put his rifle on "safe." *I think it's maybe time to send Faraudo to Cazador School,* thought Cruz.

Another blast of the centurion's whistle sent a search team out into the kill zone to gather intelligence from the bodies. A small pile of useful tidbits grew near the center of the kill zone. These had been placed in the uniforms draped on the targets before the exercise. Another pile, of plastic weapons carried by the targets, grew nearby. Cruz, accompanied by Jan, stood and followed the search team out. He observed the search team without comment, until he saw one man turn over a target carelessly. Then Cruz took a hand grenade simulator from a pocket, pulled its fuse, and dropped it on the spot where the target had lain. An explosion followed in a few seconds.

"You're hit, dumbass! Deader than fucking chivalry." Cruz pointed at two men nearby. "You're hit, and so are you. Now lie down and *scream* for a medic, both of you. And blame 'dickhead' here." Cruz's stick pointed at the careless soldier. "And YOU! Boy, next time be *careful* as you turn a body over."

"*Si! Sergento-Major. Perdoname, Sergento-Major!*"

"I could forgive you, son," answered Cruz, "but what about the wives and mothers and children of the men your careless-ness might kill?"

"It won't happen again, Sergeant-Major. I promise."

Through the mind of every man flew a single word, *Shit!* The platoon had thirty-seven men assigned and two attached. They'd just lost three plus the one from the mine fragment. If they lost

even one more they would go over the ten percent casualties—
rounded up—permissible under legionary training standards for an
ambush. Then the platoon might have to stay past their twenty-
five days to train to standard. That meant both more misery and
less money. *Shit, indeed.*

Jan was unusual among Anglian military women in the number
and type of courses she'd been allowed to take. These included at
least two where night ambushes were part of the curriculum. She
was used to a well-run ambush. Even so, she was shocked at the
speed and violence of the exercise, and maybe even more shocked
at the short shrift given to safety. Her army, in any case, didn't
think that a couple of sandbags placed behind a directional mine
were quite safe enough, when the mine's pound and a quarter
of high explosive was set off a meter in front of the firing line.

We could do it better, she thought, *at least a little. But... but
we're professionals and these are citizen-soldier militia. Most of
them haven't had a uniform on in the last six months, and that
only for some minor administrative crap. And, okay, sure; they
rehearsed this most of yesterday. But they didn't rehearse it here, on
this spot... like we might or probably would. Their... centurion...
told me the unit has never been on this spot, doing the same mission, before tonight. And I think I believe him. Even if I don't, it
was a good job. So how the fuck did they do that with part-time,
citizen-soldier militia?*

It's an important question and I need an answer to it.

Perhaps twenty feet from Campbell's musing, the platoon leader
used a red-filtered flashlight to inventory the pile of intelligence
items as they were deposited. When he was satisfied that he had
everything he might find—radio, a small book of frequencies and
call signs, two maps, and sundry other pieces, including one little
book marked "journal"—he blew his whistle for the fourth time
that morning. The search team ran back to the ambush position.
Two of its members paused by their platoon leader to divide up
and carry off the pile of intel items. Three others carried the men
Cruz had declared as casualties over their shoulders. Another
blast of the whistle and the assault team, until now waiting as
security on the far side of the kill zone, likewise picked up and
ran to the ambush position.

Calling "Fire in the hole!" three times, loudly, the platoon leader dropped a simulator onto the pile of captured "weapons." He then ran, Cruz right behind him, to rejoin his platoon. They managed to get down just before the simulator exploded. At that moment every soldier in the platoon opened fire again, more or less generally spraying in the direction that any survivors of the ambush might have fled, had it been real. The theory was that this would drive them back to ground long enough for the ambushing unit to make an orderly and safe getaway.

This they proceeded to do, though it was possibly not quite as orderly as the ideal.

Cruz let them return to the last place they had occupied before moving to the ambush position, then halted them to make absolutely sure all weapons were unloaded and to conduct an after action review, a critique of the platoon's performance. Twice during the AAR, he had to stop speaking and questioning as the other two platoons of the company opened up their own ambushes some kilometers away.

When the after action review was over, Jan—whose Spanish was improving by the hour—asked Cruz, "Sergeant Major, is there going to be a stink over that one man whose arm was scored by the mine fragment?"

Cruz snorted. "Ma'am ... you aren't serious, are you? There wouldn't be a stink if we killed him, as long as the exercise was reasonably well calculated—that's a bullshit term meaning guessed at—for the state of training of the unit at the time. We don't have a stink unless we kill too many legionaries too often, where those are defined as more than three or so for a cohort per year."

Yeah, she thought, *these people need a serious dose of figuring out.*

Cerro Urraba (Urraba Hill), Balboa, Terra Nova

On the impressively steep, jungle-clad hill, the sound of picks and shovels rent the air, accompanied by the steady *oogah, oogah, oogah* of a two-man saw.

Campbell, in whose breast was growing a considerable admiration of the scrappy little Balboan legionaries, mused, *Last night another mission, a raid. Now digging in like maniacs for platoon defenses. The Balboans are really starting to get frazzled. But their spirit and morale are still pretty good, considering.*

She realized, not for the first time, *I like these kids. They're not like most part-timers. They're not worried about when their next "fuck-off" time will be.*

As she watched, the maniple's centurions walked the line, pointing with their little sticks at deficiencies in the troops' preparations. Details were stringing barbed wire between the trees and also between some steel stakes that had been driven into the ground.

A centurion jumped up and down on the overhead cover that shielded one fighting position. The centurion stepped off and bent low to look at the tuberculoid "logs" that had gone into the cover. Campbell smiled as the centurion exploded in rage. Two privates and a sergeant quivered in fright at the tongue lashing dished out to them. The centurion said something too low for Jan to hear, then tapped the sergeant twice, each time hard enough to raise welts, on the chest with his stick. As the centurion walked to the next position the sergeant began his own verbal beating of the privates. Within a few minutes the inadequate overhead cover had been disassembled, the logs removed to a draw behind the line. Then the two men trotted off in the direction of *oogah, oogah, oogah* seeking more and better ones.

Campbell glanced to her right. A sergeant, standing a hundred meters in front of where his squad was digging, was pointing out to a corporal how easily his fire team's two fighting positions could be seen. The corporal hurried off to see to the camouflage.

Good. The privates are relatively weak in skills, not so well-trained as the Tauran Union's norm. Or maybe not nearly. *The leadership is...* Campbell hesitated at a painful thought... *maybe... if only a little... better than ours. Better than most of ours for sure. Tougher... more demanding anyway.*

And this promises to be an interesting problem. The platoons have until 0900 tomorrow to finish digging in. Then the maniple CO will have two platoons plus the weapons platoon attack one platoon. He's letting his junior signifer command the attacks. A good experience for a brand new lieutenant. Then they're going to switch off platoons; one of the former attackers will return to its position and become the defender while the previous defending platoon will join in the attack. Should be fun.

CHAPTER FOURTEEN

When women are depressed, they eat or go shopping. Men invade another country. It's a whole different way of thinking.

—Elayne Boosler

Cedral Multiplex Shopping Mall, Aserri, Santa Josefina, Terra Nova

Cedral was one of those places—they existed over most of Colombia del Norte—where the terribly wealthy went up on cool, pleasant, and green hills, to lord it over the peasants in the slums below. Naturally, since that was where the money was, it was also where some bright developers got together to build the largest and most exclusive—to say nothing of most expensive—shopping mall in the country. Even the resorts of the *Mar Furioso* and Shimmering Sea had nothing to match.

Estefani, the ambassador's personal secretary, was older, lighter, and taller than Esmeralda, all three being signs, in her world, of superiority, however unjustified. Even the Castro-Nyeres were approximately as white as High Admiral Wallenstein. Estefani was certainly also better educated. That made her fright at having to escort Esma around more than a little disturbing.

I wonder what she'd say if she knew I grew up as the daughter of a serf and was a slave in the market for a while? No matter what she'd say, really, since I can't tell her.

The secretary licked her lips nervously as the embassy staff car pulled up to the main entrance to the mall. "There are three of these that I know of, ma'am," she said. "This is the second largest."

"Where are the other two?" Esmeralda asked.

"Ma'am, there's one in Lempira and another in Balboa. I believe the one is Balboa is the largest, though they're always adding more stores, so that may have changed."

That "ma'am" thing is bothering me, Esmeralda thought. *But how to get her to stop . . . ah, I know.*

"Estefani," she said, "I am here incognito. I am darker than you and look younger than you. Tell me it's not suspicious for you to be calling me 'ma'am.'"

The secretary switched from licking her lip to chewing at it. "I can't," she admitted.

"Thought not. Call me Esma and I'll call you . . . what do you prefer?"

"Stefi, ma— Stefi."

"Stefi, it is. And it's a nice name, too."

The secretary blushed. "Thanks, ma— Esma."

"Okay. Now that that's out of the way, let me tell you one thing about me, incognito or not. That is that I've spent my entire adult life in the fleet." *Which is absolutely true. You don't have to know I haven't been an adult very long.* "I haven't the first clue about how to dress here and, since I haven't seen anyone on the streets dressed like me, I'm not sure that what the fleet gave me is entirely suitable."

Stefi really didn't want to address that. Fortunately, by that time the driver had come around and opened the door for the two women. "Go find someplace to park, Pedro," Stefi said. "Don't go to sleep and keep your phone on. I'll call when we're done."

As the car pulled away, Esma asked more directly. "Is what I'm wearing suitable?" Seeing Stefi start to chew her lip again, Esma added, "I will not report you."

The secretary sighed. "They're too severe," she admitted. "You look like a lesbian, a mannish lesbian. Especially with the short hair."

"Ohhh. They recycle the water aboard ship, but it's never enough. Most of us keep our hair short. Plus long hair gets in the way in the low grav areas.

"Thank you," Esmeralda said. "Now take me to wherever I need to go to get things that make me look like a regular woman, and not too noticeable."

"That won't exactly work here, either," Stefi said. "Women here dress to be appreciated. It's a fine line we walk; one step too far in a sexy direction and you're a slut...too much in the other and you're a matron or a lesbian, depending."

She looked Esma over appreciatively. "But we can do something with you, I think."

They first saw it between *Joyeria* Haarlem and Veronica's Passion, a recruiting station from the legion in Balboa. A cloth banner over the entrance proclaimed it as such.

Embarrassed, Stefi tried to push on past it. Esma would not. She stopped right in front of the station and put the two stuffed shopping bags she carried down, reading the posters on the front windows.

"Isn't it a little unusual," she asked, "having a foreign country recruiting inside another? Your president told me that traditionally young Santa Josefinan men have joined revolutionary movements all over this quarter of your planet. But one country recruiting inside another just strikes me as different."

"Well," said Stefi, putting her own couple of bags down, "of course on Old Earth there isn't any war or anything like that, and you're a unified planet—as I wish we were—so I guess you couldn't really know, but, yes, it's unusual. Only the Balboans do it, I understand, and they have recruiting stations all over Colombia Latina."

Actually, my dear guide, thought Esmeralda, *there is something a whole lot like war going on back on Old Earth. And with whole swaths of the surface reverted to barbarism, we're not as unified as all that, either.*

"Hmmm," murmured Esmeralda, just loud enough for Estefani to hear, "my commander wanted broad intelligence on this place. I think this qualifies. Guard the shopping bags. I'm going in."

She was lying; neither the high admiral nor any of her staff had suggested that Esmeralda was to gather anything but President Calderón's agreement to denounce Balboa and ask for protection.

"How can I help you, miss?" asked the sergeant at the desk. Though the name tag on the desk said, "Centurion Chavez," the sergeant's name tag read "Riza-Rivera." She decided the latter was probably his name.

There was another one, at a different desk, but he had a phone stuck to his ear and his head bent down over an open manila folder. Three more desks, all empty but showing signs of normal occupation, suggested the recruiting station was much bigger than a two-man deal. There was also a corridor that led off into the recesses of the station or the mall, but there were no signs to say what lay down that way. There was an office door labeled "Doctor Arroyo," but that door was closed.

"Miss?" he repeated.

Esmeralda tore herself from visually scanning around the room and apologized. Then she asked what the sergeant could do for her.

The sergeant shrugged, saying, "Probably not much. We have women in the legion, but, frankly, enough of our own women volunteer from the limited positions available to them that we really don't have a lot of need for foreign women. There's a rumor that this is going to change someday soon but, near as I can tell, that's only a rumor."

"Oh," she said, somewhat dejected and perhaps a little annoyed. Whatever failings the Peace Fleet might have, they were pretty egalitarian as far as gender went.

"Don't look so glum, miss. If you really wanted to join we'd make an effort to try to find you something to do. Good chance though that it would be something miserable."

The sergeant looked her up and down.

He's seeing what Stefi said people would see, a lesbian.

That, in fact, was not what the sergeant saw at all, since Esmeralda's clothing would not have sent the same signal in Balboa as it did here. No, what he saw was a woman too well dressed to be happy scrubbing pots in a field mess.

"May I see your hands, miss?" the sergeant asked.

Esmeralda held them both out, palms down. The sergeant took them in his own hands, running his fingers over what a palm reader would have called her "planetary mounts"—Jupiter through Mercury.

"Odd," said the sergeant. "You're not dressed like a girl who would have much callous. But you do."

"Looks can be deceiving," Esmeralda replied.

Nodding, the sergeant agreed. He opened a drawer in his desk and took from it a cheaply bound volume, about the size of a Catholic missal. He held it up so she could read the cover, "*Historia y Filosofia Moral,* by Dr. Jorge and Marqueli Mendoza. Abridged and annotated."

"We give these out sometimes," the sergeant said, slipping a business card between the pages and handing it to her. "They're special editions printed up expressly for foreigners and high school students. You can have this one to keep. Who knows; it might do you or someone else some good."

"How many stations like this are there?" Esmeralda asked.

"Total, I'm not sure," the sergeant answered. "I know our recruiting maniple for Santa Josefina has eleven, three of them here in the city, and two more in well-populated suburbs. The only other country I know of with that kind of density is Santander, which has four or five times more of them. Well . . . it's that much more populous, after all.

"Other places? Dunno. Some I do know operate out of the embassy. Others are clandestine. Most of them are somewhat subdued.

"Not all of us are recruiters, either." The sergeant jerked a thumb at the man still talking on the phone. "Sergeant Morales' job, for example, is setting up transportation for Santa Josefinan reservists and militia who live here to get back to Balboa for training."

"Well, *that* was interesting," Esmeralda said to Stefi as she slid the booklet she'd been given into her own bags, picked them up, and started to walk again in the direction they'd been going.

"I think it's disgusting," said Stefi. "Recruiting our young men and using them as cannon fodder in their mercenary wars."

"Are they mercenaries?" Esma asked.

"They claim a distinction. They claim they're auxiliaries, currently unemployed. But it's not a distinction that means much to me. We've had several hundred of our boys butchered for their profit. And many times that in wounded and crippled. It's a filthy bunch."

Esmeralda didn't comment on that one way or the other. Instead she asked, "What's next?"

"Makeup!"

Casa Presidencial, Aserri, Santa Josefina, Terra Nova

There was a young black man in a light linen suit with the president when Esmeralda returned. President Calderón introduced the man as "Lieutenant Blanco of our Public Force. He speaks English and French along with our native Spanish."

After spending a few minutes on pleasantries, sincere ones insofar as they reflected Esmeralda's new, more feminine and tasteful appearance, the president cut to the chase.

"If your Admiral Wallenstein wants my cooperation, then she needs to see to it that the Taurans in Balboa admit Lieutenant Blanco into their confidences and show him that they are ready to move at a moment's notice to put troops in place to defend us. When Blanco can assure me that this is ready, *then* and only *then* will I speak out in public against the military buildup in Balboa."

"I'll bring your proposal to her, Mr. President. What you want exceeds my instructions. I cannot agree to it on my own."

"Very well. Blanco will be available as long as needed. Go back to your admiral and get her agreement. For the peace of the planet.

"Now, can that device you played the high admiral's words on for me also record?"

"Yes, it can, Mr. President," Esmeralda said. Khan, male, had taught her how to do that, too.

"Good. I have a prepared statement I would like you to bring to your chieftainess."

High Admiral's Office, UEPF *Spirit of Peace*, in orbit over Terra Nova

With her middle finger resting on her upper lip, her ring finger on the lower, and her pinky on her chin, Marguerite's index finger tapped her nose contemplatively, mostly ignoring the mufti-clad girl who sat opposite her, with a finger poised over a replay button.

She looked down at the small hologram of Calderón Esma had brought back, tapped some more, then muttered, "You are adding complexity, young man, where I neither need nor want it. Actually, you are adding both complexity and scheduling issues."

She sighed. "But, I suppose, in your shoes I would demand no less. Now, the question remains, can I deliver? What would actually be required to defend you from the Balboans, if they decide you need to go?

"Time to go consult Janier again, down below, I suppose. Ground combat I know very little about, and he is supposed to be expert."

She looked in the direction of her cabin girl. *She's showed already some unusual ability. Let's give her another, technically more complex, mission and see how she does.*

"Esma?"

The girl looked up, "Yes, High Admiral?"

"You and I are going to be going back down below, but only to Taurus. Make the arrangements, please, and have signals get a message to General Janier to meet us in..." she consulted her computer for a suitable unobtrusive but comfortable town below "...let's go for someplace with a lot of tourists this time of year... preferably someplace I can fly to directly without screwing around with local airlines.

"Yes, set us up to fly directly to the island of Teixeira, and have Janier meet us there with a small staff. Have him arrange to bring with him whoever is needed to authorize a sufficient force to defend Santa Josefina."

"Yes, High Admiral."

"And get a rejuvenation screening medical team to come with us. I wish we had full capabilities within the fleet, but the Consensus keeps that at home. We'll make do with what we have. We can prepare to deliver on the twenty to twenty-five years I've promised, at least.

"Also get with our ambassador to the World League, below, and have him get us a representative with a little clout."

"Yes, High Admiral."

"And, by the way, Esmeralda, you look very lovely in your new outfit, and properly made up."

"Thank you, High Admiral."

"Who taught you to put on makeup?"

"The ambassador's secretary, in Santa Josefina. She's very nice. I would count her a friend if I could be truthful with her."

"You can't."

"Yes, I know, High Admiral."

Hotel Edward's Palace, Island of Teixeira, Lusitania, Tauran Union, Terra Nova

"The question's a lot more complex than you might think," said Janier to Marguerite, alone, without aides, and before they allowed in Janier's nominal political masters. "And, like many things, it's a political question as much as a military one."

He took a map from a pocket and unfolded it so she could see that it was of the Balboan-Santa Josefinan border, stretching back to Aserri.

"There are two regiments nearby on the Balboan side of the border, both with heavy increments of Santa Josefinans. Of course there are a lot more farther in, thirty-five or so, I think, exclusive of support.

"But to get those up to the border requires time and effort, which means warning. So it's really only the two close by we need to be able to deal with. As for those...they're not really two regiments. They're really two big companies of professionals—though, since they are not Taurans, they are, at best second rate—with another six company equivalents of barely trained reservists, and perhaps sixteen or so companies of rabble they call 'militia.' I discount that last, but I think we can say that the professionals and the reservists probably form two modestly capable battalions."

Janier's finger traced along the main highway, that ran from *Ciudad* Balboa, along the coast, then to Aserri. "This is the only practical invasion route for them." His finger tapped some high ground, not too far from the border. "This is easily defended by one battalion against two of theirs. Indeed, I think a single company, and not necessarily an elite one, could hold it against two of their battalions, except that a single company could be too easily outflanked."

"I don't know how that works," admitted Marguerite, "so I will take your word for it that a single battalion can defend that road. Why so far back though?"

"Out of artillery range. Enough distance to give time to pursue and destroy any Balboans who come that far. Enough distance for patrols to give warning of an incursion. Also it's the most defensible ground in the area that suits those criteria."

Such a wonder to report to someone who knows what she does not know, thought Janier. *How rare is this world, and probably on hers as well.*

"As for a single battalion defending it, no, not indefinitely, not against everything they might throw at us, but long enough for us to mass the airpower to make it impossible to supply any large force assaulting that battalion, yes. And provided that battalion includes at least one battery of artillery and a company of tanks.

"However, that is not the only problem." Again, his finger

began tracing, this time along the lengthy border between the two countries. "This is a much less tractable problem," he said. "It simply cannot be defended. Fortunately, as a logistic matter, only trivial attacks, mere pinpricks, can come through the jungle. To deal with that I need aerial reconnaissance assets, information from your own ships, overhead, a battalion engaged full time in security and anti-infiltration patrolling on the ground, and another battalion's worth of reaction force, with helicopters, engineers, and artillery but no armor. And I'll need a fourth battalion to allow rotation of the troops for rest and training. Plus service support. In total, I need about six to seven thousand men on the ground, and perhaps twelve hundred in aviation assets."

"What about naval?" she asked.

Janier shook his head. "No, High Admiral. The Santa Josefinans have no real ground forces, but they never disbanded their small navy since it never took part in a coup attempt. They're adequate to screen the seas nearby."

"The Balboans have a not inconsiderable little fleet of their own," Wallenstein objected.

"Yes, I know, including the last true heavy cruiser at sea on this planet, as well as an old aircraft carrier. But the aircraft carrier isn't really capable of contesting with modern air forces, and the cruiser is not really all that heavy. Airpower can secure the seas, provided we know they're coming. That also allows us to avoid those peculiar plastic coastal submarines they've built, the exact capabilities of which has my naval staff at each other's throats."

"How will you get forces to Santa Josefina once President Calderón makes his announcement?" Marguerite asked.

"Well, not from the Transitway Area," Janier hastened to say. "That would be the worst possible time to weaken ourselves in Balboa."

"I agree," she said. "Airship direct from Taurus?"

"That would be my preference," he said. "Six airships for several days, two of them heavy-lift capable, should suffice. The only problem is they will have to be in the air *before* Santa Josefina even asks or there will be a day's worth of window of vulnerability. I want troops debarking the moment Calderón stops talking."

"I concur. Now give me again your troops list."

Janier reached into another pocket and withdrew a small, folded and stapled packet of printed sheets. "It's all there."

"Very good," said Wallenstein. "Now let's go meet our public."

CHAPTER FIFTEEN

Safety is an illusion. Bad things can happen to anyone
at any time, whether you follow the rules or not. You
can check left, check right, check left again before
you step off the curb and into the crosswalk, but that
won't stop an anonymous asshole in his shitty pickup
from putting you in intensive care...

—Megan McCafferty, *Perfect Fifths*

Range 4, Imperial Range Complex, Balboa, Terra Nova

Hendryksen and Cruz observed as a platoon from Third Maniple,
by squads, went through a remarkably ugly structure built of wood,
dirt, and—mostly—tires, clearing it room by room with hand grenades and rifle fire. Hendryksen was alone, today, since Campbell
had semi-attached herself to the cohort operations officer, the I, for
a couple of days, splitting her time between watching the operations,
logistics, and intel office and looking at training close up.

Two men crouching on either side of a window nodded at
each other, pulled the pins from grenades, released the spoons,
and counted: "One...two...throw!"

The grenades sailed through the windows, exploding a couple
of seconds later. Angry black smoke spilled out of the window.
It had been preceded by a cloud of light shrapnel, serrated wire.
Following the twin blasts, first one man, then another, lunged
over the sill and into the room beyond, spraying from the hip
as they did. The first man crouched and sprayed low while the
second stood and sprayed high, just over the head of the first.

"Clear!" came the shout through the window. The rest of the squad begin piling in.

"Marine R.E.S. Mors du Char the Fourth would never approve," said the Cimbrian.

"Who's she?" asked Cruz.

"Tauran Union minister of safety," he replied. "Think: Essence of self-righteous pussy, with a heavy side order of moral cowardice, ignorance, insuperable arrogance, and massive stupidity. If you want to know what's wrong with civilization, Sergeant Major, just look at Marine Mors du Char the Fourth.

"Do you know the type?"

Cruz shook his head. "No, we don't have any of those."

Figures, thought Hendryksen. *The more I watch you guys the more frightened I become.*

The Cimbrian asked, "Sergeant Major, where the hell do you guys get all this ammunition? Or are you all putting on a show for the foreigners?"

He had seen this legionary infantry cohort—essentially a part-time infantry cohort, at that—go through more live ammunition in five days than most army units in Cimbria used in as many months.

Cruz chuckled. "Not a show, no. We were expressly counseled against that.

"No, we use about as much as another army might, but about half of another army's allocation we use for our regular and reserve increment, spread out over the year, and the other half we use when we have everybody together for annual training." He wagged his hand, palm down, adding, "Roughly.

"Other than that, the ammunition account only varies by assigned troop strength and type of unit. I could have the battalion supply sergeant gin up the cost for you, if you're that curious. It's not exactly a secret. If you don't need that much precision, I'd guess that the ammunition for this training period will cost...oh, maybe half a million drachma, give or take. Maybe seven hundred drachma per troop though, of course, some ammunition is more expensive than others."

Cruz considered. "Hmmm...I guess maybe that *is* still substantial. On the other hand, since our basic rifle and machine gun round used little brass—just the stubs for obturation—our ammunition is often a lot cheaper than yours might be.

"But I once heard *Duque* Carrera speak on the subject. He said that while other armies spent their money on computers, paper, pens, transparent slides for ornate briefings, and red carpets to make their headquarters look more civilian and less military, he would spend money on training: food, spare parts, ammunition and fuel."

Hendryksen digested that for a moment. He started to ask, "How many rounds for the twenty-five days for—" then stopped, his attention diverted by a series of unusual squeaking sounds. He turned to look.

Gaping, he asked, "What the hell is that?"

Cruz also turned around, to see a half-dozen wheelchairs carrying crippled men, along with some ten apparently mentally retarded kids taking turns pushing them up the road. Cruz smiled; he did not laugh. "*That* is the TSC, the *Tercio Santa Cecilia*. It is one of only . . . well, very few named tercios in the legions that *I* know of. Oh, they've got a number but nobody much uses it, while every tercio has a name but is almost always referred to by its number, sometimes with an honorific like 'Cazador' or 'Mountain' or 'Marine.' There's also a Tercio Socrates, for old folks who decide to join. And one hears persistent rumors that a couple more are going to be raised."

Cruz continued, "The TSC are an interesting story. It seems that, about a year and a half ago, *Duque* Carrera was visiting the building where they test new recruits for the legion. It's in *Ciudad* Balboa.

"Anyway, there was a demonstration outside the building. It consisted mostly of a number of crippled people, almost all in wheelchairs, who objected to being denied enlistment and the right to become full citizens. *Duque* Carrera listened and decided that they had justice on their side, provided the people concerned could understand the oath of enlistment. So he ordered the TSC formed. The *Tercio Santa Cecilia,* he named it himself, must find useful military work for those who cannot qualify for service in a regular tercio but insist on their right to serve. Some of them are formerly fit legionaries who were badly hurt in accidents and didn't want to take a medical discharge.

"But there's a tank turret range about two miles down that road, so those people are probably *Adios Patria* troops."

"Farewell Fatherland?"

"Yes. Those men are assigned to serve in fixed tank turrets, ones that have been taken from unserviceable or modified tanks and mounted in fixed fortifications. You can buy a tank turret for as little as a few thousand drachmas, you know. And, once mounted in concrete, they don't need a lot of care and can take a lot of killing."

Hendryksen was normally pale. He seemed paler still as he said, "But retarded kids? That's ... not to be judgmental, Sergeant Major, but I just don't have any words for how *evil* that strikes me as being, using the retarded for defense."

"Well," observed Cruz, "if you guys don't attack us then those guys will be perfectly safe, won't they?"

Hendryksen started to say something, his mouth opening and closing several times like a gasping fish.

Cruz opted to help him out. "Generally—if not always—the mentally retarded *can* be trained to do many things by rote. I understand that the para- and quadriplegics are the gunners and commanders, while the mentally retarded load the gun and hand ammunition up to the turret from a concrete bunker that's built below. They also do the scut work; fetching and carrying, and caring for their gunners and commanders.

"Nobody plans on chaining them into their positions, but there would be little chance for them to escape if they had to fight and things got bad. So ... *Farewell Fatherland.*

"I have never worked with them, personally. But they try very hard, I hear. For most of us our basic training is quite difficult. The TSC uses a more soft-handed approach ... little if any harassment; but still a lot of meaningful pain. I don't know enough to say whether that's right or wrong."

Hendryksen muttered something under his breath.

"What was that?"

"I was just thinking out loud. About what a ruthless ... man ... Carrera is; to use the mentally retarded as cannon fodder. What a waste; they can't possibly be effective."

Again, Cruz shrugged. "Well ... he certainly is ... you could say ruthless, I suppose.

"Yet there is more to the story, I think. An acquaintance of mine broke his back and went to the TSC rather than take a medical discharge. He has a crew of three retarded, all *Adios Patria* troops. He says that his 'retarded boys are smarter than dogs, just as loyal, don't slap you in the balls with their paws or drool. They let *themselves* out to go to the bathroom. And, best of all, they have opposable thumbs. They just might be effective enough.' As for ruthless...kind I should think. Kinder anyway than wasting their lives entirely."

The Tauran hid his scowl until a series of explosions within the tire house drew the two men's attention away from the parade of the "*differently abled*," as the community of the caring and sensitive might say.

A few hundred meters from Cruz and the Cimbrian, Legion Corporal Rafael de la Mesa swore under his breath. *Bad enough I am a cripple. But to saddle me with these morons is just too unbearable.*

"Faster, you idiot!" de la Mesa cursed at the retarded boy pushing his wheelchair. "We have only six minutes left to get to our gun turret!"

The boy was almost immune to insult, and was sure Corporal de la Mesa didn't mean anything by it, anyway. Well...he was *almost* sure. You never really knew with the normals. Some were kind and despised you. Others were harsh but loved you. In that little no man's land of uncertainty, he got along about as well as could be expected. And he was proud, too, proud of his uniform, proud he could take the harsh conditions and harsh language his leader sometimes meted out. And at least he didn't cry when it hurt. The boy—his physical age was twenty-three, his mental age perhaps twelve or thirteen—redoubled his efforts to push de la Mesa's wheelchair a bit faster.

"Good boy, Pablo," said the corporal, which got him a smile in return and a bit more speed as, encouraged, Pablo broke into a trot.

Range 6, Imperial Range Complex, Balboa, Terra Nova

Low berms dotted the landscape, adding some terrain to what was otherwise about a square kilometer of flat nothing-too-much. That square kilometer wasn't square in shape. Framed by a creek on one side, a mostly dead pond on the other, it formed a tongue jutting out from the road paralleling the Transitway. The whole thing was made of spoil from the digging of the Transitway.

Ahead, forming a mirror image of the rounded tip of the tongue, seven sandbagged bunkers lay, protected by wire out front and connected, one to the other, by trenches, with two more trenches zigzagging back to the tip of the tongue and its drop off to thin creek and dead pond, below.

The concertina wire was strung in a belt forty or fifty meters in front of the arc of bunker and trench. More concertina, ripped and rusted, struck up from the ground, residue of previous exercises. The sound of small explosions—they were merely firecrackers meant to simulate hostile gunfire—rattled from the bunkers. The problem had given the Balboans mortar support. Small blocks of TNT, electrically detonated on the objective, provided that. To add to the realism craters had been dug on and in front of the objective, just as would be there if real mortars and artillery had been used.

And there it is again, thought Jan, *that same overdependence on their leaders.*

What made her think so was the way in which legionary infantry clustered in small groups—with three or sometimes at little as two meters between soldiers—rather than spreading out like Tauran and South Columbian soldiers did.

"Is that wise, Top?" she asked the maniple first centurion. "Clustering up like that, I mean. What about artillery? Mortars?"

Top reminded her a little of Sergeant Major Cruz, but bigger across the shoulders, taller, and maybe a little darker.

The centurion answered, "It's a tradeoff, I suppose. Note that the cover available doesn't really support spreading out too much. Better four men in a ten-foot shell hole than one safe in it and three more exposed.

"Then there's the moral factor. Some Old Earth writer—a general, too, I think he was—said that what made men fight was the near or presumed presence of a comrade. We don't like to have the men have to presume too much...and we want them to be willing and able to fight.

"Besides, our reserves are pretty well trained, but the militia are not as good. So we get more out of the militia if we put them physically closer to their leaders in the reserves.

"One other thing, too," and here the centurion was almost quoting verbatim from the manual, "if you think about how artillery and mortars really act, you'll realize that it makes little or no difference if the men cluster. True, it is somewhat more likely you may lose an entire fire team or even a squad to a single large indirect fire round. But how often is artillery fired in single rounds to any effect?' And, of course, mines are a problem. But then, too, it is also more likely to lose men by ones and twos if you spread them out than if they are close together. And when closer together they can—like I said—sometimes take better advantage of cover... or find a narrow way through mines."

The centurion pointed down range, the front end of his "stick" catching the sun. "See how all of that squad can fit into that shell crater. We think it evens out, overall. Besides, we have little choice... Now, watch! It looks like the assault is starting to go in. Let's move forward!"

With machine guns firing to either side—which made Jan distinctly nervous—she and the first shirt walked forward in the general direction of the trench line. If the Balboan was at all bothered by it, Campbell couldn't tell. They stopped atop one of the berms where they could see all the action.

The first centurion looked around. A team of six—one was the platoon leader, Senior Centurion Umberto Minden—was moving backwards. The platoon leader was easily the tallest man in the company, towering over the rest by as much as two feet.

The first centurion bellowed, "Umberto, what is this retrograde bullshit? Post!" His stick slapped his thigh.

There followed a wait of several minutes while Minden made short dashes toward the berm on which the centurion and Campbell stood. He was delayed by machine guns and RGLs firing overhead and nearby to suppress the bunkers and trench lines. Then the gasping—almost retching, really—platoon leader came to a covered halt at his first shirt's feet. The latter's stick was tapping a tattoo against his left leg.

"We're... waiting," Minden gasped, "... for ..."—gasp—"... the ..."—gasp—"... explosion," he finally managed to get out.

"Explosion? What explosion?!"

Without warning, Campbell and Top were rocked back over a meter, barely keeping their feet as a fifteen-pound satchel charge detonated about seventy-five meters to their right front.

Top was the first to recover his equilibrium. He made sure to tuck his stick back under his arm before speaking, "I see. *That* explosion. Carry on, Centurion."

By the time Minden returned to his headquarters team, his junior centurion was already directing the assault.

Campbell's ears were still ringing. Seventy-five meters away was just way too close to set off that large a blast without people being behind cover. *Or warned to cover their fucking ears at a minimum.*

"An unusual case, Centurion Minden," said Top.

"Unusual?" prodded Campbell.

"Oh, yes. He is one of only seven men in the legion that have served in three different armies; in his case the Castilian, the Sachsen, and ours. Two armies? No, that's not unusual. We have Volgans, Southern Columbians, a few Secordians, Jagelonians... all kinds of Latins, Cochinese... Shitloads of refugees from other armies, other cultures. But three is quite rare. I expect him to go far."

"Because he's been in three armies?" asked Jan.

"No, ma'am," Top replied. "Because he went looking for the right army and finally found it. Why, had it not been for us, he might have ended up with the Gauls. What a waste that would have been!"

The maniple called a halt about the time the sun went down. They were behind on sleep, and had some serious action planned for the following day. Better still, the mess folks had turned their normal rations into something more fully resembling a real meal.

Campbell and Hendryksen had been doing pretty well on their own side's rations. After all, with about nine different cuisines, and about thirty-five different menus, to choose from, at least they weren't bored. This was an artifact of having so many different detachments in the Tauran Union Security Force. Normally, a Tauran army had anywhere from two to eight different menus. Which was sheer hell if one had to live off them for any period of time.

That night Top and Campbell spoke further. Rather, she continued grilling him as she had been, which grilling he put up with and with good humor. He'd also invited her to share a meal of legionary rations. Since that, too, was a part of combat effectiveness, she'd agreed...as long as she was invited. She wasn't about to overstay her welcome by asking.

Once she'd assented, Top made a signal to a private, two fingers held up. The private scurried off to the mess line, grabbed two metal trays, a fork and knife, and a couple of cups, then got in the line.

That's the first thing I've seen that says they're putting on any show for my benefit at all, Jan thought. *And, under the circumstances— not knowing if I was willing to eat with them—it strikes as less a show than an effort at politeness and economy.*

The private brought the two trays over, then passed them over carefully to avoid spilling the drinks. Jan sniffed and had to admit, "Smells...pretty good, Top."

"Damned well better," said the first centurion, "or I'll have the cooks *cojones* to decorate my stick... Oh, sorry, ma'am."

"I've heard the word, and in more than one language," she answered. "Don't sweat it.

"Something has been bugging me, though."

"Yes?"

"I've been with your cohort now for a while. Why haven't I seen any man have to eat the same thing twice?"

Legion rations were canned, as most armies' had been until quite recently, but came in squad packs, something like Anglian rations did.

"I've eaten a lot of other folks' rations," Top said. "And I know something about this since it's a half day's training at the Centurion Candidate School.

"We just have a lot more menus than you do. Over seven hundred daily menus, to be exact...in theory. The real number is somewhat less because some things just don't go well together. At any time there are something like forty-eight individual meal menus, with variables...starch, desert, vegetables. I say 'something like' because they change them out, so there might be more than forty-eight in the system. Usually are, in fact.

"I think this is one area where *we* outdo everybody else. Still, you needn't be ashamed. *Our* people are simpler, not so sophisticated..."

"You mean 'spoiled.'" she said.

"I didn't say that. But, since you did...Anyway, our legionaries just expect less. They'll eat what is put in front of them. So the people who designed the ration system—I understand General Carrera took a personal hand in that, too; oh...and he taste tests every one—don't have to worry so much about making meals that everyone will eat. Everyone will eat pretty much everything. It allows us more... latitude?... in planning meals. And we don't try to worry about each individual meal being balanced; as long as the average is balanced. On the other side... it's also kind of demoralizing, you know... when a soldier can tell what day it is by what he's eating? That's almost impossible with our rations."

Illustrating the point somewhat, Top picked up his fork and dug in.

Jan dug in herself. *Well,* she thought, *at least Balboan cuisine didn't start on a dare. Not bad, really.*

She heard a series of harshly barked commands interspersed with thumps and pained grunts coming out of the jungle behind her. Setting her fork down she turned to look. Walking upright, stick under one arm, a tall and slender junior centurion, as black as the end caps to his stick, gave an order.

"Centurion, J.G., León," Top volunteered. "A hard ass even by our standards."

León gave another command. Four unfortunates arose from the ground, rushed forward, and flopped down.

"*Tsk,*" said Top. "How sad?"

León's loudly voiced opinion was that it wasn't sad and they were not unfortunate. "You lazy shits will do this to my utter satisfaction or your own death, whichever comes first. Again!"

"Who are they?" Jan asked in a hush.

"B team, Third Squad, Second Platoon," Top said. "They're short a man so it's one reservist corporal and three militia privates. They got sloppy... yes, lazy, too, while the platoon had run through the range. Were too slow in their rushes. Maniple commander had assessed them as casualties, which—with other casualties—had caused the platoon to fail the mission even though they had taken the objective. So León's going to fix it so they don't get lazy again. Cause *his* platoon to exceed the standard for casualties, and fail? Make it so everybody had to do the problem again? Only right they suffer for it."

At another of the junior centurion's orders the four flung themselves to the rock-strewn ground. León gave them only a scant second's breather before sending them off again.

The four boys had been doing short—three to five second—rushes, without a serious break and certainly without dinner, since well before sunset. They were cut and bruised from the many rocks that littered the ground. Jan turned away, embarrassed, as

León smacked the corporal across the shoulder with his "stick." "Maggot! This is how you lead my boys?"

A cook brought over two large mugs of coffee, handing one each to Jan and Top. Jan sniffed at hers as the first centurion offered simple, "Thanks." One sip and Jan started to choke, much to Top's amusement.

"What the hell is *in* this?" she demanded.

Top sipped and answered, "My guess would be about two ounces of straight grain alcohol. But you're a guest and we have some extra so yours may be a little stronger than that.

"It comes, canned, with the ration packs. Roughly two ounces per man per day. Sometimes we withhold it, for punishment . . . or to save for a special occasion. Although ordinarily the squad leader has the power to dispense or withhold the daily alcohol ration, in this case, because they all failed, the platoon won't get any."

"You aren't afraid of one of them going wild; what with all this ammunition?"

Top quoted something he had heard the late Sergeant Major McNamara say at Centurion Candidate School. "'You can *never* teach men not to drink. You *can* teach them to drink responsibly.' We try to. Mostly, it works."

As Campbell again sipped, more carefully, at her coffee, León's voice, and slashing "stick," cut the night. "*Gusanos! Maricones! Otra Vez!*" Worms! Fags! Again . . . And again. And yet again. The thuds of bruised and bleeding bodies, self-tortured, sounded faintly in the distance.

CHAPTER SIXTEEN

> 'Tis pleasant purchasing our fellow-creatures; And all
> are to be sold, if you consider Their passions, and are
> dext'rous; some by features Are brought up, others by
> a warlike leader; Some by a place—as tend their years
> or natures; The most by ready cash—but all have prices,
> From crowns to kicks, according to their vices.
>
> —Lord Byron, *Don Juan (canto V, st. 27)*

Teixeira Island, Lusitania, Tauran Union, Terra Nova.

The promise of limited rejuvenation hung in the air. Still, Marguerite couldn't mention it openly; there were politicos and diplomats present who really were principled, who really thought they were working for mankind, not for themselves. This, of course, didn't stop them from living pretty well as they worked for the betterment of mankind, but that made them only human.

Fortunately, she thought, *there are also plenty of people here who are unprincipled, who know exactly what's on offer and would gladly kill their mothers for the reward. Oh, we are so obviously of the same species... and I see my own government in proto form right here.*

Marguerite had looked to ensure that her predecessor's former occasional lover, Unni Wiglan, was not present. *I wonder if she figured out where one of the nukes she arranged to provide to Martin ended up. In any case, I'm glad she's not very prominent anymore; the idea of increasing her lifespan is just too wrong on so many levels.*

On the other hand, now that I think about it, it might be worth finding out, if possible, if she has guessed where the nuke for Hajar came from. If so, she's got a very dangerous piece of information.

That's for the future, though. For now I have other problems.

In one corner, over a table, Janier and the small staff cell he'd brought with him were arguing with half a dozen representatives of both Tauran Union and national ministries of defense over just how big the slice for Santa Josefina must be.

At least, thought Marguerite, *they're not still arguing over the* principle *of sending troops to guard Santa Josefina, just the numbers.* For the tenth or twentieth time, she once again looked over the force list Janier had given her.

I think Janier's got a defensible force package. Combat forces: Four light infantry battalions, one commando company or equivalent, one tank company. Combat support: One artillery battalion, one engineer battalion—clever bastard sold them on that one already with his "they will be invaluable for civic action and public works" routine—one MP company for route security and prisoner guard, and an air defense artillery battery. Aviation: A helicopter squadron, a fighter-bomber squadron, and a recon squadron, with a maintenance squadron and a headquarters and support squadron. Headquarters and service support: One forward support battalion, one rear support battalion, plus medical and transportation companies extra. And a headquarters battalion with signal, PSYOP, and intelligence companies.

One of Janier's underlings, a short and stocky type, running to fat, named Malcoeur, walked briskly over from where he'd been scribbling on an easel with butcher paper. "Madame Admiral," he said, "the general could use a little moral support."

Something in Malcoeur's tone suggested that he'd be perfectly happy if Marguerite just let the general stew. She let that pass for the nonce. Folding the force list packet up and putting it away, she stood and walked to the corner table where Janier argued with the ministerial representatives.

"What seems to be the problem, General?" she asked of Janier.

The latter theatrically held clenched fist to forehead. "The world prepares to burn," he said, full of self-righteous fury, "and these . . . these *people* argue over who is going to pay for the water."

Thinking, *He's a little too melodramatic to make it in the theater, but not bad for a military or naval officer,* Wallenstein raised a scornful eyebrow and glared at the assembled bureaucrats. "In all of my roughly *two hundred* years"—she emphasized the number, then paused to let that emphasized number sink in—"I have never seen such a shortsighted, narrow-minded group of... Oh, *words fail!*"

Maybe I should have petulantly stamped my foot. Or is the Gaul's overacting affecting my judgment?

"Madame High Admiral," said the middle-aged representative of Tuscany, "our problem is that we have to go back to our masters in our own capitals and justify why we offered X, while Anglia or Gaul or Sachsen offered only Y. Ask them and they'll tell you exactly the same things, only substituting their country for Tuscany."

"And the perfidious Castilian," said the Gallic representative, "offers nothing but some medicos and propagandists."

"I told you before, gentlemen," said the Castilian, "the defection of Colonel Muñoz-Infantes and his entire battalion to the Balboans has tied our hands. We cannot give a penny, we cannot offer so much as a round of ammunition, to anything that endangers our men there directly, even if they are defectors." The Castilian glared at Janier and then at the other Gauls, in turn. "They should perhaps have realized that when they tried to have Muñoz-Infantes killed...and *failed.*"

"No more than arrested," countered Janier. We would never have killed an allied officer.

"*Nobody* believes *that*," said the Castilian.

Replied Janier, "I cannot be held responsible for the paranoid delusions of others."

Of course, General, thought Marguerite, looking directly at Janier, *you absolutely* did *intend that Muñoz-Infantes would be killed.*

Well of course, said Janier's return glance. *I only look stupid and even then only when I drink. To excess.*

"Who is offering what?" asked Wallenstein.

"The republic of Gaul," said Janier, most self-righteously, "has offered two infantry battalions, a service support battalion, and a headquarters company with a brigadier general to command the force."

"Funny," said the Anglian representative, Mr. Crewe, short, plump, and clever-looking. "Funny how the bloody Gauls are always willing to provide a commander."

"And Anglia has offered?" asked Marguerite.

"Ummm...one infantry battalion and...ummm...a brigadier to command."

Janier laughed aloud, calling to the entire room, "Hypocrites. Oh, perfidious Anglia."

Marguerite scanned over the assembling Taurans. "Will you accept," she asked, "my judgment of who should command?"

"Somebody has to decide," said Cimbria. "And we'll never agree on our own. Madame High Admiral, will you *please* be the one to decide?"

This was greeted with murmurs of approval, generally, with only the Gauls and Anglians remaining silent. "Oh, all bloody right," said Crewe, relenting.

Janier didn't wait for the civilian from Gaul to say a word. "Gaul agrees," he said, earning himself a glare from the civilian. "Malcoeur, show the high admiral what's on offer."

The aide went back to the butcher paper and flipped several sheets back. "Here, High Admiral."

Wallenstein read:

Formation	Approx Strength	From
Inf Bn 1	800	Gaul
Inf Bn 2	800	Gaul
Inf Bn 3	800	Anglia
Inf Bn 4	800	Sachsen
Eng Bn	650	Tuscany
Artillery Bn	380	Haarlem
Commando Comp	120	Cimbria
Tank Comp w/Maint	80	Hordaland
MP Comp	180	Sachsen
ADA Battery	160	Götaland
CS Bn H&S Comp	210	Mixed
Helicopter Sqdrn	470	Tuscany
Ftr-Bmbr Sqdrn	90	Anglia
Aerial Recce Sqdrn	90	Sachsen
Avn Maint	290	Mixed
Avn Grp H&S Sqdrn	190	Mixed

Forward Support Bn	330	Lusitania
Rear Support Bn	420	Anglia
GS Trans Comp	180	Mannerheim
GS Med Comp	110	Castilla
Svc Spt Group HQ	80	Mixed
Intel Comp	100	Anglia
Signal Comp	150	Mixed
PSYOP Comp	90	Castilla
HHD, Bde HQ Bn	95	Mixed
Headquarter, Bde	130	Mixed...???

"That," pointed out Malcoeur, "is merely tentative, High Admiral. No one has yet definitively agreed to anything."

"It's heavy on multilingual people in a number of places," added Janier, "some of the headquarters, the signal company, the intelligence company, and aviation maintenance and air operations support, especially. It's unavoidable, really, with this many languages involved."

"This isn't entirely based on population or wealth or size of military, is it?" asked Marguerite.

"No, High Admiral," Janier admitted. "Those were factors, of course, but one of the big drivers, as especially with Castile, is willingness."

"High Admiral," said the representative from Hordaland, "we can't offer anything in good faith that our governments won't, in good faith, honor.

"Will they honor that?" she asked, pointing at Malcoeur's easel and butcher paper. "And the sticking point is who's to be in charge?"

"Yes, High Admiral," said all the representatives of the big four—Gaul, Anglia, Sachsen, and Tuscany—together.

"Will Anglia accept a Gallic commander?" she asked.

"Under no circumstances," answered Crewe. "Been there. Done that. Didn't like it the first time."

She looked past Janier for the representative of the Republic of Gaul. "No Anglian commander," he said, without being asked.

She looked for the Sachsen rep. Even before she found him both Gaul and Anglian said, "No, no Sachsen commander."

"We've both been there before," said the Gaul, "and we liked that even less."

"Is there a brigadier or major general in the Tuscan army everyone could approve of?" she asked the Sachsen, who was surprisingly not very put out that the Gauls and Anglians had nixed a Sachsen general.

"Claudio Marciano," the Sachsen said. "I think he's retired now..."

"Semi," said the Tuscan rep. "He's working for the World League."

"Available then?" Marguerite asked.

"The World League would be happy to send him to command this force," said Mr. Villechaize, from the World League, "but for him to have command authority the Tuscans, or someone in the Tauran Union, would have to recommission him."

"We could recall him to duty," said the Tuscan.

"Objections, Anglia? Gaul?"

"Not really," answered Crewe. After all, *Anybody but the bloody Frogs.*

"None," said Janier. After all, *At least Italian is a related tongue... and not English.*

"Let's call that settled then," said Wallenstein. "That force list. The Tuscan in command, certainly for the first iteration. Now how do we transport them? And remember, there's not a lot of time to waste here."

In a private dining room she shared with the general, Marguerite rubbed at her temples. *There are some kinds of headaches even Old Earth medicine can't do a thing about.*

Janier clucked sympathetically.

"It comes with dealing with a certain kind of bureaucrat," he said. "On the other hand, without your moral authority as the representative of Old Earth and commander of the Peace Fleet, we'd still be arguing, we'd have gotten nowhere, and my headache would be even worse than yours, I assure you."

He didn't mention the implicit major bribe. By common understanding that was an unmentionable.

He managed to raise a reluctant chuckle out of the high admiral. Sadly, the chuckle raised her pain level.

"Will the rest uphold their part of the bargain?" she asked through the curtain of her pain.

He nodded sagely. "I think so. After all, it's not as if we're trying to get them to, say, actually agree to and follow through on sub-stantially larger defense budgets. The forces they've agreed to are already in existence and won't cost more—rather less, actually—to maintain in Santa Josefina than in their home countries."

"Does it leave you enough to reinforce the Transitway Area as we've discussed?"

"Yes, though if you think they whined and moaned about the less than eight thousand troops going to Santa Josefina, under Tuscan command, wait until they have to produce fifty thousand, plus another twenty in follow-on forces, under my command." He hesitated, then reaching into a pocket said, "Oh, that reminds me." He pulled a fax from the pocket and handed it over, but said what it was anyway. "The Republic of Gaul is promoting me to a rank commensurate with command of the corps I intend to raise in the Transitway Area."

"Good," she said, "because I can already hear the rest whining that you are too junior and using that as an excuse to withhold troops."

"My thought, precisely, which is why I expended a few tokens to arrange the promotion."

Again she laughed and again she winced. "Oh, we are so *obviously* the same species and culture."

"Indeed?"

"Oh, I think so."

"Old Earth must be a very fucked up place then."

"In some ways, sure," she admitted. "Where is that not true?"

"What—" The waiter's knock on the door interrupted Janier in whatever he'd been about to ask.

"How do you think the other side is going to react to this?" she asked.

"Shock," said Janier. "They've had the initiative for a while now, long enough to have gotten used to it. Even when they started to back off from their provocations, that was them exercising initiative they were sure was theirs, probably forever.

"This will be the first time in that same while that we've taken the initiative. That we're taking it in a place they consider mostly theirs—a friend, a cultural ally, and a recruiting ground—is going to shock them silly."

"What will they *do* though?" Wallenstein asked.

"Mobilize one of the two regiments they have near their eastern border with *Valle de las Lunas*," Janier said, definitively. "I doubt they can keep both mobilized without wrecking the local economy. We can probably anticipate a border incident or two, but even if not those defensive preparations of theirs can easily be presented as offensive. *Then* I can start the provocations around the borders of the Transitway Area that, to date, my political masters have not permitted."

"Because it will keep the Balboans focused on defense rather than on an invasion of Santa Josefina?"

"Precisely. And our provocations will keep the Balboans half mobilized, hence more threatening looking than ever. And that, too, will mean firmer grounds for me to demand more troops.

"Eventually, the need to keep mobilized, plus the threats from our provocations, plus fear and fatigue, will have them—rather, their ill-disciplined troops—do something to justify an invasion."

"How soon do you think the force for Santa Josefina will be ready to move?" she asked.

"I talked to a friend," he answered. "The two Gallic infantry battalions and a temporary command element can move in three days. That's important because, once we move, the others will have to follow along quickly. Three airships are loading now, as a matter of fact. Everyone else will be rather slower, of course."

"Speaking of faster and slower," asked Wallenstein, "do I need to restate how key timing is going to be to all this? The troops must be in the air and ready to land within just a few hours of Calderón's request."

"Yes, I know," agreed Janier, adding with a smile, "But timing, in love or war, is a Gallic strong suit."

Wallenstein mentally sighed. *Dammit, I could enjoy bedding this man in any other circumstances. Rather, being bedded by him. He's just the sort to take me away from responsibility and put me in my place. Damn duty.*

Southeast corner of Santa Josefina, above the Chelonia National Park, Terra Nova

Though the Noahs had transplanted nearly every kind of animal found on Old Earth, half a million to five million years prior, to Terra Nova, and done whatever could reasonably be done to prevent intelligent, hence dangerous, life from arising on the new world, once man had shown up a great many of those salvaged species went into precipitous decline. Sabretooths? Some species still lived. Others existed only as trophies on walls or rugs in stately homes and palaces. The phorusrhacids, the giant terror birds of Colombia del Norte? Some lived in zoos, but none were believed left in the wild. Megs still roamed the seas, but it was believed that their numbers had dwindled almost to the vanishing point as their food supplies were hunted out by man.

The giant turtles and tortoises, however, if not precisely thriving still were a ways from extinction. For one thing because they lived a long time, this could, food permitting and a mate being available, fill up their ecological niches even after a severe period of being hunted. For another, they were rather magnificent, where magnificence equaled tourism, tourism equaled money, and money meant someone thought them worth protecting.

Santa Josefina's major industries included the production of "oohs" and "aahs" from the environmentally conscious. Thus, despite being slow prey, the giants of the Chelonia National Park, after a fashion, thrived.

Several of them, at least two engaged in copulation, looked up at a strange thrumming sound never before heard above their little protected homeland. Since terrestrial chelenoids tended to have their eyes set downward, the better to find food on land, they—all but the male engaged in copulation—had to really strain to look up.

Had the tortoises been of a religious bent, they might have bowed in awe and wonder, and maybe even a little shock, too, at the spectacle of three huge forms, as turtlelike as made, to them, no difference, flying through the air.

For good or ill, however, the shellbacks were not noted for their religious sentiment.

Like turtles, the airships were slow, no doubt about it. The early ones were also far too dependent on ground support. The newer versions, though, hybrids that obtained about three fifths to two thirds of their lift from gas and the rest aerodynamically, didn't need a lot of ground support. Better, they were cheap to run. Better still, they could carry loads that airplanes couldn't really hope to; eighteen or twenty tanks, say, or a battalion of foot infantry with its forty or so vehicles, say.

There were three of them, cross loaded so that about a third of each of two Gallic infantry battalion rode in each, with the remaining lift devoted to necessary supplies until arrangements could be made for local purchase. There was, of course, no known reason to take the precaution of cross loading. Even so, and even without enemy help, airships had been known to go down. And the Gauls, whatever their other failings, still planned for the unlikely but potentially disastrous.

With tortoises, huge ones, visible below—"Hey, Jacques, look at those two monsters screwing!"—the three airships from the Republic of Gaul Air Force crossed the shore at modest speed and low elevation, then lifted their noses and applied power to their under-mounted fans, to fight their way over the central cordillera common to all the states of Colombia Central. The spot they were to cross had been carefully worked out prior. Near that spot, Lieutenant Blanco of Santa Josefina's Public Force watched the three pass. Then, reasonably confident that they represented the Taurans upholding their side of the bargain, he called his president to say that the cavalry was riding over the hill in the nick of time.

CHAPTER SEVENTEEN

In war, an approximation of the truth may best
be reached by a comparison of the lies.

—Leon Trotsky

Range 4, Imperial Range Complex, Balboa, Terra Nova

The shell had come down without warning. Where it hit and
blossomed into an angry black flower, men, several of them, were
scythed down, screaming in pain. Jan had seen it hit, and had
seen the maniple's reaction to it, too.

She shook her head now, half with disgust. A medical Cricket
was taking off, laden with two wounded, one of them seriously.
The Crickets were the legion's light STOL aircraft, used for many
things that other armies used more expensive helicopters for. The
Cricket couldn't get in as many spots as a helicopter could, but
it was more likely to be ready to go in those spots it could get
into. As that one took off with its bleeding cargo, another one
was settling down a few score meters from where the first had
been. Immediately three medics, one holding an IV bag above
his head, began loading another wounded man into the back of
the thing through a lowered ramp.

It was one of those things; a defective mortar round had
landed where it should not have, right by an infantry squad. The
remainder of that squad, and the rest of its platoon and maniple,
were continuing on with the attack, as if there hadn't even been
an accident.

Jan found that disgusting, too.

"Why do they put up with this, Sergeant Major?" she asked of Cruz. "Our reservists never would. Maybe not our regulars anymore either."

Nor should they, she thought.

Cruz shrugged just as if he didn't understand the question. "Why shouldn't they put up with it, ma'am? They're soldiers, and well-paid ones, too, by my poor country's standards. And most of them work in jobs *Duque* Carrera and *Presidente* Parilla created for them. Or they have businesses they set up or farms they bought with loans from the legion. Or they are going to school on the legion ticket."

Cruz continued, "And we are a close group, you know. Even when we're not training together. That corporal that León was, ah...counseling the other night? He's León's little brother. And the reserves and militia are full members of the tercio, even if they're only on duty less than a month a year. Or about two and a half months for the reserves. They're welcome at our troops' clubs, and they come because girls come...soldiers are very popular in Balboa now. The soldiers are bigger, stronger, and they have more money to spend—on a good time...or on a home, food, cradles, and diapers. Because of that, and—frankly—in some cases, because the booze is cheaper. If they're married, their wives can shop at the tercio commissary and exchange. Most attend our chapel quite often. A lot of them are allowed to live in the barracks free of charge if they wish, and if we have room. That lets them save money while going to school or getting established in their civilian jobs. They can pay to eat in the tercio mess to save money too, if they want to. It gives our cooks training without costing the government much.

"Even when they are not so involved in the tercio their friends tend to come from the tercio. They hang out at bars off of the post that men of the tercio frequent. If you ask one of them who or what he is, the likely first answer is something like 'I'm a soldier in Second Tercio.' Although the Tenth Tercio men would say 'Caesar's Tenth,' the arrogant bastards.

"This is true even if they manage a bank, as at least one of our Reserve centurions does. Although *he* is in Number Three Company. And the boys are proud, very proud, of themselves. So are their families. When we have the full Tercio parade, there are usually ten or eleven thousand family members and well-wishers who come to watch. Sometimes—even—we actually bring some of the wives and girlfriends to watch the training, if the 'Old Man' thinks it will be exciting enough for them to want to see."

The second Cricket took off in a cloud of dust and with its engine roaring...insofar as such a small engine, less than one hundred and twenty horsepower, could be said to "roar." Cmpbell went silent for a few minutes, which silence Cruz chose not to break.

Once the Cricket was out of earshot, Campbell heard a maniple swinging by on the road, maybe two hundred meters to the rear. They were singing a very sad sounding song. She listened long enough, long enough to determine that the lyrics weren't all that sad, but rather uplifting.

"I see," she said. "Then you get most of the benefits of having men serve together as regulars, at a fraction of the price."

"That's about it, ma'am. Then, too, these men will be the future rulers of this country. They will *never* have to share their votes with people less worthy. They probably could not articulate it, most of them. But it means something that their sacrifices are recognized and rewarded."

"And yourself? Doesn't it bother you that you will be old and gray before you can vote?"

"Me?" Cruz laughed hard enough he had to stop to catch his breath. "Me? Why should *I* be allowed to vote? At least until I'm so old I can't screw things up for long. I've made no sacrifices. I *like* this shit. It's the life for me. But I will be confident for our future...for the future of my wife and children...when the country is run by those who absolutely did *not* like this shit... but did it anyway. Because they cared more for the *Patria* than for themselves."

"How have you come so far? Why fifteen years ago you didn't even *have* an army."

Cruz answered with a single word. "Carrera."

"You think a lot of him, don't you?"

"Ma'am...I'd make the fucker king if I could; if I thought he'd accept. Most of us would."

"King? I don't think you mean that."

Cruz gave Campbell a look that said, *Oh, yes, I do.*

Cruz jerked his head in the direct of rustling leaves and branches. Tribune Porras stepped out of the shadows. "Sergeant Major? The 'Old Man' wants to see you at the command post."

Cruz nodded and took his leave of Campbell, leaving Porras to take his place.

The command post was about half a kilometer away, mostly hidden under a spreading tranzitree, and mostly surrounded by thick reedlike grass with tufts at the end, the technical name for which was *Saccharum spontaneum*.

Legate Velasquez was seated on a folding wooden campstool, just outside of the small hexagonal tent that served as the cohort command post. From the look on his face, Cruz was pretty sure what the news was, even if he didn't have a name to attach to the news.

"That medevac included Corporal León, Sergeant Major. He didn't make it. They pronounced him dead on arrival."

"Shit!" Cruz exclaimed, stomach lurching and heart sinking. "But how? I mean specifically how, sir."

Velasquez shook his head, saying, "That awaits an autopsy. To be sure, it does, anyway. But what difference does it make, really? We know what killed him, one or more fragments from a 120mm mortar."

"Do we know what caused the short round?" the sergeant major asked.

Again Velasquez shook his head. "No. I've got the platoon leader counting charges, to see if they took off one too many. But my guess is a bad charge, not a short one."

"Most likely," Cruz agreed. "Does his brother know yet?"

"No. That's why I called you."

Cruz nodded. "I'll tell him, sir."

"No, you don't understand. Gonna be the hardest thing I've ever done, but I'll tell him. I just want you there for moral support."

"Yes, sir."

Porras said nothing to Campbell; he was far too young and far too shy to initiate a conversation with a foreign officer. That she was an extremely well put together and attractive woman made this worse. Thus, if anyone was going to break the ice, it fell to her.

"Tribune Porras," she asked of the boy who wasn't a lot more than half her age, "aren't you a little young to be a commissioned officer?"

Startled at first, but pleased that someone had had the courage to break the ice when he lacked it, Porras answered, "Maybe, ma'am. I'm a month shy of nineteen. It makes me feel pretty young sometimes."

Jan was aware of Carrera's junior military academies. She asked, "And were you commissioned out of one of the new schools?"

"Ma'am? Oh, *no,* ma'am. We *never* commission anyone straight out of school. I graduated at seventeen after almost four years, then enlisted like everyone else. All my classmates who made it through four years did, except for one. No, ma'am, all the schools do for you is give you a little leg up on the others. You know how to march in step, for example."

Porras was quibbling here, as he'd been ordered to do with anyone not in the legion, or in the legion but below the rank of Centurion, J.G. Anyone who had been through the academies knew they taught a lot more than just marching in step.

Porras continued, "You still have to enlist, get picked for the Reserves in basic training, then impress your tercio cadre in your advanced training and utilization tour. Then it's the basic Noncom Course, Cazador School, and Officer Candidate School. That...or real combat sometimes, though even there you don't get out of much."

Jan, who had risen to senior noncom rank in the Anglian army before being commissioned answered, "I can see merit in that."

"Ah, yes...ma'am. So do we. There are also two other advantages to having been a cadet. Some of the time at the junior military schools counts against the time you would normally have to wait for a school. So, while most of the soldiers might have to wait as much as three or four years for Cazador School and OCS, I was able to do them one right after the other...almost. But, no, ma'am. No one gets commissioned in the legion without following the same road as the soldiers must. You *do* get paid at a slightly higher rate for longevity; the last two years in school count as years of service for pay."

Per prior instructions for dealing with inquisitive gringos Porras added, lying outright, "We don't really get all that much tactical training at the academies."

"But what about the university? Don't you need a degree to become an officer?"

That gave Porras a laugh, which laugh caused Campbell to wonder, *Why do so many of my questions seem so funny to them? Hmmm...think about this possibility, woman, they are even more ignorant of us than we were of them.*

Once recovered, Porras continued, "No, ma'am. About the time you make tribune II—you would say, 'captain'—the legion will pay for you to go to school, at least part time. But civil education is not so important to us. A legion officer is expected to have a baccalaureate by the time he makes legate I, the equivalent of lieutenant colonel. But it is not an absolute requirement. Of course we *do* read a lot... and both Legates Chin and Suarez have very time consuming programs for Officer Professional Development.

"But, for those of us in the regulars, since we spend only about a hundred days a year training troops there is a *lot* of time for OPD. But nobody really cares about having a *degree*."

Porras paused. "There is one exception I can think of. The engineers have to have at least a four year degree in—usually—civil engineering to be commissioned. But that's it."

"But what about doctors, medical doctors, and such?" she asked.

"They don't even become officers unless they go through Cazador School and OCS. In any event, we don't have enough doctors to waste their time making them leaders and commanders. Although that situation is improving, I understand. The force has hired enough Volgan doctors to start a legionary medical school."

"Why not just send them to the Federated States for medical school?"

Again, Porras laughed out loud. "Because we'd probably never get more than a fraction of them back. There's just too much money for a doctor in the Federated States. Or the Tauran Union. Or in the Islamic parts of the world, some of them. Carrera won't even let someone go to medical school who so much as speaks English. Why, did you know—"

Campbell lifted a gentle finger to silence Porras. As they'd been talking, the sun had gradually slipped down the arc of day, and was about to touch the far ends of the earth with fire. Already it seemed to be setting afire the thick stands of *Saccharum spontaneum* that grew pretty much everywhere not covered by building, road, or thick jungle canopy. With the setting of the sun, the angels' candlelight vigil in memory of the dying day, a lone piper, unseen but not so distant, had begun to play a soft and sad—painfully sad—melody while standing on a low pile of earth on the range. Even the birds stopped their nighttime calls, as if to listen.

"Very beautiful," said Campbell. "I love the pipes."

"So do we, ma'am. So do we. Is there a soldier anywhere who does not?"

"Pity his soul, if so," she said.

"Yes, ma'am, I agree. But it also means that I'd better get to sleep now, since I have the evening watch. Good night, ma'am."

After Porras left, Campbell stayed awake for a while, waiting for Hendryksen to return from his ventures with the cohort's scout platoon. She hadn't been invited to dinner again and so dug through her pack for one of Gaul's finest canned bits of culinary artistry.

"Shit. I despise *escargot*."

"Upset that their cuisine didn't start on a dare?" asked Hendryksen from the shadows.

"No one can tell me *escargot* didn't start on a dare," she replied, pulling the ring that let her peel back the top of the flattened, squarish can.

"Well ... per—"

Hendryksen was interrupted by a wail of unspeakable anguish, so profound that neither the jungle nor the thick grass could muffle it.

"What the hell was that?" she asked.

"I heard over the radio," he said. "That mortar accident? It killed somebody."

"Dreadful," she said. The tone of her voice said she meant it, too. "I saw the accident, from a distance. They didn't even stop training."

"No, they wouldn't, would they?" Hendryksen looked around, then closed his eyed and seemed to be listening carefully. Finally, apparently satisfied that none of the Balboans were around, he said, "These people have to be stopped."

"But I thought you liked them," Campbell said.

"Unreservedly," he admitted. "They're just the kind of folks I would like on my left or right flank, were we allied, or charging to the rescue if I were in trouble. But they've got to be stopped."

"I don't necessarily disagree," she said. "But why do you say so?"

"It's the lack of civilized restraints," he said. "Nothing civilized, nothing civil, holds them back. We could live without that cowardly whore, Marine Mors du Char, as safety minister for the Tauran Union, yes. But someone like her would not survive a day here. Perhaps literally not survive and certainly politically she would not.

"I never realized it before we came out here, but this whole country is fucking insane." He reached into a pocket and pulled out a little booklet, indistinguishable from the one Esmeralda had been given, though of course he and Wallenstein's cabin girl didn't know of each other's existence. He opened the book to the first page, then read off, "*Hoy tenemos Balboa; mañana el mundo; pasado mañana el universo.*

"Do you know what that means?" he asked. Without waiting for an answer, he supplied, "Today we hold Balboa, tomorrow the world, the day after tomorrow the universe.

"Now tell me, what kind of fucking maniacs, no more than three and a half or—max—four million strong, and not especially wealthy, think they can take a world, or two of them? Or an infinity of them."

"This kind, I suppose," she said, very softly. "Where did you get the book?"

"Their recon platoon leader loaned it to me. It's an issue item, apparently, accountable and inspectable, for all ranks. I suppose I'll have to return it."

"Do you really think they think they can take the world?"

"Not them, exactly. They think their political and social philosophy is unconquerable and, once on the road, will inevitably reach the end of the road in charge of all human beings, everywhere.

"And the scary part of that," a highly agitated Hendryksen continued, "is that unless stopped here and soon, it just might."

"*It just might*," Jan Campbell quoted to herself, as she lay awake under her mosquito net and poncho shelter. Outside the net, hordes of ravenous anopheles slammed repeatedly against the mesh. Past that, the *antaniae* seemed to have cleared out in fear of the presence of so many adult humans.

Thing is, though, I feel fairly at home here, for all that these people are bloody maniacs. And isn't it strange that I should feel so much at home in the company of this foreign army? It should not be true that I do, especially considering their arcane rank structure and bizarre organization, to say nothing of the trivial value they seem to assign to human life. And yet I do feel hugely at home among them. I value them. Which is why, I think, I take it badly when they show no value for their own lives.

And it is no mean thing to be surrounded by men training, and ready to die, to defend their homes.

Campbell, lying under her poncho shelter reviewed her time with the legion, now drawing fast to a close.

They have almost no set drills. And yet, based on the way the platoon leaders and maniple commander face, analyze, and overcome very new tactical situations, they seem quite innovative. And their innovativeness is enhanced—or exacerbated, maybe—by their frightful willingness to risk losses in training.

I mean, really . . . having the machine guns and antitank weapons fire at the objective from the front, then using the dead ground behind to come upon the "enemy" from almost the exact rear . . . that was not something we would do; ordinarily. Not in training with live ammunition. And even the militia privates have considerable determination. Witness those two troopies in the other platoon who cleared the objective after every other man in their platoon was declared killed.

Yes, they are not so intricately trained as we are. But they have a fine grasp of keeping things simple and going for the jugular. Admirable and disturbing, both.

Casa Presidencial, Aserri, Santa Josefina, Terra Nova

Calderón really didn't trust the Old Earthers for beans. He didn't trust the Taurans, either. And for all that the high admiral's no doubt century-old assistant had been both attractive and charming, he didn't trust that little bitch either.

But he trusted Blanco, when the latter had informed him the Tauran airships were crossing the shore. He trusted Blanco's assistant when the latter informed him the Taurans were landing troops just north and south of the highway between *El Carman* and *Rio Clara*, the troops fanning out to what looked to the assistant like defensive positions.

"And very sharply they move, too, Mr. President," the assistant said. "Real professionals they look like, to me."

Marguerite, who didn't know but might well have guessed that the president had his own people out watching, called. "Satisfied now, Mr. President?"

"Not entirely," he answered. It didn't surprise him that she could call. Everyone knew the Old Earthers had tremendous technology and power. "Why are they taking up positions so far from the border?"

"I asked the same question," she said, then proceeded to parrot Janier's answer.

"Okay," said Calderón then, "I shall speak within the hour."

Now, seated in his main office, behind the presidential desk, with the flags of his country and of the office of the presidency upright on staffs in stands behind him, he waited for the director of the production to signal, "*Ahora,* Mr. President."

"People of Santa Josefina," Calderón began, "we are under a grave and growing threat. Before I explain that, a little history. Some of it you will know. Bear with me on that; I am also speaking to the world on your behalf. Some you may not know or, if knowing, may not have thought about.

"This part you know: Three-quarters of a century ago, the people of Santa Josefina forever rejected the prospect of being a normal state, with a normal army. There were sound reasons for this; our old army had never been large enough—we never could have afforded for it to be large enough—to really defend us from a foreign aggressor. Conversely, it was always available to defend the people from such threats as free speech, freedom of religion, freedom of assembly...

"In short, our army was never anything but a tool of repression at home and a wasteful indulgence as far as foreign affairs went. Add in the costs of the civil wars we fought about every other generation, and...well...good riddance.

"Was this a form of moral welfare, with us totally dependent on the good will of others and their willingness to defend us? Absolutely. No question about it. Remember that as I continue to speak."

Calderón stopped to take a sip from his water glass. Then, glaring into the camera, he continued, "Now is not three-quarters of a century ago. Yet still we are not and never shall be capable of defense against a powerful foreigner with a malignant heart.

"And that foreigner, and those malignant hearts, have grown up right next door. Balboa—they call themselves 'The Timocratic Republic of Balboa'—has armed itself such that it has become one of the eight or a dozen most powerful armies on this planet.

"Some may say, 'Well, of course; the middle of their country and their most precious resource is occupied by thirty thousand or more foreign troops.' And yet, they should need ten times that many? I think not.

"And we, to our shame, have helped them raise this force. Fully eight percent of their soldiers are *our citizens.*

"I can no longer sleep at night, I can no longer keep silent, about this threat that has grown up on our doorstep. Thus, I have made the following request, I issue the following decree, and I make the following demand.

"The world cannot sit still. I demand that Balboa lay down its arms or that it be made to lay them down.

"I request the help of the world community, which assistance the peace-loving Tauran Union has already begun providing, to defend us until the Balboan threat is put to rest.

"And I order our young men, now in Balboan service, to return home or face criminal prosecution."

PART III

CHAPTER EIGHTEEN

Discipline can only be obtained when all the officers are imbued with the sense of their awful obligation to their men and to their country that they cannot tolerate negligence. Officers who fail to correct errors or to praise excellence are valueless in peace and dangerous misfits in war.

—General George S. Patton, Jr.

Fort Guerrero, Balboa, Terra Nova

The annual training period was over. Now the cohort stood in a "C" formation, the maniple first centurions out front, and Sergeant Major Cruz, gold tipped stick under his left arm, facing them. They reported to him in sequence.

The report from the maniples having been taken, Cruz faced about and saluted Legate Velasquez with the right hand, reporting, "Sir, Second Cohort, Second Tercio is formed and ready."

The legate returned the salute, then commanded, "Post!"

Cruz marched off to the left side of the formation, not far from where Campbell and Hendryksen stood. There he came to attention, facing toward the cohort front. The maniple first centurions did likewise, marching off toward the left of their units, while the tribunes commanding strutted out from the right.

Once Cruz was out of the way, Velasquez ordered, "Soldiers to be recognized, front and center."

Two small groups came forward, one each from the left and the right. On the left were two guards, plus Carillo, he who had failed to show up for training, and another boy—Private Salazar, aged seventeen. Salazar marched behind Carillo and apparently without a guard. Carillo wore leg irons and shuffled forward awkwardly. Salazar walked proudly, unrepentant and unrestrained.

Salazar had violated tercio policy just that very morning by washing his maniple commander's vehicle at another tercio's wash rack despite specific orders not to do so. Since that other tercio was "Caesar's Tenth," them being assholes about it was only normal.

The commander of the Tenth had chided Legate Chin on his unit's lack of discipline. Chin had, in turn, very mildly chewed out Velasquez.

Once the prisoners were in front of him, and their charges read off, Velasquez announced Carillo's and Salazar's punishment; for Carillo the thirty days at half pay in the disciplinary platoon previously decided on. Salazar was given three days. Both sentences were to begin at 0600 the following morning. Carillo would spend the night in the tercio guard house; Salazar, however, was free until it was time to report to serve his sentence.

Some minor medals for achievement were given to three soldiers from the other group. Then Velasquez called the cohort back to attention and turned the formation back over to his sergeant major. Once Cruz was in position and salutes exchanged, Velasquez, himself, took a place behind the formation.

Cruz put the cohort "at ease" and read off several more things from his clipboard. Among these were time rewards—rare, monetary rewards—rarer still, promotions, and elevation to the reserve echelon from the militia or regular from the reserves.

Last of all he read, "By personal and direct order of the commanding officer—Manuel Velasquez-Boyd, Legate, Infantry, Commanding...Private Salazar-Luis, Emilio F.—for initiative and determination beyond that normally expected of a soldier of the Republic in time of peace—is elevated from the militia to the reserves. Private Salazar is further raised in rank from Private to Private First Class. In addition, PFC Salazar is put on paid pass, for three days, effective tomorrow at 0600." Every man present, excepting only Campbell, understood that Salazar's pass covered the period when he would have otherwise been serving his three-day sentence in the disciplinary platoon. The soldiers laughed at their commander's little joke. She asked Hendryksen, who also got the joke, what had just happened.

"An officer just showed some judgment and some moral courage," he answered. "How often does that happen?"

"Cohort!" The five first centurions, turning heads over right shoulders, echoed, "Maniple!"

"Until seventeen hundred hours," said Cruz, "which means you're to have your hair cut and your brass and shoes polished by then, motherfuckers... DISSS...missed!"

The legion actually had a mess dress uniform. It was white with gold piping. It wasn't an issue item but was available and authorized for individual purpose and wear. Most senior officers and centurions along with a few of the middle rankers bought a set. For the troops the dress uniform was created by the addition of a lightweight, olive-colored jacket to the normal undress khakis.

That's what they wore and, Campbell had to admit, it was better than, say, in the Anglian Royal Artillery where, if a senior officer and a junior officer showed up at an event dressed the same, the junior had to leave and change.

Since Campbell and Hendryksen had spent so much time with the cohort, they were invited guests at the farewell banquet's head table. Campbell sat between Legates Suarez and Chin, while Hendryksen, on the left side of the head table, was situated between Cruz and an even more senior sergeant major, Arredondo, nicknamed "Scarface."

Behind them, in racks, stood the Eagles of 2nd Legion: Gold, 2nd Infantry Tercio: Silver, 2nd Cohort: Bronze, and below those, as if on guard themselves, the five blue guidons for the cohort's five maniples.

The dinner began with a recitation of the oath of enlistment for the legion: "...against all enemies, foreign and domestic." After that, the tercio chaplain—he was a Roman Catholic priest, and a reserve warrant officer—blessed the meal, the eagles, the guidon, and the cohort. Then one of the junior privates of the cohort solemnly read off the names of those of the tercio who had been killed in action...or in training, and their honors, since its parent formation had been founded, about fifteen years before. The list was fairly long. The men bowed their heads as the names and circumstances were cited.

Velasquez made a short speech, as did the other commanders. The CO invited Campbell to say a few words, which she begged off from, citing crappy Spanish. At the legion commander's order to "Take Seats!" the men of the cohort shouted their motto "*Improviza! Adapta! Gana! Ataque! Ataque Ataque!*" Improvise, adapt, overcome, attack, attack, attack!

Palacio de los Trixies, *Ciudad* Balboa, Balboa, Terra Nova

Downstairs and around the corner, the courtyard fountain splashed while raucous trixies scurried away from the fight.

"I tried to warn you, Raul," said Carrera, head outthrust on his neck, glare on his face, and his fingers turning white from his grip on the arms of his chair, "that this was not the time to show the slightest weakness."

Parilla didn't answer right away, his eyes locked in a hate-filled glare at the television screen on which was frozen the countenance of Santa Josefina's Calderón. "Son of a bitch," Parilla muttered. "You could have come to me and asked me why we needed what we had, but nooo...you went to our fucking enemies."

"Well...he wants his soldiers back, does he?" Carrera asked, rhetorically. "I think we can arrange to send him a few thousand at least."

Parilla held up a restraining hand. "You mean send an expedition to Santa Josefina? Maybe plunge the place into guerilla warfare? No. Or, at least, not yet."

Patience almost at an end, Carrera shouted, "Why the fuck not?" He stood up, walked to the television, and slapped it, setting the thing to teetering dangerously. "Why the fuck not? That motherfucker has opened up our entire eastern flank. Half my plans for defense are in a ruin now. Do you fucking hear me, Mr. President? We're fucked! Fucked!"

"Calm down, *Duque*," Parilla said, with heat.

"I'm...sorry, Mr. President," Carrera forced out. He sat.

"Now what's this going to do to us?" Parilla asked.

"It's so fucking brilliant I can't even say," Carrera admitted. "Leave aside that it opens up a flank I'd considered secure. I'll find a way to close it again. But this is going to put pressure on damned near everybody we do business with to stop. Everyone in the international community of the very, very caring and sensitive is going to jump on the bandwagon: 'Disarm those beasts in Balboa.' And mark my words, that very phrase is going to be used.

"And the border provocations Fernandez warned us of? They'll be starting soon. Very soon. We can expect embargoes, fund raising concerts, condemnations in the world league, a veritable orgy of denunciations."

The heat in Parilla's voice cooled to sadness. "And all of that, ultimately, leads to the war I wanted to avoid."

"Well...to be fair," Carrera admitted, "I was speaking out of my ass. I don't know that anything you ordered me to do or not do made a trixie's shit of difference. Maybe it did but...I don't know that it did. And I kind of doubt it.

"And besides, maybe *this* is the war that has to be fought. Maybe when the other side has martialed everything it has against us—from the World League to the UEPF to the Tauran Union to the shitbird idiot actors and actresses of Wilcox's Folly—and they either lose to us or win in the worst way, with casualties that discredit all the above—"

"You're speaking of good to the world," Parilla observed. "Fuck the world; I only care about Balboa. That's why I wanted to avoid the war in the first place."

"Raul...I've said it before. I don't think we can avoid it. But... that doesn't mean that there aren't better and worse ways of fighting it, for greater and lesser goals. Neither does it mean that your ways won't give us the better way of fighting it and the greater goals."

Parilla looked intently at Carrera, searching for truth in his face. *Are you blowing smoke or sincere? I used to be able to read you better but the more time you spent with us the murkier your thoughts became.*

"I mean it," said Carrera, which pretty much settled that.

"What do you want to do now?" Parilla asked.

"Step one is ready," Carrera said. "Has been for a while. When it began to look like the Taurans were going to start fucking with us along the Transitway border, I started putting some things into place to humiliate them. Those are ready now.

"Step two is going to be a little harder. We're going to cull the legion of Santa Josefinans. Those cullings are going to fall in on the two *Valle de las Lunas* tercios for reorganization and training as guerillas. I'm going to have the training center on the *Isla Real* send some cadre for that, and maybe do a little recruiting in Cochin. They were probably the best guerillas in our history, so ought to have something to teach."

"Don't send them into Santa Josefina any time soon," Parilla cautioned.

"No," Carrera agreed. "But when we need them I want them ready."

"I concur," Parilla said.

Carrera relaxed his fingers from the arms of his chair. His left hand waved at the TV screen, still bearing Calderón's frozen face. "But that son of a bitch is going to get his soldiers back, eventually, just as he demanded."

Forming that left hand into a loose simulacrum of a pistol, index finger pointed toward space, "And that clever bitch overhead is going to pay for the trouble she's caused." The palm flattened. He swept it across the general direction of the Transitway Area. "And so are those oh-so-fucking clever Tauran bastards."

Tauran Union Security Force-Balboa, Building 59, Fort Muddville, Balboa, Terra Nova

"Oh, those stupid fucking bastards," said Captain Jan Campbell. She held two sheaves of papers loosely, one in each hand. Her lower lip was quivering as if she were about to cry. *That* was nearly enough to induce panic in Hendryksen.

"What is it?" asked Hendryksen. In reply all he got was an inarticulate shriek and a blizzard of white papers being thrown across the office. This was followed by Jan putting her head down onto her arms on her desk. From the shaking of her shoulders, Hendryksen was quite sure that "about to" had become "oh my God the world is going to end Campbell is crying."

He raced across the floor and began recovering the sheaves she'd scattered. A little shuffling of his own and he had them back in something like proper order. He began to read from one sheaf, labeled, *Campbell Report:*

> "The Legion has a developed Staff function, based primarily on historic Sachsen principles, which in their turn closely mirror Old Earth German doctrine. Staffs generally are significantly smaller than is the norm in the South and East and generate far less routine work, operating as a norm in wartime mode. This is a general characteristic of the Legion, in fact—its active elements sense and display no appreciable difference in attitude

between "peacetime" and "wartime." How much of this comes from the threat we present is arguable. It is this observer's suspicion that they would be exactly the same if we and the Transitway sank into the sea."

"That's about right," Hendryksen whispered. Then he shifted his attention to the other sheaf and read silently from it:

Chief of Intelligence Directorate's Version of the *Campbell Report*:
"The *Legio* has a minimal Staff function, organized on an inefficient basis, with few key staff officers and little capacity for the wide engagement with units under command. *Legio* headquarters will thus have a minimal understanding of the posture and readiness of the units at their disposal and little free capacity to make the transition to combat operations."

"Pure bullshit," said the Cimbrian, loud enough for Jan to hear. "That's not...the...fucking worst...of it," came from the desk.

Campbell Report:
"The *Legio* maintains a small Regular component, which leads and administers a larger Reserve component, which in its turn leads and administers the wider Militia component. This permits both rapid mobilization of formed units, each successive mobilization wave building coherent units from cadres from previous waves, without creation of new or scratch units and formations. While a fully mobilized militia force would be in no way comparable to the effectiveness and flexibility of an all-Regular or mobilized Reserve formation, it would be considerably more than an untrained mob and would have a common skill base and extant unit cohesion through the tercio system.
"Though in theory conscript, in fact every man and woman in the legion is a volunteer. To the extent bravery can be measured by peacetime training, it is this observer's opinion that the soldiery would prove brave enough in combat."

"You understated that," he said.

Her head popped up over the desk. She made a quick wipe of her face then said, "You're fucking right I did. Now look at the lies de Villepin is passing on."

> Chief of Intelligence Directorate's Version of the *Campbell Report*:
>
> "The *Legio* maintains a small mercenary cadre, which dominates the extended Reserve and the wider popular Militia. All adults are subject to conscription into the military and those responding to the draft are given at least a cursory basic training before release back into civilian life. No sanction is currently applied against those failing to report for conscription, but successful completion of extended military service is currently the only route to enfranchisement, so the politically engaged will tend to accept conscription in order to become politically active. Progressive views are discouraged during service and are thus not represented to any marked extent in active politics in the illegal entity in Former Balboa.
>
> "The fully-mobilized militia force would produce an impressive proportion of the population in uniform, but it is considered unlikely that the dominant Regular and Reserve cadres in overall command will be able to sustain combat operations on the part of their militia charges, whose state of training and preparedness is significantly lower than the higher echelons' and whose unit cohesion is questionable, given the coercive nature of militia service."

The whole report, rather both whole reports, were considerably lengthier that that, Jan's running to fifty-two pages and the official version weighing in at seventy-seven. Rather than reading all of both, Hendryksen asked, "Is it all like this?"

"Some parts are worse," she replied, this time not bothering to lift her head up.

"Is there any truth anywhere in what is going to be the official version?"

"Maybe around the margins," she said. "It's tough, you know, even for the fucking Gauls, to paint your enemies both as incompetent and as a real threat."

"Where's the painting that's labeled, 'real threat'?" he asked.

"Appendices A through G."

"I see... What do we do about this, Jan?"

"I'm sending a copy of mine to a friend in MoD, back in Anglia," she answered. "Hopefully he can kill our participation in the TU's madness. If you care for your comrades in Cimbria, I'd suggest you do much the same."

University of Balboa, *Ciudad* Balboa, Balboa, Terra Nova

One of the things that Calderón's denunciation of the regime had done, besides bringing more TU forces into the area, was to give a much needed shot in the arm to Balboa's remaining dissidents. Now, with the possibility of the regime being extinguished, and the chance to return to business as usual, these came out of the woodwork of the university, the place that had always been their shelter and natural manure. They weren't a majority even there, not anymore, but they had a minimal critical mass there. Meetings could be held, if anyone could be made to see the point. Rallies could be mustered, if enough meetings were held.

In a little used and more than a little run down auditorium, twenty-year-old Manuel Darias-Rocaberti listened as, one after another, fellow students mounted the rostrum to denounce the current regime. Some were liberal, some libertarian. More than a few were leftists: anarchists, socialists, Marxists. Whatever their political persuasion, each speaker had a common theme: the need to overthrow the dictatorship of Raul Parilla and his "pet" gringo, Patricio Carrera.

Manuel wasn't all that impressed. *The thing is,* chicos, *that the country is becoming less of a dictatorship all the time. What you want to see happen? Will it mean less of a dictatorship, sooner, or more, forever?*

Manuel's family was not of the highest among the Rocaberti's many-sided clan. In fact, his father was a modest businessman of no great wealth or pretensions; his mother, a simple farm girl brought to the big city. These facts had much to do with their having been spared any taste of the follow-on results to the attempt to get rid of Parilla and Carrera. For his own part,

Manuel had a certain distaste for military regimes, but was not fanatically opposed either.

Still, Manuel listened politely to the parade of denunciation, perhaps made especially bitter by the fact that his class had just received their conscription notices. He caught on quickly to the common theme. Bored, he still applauded with the others. At the same time he attempted to catch the eye of Vielke, a lovely blond coed. When he realized he would not be able to do so, he turned his full attention back to the "rally."

It was not much longer before Manuel realized that there was another theme, or rather a lack of one, in what was *not* being said. They all wanted to change the government. Each vowed resistance. And yet none had the slightest idea of what resistance meant. Looking at them, Manuel was fairly sure that none had the fire, the determination, the...courage...to resist with arms.

And why should they resist with arms, when it is an infinitely safer path to political influence to join up? And how could they, when—if they had the determination to fight—they would have the determination to organize and train to fight? I don't think that's going to happen with this bunch.

Bored and disillusioned, Manuel left the meeting and returned to his rooms. He dug through his personal papers until he found his "draft notice."

He read:

> Greetings from the President and People of the Timo-cratic Republic of Balboa:
>
> You have reached your 18th birthday. As such, you are eligible to be conscripted into the Legion of the Republic. Under the law, the government is required to inform you of your choices.
>
> 1. You may do nothing. If you so choose, the citizen-ship rolls will be amended to place you on suspended status. This means that you will not be entitled to vote in elections for public office, or to run for election to public office. You are also denied any government funded job training, or educational assistance. You will further be prohibited from being selected for any of the "reserved" jobs—police, fire, weapons manufacture, teaching certain school courses, some few others. There will be no other

negative effects from a failure to serve. Your taxes will remain the same. Your standing in a court of law will remain the same as that of any citizen, veteran or not.

2. You may write, call, or visit your nearest tercio to enlist. In such a case, and only after successful completion of training, plus the mandatory ten years' reserve or militia service, or twenty-five years if you are selected for, and elect to change over to, regular status, the above constraints shall be lifted.

Choose well.

Signed,
Raul Parilla
Presidente de la Republica

Manuel reread the notice. After some hours of thought, he picked up the phone book and dialed a number.

After two rings the other phone was answered: "Third Infantry Tercio, Recruiting Sergeant Barrios speaking."

CHAPTER NINETEEN

I am only one, but I am one. I cannot do everything,
but I can do something. And because I cannot do
everything, I will not refuse to do the something that
I can do. What I can do, I should do. And what I
should do, by the grace of God, I will do.

—Edward Everett Hale

Casa Linda, **Balboa, Terra Nova**

In Ham's bedroom, in a rack over the bed, sat a highly engraved,
highly gold plated, custom F-26. The F-26 was the legion's standard
battle rifle, a very high rate of fire, fairly low recoil job, feeding
6.5mm bullets with semiplastic casings from large rotary magazines
and firing them at a ripping cloth rate of fire. This particular one
had been an eighth birthday gift to Carrera's boy from the Balboa
Arms Corporation, over in Arraijan. It was nonstandard, a one-off
job, shortened and with a muzzle brake to reduce recoil, plus with a
pistol grip slimmed down to fit the hands of an eight year old boy.

Of course the gilt and the engraving weren't readily visible, as
Hamilcar's very practical Pashtun guards had covered the thing
with dull black paint as soon as they could. The rotary magazine
in it was empty, but left there to keep dirt and dust out.

Pililak stood in stocking feet on Ham's bed, running her slim
hands over the rifle's stock lovingly. The pistol grip was too small
for Ham, now, but fit her dainty little digits perfectly.

*And when I leave this place, and rejoin my lord, his rifle will
go with me. He can always get a better grip made. I just have to*

figure out how to get some ammunition for it with nobody notic-ing. I can't steal or borrow a few rounds at a time; the magazine can't be reloaded outside of at the factory. I have to steal a whole magazine or, better, three or four of them. Which, so far, has not proven easy.

The rifle was almost the final obstacle in Ant's quest to join Ham. She could swim now, maybe not superbly but well enough. Moreover, she'd had one of the guards teach her to make a pon-cho raft, so she could float any gear and supplies she would need across bodies of water. She had boots and clothing in her own size suitable for trekking the jungle. The boots had been a pair of Ham's old castoffs, still serviceable, while the clothing she'd sewn herself from some old uniforms she'd found in a closet in a room nobody used anymore.

The boots had been broken in, but not to her feet. Getting them broken in to her own feet, or her feet into the boot—depending on how one looked at it—had been an agony, while keeping a smile on her face while she broke them in had been most difficult. She had downloaded and printed out maps. A compass she had, since she hadn't been able to get her hands on a global locating system receiver. She knew how to use it, too, to include with a map.

Months of stealing relatively nonperishable food had been a problem, made worse when some damned rats got at her stash. There went four pounds of smoked sausages; *poof!* Now she had about fifteen pounds' worth of food in a waterproof, airproof case borrowed from household supply. To carry it and her water bottle she had a bag and some straps, since she hadn't been able to steal anyone's load-carrying equipment. That was all hidden in a closet down in what some of the visitors called, "the staff room." She didn't know why they did; the household staff rarely went down there.

And it had all gotten tougher lately. Alena the witch had gotten nervous and fidgety as could be. Pililak didn't know why, precisely, but gathered that it had something to do with something some foreigner had said on the television.

Then again, Ant thought, *the witch often doesn't know why certain things bother her.*

Ant wrapped her slim fingers and palm around the pistol grip for perhaps the hundredth time, a thrill coursing through her at the vicarious contact with her lord.

Hmmm, she thought, *these will never fit my lord's hands again. I wonder if I could get a measure of his hand size and have the household armorer carve new ones?*

Dido, Alena's baby, shuddered in her sleep, then gave off a single loud cry, almost a shriek. Bending over the crib and picking the child up, Alena clasped her to her breast, then sat and rocked. She didn't bare that breast, it hadn't been a hunger cry. Besides, the child was getting almost ready to wean, and Alena's milk was beginning to fail.

What is it, baby? she silently wondered. *Are you in fear for our lord, as I am? I'd say that it's all the fault of that evil bastard from Santa Josefina, but my instincts say no, that it comes from far higher.*

The unvoiced question was a valid one. No one, least of all herself, really knew if Alena was a witch. But it was said, back home, that the pistachio never fell far from the tree. If Alena was a witch, and if the knack passed on, there was no reason her daughter had to be able to articulate words to know when something threatened their Iskandr.

Looking up at the ceiling, Alena thought the vilest curse she knew at the Old Earthers who were bringing peril to her god.

He will punish you, she thought further, at the vultures in space. *With fire shall he burn you. With scorpions shall he chastise you. In blood and smoke your entire corrupt order shall fall. And he shall stand in his booted feet on the looted, smoking ruins of your world.*

So it is written. So it shall be.

As if sensing her mother's determination—as, perhaps, she did—Dido relaxed and made sucking motions with her mouth. "Aha, greedy thing! So you are hungry after all." Alena dropped a flap on the front of her dress and presented herself for feeding. "And if you are a witch, then perhaps your hunger is a sign of confidence that our Iskandr shall come through."

Paintball Facility, *Academia Militar Sergento* Juan Malvegui, west of *Puerto Lindo*, Balboa, Terra Nova

Centurion—*No, it's Sergeant Major now isn't it?*—Cruz had certainly done his part in getting Ham fit in and accepted. But running the boy ragged to get everyone in his section and platoon to see just how useful Ham could be—if he was on your side—only carried things so far. It took an enemy to really bring the rest of the boys around.

And who was the enemy? The treacherous Santa Josefinans? Not on your life. There were dozens of Santa Josefinan-descended boys at the school, no different from anyone else. How about the Tauran Union? Nah. Too distant. Too adult. Too off the scale. The United Earth Peace Fleet, perhaps? What? Old Earth? What did they ever do to us?

No, it was those bastards from third platoon waiting in the nine buildings of the paintball facility that Ham's crew wanted to come to grips with.

Generally speaking, the academic week at one of Balboa's six military schools went Monday through Thursday: Academic subjects, including history, Spanish, mathematics, some science or other, a foreign language, physical training, and such. "Such" included things like music, art, and public speaking . . . and such.

Thursday evening through Saturday late afternoon or evening were more military subjects, ranging from marksmanship to land navigation to special weapons and minor tactics. This included operating armored vehicles.

Saturday nights and normal Sunday afternoons were given over to studying, while Sunday mornings were for nonoptional religious services and a rather lavish breakfast. Some Sunday afternoons, it should be noted, were spent walking off demerits on the parade field in full kit.

Since there was no leave for the first two and a half years at the school, this meant that the cadets, before beginning their second year, had had on the order of two hundred and forty or so days of purely military training. This figure increased with subsequent years, albeit only at a rate of about another ninety to one hundred days per year.

In short, although young and immature, with their bodies not yet fully formed, and not being as strong as adults would have been, from a moral, technical, and tactical point of view the cadets were probably better trained than any reserve force on the face of the planet.

Ham was serving as section leader for the exercise. The other two squads in the platoon—there had been four total but washouts had forced them to consolidate into three—flanked his squad, all three being under cover in a concrete lined drainage ditch, about mid-thigh deep in murky water. The whole platoon was under the control of two upperclassmen, each fifteen years old, cadet sergeants Delgado and Vega. The former was the senior of the two. If he had not been a cadet, his rank equivalent would have been something like Centurion, Junior Grade. There were, however, no cadet centurions or warrant officers, even though there were cadet corporals and sergeants, as well as cadet signifiers, tribunes, and legates.

Ahead, standing on walkways above the roofless buildings, Sergeant Castro and his best friend, Corporal Salazar, waited for the boys to begin their assault. This was their particular bailiwick; they'd do the judging for weapons that had to be too simulated or occasions where someone flaunted the rules, by taking a shot after being hit in a fatal spot, say.

Castro was not too far from the building nearest the ditch, but deliberately facing toward another. Salazar stood atop the walls of a building three around, going counterclockwise. It was about the best they could see to do to give the boys assaulting a chance at surprise.

The paintballs tended to be painful enough, most of the time, that a hit meant there would be no immediate return fire. Fistfights following a hit, however, were not particularly rare. Stopping those before they got out of hand was Castro's and Salazar's *other* job.

The boys were "armed" with pretty close simulacra of the legion's standard F-26 rifle and M-26 light machine gun. Being paintball markers, the rate of fire was much less, and range was very much less, than the real things. Even so, they were still adequate to clearing rooms and buildings. The boys had "grenades," but those were heavy-duty plastic bodies with practice fuses. Assessing casualties from those, or from the directional mines third platoon had, no doubt, emplaced, was on Castro and Salazar. There were also smoke grenades and "demolition charges," the latter being not a lot more than big firecrackers inside bags of flour on shorter than normal fuses with standard issue pull igniters.

The big advantage Ham's platoon had, under Cadet Sergeant Delgado, was that third platoon didn't know from which direction the boys would be coming. There was either a ditch, or low ground, or thick foliage, or ruined automobiles in every direction. Thus, third had had to outpost the eight exterior buildings with a couple or three boys each, while keeping one section, one-half of another, and the third platoon headquarters in the central building as a reserve.

At least that was Delgado's intent and, so far as Ham could see or, rather, hear, it had worked. Of course, he hadn't yet tried sticking his head over the lip of the drainage ditch, either, to find out. He'd seen the target building earlier, from a leader's recon with Delgado. Things could have changed though.

Thing that bugs me about it, thought Hamilcar, heart beginning to pound in his chest as the time for action drew closer, *is that if they did hear us, they'll be waiting for us en masse. Delgado didn't include a deception plan, but is relying entirely on stealth. And I don't know if we were all* that *quiet.*

He began drawing breath more quickly and shallowly, almost as if he were trying to jerk air into his lungs. So did the other boys in his squad. The rushing air made a hurricane sound as it passed through the mouthpiece of the durable plastic mask covering his face.

Which is fucking ridiculous, for me if not for them, thought Ham, trying to calm himself and breathe normally. *I've done this sort of thing for* real . . . but . . . aha! . . . but never with people who didn't think I was a god. So . . . I'm afraid that I'll fail them or they'll fail me.

Yet another little piece of evidence that the old man knows what he's doing, isn't it?

Delgado, walking down the ditch as quickly as thigh-high water would allow, while maintaining quiet, interrupted Ham's reveries. Delgado, despite the name, was pretty stocky and maybe two inches taller than Ham.

"Sir?" Ham asked, in a whisper.

"Just checking if you're ready," whispered back the senior cadet.

"At your command," replied Ham.

"Right. Figured. But best to see for oneself, no?"

"Yes, sir."

Delgado looked down at the water with distaste, then said, "Okay, assume it will take me about three minutes to get to the left flank squad. If I find nothing there wrong. We'll start supporting from that side. The right will kick in as soon as the left does. Ammunition's not limitless, so as soon as you're fairly confident you can make it across to the windows, pop smoke and move out."

"Yes, sir," Ham said. His breathing grew strained and jerky again, even as he said it.

Delgado squeezed the younger boy's shoulder. "Hamilcar Carrera," he intoned solemnly, "relax. You'll do fine."

Ham gave a jerky nod even though his breathing did, in fact, grow more regular. And then Delgado was gone off to the right as Ham signaled with his hands for his section to line up on the enemy side of the ditch. Ham, himself, crawled up the concrete until his head was about two feet below the lip. Then he listened for—

Phhhtphhhtphhhtphhht . . . *That was from the left . . . faint but audible . . . now what the hell is going on on the right?*

He strained to hear but . . . *Nada. Dammit! Did Delgado overestimate how far away they could hear the paintball markers? Shit! Send someone to the right to tell them to engage or just cross? No time . . . limited ammo . . . Okay, change the plan.*

Ham pulled the pin on a white smoke grenade and sailed it as far as he could toward the target building. His two team leaders, keying on him, did likewise, then repeated the barrage with less force. To either flank, a thin screen began to build.

"Francisco," Ham called to the right. "Do not follow. Stay and support by fire. Send one man to find out what happened on the right." Head swiveling left, he called, "Ramon! Follow me."

Ham sprang up and over the edge of the ditch, with five more boys following. They fired from hip and shoulder both as they emerged. Ham caught something flying slowly from the right to splat against the target house wall in front.

NOW, they fucking get into it?

"Francisco," he shouted over his right shoulder as he raced forward, "fuck it. Come on!"

"With ya, Ham! A Team . . . foll—owwwowwoww . . . motherfuckers!"

From the building just to the right of the target, a gas-powered "machine gun" lay a heavy barrage down on the edge of the ditch from which Francisco had tried to lead his boys. He took one in the face and two more in the chest—though not in that order—then fell and rolled backwards into the ditch. The resultant splash could heard even if not seen. At seeing him bowled over, his boys simply froze in place which the third platoon machine gun searched across the top of the ditch.

Ham didn't see any of that, not in any detail. He heard the

third platoon gun *phhhtphhhtphhhtphhhting*, and dimly sensed the flight of its round projectiles. But where they came from, precisely? That he couldn't see.

On the other hand, he added that to Francisco's cursing and came up with the mathematically perfect answer of, "Shit."

But by then he and Ramon's team, unscathed, were at the wall on either side of a waist-high window. Ramon beat Ham to pulling a grenade from his harness. He pulled the pin but held onto the spoon, the safety handle, until he saw Ham was likewise ready to toss.

"On three," said Ham. "*Uno...dos...tres!*" Both grenades sailed through the window more or less together. From above they heard Sergeant Castro shout, "You and you! Lie down. You're dead. You! Yes, you! You're wounded. Scream. You can try to crawl out. Or you can stay and fight. But if you crawl, son, *crawl.*"

Ramon wasn't giving whoever it was a chance for that. In an instant he was on his feet and surging across the window sill. He fired once at one of the bodies, then again at another. By the time he got around to the third—

Phhhtphhht. "Owww...shit. That fucking hurts!"

"Lie down, Cadet," ordered Castro. "Not a word out of you; you're out of it. And three demerits for language unbecoming."

"Ramon? Ramon? Who's dead?"

Ramon didn't answer.

"Crap." Ham took another grenade from his harness. *No... no...can't do that. Castro didn't say "dead," he said "out of it." Can't use a grenade where one of my own men might just be hurt. That means...*

Ham didn't try to sail through the window. Instead, he dove through head first, "rifle" and grenade out ahead, body as low to the sill as possible without catching his buttons on the wood. When he hit he rolled. It still hurt.

And there was Ramon, sitting there, cross-legged with his chin resting in his hands. He was forbidden from saying anything, of course, but the eyes he rolled toward the other side of the room were eloquent: *The bastard crawled out the door and is probably still in the corridor.*

"I saw that, Cadet," said Sergeant Castro. "Three more demerits."

"But Sergeant..."

"Four more. Shall we go for five?"

Five represented a whole lot of marching alone around the parade field. Ramon sighed and looked down.

No matter; Ham took the grenade, pulled the pin, and tossed it into the corridor. *Bang.*

"You're out, Cadet," said Castro, from above.

"Clear," shouted Ham, to the waiting troops outside. One by one they piled in and took up defensive positions in the room, just the four of them and Ham.

Ham emplaced two of the four remaining cadets to cover the one door into the room, and the other two to cover the two windows through which they had not entered.

"Stay well back from the windows," he said, then trotted to the window of entry and tossed a flash signal out of it.

KaBoom!

The nine buildings of the facility weren't regularly shaped. Neither were they regularly placed. Neither were they of the same height. Some were at an angle to others. Others had little projections sticking out. Some were one floor, some one and a half, and one in the center was a solid two floors. Worse, there were internal partitions that could be moved around, plus furniture in some rooms that could be moved around, plus entrances and passages that could be closed with barbed wired while the cadre—Castro and Salazar—could open up still other passages on request.

What that meant, given that the defender was about as strong as the attacker, was that before three buildings were cleared, the platoon was down to Delgado, Ham, four of Ham's boys, three from one of the other sections and four from another.

And the worst part of that was that the defenders had, overall, killed the attackers at about two to one. That meant that the three buildings held by Delgado's boys were under heavy attack by the defending third platoon which now outnumbered them two to one.

Delgado looked pretty down about the whole thing. At least, in the lulls in flying paintballs he looked down. Most of the rest of the time he was looking all around for wherever the hell the firing was coming from.

"Oh, knock it off, sir," said Ham. "You did fine and when it comes time to switch over, just you watch us kick the crap out of whoever attacks us."

They were in the center building of the ones they'd managed

to capture. Ham was serving as platoon sergeant, since Vega was lying out somewhere between the ditch and the buildings, no doubt twiddling his thumbs.

"Maybe," said Delgado. "As is, we got the crap kicked out of us."

"Not yet, sir," answered Ham.

"You have an idea," Delgado accused.

"Well . . . maybe. But it's going to take a little timing and we need to make a shelter for somebody . . ."

Ham looked up at Sergeant Castro, standing with arms folded at the top of the wall. "Go on," said the sergeant, first squatting and then lying down on the wall, while keeping his voice low. He cupped his hands to deaden the sound still further. "I'm not going to tell anyone."

Ham's trooper, Belisario, lay in a corner in a shelter they'd made for him from the furniture in one of the buildings. This consisted of little more than a shambles of a dresser, a dingy yellow stuffed chair with the springs sticking out, a box spring, and an old and moldy mattress. Like every other bit of furniture in the facility the things were all so ruined not even the poorest people in the country, or at least in the country nearby, would want them.

In his hands Belisario clasped one of the two remaining "satchel charges" the boys had for the exercise. His finger was curled into the pull igniter.

"The important thing," Ham had said to Delgado, "the really *key* thing is that we've got better communications than they do."

And it was true, when nobody had a radio or telephone, the people who could get a verbal message across more quickly and more securely *did* have better communications. Using that, they'd been able to coordinate moving the troops, except for Belisario, out of the rightmost building they held and into the central one, all except for Ham who took a position next to but below a window near that central building. They'd also been able to coordinate making that move just about noisily enough that the third platoon folks in the next building over thought they heard an opening. When Delgado renewed the firefight with the other half or so of third platoon, that was the signal the rest, the ones to the right, took to mean they could storm the building.

This they did, a baker's dozen of them swarming in through

doors and windows. And then Ham and Belisario ignited and
heaved their short-fused "satchel charges" into the room.

Boom. Boom.

"You're all dead," said Sergeant Castro, from on high. He had
to shout, because as he was speaking Delgado led the remnants
of his platoon away from the leftmost building, through the
middle building, past the rightmost building—picking up Ham
and Belisario on the way, and right into the building past that
from which third had launched its baited assault.

Panting with the effort, they ran right over bodies, buildings,
alleys and openings, then cut left and charged, en masse, into
the central building.

"Fan out!" shouted Cadet Delgado. "One man per window.
Ham?!"

"Sir!"

"Up on the roof with you and yours."

"Sir!"

Sergeant Castro was all smiles as he ran the after action review
for both platoons. "Don't be hard on yourselves, third," he insisted.
"You thought you had an opening. You had reason to think so.
And you took advantage of it. It didn't work out, no, but in war,
sometimes, things don't work out. What could have made it better?"

"A couple of radios," muttered the third platoon leader.

"Yep, would have helped," the sergeant agreed. "What did you
need, Delgado?"

"About three times as many people as I had."

Castro laughed, though without a lot of mirth. "If we were the
Volgan army, we'd say you needed ten times as many people, and
you could have expected to have lost nine-tenths of them. See
what I mean about really doing pretty well?

"I'm pleased," the sergeant said, "that both of your groups put
on a creditable show. You see, this is my and Corporal Salazar's
last run through of this facility. From now on there are going to
be a couple of Volgans running it, courtesy of Legate Chapayev's
connections—"

"Where are you going, Sergeant?" Ham interrupted.

"*Duque* Carrera—bless his heart and if you tell him I said that I'll
come back and kick your ass, young Carrera—is setting up a new
unit, a new kind of unit, and Salazar and I are both going to it."

CHAPTER TWENTY

By my counsels was Sparta shorn of her glory,
And holy Messene received at last her children.
By the arms of Thebes was Megalopolis encircled with walls,
And all Greece won independence and freedom.

—Inscription on the tomb of Epaminondas,
Pausanius IX, 15, 6

Parade Field, Epaminondas Caserne, *Ciudad* Balboa, Balboa, Terra Nova

The caserne, formerly a police barracks outside the southern outskirts of the city, farthest away from the sea, had taken a bit of refurbishment. Due to the Senate's refusal to fund Carrera's latest little project, he'd paid for the refurbishment himself. It hadn't been all that expensive, really; the caserne was a single main building, surrounded by a concrete wall, both of those painted a shade of tan with a darker brown trim. The barracks was suitable for housing perhaps eighty or a hundred men, full time, and adequate for weekend training, in rotation, for four or five times that. There were a couple of outbuildings, and a PT field that had been redesignated the parade field. Occupying perhaps five acres, it had no rifle range, though there was a subcaliber range in the basement of the barracks.

The parade field was, at the moment, graced with about a hundred dignitaries and high ranking officers, in bleachers that normally served as an outdoor classroom. To either side of the bleachers were TV cameras from *TeleVision Militar* and *Canal Siete*, there to transmit the news and the ceremony that would mark it.

Not all of the dignitaries or senior officers really wanted to be there. Many and possibly most didn't approve, either.

Has the Duque *lost his goddamned mind?* fumed Legate Suarez. *A tercio of fucking mariposas?* Standing on the reviewing stand with Carrera and the other legion and corps commanders of the *Legions del Cid*, the legate consoled himself, *Well... good riddance to the cocksucking bastards. I always had my doubts about Silva anyway.*

On the field, itself, in serried ranks, under the scrutiny of cameras and rank, were four hundred and forty-eight soldiers gleaned from almost every other tercio in the legion. That was all that Silva could find of suitable homosexual men, already in pairs, of suitable rank each. At that, some had had to take reductions in rank—not pay, however. When asked, Carrera had judged against that—to find a slot in the tercio.

Still, Silva had done his work well. The *Tercio Gorgidas*—named for an ancient Greek commander of some note—was recruited and organized. A few necessary special regulations were written. Training needed work, since few of the men had worked together. Discipline was mostly a matter of wait and see. It had never been successfully done, the creation of this kind of unit, since the fourth century... BC. And, back then, when slaves did the scut work and reward was being posted at the place of danger, when there really was no other benefit a chain of command could incur...

Still, tomorrow could deal with tomorrow. Today, the tercio needed to be officially formed. That was the purpose of the parade: to read the words that would call the unit into official existence... and to conduct the ceremony that would lay the groundwork for their future discipline and leadership.

A bugle called. The adjutant read off the orders. *Tercio Gorgidas* had an official existence. Then came a peculiar, indeed a unique, ceremony. In front of their newly silvered eagle and the many witnesses, the men—all but twenty-two of them—swore fidelity to a single comrade, unto death. The remaining twenty-two, including the chaplain, to whom it really wasn't a big deal, swore an oath of celibacy instead, the oath to last until either discharged from service or willing and able to take the other oath.

At a nod from the adjutant that he was finished with calling the unit into existence, Carrera, carrying a very old and very small green-bound volume, went to the microphone and began to speak. "At ease."

He opened the volume and, after a brief explanatory note, read from it:

"The ancient writer, Plutarch, tells us of an extraordinary military unit of his times, its life . . . and death. Listen: 'Gorgidas, according to some, first formed the Sacred Band of three hundred chosen men . . . It was composed of young men attached to each other by personal affection . . . For men of the same tribe or family little value one another when dangers press, but a band cemented on friendship grounded upon love is never to be broken, and invincible; since the lovers, ashamed to be base in the sight of their beloved, and the beloved before the lovers, willingly rush into danger for the relief of one another . . . they have more regard for their absent lovers than for others present, as in the instance of the man who, when his enemy was going to kill him, earnestly requested him to run him through the breast, that his lover might not blush to see him wounded in the back.'

"'It is stated that the Sacred Band was never beaten till the battle at Chaeronea; and when Phillip, King of Macedon and Father of Alexander the Great, after the fight, took a view of the slain, and came to the place where the three hundred that had fought his phalanx lay dead together, he wondered, and understanding that it was the band of lovers, he shed tears and said, 'Perish any man who suspects that these men either did or suffered anything that was base.'" Carrera turned slightly to send Suarez a dirty look.

"'Gorgidas distributed this Sacred Band all through the front ranks of the infantry, and thus made their gallantry less conspicuous . . . But Pelopidas, having sufficiently tried their bravery at Tegryae, never afterward divided them, but keeping them together, gave them the first duty in the greatest battles . . . thus he thought brave men, provoking one another to noble actions, would prove most serviceable, and most resolute, when all were united together.'"

Carrera shut the small book from which he'd been reading, then said, "Your tercio has a glorious ancestry; quite possibly a glorious future. Don't fuck it up."

The Tunnel, Tauran Union Security Force-Balboa, *Cerro Mina*, Balboa Transitway Area, Balboa, Terra Nova

Building 59, over on Fort Muddville, was more or less an administrative headquarters. Oh, it was perfectly capable of overseeing combat operations, having all the office space, radios, telephones, map boards, and computers to do so. To say nothing of sufficient coffee makers, without which military operations all over the planet would have ground to a halt.

What it was not, however, was *secure*. Why, one little five hundred pounder in the portal under Janier's office and the good general would be left wondering why they spoke English in Heaven. If it was Heaven.

No, for *real* security there was the tunnel, which had all the required office space, map boards, radios, telephones, computers, and about three hundred feet of solid rock and concrete overhead. And coffee machines.

It was immune to bombs, even the latest Federated States Air Force deep penetrators. It was immune to fairly large nukes. It even had a complete suite of defense against biological and chemical attacks. The Tauran Union Minister of Safety, Marine R.E.S. Mors du Char IV, had insisted that that be restored, lest her own ever so precious hide be potentially endangered.

But then, thought Janier, *Marine R.E.S. Mors du Char the Fourth is a pussy, even by her definition.*

Best of all, thought the general, walking from his staff car to the *Tunnel's* entrance, and with Malcoeur following along like a loyal dog, *we didn't have to pay for anything but restoring the chemical and biological defense suite. The rest the Federated States paid for. About seventy years ago.*

About thirty feet from the Tunnel's entrance Janier paused to look upward at a large rectangle of blue. There, at the very topographical crest on the hill, on an enormous staff, a huge Tauran Union flag fluttered in the breeze. It inspired in Janier the most profound sense of indifference. Indeed, it didn't just mean nothing to him; it meant less than nothing, a net negative, the focus of contempt, not filial piety or adoration. He was a son of Gaul, not a Tauran.

However, he admitted, *I do thoroughly enjoy the feelings of helpless loathing it inspires in the wretched locals. That, and the authority it provides me to call on foreign troops at need.*

Though beginning to get on in years, Janier's walk was brisk. Malcoeur, still following behind, also panted like a dog in the heat as his chubby body strained to keep up.

✧   ✧   ✧

Two military policeman, one Sachsen, *Gefreiter* Czauderna, and one Anglian, Private Stalker, stood inside an air conditioned, glassed sentry box, outside the Tunnel's entrance. They snapped to attention and saluted at Janier's approach. They'd have been more professional, demanded his identification, at the least, but the word had gone out from their *Hauptmann*, David Lang, to the mixed Anglian-Sachsen MP company that guarded *Cerro Mina*: "As far as the Frog general's concerned, rules are for lesser beings. When he shows up, pass him through without hindrance."

Said Stalker to Czauderna, in basic German, "Moritz, tell me again why we're not allowed to shoot the Frogs?"

Moritz Czauderna, six feet tall, mild belly brought on by the normal Sachsen diet of noodles, lard, and beer, with his skin reddened and sloughing off from the harsh Balboan sun, answered, "In the first place, be careful speaking even German around the general. He's been known to pretend he doesn't understand languages he can speak perfectly well in."

Czauderna stretched, awkwardly, as if the long stint of sentry-go were hurting his back.

"Shitty bastard," Stalker observed.

"Indeed. But in the second place, it's just sort of gone out of fashion.

"Fortunately," Czauderna added, "fashion is cyclical, so maybe someday."

Ignoring the MPs, Janier descended into a tunnel dimly lit with blue light. The floor was mostly short platforms followed by a few steps. Occasionally this pattern was broken by longer platforms from which side corridors radiated. His and Malcoeur's footsteps echoed off of the concrete walls as they walked. At length they came to a longer platform with a pair of side corridors. Turning down the right-hand one, they came within exactly thirty meters to the most secure conference room in Balboa. Even Carrera's was not so secure.

Janier's entrance caused the first officer to see him to announce his presence. Chairs scraped the floor as officers of all services stumbled and scurried to come to attention. The Gallic general swept them all with a baleful eye. It was his way.

Without a word Janier walked to his chair. "Begin," he ordered. Immediately, the screen on the far end of the conference room, opposite Janier's own chair, was lit up by a projection screen linked to a laptop computer.

His underlings had rehearsed this briefing many times. It could be fairly said that they'd spent more time rehearsing the briefing than in actual planning for the proposed operations the briefing was intended to discuss. Janier did not know of this. Neither did he much care. He was a General Officer. He gave orders. Lesser beings worried about the details.

Though now promoted to brigadier general, de Villepin was still the intel chief, the C-2, for the TUSF-B. "C" referenced "combined," military groupings from more than one nation. Hendryksen was there with him, as an assistant. Jan Campbell had been pointedly noninvited.

Stepping to the podium, de Villepin opened a loose-leaf notebook labeled to indicate its contents were ultra-secret. It had come from a shelf in a walk-in vault in the intel office in the Tunnel and would return there following the briefing.

At de Villepin's first word, "*Mon,*" the screen behind him changed to a map of Balboa. By the time he got to "*General,*" the map had changed to show every major formation of legion troops within the country.

"I have never been entirely satisfied that we know every legion formation," said de Villepin. "I am satisfied that we know of every formation with a caserne, a headquarters, and a flagpole. This includes that new formation of gays"—the entire conference room, including Janier, erupted in laughter—"that the locals have raised."

"It's a measure of their desperation," said Janier.

"It is, of course, *mon General,*" said Janier's public affairs officer. "But it does represent a public relations problem for us."

Janier looked at the PAO as if he were stupid or diseased or both.

"Gays, sir?" The PAO said it as if he couldn't believe Janier didn't understand the problem. "They're a protected class. There will be a lot of good public relations for the Balboans for this, whatever their reasons and however silly real professionals know those reasons to be."

"Fuck 'em," said the general.

"But they *like* that," said de Villepin, raising another barrage of laughter.

Forcing the grin from his face, Janier made a hand signal,

basically twirling his right hand, index and middle finger joined and extended, for de Villepin to get on with it.

The C-2 went down the list of known formations, interspersing key terrain details as he did. The really key ones here were First Mechanized Corps and Third Infantry Corps.

The former was dangerous because it contained the overwhelming bulk of Balboa's heavy forces, two short legions' worth, with hundreds and hundreds of tanks, infantry fighting vehicles, armored personnel carriers, self-propelled guns, and the like. Tenth Artillery Legion was also based there, and that had further hundreds of guns and rocket launchers. A reserve formation, like almost all of the rest, First Corps' cadre was stationed at *Lago Sombrero,* just off of the InterColumbian Highway, and with a fairly good hard surfaced airfield intersecting the highway and bisecting the base. There was also a huge ammunition supply point near *Lago Sombrero* that was worth capturing if only to ensure that Balboan resistance couldn't be extended indefinitely.

Located near Herrera International Airport, which was key to the efficient buildup of Tauran forces in Balboa, Third Corps, of two infantry legions, was considerably less powerful than First Corps, but also much closer, hence equally dangerous.

Second Corps was the city corps, basically. It had dozens of small casernes all over *Ciudad* Balboa. Headquarters, however, was in the old *Comandancia,* which was reachable.

There was also a known Balboan Fourth Corps, the center of mass of which was the city of Cristobal, on the Shimmering Sea, which had formations all along the highway between that city and *Ciudad* Balboa.

Some independent tercios were covered, though some, like the Forty-fourth Tercio of Indios over in la Palma province, could be generally discounted, while others, notably Fifth Mountain and the bulk of Fourteenth Cazador, in *Valle de las Lunas,* facing Santa Josefina, were a definite threat to that place.

"And speaking of Santa Josefina, it seems that the other side is combing its ranks for troops from there. Whether that is a defensive move or an offensive one I cannot say."

"Obviously it is offensive," said Janier. He looked pointedly as his PAO. "Is that not right, Colonel?"

"Oh, most certainly," the PAO agreed.

There was actually a Fifth Corps, which de Villepin could be forgiven for not knowing about, since it was based out on the *Isla Real,* anyway, and was openly composed of the school and training formations. He discounted those training formations as, without some substantial preparation time, they would not be combat capable. For that matter, even with that time, they had no chance of intervening on the mainland once the TUSF-B had established air and naval supremacy.

"And speaking of air and naval forces, they are strictly fourth rate," said de Villepin. "But even a rock can be dangerous..."

"Don't worry about it," said Janier. "Once we have the major airbases and airports, they won't have anywhere to fly from. C-3?"

"*Mon General?*"

"You *have* planned for a disarming attack on the air forces, have you not?"

"Of course," the C-3 replied. "We further intend to strike their two major naval facilities, out on the big island and at Balboa Port."

"Very good," said Janier, telling de Villepin to continue.

"Lastly, and it is a political question beyond my ability to deal with, General, is the Castilian Battalion under Colonel—though we should probably call him 'Legate'—Muñoz-Infantes, at Fort Williams.

"That's all I have, sir. I will be followed by the C-3."

The C-3, Combined Operations Officer for the Tauran Union Security Force-Balboa, moved gracefully to the podium. "Sir, the purpose of my portion of this briefing is to get your approval for the course of action we will use to change the government of Balboa. We begin with a list of forces available to us."

A slide showed on the screen against the wall. It showed the nine infantry, one commando, one engineer, two artillery, one tank, and two aviation battalions the TUSF-B had been built up to, so far. A side box showed the composite wing from most of the air forces in the Tauran Union.

"In addition," said the C-3, "we have been promised reinforcement by air with the Anglian Para Brigade, the Army of the Republic of Gaul's Para Brigade, reinforced with a commando regiment, a Mountain Infantry Brigade each from Sachsen and Tuscany. The Anglians have further promised the shipment, mainly by sea and in advance, of an air assault infantry brigade, as soon as proper billeting can be found for them. In the interim, we'll be getting out own airmobile brigade. We will also be reinforced beforehand by four aircraft carriers, two Anglian and two of ours. The Zhong have indicated they will be sending one also, not to take part in hostilities but to evacuate their civilians. And, before you ask, sir, no we have not informed the Zhong of anything. But they can read the probabilities and they are perfectly capable of tracking something as big as four aircraft carriers even with their own, substandard, satellite reconnaissance capabilities.

"Moreover," said the C-3, "a short division of Marines will set sail two days before we strike, and will arrive here, mostly by assault transport or fast merchant vessel, within one week."

"Composition of the Marines?" asked Janier.

"One commando—think 'brigade,' *mon General*—of Anglians, with Haarlemers attached, one brigade of ours, and the Santa Martina regiment—really just a big battalion—from Tuscany. Command remains to be worked out."

"A week before they arrive? Toss it to the Anglians as a sop," said the general. "It will mollify their pride and keep them from whining too much about more important commands going to us."

"*Oui, mon General.*"

"What about the two enemy regiments out in *Valle de las Lunas*?"

"Marciano will be ordered to strike across the border to deal with them," said the C-3. "He's got more than enough force for the purpose."

Janier thought about the oversized brigade or perhaps short division they had covering Santa Josefina. Finally, he nodded satisfaction. *Yes, they should be able to take out a mere two or three active companies in Balboa's eastern province.*

"Now, how are they all getting here, and where are they going?"

The C-3 nodded. "As mentioned, sir, the Tauran Union Security Force-Santa Josefina, or TUSF-SJ...I hope we'll be forgiven but the Operations cell has taken to calling it Task Force Jesuit..."

"That works," agreed a grinning Janier.

"Yes, sir. Phase I: Airstrikes on all Balboan air forces and naval forces." The projected map showed drawn explosions over about twelve places. "The Jesuits strike across the border..." The projected map swirled and then stabilized showing a split arrow lancing out from somewhere in northwestern Santa Josefina to the two casernes for Fifth Mountain and a chunk of Fourteenth Cazador. Again the map went fuzzy before clearing up with two more arrows coming in from outside the mapped area. "Anglian

Paras to *Lago Sombrero*. Ours to Herrera International." Five
more, but much thinner arrows, began twisting through the city.
Two more did the same toward and through Cristobal, while two
solid ones aimed directly for Fort Williams. "Our *Mar Furioso*
side based battalions engage and eliminate the headquarters for
Second Balboan Corps and its subordinate legions. On the Shimmering Sea side, two battalions fix and isolate the Fourth Corps'
Headquarters, while two eliminate the Castilian traitor battalion.
Once that is done, those last two move to eliminate the Fourth
Corps' various headquarters and casernes." The map fuzzed and
swirled and reappeared with seventeen more explosion marks,
though these were in green. "We have also planned a number
of strike missions for the commandos to eliminate the Balboan
radio and television system."

The C-3 paused to fill his water glass from a picture just inside
of the rostrum from which he spoke. Once he had, and had
taken a brief sip, he continued, "At this point, *mon General,* it's
worth explaining the end state of Phase One. We began with the
Balboans able to mobilize about twenty-five or so regiments of
perhaps eighty battalions of ground gaining maneuver troops, well
armed and modestly well led. We have eliminated the leadership
of all of the regiments, legions, and corps, and for most of the
battalions as well. At the same time, in terms of manpower, we
will have physically eliminated only about five battalions' worth.

"It is my suggestion, if it can be arranged, that the Balboans
be given enough warning to mobilize their second wave, their
reservists. That will make our job tougher though we will still have
more than sufficient local superiority to eliminate those increased
forces. Since the reservists provide the middle leadership for the
enemy force, we are talking about getting rid of the equivalent
of twenty to twenty-four battalions, and leaving the remaining
rabble totally without leadership. In the long run, though it will
be initially higher casualties, I believe this would give us a shorter
war and fewer men lost."

"Is the end any less certain if we do not provide the Balboans
that warning?" asked Janier.

"No, sir," admitted the C-3.

"So it's a chance we don't really have to take?"

"No, sir."

"Then forget it. Maximum secrecy. Maximum surprise."

"Yes, sir."

The C-3 continued speaking as chart after chart, slide after slide, was presented and removed. Meanwhile Hendryksen, stomach upset after the first two hours and in absolute psychic agony now, thought, *There ought to be a test for senior commanders. Hook them up to a polygraph and make them sit through a long, long meeting or briefing. If they don't show signs of physical distress... never, never, never let them command; they'll waste too much time.*

At length Janier was satisfied with his staff's presentation. There were weaknesses in the plan, surely. Notable among these was that combined arms was, in several places, highly problematic. That weakness, however, was balanced or more than balanced by the staff's diligence in keeping friendly fire incidents down by keeping away from each other's units that didn't speak the same language.

He indicated he had seen enough. Then he gave further guidance. "This is one of the most complex operations the Tauran Union's armed forces have ever undertaken. Indeed, it is the first real war operation the TU has ever undertaken, on any scale, without being under the leadership of"—Janier let a note of contempt creep into his voice—"the Federated States. It will not work unless properly prepared and rehearsed. For that reason, also to keep the Balboans on edge, and also to develop in them a sense of inferiority, we are going to dress rehearse this to the Nth degree. Beginning next week I intend to start ordering our companies, battalions and brigades to practice moving to the very assault positions they will occupy prior to the invasion. This will be done without prior notice... either to our men or—and my word is *law* on this—the Balboans or anyone who might inform them.

"We'll call the small exercises '*Mosquitoes*'; the larger ones '*Green Monsoons.*'

"Further, since nothing works that the commander does not personally check, these exercises will also allow me to check our readiness in person."

One of Janier's subordinates, *Oberstleutnant* Meyer, from the Sachsen tank battalion, had a question. "Sir, what are our priorities? General purpose training for general problems... or preparation for the specific mission for the invasion?"

Janier scowled. "Train for the specific mission. *Obviously.*"

Typical boche.

CHAPTER TWENTY-ONE

I call Christianity the one great curse, the one great intrinsic depravity, the one great instinct for revenge for which no expedient is sufficiently poisonous, secret, subterranean, petty—I call it the one mortal blemish of mankind.

—Nietzsche, *The Antichrist*

Building 332 (Barracks, Company B, 420th Gallic Dragoons), Fort Muddville, Balboa, Terra Nova

"Mosquito!" cried the company duty NCO. In other armies he might have been called a CQ, for Charge of Quarters, or an U von D, for *Unteroffizier vom Dienst*. "Mosquito! Mosquito! *En tenue! En tenue!*" Kit up.

Storming along the tiled corridor, the duty sergeant beat his baton against the troops' doors to help roust them out. Troops began spilling from the rooms, some grumbling, a few swearing against their commanding general. All struggled to pull on shirts, trousers and boots in the anarchic hallway of the barracks.

Even in the TUSF-B, few NCOs lived in the barracks anymore. Instead, they were typically off in family housing. Those few who did still reside with the rank and file, albeit in private rooms, took charge, chivvying some soldiers to the motor pool to precheck and start the tracks, ARE-12P infantry fighting vehicles, and still others to the arms room to draw heavy weapons and breach blocks for the IFVs. Still other soldiers carried bulky company equipment outside of the barracks to where the tracks would pull up for loading. An immaculate staff officer consulted his stopwatch near the main entrance to the billets.

Already the battalion supply and transport platoon was pulling up with pallets of ammunition, four heavy trucks about half-filled with small arms, guided antitank missiles, belted 25mm in staggeringly heavy cans for the dragoon's cannons. Shouting, sweating, groaning under heavy loads, tearing their flesh on all the sharp projections found on military equipment of all types, from all countries, gradually at first, then faster and faster still, Company B made ready to roll to their assault position just northwest of the main hospital.

A military police car showed up, flashing lights. For a real attack it wouldn't be there, the MPs having other things to do and noncombatant life becoming much less precious once the bullets started flying. For now, though, the company couldn't move without them, lest somebody get hurt playing footsie with the heavy armored vehicles.

It only took a couple of hours, which really wasn't bad considering it was the first time, before the unit commander, Captain Bruguière, gave the order: "Roll." Then, flashing MP in the lead, the company surged down the street, hanging a left to go out the main gate before reaching Building 59. The MP waited just past the gate, letting his flashing lights warn off civilian traffic. Once the company's last track had passed, the MP raced to get ahead of them and then farther on to the next intersection.

Rain, not a serious downpour but just a dry season sprinkling, began coming down as the tracks of B Company passed by Brookings Field, a long abandoned Federated States air base, now used to house commandos and a squadron of helicopters, along with diverse support.

Well past Brookings, and just before commencing an unauthorized invasion of Balboa, the column swung right, with the MP car flashing away frantically on its left as it turned. The troops rolled about another half mile, then halted in place in front of *Cerro Mina* before pivoting left. At that point, Captain Bruguière walked the line to ensure he was satisfied with their spacing—there wasn't any cover out there on the road—then called in to 420th Headquarters that he was in position. Battalion then sent back, "Come on home."

✧   ✧   ✧

Not far away, perhaps a kilometer as a trixie would fly—presupposing the quasi-intelligent bitch didn't stop off somewhere to hunt *antaniae*—Signifer Porras, duty officer for Second Cohort, Second Tercio, on *Fuerte* Guerrero, trying to catch a half hour's nap between rounds, was awakened by his runner.

"Sir! Sir! Signifer Porras...for God's sake, wake up! The duty centurion's gone to wake the troops. The Gauls are moving toward the *Comandancia* and the fort, sir, and the police told us they look ready to fight. They're lining up on *Avenida Ascanio Arosemena* just before it becomes *Avenida de la Santa Maria!*"

That was a portion of the broad and lengthy boulevard that separated Balboan territory from de facto Tauran Union ground. The street had gone through many name changes and a couple of minor changes in route since it had first been founded by Belisario Carrera as *Avenida de la Victoria*, following the driving out of Old Earth's then United Nations, centuries before. Sometimes it was still called that, for its entire length.

"What? Shit!" Porras rubbed sleep from his eyes, trying to gather his thoughts from his dreams. The signifer asked, "From where are they coming? How many? Tracks or infantry?"

"We don't know, sir. The police sub-station on their way just made a call to tercio that they are moving. Tercio called cohort; cohort called us."

"Well, dammit, man," said Porras. "Call them back. And start the mobilization recall, level two. And remind them to Second Legion, the *Estado Mayor*, and those assholes in Tenth Tercio. They may not know yet. Hmm...on second thought, I'll call legion and *Estado Mayor*. *They* can call the Tenth. You get the recall going."

"*Si*, Signifer." The orderly snapped to attention, then scurried off to obey.

A junior sergeant, one of the cohort's supply section, stepped up to Porras, reported, then asked, "What's the word, sir?"

"Fucking Gauls," Porras answered. "Coming toward the *Comandancia*."

"Shit! I'll get the arms room open, sir, for the crew-served weapons. Shit!" The corporal hesitated, looking worried. After a few pained seconds he admitted, "Ah...sir? Umm...I issued half our alert stocks of ammunition for training last drill."

"And you haven't made them good *yet*?" Porras snarled.

"Hell, sir, it was only two weeks ago. I put in the request, but it hasn't been filled. That's all."

"Then why the fuck didn't you tell someone before now?"

"I'm sorry, sir. I just didn't think it was that important."

"Assuming the gringos don't attack tonight, this will be the last time you make that mistake. Clear?"

"Clear, sir."

Porras, thought, *It really doesn't make all that much difference, I suppose. The reservists have a fighting load of small arms ammunition at home. But it rankles.*

Then Cruz, unshaven, boots untied, and trousers hanging loose, burst into the headquarters. "Status, sir?"

Porras began briefing the sergeant major, as he dialed tercio headquarters. When someone there answered, he held up a finger toward Sergeant Major Cruz: *Hold one and listen. You'll learn as much as I know from what I ask higher.*

While Cruz listened and tucked his shirt in, then bent to lace his boots, a cacophony arose in the hallways of the barracks. There just might have been a note of hysteria in the men's shouts.

Changeover from *Avenida Ascanio Arosemena* to *Avenida de la Santa Maria, Ciudad* Balboa, Terra Nova

Legate Suarez pointed at the black rubber skid marks on the asphalt of the road. "The fuckers were here, all right. Pulled up and pivot steered, right fucking *there*, then pivot steered again and took off."

Porras, somewhat overawed at being in the presence of his legion commander, said nothing. Conversely, Cruz shook his head, saying, "And for the cost of pulling one of their companies out of its bunks, twenty thousand of our people had to respond."

With a wicked, nasty smile across his face, Suarez asked, "There's a certain elegance in that, don't you think, Sergeant Major?"

"Yes, sir. And if we let them keep it up, they'll frazzle the troops' nerves to bits."

"Just so. That's why they're doing it."

Both men stopped speaking as Carrera's jeep rolled up. They saluted and reported.

Carrera scowled. "So it begins again," he said.

Porras, Cruz, and Suarez stood silent.

"Are you ready to fight them, Suarez? Sergeant Major?"

Suarez didn't answer immediately. Cruz did.

"Sir, we aren't quite ready yet. Two more years, if we can delay it that long. At least a year. Or buy us six months. But not today. Not and win more than one fight. Sir, it isn't that the men won't or can't fight, sir. But we need just that little more time to fill up our ranks and train."

"I agree with the sergeant major, sir," said Suarez.

Carrera exhaled audibly. "Yeah...so do I."

Suarez, looking down, said, "There's another thing, though. The boys aren't sure they can beat the Taurans. But they're not sure they can't either. Every time they do this to us and we don't fight, our men are going to be a little more sure that we can't win, that *you* don't believe we can win. We can't delay forever."

"I know."

Fort Nelson, Tauran Union Security Force-Balboa, Balboa Transitway Area, Terra Nova

Named after one of the most successful, most courageous, luckiest, and least principled officers in Federated States military history, Fort Nelson and its next door neighbor, Arnold Air Force Base, formed one of the strongholds of foreign power in Balboa, dominating the northeastern exit from the Transitway. They had done so for the Federated States, for decades; they did so now for the Tauran Union. That Balboa held Fort Guerrero, on the other side of the bay, didn't change this. Whoever held either post could prevent anyone from using the Transitway, at will.

Fort Nelson and Arnold AFB were, in turn, dominated by the hills to its east. Those were recently fortified by the Taurans, but lightly held. On the post three lines of substantial, white-stuccoed barracks ran north to south. Two of these, of five each, held one battalion of Gallic commandos, one of infantry, an engineer company, and a light artillery battery, with one large, centrally located mess hall for all ten company-sized units.

Opposite the barracks that held the mess hall, which—being a much larger building—housed the headquarters for both of the other battalions, another barracks sagged dangerously in the middle where an idiotic Federated States major had once had a load-bearing wall knocked out to put in an unneeded chapel.

The last line, of three barracks, housed a large aviation squadron, most of whose helicopters sat at nearby Arnold AFB. That last line of three was separated from the other ten by an athletic complex and parade field.

Out on the parade field, stopwatch in hand, a starched and spit-shined staffer observed the last of Company B, 35th Commando Battalion (Airborne) board helicopters. The other two commando companies likewise boarded helicopters, on different parts of the field, but those were not that particular staff officer's problem. To the northwest and southwest, in two open fields, the artillery battery—split into two firing sections—blasted away with signal blanks, simulating fires on Fort Guerrero, a few miles away across the bay, and at the old *Comandancia*, now serving as Second Corps Headquarters. The staffer jotted down the exact time the helicopters lifted from the open athletic field between the Thirty-fifth's barracks and the helicopter squadron.

Turning north, the helicopters passed low over the two old and abandoned hemispherical coastal artillery bunkers of Batteries Henry and George, then across Nelson Beach and out to sea.

Once past the pounding surf, the helicopters veered east toward Fort Guerrero, flying only a few feet above the waves in V formation. A kilometer out from the Balboa Yacht Club the helicopters closed that V into a trail formation, one behind the other. In the next few seconds the commandos of Company B felt their stomachs sink as the pilots, one after the other, pulled pitch to raise the aircraft safely over the trees that fronted the coast.

As soon as the trees were cleared the pilots dumped altitude to come low again, even as they pushed pedals to change direction. Troopers' stomachs heaved. Then, engines roaring and blades chopping the air, the birds were down, landing in trail on the south side of Fort Guerrero's parade field.

With shouts the commandos leapt from the open doors to take up a perimeter around the helicopters. No sooner had the helicopters been unloaded than they took off once again, then headed to Arnold again to refuel. There was a short halt while the company's leaders got the troops on line. Then there began a series of short rushes by individuals and small teams, moving toward the 2nd Cohort, Second Tercio barracks. The troops shouted "bang" ... "bang" in between rushes. They could have used blanks, of course, but blanks could be mistaken for real rounds, which might have invited real return fire. It was not the time for that, not just yet.

I am getting so *sick of these games,* thought Sergeant Major Cruz, standing with arms folded on a second floor balcony to catch a bit of sea breeze against the heat. *Of course, that's their objective.*

"Duty Sergeant," shouted Cruz. "Get the boys outside and on line. No weapons. I have an idea."

"*Si,* Sergeant Major." The sergeant didn't have a clue what Cruz intended, but wasn't about to question his cohort's sergeant major.

Over the next few minutes, as the skirmish line of commandos drew closer, the available men of Second Cohort, Second Tercio formed an even line on the pavement in front of their barracks. When Cruz saw that he had about as many as he could expect he gave the command "Cohort...Atten...shun!" Still sleepy, the response was ragged.

The Gallic troops barely hesitated in their movement towards the barracks. In seconds, the pace of the advance had resumed. As the "bang...bang...bangbangbang" grew louder, the Balboan soldiers awoke quickly.

"About...face!" The legionaries seemed still ragged, but it was mostly reluctance to turn their backs on an armed, advancing enemy.

"Drooop!...Trousers!

"Bennnd...over.

"At My Command...Fart.

"Ready...Fart!"

With the Gauls a bare fifty meters away the Balboans gave a Bronx cheer that just grew louder and louder with time. Faster than if mowed down by machine guns, the Gauls' assault line broke down in laughter.

Cruz gave the order to his men to recover and go back to bed. Before retiring into the headquarters, himself, he gave a single upraised finger towards the men on the parade field.

As the screen door closed behind him, and the Gauls shuffled off to where the helicopters could get in to pick them up, Cruz thought, *And "on each end of the rifle we're the same."*

He shook his head. *It won't do much good, not for long. But anything positive is better than nothing.*

Gatineau, Secordia, Terra Nova

Emotionally, substantial sections of Secordia, south of the Federated States, felt as one with the Tauran Union. Moreover, they'd put their traditionally excellent army to use for decades toadying to the World League in peacekeeping missions in sundry undeveloped hell holes. If there was a spurious, recently invented human right held sacred anywhere on Terra Nova, the odds were good the notion had been birthed right here in Gatineau. Occasionally, the United Earth Peace Fleet had acted as midwife for the birth.

Among those sacred human rights, and one where the UEPF was not merely midwife but father, as well, was the right not to be blown up by the small explosive devices called "antipersonnel land mines." It might further be noted that while the UEPF was the father of the treaty, its mother was an Old Earth princess, long deceased.

Mind, it was a right only among some nations whose armies were really quite careful with the use of land mines, and who could have been counted on to recover mines once emplaced but which were no longer needed. For the major powers, the Federated States, *Xing Zhong Guo*, the remnants of the Volgan Empire, along with some of the lesser states around some of those, people who took war seriously, in other words, that "right" and the treaty which sanctified it, were studiously ignored where not actively sneered at.

Among serious war making powers, only Anglia and Gaul had ratified the "Gatineau Treaty Against the Manufacture, Stockpiling, Sale, and Use of Antipersonnel Landmines." And of those two, the Gauls totally ignored it whenever ignoring it was convenient, while castigating anyone who used mines where such use was inconvenient for Gaul.

And yet—oh, the *thrill*—another serious military power was about to sign on: the Timocratic Republic of Balboa.

Balboa did, however, insist on certain codicils of its own. First, it accepted only a ban on undetectable *plastic* mines. Second, it reserved the right to use any device on hand, or obtainable, in self-defense. The country cited its unique importance to world trade in defense of its position. The Balboan codicils were simply stated at the moment of signing; the treaty itself did not permit national reservations in the text. Still, the international community of the very, very caring and sensitive assumed that, once signed, the Balboans could be legally forced to ignore their own codicils and their own domestic law.

Balboa's ambassador to the World League signed the treaty on behalf of the Republic. From the conference room under the Curia, the Senate House, Carrera and Parilla laughed.

As Carrera told Parilla, "And why not, Raul? Isn't it wonderfully ironic, a really perfect memorial. Think of it. A woman dies. She was fairly vapid and, though merely somewhat attractive, she convinced the world she was beautiful. She led a fairly meaningless life as a mere clothes-horsey ornament to a purely symbolic royal family. She went through an artificial marriage in which both she and her husband cheated nearly from the outset. So we, and the rest of the deluded world, are memorializing her with a vapid, only apparently lovely, meaningless, ornamental, symbolic, and artificial treaty which, when put to the test, will have both sides cheating shamelessly. What a wonderfully fitting piece of international and interplanetary lawmaking *cum* eulogizing.

"Certainly, *we're* going to cheat, mercilessly. And that's hilarious, too."

"She meant well, you know," said Parilla, uncomfortable with maligning the dead.

"She meant to make herself feel good and get applause from all the right people, never mind those who might die for lack of a minefield defense," Carrera answered. "To Hell with that."

Barrio San Miguel, Ciudad Balboa, Balboa, Terra Nova

Not every cohort had a sergeant major with quite the force of character or self-discipline, to say nothing of the imagination, of Ricardo Cruz. Not every tercio in the legion was as disciplined as Second, either. But every unit, every maniple, every cohort, every tercio, every legion and corps had been seriously inconvenienced and annoyed by Janier's "Green Monsoons" and "Mosquitoes."

But even if they had been, every unit contained a few marginal characters. A couple of those, Corporal Bairnals and Private Castillo, were from Tenth Tercio. Half-drunk, the two were leaving one of the brothels where they'd been unsuccessful in negotiating from one of the local professional ladies the precise services they desired at a price they were willing to pay. They might have had the money she demanded, had they not drunk up such a large percentage of it before entering into negotiations. She, on the other hand, might have come down on her price, had they not been quite so drunk.

Knocking around a whore in one of the city's many brothels, always well-guarded, was a good way to end up dead in some painful fashion. Drunk the Tenth Infantry legionaries might have been. *That* drunk they were not.

Sure, they were armed, with their wire-cutting bayonets. The Republic didn't have many rules against carrying firearms; it would have been silly in a place where over half the households had a fully automatic weapon. The bordellos, however, did. In the interests of protecting the girls, the atmosphere . . . such as it tended to be . . . and making money, they never permitted firearms. Knives or bayonets? Some were okay with that. The key thing was that security had to be better armed than the clientele.

Those better armed guards had shown Castillo and Bairnals the door.

Filled with a sense of the injustice of it all, the Tenth Tercio troopers had staggered to the curb and sat down, nursing their grievously wounded egos. The street was *Avenida de la Santa Maria.* On the other side arose *Cerro Mina,* with the Tauran Union sitting atop it, but also some families of the officers and senior noncoms residing within its chain-link fence.

Sometimes, not unlike some married couples, soldiers who have trained long together can read each other's thoughts, even when drunk . . . or perhaps especially when drunk . . . or aggrieved . . . or both.

Add to the injustice of being turned down by a Santandern whore the nearly nightly disruptions from the Taurans, and the near presence of Tauran family members . . .

Bairnals lifted his shirt and took the bayonet from its repository in his waistband. Flipping it a couple of times, he slurred, "Let's go get us some Tauran pussy, my friend. Teach them to wake us up in the middle of the night . . ."

"Right," agreed Castillo. "Go teach them motherfuckin' Tauran pigs a lesson."

The two staggered across the street, then walked along, on the Tauran side, until they came to some thick bushes. Into these they ducked, then moved on all fours up the hill. Occasionally, since the hill was quite steep, one of them would lose his footing and slip back a few feet. Still, progress was generally upward.

They came to the chain-link fence. Bairnals took off his shirt to muffle the sound, then connected his bayonet blade to its scabbard, forming a set of wire cutters. They were, to be sure, not the best wire cutters in the world, but for mere chain-link fence they would do.

Muffled by the shirt, snip-snip went the wire cutters. In short order Bairnals had worked a passage through the fence, about two feet on a side. Unfortunately, his shirt was both cut by the bayonet and torn by the wire.

"Fuck it," he said, and crawled on through in just a T-shirt.

There was a dimly lit house ahead, one of a line on a jungle shrouded street. Where there was a house there would be a woman, since the Taurans only gave housing to families. Where there was a woman there would be revenge on all women, and where there was a Tauran woman there would be revenge on all Taurans.

CHAPTER TWENTY-TWO

I believe that the rape-is-not-about-sex doctrine will go down in history as an example of extraordinary popular delusions and the madness of crowds. It is preposterous on the face of it, does not deserve its sanctity, is contradicted by a mass of evidence, and is getting in the way of the only morally relevant goal surrounding rape, the effort to stamp it out.

—Steven Pinker, *The Blank Slate:*
The Modern Denial of Human Nature

Carcel Modelo, Ciudad Balboa, Balboa, Terra Nova

The court-martial had been very quick. With the evidence of the shirt, DNA collected from the shirt and the victim, the eyewitness testimony of wife and husband, whom the drunken creeps were stupid enough to leave alive, the jury had deliberated for about half an hour, about twenty minutes of which was pure and idle posturing, then returned a verdict of guilty.

The judge, quite conscious that Carrera would arrange an early demise (because Carrera had had one of his aides bring the judge just that advice) if he failed to give the maximum penalty, had duly sentenced the pair of them to that maximum penalty for rape: public impalement...right up the ass. Under the circumstances, and given that they'd inflicted on the wife what the whore had not agreed to, that seemed very appropriate to everyone except the culprits, Bairnals and Castillo. But they didn't get a vote.

The wife, on the other hand, just couldn't deal with that. "No, no; no matter what they did to me, they don't deserve that."

Carrera, who took a personal interest in the case, disagreed. But, the law was the law. She had the right to partially forgive. The bastards were still going to die, but their deaths would be less exacting.

To Carrera's left stood a Sachsen serviceman in mufti. To the left of the soldier was the soldier's pretty, young, blond wife. To the right were Suarez, flanked by the commander and the sergeant major of the Tenth Infantry Tercio. All six looked on with emotions ranging from distaste to hate as a like number of prison guards led out two men in striped garb. After the beating administered by the staff of the *carcel,* the broken-nosed, swollen-eyed, limping human excrements didn't look a lot like they had at trial.

Bairnals and Castillo were handcuffed and chained at the ankles. They could make only short steps, and even those were awkward. An accompanying Roman Catholic priest muttered prayers on behalf of the condemned.

The senior of the guards took a position in front of the prison's gallows, a simple crosspiece mounted on three uprights with clamps for a half-dozen ropes. He waited silently while the other four guards prodded the condemned onto stools and affixed ropes around their necks. Above, poised on the crosspiece, the hangman pulled the ropes almost taut through the mechanical clamps, then stepped on the clamps to lock the ropes in place.

The hangman then descended and, picking up a stool of his own, set it beside Bairnals'. He shot Carrera a look, *Mercy?*

At Carrera's headshake, the hangman twisted Bairnals' rope so that the noose rested just under his chin on the left side. He stepped down, moved his stool, and did the same for Castillo, but without bothering to consult Carrera.

The senior guard consulted his clipboard and began to read the charges and sentence aloud. The two men had been found guilty of kidnapping and rape of the Sachsen soldier's wife. They had used their legion-issue bayonets in their break in. They had beaten the husband using the pommels of the same bayonets, then tied and gagged him. They had then used the blades to threaten the wife into a weeping acquiescence. The husband had been able to hear every small detail, every plea, every time his wife had sobbed or—turned on her stomach—screamed.

The senior guard turned to Carrera, saluted, and asked a question of the wife. Carrera translated, "He is asking you who you choose to be your avenger . . . or if you wish to execute sentence yourself. It is our law that, once a capital crime has been adjudged, the victim may personally take revenge, with the sanction of the state . . . or may choose someone to represent him or her. If you wish the Republic of Balboa to execute the sentences just say '*el Estado.*'"

The wife shook violently. "I . . . can't do this. No matter what they did to me. I just can't kill anyone." She began to cry.

Carrera pretended not to notice the tears. He spoke to the husband. "Sir, your wife appears incapacitated. In such a case—as you *are* her husband—the choice of being her avenger falls to you . . . if you choose to take it."

The Sachsen went even paler than he had been. He said nothing.

Carrera continued, sternly, "Do *not* be weak! These men committed the vilest of crimes against your woman and the mother of your children. It is your *duty* to avenge her!"

His own will overborne by Carrera's, the Sachsen nodded slightly. Then, in a weak voice, he said, "I'll do it." Carrera put a steadying hand on the soldier's shoulder and instructed the guard that the husband would be the executioner. The guard saluted again and marched away from the gallows. Carrera led the soldier forward.

The Sachsen looked up at a Balboan whom he had seen but twice. The first time had been during the crime. The second had been at the trial, just days prior. The Balboan tried to spit but his mouth had gone dry.

"Kick the stool!" Carrera commanded. Without thinking, the Sachsen complied. Bairnals dropped less than three inches and then began to dance on air. The sound of gagging came past the slowly tightening rope. Since the noose was set so as not to cut off blood to the brain, Bairnals would be conscious and suffering for quite some time. And it would seem even longer to him.

Carrera then led the Sachsen to the second stool. The soldier didn't need to be told the second time. He kicked the stool on his own. Carrera guided the man back to his wife.

Thirteen minutes later, when the last twitching foot had stilled, Carrera tendered the apologies of the Republic and dismissed the couple. The husband had been almost worshipful as he shook hands goodbye. The wife had cried without cease during the lingering deaths and for a while thereafter. After they'd left, Carrera walked away briefly to vomit in a corner of the *carcel*.

When the Sachsens had gone, chauffeured back to *Cerro Mina* by Soult in Carrera's limousine, Suarez asked Carrera to speak privately.

"There's going to be more of this, you know, sir. If we don't do something."

"Meaning precisely what, Legate?"

"Sir...you know exactly what I mean. Those two idiots"—Suarez pointed a finger at the still dangling corpses—"only raped that woman to hurt the Taurans. Well, mostly that. Because that was the only way they could hit back. If we don't start fucking with them like they're fucking with us, more troops will decide to take measures into their own hands."

This wasn't precisely what Carrera believed, but it was close enough.

Suarez grew thoughtful. "Sir, the same thing happened with Piña. When the gringos were provoking us, he didn't have the balls... well, to be fair, we didn't have the power then even if he'd had the balls... to provoke back. So the troops—some of them—took matters into their own hands. And Piña, since he was dependent on the troops, couldn't really discipline them."

"I know the story, Suarez. I was on the other side, remember?"

"Oh, yeah. Sorry...you've become so much one of us I forgot."

Carrera removed his hat and ran fingers through his hair. "Did you ever hear of My Thang Phong, Suarez?"

The blank look on Suarez's face said he had not.

"It was a village...rather a series of tiny villages. During the Cochin war it was the scene of a particularly horrible massacre of 'civilians' by Federated States soldiers. Most *Sur Colombianos* could tell you that. What isn't well known is the background. The unit that did it...well, I had a platoon sergeant once, back when I was in the FS Army. He told me that he had been in not that battalion but a sister battalion. He also told me that he had been in his platoon all of three months when he became the most experienced soldier there. The rest had all been hit. By booby traps. This platoon sergeant said that he'd never so much as seen a guerilla. Never even heard a bullet fired.

"Think about it. Always hit and never able to hit back. Of course the 'civilians' were making the mines and booby traps that were killing the troops. Everyone knew it. But the FS Army didn't have the moral courage to investigate these 'civilians,' find the ones who made the booby traps—it was possible to find them, just good police work really, although it would have taken a lot of it...and then try and—in front of the troops—hang them. So the troops—seeing that policy wouldn't save them or avenge them—took matters into their own hands, sadly...indiscriminately. And thereby did a lot to help the Federated States lose the war."

"I see...sir," Suarez slowly answered.

"Just as you've said, if we don't give our men an outlet for their anger, a chance to get 'even,' they'll do it in ways we would prefer they didn't. I'm going to go see the president and say it's this or I resign. I think he'll go along. And then I'll issue orders tomorrow. We're going to start fucking back."

Not far from the Shimmering Sea, *Campo de los Sapos,* Balboa, Terra Nova

Among other assets available to Janier's forces was a company of old-fashioned landing craft, based at Dock 54, a sub-base of Fort Williams not under Muñoz-Infantes' control. Even then, the craft tended to spend the bulk of their time either at the lagoon at Fort Tecumseh or at a different set of piers at Fort Melia, both Fort Williams and Fort Melia backing onto the same man-made lake.

This particular set of landing craft—two of them, enough to hold an infantry company comfortably and two companies with a little pushing—had started the evening's journey at the lagoon at Fort Tecumseh. There, they'd picked up their one infantry company, C Company of the 14th Anglian Foot, stationed at Tecumseh on the Shimmering Sea side because there the Gauls need have as little contact with them as possible.

Other landing craft had picked up A and B companies. Those could be seen, as could C Company, across the water by anyone with night vision. Among those with night vision were some Cazadors posted in a commandeered room in the top floor of the Hotel Franklin on Cristobal's extreme southern side. They immediately reported to Xavier Jimenez.

The landing craft had been spotted almost as soon as they'd departed the lagoon at Tecumseh. For the companies going outside the sea wall that protected the great bay east of Cristobal, the journey on the slow-moving landing craft was about forty minutes. For C Company, staying inside that sea wall, it was a bit shorter, at thirty minutes.

That was much time for someone like Jimenez to prepare a reception, especially when he'd been working on the reception for some days.

The landing craft cut their engines to a dull gurgle as they approached the concrete faced seawalls that guarded the shore. Inside, the Anglian infantry—not Marines—tensed expectantly, as did the more exposed boat crews. At the front of each boat special crews prepared to fix the ladders that would allow the soldiers to scale the boat ramps without dropping them, then go over the sea walls, and emerge onto dry land.

A lone private began the Company C chant, softly so none outside the boat would hear. "CC...CC...CC." The chant stood not for "Charlie Company," but rather for "Cimbrian Club," the vodkalike semi-onomatopoeic drink of preference of Company C. The chant grew as the boat angled in closer to the wall. The Charlie Company motto was met by a faintly heard answering chant, "Mad Dog...Mad Dog...Mad Dog," from Company A, "Mad Dog Alpha," a hundred meters across the water. "Mad Dog...CC...Mad Dog...CC..."

Jimenez heard the chant without being able to make out the exact words. He didn't criticize. It was true—so Carrera had said and so Jimenez believed—that morale was often more important than stealth or surprise. Had it not been for a scout team carefully planted in the Franklin, Jimenez might not have known that any of his tercios were to be probed that night. Even so, he had better than five thousand men on alert. Arguably, this was overreaction.

He didn't know for sure where the Anglians were going, even if the fact that they were coming there could be no doubt of. But...

"*Campo de los Sapos,*" Jimenez had said to himself. "Once the two landing craft left the breakwater that was the only logical objective."

Jimenez listened as the ramps of the LCMs ground against the concrete wall. "Fire," he ordered.

Inside the landing craft the men of the two companies tried to flatten themselves against the bottoms of the boats. Given the crowding this was impossible. Well above each lightly armored side, directly over the heads of the troops, tracers drew solid lines in the night sky. One man—from Company A—cried out in fear before being cuffed to silence by his sergeant.

After the first brief warning bursts Jimenez gave the order to cease fire and standby.

Company A's men looked expectantly backward at the commander, riding high on the boat's deck. To either side of him the boat's machine gunners fumbled with their .50-caliber, heavy-barreled guns. The leftmost gun had no trouble. On the right, however, a female crew*person* simply lacked the strength of arm to pull the bolt against its heavy spring. The boat's assistant walked over and contemptuously cocked the gun for her.

"Don't shoot without orders," he said.

The commander spoke on his radio to his own battalion headquarters. At the answer, he let his arm relax and his radio's microphone sink with it. Then he gave an order to the boat's skipper driver. Slowly, almost reluctantly, the two boats backed water and headed out to sea. The other two, bearing A Company, did as well.

La Comandancia, Ciudad Balboa, Balboa, Terra Nova

While the plan was for the Tauran Union forces to attack the *Comandancia* on the ground, that would have been so inarguably an invasion of Balboa that it was not to be attempted until *The Day*. Still, it just wouldn't have been right to let Suarez's corps headquarters sleep regularly and reliably. So...

Helicopters, small agile gunships, buzzed over the heads of men attempting to bring order from chaos. It was always chaotic when the reservists were called up without notice. It was also demoralizing for them to be pulled from wife and bed, never knowing for certain if this would be the real event.

Video cameras recorded the event.

"The bastards are practicing how they'll attack us when they get the go-ahead," fumed Signifer Torres to no one in particular. He turned his attention back to where an antiaircraft gun crew was hastily breaking out ammunition in case the provocation turned out to be more than that. They already had two fifty-round boxes emplaced and the conveyor feeding the first rounds to the load position.

As one little gunship passed overhead, a gun crew swiveled to track it. Torres asked a gun leader if he thought he could hit the helicopter if the order was given to fire. Torres had to shout to make himself heard over the helicopter's angry roar.

"You heard the man...Fire!" someone shouted. The gunner depressed the firing trigger. A line of tracers arose just ahead of the gunship. The helicopter veered wildly to avoid the stream of tracers passing to his front. Too late, four rounds passed through it.

One passed through the body of the aircraft without exploding, doing no harm. One hit the tail boom, ripping it fatally. A third hit the transmission. The pilot and copilot didn't care, however, as a fourth had exploded inside the crew compartment, killing one and wounding the other.

The helicopter dropped like a stone to crash on the far side of the compound, bursting into flames. Immediately, the other guns in and around the compound opened fire at what targets they could see, but without success. The other Tauran helicopters pulled back out of range, seeming to await orders. At length, the sound of whopping rotors receded into the night.

Cerro Mina, Ciudad Balboa, Balboa, Terra Nova

"Get me that fucking son of a bitch on the phone," demanded Janier.

After an interminable wait, an orderly announced, "*Duque* Carrera on the line, sir."

Janier took the phone. "Carrera, you bastard! Your murderers just shot down one of my helicopters!"

"Pity," said Carrera, dryly. *A pity, indeed,* he thought.

"Well, what are you going to do about it?"

"Do? I'll have to think. Decorate the gunner? That seems appropriate."

"Listen, asshole. You only think you know what tough times are. You better hang that son of a bitch or I'll—"

Carrera interrupted "You'll what? Harass my troops. I suspect you're doing all you can in that department. Start issuing live ammunition? If you aren't already I'd be surprised; my Intel people tell me you're not *precisely* stupid—merely...somewhat... oh, anal retentive. Now I really must go, General. And by the way, my boys are mobilizing as we speak—merely a defensive measure, I assure you. However, if so much as one more Tauran soldier, armored vehicle, or aircraft enters the Republic today I will personally feed your stinking corpse to the *antaniae* in the Transitway. Have a pleasant day, sir."

La Comandancia, Ciudad Balboa, Balboa, Terra Nova

When Soult and Carrera arrived on the scene, the wreck of the helicopter gunship still smoked slightly. A substantial crowd of civilians looked on from a distance. Carrera gazed—not quite dispassionately—at the charred bodies of its two Tauran crewmen. The Balboans had been unable to recover the corpses until long after they had been burned beyond recognition. Despite the constraints in their helicopter, fire had twisted the bodies into fetal positions. *Did I know you once, I wonder? After all, you were allies for many years. Were we comrades? Have we ever talked shop in the O Club over a friendly beer? Did your teachers and mine ever share a friendly beer? Might you even have been one of mine once? If so, I'm sorry, Friends. Even if not, I'm sorry. For your families most of all.*

An ambulance pulled up. The medics on board assembled two litters and roughly placed the corpses on them. The arm of one of the Taurans came loose and fell to the ground, burnt splinters of bone and fragments of flesh sloughing off, at the coarse handling. Carrera flew into a rage. Barely restraining himself from soundly slapping one of the medics, he shouted, "Those were brave men, good soldiers, and you will treat their remains with respect. Understood?"

The medics cowered, mumbling apologies. Carrera turned away to walk to where the gun crew, and Signifer Torres, waited.

Torres stood the crew to attention and reported. Carrera returned the salute and asked what had happened.

Reluctantly, half-ashamed, Torres admitted, "Sir, it was a mistake. My fault. For whatever it's worth, sir, the men did well. They just were following what they thought were my orders. My fault, sir."

Carrera exhaled. "No it wasn't, son. And who knows? Maybe it will turn out to have been a good thing, for us if not for those pilots." He clasped a hand on the officer's shoulder. Torres bowed his head slightly, in thanks.

Carrera continued, "But, with orders or without, these men did their jobs well. And that deserves to be rewarded."

Carrera motioned an aide to his side. The aide drew five badges from a satchel. One by one, Carrera decorated the crew with antiaircraft "kill" badges, shaking each man's hand after pinning on the award. These were only the second crew in the entire legion ever to receive the badges, the first having been the crew that had shot down a Federated States Air Force jet during the war in Sumer.

As Carrera walked back to his automobile a little Balboan girl of perhaps five or six broke from the crowd. Before her mother could restrain her she rushed across the street to Carrera's car. When she reached it she stood, silent and suddenly gone very shy, by the door. The girl kept her hands behind her back.

Carrera looked down and smiled at the child. *So like my little Milagro. Are you going to end up like those poor pilots, little one? If you are, it's going to be my fault, too. Then who will avenge you? Who will be left to avenge you? Who will the revenge be against? I know who it should be.*

The child, still silent, pulled her hands from behind her back and presented Carrera with a bouquet of flowers such as any child might pick from among the weeds found in a still downtrodden part of the city. Her own sweet smile answered Carrera's.

Carrera picked the girl up in one arm, taking the bouquet in the other. He walked in the direction from which she had come, speaking so softly to the child that no one could hear but she.

Seeing the young woman who, from her fretful face, had to be the little girl's mother, he passed the girl over with as much grace as a man could be expected to. He'd guessed from the lack of a ring on the woman's hand that she wasn't married.

"I take it this is your little girl, Miss . . . ?"

"Fuentes, *señor*. Maria Fuentes."

Carrera consulted his watch. "Well, Miss Fuentes, little Alma here has brightened up my day considerably. Would you do me a *big* favor and let me take the both of you to lunch?"

One does not refuse an invitation from someone who is not only the second most powerful man in one's country, but also has a reputation Attila the Hun would have been proud to own. Still, it was the strangest thing to Maria, walking through the streets of the City, Carrera carrying her daughter, and all of them surrounded by big men carrying guns.

The owner of ice cream shop and delicatessen blanched. Of

all the people he never expected to see enter his establishment, Carrera was probably the last.

Carrera bought Alma a sandwich and then an ice cream cone. It was painful to watch, actually, a beautiful little girl who just possibly had never had ice cream in her life before.

Maria tried to refuse out of sheer pride but Carrera was having none of that.

"I insist," he said, "at least a sandwich."

He, conversely, settled for coffee. Patting his stomach he said, "My wife overfeeds me. And I don't get out as much as I used to. If I didn't watch myself, I'd get fat."

Carrera asked Maria a little bit about herself. She told him as little as possible, consistent with that pride.

"You know," he said, "I never get a chance anymore to just sit down with someone and talk. Where do you work?"

At that point Maria was certain he was going to offer her a job as a mattress. He was old enough to be her father but in Balboa that was not such an obstacle.

"Well...I'm sort of between jobs right now," she admitted.

He asked Maria about her future plans but she didn't have any beyond seeing Alma grow up to a better life. "For myself," she said, "I have no hope for the future."

After a while, she asked a question of her own. "Sir," she asked, "why did you and *Presidente* Parilla exterminate the opposition government?"

He put his hands behind his head and leaned back in his chair, his eyes staring into space. At length he answered, "Self-defense, I suppose; they were trying to exterminate us."

Seeing she didn't understand, he elaborated, "The old, rump government tried to get rid of us on some trumped up drug charges. Many of my friends were killed; my new family threatened. My wife, Lourdes..." He stopped talking for a moment, his eyes filling with pure hate. Maria had never seen that much hate, not even her own after some particularly bad days.

"Anyway," Carrera continued, "Lourdes saved us. You probably knew that; it's become the stuff of national legend. When our side had won out, Parilla and I determined never to let anything like that happen again. We stamped out the oligarchs to let the country start over fresh.

"Mostly, it's working," he said. Then he looked at her threadbare clothing, looked at Alma's too thin frame. He looked at Maria's face and sighed. "Unfortunately," he added, "a lot of decent people have been cut out. We only have so much money to go around, despite some help from some friends who have the same enemies we do. There's only so much we can do. By concentrating only on those with military power, we've left a lot of folks—people like yourself—without any recourse at all. This seems to be especially true of the women of the country. I'm sorry. There's only so much to go around," he repeated.

"God knows," she told him, "I could use some help. One decent break, that's all I need." He was impressed that she *didn't* cry, though clearly her voice was breaking and ready to.

He looked at her very intently, then he asked her, if it were possible for Alma to be cared for, if she would be interested in joining up. He said he couldn't do more for her than that. "The benefits of society are for those who benefit society."

Maria hesitated. Carrera reached over and pulled Alma onto his lap. She immediately settled in nicely, still intent on her ice cream. He asked her, "Don't you think this beautiful little girl deserves every chance you can give her?"

"I might be interested," Maria admitted.

Carrera reached into a pocket, pulled out a business card and wrote something on it, signing "C."

"Call that number if you think you would like to try."

Before leaving he reached into a pocket and pulled out some money, saying, "Buy her a birthday present from me." He turned his body, too, so no one could see the money.

Then he set Alma back down, paid the bill and left, his entourage of guards following in his wake.

He stopped, turned, and then waved to Alma from the door.

CHAPTER TWENTY-THREE

The confession of evil works is the first
beginning of good works.

—Saint Augustine

Iglesia de Nuestra Señora, Via Hispanica, Ciudad Balboa, Balboa, Terra Nova

A noonday sun beat down on the city with its customary lack of mercy. The only shadows were under the many trees lining the boulevard. Even there, sun reflecting off of red tile roof and white stucco reflected painfully to the eyes. From that the only shelter was indoors or behind sunglasses or tinted automobile windows.

Carrera consulted the calendar on his watch, then pointed, ordering, "Over there, Jamey." His finger was aimed down a side street that paralleled a large, gossamery church, mostly in white, and more particularly at a reserved parking spot, marked with a yellow sign, next to a lacelike projection from that church.

Nuestra Señora was not the largest church in Balboa, nor remotely the oldest; there was one still in use in *Valle de las Lunas* that claimed—right out front on a bronze plaque—that Belisario Carrera had laid its cornerstone. It was, however, the grandest, the prettiest, and the one where, when he found time for services, he preferred to go.

"Sure you don't want to swim the Tiber?" Carrera asked, with a smile.

"Eh?" Warrant Officer Soult shrugged, with a mirroring grin. "All you bloody papists are doomed to hellfire."

"Well," Carrera half agreed, his smile disappearing, "surely some of us are."

Dammit, Jamey, thought Soult to himself. *You dipshit, you know how freaking sensitive he's been about some things ever since he nuked Hajar.*

Not that he doesn't have some reason.

Carrera let himself out of the armored sedan—today, in the city, he was using an unmarked one, and had dispensed with his usual armored car escort, in favor of a team of bodyguards—then closed the door behind him. The heat struck him like a blow, except uniformly all over his body.

Note to self: tell Jamey not to run the air conditioning in the car quite so cold. The transition is too tough.

Under the shadow of the projection, the door was closed. Air conditioning for something so large was not, after all, especially cheap. The door was not, however, locked nor did he expect it would be. He slid inside, as a welcome bath of cool, dry air washed over him.

He dipped three fingers in holy water, then made the sign of the cross. A half-dozen steps along the tiles, under the vaulted arches above, a left-hand turn, and a few more steps, and he took a seat outside one of the confessional booths. There were a couple of well-shaped, well-coiffed, well-dressed, and rather pretty women of about ten years less than his own age there ahead of them.

Carrera was most flattered when the women checked him out. Surely they recognized him—no one in Balboa could fail to—but they might not have been aware he was married. They might not have cared, either. So, to spare both them and himself any embarrassment, he began nonchalantly playing with his wedding band with the fingers of his right hand.

Best I can do under the circumstances.

The women took the hint with good grace. They were still, after all, quite attractive and they knew it. Plenty more fish in the sea...even if...none quite so replete with such a thrilling air of infinite menace.

And then it was Carrera's turn at bat. He entered the confessional, knelt, and began, "Bless me, Father, for I have sinned grievously. It has been...oh...lemme think...nine weeks? Yes, that long...since my last confession. My theology was unsound then; it is unsound now; but there are sins on my soul I cannot confess."

Recognizing the *surcolombiano* accent, the priest, a Spanish-speaking expatriot named Murphy, asked, "It *is Duque* Carrera, is it not?"

"Yes, Father; Carrera." Not to be outdone, Carrera asked, "And you would be Warrant Officer Father Murphy of the Tenth Infantry Tercio, would you not?"

"I would," the priest admitted, "though why you won't commission men of the cloth...never mind, never mind. That's for another time and place. What sins have you committed that are not common knowledge, my son?"

"The sins that are common knowledge, Father, I feel no repentance for, and cannot, in good faith, ask for forgiveness for them. There are other sins for which I am truly sorry but which I do not have the right to confess, even to a priest. There are sins of mine that innocent people might pay for, were I to confess them."

"You don't feel repentant for the murders, the torture, the overthrow of the government?"

"No, Father. And, speaking of torture, that's why I cannot confess them. If the Gauls got their hands on you, say, and put you in the hands of a skilled and ruthless interrogator, there is nothing you would hold back. As for the old government—getting rid of them has worked out well for the people, and so I will take my chances that God will count the benefits against the harm and forgive me anyway. I am sorry for the innocents that suffered—I know there were some—but when I can forgive myself, I'll ask God to forgive me."

"Then what sin do you seek forgiveness for?"

"I've caused a great war, Father."

Misunderstanding, the priest said, "There is no war here. Yes, I heard on the news about the Tauran helicopter. But that was not a war...a skirmish perhaps, even an accident of sorts, so I've heard."

"An accident only in its details, Father. I shot down that helicopter as surely as if I'd pulled the trigger. It was inevitable the day I returned to Balboa. The day I let my pride—and my anger and hate—set me on the road I'm on...the road I've forced Balboa down. It's a one-way road with no going back."

"How could you force this country to war? You're just one man."

"No, Father, I'm not *just* one man. I wish I were. Then I could not have done what I've done. You could not know all

the details—no one but myself does—but I've given Balboa the
means to fight the Tauran Union and even more, very likely with
success. And I have arranged things so that fighting is inevitable.
I knew what I was doing from the beginning, at least from the
time when Parilla recruited me. Almost every step, and every
important one. Even when the old government tried to get rid
of me—it was not my plan, but it was certainly within my intent
to get rid of it, eventually, so the Taurans and the internationals
would back Balboa into a corner from which it had to fight."

"Why?"

"Because I *hate* them. Because I detest their decadent society. I
despise their arrogant, ignorant view of the world. I have nothing
but contempt for their whining self-pity, their glorification of the
worthless. I detest their preference for form and appearance over
truth and substance.

"I hate them for giving aid and comfort to the people who
murdered my last family. Even then, though, I think that—deep
down—I may have hated them even before that.

"But maybe not... It's hard to remember now what I felt back
then."

"And what has changed?" asked the priest.

Carrera sighed, "Hate pales, Father. It grows old and stale. Bitter on the tongue. And... then, too... I don't want my people,
my real people, hurt anymore. It just isn't worth it. There was a
little girl this morning, Father. Not far from where the helicopter
was shot down. A sweet little child. I don't want *her* hurt. I don't
want my new family hurt. I don't want any more of my soldiers
hurt. I don't even want any more of *their* soldiers hurt."

"'Th' unconquerable will and study of revenge, immortal hate
and courage never to submit or yield'?" asked the priest.

"Yes... well, Father, hate may have paled, but back when it
was fresh and new I studied well, planned well. And so, in my
pride, I laid all the groundwork needed to ensure revenge. Even
if I don't want it, or don't want it enough, anymore."

"Can you not stop the war?"

"How? If I leave Balboa, I leave behind me a fine little army of
citizen soldiers; well trained, well led and brave... and patriotic,
too. Their patriotism will make them stand firm to the time of
fighting, their training and courage will make them fight hard.
Although they'll lose... without me."

"And with you?"

"They could win. I've planned for them to win. But it will be costly; bloody beyond even what they *can* believe."

"And you were ready to let them bleed for your revenge?"

"I was. No more. I'm sorry. But it's too late to stop now."

"Could you go back to the old government? Would that make the Taurans back off?"

"I actually didn't plan for this. I didn't because I knew it would happen; the soldiers will not permit us to go back to the old ways. Why should they? They run the country now, or will when their time of service is up. They benefit from the arrangements I have made. They'll follow me as long as I lead where they want to go. But they won't willingly go back to the way things used to be."

The priest went silent for a moment, on his side of the darkened cubicle. Carrera could barely make out the shadow through the mesh that separated them. When the priest spoke again, he said, "There is pride in your voice. More perhaps than you know. You said Balboa can win. What I think you mean is that you believe they *will* win. Is that so?"

"Yes, Father. Balboa will win, if I lead."

"Can't you convince the Taurans States of that? It seems to me the only hope for peace, for them to back off since you . . . we . . . cannot."

In the darkness of the confessional, Carrera shook his head. "No. Not without revealing things that, if revealed, would ensure that Balboa cannot win. I've tried certain things but . . . no, they don't seem to want to believe."

"Can you bluff, make them believe that they would be taking a great risk if they attacked. I assume you have no plans to attack the Tauran Union."

The way Carrera started when the priest said that told that he did, indeed, have some such plans. The priest, with some regret, didn't ask for information he knew would not be given.

"Even a bluff has great risks, Father. People can bluff each other into war, no matter that what they intend is peace."

"Yes. I see," the priest agreed. He considered a while. "You seek penance and forgiveness for a sin—and it was a sin—the results of which have not yet come to fruition. Ordinarily, the token penance of prayer is sufficient to obtain God's forgiving grace. But the ordinary sin is complete in its essentials before the penitent seeks that grace. Your case is special and no amount of praying seems to me sufficient. I mean, in a sense, that God helps those who help themselves. Prayer there must be, prayer for guidance, divine assistance, wisdom. And I shall assign you much. Yet works have their place along with faith. You said that there are great risks in bluffing. But you've also said, and I believe you, that war is otherwise a certainty. You must take the small chance for peace, rather than the certainty of war. You must actively try to prevent the outbreak of war. How you will do this, I do not know. God, however, will. He will know also if you have sincerely tried to prevent the impending harm you have caused."

"I will do so, Father, but only to this point: I will reveal nothing to the Taurans that will make it more difficult for Balboa to survive and prevail if it comes to a fight...as it almost certainly will anyway."

The priest started to interrupt, but Carrera cut him off. "No, Father. Don't bother. If the price is my soul, then I deserve to lose it. I have used these people and abused their trust shamefully. A single soul is not too great a price to pay to redeem that trust.

"Even so—up to the point of further betrayal, not an inch beyond—I will try."

La Comandancia, Ciudad Balboa, Balboa, Terra Nova

The compound was walled, but more for show than defense. That said, there were machine gun towers on the walls, as well as hidden firing ports at street level, and several antiaircraft positions sandbagged on the roofs of its buildings and a few more in the open spaces. Still, the obvious defenses couldn't do much beyond preventing either clandestine infiltration or a *coup de main*. The *real* defenses of Second Corps' headquarters was outside the compound, in rehearsed positions, some of which had already been fortified, out in the town.

This time, Carrera came with full escort, a marked armored sedan, two armored cars mounting cannon, and a platoon of infantry in two trucks. The infantry were from Ham's Pashtuns, though the armored cars were manned by legionaries.

Second Legion's bagpipe band was standing in the open area as the guards on the gate waved the first armored car through. As Carrera's sedan's grill made its first appearance at the gate, the band struck up what was widely believed to be Carrera's favorite march, which had been adopted also by several tercios and legions: "*Boinas Azules Cruzan la Frontera.*"

An escorting officer and centurion were waiting about in the middle of the yard. Soult aimed for a spot next to them, then gently applied the brakes to come to a halt. The centurion had Carrera's door open within a small fraction of a second of the car's coming to a halt.

How the hell did he do that? Carrera wondered as he returned the escorts' salutes. They then led him off at a brisk step toward the conference.

This really wasn't necessary, he thought. *I know the way. Then again, the pipes are always nice.* Carrera sniffed a bit. *Ah, good. Last time I was here the place reeked of spilled gasoline and burnt flesh and plastic. Now ... somewhat better. Hmmm, I wonder if that young mother with the little girl will ever work up the gumption to call my aide?*

Suarez and his senior officers and sergeants major stood to attention as Carrera entered their conference room. The room only held twenty at the table and about one and a half times that on a stepped platform in the back. An air conditioner mounted in a window strained without much success against the heart of bodies and the heat radiating down from the roof and through the windows.

Fifty men—or forty-nine, minus Carrera—just about worked out to legionary and tercio commanders and sergeants major, Suarez, his corps staff and sergeant major, and either the executive or operations officers for those. The one centurion present had a misery in his bowels; he was pretty sure he'd been delegated to piss boy.

"Seats, gentlemen," Carrera began. "I've been giving a lot of thought lately to our problems with the Tauran Union. Every day, it seems, there is some new incident. We've done a few things to make them back off—on those occasion when we've had enough warning to be in position to make them back off. And you people shooting down their helicopter may pay dividends.

"Still, I wonder if it isn't time to increase the stakes a bit. We ... none of us, I think, want to fight if we don't have to. The Tauran Union is powerful, not an enemy to treat with contempt. But, given their overarching political and philosophical outlook, they're a power much given to delusion. They may not realize, yet, that they could face a serious fight here. We should show them, I think."

Suarez grew grim-visaged. "Take them on the next time they come near our borders?" he asked.

Carrera shook his head. "No, we don't fight...yet. Let's play some more games back, though, shall we? How hard is it," he asked Suarez, "to come up with forty or fifty really beautiful girls in Second Corps' area? I mean here *stunners,* the kind of women who don't just suck all the oxygen out of a room when they enter it, but can leave entire city blocks gasping for air as they pass by. Being photogenic counts."

"Not so hard," Suarez answered. "Even without going to the foreign help in the bordellos. Though a small budget for clothing, makeup, and makeup artists might be a good idea. Most of our grid area"—the seven layered complex of grids that drove Balboan recruiting—"is fairly poor, after all."

Carrera thought of the poor girl, Alma's mother, and said, "I'll cover it myself. How much?"

Suarez, after a moment's thought, answered, "Fifty girls? A hundred thousand drachma. Maybe not even that much."

"Fine. Make it two hundred thousand and have polleras made for them, too. *Nice ones.* With lavish silver for their hair." The Balboan national dress, the *pollera,* or "bird cage," included, indeed derived its name from, the ornate arrangements of silver ornaments in a Balboan girl's hair.

"Might even let 'em keep the silver if they do a good job."

"Pay them?" asked Suarez.

"Yeah, sure. Standard, not drilling reservist or militiamen's, daily pay, to include when they're on alert."

"On alert?"

"Oh, *yeah,*" said Carrera, and his voice was full of malicious mischief. "After the girls are ready I want parties of them on continuous alert, whenever the Taurans roll out, to meet them at their assault positions...with coffee, and doughnuts and other pastries, maybe empanadas if it's mid-day or early evening. Cold drinks, too, at noon. Whatever's appropriate.

"And I want cameras there to record the whole fucking thing. And prominent banners that say, 'Balboa es Soberana en la Area del Transitway,' and, 'Taurans out of *Our* Country,' just in case anyone thinks those girls are out there in support of, rather than to undermine, the Tauran Union."

"Ooooh...that's evil," said Suarez. "I *like* it."

"Me too, but I don't trust the Taurans, so trailing along after the girls, just in case, I want fully armed maniples . . . or cohorts, if you think it's necessary. And police, of course, to chaperone the girls."

"How old?" asked Suarez. "Is there a bottom age?"

Carrera thought about the Balboan notion of the *quinceñera*, a girl's fifteenth birthday party, the time when she was officially available for (escorted) courting. "Fifteen on up, provided they look *exquisite*.

"Oh, and Suarez?"

"Sir?"

"Tell the girls, from me, that everyone who is a patriot fights for their country in the best way available to them."

"Sir."

"Note, also, gentlemen, that I'm going to be giving a similar mission to Third Corps. I trust the girls of Second will not be content with second place.

"One last thing, Suarez. I'm having the propaganda department print up copies of *Historia y Filosofia Moral* in every language present among the Taurans here. I'd like it if the girls could get the Tauran troops to take copies."

Alfaro's Tomb, *Ciudad* Balboa, Balboa, Terra Nova

News stations' video cameras whirred, taking in the aspect of lovely olive skinned Balboan women, in ornately frilled, colorful, dresses, pouring coffee, passing out doughnuts, and chatting amiably with befuddled Tauran soldiers, most of whom had already picked up the minimum of Spanish since that was, after all, *what the local women spoke*. The women's smooth and rounded sleekness stood in stark contrast to the angular, squat, ugly lines of the armored cars they surrounded. A hastily erected banner proclaimed, "Balboa is sovereign in the Transitway Area."

Politely refusing a gracefully proffered cup of coffee from an angelic faced girl, the frustrated Tauran company commander spoke into his radio handset. "No, sir. I tried to pull out. Four of these women, with six TV cameras to watch, blocked the way. . . . Sir, I think the little bitches would have let us run them over before they moved. I had to stop my tracks. And now there are police passing out tickets to my squad leaders. . . . Oh shit; they're hooking up a wrecker to one of my tracks!"

The captain stormed over to where a crew of wrecker operators were attaching the last cables needed to drag the armored
vehicle away. The captain unholstered his pistol. Immediately,
two Balboan policemen drew their own, pointing the firearms to
the captain's chest. Women stiffened—a few suppressed cries—as
vehicle turrets swiveled to cover the policemen. Two trios of the
girls moved—they shook with fright but they still moved—to
stand beside and behind their police. Their chins lifted, defiant
and proud. At the moral reinforcement, the policemen cocked
their pistols. The cameras caught that, as well.

Shit, thought the captain. *I can't start anything. If I do, the
police will shoot. I might survive that, but my boys will fire at
the police. Then we'll hurt these innocent girls. With the cameras
watching . . . the whole world watching. And two cops with pistols
against what everyone will say are tanks. Shit!*

Casa Linda, Balboa, Terra Nova

Carrera held his sides and rocked, he was laughing so hard at
the afternoon news. It was especially delicious since, many years
before, during preparations for the FSC's invasion of Balboa, he
had, for all practical purposes, *been* that Tauran *Panzergrenadier*
captain.

"That dipshit, Piña," he said. "If he'd had two brain cells to rub
together, he could have done that to us, and wouldn't that have
frosted the old Northern Command's collective balls?"

Lourdes, sitting beside him, didn't say anything. It wasn't until
Carrera had been able to bring his own laughter under control
that he'd been able to feel through the structure of the sofa that
she was shuddering.

He turned his head and looked at his wife, who was almost
as tall as he was. She was crying, tears running down her face
and chin lifted in defiant pride—an unconscious imitation of the
girls, perhaps. She stood and began to walk out of the room, in
the general direction of the front door.

"Where are you going?" he shouted after her.

She sniffled, then sniffled again. Turning, she answered, "To
find Suarez and volunteer myself. I'll be damned if my country-
women will stand against armored vehicles without me there to
stand with them."

CHAPTER TWENTY-FOUR

The press should be not only a collective
propagandist and a collective agitator, but
also a collective organizer of the masses.

— Vladimir Lenin

The press is the enemy.

— Richard M. Nixon

With the press there is no "off the record."

— Donald Rumsfeld

The Tunnel, Tauran Union Security Force-Balboa, *Cerro Mina*, Balboa Transitway Area, Balboa, Terra Nova

Janier, plus his C-2 and C-3, watched the very same news film as had Carrera and Lourdes. The difference was that theirs was beamed in via satellite from a channel in the Tauran Union. It was also, unlike the ones broadcast in Balboa, accompanied by shots of a series of, so far, small protests across the capitals of the Tauran Union.

"And I wonder whose idea that was," said Janier.

His intel chief, de Villepin, shrugged. "The protests back home? Might have been spontaneous, for all I know. For that matter, the use of the—let us admit it—lovely girls here might have been spontaneous or, at least, low level."

"No...no," Janier disagreed. "There's organization there. Otherwise, no police, no military backup just behind the girls. And

I would not be the least surprised to discover there's some organization back home behind those protests."

"It doesn't sound like the kind of thing Carrera would do," de
Villepin said. "For all his myriad faults, he's always struck me as
a pretty unsubtle man and up front soldier. If I've been wrong
about that..."

"You mean if he's as much an unprincipled hypocrite as we
are?" Janier asked.

"Exactly."

"It requires thought," Janier said. "But what I want to know is
how have the bastards been keeping such good track of us. How
do they know every time we make a move?"

"They don't," de Villepin said. "Yes, I had the same impression
as you, sir. But I've counted the numbers and tallied the incidents;
they've intercepted less than a third of the probes we've made. I
think if they knew more they'd have intercepted more.

"And yes, they have their spies in our ranks, as we have some
in theirs. It's tougher for us, by the way. If we catch one of ours
spying for them, we have to send them home where their home
countries never have the moral fortitude to do much about it.
When the Balboan, Fernandez, catches one of his people spying
for us, the fate of that man or woman is grim, indeed."

The C-3 interjected, "Sir...no one knew in advance...except for
you, me, and the C-2. And sure as shit we didn't tell the locals.
No, sir. The early Mosquitoes warned them. And they set up an
ambush—a public relations ambush—for this last one. And they
are watching us. As de Villepin said, they have a few spies here,
but this has all been too close hold and short notice for that to
work. They're just using recon, all kinds of recon, to get warning,
then reacting only to those they have sufficient time to react to."

"*D'accord,*" said de Villepin.

A messenger knocked on the door to Janier's office, then hurried over to hand a message to the C-2. De Villepin's face went
ashen as he read.

"Sir...it seems the Balboans are mobilizing and moving towards
our facilities."

Janier blanched. "Who? Where?"

De Villepin looked down at the paper in his hand. His first
glance had been at the headline paragraph. Now he began to
read in more depth. "The information is incomplete, General.

However, indications are that two tercios are forming up just north of here... it looks like they intend to assault this hill. That's probably Second Legion's Second and Tenth *Tercios*. Third Corps' Third Legion is not making offensive moves, but to be taking positions to defend Herrera Airport. Fourth Mechanized Tercio is moving—in dribs and drabs—toward the City. On the Shimmering Sea side there is a tercio—Eighth Marines would be my guess—inflating rubber rafts in Cristobal opposite Fort Tecumseh. Another is moving on the locks on that side. And, sir... there is artillery setting up all over the place."

Janier ran to the door to his office. "Get me the goddamned Air Force!" he shrieked, near panic.

"Sir," an airman piped in, "Radar at Arnold reports numerous previously unidentified radar sources blanketing the Transitway. They say these are air defense radars, sir."

"Get me the Air Force!" Janier demanded again.

Before anyone could respond to his double demand, a French-speaking Anglian Army private walked up with a portable phone. The private hesitated, then held the phone out. "Sir... the enemy commander, *Duque* Carrera, wants to speak with you."

Janier took the phone. "Janier here." He struggled to keep his voice calm.

From the other end Carrera spoke calmly. "General Janier? This is Carrera. How good to speak with you again.... Yes, General, we are engaged in harmless maneuvers as well. It would be a pity though, don't you think, if someday I neglected to give my boys a limit of advance? Why... they could overrun the Transitway area before I could order them to stop.... Well, of fucking *course* they have ammunition, General.... Oh, yes; we'll return your armored vehicle to you as soon as the Tauran Union pays off the fines for that infantry company that trespassed onto our territory. The fines will be heavy. Good day to you, General."

After sober reflection, much reflection, Janier went to his office and took out the communications device Marguerite had given him. He suggested very strongly to her, and said he would be going to the Security Council for the Tauran Union as well, that it might be better to let things cool down in Balboa for a while.

"But what if," asked de Villepin, "they do this to us someday and don't give us an early indication that they won't go past a certain point? Things could easily spin out of control."

Casa Linda, Republic of Balboa, Terra Nova

Between the shot down helicopter, the pretty girl ambush, and the dramatic increase in tensions brought about by Carrera's policy of active confrontation, Balboa suddenly found itself once again newsworthy in the Tauran Union, and for something other than being denounced for war crimes. Accordingly, a popular Tauran television news "magazine" asked permission to interview Patricio Carrera and Raul Parilla. Parilla declined the invitation as his English was wretched enough to make a bad impression on the viewers of Tauran television. Carrera, however, was tempted.

Fernandez, bound to his wheel chair, had objected strenuously. "Sir, you cannot trust them. They will twist what you say. They will *lie*, they will make you appear to be a liar. They will edit and splice to put words in your mouth that you never said. When it is shown on television you will find yourself answering questions that were never asked. Please don't do this."

After reflection, Carrera had overridden his chief of intelligence and security, even after Fernandez brought in Professor Ruiz, chief of propaganda, and Maya Delgado, a distant relation of Cadet Delgado and the CEO of the largest national news service in the country, to plead his case.

"It's up to you gentlemen," Carrera had said, "and you, too, Mrs. Delgado, to protect me and the country from that kind of journalism. So do it."

As part of that, Fernandez insisted on making separate tapes, from three hidden cameras that could see both participants to the interview. Also he had the furniture moved around a bit. Then he, Mrs. Delgado, the Balboan newsie, and Ruiz had drilled Carrera numb on some of the tricks the press could and would use.

Wally Barber, the interviewer sent out by the TNN, was a black Anglo-Secordian news correspondent with fierce white whiskers. The maid met him and the camera crew at the door, then showed them into the living room where he and Carrera shook hands amiably. From there they went to the office where a single camera was set up facing Carrera only. Behind Carrera stood a flag of Balboa in a stand, plus the golden eagle of all the legions, temporarily removed from its secure cage at the *Estado Mayor*, in the City. There was no flag behind Barber, though there was a bookcase with many distinctive titles contained on its shelves. The Balboan newsie, Mrs. Delgado, sat slightly behind and to the left of Barber.

A red light started blinking on the camera. The cameraman said, "Damn. I'm sorry, Mr. Barber, the tape's run out on this one. It was those shots we took of the City and the countryside on our way here. It'll just be a minute while I run down to the van and get a new tape."

"That's all right, Phil. *Duque* Carrera and I can use the time to get acquainted, off the record. Would that be all right with you, *Duque*?"

From behind Barber, Mrs. Delgado shook her head violently. What she knew, along with Barber and the cameraman—but not Carrera, some things in the prep they'd missed—was that the video camera had a built-in fifteen minutes' worth of recording time. This was an old trick for the unwary; get the subject of the interview to chat without thinking for fifteen minutes so that the unwitting answers could be used for questions that had never been asked. Carrera told Barber, "I think it might be better if we wait for your assistant to return with the tape."

Hiding a snarl, Barber answered, "As you wish, *Duque*." *You may avoid that trap. But I'm a professional while you're just an amateur with a second-rate newsie as a handler. I'll still make you look a fool.*

When the cameraman had returned, and the tape had been installed, Barber began his questioning. The camera stayed focused on Carrera, as it would throughout the interview. "*Duque* Carrera, people in the Tauran Union are...well, frankly, worried. They're worried over the growth of Balboa's armed forces, over the increasing tension you have created by your violent provocations of Tauran forces here in Balboa, over the trade in illegal drugs which passes through Balboa. What would you tell them to calm their fears?"

"In the first place, Wally," Carrera replied, "to the best of my knowledge and belief, no drugs are passing through Balboa. I know you find that hard to believe, because you still have a drug problem in the Tauran Union, but that's *your* problem, not ours. As came out during the coup launched with Tauran Union aid against the democratically elected government of Raul Parilla, we fought a mostly secret and very bloody war with the drug lords of Santander and broke them.

"In the second place, I join in grieving with the families of those two pilots killed recently. They did not have to die. None of my people wanted to kill them. It was, sadly, just an accident of the kind anyone could predict when Tauran forces are continuously sent to impinge our borders and threaten our troops. And lastly, Balboa's regular armed forces are, as a percentage of our population, no larger than those the Tauran Union maintains. Also, in absolute numbers, you outnumber us by about one hundred to one in regular forces."

Barber made a strong effort to keep a supportive and friendly look on his face as he said, "And yet, *Duque*, Santa Josefina—your eastern neighbor—has no armed forces. Don't you think they have a right to feel threatened. You have—after all—soldiers, tanks, artillery, a reasonably modern air force."

Carrera shook his head, "Perhaps...if we had anything but friendship and kinship for Santa Josefina, they might have cause to fear. Although, if you were to ask one of your own military, they would tell you, I'm sure, that Balboa hasn't the logistic capability, the ability to move supplies, to support any operations in Santa Josefina. Certainly not against Tauran interference.

"Moreover, whatever the government of Santa Josefina might say, the people there don't fear us. After all, they send us their sons to serve in our legions by the tens of thousands."

"Can you conceive," asked Barber, "of any circumstances under which you would send Balboan troops to Santa Josefina?"

"No." Which was not entirely honest of Carrera. He fully intended to send troops into Balboa's eastern neighbor, as soon as politically practical. He intended, though, to send Santa Josefinan troops.

"Back to the world trade in drugs, for a moment," said Barber. "It is said that you have financed this huge army for Balboa by taking control of the drug trade. Your wife, during the attempted restoration of democracy to Balboa some years ago certainly admitted that you took money from the drug lords. Isn't it true that you do, in fact, take money from known drug criminals?"

"Yes. Or rather demand it, war reparations so to speak. They fought us in a dirty campaign of terror for the right to move drugs though Balboa. They lost, and that was part of the price they had to pay for peace. And I might add that I've done something which neither your drug enforcement agencies nor that of the Federated States has never succeeded in doing. Balboa's actions have measurably raised the street price of those drugs in the Tauran Union. You should thank Balboa for that.

"As for an attempt to restore democracy?" Carrera guffawed. "You don't really believe that that cabal of old, corrupt oligarchs the Tauran Union tried to foist back on us was a democracy, do you? That's *preposterous*."

The interview continued for hours, interrupted by lunch in the kitchen. The redundancy of the questions sometimes strained Carrera's patience, which was most—not all—of the reason for the redundant questions.

This was not, however, the way the tape was aired, a few days later.

"This is Walley Barber, for One Hundred Minutes, speaking to you from the *Casa* Linda, Balboa's labyrinthine and secret military headquarters."

Curiously, although the camera had been focused on Carrera the entire interview, Barber appeared as a face, not just a voice. There was also a blue Tauran Union flag behind him, although none had been present at the interview.

"General Carrera, people in the Tauran Union are...well, frankly, worried. They're concerned that you have the ability and the will to attack Tauran interests, even to conquer your neighbors. Do Taurans have reasons for these fears?"

Carrera's image answered, "They might have."

That camera's view cut back to Barber's flag-framed face. "Can you conceive of circumstances under which Balboa would attack... say, Santa Josefina, the Transitway Area, or even the Tauran Union?"

Again Carrera's image answered for him, "Yes, it's certainly possible."

Back to Barber. "General Carrera, really you are—though you've denied it repeatedly—intimately involved in the world drug trade, aren't you?"

"Balboa's actions have measurably raised the street price of drugs," Carrera admitted.

Only Barber and his regular crew knew that he had made thirty-two takes, back in his studio in the Tauran Union, of what he said next. With an admirable mixture of shocked disbelief, outrage, and disgust, he said, "Well, at least you admit to your complicity."

An Tauran viewer might not, probably would not, know or care that all Carrera had admitted to, even on the doctored tape, was to accomplishing the Tauran Union's Drug Enforcement Administration's mission for them, raising the street price of illegal drugs. Framed by Barber's question and comment it was made to sound as if Carrera had admitted to a great crime.

Barber continued, "And if the Tauran Union tries to restore democracy to Balboa, eliminate the military threat your armed forces pose, and combat the drug trade?"

"That's *your* problem." The warped interview continued, ranging back to the military threat posed by Balboa to the Tauran Union.

"You do admit then, that your soldiers fired on an unarmed Tauran helicopter engaged in a routine training mission, killing two Tauran soldiers."

"To the best of my knowledge and belief," answered Carrera. "An [in]cident of the kind anyone could predict." Barber's crew had had to use a voice synthesizer and a minor bit of computer wizardry to alter the last statement.

In their living room Lourdes and Carrera watched the airing of the interview with disgust. "Patricio, I know you wouldn't have said any of those things."

"Wouldn't and didn't. I should have listened to Fernandez."

The phone rang. "Carrera."

"Sir, I've watched the interview. I did warn you."

Carrera grunted.

Fernandez's voice seemed almost chipper. "However, all is not lost. We might even be able to turn this to our advantage."

"Really? How?"

"I made tapes of the actual interview, you know. Hidden cameras; that Secordian bastard never knew. With your permission, I'll release them to all the large broadcasters. Colombia Latina, a good part of Taurus and the undeveloped world, maybe even some in the Tauran Union will believe the real version."

"Maybe they will. I want something else, too."

"Sir?"

"Taurans will not believe we would be really angry over airing a true interview. Therefore, they will expect no retaliation against the bastard. On the other hand, if we eliminate him, at least some of them will believe we are really angry and that the interview was doctored. So get him here. I don't really care how. Then we're going to try the son of a bitch and maybe hang him for attempting to foment an aggressive war. Check with the legal staff. If it is already a crime to foment war under international law we'll use that. If not, tell the legislature I want a retroactive law to make it illegal and a capital crime. Then get him."

A few hours later, when the actual interview had been broadcast on Balboan TV, then rebroadcast on CNN, the *Casa* Linda received a curious call. Lourdes answered the phone initially, then, perplexed look on her face, called for her husband.

"Carrera?"

"This is Janier. I hesitate to say this, but my congratulations on the way you trapped that son of a bitch."

"General Janier?" Carrera asked, disbelieving.

"Yes, and if you say I made this phone call, I'll deny it. But all the same, well done." Janier hesitated briefly, undecided as to whether to go on. "There is one other thing. I've told the Tauran Union Security Council that I consider it unwise at this time to continue the policy of confrontation with Balboa. Until I am ordered differently, I am suspending all Mosquitoes and Green Monsoons."

"It is kind of you to tell me, General."

"Just remember this, *Duque* . . . I'll still carry out my orders, whatever those may turn out to be."

"Forewarned is forearmed." Now it was Carrera's turn to pause. "General, do you think it would be possible to meet, to see if there isn't some way that, as soldiers, we can defuse this mess?"

"Perhaps. Do you have access to a boat?"

"Yes. Private and public, both."

"I will meet you then, at sea, no more than four guards." Janier brought up a mental image of the map of Balboa. "Four miles north of the airfield at *Isla Real*. Say . . . three days from now?"

"Done."

PART IV

CHAPTER TWENTY-FIVE

Diplomacy is the art of letting someone else have your way.

—Sir David Frost

Headquarters, Tauran Union Security Force-Balboa, Building 59, Fort Muddville, Balboa, Terra Nova

With the increase in tensions, Janier had been spending a lot more time down in the Tunnel than in the more open, airy, and civilized situation at Building 59. His mistress, a local girl, wasn't a bit happy about it, either. But between military demands emanating from both headquarters, his wife, and the mistress...

Well, there are only so many goddamned hours in a day.

Of course, the good thing about all that, he thought, was, *At least my frigid, useless bitch of a wife never knows where I am at any given time, which allows me more time with Isabel.* He looked over at the sleeping woman and thought, *May as well admit it; I'm fond of her. Another shot at it, though, or back to work?* Janier looked at the woman again, then down at his apparently disinterested penis, then over at her, with particular attention to her resplendent breasts. Then finally, and hopelessly, he looked back down again. *You miserable bastard,* he thought, generally southward, *years, decades, getting into a position where I could get nearly any woman I want into any position I want and* now *you fail me? At last I know why they call you a "prick."*

With a sigh the general stood and began to dress.

He wasn't at Building 59 merely for the woman, in any case. In

267

less than three days he had a meeting with Carrera. He wanted ammunition for that meeting.

Thus dressed in normal Gallic khakis, he looked wistfully at the reproduction Napoleonic marshal's uniform he kept in the woman's apartment. *If I make real peace, there goes any chance of earning that, I suppose. On the other hand, it beats being cashiered if I fight and lose.*

There was something else, too, something Janier could barely admit to himself and could never have admitted to anyone else. He'd begun to sense it during the naval battle between one of the legion's submarines and his own country's navy, a battle that had ended with a Gallic physical victory and a Balboan moral one. *I just don't have the nerve for this, not to gamble like this. Oh, that knowledge comes hard.*

Ah, but what about the extra twenty or twenty-five years of youth Wallenstein promised me? That caused him to look more wistfully at the woman on the bed than he had at his marshal's uniform.

"Well, what about it?" he asked aloud, causing the woman on the bed to stir and to adjust the sheet downward, exposing to view those magnificent breasts. "It's only a couple of decades, not immortality . . . and I was always willing to die young for glory. Although . . . if ever there was an argument, or a pair of them, for twenty-five more years of youth, she has those arguments all sewed up.

"Oh, well, speaking of magnificent breasts, that Anglian female in intel has some information for me that perhaps de Villepin has been keeping under wraps."

Through the windows could be seen a very large freighter, rising as water entered the Florida Locks. Inside, Campbell could smell the scent of Janier's mistress hanging about him. It was a female thing, both the smell and the ability to detect it. Few if any men could have.

Wonderful, thought Janier and he was only half thinking of Jan Campbell's chest. *So de Villepin has been holding out on me, has he?*

Janier sat at Jan's own desk while she stood to one side, hands clasped behind her back. She was in uniform, and dressed and made up even more severely than that required. It wasn't enough to hide or distract from all the things that made her such an attractive woman, not least her brainpower.

On the desk, in front of him, Janier had the *original* of the report she and Hendryksen had prepared, the report that had been extensively altered by de Villepin's directorate.

"Can this be true?" he asked her. "Are they really this good?"

"They've got all kinds of flaws and weaknesses," she said. "The rank and file, for example, are not especially well trained. But they are willing. They are far more morally fit for war than we are; they won't blanch at the thought of casualties and in their entire country there is no person like TU Safety Minister Marine R.E.S. Mors du Char the Fourth—"

"That pussy!" Janier exclaimed.

"Quite," she agreed, "and everyone knows it, and yet the silly twat *still* exercises her baleful influence. But never mind that, sir; the point was that marginally trained or not, the rank and file are willing to bleed and the country is willing to let them. And their leadership is every bit as good as I've said, on a par with our own or, in many cases, superior."

"What else?" Janier asked. In response, Jan walked around the desk and pulled something, a bound file, from a side drawer. She opened the file and handed it to him. He read:

Balboan Legion VXI, the Air Forces...

Skipping ahead, Janier read:

The Artem-Mikhail 82, also called Mosaic D, is an ancient jet fighter of Volgan design, highly modified to operate in a special environment with some effectiveness. It is geared to fly at extremely low altitude, going high only for brief engagements at targets of opportunity. From above, its radar signature is so low that, combined with clutter from the ground, it is nearly undetectable. From below it can be picked up by its IR emissions. However, its very brief moments of vulnerability when operating over its adopted jungle home make a successful engagement with IR seeking SAMs most unlikely. The Mosaic D can carry just over 1/2 ton in ordnance (bombs, rockets, air to air missiles, 37mm cannon ammunition) which it can deliver with an acceptable degree of accuracy.

Known modifications for at least some models include: Upper wings and fuselage replaced by low radar signature metal/carbon fiber/plastic composite; avionics package with modern GPS and fire control; underside redesigned for minimal IR signature; tail replaced by V form low radar signature metal/carbon fiber/plastic composite. The Mosaic D has an improved, low maintenance engine (Zioni), nap of the earth radar (Volgan), a low light long range TV camera (Zioni), and a low radar signature canopy (local). It retains one 37mm cannon and can carry up to four air to air missiles, which are normally partially encased in a radar defeating sheathing.

One great advantage of the Mosaic D is its ability to take off from and land at very austere airfields. This, coupled with the Balboans' penchant for bunkerizing nearly everything makes it extremely unlikely that any large numbers can be destroyed on the ground without undue effort.

The Mosaic D is flown by exceptionally well-selected and well-trained pilots. It is not believed that the plane can take on even second line modern fighters with anything like equality. It is believed that its mission is engagement of transports, attack aircraft, and EW aircraft, along with ground attack and naval attack.

Suspected vulnerabilities include: degraded flight characteristics due to modification of wings and tail assembly; low availability due to inexperienced ground crews; lack of modern IFF; limited all weather capability (though it can fly reasonably well in the rain); poor pilot visibility except to the front; EXTREME vulnerability to damage due to almost complete lack of redundancy in systems. The use of small arms for air defense may be the best defense.

It is not known how many of the legion's Mosaics have been upgraded to this model. Based on Zioni reports, the number may be anywhere from twenty-one to sixty. However, we believe the Zionis are lying and the true numbers are on the order of ninety.

"What do you think that means?" Janier asked.

"Sir," said Campbell, "we think it means they can engage current TU air forces within the Transitway Area at parity."

"Fuck," he said, then added, "that was not an invitation, tempting though the prospect may be.

"What else?"

"They haven't brought them home yet," Campbell said, "but after piecing together a great deal of information of ours, plus some that the Federated States makes available to Anglia and Secordia, and nobody else, I've come to the conclusion that twenty-four one-seat and seven two-seat Artem-Mikhail-23-465 Gaur jet fighters are somewhere, crated and in shipment or being modified, perhaps in Zion."

"Why?" he asked.

"I can't tell you, sir," she replied. "Really. Please don't ask."

"All right," the Gallic general agreed. *Would I have had she not such a marvelous chest? Maybe not.*

"Read the chapters on their artillery park and air defense artillery park," Campbell suggested. "Note their batteries are fully manned but only have three guns, typically. Ever wonder if the other guns weren't around somewhere?"

"Some of this did get to me," the Gaul said.

She replied, "Some of it was so obvious it couldn't be hidden. But let me tell you what bugs me about it, sir: I think that's only a large fraction of what they have. Too much Volgan, Cochinese, etc., material has disappeared into the cracks. What we show there is just what's in country, not what might be hidden elsewhere. Then, too..."

"Yes?" he prodded.

"Hendryksen and I go 'round and 'round about this daily. Personally, I suspect they show us just enough to attract our fears and our attentions away from other things."

"Like their 'hidden reserve,' you mean? We know about them."

"Just what I was getting at, sir. They let us see enough of the hidden reserve that I wonder if it isn't deliberate, if there isn't even a more hidden, a more deeply hidden, reserve somewhere."

"But no evidence?"

"No, sir, none we've been able to find."

Janier nodded somberly. "Dangerous... dangerous," he muttered. Then he asked her, "Are you available for a boat trip tomorrow?"

Before she could fly into a rage at the suggestion of impropriety, he amended, "Just to accompany me as an advisor for a negotiating session? You would be one of four guards I am allowed."

"Who with?" she asked. "Where?"

"Carrera. On his yacht."

"I'll wear my skimpiest bikini."

Janier laughed, which may have been the first time in his life he'd found humor in anything having to do with Anglia. "May I ask you for some advice, Captain?"

"Surely, General," Campbell replied.

"What, in your opinion only, of course, should I do about Balboa?"

Without hesitation, she answered, "Leave them be. Just leave them be."

Explaining further, she added, "My comrade, Sergeant Major Hendryksen, is of the opinion that they need to be taken down because they are so unconstrained by civilized morals and values. And he, be it noted, sir, likes them.

"I agree with him that that makes them very dangerous, especially while Carrera lives.

"But, he will not live forever. So the problem is one that will mitigate itself in time. On the other hand, if we fight them and lose, as we may, they will not only be unconstrained, they will—after defeating someone a hundred times bigger and a thousand times wealthier, and much, much better armed—be convinced that there is nothing in the universe than even *can* constrain them.

"They will be impossible to live with, then. Contemplate how regularly the Cochinese flout and frustrate the Zhong after defeating the Federated States and Gaul. Then multiply that by fifty. Or a hundred and fifty while that psychotic bastard Carrera lives."

Four Miles North of the *Isla Real, Bahia de Balboa, Mar Furioso*

Janier came in a not too ostentatious boat he'd had Campbell rent. She, being of fisherfolk, herself, steered. Since that made her, in Janier's opinion, crew rather than guard, he also had four armored and armed guards with him. Ahead, bow on, rolled the considerably larger yacht he recognized from a target folder as Carrera's. Even if he hadn't recognized it, the mean looking, gun bristling patrol boat a few hundred meters off would have told him.

And, no doubt, he would claim that the boat doesn't count against the four guards limit, and, equally doubtless, the fully combat trained and equipped crew for the yacht won't count either. Only the ones in battle dress and armor count. Naturally. Because he has the nerve to push.

It was said Carrera virtually never used the thing, but allowed his personal staff to borrow it. There was a very faint discoloration at the bow, which Janier thought he recognized as repaired damage from when Carrera's wife had run the thing into a dock during her flight for help against the late Legate Pigna's coup.

Odd, thought the Gaul, *if we had taken out that boat in the course of the coup, Carrera's wife could never have gone for help. The coup might have worked and I would not be out here now, but back in Gaul with accolades galore. Why I didn't order that—it could have been discreetly done by us—I will never know.*

Oh, be honest, Janier, at least with yourself in the confines of your own mind: Yes, you do know why. You lacked the nerve.

The general found it strangely refreshing to admit this, if only to himself, refreshing...and a relief, as well, not to have to pretend even to himself.

Campbell guided her small craft with an ease and expertise learned as a child. With barely a thump, and not much of a scrape, she eased it right up to the ladder hanging off the side of Carrera's boat. The boat transmitted both the waves and the little bit of bump almost directly to her barely contained breasts.

Watching from the yacht's gunwales, Carrera thought, *She doesn't have to flaunt them a bit; they flaunt themselves.*

Then he was reaching a hand over to help Janier aboard, while one of the Gaul's guards tossed a line to one of his. Campbell came aboard last, and Carrera waited, helping each Tauran up in turn, just for the chance at an eyeful. As Carrera took her hand to help her up and over, Janier introduced her as, "My aide de camp, Captain Campbell."

Jan sat behind Janier, on the rear deck of the yacht, occasionally stretching or shifting position every time she thought Carrera's mind was in gear. Not for the first time in her life she recalled what her mother had told her were the purpose of breasts: *Ta feed bairns and ta turn grown men into bairns.*

Finally, Carrera had had enough. He stood, walked off, then returned with a bathrobe. "Put this on, please, Captain," he said. "Take it as a compliment, also please, but I simply cannot get a clear thought in my head while you parade yourself."

Oh, well, she thought, as she directed a knowing smile Carreraward, *didn't figure I could get away with it indefinitely. And you're more reasonable and at least somewhat less of a psycho than I had thought.*

"And now that I can think," Carrera said to Janier, "let us continue our negotiations with all the good faith we've come to expect...hmmm...no, scratch that, with genuine good faith."

"You are *not*, despite your words, negotiating in good faith," Janier said. "I have offered to stop the rehearsals—yes, we both know that's what they were; rehearsals and opportunities for you to give us a *casus belli*—for invading your country. But, throw me a bone, here. I am trapped by our own propaganda. We've painted you as a major threat to the peace of the region; I simply can't back off from that without something to show for it."

"How," replied Carrera, "can I show good faith to what is essentially a lie? You know I have no designs on Santa Josefina or Santander, and those are my only neighbors. I couldn't attack either one. Oh, sure, I have the tanks and tracks, and all of that. But I don't have the ships to attack Santander, even if I wanted to, which I don't. Neither do I have the trucks for Santa Josefina. As a professional, you should understand that."

"That's not true," Campbell said, interrupting for the first time. "Oh, it's true that you don't have a dedicated transportation division able to support your entire army in Santa Josefina. But a), *Duque*, you don't need your entire army to take Santa Josefina, even with the troops we've sent there, and therefore, b), every other truck in the legion is available to be taken out of their parent formation and used to support the—what, maximum two legions?—you would send there. And that is not even counting that you, you personally, own a trucking company able to move a thousand tons a day all the way to the border. At *least* one trucking company. And while it is impossible to track just who owns what in terms of shipping, I note a tendency to move your arms shipments on the same vessels, over and over."

"Just a habitual relationship with someone who gives us a good deal," Carrera lied.

Then, obviously caught in that, he said, "I cannot trust you. Or, rather, even if I thought I could, I cannot trust the Tauran Union *precisely* because of the propaganda you've painted yourselves into a corner with. That said, what might constitute a sufficient bone?"

"*Duque*," said Campbell, "you need to concede more or the general will be replaced and all your negotiations will be fruitless."

Carrera nodded. "All right, I can see that. But by the same token, if I give up too much my troops will ignore me. Really. So what do you really need that I can live with?"

"For starters," said Janier, "you could leave those—what was it, Captain, thirty-one?—Artem-Mikhail-23-465 Gaur right where they are, in Zion or on their way there, I believe, and not repatriate them to here."

Carrera felt a moment of almost panic. *If they know about those, what else do they know about?* He pushed it aside with the thought, *If they knew about the other things, they wouldn't be asking for is us to give up those.*

"All right. I'll leave them with the Zionis. But that doesn't mean I'm giving up ownership or that I won't continue to train pilots. It only means they won't come here. For now."

Janier looked at Campbell for confirmation of his instincts. At her subtle nod, he said, "That's fair, as far as it goes. Can you disband that newly created, outsized regiment of Santa Josefinans?"

"You don't want me to let them go," Carrera said. "If I did, and if they went home, there would be no end of troubles for Santa Josefina."

"Then don't let them go," Janier said. "Reintegrate them back into the units you pulled them out of." He cast Campbell an appreciative glance. "Yes, we caught that that was how you raised them. You haven't lost anything by it and then we can say we've gotten you to eliminate a formation that was clearly intended to wage aggressive war in Santa Josefina."

"It wasn't, you know," Carrera said. "What it was intended for was to make it necessary for you to keep so many troops in Santa Josefina in the event of war that you wouldn't have a lot more left to spare for us. Five thousand guerillas, acting as cadre for twenty thousand more, would have sucked up the bulk of the maneuver forces the Tauran Union can field. I am surprised you never keyed on that."

Janier said nothing but thought, *So am I. It is obvious, isn't it, that you were making Santa Josefina a bad investment.*

"I'll do it; I'll disband that tercio. But I want the force in Santa Josefina reduced. You don't need half of what's there."

"Agreed," said Janier, "to a point. But we'll have to keep more than half. It's a shape issue. Isn't that one of Balboa's principles of war: Shape? The shape of the bloody border, and its length, and the road net, means that we can pull out the one battalion that is there resting and training, but the other three, with their support, must stay.

"And another thing..."

CHAPTER TWENTY-SIX

> Almost all of our relationships begin and most of
> them continue as forms of mutual exploitation, a
> mental or physical barter, to be terminated when
> one or both parties run out of goods.
>
> —W. H. Auden

UEPF *Spirit of Peace*, in orbit over Terra Nova

Wallenstein was alone in her office... well, alone but for a bottle
of the good stuff, flown up from the Kingdom of Anglia. The
bottle was emptying fast, which was remarkable in someone who
rarely drank to excess. But then, Marguerite had her reasons.

*The difference between myself and the late High Admiral Rob-
inson*, thought High Admiral Wallenstein, *is that he tried to use
two opposed forces, Islamic barbarism and modern cosmopolitan
progressivism, to do two opposed things. It was never possible
for the latter to win and castrate all their atavistic tendencies
toward aggression out of the new world. It was never possible
for Islamic barbarism to triumph over the power of the modern
state. Neither was it possible for both together to have achieved
this, even if they'd been able to really work together, which they
were not.*

*My approach is different. I don't want to—because I don't
think I can—knock down Terra Nova. Instead, I want to build
up first the Tauran Union, using a can't-lose war with Balboa
as a catalyst to create a real country from the hate-each-other's
guts collection that exists. Then I'll create a union in Colombia*

Latina, which will use driving out the Taurans as its mechanism for unity. Then a combined Islamic-South Uhuran state that I will usher into the modern universe. And lastly, I would push Xing Zhong Guo—New Middle Kingdom—into trying to exercise hegemony over its end of Taurania. All the while leaving enough could-go-one-way-could-go-another territory between all of them that they're perpetually at each other's throats, while the UEPF keeps in position to help whoever was the underdog, to ensure perpetual conflict, and all those eyes down below focused on their own problems and their own hates ... because as long as they were doing that, they wouldn't be thinking of how to get at us and they wouldn't have the resources to spare to build a fleet to come after Old Earth.

And five, historically, has been the perfect number for great power stability.

Meanwhile, back home, I could use the fact of perpetual war here to get the bleeding heart tendency—which normally detests the Peace Fleet—to support us for the humanitarian work we'd do.

It was perfect ... and then that fuck-faced piece of French-speaking shit had to go and fuck it all up one me. The pussy. One would almost think he was the brother of that cowardly bitch, Marine R.E.S. Mors du Char the Fourth.

And the crawling filth won't even answer the communicator I left him so that I can chew him out properly.

Awkwardly, she plucked a few ice cubes from the bucket left by Esmeralda and dumped them in her glass. Just as awkwardly, she pulled the cork from the bottle and poured about four fingers' worth over the ice. In putting the cork back in the bottle she managed to tap the glass with the bottle's base, spilling ice and scotch all over the desk. Coriolis force made the scotch run across the desk rather strangely.

"Fuck!"

Esmeralda appeared instantly at the office door. "Are you all right, High Admiral?"

Wallenstein looked up, mildly slack faced. She wanted to say, *No, I'm not all right. All my plans have been ruined by the weakness of a Gallic barbarian, below. I am lonely. I am desperately horny. I think you are beautiful and sweet and I wish I could take you to bed. But that would be rape, on my part, even if I made you get on top ... which I would, since I'm a submissive precisely so I can unwind from the stress of being in charge and responsible. But never mind the details; it would also be a betrayal of Richard, who adores you. And that betrayal might be even worse than the rape.*

Some looks come through even the slackest, most drunken face. That one was easy to read. Esmeralda's answering look was, *I will, if you want.*

Oh, I want. But it would still be rape. So, no. I know what that's like and you deserve much better. Just in case the cabin girl and sometimes brevetted officer didn't understand, Marguerite shook her head most reluctantly.

"Just toss me a towel, please," the high admiral slurred. "I can clean up after myself. Then you go to bed." *Before I weaken and change my mind. Because you make me very weak...very...*

Esmeralda left the light on in her narrow bunkroom next to the high admiral's. Lying on her back, with a light sheet and comforting blanket pulled up to just over her breasts, she looked over at and thought about the connecting door that led from her tiny cabin to the high admiral's. She realized that the reason for the door and the proximity was precisely so that cabin boys and girls could be of greatest use—which had nothing to do with pouring drinks or cleaning spills—to whoever held the office for the time. She felt, as she had felt before, tremendous gratitude toward Wallenstein for not putting her to use as the high admiral had every right to put her to use.

And that's what makes what I am planning—if I can be so bold as to call it a plan—so difficult, that you, beautiful High Admiral Dear, saved me from the chili pot and have since treated me with every kindness. You are so much better than the system you support, how can *you support it?*

Esmeralda pulled out from under her mattress the small book the recruiting sergeant had given her in Aserri and began to read from where she had left off. Somehow, without ever having been to Old Earth, the writers of the book, Dr. Mendoza and his wife, still saw the Castro-Nyeres in all their wickedness, still saw the slave pens of Razona Market, still saw the hearts of young girls being cut out on the *Ara Pacis.* The names they didn't get, of course, but the trends they saw clearly.

And there are larger factors, High Admiral, than you and me and chili pots, neo-Azteca, and orthodox druids. You represent an evil system, or perhaps a good system gone bad, and I will fight that when I can and destroy it, or help to, if I am able.

Hotel Edward's Palace, Island of Teixeira, Lusitania, Tauran Union, Terra Nova

Marguerite had really liked the place the last time, not least because, with cliffs on three sides it was easier for the couple of guards she felt safe bringing to watch the ins and outs.

This conference was much smaller than the one earlier. It was smaller by one Gallic general, and his staff, and it was smaller by any number of political and bureaucratic minions. It had Marguerite, though, and her charming AdC, Lieutenant, JG, Miranda. It also had the Five Permanent Members, the FPMs, of the Tauran Union Security Council. These were from Gaul, Anglia, Sachsen, Castile, and Tuscany. These had the power to order Janier. These had the power to remove him if he disobeyed those orders. And the Gaul, Monsieur Gaymard, had the influence, if not the official power, to have Janier run out of the Army of Gaul.

The ministers were there to listen, not to argue. While some of their constituents may have been interested—indeed, probably were interested—in peace, prosperity, fairness, and any number of other feel-good words, this crew...

They want power, time to enjoy it in, and youth to enjoy certain aspects of it with, thought Wallenstein. *I can work with that.*

"Ladies and gentlemen," Wallenstein began, more politely than was strictly necessary, "I'm afraid we have a terrible problem. And I'm afraid you're going to have to fix it. Or... ah, but wait. Before we get to serious matters, we have a birthday girl among us. Esmeralda, my dear, which birthday is this?"

"Why, my eighty-seventh, High Admiral," the young girl lied, just as she'd been coached. Not that she couldn't have kept the same looks, of course; Wallenstein had and she was more than twice that age. But there was a freshness and loveliness about Esmeralda that Marguerite really wanted to rub the Taurans' noses in.

"Ah. Well happy eighty-seventh, my dear. And in honor of your birthday, why don't you take the rest of the day off. I'm sure the representative of the Gallic Republic"—Marguerite's voice took on a nasty tone—"whose general has betrayed us"—and rose in volume and viciousness—"and led to the ruination of all our plans"—then quieted—"would be glad to pour the water. Run along, dear."

"Yes, High Admiral."

Esmeralda was armed only with her little book from the recruiting sergeant in Aserri, Santa Josefina. But the book had an address in it, plus several phone numbers and an e-mail address. But how, how in a world so thoroughly documented, and from a star fleet even more thoroughly documented, was she to get a message to someone in the Balboan forces who could make use of her willingness to serve the cause of freedom? She didn't even think she had the right names. In fact, the only name to which she could put a number or a digital address was Sergeant Riza-Rivera back in Aserri, and that from the business card he'd slipped into the book.

Everything cost, she knew, except back on Old Earth where everything cost unless you were a member of the elite, in which case a number of things came free. But what would it cost to call Santa Josefina from here? The only money she had were the remnants of the per diem she'd been given when acting as the high admiral's messenger girl pretending to be an emissary. Was that enough?

Twice she went up to the desk and twice she skirted back in fear. The first time was over the cost, when she had no clue what the cost would be. The second time...

What if the Peace Fleet is monitoring communications? What if they hear me trying to betray them? It'll be out the air lock for sure. And that's worse than being a bowl of chili. At least the neo-Azteca would have cut my throat first for that. And my body, even if in the form of shit, would have stayed home. But pushed out to suffocate, freeze, and then explode... slowly? Ugh. And my body never to return? Would God bother to even look for such a little insignificant thing as me, in the vastness of space, on the wrong side of the bridge between the stars? Floating forever... no one ever knowing or caring...

Pushing back on and defeating that nascent attack of panic was one of the tougher things Esmeralda had ever had to do. But once she had, she found that the next step, going to the desk clerk, was easier than it had been. She walked up and asked, "Is there a way I can call Santa Josefina from here? The only money I have is this." She held out about a thousand drachma's worth of Josefinan currency.

"You're a member of the Miranda party, aren't you, miss?" the desk clerk said. Wallenstein was too well a name for the high admiral to book on her own. For that matter, the five members of the Tauran Union Security Council were too well known. Thus the name of little Esmeralda Miranda had acquired a debt she probably could never pay off.

"I'm Esmeralda Miranda, yes," she replied.

"Ma'am," said the clerk, "your calls are free with your suite."

"Oh...oh, I didn't know."

The clerk smiled and shook his head. These super rich types were just so out of touch.

"If you have the number in Santa Josefina," the desk clerk said, "I'd be glad to put the call through for you, ma'am." His finger pointed at some booths with sliding doors. "You can take the call over there. I'll have it sent direct to number seven."

"Thank you," Esmeralda said.

"And...ummm...the number, ma'am?"

She read it off from the card. Then she had a horrible thought. *The clerk will call and wait until he had a connection. Then the sergeant is going to answer with,* "Legion del Cid, *Recruiting Station Cedral Multiplex Shopping Mall." And that will raise too many questions.*

"Can you talk me through dialing?" she asked. "I'm just not used to these but..."

"No need to explain, ma'am. Surely I can."

"Recruiting Sergeant Riza-Rivera," came the answer. "*Legion del Cid*, Recruiting Station Cedral Multiplex Shopping Mall."

Damn, can I call them or what? thought the girl.

"Sergeant," she said, "my name is Esmeralda Miranda. I don't think you'll remember me but I came into your office and you gave me a little book."

"Well," said Riza-Rivera, "I can only think of one girl...short, brown, don't get a swelled head but really pretty..." *Though my first guess when I saw her was "lesbian."*

"Thanks, that was probably me. But there's something you don't know."

"And that would be?"

"I'm from Old Earth. I'm with the Peace Fleet. And I want to...what's the word? Oh, yes, I remember. I want to defect."

"Miss, this is way above my pay grade," the sergeant said instantly. "Way, WAY above. But if you will give me where you are staying, and a way to contact you, I'll do whatever I can figure out how to get you in touch with someone who matters. And how long will you be there, miss? That matters, too, I suspect. And...ummm...crap. Okay, whoever finds you will say 'foxtrot lima.' You answer with 'alpha tango.' Oh, and your room number. If I have to call you back I'll say, miss, this is Mr. Riva, the desk clerk. I'll try not to do that, though."

The sergeant was thinking frantically. Opportunities like this didn't come along once in a hundred years, he knew. "Ummm... ummm...spend as much time as you can wandering public areas but alone. Put a flower, preferably red, in your hair if you think you can get away with it. And that's all I can think of for now, miss. If it weren't for the spy movies I couldn't have gotten this far."

Turonensis, Republic of Gaul, Tauran Union, Terra Nova

Khalid wasn't living in Turonensis, but he passed through often enough, and was known by Fernandez to pass through often enough, that Fernandez contacted him immediately upon receipt of the message—after much filtration—from Sergeant Riza-Rivera.

Khalid didn't have a photograph of the girl. Riza-Rivera had already checked and found that the security cameras in the recruiting station had long since erased their old recordings. Fernandez had sent the sergeant to an old acquaintance in Aserri, a forensic artist who did work for the Aserri Police Department. The artist, using the more old-fashioned sketching technique, aided by facial design software, was able to produce a reasonable likeness of the girl in a few hours.

As with many things, the fact that nobody could really be sure just what the Peace Fleet was capable of meant that the composite couldn't be faxed to Fernandez's office in the plain, nor did a mere recruiting station and sometimes mobilization coordination point have the requisite encryption capability. It had to be hand carried by the sergeant to Fifth Mountain Tercio headquarters, in *Valle de las Lunas,* then encrypted and faxed to Fernandez's office, then immediately transmitted to Khalid, who did have decryption capability, along with the order to proceed to Teixeira, Lusitania, to contact the girl at the Hotel Edward's Palace.

"Khalid," Fernandez had written, "you're my best man for direct action, but I've never had you do anything remotely like this. Still, of what I have who might be able to do this you are the closest.

"The most I hope for is that you can contact the girl, confirm she is who she says she is, and somehow arrange a way for her to contact us. Do that, and you'll have earned your pay for the next month."

I'll have earned my pay for the next fucking year *if I get you a mole inside the Peace Fleet,* thought the assassin, flying to the island on an airplane rather than a cheaper but slower airship. But even the girl was unable to say how long she'd be there. Time was a wasting asset.

The airship touched down without accident. The island lived off of tourism these days, so there was no shortage of a taxi to take Khalid to the hotel. The hotel had been a problem, largely because they had no cheap, unostentatious rooms. Khalid had at least been able to wrestle a *small* suite from them, where they had tried to saddle him with a large.

In the plane and in the taxi, he alternated his time with studying the composite drawing of the girl and trying to figure out a way for her to keep in contact once contacted by him.

The best he'd come up with was a dead drop e-mail account, with only the draft folder being used, and that only if she came back to Terra Nova again. In the airport at Turonensis he picked up half a dozen novels, in the sure and certain expectation that the very same half dozen would be available at the airport on Teixeira. He wrote a single number inside the cover, one through six, in each of the ones he'd bought in the former airport, then repeated those for the ones he purchased in the second.

"Best I can do, under the circumstances."

Hotel Edward's Palace, Island of Teixeira, Lusitania, Tauran Union, Terra Nova

Clever girl, though Khalid, *clever sergeant, too.*

The picture was fair, but less than perfect. Even so the large red flower in her hair, that was a dead giveaway. And she was alone, sitting in the hotel restaurant, reading a magazine. She wore a very attractive ecru silk dress, empire waisted, with a thin, red, tubular trim.

Khalid, always a mix of caution and boldness, tossed caution to the winds. He walked to her table as if he belonged there, sat down, and said, "Foxtrot...lima."

"Alpha tango," she replied. Even though she'd rehearsed this meeting in her mind fifty times, the knowledge that she had just come so much closer to her goal set her voice to quivering and her heart to pounding.

"Wonderful," said Khalid. "If anyone you know comes over, or even gets in a position to see us, say, 'How dare you sit down with me uninvited? Get away.' Got it?"

"I think so."

"How long do you have here?"

"I'm not sure," she answered. "My high admiral—"

"What?"

"My high admiral."

"There is only one high admiral."

"Yes, I know. I'm her cabin girl."

"Oh, dear God." Now it was Khalid whose heart pounded. "I don't think Fernandez has a clue who he sent me to meet." In most unKhalidlike fashion, the assassin threw his head back, softly crying, "Oh, God! Oh, God! Do I just rush you out of here for debriefing or send you back for whatever purpose Fernandez might think of. Crap. Crap. Double crap!"

Being flustered was not something that came easily to Khalid. He recovered and said, "No matter. Keep going. Your high admiral...?"

"She's beating the locals into submission, the Tauran Union Security Council. I think they're about ready to fold. So I could be leaving within a few hours."

"All right," Khalid said. "Do you have bags sufficient to hold these?" He pulled one of the two sets of novels he'd picked up out of a bag and set them on the table.

"Sure. I overpacked a little, because we didn't know how long this would take. I can leave something behind if I must."

"Okay," he began to explain. "These books are novels, fictional writings. Inside the cover of each I have written a number. I have a matching set I'll send to my chief. For you to compose a message, you need to write the number I have written, then find the word you want. You write the page number, the line number, and the number of the word in the line. You can mix and match across books, if necessary, so long as you put down what book it's coming from." He opened one of the books and showed her how to do it.

"Then you underline or cross out that word so it cannot be used again. If we see that word's number used again, for the same book, we will assume you are compromised and probably just cut you off.

"There are better codes," he explained, apologetically, "much simpler and quicker ones, but none I could come up with quickly, that looked so innocent.

"It may happen that there is no word. In that case, use the same system, but only count the first letter of the words you find and spell out the word you want that way. The message will make no sense so we—my side—will automatically look for the first letter."

"Okay," she agreed.

"Now...I suppose there is no way for you to send a message from the ship you are on?" he asked.

"The *Spirit of Peace*? No. Or nothing that wouldn't be too suspicious."

"Okay...I wish..." Khalid let the thought trail off. He knew, or at least, guessed, that Fernandez had some kind of limited intelligence source on the ship, some kind of bug. If he knew what it was and where it was he could have her go and simply talk. But he didn't know so..."The less said about that the better."

He passed over an e-mail account, a password, and some hastily written instructions. "When you get back here, if you do, get to a computer and access that. My chief will have more clear guidance in the folder labeled 'draft.' Do you understand all this?"

"Yes," she said. "I think so."

"Clever girl!" Khalid enthused. "And now, to protect you, I am going to disappear. My suite number is Five-two-seven. I will hang around a couple of days and if I get better guidance I will contact you again, if I can. If not, good luck and contact us if you are able. God go with you, child."

Later that afternoon, an exhausted High Admiral Wallenstein joined Esmeralda in their suite.

"Honey," said the high admiral, "I need to sleep for a few hours. Please make the arrangements to get us back aboard ship."

"How did the...negotiation session go, High Admiral?"

"The bloody Gaul gets his marching orders tomorrow and either obeys or is relieved by the end of the local month."

CHAPTER TWENTY-SEVEN

Pity not! The Army gave
Freedom to a timid slave.
In which freedom did [s]he find
Strength of body, will and mind.

—Kipling, *Epitaphs of the War*

Hovercraft Ramps, Port of Balboa, Balboa, Terra Nova

Centurion Rafael Franco, assigned *Tercio Gorgidas* and seconded to
Training Maniple, *Tercio Amazona*, watched as an elderly woman
showed her pass then drove her van past the security gate and
into a parking spot. *One of the Tercio Socrates types,* he thought,
*the ones who are going to provide dependent care in their homes
for the girls' children.*

Franco did a quick estimate of the head count under the bright
lights, each pole-mounted light surrounded by a cloud of flying
insects. *Maybe two hundred and forty,* he guesstimated. *A bit
under half of those who signed up. With any luck, the rest will get
a sudden rush of brains to the head and not show up.*

Franco mostly stayed back near, if not quite in, the shadows,
himself, while noncoms, sergeants and corporals, tried—*What
the fuck is the point of being so gentle? I know Silva said to be,
but why?*—to get the girls to one or another of the holding areas
marked with the number of their future training platoons.

Oh, all right, Franco silently conceded, *I actually know why.
So that the shock will be that much worse. Man, I shudder. Poor
little shits have no idea what they're in for.*

A couple of the cadre of the platoon that would be led by Franco and his partner (and, for military puposes, boss), Centurion Baltha-zar Garcia, were taking girls' names, as they reported, and direct-ing them to one of the seven holding areas set up. Those two were Sergeant Castro and Corporal Salazar. Castro, always a nice sort, wasn't having any problems with it but Corporal Salazar, Franco could see, was visibly trembling with the difficulty of restraint when he longed to shake some of the girls by the scruff of their necks.

I see trouble from that one, Franco thought, *trouble in one form or another.*

The door of the van he'd seen park opened up. Emerging from it was a woman Franco didn't recognize, though she reminded him slightly of his mother. She had a few folders under her arm as she went to stand under one of the seven signs for the seven holding areas. Every now and again, the woman would open one of the folders and scan it against the face of a nearby woman or girl. Every now and again, too, she would look around at the disorder and either shake her head or shrug.

I wonder, the centurion mused, *if she has some experience of the military or is just the orderly sort, like my own mother was. Now* there *was a woman, altogether too good for my tyrant of a father.*

Franco was slightly startled as a loudspeaker began to blare out names and instructions. All talk from the women ceased. Castro and Salazar, along with the other noncoms, continued to direct and sort them as best they could, being as gentle as they were.

Franco heard a name announced. He already recognized it from the roster he and Garcia had been given. "Fuentes, Maria. Fuentes, Maria. Report to Load Ramp Seven. Fuentes, Maria, report to Load Ramp Seven." Again the old woman checked an open file.

The other reasons Franco noticed that particular name were twofold. One was that the *Duque* had apparently taken a personal interest in the girl. The note he'd scrawled into the file suggested as much, anyway. Franco didn't have the sense, though, that Carrera was looking for a mistress. The other was that the same personal file practically had "toughness, but worn to a nub" written all over it. Looking the girl, Fuentes, over, Franco decided he'd been right in his estimate of what the paper suggested. Fuentes looked already defeated somehow, with no happiness, nor perhaps even the capacity to feel it, left in her.

The young woman carried a child on her hip and a battered

suitcase, or perhaps more of an overnight bag, in the other hand. Her expressions didn't change as the old woman walked up and introduced herself. The child, however, also female, opened her mouth into an "O" of wide-eyed surprise and asked something Franco couldn't quite read. He'd guessed it was something nice, though, since the old woman passed over an oversized lollipop.

Get them while they're young, thought the centurion.

Franco turned away from the two women and baby girl at the sound of seven hovercraft skimming the water at high speed as they approached the long ramp that led up to the land adjacent to the pier. One by one, the hovercraft climbed the ramp from the sea to the land, before settling down at marked spots on the asphalt. As each settled, the sound pouring from it dropped down to a comparatively low whine.

We could use a boat, Franco thought, *and we do for bulky non-perishable cargo*. But transport by hovercraft was almost as pricey as by aircraft, so they only moved the island's most important cargo, people. And they were used for that, at least half, because they were so strange, providing the same sense of passage, of break, that airplanes did, but at less cost.

Turning away from the sea, Franco let his attention rest back on the three females. Words passed between the two older ones, then the child was given a last hug by her mother before the mother began to trudge toward the nearest hovercraft. Franco thought he saw tears falling to the asphalt, marking the young woman's passage.

For what I am about to do to you, young lady, may God forgive me.

Franco followed the last of the girls up the loading ramp, then found himself a spot where he could listen and not generally be observed. He was enough bigger than the girls, though no giant, that they instinctively cleared a way for him, except for the half dozen who tried to get closer.

And you're operating off of instinct, too, aren't you, chicas?

Franco was, in the vernacular, a handsome son of a bitch, knew it, and was mildly embarrassed by it.

A horn sounded three times in warning, then the foot ramp whined its way up to the vertical. The engines of the hovercraft began to whine and strain. By fractions of inches, the big machine lifted, then began to turn back towards the ramp and the water of the bay past it. On that water shone one of Terra Nova's three moons, named for Eris, goddess of strife.

Franco was gay, totally, completely, utterly gay. There was no doubt in his mind of this, nor in the minds of anyone who knew him. But...

But I've always approved of the female aesthetic. Let's face it, when we are talking "beauty" we are talking feminine. Beautiful mountains that remind one of a woman's breasts. Beautiful valleys that bring forth life, as women do. Hell, there was a time I thought or wanted to be one, or wished I had been born one. I was even married once, and I wish I could explain to my ex-wife that it was NOT her fault. God knows, I've tried.

Three girls, none of them apparently aware of his presence, formed one of those immediate groupings found rarely outside of the military and almost never as strongly as within the military. One was tiny; one the girl, Fuentes, he'd seen give up her daughter to the old woman from Tercio Socrates; and one—he knew from the file—the ex La Platan whore with the medal for bravery under fire.

Besides the one risen moon, Eris, there was really nothing to see but water and wave and the lights of the city, receding behind them. Most of the girls, Franco suspected, and all the ones he could see, began staring backwards at the city's lights, and the loved ones being left behind. Several of them, two that the centurion could make out clearly, began to sniffle, though at least it didn't turn into a crying jag.

He heard the tiny girl introduce herself as, "I'm Inez, Inez Trujillo."

"Maria Fuentes," said the other, the one Franco had seen turning over her daughter to the old woman.

A third introduced herself as, "Marta Bugatti. And, yes, I'm a bloody foreigner. Moreover, I've been in the legion for a while, with the *classis*." The girls kept talking, but Franco turned his attention away from those three, concentrating instead on another who was quite possibly the most beautiful woman he'd ever seen, and this in a country noted for stunning women.

"Just listen to me," the stunner declaimed, over the hovercraft's whining. "Stop worrying. This is going to be *easy*. Don't fall for the men's lies. We are smarter than they are. We are tougher than they are. Why, if a man had to go through childbirth, he'd cry like a baby. But *we* can and we *do*, all the time."

Like that one knows anything about having a baby, Franco thought.

The tiny one near Franco muttered, "We're *not* as strong as they are."

Whether the stunner had overheard or not, Franco couldn't say and rather doubted. Instead, he thought it likely she was just parroting the female supremacist mantra in cadence. *Hmmm . . . I wonder if she's studied under Professor Torres.*

In any case, in accordance with the approved mantra, the stunner continued, "What difference does it make if men have bigger muscles? They have tinier brains. After all, how much of a brain can you stuff into something about six inches long and usually far, far too thin." That raised a laugh.

Franco thought it was endearingly funny, too, but then mentally amended, *You wouldn't say that, girl, if you had ever seen Balthazar in the flesh . . . very in the flesh, as a matter of fact.*

"And besides," she continued, "strength is overrated. I've seen it on TV; you all have. These days technology is what wins wars. And if men weren't so stupid, they would realize that, too. Just let us show them."

Some of the other girls who had gathered started to drift away. Franco overheard the large breasted La Platan ex-whore say, loud enough to be heard over the stunner's speech, "Amazing. Imagine how seldom women would be hit by their husbands or boyfriends if they only knew that muscles don't matter."

The La Platan former hooker was one of a few on the hovercraft who had spent time on the island before. Of course the noncoms and Franco had, but they—and he, especially—were keeping their distance. As they neared the *Isla Real,* its barely moonlit peak rising from the sea, artificial lights, too, began to appear. Some shone from several places near the summit, while one set seemed to stand several hundred meters above that.

"It's a solar chimney," the La Platan explained. She was easily recognizable by her more than half Tuscan accent. "They saved a bundle by running it up the side of the mountain, but it goes straight up even from there. All the power for the island, enough for two hundred thousand people or more, so I've been told, comes from that. They've got it marked so that helicopters and airplanes don't run into it at night or in fog or rain."

"That's right," observed another, the tiny one Franco thought, "you've been out there before, haven't you?"

"A few times, yes."

"You were navy?" the tiny girl asked. "Why did you switch?"

"Bad memories," the La Platan answered, then wouldn't say more about it.

The hovercraft began to veer, causing them all to lean to the side away from the turn. Except for the marking lights, there were no others to be seen. Then, suddenly, a battery of overhead lights, powerfully bright, came on to illuminate a large concrete pad. The hovercraft eased itself over a strip of sand, then came to a gradual stop before descending to land on the pad. The engines gave a last whine of protest at being put to rest.

With a whine of a completely different pitch, the foot ramp went down on one side before settling to the concrete with a jarring clang. Up the ramp trotted a man, close-cropped, uniformed, bemedaled and just flat mean looking. He had a sneer of complete contempt engraved across his face. He carried a small portable loudspeaker in one hand. He pushed aside any women who didn't clear out of his way quickly enough. The stunner went to her rear end with an outraged shriek.

Oh, Balthazar, thought Franco, *you always did have an amazing degree of charm and grace about you.*

The man stepped up to where the stunner had been sitting, then lifted the loudspeaker to his lips. "All right you stupid twats, get your fucking high heels off." The man waited for all of ten seconds for the women to complete that task. "When I give the order you will have thirty seconds to clear your worthless smelly hides off this hovercraft. When you get off, the men standing below will put you into formation. Then Tribune Silva, your maniple commander, will speak to you. You will keep your foolish mouths shut. Now *GO!*"

Pushing each other and scrambling, the women crowded the single ramp. Many tripped and fell, to be trodden on by the others. At the concrete base, a number of noncoms, none of them with a kindly face, slapped and pushed and prodded the women into a single block. To the right, other groups were receiving much the same treatment as they debarked from their hovercraft. Being so far from the center, the men herded the women to their right. At the other end, women were being herded to the left. The end result was a mob of prisoners, surrounded by guards, standing fearfully before a dais that rose about ten feet off of the concrete.

Franco, Castro, and Salazar walked up and joined the "guards."

A very handsome man—he introduced himself to the women as "Tribune Silva, and your commanding officer"—walked briskly up the steps of the dais. Silva made a little welcoming speech— sort of a welcoming speech. Had they been asked, most of the women would likely have confessed that they had been made to feel more welcome. After all, few welcoming speeches in history had begun with, "You fucking whores," nor ended with, "Centurions, take charge of your sluts."

Silva then departed in a legion vehicle, leaving the women to the none-too-tender care of their senior centurions.

Franco could see and feel it, both, as the girls involuntarily leaned back from the charging malevolence of their common chief, Garcia.

"I am Senior Centurion Balthazar Garcia. You are shit. Introductions being finished, we will get on with business."

Garcia began to walk slowly from one side of the group to the other, distaste shining in his features. He did not smile. He spoke dispassionately as he walked the line, commenting on each of the women. "Too scrawny...You'll want to see the docs about getting a breast reduction, swabbie; those things are going to get in the way...No arse...Legs too skinny...Nose? Or is that a bus stuck on the end of your face, girl?...Stringy hair...When did you last douche, pigpen?...Bimbos. You! Bitch! Dry your silly fucking eyes. That's right, sniveler. That's right, crybaby..."

It was a ritual that hadn't changed, couldn't have changed, since long before the days when some Roman centurion had first taken charge of a group of new recruits. It made a sort of cruel sense, actually, though none of the women understood it at the time. There was only so much time—which is almost the same thing as only so much money, but harder to come by—any army could afford to spend on basic training. The kind of rule that Garcia was establishing cut down on the silly questions and complaints. That saved money and time. Since the time and

money thus saved could be spent training soldiers to fight and
live, it also saved lives.

It is often better to be insulted than dead.

Even so, Franco took it hard. These recruits weren't raised for
this. They were, most of them, gently raised, raised to be loving
wives and devoted mothers. This was just fucking cruel. There
had to be a better way.

Then, too, the best thing about beating your head against a
wall is that it feels so good when you stop. A moderately kind
word from someone who mostly tells you that you are animate
pond scum means more than the same word from someone who
routinely says that you are God's gift to the world. It was defla-
tion of the currency of praise.

Mentally, Franco went over the introductory speech he'd worked
out with Balthazar: Now, is there among you tramps even one bitch
gutsy enough to duke it out with me? Two of you? How about ten
of you? Come on, surely ten of you plumped up sluts can outweigh
me by a factor of five. What? One man is five times better, pound
for pound, than you twats? And you think you've got what it takes
to be legionaries? My fucking ass. You cunts are just garbage.

Interestingly, for reasons he'd no doubt explain later, Garcia
used none of that. Instead, he just went on with the insults for
quite some time.

Once Garcia had finished engraving their faces on his memory
he shouted out. "Franco?"

"Here, Centurion," Franco answered.

"Take charge of this garbage."

"Yes, Centurion." Franco then walked from behind the formation and took a position in front of the new meat.

"I am Centurion, Junior Grade, Rafael Franco," he announced.
Showing a smile neither friendly nor unfriendly, but ripe with
anticipation, he continued, "You are going to be seeing a lot more
of me than you are going to like over the next several months.
Just to be up front with you, I do not like you. I do not care
about you. You are just things. Someday, perhaps, unlikely as it
seems right now, you may become more. For now, you are using
up oxygen that you don't deserve. Keep your mouths shut and
your ears and eyes open and we might—just possibly—learn to
get along. Cross me and . . . well, don't."

"Now, you silly little girls, I know you are far, far too stupid to know your right from your left. Take my word on it; that bus over there is on your right. When I give the command 'Right, Face' I want you to turn those stupid looking things you hang in front of what passes for brains in the direction of the bus. Got it? Right . . . face."

Though it started with the La Platan, the entire bus gave a collective groan and said, simply, "Oh, shit." They had arrived at Camp Botchkareva.

The camp looked more like a prison than a school. It consisted of fourteen large metal huts, some open fields the women couldn't guess the purpose of, and about fifty or sixty tents. At the edge of the camp the perimeter was defined by a fence of triple concertina, rolled barbed wire, with two rolls along the ground and one resting above those two. Guard towers and searchlights were at each corner and the solitary gate.

"Off the bus, twats," said Franco. With the help of a few others, they pushed the women into a kindergartenish double line, that being about the limit of their ability at the time. Then Franco led them through one of the metal huts. There, their clothes and suitcases were taken from them and locked in tiny double-locked compartments. They left the hut bare-ass naked, with only a wallet to call their own.

Franco saw the intensely beautiful one arch her back to show off her bare breasts. *Oh, puhleeze. Don't you have any idea what it means to be in my unit? Silly girl.*

There were a few women in the group who seemed . . . interested. *Oh, shit,* thought Franco. How fucking stupid can we have been? We forgot about the lesbians. Damn, damn, damn.

"Get your fucking eyes off me," the La Platan told another woman, bunching her fists. That woman made some apologetic sounds and backed off, keeping her eyes carefully away.

Then came the buzz cuts. That, more than most things, struck Franco as cruel. Even a raped woman doesn't become less of a woman by being raped. She may be a thing while it's going on, but at least it's a fully female thing. Taking their hair away, though . . . that's about half as bad a removing a breast.

Has to be done of course; they're going to be too filthy for hair for a long time to come.

Whatever he felt inside, it was a smiling Franco who gave the order, "Buzz 'em, Pedro."

He kept smiling, even as some of the girls, looking in the mirrors, began to cry.

Before they were issued any clothing, the women were marched into some mass showers, where they placed their wallets along a shelf on the way in. Most everyone in Balboa took cold showers, at least sometimes. It was no big deal in a place so *hot*. The water for these showers, it turned out later, was specially chilled to be *icy*. The women all screamed when Castro turned on the water.

As the women left the showers, they were asked for their sizes. Each woman was then handed one sports bra, in approximately her size (Marta was a tight fit even in the biggest size they had; the man passing out the bras made a note of it), two pair of boxer shorts, physical training shorts, two pair of socks—not stockings—and running shoes. It wasn't such a bad outfit; except for the boxers.

Franco gave the women a very few minutes to dress. Then he lined them up again and led them to their barracks. This was a long low arching metal hut with few amenities to speak of; three bare light bulbs and forty pairs of bunk beds. On each bed were a thin, useless pillow, a pillow case, two sheets, and a very light and unnecessary blanket.

This is so going to suck, thought the centurion, *and not in a nice way.*

"Gather 'round, girls," Franco ordered. The women, all of them still in something like shock, clustered in a circle. "Sit down."

He began to pass out red felt-tip markers. When everyone had received one, Franco began to speak.

"Okay. I want you to take your markers and I want you to draw a dotted line just like the one I am drawing on my wrist." Franco drew a six-inch-long series of red dots lengthwise down his left wrist. "Everyone done with that? Good. Now draw another one on the other wrist...Done? Good. Let me see. *Very* good. Now there's no excuse.

"You see, women threaten suicide and even act it out rather frequently, but you fail so often to carry through that I am forced to question your sincerity and competence as a sex. Therefore..."

Franco turned toward the door. He tossed a package of razor blades to the floor on his way out. "Trujillo!" he called over one shoulder. "Collect up the markers in that box and put them by my office door. Anybody who wants a razor blade, just help yourself. 'Cut along dotted line.'"

CHAPTER TWENTY-EIGHT

The minstrel boy to the war has gone
In the ranks of death ye will find him
His father's sword he has girded on
And his wild harp slung behind him.

—Thomas Moore, "The Minstrel Boy"

The medium *is* the message.
—Marshall McLuhan

Janier's Office, The Tunnel, *Cerro Mina*, Balboa, Terra Nova

I am not a good man, Janier said to himself, in the confines of his office and his brain. *Never have been. I am selfish, self-centered, arrogant, overbearing, abusive toward subordinates, and even occasionally treacherous. But what the politicians are demanding is so wrong on so many levels that even I have problems with it.*

That it's intensely stupid only makes it worse.

So what do I do? I can refuse the order to recommence the provocations. Then I am relieved and they put in somebody else—someone probably not as competent; whatever my failings, I am, at least, competent—who does their bidding and loses badly.

I suppose I must go along. At least, I see no good coming from refusal . . . unless I simply defected to the Balboans with my entire force. Tempting . . . oh, it is tempting. But I am not humble enough for that, so no, I can't. And besides, the troops might not go along and I'm sure most of my senior officers would not. So forget that one.

But what I can do is what I agreed to do. I can give Carrera the warning I promised.

Oh, what the hell? Détente here was never more than a forlorn hope, anyway. He picked up the phone on the desk and dialed Carrera's private number.

Fuerte Guerrero, Balboa, Terra Nova

After a call from his commander, Ricardo Cruz left the Centurions' Club with no more than a lightened walk. He'd drunk little—he rarely drank much—and that little only for sociability. He certainly wasn't remotely drunk.

From the club he went straight to Second Cohort. There, upstairs, in the operations office, he found all the cohort's officers and centurions assembled in the conference room. At the long table Legate Chin and (since he was at nonmobilized rank) Tribune Velasquez hunched over a map, along with Velasquez's Ia, or operations officer, and the Second Cohort executive officer. Fingers jabbed at the map, while querulous voices traded words. Finally, Chin turned from the map.

"Gentlemen," he said, "I have just been notified of a change in the rules of engagement." Chin let the words hang in the air for a few moments. "Effective tomorrow, at 0600 hours, no more Tauran incursions outside of their designated treaty limits will be tolerated. Each parcel of land surrounding their areas has been divided up. The Taurans have been warned. When next they violate our territory, we fight."

Again Chin halted briefly. His next words were spoken with a degree of disdain. "However, our leaders have decided that a general war to expel the Taurans would be unwise at this time. So, if—when—they enter our area of responsibility, it will be our task to expel them, almost alone. Other units will mobilize, but will neither assist us nor attack on their own. The same holds true if the Taurans move into some other unit's area of responsibility."

He said with chagrin, "Second Tercio if called, gets 42nd Artillery Tercio in support. Which is better than nothing, though it only has twenty-seven guns. And here may be some diversion for you, or for any of us. Carrera says that some undefended point within Tauran-controlled land will be seized also, if possible. And, he says, too, the Aviation Legion will scramble to keep the

Taurans' air off of our backs. Although they will not fight unless the Tauran Union Air Forces get involved.

"I know you don't like it," Chin said. "Maybe neither do I. But it has this justification. If we can prove that we can stand up to the Taurans man to man and cohort to battalion, maybe, just maybe, they'll decide we're 'too hard' and go home. The *Duque* and *Presidente* Parilla think it's an acceptable risk for peace with dignity and freedom. What we think doesn't matter.

"In any event, forget about sleep tonight. We worked out hidden mobilization points for all our reservists years ago. Tonight, I want you to check out your target folders from the Ic and recon each of these mobilization points. Go!"

Headquarters, Tauran Union Security Force-Balboa, Building 59, Fort Muddville, Balboa, Terra Nova

It was long past lights out, with the troops in bed and the headquarters and the post under the control of the field officer of the day, or FOD, for the Tauran troops. That officer, an Anglian major by the name of Key, Christopher Key, was trying to catch a few winks before trying to type the evening log in grammatically correct French. Since his French was actually quite poor, he relied on his NCO for the evening, Sergeant Major Hendryksen, who spoke and wrote quite decent French, to actually translate the log.

"Sir," said the sergeant major, after knocking politely. "Sir, there's a Balboan tribune at the door."

"Well, see what he wants," said Key.

"Okay, sir." The sergeant major left. When he returned he looked puzzled and worried.

"What did the tribune want, Sergeant Major?"

"I'm not quite sure how to put this, sir, but . . . well . . . he just wanted to give us a list, sir."

"A list?"

"Yes, sir. It's from their *Estado Mayor*, the Balboan general staff. Ummm . . . sir, it's a suggested ammunition load for our next 'Green Monsoon.' All live ammunition, they suggest."

"Arrogant bastards." The officer threw the list in the trash.

Approximately twelve hundred feet above Florida Locks, Balboa Transitway Area, Terra Nova

Montoya's was, so to speak, the "full monty" of Condors, the latter being gliders, some models of which were auxiliary propelled, some were drones, some recon, some light courier, and some antiaircraft. They were all highly secret, except the totally non-stealthed versions used ostensibly for training on other aircraft.

The Condor was an attempt, so far a successful one, to create a low performance aircraft stealthy enough to be essentially indetectable by either Federated States, Tauran Union, or United Earth Peace Fleet means. It had been tested against all three, and against the UEPF by conducting overflights of their base on Atlantis Island. Performance was important, of course, but cheapness, to Carrera's *Legion del Cid,* was even more important. The nice thing about the Condors, the impressive thing, was that they were quite cheap.

They were built around a spun carbon fiber and resin shell and tail which projected out struts for the wings. That shell and those struts were "lossy," lossiness being a chemical property that referred to the conductivity of a material. In layman's terms, the shell and struts absorbed radar energy and converted it to heat.

Around the shell and struts were built up—rather, sprayed on—layers of polyurethane foam. Within the foam, which grew less dense the closer to the outside it was, were tiny convex-concave chips. The effect of this was twofold and complimentary. The foam, fairly tough stuff even in fairly low densities, tended to act as an energy manager for incoming radar, with the low density outer foam radiating back too little radar energy for the receiver to notice, the next inner layer radiating back no more than that, and so on.

The chips, on the other hand, attempted to do randomly what the Tauran Union and Federated States spent hugely on to create deliberately. They pointed in all directions, such that radar hitting them was typically bounced anywhere but the direction it came from, while their shape tended to either concentrate and diffuse, or just diffuse, that energy.

The most expensive part on the basic design was the bloody gold-plated pilot's canopy.

After manufacture, all Condors, along with replacement bottom sections, were subject to testing for radar signature. Some, the random process being, after all, *random,* were not stealthy enough. Of these some were stripped of their polyurethane and canopy and had a highly radar reflecting coat of paint put on. That was one way of getting an enemy to simply not worry about them. Others, conversely, had the canopies stripped but were modified with auxiliary power and turned into Global Locating System and TV-guided, high explosive and/or propaganda-carrying, drones, then packaged up in shipping containers for launch via lighter than air balloon.

Most of those shipping containers were already in the bottom of one or another of the container ships the legion owned and ran. Every month a few or a few dozen more might be added.

There were weaknesses, of course. Landing tended to ruin the stealth qualities of the underside, since useful wheels were right out. There were some techniques to mitigate that, but they were always a bit iffy. Speed and payload were both quite low. For the auxiliary power versions, a thin tube ran along the top of the wings, to mix hot gasses with cool air, then let them out where they were least likely to be detected. From above, that could sometimes be seen. Though even there, the Condor was so slow that it really existed in a different tactical and technical universe from the aircraft that would have wanted to engage it. There was a certain amount of safety in that.

Montoya's Condor was as stealthy as design and randomness could make it. Under auxiliary power, Montoya had the engine shut off to make himself completely silent to the mostly sleeping Taurans below. He looked occasionally at his low light television, or LLTV, screen. As expected, there was no unusual activity around the locks. Even the swing bridge was in its normal, retracted position.

Montoya veered northwest, heading for the airfield, Brookings Field, that was a next-door neighbor to Fort Muddville. He lost a little altitude in the process, about a hundred feet, but was able to pick that up and a hundred or so more, from the mini-mountain wave surging over the hills southeast of the field. In the course of that he swept over the barracks that supported the field. Other than somebody getting a blowjob while leaning against one of the stuccoed walls of the barracks there was nothing.

The Condor's wing dipped as the glider rolled and turned gracefully toward nearby Fort Muddville, home base of, among other units, the Gallic Army's 420th Dragoons. With no ordnance aboard, and only a half load of fuel, the glider sank slowly as it flew to the southeast. Even so, by the time Montoya reached Building 59, the administrative headquarters of the Tauran Union Security Force-Balboa, his altitude had dropped once again to about eleven hundred feet. It would have been less but for a chance updraft that pushed him a *little* higher.

"Oh, oh," Montoya said, looking at his screen. "What have we here?"

The LLTV screen showed a line of fourteen turreted infantry fighting vehicles, ARE-12Ps, pulled up next to what Montoya knew was Company B. Having studied Fort Muddville's map extensively and diligently, he knew all the barracks' usages.

As Montoya watched, another four vehicles—*Crap, tanks!*—swung around a corner and joined the IFVs, moving past the latter to take point. One of the IFVs moved out of its position, fifth in order of march, trundled along the concrete road, and slid in behind the tanks.

Montoya waited until he had flown on an additional two kilometers before restarting his engine. Confident that he'd have power to climb, if needed, he ducked into a jungle-shrouded valley and made a radio call to Second Corps headquarters, at the old *Comandancia*.

Second Legion Headquarters, *Fuerte* Guerrero, Balboa, Terra Nova

The Second Legion's field officer of the day at the *Comandancia* read the hastily scribbled down message from Montoya. Then he checked B Company's known invasion mission—known because it had been rehearsed dozens of times on Green Monsoons and Mosquitoes—against the cohort and tercio that was responsible for repelling them. He also checked the units that were to assist that tercio. Then he made a phone call to the homes of Legates Chin and Velasquez. Chin then made his own call to Carrera.

Second Tercio Headquarters, *Fuerte* Guerrero, Balboa, Terra Nova

"It's us, all right," announced Legate Chin, "Or rather, it's you, Velasquez."

In the otherwise still night, and with the surging waves on the nearby coast for backdrop, Sergeant Major Cruz's voice arose, chivvying the legionaries of Second Cohort through their preparations. The men had come with their rifles and machine guns, likewise ammunition for same, but there were other weapons—mortars and antitank guided missiles—and other ammunition—grenades, mines, rounds for the rocket grenade launchers, mortar shells, shoulder-fired antiaircraft missiles—that had to be passed out. Some of that, or more of that, was hidden farther forward, in secret caches.

Cruz's voice was insistent and demanding, and loud enough to be heard over wide swaths. Yet still it retained a sense of calm purpose, which sense both Chin and Velasquez knew would be imitated by the cohort.

By ones and twos, tens and twenties, the reservists and militia of the cohort made their appearance. Some came on foot, others by automobile. In one case thirty-nine of them showed up on a commandeered bus. The driver of the bus was Eleventh Tercio but, as he said, "What the hell? Same army, same legion, same enemy. You guys got a rifle and some ammunition to spare? Mine's all at home."

The rest of the tercio was being mobilized as well, along with a hefty chunk of the combined force. Yet it was Second Cohort whose job it would be to pin the Taurans in place and destroy them. The rest would only join if the Taurans reinforced.

Carrera arrived by helicopter a few minutes before Second Cohort began its march to the south. The chopper touched down on the parade field, as close to the formed maniples as the pilot thought safe. Carrera made a hand signal to the pilot to lift off and move away. The pilot assumed, correctly, that that meant far enough away that the motor and rotors wouldn't be heard.

Carrera absolutely *hated* making speeches. As he trotted from where the helicopter had let him off to take over the formation from Velasquez, he thought, *No coward's ever been made brave by a speech, though plenty of brave men have been demoralized by them. Ah, what the hell, the boys deserve to know that what they're doing matters.*

Salutes being exchanged, Carrera called, "Post," which caused Legate Velasquez, but only him, to march off to the side. The cohort was already in a C formation, in front of cohort HQ, with Headquarters and Support Maniple to Carrera's left and Combat Support to the right. The three rifle companies, which looked to be at about seventy or seventy-five or eighty percent strength, made up the center. The men looked gorillalike in their bulky, liquid metal and silk, loricated body armor. Each maniple had a piper off to its flank.

Not bad, thought Carrera, *not bad. No unit ever took an objective at one hundred percent.*

There were also six Puma tanks from the tercio tank maniple, plus the cohort's own platoon of light armor, Ocelots. Those were all lined up behind the cohort.

Carrera turned and made a quick trot up the steps leading into cohort headquarters then stopped and faced the troops.

He raised his voice and said, "I figured it would be good for you men to see if I'm as big a bastard as I'm reputed to be." He made a gather-in motion with his fingers, saying, "Now that you've seen, come in closer boys, I'm getting old and my lungs aren't what they used to be."

He gave them a few minutes to break ranks and gather in. Then he said, "Second Cohort of the Second Tercio . . . '*Segundo a nadie.*' I know you of old, gallant Two-Two. Decades ago I watched your fathers and your uncles and your older brothers storm up a steep ridge in Sumer. Neither river nor ridge, nor machine guns, nor artillery, nor wire, nor mines could stop them then. As nothing is going to stop you today.

"Those fathers and uncles and older brothers are still with you, of course. They're your legate and your sergeant major. They're your senior tribunes, centurions, and senior sergeants. They're the men who've fought from Sumer to Pashtia to Kashmir to here at home, over in the Province of La Palma. They have *never* known defeat. Neither shall you."

Carrera looked in the direction of *Cerro Mina* and sneered, saying, "To the south of here, the Taurans are rolling out. They think they're better men than we are. They think we're afraid to meet them, man to man and tank to tank.

"I want you to give them a *very* rude awakening. Meet them. Pin them. Trap them. Destroy them. Let none escape. *Prove* to them that this is *our* land, *our* country, *our* sacred soil and sacred trust, and that *none* may profane it except at the cost of their lives.

"Now don't cheer. And no pipes until you make contact. No need letting the enemy know what's coming for them. Just go do your duty. And God go with you."

Carrera then trotted off, calling, "Legate, take charge of your cohort and move them to battle."

"I'm a little surprised," said Cruz to Signifer Porras. "He normally hates speeches and doesn't do a great job with them. But that one wasn't bad."

Porras nodded. "I know what you mean. But never mind that. The legate's making the signal to get the boys moving. We'd better do our parts."

"Yes, sir."

A quiver in Porras's voice caused Cruz to study the young officer's face. The boy looked grim and, under the fixed lights outside the headquarters, visibly pale.

"Nervous, sir?" the sergeant major asked.

"Not for myself, Sergeant Major, and that's the truth."

"I believe you, sir." For the most part, Cruz did believe the boy.

Porras continued, "I'm just afraid of letting the men down. Or rather, I'm afraid of being afraid of letting the men down."

"Well, duh, sir," the sergeant major said. "That's all any good soldier worries about. But don't you worry much; you're going to be all right, sir, and you're going to do just fine. We have a good group. You won't really even have to do much."

"'But the simplest things are very difficult,'" Porras quoted from a book both he and the sergeant major had studied.

"*Tsk*, sir. Pulling a Clausewitz on me? For shame. But even so, I understand, sir. Trust me, you'll do fine. There's nothing worse going to happen than what you did in Cazador School."

"Intellectually," said the signifer, "I know that. Emotionally? I'm not convinced."

The conversation was cut off as the platoon leader for one of the infantry platoons, Senior Centurion Figueroa, motioned to request that the two come to his side.

Avenida Ascanio Arosemena, Ciudad Balboa, Balboa, Terra Nova

Bored Gallic dragoons—calld mechanized infantrymen in other armies—stood around their fighting vehicles casually and unworriedly. Some of the dragoons smoked cigarettes. Others slept inside the cramped vehicles, their bodies twisted unnaturally to fit as well as possible against or around the ARE-12Ps' various sharp and unyielding projections. Turret crews scanned their sectors—when they did—idly, without interest.

"Why the hell did they have to start this shit again?" asked a nineteen-year-old private of no one in particular. "I had a date with a really hot local girl. Who knows when I'll get a chance to see her again?"

Some of the men remounted the tracks as a heavy rain began to fall, ignoring the protests and curses of the men inside who were rudely awakened. Others just stood, bored, in the rain. Balboa was so warm that rain was no discomfort.

CHAPTER TWENTY-NINE

The patriot volunteer, fighting for country and his
rights, makes the most reliable soldier on earth.

—Stonewall Jackson

Old Balboa City, Balboa, Terra Nova

The neighborhood, which also held Second Corps Headquarters,
had once been an eclectic mix of ritzy, once ritzy but now run
down, and outright stinking slum. The first two still existed,
though ritzy had taken a lead on run-down. More important, for
more people, most of the slum had been cleared, and nearly all
of the people who'd made it such an unpleasant place to live were
now dead and, generally speaking, buried in unmarked graves or
dissolved in lime. A healthy population of trixies, too, had been
encouraged to settle, which had done for most, if not all, of the
former *antaniae* problem. And the new sewer system the legion
had put it hadn't hurt matters any.

There'd also been a fair amount of demolition and rebuilding.
Oddly, some of the rebuilding had been to standards that nobody
but the legions really understood.

Cruz, Porras, and the platoon leader, Senior Centurion Figueroa,
arrived at the safe house where the regulars, reservists and militia
of the platoon had gathered. Although its authorized strength was
forty-eight, at eighty-one percent present for duty, the platoon had
only forty men of its own. It was, however, reinforced with two
medics, an engineer squad, a forward observer team, and half the

fully mobilized cohort's antitank platoon. The strength present
was seventy-seven, which made the safe house *cum* ammunition
cache a very tight fit. Fortunately, that number included Porras,
Cruz, and an RTO, a radio telephone operator, from the cohort
signal platoon.

Figueroa quickly briefed the men. They listened, hoping that
their mission had been called off. When told that it was going
forward, they stopped paying attention for a moment, lost in individual thoughts. Most of which corresponded roughly to, *Oh, fuck.*

No matter, they had been given the essentials of the plan long
ago. It was just luck that fate had chosen that particular Tauran
unit to restart the harassment. Damned bad luck.

A Balboan trooper muttered, "Christ, why us?"

The boy thought his question had been too low to hear, but
Cruz had heard it. "Because it's our job, boy, and no one else's,"
he answered.

Consulting his watch, Figueroa gave the order to move out.
Silently, columns of men padded from the safe house and began
to move up the tiny back streets and alleys of one of *Ciudad
Balboa's* less desirable neighborhoods.

The legionaries were stripped down for fighting—no rucksacks,
just weapons, armor, ammunition, and a single meal per man.
Some of the soldiers looked at where areas that were burned out
in the Federated States invasion, decades before, had been rebuilt.
Some had participated in the rebuilding. To the west, unheard
and unnoticed amidst the rain, other columns moved forward to
Avenida de la Santa Maria.

Leading from the front—only he, Porras, and Cruz had ever
followed this route—Figueroa opened a door and moved through
the hallway of an apartment building. The platoon emerged from
the hallway into a fenced yard. Passing through an unlatched gate,
they walked up a very dark and narrow alley between two buildings. In the alley they were almost completely sheltered from the
rain and partially sheltered from its sound. From overhead came
the sound of a serious domestic quarrel. A slap was followed by
a woman's cry. Hands tightened on rifles, but there was more
important work to be done this morning.

Halting the platoon inside yet another fenced-in area, the
platoon leader spoke into his radio. "Bloodhound," he said. *In
position and awaiting orders.* The men waited in the rain. They

heard the distinctive sound of cars passing by a few feet away on the wet pavement of *Avenida Ascanio Arosemena*, near where it joined *Avenida de la Santa Maria*.

The answering call came back. "Wait, Out." Other platoons were still moving into position, onto the roofs and into buildings opposite the Tauran company across the broad avenue. Other leaders' and commanders' voices broke radio silence to inform headquarters they were ready. At length the encrypted radio came to life again. It was the cohort commander's voice.

"To all officers, centurions and men of the Second Cohort, Second Tercio. This is Velasquez. Begin Phase Two...and God bless you on this day. Velasquez...out."

Headquarters, Tauran Union Security Force-Balboa, Building 59, Fort Muddville, Balboa, Terra Nova

Oh, shit, thought Campbell as she replaced the phone's receiver in its cradle. Then she said it, loud enough for Hendryksen to hear, "Oh, shit."

"What is it?" asked Hendryksen.

"The radio intercept people...there is a huge surge in Balboan radio traffic. They say they've never seen anything like it before.... It's coming from everywhere. Mostly encrypted and the little that isn't sounds worrisome, too."

"Where are we doing a Mosquito?" he asked. "Is it just down on *Avenida de la Santa Maria*?"

"That's all I know about," she replied.

"Then the Balboans are seriously overreacting," said the sergeant major.

"That or they intend to drive us into the sea."

"Shall we?" he asked.

"Maybe we'd better," she answered. "I'll go get our weapons. You draw the vehicle."

"We'd better hurry," said Hendryksen.

Old Balboa City, Balboa, Terra Nova

"That's our cue," announced the platoon leader. "Let's go."

Getting to his belly, the platoon leader began to lead his men in a long crawl across the potentially deadly wide open space of the street. A half mile or so to the east and west small teams of military police stopped traffic on the otherwise busy avenue. It wouldn't do to have a too fast driven car take out half of a squad. Cars quickly built up all the way to the Bridge of the Columbias. With luck, Figueroa's platoon would be across before the Taurans got the message.

It was fortunate that the police had long since taken to blocking off the sites of Mosquitoes, in the interests of preventing the kind of accident normal when civilian cars and heavy armored vehicles try to use the same road.

Unseen by anyone, a lone man in civilian attire made a tape of the scene with a video camera. He was so engrossed with the ARE-12Ps that he didn't notice the legionary infantry crawling twenty feet below his window.

The Tunnel, *Cerro Mina*, Balboa, Terra Nova

As often as not, during Mosquitoes and Green Monsoons, Janier slept in his office in the Tunnel. Since this was the first one in a while, he especially wanted to be there.

Malcoeur, Janier's aide de camp, shook the general awake. The aide was already in uniform. "Sir, we have indicators that the legion is calling up their reservists *and* militia."

Groggily, Janier sat up, then spent a few moments rubbing sleep from his eyes. "Funny," he said, "they've never called up the militia before. How many? Who?"

"It looks like everybody, General. Sir, they've even got about eight Mosaic fighters in the air. Eight the air element have detected anyway. Could be more."

"Call C-3. Alert all three brigades . . . and the battalion going through the Jungle School." Janier considered a moment. "And the Air Force."

Alert them, yes, we'll alert them all. But I hope my opposite number understands the concept of human sacrifice.

Parade Field, *Fuerte* Guerrero, Balboa, Terra Nova

Nine drivers in three groups turned their steering wheels violently, chewing up the neatly manicured turf. Behind the trucks, towed 85mm artillery pieces swung to point to the southwest. The trucks stopped suddenly, almost as a single man, then began disgorging seven or eight men each. Some of the gunners frantically disengaged the guns' towing pintles while others turned elevation cranks. Gunners slid sights into slots, then looked through the lenses.

"Aiming point this instrument," announced one soldier standing behind a tripod with an optical device mounted atop it. Gunners swiveled their sights and announced, one after the other, "Aiming point identified!"

Behind each group of three guns another truck pulled up. From it artillerymen began running wire to the guns, while the fire direction center personnel unzipped plotting boards and prepared their game of charts and darts. Two other trucks began rolling from the flanks inward, dropping off loads of 85mm ammunition at each position.

A few towed antiaircraft guns took up positions to defend the artillery pieces. A column of four Ocelots, three Puma tanks, and six SPATHA tank destroyers rolled up the street. This was Third Cohort's slice of tercio and legion armor. Eight trucks carrying six heavy mortars and their Fire Direction Centers followed the armor. A bronze statue of Belisario Carrera stood calmly by. The tank commanders, standing in their hatches, saluted the statue as they passed.

Behind the guns, to the left of the tanks, the rest of the tercio's men, the stragglers who got the word late, who lived farther out, who were stuck on the wrong side of the bridge—and twelve of those landed by the yacht club on a commandeered boat—or who had had to struggle with their fears, before overcoming those fears, were reporting in.

Avenida Ascanio Arosemena, Ciudad Balboa, Balboa, Terra Nova

"Sergeant!" exclaimed the Gallic gunner into his microphone. "Sergeant! I have movement in the street."

Suddenly jerked to alertness, the gunner traversed his turret to sweep his sight over the prone figures crawling through the night. The movement of the vehicle's 25mm cannon did not go unnoticed by the Balboans. One of them, who didn't bother to announce why, simply took the initiative. Raising himself to a kneeling position, bringing an RGL to his shoulder, he took aim.

The Gallic gunner was just that little bit faster. Reacting to the threat, he made a slight aiming adjustment and pressed the firing button for his coaxial machine gun and, in his fear, held it for nearly two seconds.

As half a dozen bullets, of the twenty-one launched, tore through his body, the Balboan screamed and threw his arms to the sky. The finger on the trigger of the antitank weapon twitched enough to fire it. The RGL's rocket motor burned almost straight down, gouging a dent in the street, as the warhead shot upward, uselessly.

The gunner's body twisted back to fall in the street. Blood welled from his wounds and ran across the bow of the asphalt into the gutter. The single long burst also hit two other men, one fatally. The wounded soldier writhed in anguish, crying aloud for his mother . . . for a medic . . . for any help at all. One of the platoon's medics pushed himself to his feet and ran to the wounded soldier's side, aid bag slapping at his back. Unable to tell the difference between a medic and a machine gunner, even with a thermal sight, the Gaul fired again, with another too long burst. His fire nearly cut the medic in two.

Almost as quickly as the Gaul had let loose with his second burst, the opposite side of the street erupted in fire. An RGL flashed on a rooftop, its missile lancing down to strike the vehicle on the glacis. The hot jet of gas and molten metal burned through the armor, then melted the driver's face as it slashed into his brain. The driver died instantly, without even the chance to scream. His death immobilized his vehicle until his body could be removed. A few Taurans, caught outside their armored protection, were cut down by rifle and machine gun fire, much of it coming from the *Cerro Mina* Inn—a notorious prostitute bar, much favored by the staff of the Tunnel for the odd afternoon quickie. Other Taurans took whatever cover was available, remounting the tracks if possible.

The on-line ARE-12Ps returned fire, knocking chunks from the walls, shattering windows, and in the process killing some of the Balboans. Still, they could not suppress everyone engaging them. Lone infantrymen, carrying RGLs, popped from cover to fire at the tracked vehicles. Sometimes they hit; mostly—too frightened to aim properly—they missed. Still, with each effective hit on a Gallic infantry fighting vehicle the amount of fire the Balboans had to brave decreased. Correspondingly, the amount of fire directed against the Taurans increased. It also grew more effective.

The Tauran company commander, Captain Bruguière, frantically worked his radio. What had happened, he wanted to know. Who had shot first? Why? Who was hit? His platoon leaders, such as were still unhurt, passed what information they could. In the surprise and confusion, this was not usually much.

The immobilized ARE-12P that had first opened fire swept its machine gun over the prone figures caught in the street. A half dozen were hit, including the Balboan platoon leader, Figueroa. On the far side another RGL gunner took aim and fired. The rocket propelled grenade sailed across the street, exploding against the turret. A thin stream of superheated gas and metal burned through the light armor. The gunner and squad leader were killed instantly. The infantry, sitting in the compartment below the turret, were stunned by the sudden overpressure, eardrums bursting. Outside, two guided antitank missiles exploded in sympathetic detonation. A third RGL hit, then a fourth. The vehicle began to burn. Over the flames screams could be heard, as if from a great distance, as some of the men in the back began to burn alive.

Some dragoons, even some whose uniforms had caught fire, tried to abandon their vehicle. However, when they opened the small combat door and tried to leave, a machine gunner who had taken position on the hill behind opened up on them. Bullets ricocheted menacingly off the door, but couldn't prevent the men from getting to the ground and behind the cover of the road wheel.

They had just barely escaped the track but could not leave the area. Pinned to the protection still afforded by the hulk, they waited for either the Balboans to cease fire, or be destroyed... or for the flames to set off the internally carried ammunition. They were too badly shocked and stunned to even think about returning the fire.

Suddenly one of the Taurans clutched at his throat and began to convulse. His feet began to beat a tattoo on the asphalt as he began to die in misery.

"What happened?" asked one of the dragoons of his corporal.

"He'd probably been inhaling when one of the enemy weapons hit," said the corporal, as he pulled a pen from his pocket. He removed the ink cartridge, leaving just a clear plastic tube. Speaking as he worked, he said, "The hot gas entered and seared his throat. He might not even have noticed right away." The corporal used his fingers to find the spot on the front of the man's throat, then he used the point of his bayonet to cut that open. He continued talking, "Then the damaged tissue swelled up to the point of cutting off his airway. But..." the corporal inserted the tube through the slice he'd made. Instantly, the thing whistled as the formerly strangling trooper sucked in air at a furious rate.

Man, that is one cool son of a bitch of a corporal, thought the dragoon who'd asked the question.

With the Tauran fire that had pinned them suddenly cut off, the Balboan platoon should have rushed to their feet and across the street. But, with the platoon leader down, no one gave the command. Every man knew what they should do, but no one wanted to be the first up and the first to draw more fire.

Porras, not knowing why no one gave the command to rush, decided that it was up to him. Screaming "Follow me!" he lurched to his feet and began to run to the shelter of the far side. The Balboans followed, Cruz and the platoon sergeant kicking the slower ones into motion to support their officer.

Reaching the far side first, Porras flung himself to the ground. Frantically, he looked to the Gallic IFV that had fired upon his platoon. A few Tauran soldiers huddled behind its sheltering bulk, the flames of the track casting strange shadows on the ground. Porras did not hesitate. The footbeats of his soldiers echoing in his ears, he aimed and fired, the F-26 rifle vibrating against his shoulder. The Taurans fell in a heap. Porras did not release the trigger until his entire magazine of ninety-three rounds had been emptied.

Naturally, some wounded were killed as well. It was impossible to distinguish the hale from the hurt. The unconscious but still breathing dragoon the corporal had saved, for example, suddenly spouted many more holes to allow his lungs to draw air. That would have killed him, eventually, if blood loss and damage to his organs had not.

Quarters 20, Family Housing, Guerrero Road and Firth Street, *Fuerte* Guerrero, Balboa, Terra Nova

Back in the day, under Federated States ownership, then *Fort* Guerrero had had a number of really very nice, spacious, attractive, and solid-as-a-rock family quarters for officers, mostly senior ones, and noncoms, all senior ones. Somewhat like Imperial Range, these had been split between Balboa and the FSC with the Tauran Union taking over those that the FSC had retained, under their mandate from the World League.

The housing areas sometimes represented intelligence sieves, for both sides, as wives gossiped across political lines and men engaged in figurative cock-measuring contests, generally in support of political lines. Sergeant Major Cruz, for example, had his family in one of the larger duplexes, while he had Scarface Arredondo in the other half of the duplex. On the north of those two, however, were a Major Michael ("Mad Mike") Tipton, Anglian Army. To the south was an Italian family, the del Cols.

Not particularly surprisingly, the soldiers—cock-measuring contests notwithstanding—got along famously well, as soldiers will, while the wives, in those three buildings and the other eighty or so on the installation set aside for families, had a pretty nice informal club going, watching each other's kids, trading recipes, sharing maids, and just generally doing what soldiers' wives did best, being good women.

In Quarters Twenty, however, Major Tipton—Anglian Army, seconded to the TUSF-B—awoke to the twin sounds of his wife screaming hysterically and the steady drum beat, impossibly loud, coming from the parade field just in front of his house. Tipton went to investigate, then came back to his wife saying, "There's a big fucking artillery battery on the field! They're shooting like crazy!"

The hysterical screaming converted into a single, amazingly drawn-out shriek, that rose and rose until Tipton grabbed his wife, shook her vigorously, and said, "Honey, shut the fuck up and let me think."

Tipton tried frantically to think, but the steady, "*Cañon! Fuego!*" followed by *kaboom* after gut-wrenching *kaboom* made that an exercise in futility. "Shit! Shit!"

He did have one good thought though. "Honey, grab the kids and head toward the water. There should be some dead space down there. Just do it! Now!" Coming partially to her senses, Tipton's wife, Judy, got out of bed naked.

I wish I had a couple of guns, thought the major, *but* nooo, *the wife wouldn't let anything so evil into her house.*

The doorbell rang, barely heard above the pounding of the nearby guns. Tipton answered. It was their next neighbor over, Caridad Cruz, carrying a whimpering baby in her arms, a Balboan chaplain, and four armed men. Though Tipton didn't know the chaplain by sight, he could see by the man's collar, with its warrant officer's insignia on one side of his lapels and a silver cross on the other. Looking past the chaplain, Mrs. Cruz, and the four armed men, Tipton saw several dozen more soldiers standing in the street.

Looking past Tipton, on the other hand, the chaplain saw a buck naked Judy Tipton standing in the middle of the foyer, in obvious shock. Caridad bustled past warrant officer and major, then took control of the naked wife, turning her and leading her to her bedroom to, "For God's sake, Judy, get some *clothing* on!"

"Excuse me, *señor*," said the chaplain. "I have been detailed to go to each residence here and advise the occupants that portions of the legion have been—rather, are—engaged in battle in response to Tauran incursions upon Balboan soil. The legion regrets and apologizes for any inconvenience or fright this may have caused you or your family. Mrs. Cruz has volunteered her place as a safe house for you and yours. Please go with her and stay indoors with your family until the situation is resolved. These men will guard her house and the RSMs. Be advised, too, that operations are ongoing in this area as well. We cannot guarantee your safety in the open."

Tipton, nonplussed, merely said: "Thank you . . . uh, Father." He closed the door as the priest turned to leave. The four soldiers waited at the door until Tipton, his now dressed wife and their children, and Cara Cruz, came out. Then they escorted them to the Cruz residence before posting themselves around the house.

"Where's Ricardo?" asked Judy Tipton, though she was pretty sure she knew the answer.

"He's *out there*," Cara answered. Then she began to shake.

CHAPTER THIRTY

A thousand shall fall at thy side, and ten thousand
at thy right hand; but it shall not come nigh thee.

—Psalm 91:7, King James Version

Carretera Gallardo, Balboa Transitway Area, Balboa, Terra Nova

The northern tip of Brookings Field wasn't actually visible from
the highway, as Campbell and Hendryksen sped by it. What was
visible was the brace of Sachsen *Luftwaffe* Cyclone fighter-bombers,
taxiing to the southern takeoff point. Thirty-two seconds after
the first of those Cyclones reached the spot, it was deluged with
artillery fire—or possibly heavy mortars...or both—coming from
somewhere inside the city. Neither plane nor crew had a chance,
as shrapnel tore both men and their plane to shreds, while the
mix of high explosive and white phosphorus set off the several
tons of ordnance slung underneath the plane. It was that, the
secondary explosions, that both destroyed the second Cyclone
and tore the runway at the end into smoking, jagged ruin. All
over the base, airmen and security personnel were wounded by
shattering windows.

"Holy fuck!" said Campbell, shuddering at the explosions. Even
at a distance of nearly a mile, the concussion from the blasts was
staggering. It staggered Hendryksen, who barely managed to keep
their vehicle on the asphalt.

What was also visible was a mass of tracers, arcing over *Cerro
Mina* in a madman's conception of a fiery waterfall in reverse,

as the bullets struck metal or asphalt or concrete, then either ricocheted upwards or split off their tracer elements to fly alone toward the heavens.

"Take the back road," Campbell shouted. She needn't have. For one thing, between damage to his eardrums from the Brookings blasts, and the roar of the vehicle engine, Hendryksen wasn't hearing much of anything. More importantly, however, he lacked a death wish. Anything heading toward *Avenida Ascanio Arosemena*—or its continuation, *Avenida de la Santa Maria*—needed either a death wish or steel-hard discipline. That many tracers, careening across the sky at random, suggested a staggering amount of aimed fire below them.

At the back gate to *Cerro Mina* they found an MP quivering behind sandbags laid around the base of the guard shack. The policeman seemed in shock. When asked to move the barrier gate, he couldn't articulate and answer beyond some hysterical shaking of his head. Campbell had to get out, herself, to move the gate. Then she and Hendryksen stormed their vehicle through ... to be met by barely aimed fire coming from the tree line to the west. Neither was hit, but the 6.5mm bullets shredded the front tires of their vehicle in an instant, dropping the steel rims to the asphalt as they shed the scraps of rubber that had once been tires. There was no controlling the vehicle then. Despite Hendryksen's best efforts the car skidded off the side, slid into and then out of a drainage ditch, slammed into a thick tree and came to a halt in a cloud of steam from the ruptured radiator. Shards of safety glass from the shattered windshield covered the two Taurans, the hood, and was scattered all over the ditch and jungle. Headlight glass, too, was gone. The lights, one after the other, gave a defiant glow and then died out.

"Oh, my tits," groaned Campbell. The seat and shoulder belts had cut into her "girls." Then she looked left—*Why the fuck did they have to go with Federated States rules for driving and car design? Oh, yes, I remember, they built this place*—and saw Hendryksen slumped over the wheel, blood oozing from a deep gash on his head. He seemed more stunned than unconscious. At least, his eyes were open.

The side where they'd come to rest was a bit low, relative to the ground from which the fire had come. Bullets chipped the trees overhead, cut branches, and sent down showers of bark.

Campbell shuddered from the close call, then reached over to unbuckle Hendryksen.

Under the circumstances he couldn't resist saying, "You have no idea how often I've wanted to get you into very much this very position."

"Ya dirty bastard," she answered, "undo your own belt."

"And I see you're getting into the precise spirit I had in mind..."

"Ah, shut up, ya pervert." She finished undoing the seat belt, then pulled him behind her as she scooted back out of the vehicle. She got her feet to the ground, then continued pulling him out, easing him to the dirt until he could recover.

She leaned back into the vehicle to retrieve her submachine gun and the Cimbrian's, along with a broad flat pouch holding six magazines. She should have been wearing it, she knew, but, outside of her chest, she was a *little* girl and the damned, bloody thing didn't fit. As she was pulling back, she became aware of an enemy soldier, barely visible in the dank jungle, what with his pixelated tiger stripes blending in so well. The legionary had possibly been blinded by the lights before they died. She wasn't taking any chances. At a range of maybe twenty feet she opened fire.

The first four bullets either missed or, impacting on the legionary's armor, failed to penetrate. The fifth passed through his neck, blowing out a large chunk of meat and letting his life's blood gush out in a fountain.

The volume of return fire was, in Campbell's experience, simply amazing.

Never saw them fire so lavishly when I was with them...and they fired pretty lavishly compared to most, then.

She'd have been deader than chivalry but for the cover of the auto and the lip of the drainage ditch.

"Can ye walk yet?" she asked Hendryksen. If he'd been more alert and thought about it, he'd probably have realized that her starting to drop back to the accent of her youth was not a good sign.

"Get me to my fucking feet and I can *run*."

She did, then started to help him up the side of the ditch. Big mistake, way big; the area immediately around where the crown of his head first made its appearance took about two hundred rounds from half a dozen or more sources, in a fraction of a second.

"Holy shit. Forget escape that way," he said. "Follow the ditch."

She followed his advice, but it only worked for a while. As

drainage ditches sometimes do, this one bent. And the bend was covered by enemy fire.

She returned the fire, though the enemy probably had better vision of her area than she did of his. This time, as she spoke, Hendryksen *did* see the change in accent as a bad sign. "See youse Spanish sodomites, you"—the soliloquy was interrupted by several short bursts of fire—"wee baldy cunt, just you shaw yir heid wan mair time—there y'go, fuckin huv some a that—heh, Hendryksen, see's anither mag over, wid ye—right, they're a shoat tae shite, fuck, ah broke a fuckin' nail, youse fuckin Latin bastards..."

What made the whole thing *really* horrifying is that it was all said in the kind of tone of voice a normal person might use in asking a waiter at a restaurant for a glass of water.

But the fire was definitely coming closer, driving Campbell and Hendryksen more and more behind cover. It was only a matter of time before whoever it was shooting at them was in a position to donate a grenade.

In anticipation of that grenade, or some other manner of grisly death, Hendryksen, not normally among the most spiritually driven of men, began making the sign of the cross on the theory, *At this point it can't hurt and might just help.* He was at the "filioque" when, from off to their right there came a very long burst of fire—from weapons that weren't designed to spit out eighteen hundred rounds a minute—and that, for a change, didn't impact around them.

"It's the cavalry," Jan said, "and aboot fuckin' tahm."

Combat in cities and jungles tends to be rather short ranged, anyway. Night only makes this more pronounced and common. The relief that came to Campbell's and Hendryksen's rescue had, in fact, emerged from the entrance to the Tunnel, which was a scant two hundred meters from the scene of the action. A few hundred feet below, and a good distance inward, Janier fretted some more.

Will that South Colombian bastard understand the whole point of the exercise or will he, as usual overreact? I should have worked this out in advance, the limited provocation once I was overruled, the counterattack, the letter written in blood to the politicos back in Taurus...

Janier's headquarters was a riot of confused activity. Reports—often contradictory ones—flowed in all directions, to include into little muddy eddies of disinformation that led nowhere. So far the only positive steps taken had been to recall the staff, to order the engaged company to withdraw if possible, to tell the aviators to get something into the air, and to order the rest of the dragoons to roll to relieve the company.

Janier heard over the loudspeaker the sobbing report from Brookings about what had happened to the two planes they'd tried to send up, and what that had done to the base and its personnel. He was about to order Arnold Air Force Base to fill in for Brookings when he looked at the map and realized, *No, no point. There's a regiment's worth of artillery in the town east of Arnold, Santa Cruz. They'll just blast the base if we try to lift anything.*

"Sir?" It was the AdC, Malcoeur, holding up an old-fashioned black telephone receiver, actually a relic of when the FSC had ruled here. "Sir, it's the Balboans...the chief...*Duque*...or whatever he calls himself. He wants to talk with you. He says it's very important."

Oh, I imagine it is. Janier took the phone from his aide and covered the mouthpiece with his hand. *Note to self, remember to put on the right show for the audience. Wonder if Carrera's thinking the same thing? Likely he is, so don't take anything he says too personally.*

"Has there been any word of what the rest of the legion is doing?"

"Moving to dispersal areas, sir. They're taking no aggressive moves, barring a couple of artillery strikes anyplace we've tried to escalate or made some move in that direction."

Janier nodded understanding, then took his hand from over the mouthpiece, placing the phone to his ear.

"Janier."

Carrera's voice was strained as he said, "It would appear that some fighting has broken out between elements of our forces."

"Are you implying that you didn't order this?"

"No...no, I ordered it."

"In heaven's name, why?" *Because you understand the issues, I suspect.*

"Because," Carrera answered, "the people in Taurus are most likely under the illusion that the legion of today would be the walk-over everyone thinks it was when the Federated States invaded. I hope to prove differently. Of course, if we cannot, at the kinds of force levels committed, then I will know we cannot win. In that case I will step down and surrender myself to the Tauran Union.

"Of course, that depends on the levels of force involved. If you throw in everything, and I throw in everything, you will lose but it won't prove much since you have only about one division here while I have the equivalent of six and change within striking range."

Janier, suspecting the possibility that his words were being monitored and possibly recorded, said, disingenuously, "I don't understand. You have your entire force mobilized, but only one group is fighting. That makes no sense."

"Yes it does. Think. If one of my battalions can take on one of your battalions in a great, bloody skirmish, then you can tell your political masters that we're too tough a nut to crack. And then you'll be believed. And the rest of my tercios won't have to fight."

Janier didn't answer for a moment, pausing for dramatic effect on those presumptive listeners and reviewers. "A blood sacrifice? You're offering up some of your troops as a blood sacrifice?"

Carrera sighed. "That's about it. And it can stay at that level, too. If you don't send any more troops into the fight than your mechanized battalion, I will not reinforce Second Cohort Second Tercio, beyond their normal supporting artillery."

"And if I do send more?"

"I will meet every attack equally. Although at some point, I'll have to decide that general war has begun. At that point I won't hold anything back."

"Air power? You can't meet me equally there." *No, in sheer numbers, at least barring* Avenida Ascanio Arosemena, *you surpass me by far.*

"I know. But I will have my heavy rocket launchers mine the runway and shell Arnold Air Force Base out of existence as soon as a single aircraft takes off. You must know I have it under constant observation. If you need proof, consider what we did to the aircraft you tried to lift from Brookings."

Carrera hesitated before continuing. "Speaking of being under observations, I'm also getting reports from just about every place in the Tauran Union that has light infantry, airborne, or special operations troops and every place that bases transport aircraft and airships. It would be better, perhaps, if they didn't mobilize for this."

"And what am I supposed to tell my government?"

"The truth. That it *appears*—and it does appear that way, I made sure it would—that a single Balboan unit and a Tauran unit, both engaged in provocational maneuvers, ran into each other in the night and engaged in a fire fight. That you don't know who fired first...not that it really matters. That, since you are very badly outnumbered and outgunned, the mobilized legion could throw you into the sea if it attacked. That you and I are trying to limit the fighting.... That this is a predictable result of the kinds of stresses we've been throwing at each other."

"You really expect me to hang Tauran soldiers out to dry?" *You had better expect it; it's precisely what I wanted to happen.*

Unseen by Janier, Carrera shook his head. His voice when he resumed had a strained quality. "I know it's a hard thing to do. But harder than losing many times more? I don't know. In any event, you don't have to give me an answer in words. I'll know what decision you make by your actions. And now, I really have to go. But think about it—*please think about it*—before you do anything rash. Carrera out."

Avenida Ascanio Arosemena, Ciudad Balboa, Balboa, Terra Nova

Half of Captain Bruguière's tracks were wrecked, along with three of the four tanks. Some still burned and others had burned out, with thin smoke seeping from their ruins. The smoke stank of overdone long pig.

He had wounded all over the place, although the dreadful Balboan artillery and mortar fire reduced the numbers of wounded steadily, by killing them where they lay. The company commander tried desperately to think of some solution while directing his own gunner's fire.

I can't attack into those buildings. I can't leave my wounded behind. I can't stay here or my whole company will be destroyed eventually. I can't stop fighting to recover the wounded or the locals will murder us. The commander considered something, then rejected it. *And I won't surrender. Let's pray for the cavalry then.*

Cerro Mina Inn, *Ciudad* Balboa, Balboa, Terra Nova

The senior surviving and unhurt leader in the building, a staff sergeant of Third Platoon, Number One Company, Second Cohort, Second Tercio shouted encouragement and orders to his remaining men. Both the centurion and the platoon sergeant were down; killed by the tungsten penetrators of the ARE-12Ps' cannon, punching through brick and concrete walls. They'd torn through the *Cerro Mina* Inn's walls as if they were tissue paper. Whether they hit anything after punching through was largely a matter of luck, though, when each penetrator carried its own luck, and there were thousands of penetrators....

Well, luck had been against over half of the platoon, and both the radios, so far as the sergeant could tell. He stepped carefully over a legless body as he moved down a hallway to check on a position set up in a whore's room and that had gone silent. Blood made the floor tacky to his feet.

Of the three men in the whore's room, he found only one alive. The others had been torn to pieces, their blood and brains sprayed across the floor and against the walls. The terrified survivor huddled against a corner, covering his head with his hands. That sole survivor moaned and wept continuously, rocking back and forth against the wall.

The sergeant wiped a hand across his face and chin. He couldn't bring himself to order the broken man back into the fight. And he couldn't just leave him there, either. Bending low, the sergeant said, "Sanchez, I need you to carry a message to the commander. Can you do that for me?"

Sanchez stopped weeping and looked up. "They're all dead sergeant? Do you want me to tell the commander that they're all dead?"

"Something like that," the sergeant said, as gently as he could. "I'll write it out for you and then you head back and find the CO."

Avenida de la Santa Maria, Ciudad Balboa, Balboa, Terra Nova

The Ocelot platoon leader and track commander ordered, "Gunner! Armor Piercing! Track."

"Target," the gunner announced.

"Fire!" The track rocked back on its suspension. Even a 100mm gun generated a significant amount of recoil for a lightly armored IFV pressed into duty as an armored gun system.

"Shit. Miss."

"Repeat."

✧   ✧   ✧

It had taken quite a while for the Ocelots to get into action. In the first place they'd been held back, to allow the infantry time to get into position. But when called up, the fighting had already commenced, which set thousands of the urban poor to flight, blocking the streets. Then, too, the streets of the old city were narrow, and made worse by automobiles parked a lot more densely than a maneuvering armored vehicle driver would prefer. Then, worst of all, just before breaking out, the first Ocelot had been hit by a missile launched from by either one of the ARE-12Ps or a dismount with an antiarmor missile. The only ones who could have told were the turret crew and driver and they were all dead.

Yes, the Ocelot had had reactive armor, blocks of explosive that deformed the jet stream formed by antitank hollow charges. These had proven inadequate against the tandem warhead of the missile system.

The second Ocelot, the platoon leader's track, had taken partial cover behind the first and trained its gun on the Gallic armored vehicle. That had fired a missile, but that missile had been a waste, hitting the destroyed Ocelot a second time. There had been no time for another shot; with its autoloader, the second Ocelot had been able to fire, miss, fire again, and hit too quickly. A solid shot at close range struck the Gallic IFV. The shot punched through the armor, then careened down the missile rack, destroying three of them and setting the rocket of a fourth alight. The flame from that touched off the other three, then caused all four warheads to detonate, essentially simultaneously. The rear door blew open, flames from the ruptured fuel tank shooting out. One poor bastard emerged, shrieking, a walking mannequin of flame. He fell and rolled, in absolute agony, until a bullet ended his pain. No one could say later if it had been a Balboan bullet or an Tauran one that had put the man out of his agony. No one bothered to ask, either. Sometimes one's enemy can be one's best friend.

"The CO's track's been hit!" the Gallic company exec shouted into his microphone. His next words were spoken more softly, mournfully, disbelievingly. "Shit...it's burning. Boys, we can't stay here much longer." The exec forced his brain to formulate a plan that might save them. He came up with something only a little better than, "*Sauve qui peut!*"

"All right," the exec said, "we're getting out of here. Two minutes to recover what wounded and dismounts you can. Then we pull back by platoons. Pop smoke, now!"

From either side of the turrets of the ARE-12Ps that were still intact phosphorus smoke grenades flew to impact in the street. A dense cloud of white, choking smoke began to billow up. Unable to see through the smoke to identify targets, the Balboans either ceased fire or kept it up at the last known locations. Both Ocelots and ARE-12Ps had thermal sights. But the Volgan-built Ocelots' sights were fairly marginal, while the Gauls' were first rate. The latter had no problem with seeing through the smoke. Their rate of fire increased. Back doors opened to let men out to recover wounded and to allow soldiers trapped outside to get back under cover. Still, the Balboan artillery fire coming from Fort Guerrero—now slackening as the gun platoon displaced by sections to another position—made even the brief trek to the armored vehicles a hazardous one.

Balboa City Train Station, *Ciudad* Balboa, Balboa, Terra Nova

Inside the light brown stucco of the mostly open-sided building, Porras sucked air, as did most of *his* remaining men, some thirty-three of Figueroa's platoon, a half-dozen combat engineers and fifteen men with four smoothbore rocket launchers from the antitank section. There were also two FOs and a medic left. Cruz flopped down beside the lieutenant.

"No time for a break, sir. You've got to get the men into position! That's what you get the big bucks for!"

"Sergeant Major," said the signifer, weakly, "you make twice what I do."

Cruz grinned broadly and said, "Yessir, and I'm worth every *centavo*, too."

Porras's weakness came partly from fatigue, partly from fear, and in good part from the horrors the platoon had, so far, fought through. Weakly or not, though, Porras nodded. He arose to his feet, stumbled once, and then began to shout orders. Cruz joined him in moving the men into a position from which they could dominate the only safe routes for reinforcements from Fort Muddville to reach the *Avenida de la Santa Maria* or for the Taurans engaged there to retreat to Fort Muddville.

The rain began to fall again as engineers laid mines across the street. There weren't many mines, perhaps fifty in all. About half were laid on the other side of the street, half laterally in front of the ambush position. Exhausted from lugging the little five-pound track killers, the engineers moved more slowly than was usual. On the tree covered hill behind the station, Cruz and Porras pushed men into hasty positions, taking advantage of what cover was available, mostly thick tree trunks and shallow depressions.

CHAPTER THIRTY-ONE

Blessed *are* the peacemakers: for they shall be
called the children of God.

—Matthew 5:9, King James Version

Avenida Ascanio Arosemena, Ciudad Balboa, Balboa, Terra Nova

Shocked with the fury of the battle just ended, the remnants of
Number One Maniple slumped in exhaustion or shuddered with terror, each as the feeling struck. They were all, in any case, completely
incapable of pursuing the fleeing shreds of the Tauran company.

Recovery—the first baby steps in recovery—began with an acting
platoon leader; he was a corporal and the fourth man to hold the
job in forty minutes. His first step was finding the presence to
order what was left of his platoon to begin to fight the smoldering
fires threatening to burn the *Cerro Mina* Inn. He also directed
that recovery and evacuation of the dead and wounded begin.

Should have been done sooner, thought the corporal. *Then again,
who was responsible at any given time to give the orders? And
did they even know? I didn't until a private pointed it out to me.*

Farther to the west, another replacement chief had the presence of
mind to lead a squad across to begin the search for Tauran wounded
and to take prisoners . . . if possible. A half-dozen men, and all that
remained of a twelve-man squad, fanned out to search for survivors
or to silence any Taurans who might resist. In this sector, wounded
were already being carried back to casualty collection points.

Farther into the city, ambulance sirens, some civil, others

military, echoed off of the walls of buildings and down streets and alleyways. The ambulances forced their way to the casualty collection points scattered throughout this portion of the old city. No helicopters were available; the Taurans weren't allowed to overfly while the Balboans had mostly fixed wing *Crickets* for dustoff, which couldn't land in the narrow confines of the city.

From the sounds of it, the battle moved on farther toward the Transitway. Even there it was now usually single shots—albeit sometimes very *large* single shots—rather than the deluge of fire that had been the norm for the morning. Some of those large single shots came from the Ocelots, tanks, and SPATHAs whose crews, once they realized that the Gallic armor facing them had pulled out, had begun a cautious pursuit. Because they were buttoned up, that realization took a while.

Balboa City Train Station, Balboa, Terra Nova

"I just got the word over the radio, Sergeant Major," said Signifer Porras. "The priority of fires for the artillery and heavy mortars has switched to us."

"Good, sir. I don't like being left out on our own. Any word from Intel?"

"Just that the rest of the mechanized battalion's readying at Muddville; almost a full tank company, two mech infantry companies, an antitank and part of a headquarters company."

"Did they have any idea of how long the Taurans will take?"

"No. I asked. But we'll get word as soon as they move."

Cruz stopped for a minute, then said, "Just in case I don't get a chance to tell you this later on, you did well back there, sir."

Porras flushed, unseen by Cruz in the darkness. "Thanks, Sergeant Major. Seemed like the thing to do. And...ah, Sergeant Major, if I don't make it..."

Cruz frowned and waved the nascent comment off. "Don't even start that shit, sir. The somber morose crap is *my* job, not yours. Besides, you'll come through just fine."

Porras gave a noncommittal grunt. The radio crackled to life. It was a two-man team that Porras had placed on flank security toward *Avenida de la Santa Maria*. "Five, this is two-three," announced the caller. "Five Tauran tracks, one tank, heading your way...maybe three minutes. They're moving fast."

"Damn!" cursed Cruz. "First Maniple wasn't supposed to let them get away. We're not set up to handle someone coming from that side. Not as well anyway."

"Two-three," answered Porras, "this is Five. Roger."

"It was a calculated risk, Top." Porras recalculated—picturing the layout of his platoon in his mind—then decided. "All right. Take one of the rocket launchers. Cut left and get in position on the other side of the station. They won't see you there. Toast the first track. I'll take the other gun and we can handle the last. On your way pass the word that the RGLs are not to fire until one of us does...or an antitank mine goes off."

Cruz jumped to his feet and ran to the left, shouting Porras's instructions to the rocket grenade launcher gunners.

300 Barracks Block, Fort Muddville, Balboa, Terra Nova

Compared to this morning's frantic pace, the usual alert was positively lackadaisical. But their comrades of Company B were in battle, rumor said desperate battle, and the men of the other companies in the 420th Dragoons fairly flew to go to their aid.

Ammunition was short, although not desperately so. Each company arms room and the ready battalion stocks held something less than a full load. There were safety regulations, by and large sensible ones, that restricted the amount of ammunition that could be held on hand. It was only through bending the rules that the dragoons had as much as they did. A convoy of trucks had been dispatched across the swing bridge over Florida Locks to the main Ammunition Supply Point. They had yet to return. Most worrisome was that the battalion had no mortar ammunition. If they fought it would be without the ability to suppress enemy infantry with high explosives from the battalion's heavy mortar platoon. Supposedly the artillery battery on Fort Nelson could range, but who trusted that?

Some of the men of the battalion had begun to breathe easier when the sounds of firing had died out, a few minutes before. Others, knowing what the cease fire most likely portended, grew furious.

The Battalion Commander's ARE-12PC squatted at the head of the line of tracks, nearest the usually locked gate that was the 420th's standard egress. The commander, Lieutenant Colonel

Michel Koenig, a Gaul, despite the name, stood in the commander's hatch. He had his internal coms tuned to higher, and couldn't hear anything outside of what came through the combat vehicle crewman's helmet. Down below his radio telephone operator monitored the internal nets.

Koenig felt a tapping on his leg. Looking down, he saw his RTO holding a microphone up to him. Koenig tore his helmet off, then reached down for the mike.

The RTO said, "Sir, it's B Company's XO."

"Six, over!"

From the other end, broken by static and distorted by the roar of the engine, B Company's XO sounded nervous and fearful. He was clearly near—if not quite at—panic. "Six; Bulldog Five. We have broken contact and are returning to base. Losses are heavy..." the XO paused and swallowed. "Very heavy."

"What the fuck happened, Five?"

"Don't know," the Exec replied. "We were in our assault position. Firing broke out from the right. I think we might have started it. Then all hell broke loose. We had Balboans in the buildings within twenty meters of our front and didn't know it. The CO's dead, sir...I saw him burn!"

Koenig swore before keying the mike. "Calm down, Five. We're just about ready to roll. If you think you need to hunker down 'til we get there, just say so."

"Six, Five. No, sir. I just want to... Shit! Shit!" The XO began relaying orders to his driver and gunner without flipping the communications switch on the side of his helmet. Koenig heard confused commands interspersed with machine gun and cannon fire. The static from the radio cut out.

Face a mask of rage and hate, Koenig dropped the mike, climbed on top of his track and spun his finger in the air. "Fuck the ammo! We roll!"

Balboa City Train Station, *Ciudad* Balboa, Balboa, Terra Nova

Porras—in the grip of terror-induced exhaustion—took off his helmet and ran his fingers through his stubble of hair. The lieutenant's back and head rested against the tree behind which he had taken cover during the ambush. Spaced 50 to 150 meters away the remains of five ruined tracks and a single burning tank littered the road and a nearby parking lot. The building the parking lot serviced had once been the headquarters for a Federated States veterans organization. Since the FSC had pulled out of Balboa, the building had kept the name and the number, Post 3538, but transitioned to other uses. The organization, itself, had moved to lesser quarters in the city.

Cruz sat on the wet ground opposite Porras. Two radios were propped against the tree between them.

Out in the kill zone, among the smoldering tracks, a dozen Balboans searched for survivors. The sole remaining medic gave what aid he could. The horrible burns and ripped guts he found were beyond his small skill and lesser equipment. Already, on more than one occasion, he had felt compelled to administer a fatal dose of morphine to a hopelessly burned gringo. It was a cleaner end than letting one of the infantry put a merciful bullet in their brains.

The dial light on the radio lit up. Cruz picked up the microphone. He heard the cohort commander's call sign and another that Cruz didn't recognize. The speaker reported the imminent arrival at the train station—"within ten minutes, probably less"—of the rest of the Gallic mechanized infantry battalion.

Cruz thought he recognized the speaker's voice. "Montoya? That you?"

High above, Montoya laughed to himself. "'Oh, Cazador buddy.' Cruz, we have got to stop meeting like this.

"Anyway, how you doin', pal? You the one toasted those tracks I see?"

"Okay," answer the sergeant major. "And yes. Well, I mean, the people I'm with did."

"Looks like good work from here. Anyway, *compadre*, you've got company coming. Good luck...and out."

Cruz relayed the warning to Porras, who wearily arose from the tree and began to issue orders. The platoon, instead of retreating, moved forward a few hundred meters. The oncoming Taurans should not expect them to do that. The cohort commander, maybe two miles away, approved the move. The maniple commander piped in, giving some orders to his other two platoons that would put them in position to support each other across the northern end of Brookings Field.

Tauran News Network, Headline News Studios, Lumière, Gaul, Terra Nova

"Newsflash! Heavy fighting in the Republic of Balboa. More in a moment." The camera cut out to allow the newscaster to mop his brow and collect his thoughts over the advertising break. When the camera returned, the 'caster reported, "Heavy fighting in the Republic of Balboa between Tauran Union Forces and the Balboan *Legion del Cid*, the mercenary organization that has taken over the country. Reports indicate that this is a localized battle, centered on the area between *Avenida de la Victoria* and Brookings Air Base."

A map showed behind the 'caster, a marker for an explosion superimposed on the image. Though the name, *Avenida de la Victoria*, was rarely used, the map did, in fact, show the old name given the avenue by Belisario Carrera.

"Casualties, to both sides, are said to be heavy. TNN has also been able to obtain this exclusive video of the outbreak of the fighting. We turn now, to Brent Strider in the Republic of Balboa. Brent?"

"Good morning, ladies and gentlemen. This is Brent Strider reporting from the Republic of Balboa." The camera backed off to show Strider standing next to a diminutive, elderly Balboan. It also showed ambulances carrying away the many wounded, as well as a long line of the plainly dead, lying side by side under ponchos along the sidewalk. "I have here *Señor* Eduardo de la Mesa. Mr. de la Mesa was an eyewitness, a video eyewitness, to this morning's unfortunate events. *Señor*, if you please, tell our viewers what you saw happening this morning at about quarter to three."

As de la Mesa spoke, a simultaneous translation was dubbed over his words. "I was woken up at about midnight by the sound of many engines and a funny squeaking. It—a Tauran unit taking up position near my apartment—has not happened in some time and so I thought I would videotape it. I was filming the *tanquito* nearest where I live when suddenly it turned its guns and began firing a machine gun. I turned my camera to record what the machine gun was shooting at and saw several dozen Balboan soldiers lying helpless in the street."

Strider asked, "*Señor*, do I understand you correctly? Tauran forces opened fire first."

"Yes, sir. That is what I saw."

A technician caught Strider's eye and gave a thumbs up signal. "We turn now to what Mr. de la Mesa saw through his video camera a few hours ago."

Strider's image cut out, to be replaced by a grainy, erratic video shot, illuminated initially only by street lights, then only by muzzle flashes. Those Taurans awake and watching saw an ARE-12P's turret rapidly turn and begin to fire. The camera swung to follow the tracers. A lone Balboan, without a visible weapon—his pistol was hidden by his far more prominent aid bag—ran across the street. On the videotape his medic's armband, white with a red cross, stood out. A burst of fire, heard but unseen by the camera, was made plain by the medic's "Spandau ballet." The image died, as the medic had, spinning to the end.

"What did you do then, *señor*?"

De la Mesa looked at Strider as if he were stupid, or crazy, or both. "Then? Then everybody in the world started shooting! I ducked and ran to the back of my apartment. What do you think I did?"

The camera closed again on Strider, cutting de la Mesa out of view. "Back to you, Guillaume," said Strider.

Estado Mayor, Ciudad Balboa, Balboa, Terra Nova

Sitting in his wheelchair at Headquarters, watching television, Fernandez smiled as he watched one of his better agents. *You've earned yourself a hefty bonus, de la Mesa.*

Roughly halfway between Balboa City Train Station and *Avenida de la Santa Maria, Ciudad* Balboa, Balboa, Terra Nova

"We can't hold 'em much longer, Top," said Porras. Blood seeped out from a bandage that bound the lieutenant's chest, courtesy of a near miss from an IFV's cannon. Air gurgled, frothing the blood; it was a sucking chest wound. Of the seventy-seven men the platoon had started with, assigned and attached, fewer than thirty remained. Many of those were wounded, some badly. The dead, and some of those wounded too badly to risk moving had—reluctantly—been left behind.

"Yeah, but they can't attack much longer either, sir. But... well... we're down to less than a magazine per man."

Porras nodded agreement. He spoke in a voice no louder than his collapsing lung permitted, "Pass the word, Top. Fix Bayonets! Pass it loud. Let the bloody Gauls hear."

Cruz smiled what he fully expected would be his last smile. "Maniple . . . Fix! Bayonets!" He reached to unsnap his own bayonet.

In the relatively open area here there wasn't nearly as much reason to keep the infantry in the fight. The bulk of the killing, on both sides, was being done by the armor, Puma Tanks, SPATHA tank destroyers, and Ocelots, on the one side, Roland tanks and ARE-12P infantry fighting vehicles on the other.

With real surprise lost, the fight had been much more even. Meter by meter, the rest of the 420th had pushed the Balboans back. Both sides had paid dearly, the Taurans for every meter gained, the Balboans for each minute.

Against the frontal armor of the Tauran tanks the main guns of the Pumas proved useless, although a lucky side shot had left a sixty-ton behemoth dead in the road. Even less effective were the 100mm guns of the Ocelots. Only the "demo guns" of the SPATHAs had been able to deal with the frontal armor of the Rolands. Better said, they had proven able to smash the crews; the armor remained mostly intact. In all, five Rolands had been left, burned out or smashed hulks. All twelve pieces of the Second Cohort's little armored force that had made it to the vicinity of the fighting had paid the ultimate price for those kills.

With the Balboan armor crushed, the Rolands had pushed on alone. The IFVs were too lightly armored to risk keeping up. So, when the Taurans had closed to within range of Porras's infantry, the recoilless guns and RGL launchers had had their own fight of it. The tanks had won, but at the cost of two more of their number—one to a mine, another to a side shot from an RGL. Porras's infantry had paid a higher price—a dozen men dead or wounded, but the tanks had pulled back, calling for the infantry to take the lead in the tightening terrain.

Under cover of the remaining tanks' fire, the Tauran infantry had cut left and right, one company each going after the platoons the maniple commander had pushed up to support Porras on his left and right. In vicious close fighting they had driven the Balboans back from one hastily chosen defensive position to another. Still, each mechanized infantry company could dismount no more than sixty foot soldiers. The lonely grunts had bled equally along with the Balboans once outside of covering fire from their IFVs.

They had bled so much, in fact, that a further advance was almost impossible. Still, they were Gauls and, as such, they were willing to try.

The Tunnel, *Cerro Mina,* Balboa, Terra Nova

Inside, inside where it couldn't be seen, Janier bled with his troops. *And that surprised me more than anything. I thought I was above all that silly sentimentality. Does this carnage bother Carrera, I wonder? Do people mean anything to him? I'll be they do. I'll bet he bleeds as I do.*

"General," said Malcoeur, "it's the Union Security Council, in the form of Monsieur Gaymard."

"Janier, here," said the general, after taking the ancient black phone. "No, sir, it isn't possible to defeat the Balboans with the force I have on hand here. It isn't possible to defend the Transitway with the forces I have here.... No, sir, I don't think the Balboans intend to attack the Transitway, unless we escalate the fighting.... I didn't give air support to the soldiers engaged because I had reason to believe that Arnold Air Force Base would have been shelled to ruin if the Balboan commander had been told we were getting ready to do so.... Yes, they did shell Brookings rather badly.... If you will recall, sir, I asked for two aircraft carriers to support us before we started the Green Monsoons again.... Monsieur, the Balboans had aircraft in the air and didn't use them to support their troops.... Mr. President, it was on *your* orders, yours and the rest of the Council's, that I began the provocations again.... Yes, sir, I do have copies of those orders.... No, sir, I will *not* destroy them.... Of *course* you didn't mean to suggest anything illegal, sir.

...."No, it's not possible...I have eleven maneuver battalions in Balboa now. One is practically destroyed. One is scattered across the Jungle School and can't be collected for some hours yet. One is a commando battalion uniquely ill-suited for heavy combat. For the remaining eight there are another twenty uncommitted battalions of Balboans mobilized and ready to fight immediately. There could be another fifteen here in a matter of hours; at most a day. And against my four battalions of artillery I am facing the equivalent of fifteen or twenty from Balboa immediately, thirty or forty in time.... Yes, I think that's right. If we escalate the fighting we *will* lose, badly. No, 'badly' isn't strong enough. We'll lose stinking. I think the Balboans have proven they can and will fight, sir.... Yes, sir. It *is* a pity they're not like the Sumeris.... No, sir. If you try to send me reinforcements from the Tauran Union in any form I will be ass deep in the Transitway before they get here. Our plan was only good if the Balboans were not mobilized. They are certainly mobilized now.

"Very well, Monsieur. I will order the 420th Dragoons to withdraw to base."

Roughly halfway between Balboa City Train Station and *Avenida de la Santa Maria, Ciudad* Balboa, Balboa, Terra Nova

"This Second Platoon, Second Company?" asked a dirt smudged senior centurion. In the dim light he didn't recognize either Cruz or the unconscious Porras, lying beside him. Unable to speak at the moment, Cruz just nodded his head. A rifle with a blood-stained bayonet lay across his legs, the bayonet beginning to shine a faint pink by the light of the just rising sun.

"Sergeant Major," asked the centurion, incredulously, "is that *you*?"

Again, Cruz could only nod.

"Sorry we took so long, Sergeant Major. Had to help this maniple's first platoon before coming here. Their CO's hit, but he's going to make it. We'll pass through you and move to contact as far as the boundary. There's ambulances coming for your wounded...and the Taurans."

"Good...good," answered Cruz.

The centurion said, "Hell of a job these guys did, *hell* of a job. How many they got left?"

"Twelve that I can count," answered Cruz.

"'Second to None.'" quoted the other centurion. Then he gestured for his men to advance.

Tauran News Network, Headline News Studios, Lumière, Gaul, Terra Nova

"General Bigeard, what does this all mean?" asked the vapid faced host.

"It *means*," answered the retired Gallic four star, aged, bald, with just a thin patina of the strength and force that had once carried him to the top, "that we can't have our way in Balboa any longer. It means that the Tauran Union has actually lost its first and only battle in history. It *means* that any pretense to Balboa needing us to defend the Transitway is just that, a pretense. It means that the pernicious safety constraints imposed on all Tauran armed forces by Marine R.E.S. Mors du Char the Fourth have come to fruition. We can't fight anymore."

"On the other hand," continued Bigeard. "They can obviously fight on their own."

The host turned to face the camera. "For those of you just joining us, as you may have heard already, serious fighting broke out between Balboa and the Tauran Union about six hours ago. It cannot yet be ascertained whether this will result in general hostilities, but word on Tauran casualties suggests that they are *very* heavy, at least eighty Tauran soldiers have been killed, a larger number wounded in action. Balboan losses are said to be heavier still. I have with me General Marc Bigeard, one time Chief of Staff of the Army of the Gallic Republic."

The talking head returned his attention to the retired old soldier. "General, what do you make of the videotape we saw a few moments ago that shows Tauran soldiers opening fire first?"

"The tape," Bigeard pointed out, "only speaks partly for itself. A lot of questions remain unanswered: Why did our soldiers open fire? What were so many Balboan soldiers doing in that place and time? Perhaps most importantly, why were Tauran soldiers sent in harm's way if the Tauran Union was not prepared to support them? The Tauran Union Security Council has much to answer for."

Cerro Mina Inn, *Ciudad* Balboa, Balboa, Terra Nova

Carrera walked solemnly among the wounded being cared for on the floor of the brothel. Chin and Second Cohort's Commander, Velasquez, met him and reported.

"How badly off are you, Velasquez?" Carrera asked of the cohort commander.

"Bad, *Duque*," Velasquez replied. "My cohort's been hurt badly." He gulped before speaking further. "We know we've got, maybe, a hundred and thirty, maybe a hundred and forty dead. I think another twenty or thirty are going to die. Wounded? Damn near everybody in First and Second Maniples to one degree or another.... But...we held 'em, sir. We held 'em."

"The Taurans?"

Chin answered, "We've recovered a hundred and twelve bodies, last I checked. We've also got about sixty prisoners. Almost *all* of them are wounded. They're being cared for along with our own. Then there are some *things,* piles of ashes, in some of the tracks, that might be...probably are...Gallic troops."

Carrera nodded understanding. "Okay. You and your men were splendid, Velasquez. You may have even bought us peace." Carrera reached into a pocket and pulled out a set of insignia for the next higher step in rank. He handed them to Velasquez and said, "Put these on, *Legate...Permanently.* And tell your boys, what's left of them, that the men of Second Cohort, Second Tercio, who fought here today, plus all of their attachments, are to assume their full, mobilization level-three ranks, when on duty, until they retire or are discharged. We'll work up a citation for the unit in the next few days. Now you have things to do. Go do them."

Velasquez saluted and was turning to go when Carrera stopped him again. "One other thing. Two-Two will not die. Whatever it takes to rebuild your tremendous cohort so it can continue to serve the Republic will be done."

"Thank you, sir." Velasquez left.

Carrera shook hands with Chin and left the building. Lourdes had been waiting with Soult outside. He joined her there. She had wanted to go inside but could not bring herself to do so. The cries of pain were just too horrible.

Followed by three radios and a half-dozen guards, Carrera and his wife walked south toward Balboa City's Central Avenue. Wounded were being treated and dead collected there, with Second Cohort's Medical Platoon centurion, aided by a doctor from the tercio medical company, overseeing the evacuations.

Carrera's first impulse was to walk to the wounded. However another scene caught his eye. A woman, no longer young, was searching for someone. A soldier lifted the poncho from the face of one corpse after another. At each the old woman shook her head. Finally, the soldier pulled a poncho from the particular face for which she had been searching. Putting her hands to her face, the woman fell to her knees and buried her face against the blood-stained chest of her only son, her hope for the future. Her body shook with sobs. If she cried aloud, the sound was muffled by her son's body.

Carrera turned from his intended path to go to the woman's side. He let her cry a while longer, then, together with the soldier, he pulled her to her feet. Wrapping the old woman in a hug, he heard her ask, over and over "Why? Why?"

Because of me, Old Mother. Only because of me. Your son? I feel no pity for him, he is past all pain. If anything, I feel a certain envy. All my sympathy is for you, left alone in the world as I was once left alone. Mourn, that is proper. But don't fear. I will take care of you. Or, rather, my Balboa will.

PART V

CHAPTER THIRTY-TWO

Days of quiet for us have come now,
Day of learning and of work.
So that calmly, quietly will bloom
Our villages and towns...

Soldiers on the march, the march, the march
And for you your own field mail is waiting
But hark the trumpet calls
And soldiers march on.

—"Soldat y've put,"
Volgan Traditional

Palacio de las Trixies, *Ciudad* Balboa, Republic of Balboa, Terra Nova

It was evening, with a pleasant breeze blowing from off the *Mar Furioso*. The presidential palace was quiet for the nonce as the trixies had left the roost for a while, hunting *antaniae*. To Parilla, Carrera seemed exhausted, and not from the post adrenaline let down after the battle with the Taurans. No, his exhaustion seemed to go all the way to the soul.

My friend, thought Parilla, *is in serious need of a break.*

Damn, thought Carrera, *I so need to take a couple of weeks... or months... or years mostly off.*

"You, my friend, are one lucky bastard," said *Presidente* Parilla. "So are all of us."

"How's that?" asked Carrera. Before Parilla answered he chugged down a good three fingers' worth of sipping rum then reached for the bottle to add more.

"No war. The shocked-ever-so-silly Taurans are going to give up on trying to get rid of us."

Carrera shrugged. "War might have broken out, it's true. But only if the Tauran Union had been of a single mind. Fortunately, the Tauran Union has *never*—'What, never? No, never!'—been of a single mind in its history, to date.

"Among conservative circles there was a strong feeling that nothing in Balboa—or anywhere in the world that had no oil reserves or rare metals—was worth a drop of Tauran sweat, to say nothing of Tauran blood. Revenge did not seem like a good enough reason to go to war when it *did* appear—good old Fernandez and his man with the camera!—that we had only been defending our own country."

Carrera then sneered, more or less by instinct. "More liberal groups were more radically split. Some—the remnants of those who hated their own countries and cultures so much that they had once thought it a fine thing to support any guerrilla or terrorist movement so long as its aims were anti-Tauran or anti-Federated States—cheered what they saw as a defeat of Tauran arms. Others, and I find these the more respectable by far, mourned any loss of life, Tauran or Balboan, or just plain old human, for that matter. Of course, revenge was a completely inadequate reason for any of these to want war.

"Then there are our own sorts, Latins living in the Tauran Union. They were torn between patriotism for their adopted countries and a certain cultural pride. I understand there were refugees from Tsarist Marxism, who totally hated Marxism in all its versions, who—Zhong or Cochinese or Uhuran—were still full of pride when their former peoples beat Taurans and South Columbians.

"You know," observed the president, "that the Tauran Union has renounced neither its stated right to intervene in Balboa, nor to maintain bases on Balboan soil in perpetuity, nor to avoid provoking the legion."

"They'll get sick of staying," Carrera said. "A riot here, a riot there...their own people pushing to get them to leave...and our budget to support those people isn't even especially high. They'll be gone in time and instead of losing twenty or thirty or forty thousand fine young men, and some women, too, of course, we got off with a few hundred dead and wounded."

"There are still some major issues," said the president. "The drachma embargo remains in place..."

"Sure," Carrera agreed, "in theory. But—years after unsuccessful years of trying to break us that way, our people and theirs always find a way around it. I don't think the Taurans even try to prevent it anymore." Carrera snorted, mirthfully. "Hell, if anything, the drachma embargo makes your government more popular than ever."

"Yes, I suspect it does," said Parilla. "It's also gotten us sympathy to help us form mutual defense treaties with half of the other states of Colombia del Norte."

"That's even better at the moment," said Carrera. "You need to lean on the diplomatic folks because the rest, maybe minus Santa Josefina, should be joining us very soon, too. After several hundred years of outrageously pushy and arrogant Tauran imperialism, there are pro-Balboa demonstrations in the streets from la Plata to Atzlan."

"Hmmm..." Parilla mused on the prospect of killing a couple of birds with one stone. "Why don't you and the wife take a tour? You can see some sights about this part of the world, while standing in as a national symbol in those countries sympathetic to us."

"Maybe...just maybe," agreed the *Duque.*

"I hear they're pulling Janier out?" said Parilla.

"Yeah," Carrera agreed. "Fernandez passed that to me, too; kicking Janier upstairs to some caretaker position, maybe, or maybe putting him in as Chief of Staff to the new Tauran Union Combined Staff. I'll be interested in seeing who they appoint here to take his place."

Carrera and Lourdes did take their vacation, while from his end Parilla pushed for a mutual defense treaty with all of the other states of Colombia Latina. There was already a treaty with many, but Balboa needed more. True, it was something of a rush job but in the general euphoria over Latin troops holding their own against Taurans, the treaty was ratified everywhere but Santa Josefina, where President Calderón refused to submit it to the legislature, and Cienfuegos which, as one of the last Tsarist-Marxist states on the planet, found Balboa's timocracy loathsome in the extreme.

Why it passed so easily everywhere else was a matter of some conjecture. Some said it was pride. Others fear. A few cynics maintained that the rest of Colombia Latina signed on only because there was so little prospect, after the battle, of actually having to fight Taurus.

The key points of the treaty, from Balboa's perspective, were that specific military organizations from other Latin states were identified for defense of the Transitway. Atzlan, for example, pledged its Parachute Brigade and committed to rotating its battalions through Balboa, one for a few months every year to train with the legion. Lempira and Valdivia offered highly trained battalions of mountain troops, one each. La Plata offered a regiment of Marines as did its Portuguese-speaking rival to its south. Other states offered battalions of infantry as they were able, twelve in all. To help ensure quality, Balboa began to supplement training for these units; some in their own countries, others with training rotations at the training center in Balboa's *Fuerte* Cameron. Balboan military schools, including Cazador School, were opened up rather liberally to allied Latin states.

Four extra tercio headquarters, Fortieth through Forty-third, were authorized and raised. These took over the training and partial support of the twelve miscellaneous Latin battalions under their wings. Fifth Tercio did the same for the mountain troops. In assigning allied Latin battalions to the headquarters, great care was taken to keep traditional enemies and rivals apart. Thus, for example, one newly formed allied tercio had troops from La Plata, Pizarro, and Bolivar, but certainly none from Valdivia and definitely no one who spoke Portuguese. And for the battalions from Colombia Central, one had to be most careful not to put Lempirans and their neighbors together. Since everyone in Colombia del Sur detested Stroessnerns, they were meshed with two battalions from Colombia Central.

The service support and combat support troops the new tercios would need were raised in Balboa itself, although in three different ways. Additional maniples were authorized in the already existing service support tercios of the legion, as a whole. The combat support tercios of the brigade, legions, and corps which would receive the foreign troops also added maniples. The artillery already existed in the artillery tercios of the legion.

There was also a brigade of Sumeri Presidential Guard promised by Adnan Sada, but that was a personal agreement between him and Carrera, and not a matter of treaty or diplomacy.

Despite the expense, and it was not small, of raising those new troops and supplementing the training of the foreign units, Carrera was able to cut back on military expenses to a significant degree. The primary reason for that was that, except for the Megalodon class coastal defense submarines, and the Condors—which were still coming off the local assembly lines and slipways—plus ammunition for training, Carrera had already bought and stored almost all of the equipment and supplies he believed he needed to defend the country. It had cost many billions and had a limited useful life span, but he was able—for a time—to sharply reduce capital expenditures.

There followed what was probably the greatest surge in the Balboan economy since the FSC had gone home after their invasion and the government had been able to sell off abandoned real estate to insiders. With massive investment in the economy made possible by the Cristobal Free Zone Tax, drug lords' tribute, various sources of foreign aid, some of it somewhat reluctantly given, unemployment nationwide dropped to the lowest level in Latin Columbia. Among veterans and volunteers, some ten percent of the population, unemployment was almost precisely nothing. The exceptions were the very few; rich members of the legion, and there were some, and the rather larger number going to school full time. And those last weren't precisely unemployed. Carrera's enterprises were also able to increase Balboa's exports to a healthy degree; lumber, scrap steel, canned food, clothing, footwear, minor electronics, weapons, ammunition, and other goods flowed from Balboa as far north as La Plata and as far south as Secordia. Some also went to Uhuru, Taurania, and the island country of Wellington.

Although "trickle down economics" garnered much scorn in most of the planet's progressive circles, it seemed to work well enough in Balboa. In part this was because most of the money spent by Carrera and the legion went into common people's pockets where it was reasonably sure to be spent, almost always on something that would help another Balboan stay employed. The rest was because the average resident of Balboa expected, and received, so little of his or her government in the way of social benefits that the policy caused no reduction in government income and no loss to already nonexistent income redistribution programs. The government had little in direct tax revenues to redistribute in any event.

Tourism—the Transitway was still a big draw—enjoyed something of a renaissance as well. After all, Balboa City was cheaper, warmer, cleaner, more cosmopolitan, and—especially for older and wealthier tourists—safer than anyplace else they were likely to find. Moreover, English was widely spoken. Only the capital of Cienfuegos could boast an equal degree of safety... but that capital, Batabanó, was almost entirely run down after decades of embargo and Tsarist-Marxist misrule and economic mismanagement. Also, and unlike Balboa, no appreciable percentage of the world's commerce, in fact, none of it, actually *had* to pass through Cienfuegos.

Of course, that safety came at a price. The domestic criminal code of Balboa, it was said, was written in blood, not ink. And that whole thing about cruel and unusual punishments being bad things? Yeah, completely lost on the Balboan Senate.

On the other hand, freedom of religion, the right of free *peaceful* assembly—indeed, most of the rights once enshrined in a constitution of a long disappeared major state on Old Earth— were respected scrupulously, albeit under interpretations that Thomas Jefferson would have found more understandable than did the Federated States Supreme Court. And with over a third of a million fully automatic weapons in the hands of individuals, gun control would have been something of a joke.

Freedom of the press was more problematic. The legion had always taken a dim view of people who used their position as journalists to fight for, spy or scout for, or serve as propagandists for, the other side. This had been true in Sumer, in Pashtia, in La Palma Province, and was still true in the country as a whole.

Several reporters—local and international—had been shot or hanged for espionage or some other infraction before the rest took the hint. The actual rule was quite simple: "Look at anything you want that you can get physical access to (most facilities were well guarded); report what you wish; but give up the smallest scrap of militarily valuable information, or demonstrate that you're working for our enemies and you *become* the enemy... and go before a firing squad or to the hangman if we can catch you. And we'll certainly try."

Mostly the media contented itself with reporting the allegedly widespread dissatisfaction with Balboa's government. In fact, such dissatisfaction *was* fairly widespread among certain elements of the population. At another level of society, however, among people who had well-paying jobs—by Balboan standards—and hope for a better future for the first time in memory, it was said that with Parilla there was no freedom to starve...unless one really wanted to.

Still, a small community of Balboan expatriates grew up around the capital of Hamilton in the Federated States of Columbia. A hundred or so of these were disgruntled police cast off by Carrera in the years after the attempted coup by the late (crucified) Legate Pigna. These tended to look to Endara-Rocaberti as their natural leader and spokesman. They were also obvious enough to attract the attention of the high admiral, from her perch aboard the *Spirit of Peace.*

Wallenstein could hardly help take note of a minor crisis, involving the press. This came about when, in accordance with established Tauran and Federated States jurisprudence concerning jurisdiction, a bound and gagged Wally Barker was deposited on the doorstep of the criminal court building in *Ciudad* Balboa. Mr. Barker had been kidnapped by a team from the Fourteenth Cazador Tercio while he was on vacation in Atzlan, allegedly with the aid of the Atzlan Brigade of *Paracaidistas.* The Supreme Court of Balboa, taking its cue from the Tauran Union's Supreme Court, determined that it was not its business precisely *how* the weasel reporter had arrived in Balboa. He *was* in Balboa and the Court had jurisdiction.

Barker was tried in camera within days for "Attempting to Foment Aggressive War" and sentenced to loss of his nose—some poetic justice there—one hundred lashes, death by hanging...and fifty drachmas in court costs. He was publicly flogged and the money taken from some found in his wallet, but the execution and loss of his nose were temporarily suspended. The Tauran ambassador was told not to protest and to advise his government not to interfere unless they were seriously interested in war, because if the Tauran Union did interfere Barker *would* be mutilated and hanged.

When the Tauran Union Security Council kept silent but for a couple of "*Tsk-tsk*'s," Carrera determined that the Tauran Union really had finally given up on the idea of invasion. After all, he had told them he was prepared to give them a good excuse to invade and they had not taken it. A week after the flogging Barker, his back still in shreds, was deposited on the embassy doorstep. A note pinned to his shirt advised that his remaining sentences were suspended indefinitely on condition he *never* return to—or publicly mention the name of—the Republic of Balboa.

And, outside of furious but impotent protests from the news media, that was the end of that. Even the media soon realized that in the eyes of most readers and viewers, for the *potential* magnitude of the crime, the Balboans had been fairly merciful.

With the *Legion del Cid*, an exhausted Carrera simply had to loosen the reins. As often happened with well-trained units in any army, this loosening of the reins did not mean that the legion fell to pieces. Rather, the tercios began to pick up speed in their training. Carrera had long since ruthlessly purged the force of every slug that could be identified. Now, with nearly four hundred thousand imaginations brought to bear, just as the imagination of Corporal Ruiz had come up with a unique way to hide landmines, so the legion became, if anything, tougher, smarter, and quicker.

The more than decimated Second Cohort, Second Tercio was given a massive influx of support. Recruiting boundaries were shifted slightly to give it more of a population base to draw recruits from. Both the rest of Second and Third Corps were combed for volunteers to refill the one cohort that had fought the Taurans to a standstill. There were many volunteers. In addition, Carrera authorized additional training days for the unit to allow it to bring its new men back up to the same standard as the rest of the legion. Cruz stayed on as cohort sergeant major, while Porras received an early promotion to junior tribune.

Lourdes used the extra time Carrera spent at home or traveling with her wisely and well. Her fourth child, another girl, was ushered into this world without problem about ten months after the battle with the Gauls. Unfortunately, Lourdes was slender and her babies large. On her doctor's advice, the fourth child, also named Lourdes, had to be her last.

Carrera discovered that he liked being a family man again. More to his surprise, he found as much satisfaction in dedicating a new school building, library or clinic as he did in watching a cohort go through a deliberate attack. For the first time in two decades, near enough, he found himself to be happy, and his life balanced and full. He still woke up from time to time with richly satisfying dreams of warring against the Tauran Union. He still planned and prepared for having to do so. But he did not, as he had once planned, do anything to provoke such a war.

Casa Linda, Balboa, Terra Nova

Pililak was devastated. Ham would be home on leave from the academy in just a few months and she *still* hadn't been able to escape to join him, proving thereby her devotion to him in a way that would set her apart from his other wives... or, for that matter, his sisters.

She could almost cry. She *would* have cried if she hadn't been from a people who were about as hard as nails.

Every time I thought I was ready, I thought of something else that needed doing or, if not needed, would at least be good to have ready. Or, if I thought of it early, it took much time... or it took much time and then, as with the food I stashed, the rats and bugs got to it. And then there were the things Alena the witch said, that made me think of still other problems.

And now he's coming home and I will just be one among many. I don't even deserve for him to think I'm special or important, since I've failed so miserably in this one thing I set my heart on.

"Ah, to Hell with it," Ant said, in her native tongue. "If I haven't got everything ready in the next five weeks I am going to go anyway."

Alena, who, again, was more likely to have been simply a supremely observant and intelligent woman than a witch, overheard little Ant and thought, *About time. How many suggestions did I have to give you to make sure you got yourself ready for this? Silly little girl. Go to our god soon. And make for us all the sixth sign.*

CHAPTER THIRTY-THREE

Feminism, Socialism and Communism are one and
the same, and Socialist/Communist government is
the goal of feminism.

—Catharine MacKinnon, *Toward
a Feminist Theory of the State*

Hamilton FD, Federated States of Columbia, Terra Nova

Not a lot had been heard from Belisario Endara-Rocaberti after
he'd taken Parilla's secretary Luci, and fled the country. He, and
she, had had excellent reason to flee, of course, since the assassination they'd set Carrera up for had failed and since he was
known to be unforgiving, unrelenting, and remarkably vindictive
and vicious. Thus, while the couple had initially put down stakes
in Aserri, Santa Josefina, they'd soon realized that that was far
too close to Patricio Carrera for health and safety. They'd fled
then to the Federated States, where Carrera could probably still
reach, but which he was also probably loath to annoy.

Endara'd married Luci then, in the capital city of Hamilton. A
joint meeting with the then-president of the Federated States, Karl
Schumann, had disabused him of the notion that the marriage
was going to be an exclusive relationship. At least, if he wanted
a hearing with the president, he'd best be willing to share such
a bounty. Luci? Sure, she'd been willing enough. However, when
Schumann had used her thoroughly, but never helped her husband
return to power, while his successor, Walter Madison Howe, had
done no better, she'd grown quite disillusioned.

And the last one, Howe, at least, had been true to his word. He, unlike Schumann, had listened to all petitions carefully and attentively, provided such petitions were carried by the quite beautiful and large-breasted Luci, wearing nothing but perhaps a pair of kneepads. He'd even provided a house and government-funded security for the couple. He'd even sent an official vehicle to pick up Luci for her fortnightly dates with his cock. But war? No, he wasn't interested. He'd also advised against wasting time with the Tauran Union, since they were even less interested in war than the Federated States was.

Now, with even the hope of Tauran intervention apparently gone, an unhappy Belisario Endara-Rocaberti sat with Luci in their government-provided house. He cursed his own weakness, cursed the fact that he had to share his wife with the president of the FSC, cursed life, and cursed fate. Even the coming of the New Year, normally a greater festival for Balboans than for gringos, failed to improve his mood. He drank without enjoyment. The sounds of celebration coming faintly from the street below were anathema to his ears. The delicacies spread before him tasted of ashes. He was curt and unpleasant to Luci when she tried to make conversation. He'd actually been losing some of the lard he could afford to dispense with, though his girth was still a large fraction of his height.

"Well, it isn't *my* damned fault," Luci countered. "I've done everything you wanted me to; a lot more than you have done yourself to return to Balboa." She crossed her arms over her breasts—large-breasted female sign of disapproval and rejection—in a huff.

Endara-Rocaberti relented. "I... I'm sorry. I know it isn't your fault. But it just seems we're further away from coming back to power than we ever were. Nothing works. Their fucking president won't talk to me anymore. 'Too busy,' his aides say. 'He's working on the problem,' they say. What a load of horse manure."

Luci hung her head. "He doesn't want me much either. Not since his wife—the *tortillera* bitch—caught us in bed. I really don't see any point in continuing to see him at all."

Belisario Endara-Rocaberti sat up suddenly, the beginnings of an idea forming. The mention of the first lady caused him to think hard for a few moments, then a thin smile widened on his face.

"Luci, my very dear... how far would you be willing to go to give us some influence again?"

The woman looked intently at her nominal husband but without understanding. Then, with understanding, came disgust, nausea forming from enlightenment. "Oh, I *couldn't*; not possibly. Not that! And especially not with her, for all that she licks her lips when she looks at my chest."

"Easy to understand," said Belisario smoothly, "since that skinny, dark-skinned *houri* she sleeps with has no tits to speak of. As to whether you could; of course you could. You are the finest actress in the world. You can pretend to be anything you want to ... or need to."

She was adamant, however. "But ... Belisario. I've done a lot but I've never done that. I wouldn't know what to do. Really I wouldn't."

Endara-Rocaberti walked across the room to pick up a telephone book. He thumbed to the "E" pages. "Don't worry about that. We can hire a technical expert to teach you. I'll enjoy watching the lessons."

"Listen to me!" she shouted, stamping her dainty foot. "I've done a lot for you ... for me, too. But this is too much. I will not go to bed with that woman, not if you—or she!—offered me the world. Even if she *is* more of a man than her husband. Find another way."

Belisario, reluctantly, closed the phone book. "Very well," he said, "we'll see what turns up. Maybe we should move ... to Tauran. Maybe to Anglia."

"I'd *love* to get the dust of this place off my feet," she said. "What brings up Anglia, anyway?"

"Oh, there's some female supremacist woman there, Patricia Britain, who's been complaining about Balboa not giving the vote to women."

"But they do," said Luci. "If the women finish a term with the legion."

"I'm reasonably sure," said Belisario, "that Britain could care less about men not being given the vote, gratis, but is deeply offended by the notion that women must earn it, too."

"Well, of course," said Luci. *And maybe I should have just stayed there and done a term myself. And never got involved in trying to kill the boss's right-hand man. God, was that fucking stupid!*

"Hmmm ... maybe I should send you to talk to her," suggested Belisario.

"If you mean talk, fine," she answered. "But if you mean let her lunch me, or vice versa, no."

"Just talk," he assured her. "Might be useful. You want me to make the arrangements?"

"Last time you 'made the arrangements' I ended up blowing the president of the Federated States. Both of the last two. Dozens of times each. And for no good purpose whatsoever. So I'll make my own arrangements, thank you very much."

Masque Hall, Marylebone, Anglia, Terra Nova

Luci did make her own arrangements, except that the Anglian female supremacist, Patricia Britain, set her up with a suite not too far from the old palace at Marylebone. Since Balboa was Britain's current obsession, she'd been thrilled to host the wife of the one everybody who mattered assumed was the rightful ruler of Balboa.

Patricia Britain was, it turned out, better looking than the first lady of the Federated States. This was still not particularly good looking, and certainly nothing that would have tempted Luci to consider sleeping with her. As it turned out, though, that wasn't necessary. Britain had both a husband, male, and a partner, female. The partner, Renee Feist, was also a devout Tsarist-Marxist, thus of somewhat mixed feelings toward Balboa, given its heavy increment of socialism.

Luci had been around power most of her life. She was used to cynicism, corruption, and hypocrisy. What she was totally unfamiliar with was political sincerity. Britain and Feist just oozed it, so much so that it took Luci the better part of an hour before she could be certain the sincerity wasn't an act.

She could tell they were sincere by the way the two women argued with each other, in this spacious basement office of a former government building, now gone to charitable uses.

Britain stood and paced. "If we don't go forward we must go back!" she declaimed to the walls. "We can't afford any chink in our armor. Every little place that refuses to accord equal rights to women is a bad example to men here and everywhere."

"It's not just about women, though," answered Feist, seated and calmer. "There are questions of class involved here and, whatever else they may have done or may do in the future, the rulers of Balboa have made massive strides in elevating the working class."

Feist looked at Luci for confirmation. The Balboan woman nodded her head, briskly, saying, "Well ... yes. But only for some.

There are still plenty of poor they have no interest in. And the opportunities they provide for poor women are highly limited."

"That's true, as far as it goes," agreed Feist, "but I understand they're making or may have already made a regiment to create more opportunities for women."

"I heard that, too," half-shouted Britain, still in declamation mode. "It's a sop, a token force, with no consciousness of their prime duty as women to women. They're just traitors to the cause."

"Traitors to which cause?" asked Feist, a touch of heat rising in her voice. "There are two causes here. One, the cause of the working masses, the Balboan soldier women are supporting."

"That, after tens of thousands of years of patriarchal oppression," said Britain, still more heatedly, "is secondary."

"Never!" said Feist.

"Always!" said Britain.

They're fucking serious about this shit, thought Luci. *How very odd.*

"Put Tsarist-Marxists in charge and women will rise automatically!" shouted Feist.

"Put women in charge and Socialism will come as naturally as the rising of the sun!" shouted back Britain. "Feminism *is* Marxism!"

And how many angels can dance on the head of a pin? thought Luci. *Because you two are just arguing religion.*

"Feminism is socialist and pacifist, first and foremost," said Feist.

"Bah," said Britain. "A soldier's job is to defend our rights, which means women's rights. And *our* rights are threatened by the government in Balboa. Hell, *our* rights are threatened right here and in the Federated States. Do you realize that after the battle in Balboa even the *Army* is beginning to question the degree of opportunity it has opened to women? Naturally we've beaten them into submission again, the uniformed *castrati*, but another disaster like that and we could set the clock back in the military, then in the whole Tauran Union, by decades."

Lesbian they may be, thought Luci, *but if sex were really important to them they'd be paying a lot more attention to me than they are. No, they care about religion and their religion is politics.* She suddenly had a perverse image, rather a couple of them, of the two women taking turns performing oral sex on each other. In the first image, Britain, receiving oral sex from Feist, declaimed, *"Let the ruling classes tremble at a Communist revolution. The proletarians have nothing to lose but their chains."* In the second, with Feist sitting on Britain's face, she spouted, *"They have a world to win. Working men of all countries, unite!"*

Luci couldn't help it; she started to giggle. This got her dirty looks from both Britain and Feist. She stifled the sound.

Still, the magic of argument was broken. "You really think they might start to push back?" asked Feist. "Hard to believe, as emasculated as they are, but..."

She grew thoughtful. "Hmmm. Maybe the thing to do is to fight them politically in Balboa since the Tauran Union now refuses to fight them militarily."

"How do we do that?" asked Britain.

"Well, what if we start sending missions to Balboa to rally its women, rebuild the women's movement there? If it doesn't work we're no worse off than we were. If it works partly then they'll probably repress it pretty violently—it's how their dictator and his chief stormtrooper think. A few images on TNN of Balboan women being beaten in the streets by legionary thugs might change things. And it is possible that we could succeed; swing the women back to our way of thinking and have them sway the men. It worked here, after all."

They both turned to look at Luci. "What do you think, my dear?" asked Feist.

"Might work," was all she could offer, what with having to put so much effort into the giggle suppression campaign. The twin images, side by side in her mind, just wouldn't go away.

Ciudad Balboa, Balboa, Terra Nova

But it did *not* work in Balboa. Groups of well-meaning, and often quite eloquent, Spanish-speaking feminists duly went to the Republic; about one such group a month. They were not arrested. They were not harassed. They appeared to be pointedly ignored by the Balboan government, although, in fact, some tabs were kept on them for their own safety's sake.

Not that these groups couldn't drum up an audience. The entertainment value alone was too high to permit their being totally ignored. They were also, invariably, interviewed on every television channel except *TeleVision Militar*. Then, too, local feminist groups—there were still a few that were active—bought advertising and put up posters; all to little, if any, avail.

Upon returning, the Tauran feminists did greatly play up their imagined dangers, and their almost as imaginary successes. It's possible that some television viewers in the Tauran Union were persuaded that there was a great groundswell of support for women's rights in Balboa and that their heroines in men's clothing were daily braving martyrdom. At least, they might have been if heavily predisposed toward fantasy.

However, as one member of a Balboan audience put it to one of the missionary groups: "You are missing the point. Yes, if men as a whole had the vote we could make them feel guilty enough to give it back to us, too. But they do not. And those who do, or will, will have paid a great price for it. They will not share with anybody who hasn't paid that price. And they don't feel even a little bit guilty about it, quite the reverse. Most women, here or anywhere, probably can't or won't pay that price. And the women who do, or will? They're worse than the men. So, unless the Tauran Union can force Balboa into giving us back our political rights, you are wasting your time...and ours."

Masque Hall, Marylebone, Anglia, Terra Nova

Britain and Feist exchanged a chaste kiss. After all, neither was quite as young as she'd once been and Luci had flown over for the meeting. Maybe, just maybe, if she'd shown an interest they might not have kissed quite so chastely but, alas, so many women just didn't understand what they were missing...

The three sat down to chat.

"It just isn't working, none of it," admitted Feist. She was not one of those fooled into believing there was any real progress in Balboa. "You may as well call off the missionaries. It's just good money after bad."

"Don't be silly, my dear," answered Britain. "Why, we've hardly started. Attendance at our rallies in Balboa is up by an appreciable fraction. Our surveys show an increase in the number of Balboan men who want to reenfranchise the women. It isn't all bad."

"Any of the men in those surveys have the vote themselves?" asked Luci.

"Some. A few." At Luci's raised eyebrow, Britain admitted, "Okay, two. But that's two more than we had last month."

After a moment's hesitation Britain blurted out, "Let me try one more thing before we give up. Let me go to Balboa with a few select women. Maybe we can raise their consciousness."

"Do you think," asked Feist, "that you should take someone from the government with you?"

"Like who?"

Feist thought for a moment, then answered, "I think the Safety Minister, Marine R.E.S. Mors du Char the Fourth would be willing."

Hamilton FD, Federated States of Columbia, Terra Nova

Belisario Endara-Rocaberti and Luci sat staring at the TV. Patricia Britain was making an announcement. Feist stood discreetly nearby on the screen, applauding where appropriate.

Rocaberti waited until the news was over, then looked down in deep thought, weighing probabilities.

I have the itinerary from Luci. I have the personnel from the cast-off Policia *I've been supporting. Arms and other necessities are not hard to come by, back home. It can be done.*

After a moment a smile lit his features. "Luci, bring me the telephone, would you?"

Herrera International Airport, *Ciudad* Balboa, Balboa, Terra Nova

Four men, each bearing a seemingly valid Balboan passport, processed through customs without speaking to one another. The passports had been stolen, but not yet reported as such, from the Balboan consulate in Hamilton. It had been no great feat for two former policemen, and two former criminals, to break the security of the office.

The leader of the four—his name was Arias—carried a briefcase containing many thousands of drachmas he had received from Endara-Rocaberti the day prior. A portion of the money had been passed out for expenses to the other three. Still without speaking, they parted near the rental car area at the airport's street level.

In a dimly lit back street of a fairly well-to-do neighborhood, a former car thief scanned windows for any sign of light. It had taken several passes through the area before he found what he was looking for—a van that was of the same model as those used by the some portions of Fernandez's sister organization, the National Department of Investigations.

The car thief parked his rental car in another neighborhood about a mile away and walked to his target. To open the door, then the engine cover, and hot-wire the van took about ninety seconds. The car thief then drove to where he had rented private garage space.

I'll take it to Enrique's day after tomorrow, thought the thief.

The other former policeman, and the second in command of the expedition, had been a police sergeant. He walked nonchalantly into the military surplus store on *Avenida Central.* He wore the thinnest of disguises; no more than that was necessary. He had a list of sizes and types of uniforms and equipment. In half an hour he walked out of the store with complete police uniforms for four, along with handcuffs, an electric stun gun, and some few other items.

There were to be two more stops before the day could be called complete. One was to pick up the remaining uniforms and equipment. The other was at a medical supply house.

Pedregal, Balboa, Terra Nova

Arias, the senior of the two former policemen, wore mufti. Still, his air of authority convinced the real estate agent trying to rent the small and isolated cinder block walled and metal roofed warehouse that this was official business. This was precisely what Arias wanted.

Further, Arias wanted the real estate agent to think he was a policeman of a particular bent. For this reason, he had a hired prostitute in his rental car, which prostitute he verbally abused endlessly, with special mention of "feminist cunts," "stupid foreign twats," and "international lesbian whores." He'd had to pay an extra two hundred drachma to get the whore to let him slap her a few times but, what the hell, it wasn't like it was his money, after all, nor that she wasn't used to taking money from a certain kind of client who liked slapping around women.

The realtor blanched. He was as macho a sort as anyone else in Balboa but believed in treating ladies as ladies. Still, *none of my business.*

"*Si, señor,*" said the former cop, "I think this will do nicely. Do you mind if I repaint and redecorate a bit?"

"Oh, not at all, sir," said the realtor. *I'm just glad to get this baby white elephant off my back.*

Ciudad Balboa, Balboa, Terra Nova

Firearms were generally legal in Balboa, even for noncitizens. This was something Carrera and Parilla had never had a wish to change. Weapons were, however, more expensive there, which served to keep them out of the hands of the poor except insofar as the poor were members of the legion and entitled to a legion-issue weapon.

Legal though firearms may have been, there were certain registration requirements to include presenting a picture ID, passing a minor background check, and enduring a short waiting period while the guns were test fired to obtain a ballistic sample. For these reasons, therefore, Arias's expedition could not use any legal system for obtaining the weapons they needed. Fortunately for their purpose, however, there was an illegal "system" of sorts.

The last of the party, himself another criminal, knew the people to see for such an illegal purchase. With the handing over of forty-five hundred drachma the team became the proud owners of four .40-caliber pistols of the type used by the National Department of Investigations, along with a case of ammunition and three magazines per pistol.

Enrique's Body Shop, two hundred meters west of Balboa City Train Station, *Ciudad* Balboa, Balboa, Terra Nova

The government had been pretty good about paying for the damage done to Enrique's place during the fighting with the Tauran Union. He appreciated it. He appreciated, too, that they hadn't looked too closely at some of the claimed damage. Enrique was in the business of covering up injuries to physical property. It took only a minor change of mental attitude to make damage seem much worse than it was.

Enrique, himself, was a very tall and frightfully thin dark-skinned Balboan. Almost completely nonpolitical, he minded his own business and, frankly, did some damned fine body work in this, fender-bender central of the planet. He wasn't above taking a few extra bucks for repainting a vehicle he suspected might be stolen, but he also insisted on seeing plausible paperwork to cover himself just in case.

Of course, if plausible paperwork wasn't available that didn't mean he wouldn't do the job requested; it just meant he had to be paid a lot more for his risks. Arias knew this from his days as a real policeman, which was why he'd sent his car thief to Enrique.

"We want you to do a little job for us, Enrique," said the car thief, in the body man's cluttered and greasy office. "Arias said you were the best."

Enrique shook his head. "I don't do that kind of work anymore, *amigo*. It's gotten to be too dangerous."

"My friend," said the thief, reaching a hand between the buttons of his dark *guayabera*, "you don't know what dangerous is. Now get your fucking paints and spray guns, and whatever else you need, put them in your truck, and follow me. My partner will ride with you."

Sensing that there was little point, and possibly much harm, in not complying, the painter asked, "What colors do you need the job to be?"

Pedregal, Balboa, Terra Nova

With obvious satisfaction Arias admired the work he and the others had completed. The interior walls of the warehouse were painted in the drab motifs of the NDI. Although he had never seen any of NDI's real torture chambers, which existed, as did those of Fernandez's organization, the color scheme was so uniformly recognizable as governmental and legionary that it was decided to simulate it for the effect. A reasonably soundproof chamber had been built on one end. Inside the chamber was a metal table with restraining straps. A video camera stood on a tripod, elevated above but facing the table.

There was a sound of an engine from outside of the warehouse. Shortly thereafter a knock came from the garage door. The junior policeman looked through a small security window and pushed the button for the door. After the briefest of intervals a brown, green, and black van entered the warehouse to join a white-painted rental van that already stood there.

"And now all we have to do is wait a few days...and collect a little information."

Arias, impersonating what he used to be with perfect authority and authenticity, picked up the warehouse phone and began to call all the hotels and airlines that served the City.

Herrera International Airport, *Ciudad* Balboa, Balboa, Terra Nova

"Ms. Britain?" Arias asked of the eldest of the five female supremacists who emerged from the *Aduana,* or customs. There was one better, or at least more expensively dressed, whom he knew to be Marine R.E.S. Mors du Char the Fourth. But Britain was in charge so it was to her that he addressed himself.

The Balboan seemed cheerful, and much friendlier than Britain had expected.

"Yes. Is there anything wrong?" asked Britain.

"Not wrong, precisely, ma'am," answered Arias, "but there is a counterdemonstration scheduled for the front of the hotel you have booked. We were sent here as your security."

"I've heard nothing about any such demonstration," said Mors du Char.

"It would be a surprise, ma'am, if you had," answered Arias. "We only know about it because we have infiltrated a semisecret society that doesn't want women to be allowed to serve in the legion or to become citizens at all. A very dangerous group, potentially," added the false cop.

"Now if you would join me? Please? Besides, I've already taken the liberty of changing the pickup point for your rental car reservations from here to the hotel. You can pick up your sedan there."

"But I ordered a van not a sedan."

Arias chuckled, amiably. "Yes, ma'am, but you would certainly, in that case, have been given a sedan. As I've ordered you a sedan, you will equally certainly get a van. There are some areas where Balboa is, perhaps, a bit backward." The officer gave a good simulacrum of a rueful shrug.

Britain and her companions, two of them fairly young and rather pretty, followed the false police officer out to where the NDI van awaited. A police-type radio had been installed while the team waited for Britain to arrive. It was turned off, however.

The five English-speaking people in the van chatted amiably while it was being driven. With an apology for being an inconsiderate host, the senior of the two police turned on the vehicle's air conditioning.

The van proceeded with the traffic slowly but without incident. When the driver turned south-southwest instead of northeast towards the main part of the city, the other officer explained that he was taking a short cut around the heaviest traffic.

None of the women made the slightest objection until the van turned down a narrow road with few buildings. Arias then drew his pistol and said, quite without rancor, "Shut up, bitch!"

CHAPTER THIRTY-FOUR

> If anything, my characters are toned
> down—the truth is much more bizarre.
>
> —Jackie Collins

Casa Linda, Balboa, Terra Nova

Courage, Pililak, thought Ant in her own language as she slipped out the side door, the one without a security light. On her back she had a pack, stuffed with whatever she would need to get herself to her lord. The sling of Hamilcar's rifle was attached at the small of the stock and behind the sight, on the barrel. It ran over her left shoulder and down her back, letting the rifle hang in front of her. The grips of the rifle were a little larger than Pililak was comfortable with. She'd had new ones carved to suit Ham's larger hands. The rifle had a full magazine she'd stolen personally. Another two rested in her pack. Hiding her body she had a set of battle dress, sewn herself from legionary castoffs. A hand-sewn, wide-brimmed floppy hat of the same material topped her ensemble. The girl had even put on grease paint to cover the shine of her light-skinned face and break up the outline.

Ant heard what she had hoped to avoid. "Stop, child!" It was Alena, the witch, waiting outside the door and behind some of the bushes there. The witch emerged, the wan light of three of Terra Nova's moons shining down, but with two of those in their final quarters.

"I've been waiting," said Alena, quite unnecessarily.

"I have to go to our lord," Pililak pleaded. "I must. Alena... please..."

"I quite agree," said Alena, cutting Ant off. "You must. It is written. But there is something else, something I wanted to tell you should your heart grow faint.

"Our lord, Iskandr, needs you now, as he has never needed anyone before. This I know, though I do not know how I know. Go to him. Waste no time. Let no obstacle hinder you. Bring our lord his own weapon. And child?"

"Yes, Alena?"

"Get yourself well-fucked, repeatedly, as often as possible, and give our lord his first son."

"Oh, yes, *yes, YES*, witch-mother!"

"Now go."

"You have been preparing me for this," accused Pililak, with sudden understanding.

"They don't call me 'Alena the Witch' for nothing, child. I've kept track enough to know you have what you need. Now, need I say it again? Go to our Iskandr."

Estado Mayor, Ciudad Balboa, Balboa, Terra Nova

The same moons, two of them fractional, shone down on the blocky *Estado Mayor* as they had on Alena and Ant. Inside, in the office deep in the bowels of the place where few were allowed, and fewer still since a traitor had tried to kill Carrera's intel chief, Carrera and that chief conversed.

"What do you mean the silly sluts just disappeared?" Carrera's look was more puzzlement than fear.

Fernandez, hands resting on the wheels of his chair, answered his chief with a policeman's lack of emotion, even though he was far more soldier than cop, and more intelligence officer than either. "The head of the Tauran National Organization for Upper Middle Class White Women, and her four companions, one of whom was the Tauran Union Minister of Safety, Marine Mors du Char, if I have the twat's name right, were apparently picked up, at approximately twelve-thirty, yesterday afternoon, by two uniformed policeman, driving an NDI van. They were then whisked to places unknown. My people are trying to interview and investigate witnesses but... you know how it is. No one wants to look too closely at an NDI man lest they come under some suspicion themselves. I have very little hope of getting a composite sketch but I will try."

"And your people didn't have anything to do with it?"

"To the best of my knowledge and belief, sir, no."

"And the van? Are we missing one?"

"No, sir. All are accounted for."

"Fuck!... You keep trying. I want them found. I want the people who took them found. And I'd better go talk to Parilla."

Parilla's Office, *Palacio de las* Trixies, *Ciudad* Balboa, Balboa, Terra Nova

Again the palace was quiet, but for street noises from outside. The trixies were out hunting and clever *antaniae* hid for their lives.

Carrera related the story, or rather the lack of a story, to Parilla with a fatalistic air.

"What does it mean, Patricio? What can we do?"

"We can whip Fernandez into a frenzy looking for the bimbos. But I doubt he'll find them in time. What it means? Do you remember the excuse the FSC used for invading us the last time?"

Parilla searched his memory. "It was two-part, as I recall. First the naval commandos that were spying got shot up. Then that naval officer was beaten and his wife molested and threatened with rape."

"Fair memory, Raul, but your analysis isn't quite right. The Federated States made little or no fuss about the Marines. I'm not sure they were actually commandos. That lack of fuss has always made me suspect they were, indeed, spying. But the emotional appeal of avenging one of their women who had been sexually assaulted and threatened with rape? That was what did it. We'd do the same, I think."

Carrera continued. "I don't think we'll find those women alive. I do think we have to go on the assumption that we won't find them at all. Which means..."

"War. The Taurans will invade us," Parilla summed up. "I thought we had eliminated that possibility when Second Tercio fought them."

"We both hoped it would. It could have. It should have." Carrera put his face in his hands. "There is one last chance, perhaps. Let me phone General Janier. We're not precisely friends, but we have a sort of shared outlook on a few matters. Perhaps he will intercede for us."

"Why not the ambassador?" asked Parilla. "She has the advantage to us that she's here."

"Because I don't think she'd understand the gravity of this, or care to preserve us from war if she did. She's not a big fan, you know."

"True," Parilla conceded, then asked, "You have Janier's number in Taurus?"

Carrera smiled. "Fernandez didn't lose anything but the ability to get around without a wheelchair when he lost the use of his legs."

"*We'll* call him, from here."

Tauran Defense Agency, Lumière, Gaul, Terra Nova

Nighttime in Balboa was early morning in the capital of the Gallic Republic. Janier was in his office already, with his toady of an aide de camp, Malcoeur, waiting in the anteroom.

Janier missed Balboa, as it turned out. The knowledge had come as a surprise. At first he'd thought it was his Balboan mistress, Isabel, that he felt the absence of. There was some of that; she'd refused to go with him. He understood; she was now mistress for his replacement, much like the furniture he'd left in the section of Fort Muddville's Building 59.

Odd that she wouldn't leave, he thought. *I thought she'd truly cared for me.*

The intercom buzzed to life. On the other end, Malcoeur announced, incredulously, "*Mon General,* the president of the Republic of Balboa and his military commander, *Duque* Carrera, wish to speak with you."

"There's been an incident involving Ms. Britain and her party from the NOFUMCWW, General," Carrera told the Gaul. "We're not sure who's behind it, but we expect a very unfortunate result. Her party included your own Minister of Safety, Marine Mors du Char."

"If that pussy disappears," said Janier, "it would go to show that every cloud has a silver lining."

Carrera had never found the Gaul to be especially funny, but that one struck home. "Even so, General, we—the president and I—are calling to ask you to use your influence to dissuade the Tauran Union Security Council from anything rash while we try to sort this out."

"I can't make any promises," said Janier. "Certainly not until the facts are in. I can say that I will not let them delude themselves about the basic toughness of your armed forces. Will that do, for now?"

"Yes, General," said Parilla, "and thank you."

Malcoeur was waiting with a message when Janier and the Balboans broke their connection. "Sir, the president pro tem of the TUSC is on the line. Sir, it seems that the Minister of Safety was a close personal friend of his wife."

Rolling his eyes, Janier punched a finger at a flashing light on his phone. The handset was already nestled between his ear and his shoulder.

"Janier... Yes, monsieur, I know she is a close personal friend of your wife's, sir... Yes, sir, I'm sure she is terribly upset..." Janier lied, "No, sir, I haven't spoken to the Balboans yet. I will contact the Balboan authorities as soon as we have concluded, sir.

"Mr. President, the problem is this. Right about now, I would suspect, the Balboan government and military are probably having fits. They will, they must, suspect we will use this as an excuse to attack them. So they'll mobilize. And when they're mobilized we will have to prepare to attack them, or defend ourselves, just in case. They'll see that; they keep eyes on a number of our bases here and there both. And, Mr. President, whether our preparations are offensive or defensive they'll look much the same to an observer. Then they'll have to consider: let us get in the first licks or take their initial advantage in numbers and kick us out of the country. I know what *my* choice under those circumstances would be."

Malcoeur placed a message on Janier's desk where he could see it. "Sir, let me get back to you directly. The President of Balboa is on another line."

Post Exchange, *Calle* MacKinley, Balboa Transitway Area, Balboa, Terra Nova

A white van pulled into a parking lot near the Main Exchange for Tauran forces stationed in Balboa. A nondescript sedan followed. The living occupants of the van exited. By the light turned on by the opening of the door one could see five bodies, stacked like cordwood, naked, the skin of the corpses unnaturally pale except where leakage from slashed throats had stained it red. A closer examination would show other damage: to skin, to sexual organs, to teeth, nails, tongues, and eyes. Indeed, the list of horrors inflicted on the women read like an inventory from every snuff and horror film ever made. Teeth drilled. Check. Skin partially flayed? Check. Nipples removed? Some by slicing, some by burning, check. Blinded? Check. Vaginas and anuses, hot pokers applied to? Check. Broken bones in hands and feet? Check, too many to list.

In three of the five the shoulders were totally dislocated, probably from application of the strappado.

One of the men threw on the passenger chair a bundle of digital recordings covering the vicious treatment the women had received.

The two men from the van climbed into the back seat of the sedan. The next stop was to drop off a copy of the recordings on the doorstep of a local office of a major international news organization. Then a few more to the Tauran embassy. After that, they could see to getting out of the country. Once out they'd download a copy to the global net.

Estado Mayor, Ciudad Balboa, Balboa, Terra Nova

"You've got to give me more to go with than this," demanded Fernandez of his assistant. The assistant was a replacement for the late and unlamented executive who had shot and paralyzed Fernandez. The new man was more trustworthy, but not so effective an intelligence officer. Not that his predecessor had been much. It was one of the weaknesses of Fernandez's organization that it was so dependent upon him, personally.

"I'm sorry, Legate," said the assistant. "That is it. We have a report of a stolen van which just might possibly have been repainted and used to take the women. We have no eyewitnesses who can help us make a composite sketch. We are still checking out the whereabouts of anybody who might have access to police uniforms."

"How about the uniform stores?"

"We're checking into that as well."

"Have we tried the criminal photo albums on any of the witnesses?"

"Yes, sir. But we've drawn a blank there as well."

"*Chingada!*"

Hospital, *Cerro Mina*, Balboa Transitway Area, Balboa, Terra Nova

As soon as they'd been found, and the finder had stopped vomiting, he'd called the military police. The location was close enough to their barracks, atop *Cerro Mina*, that the MPs had barely beaten the ambulance to the van. *Hauptmann* Lang, accompanied by *Gefreiter* Czauderna and Private Brickley took one look each and joined the original finder in decorating the pavement in bright Technicolor.

Even the ambulance crews, a bit more hardened than the MPs, found that accidental death and dismemberment was not so upsetting as the willful and deliberate infliction of horror.

The first ambulance driver pretty much summed up the feelings of all the Taurans present, as well as those still to learn of the atrocity: "Somebody's got to pay for this."

The stiffened and stinking bodies of the women were then taken to the *Cerro Mina* Hospital. Not that there was anything to be done for them, but medical and administrative formalities had to be followed. The tapes found with the van were impounded by the military police who made the initial investigation of the murders.

The first viewing commenced at about nine in the morning. Six hours later, the viewing was still not complete, as nobody was able to take what the recording showed for more than a few minutes at a time.

The tapes were copied then, and the copies sent to everyone with both an interest and a clearance. The clearance was needed because Janier, trying to keep a lid on things, had declared them Ultra Plus Top Secret. This was not actually a level of classification. What it was, was a statement from Janier that if anyone military leaked one of the tapes that person was soon going to be counting vanishing megafauna at the worst embassy in Uhuru that the Tauran diplomatic corps had to offer.

Janier, himself, watched the tape with a degree of detachment even he found unnatural. The scenes were disjointed. The men in the camera's view wore Balboan police uniforms but with doctors' masks and light green aprons. They said nothing. Janier studied whatever of the men's faces could be seen around the masks. *I wonder if a competent policeman could identify those bastards from the partial view?*

Janier saw each of the women raped, Ms. Britain anally, the

camera getting a close up of her tear-streaked, anguished face. He saw pliers and drills applied to fingers and teeth. One poor girl had her eyes burned out with a lit cigar for the camera. Another had an electric stun gun played over her nipples and genitals. She bit part-way through her own tongue at the pain, her chin flowing crimson. The soles of the feet of each were burned with a propane torch.

Though the general completely despised Marine Mors du Char, he thought it a bit much when a red-hot poker was slid into her vagina.

Then came the confessions. Each sobbing woman was forced to verbally confess to participation in some bizarre plot to over-throw the government of Balboa. (Even as he had taped those confessions, Arias had thought it a nice touch. After all, it was precisely what an out of control nationalist maniac might demand.)

Next, again for the camera, each handcuffed woman was forced to her knees and her throat was cut as the tape caught her beg-ging for her life. The blinded one was too far gone to beg until the stun gun was used to make her react. She said "Please. Oh, please," but that was it. Her throat was laid open last of all.

Last was a scene of the bodies being unceremoniously dumped in the white van.

Janier watched the tape again. He found the second viewing more disturbing than the first. But something nagged at him. Then he realized what it was that he found . . . wrong. *The legion tortures; it's common knowledge despite the trap they set for that stupid cunt, Irene Temujin. But they surely wouldn't paint a torture chamber in military colors. And why wear their uniforms? They're not cheap. A man wouldn't want to have them covered in blood and shit. But those men didn't seem to care about that. No, this stinks.*

Janier hit the intercom. "Malcoeur, you toad, get me Monsieur Gaymard, the president pro tem."

Tauran News Network, Headline News Studios, Lumière, Gaul, Terra Nova

Right up to the last minute, TNN's chiefs had argued about showing the tapes. It wasn't that they weren't newsworthy. It wasn't even that they were of questionable veracity—the news media cared no more about the truth than libel laws required. Rather, it was thought, the horrid content of the tapes might offend people's sensibilities. So it was decided to air a highly edited version, one with most of the actual rape and torture excised. Britain's face, for example, was left in, but the rear entry was cut out. The scenes of throats being slashed were cut out, but the piling of the bodies in the vans was left in. The blowtorch roasting feet was left uncut. In all the edited version showed just under five sickening minutes. The inconsistencies Janier had noticed were far less noticeable in what was finally shown to the world. Literally tens of millions of people around the world saw the edited tape in its first public showing.

And then people started looking on line for the unedited version. It wasn't hard to find. Once found, it spread like a virus.

The demonstrations for action began almost immediately.

Parilla's Office, *Palacio de las* Trixies, *Ciudad* Balboa, Balboa, Terra Nova

Carrera looked at the TV screen in Parilla's office and felt something he hadn't in a while, the mental *click* that said he was tossing away whatever civilized constraints and limitations he had in favor of "hard-favour'd rage."

"Well, that's that," he said. "Once the mob is in the street the Tauran Union is going to hit us. They're in the street. The invasion is coming."

There was a secure phone on Parilla's desk. It ran, basically, to the *Estado Mayor*, the Senate House, the *Casa* Linda, the *Isla Real*, and nowhere else. It began to flash. When he picked it up it was Fernandez.

"My people in Taurus," said the intel chief, "tell me they're coming. Or, at least, everybody but Castile is. 'Free beer' is being sounded at Wye, Anglia. Contracts are being let for aircraft, both heavier than air and lighter than air. Leaves are being cancelled. Even some mobilization of reservists seems to be taking place."

"What about your connection in the office of the Tauran commander, here?" Carrera asked.

"Isabel? She says she's had no contact with Janier's replacement in the last couple of days, but that the headquarters is all abustle.

"They're coming, Mr. President. Patricio, they're coming."

After Fernandez rang off, Parilla asked, "Is there anything we can do? Anything to prevent a war, I mean."

"No," said Carrera. "None. We're set up to win a country-wide ambush. I can mobilize without ordering that ambush into position. That will just convince them we mean to attack. I can not mobilize and they will sense the weakness and attack. I can partially mobilize and they will still attack."

"You know," said the president, "it's disheartening. We took some real risks for peace. We paid some high prices, too. And it's all for naught. Was Machiavelli right about all that, after all? That there's really no avoiding wars? What do you recommend, Patricio?"

"*Urraca* 2000." Carrera spoke of an annually updated plan for secret, partial mobilization, using *every* military asset the legion had available. Less than a fifteen people in Balboa even knew of its name.

"But you've told me that that is a one-time only operation, that we can't pull it off twice. We've never even practiced it for real."

"Yes, that's right," Carrera said. "And, because it is our one best chance—maybe our only chance—of defeating an invasion, if you approve it then we *must* have that invasion. Even if we have to provoke it."

"Let me think. Let me think."

"Sure, Raul. But there isn't a lot of time. We could already be too late."

"What can we do to start the thing along without raising the temperature or giving the plan away?"

Carrera had considered that question on his own many times. "I can start the twenty-seven prime supply ships moving closer without anyone noticing...probably. I can issue sealed orders with messenger guards to some key commanders; the plans not to be opened without my orders. I can have the equipment hides reinventoried, though I don't think that's necessary. Beyond that... the meat of the operation...I can't do much without doing it all."

"So what do you think we should do?"

"A partial and obvious mobilization, reservist level only, no militia. That will be enough to convince the Taurans we intend to attack. It will also cause them to feel that they absolutely must commit more than what they have here. That will take time, a week or so; they are very slow, strategically."

"And the *other* mobilization?" Parilla asked. He was one of those fifteen people who knew the name. He was one of only nine who knew all the details.

Carrera answered, "That goes forward."

"It's a heavy burden on your soul, my friend. And on mine. Start *Urraca* 2000."

CHAPTER THIRTY-FIVE

In wartime, truth is so precious that she should
always be attended by a bodyguard of lies.

—Winston Churchill

High Admiral's Conference Room, UEPF *Spirit of Peace*, in orbit over Terra Nova

In her silverwood-paneled conference room were gathered the high
admiral, the two Khans, husband and wife, Richard, earl of Care,
and Richard's lover and the high admiral's cabin girl, Esmeralda.

"What the fuck is going on down there?" demanded Wallenstein.

Both Khans, husband and wife, shook their heads. Even so,
Khan, male, offered, "We're very unclear on the details, but there's
been some kind of an atrocity. I've got someone digging those
details up, but for the nonce let's just say it looks bad. Based on
what's making the rounds, I'd have to say it looks like war. War
between Balboa and the Tauran Union, I mean."

After all my efforts to get a war going, thought Marguerite, *it
happens by a fluke? The elder gods, how many or how few they
be, are batshit insane.*

"Right," she said. "Maximum feasible sensing capability focused
on Balboa. Esmeralda?"

"Yes, High Admiral."

"Arrange a direct flight to Balboa. We need to reestablish some
of the links we let lapse with Janier's departure. Who *is* their new
commander there?"

"An Anglian," said Khan, male. "A Major General Solomon

375

McQueeg-Gordon. We've never bothered to reestablish contact since Janier left."

"Right. Tell him I'm coming and that if I am unhappy I will arrange to have him removed to . . . oh . . . one of the moons, I suppose."

Carretera InterColombiana, Balboa, Terra Nova

Only moving by moonlight had been a pain for Pililak. At first, paralleling the highway, she'd made good progress. Then she'd discovered that every passing car caused her to have to hide, since she couldn't know if her lord's father had sent people to bring her back. Worse, the headlights destroyed her night vision for a quarter of an hour or so, every time one had passed. And then, something else she hadn't anticipated, the jungle wasn't thin near the road. Rather, it was even thicker because of the abundance of light.

Young, strong, and fit, Pililak had estimated one day to get to the turn-off point she planned. It had taken three.

Now she stood on the southern edge of the roadway, right where she planned to strike out across country to go farther south. The jungle in front of her looked not so much like flora, in the country's wet gloom, as it looked like fauna, a great beast waiting to consume her.

But her lord was waiting. And Alena the witch had said he would need her. With her compass in her left hand, as the guards had shown her how to hold it, Pililak clenched her teeth against her fear and struck out toward the point where the southernmost tip of the Transitway met the man-made lake in the center. There she would have the best chance of making a crossing without being run down by one of the great ships that plied the waters there.

Casa Linda, Balboa, Terra Nova.

Lourdes normally wouldn't call her husband when he was on duty. He'd said it set a bad precedent. This, however, was more in the realm of an emergency, especially since she hadn't heard from him in several days.

A younger Carrera, then known as Hennessey, might have lashed out at the interruption. The older one took it more in stride. "Yes, Lourdes," he asked, "what's up?"

"It's Ant," his wife said. "She's missing. I just figured it out; the other girls, including Alena and our two oldest daughters, were covering for her. Though, to be sure, none of them will admit it. And Ham's rifle is missing. She's heading for him, bringing him his rifle."

"Fuck!" Carrera exclaimed. "With everything else going on this ... this ... Words fail. But, Jesus I am going to personally paddle that girl. Do we know how long she's been gone?"

"I'm guessing three days, though her accomplices will admit to nothing."

"Right, three days." Carrera knew the local jungle a lot better than the Pashtun girl did. "She's going to be somewhere near"—he mentally pulled up a map of the country—"mmm ... somewhere near Arraijan. I could ordinarily send a maniple to cut her off. Under the circumstances, though, that might be tough. Any chance she'd respond if we had a loudspeaker-equipped helicopter overfly her?"

Lourdes laughed. "That little fanatic? Maybe, just maybe, if you put her lord and master, Iskandr, in the helicopter. Otherwise, she'd ignore a thunderbolt from on high."

"Yeah ... let me think about that. This might be tougher than you would think. In any case, hon, don't bug me for a while. We've got a serious emergency going on."

"Those Tauran women?"

"Yeah."

"Awful shit," Lourdes said, which surprised Carrera, and she almost never engaged in vulgarity of any kind.

Estado Mayor, Ciudad Balboa, Balboa, Terra Nova

The *Casa* Linda was perfectly suitable as a day-to-day office. But it really wasn't equipped for what Carrera and the legion needed now.

In a centrally located and very nearly ultimately secure room, a rather large room, at that, with tables with maps, and walls carrying maps, monitors, and televisions, Carrera's long-laid plans could be seen unfolding.

Unknown to either Wallenstein, Janier, or McQueeg-Gordon, the first steps in *Urraca* 2000 were unfolding. At Carrera's coded orders, from around the world over two dozen merchant ships—big ones, mixed break bulk, ro-ros, and container ships—turned their bows toward ports closer to Balboa. Some were fully loaded already. Others had generally innocuous cargoes to pick up from various ports where those cargoes—food, medical supplies, fuel, batteries, spare parts, all the noncombat impedimenta of war— had been stored over the years. Six other ships, one very large merchant ship reconfigured as an assault transport, two medium ships that had been modified to carry Condors and antishipping missiles, and three small freighters that had been turned into mine layers, took to sea from Cochin over a period of days. Though at sea, these stayed as far from Balboa as possible.

Sealed orders, under guard, rested in the headquarters of each military academy, as well as the transportation tercio, the Military Intelligence tercio, and all the corps headquarters. Other orders, being general contingency plans and not nearly so secret, were on hand in every other unit in the legion. This included the rapidly reforming, because never really disbanded, units of Santa Josefinans, massing in the jungles near the border between their home country and *Valle de las Lunas*.

Despite sayings to the contrary, all warfare is *not* based on deception. Rather, deception is just part of the bag of tricks. That said, deception can be one of the more valuable tools in the general's kit bag. *Urraca* 2000 was based in large part on deception. This took four forms. There would be strict operational security, the guarding of what was actually going on from prying eyes, lenses, radars, magnetic anomaly detectors, sniffers, and microphones. There would be disinformation, the planting of information that might or might not be false but would serve to reinforce any preconceived and incorrect notions the Taurans might have. Most important was to make Balboa seem far less ready to fight, at the precise moment of a Tauran invasion, than was really the case.

There would be activity that could not be hidden but that would not threaten the Taurans' plans, and would attract their interest. The activation and deployment of a portion of the legion was expected to draw that attention. Such activity was expected to use up a significant portion of their intelligence interpretation assets, the human beings who actually turned the data gathered by satellite and spy plane into something occasionally useable.

Especially to catch the attention of air and space reconnaissance, the Sixteenth Aviation Legion began to disperse most of its several hundred aircraft to small fields around the country. Others had never been moved from small fields.

Similarly, of the thirteen Meg-Class coastal defense submarines, of which two were in for overhaul, the other eleven put to sea, their "clickers" advertising their presence and vulnerability to one and all. The clickers would, of course, be shut off at the first hint of hostilities.

In a program developed and implemented over the preceding decade, there were hide positions for combat equipment for forces the existence of which the Taurans were not terribly likely to suspect. An overstrength cohort's worth of armor, light and heavy, was hidden deeply in the ammunition bunkers at the *Lago Sombrero* Ammunition Supply Point. The artillery compliment to support that force was hidden elsewhere, more or less in plain sight in a scrap metal yard, next to a legion repair depot, about ten kilometers away. It had taken almost eight years to assemble that package.

Anyone could anticipate that the Taurans would attempt to seize Herrera Airport. Carrera, naturally, had anticipated it as well. There were some thirty-four houses located on three sides of the field that had been built to legion specifications, were owned by a rental company that answered to Carrera, and had stored in hidden vaults in hidden subbasements all the implements needed for about twelve hundred troops to fight. In addition, a nearby warehouse held several score of the caltrop projectors developed by Siegel in Cochin. They looked like concrete-filled barrels, such as someone might put along an airstrip to deny use to an airlanding assault. On signal, they would explode, scattering thousands of four-pointed, sharp and barbed jacks across the entire area. God pity the paratroopers who came down on that.

A half dozen similarly sited houses dominated the much smaller local airport that lay on a shallow peninsula north of and abutting the city.

On the Shimmering Sea side there was a brewery that hid equipment at *Puerto Catival*, and deeper hides at Pilon and Clay Dairy Farms.

Two construction sites at Santa Cruz and Vacamonte faced Arnold Air Force Base. Another heavy equipment maintenance facility at Arraijan also faced east toward the naval station, the Bridge of the Colombias, and the Transitway itself. The final position, a set of warehouses that seemed placed to support a shopping mall, was in the general area of Alfaro's Tomb, facing Fort Muddville and Brookings Air Force Station.

Military equipment was not remotely out of place in the maintenance facilities. And because they were maintenance facilities, with expensive military equipment present, it had not been suspicious for a constant guard to be maintained on them. And then, too, with sheds, working bays, conexes, and a constantly shifting level of "broken" equipment to be serviced, it had been very difficult for any Tauran intelligence asset to keep a very good count of what was available at any given site. In fact, the Taurans hadn't even tried. Even if they had, it would have been impossible for them to know how much was serviceable since even *Balboan* maintenance records lied. The really secret part, the provision of troop shelters proof from remote sensing, had been accomplished years before, back when there was little or no suspicion between the Taurans and Balboans.

The construction sites had been more of a problem. For one thing, tanks and artillery were not the usual denizens of such places; nor was it a simple matter to disguise a tank as a bulldozer, although it could be done and in a few cases had been. For another, construction sites move from time to time. The second problem had been handled by making them sites for major construction projects; roads, for example, in the cases of Vacamonte and Santa Cruz. Equipment had been smuggled to the place in dribs and drabs, in locked conexes where possible. Unsuspicious guards were generously provided to—in theory—secure the precious building materials and construction equipment. In practice, of course, the guards were there to secure the hidden arms. Few, if any, of the guards had any reason to believe that conexes and locked warehouses contained arms and ammunition.

All of this was for the cadets, the roughly eleven thousand children, though most were over fifteen, that the legion's military schools recruited, and thoroughly trained, against the coming day. The signs were all there to see, really, but the Taurans, even if they'd bothered to look closely, would likely have gone into apoplectic shock as the notion of using fifteen-year-olds for machine gun fodder. Thus, they'd shied away from it.

At least that was Carrera's theory. On the other hand, Fernandez just thought they'd hidden the real capability too well for suspicion.

Of course, getting the cadets from their schools to their assault and defense positions would take some doing. There were some fairly complex plans—and some rather simple ones—for that, as well. One part of both plans, that actually made things easier, was a selective call up of the reserve echelon, which attracted attention away from the academies.

All of this poured out, as Carrera watched, onto the maps, the computer monitors, and the television screens in this deepest of deep conference rooms. He did take time out to order a maniple, no more than that, to helicopter in and set up an interdiction line about three miles long to try to capture Pililak.

"The Quad," Fort Muddville, Balboa Transitway Area, Balboa, Terra Nova

There hadn't been a lot of time for farting around. Rather than try to keep her trip secret, this time Marguerite had let it be known. Indeed, she'd announced she was coming to Balboa, all in the interests of peace.

"And it's true, in a way," she told Esmeralda, on the flight down. "Peace for *our* home requires that this planet be organized into roughly equal power blocks perpetually at each other's throats, precisely five of them."

"Why five, High Admiral?" Esmeralda had asked. She was back in mufti for the trip, though Wallenstein kept in uniform.

"Seems to work well, through human history," Marguerite answered. "The average treachery quotient is such that, of five, one is certain to betray somebody, when it counts, while a three to two advantage is not enough to win before someone in the three sticks it to the other two."

"And two to one would be too great a disparity?" Esmeralda asked.

"Yes, dear; Orwell got it completely wrong."

From Atlantis Base, they'd taken the locally purchased UEPF plane direct to Brookings Field. From there, the new Tauran commander had had them whisked to his administrative headquarters—he'd barely given a thought to the combat command post in the Tunnel since his arrival in country—and met them there in the green grass rectangle south of Building 59.

"You should have met me at the field," said Marguerite crossly. "The Gaul could get away with meeting me here, but he had a style you lack. Now trot your Anglian buns into the secure conference room so I can tell you what you're up against. Nothing in the preparations we can see from space suggests you have a clue."

Fortunately the Gaul, for all his wishy-washy, nervous nellieism, is doing a fair job of prepping the invasion from his end.

Parade Field, Camp Pontfaverger, Suippe Department, Gaul, Terra Nova

One of the nice things about lighter than air craft that derived some of their lift aerodynamically or through fans, or through both, was that they didn't need much in the way of facilities. Any open field of sufficient size—a parade field, say—would do. This one was doing splendidly, with the airship holding itself in place while the Gallic 105th *Régiment de Chars de Combat* lined up along the road leading to the field. The airship, any airship of this model, could only take a maximum of sixteen of the Gallic tanks, plus their crews and minimal supplies. The other three for this regiment waited at other open fields. They'd come in for the pickup as soon as the first one was done. Loading the first one, under the eyes of the units professional sergeants, was going...fairly well.

"Hey, asshole, keep eye contact with your ground guide at *all* times! You hear me, *Garcon*?" The sergeant's shouts in fact went unheard by the tank driver, cautiously steering his sixty-ton monster across the ramp and into the hold of a far more monstrous airship. Nonetheless, with the psychic perception which most privates develop and which warns them of potentially comfort-threatening interaction with a sergeant, the driver returned his full attention to his task. A long line of other armored vehicles—and their crews—awaited their turns to load.

There was no chance that the tanks would arrive in Balboa before the invasion kicked off. Indeed, had the first of them arrived it would likely have signaled the legion that war was imminent, causing the Balboans to initiate hostilities on their terms. Instead, the tanks and the dragoons regiments loading elsewhere—along with Anglian Hussars, Sachsen Panzergrenadiere, Tuscan Carabinieri, and a host of others coming in by slow airship—were to be a third echelon of reinforcement once the legion was scattered and demoralized, with their leadership killed or captured.

It was hoped that their mere appearance on the battlefield would serve to induce holdouts and die-hards to throw in the towel, sparing both sides needless effusion of blood.

Seeing the previous tank disappear into the airship's hold, the sergeant turned around and signaled for the next to begin moving.

Camelot, Anglia, Terra Nova

The men of the 25th Regiment, known as "Paras," had taken the news of a lawful strife impending with joy almost unalloyed. The two dampers were that a) they actually rather appreciated the notion of a hot poker being, in the words of their RSM, "Shoved right up that Gallic tart Marine Mors du Char's smelly little cunt," and b) they were going to be under Gallic command.

The latter was fine, if one was a Gaul. If one was not a Gaul, however, one could be confident of getting the shitty end of the stick in every case. When the news came that while, "Yes, the bloody perfidious Gauls are in overall charge, but there's a proper Anglian gentleman, McQueeg-Gordon, on the ground now and, besides, we're going to hit far away from any of the bloody Frogs," their happiness quotient lifted by quite a bit.

There was still that issue of attacking people who, after all, had only done what every proper soldier in the Tauran Union wanted to do, but, "Eh, fuck 'em. And besides, it'll be fun."

Lautrec International Airport, Lautrec, Gaul, Terra Nova

It was pleasantly warm here, with a mild breeze that originated in the great inland sea to the north.

Khalid had never been to the Lautrec airport before. Nonetheless, the sudden sprouting of nearly five hundred tents he took as being some variant on a "tent, general purpose, medium," all in rows on one side of one of the airport's twin, parallel runways, he took as strange and unusual.

This really isn't my job, though the Druze assassin, *but I suppose I'm the only one here, so it's become my job. Hmmm...let's see, I count four hundred and ninety-five tents, give or take a few, at eighteen men per tent. That's about eight thousand, nine hundred.*

That's a little more than the Twentieth Gallic Parachute Brigade has, but subtract a few for mess tents, headquarters, medical aid stations . . . so yes, I think I'm looking at the entire half division they call a brigade. That would be the light armor regiment, which probably can't drop its gunned armored cars but can drop the troops, four battalions—oh, they call them "regiments," don't they?—of parachute infantry, a battalion of engineers, of artillery . . . yep, there's the gun line over there,

But can they lift everything? I see forty-six A-4N transports . . . thirty-three C-61s . . . nineteen Airtec-532s, I think those are.

It wasn't, as he'd thought, Khalid's job to know, but he took a healthy interest in his adopted country's potential enemies and their equipment, even so. He guestimated in his head: *Forty-six A-4Ns . . . fifty-three hundred . . . thirty-three C-16s . . . twenty-nine hundred . . . nineteen 532s . . . about eight hundred. 'Course, that's not leaving anything for outsized equipment and heavy drops. They've got to either airland some things, or bring in more lift, or send them by echelons. The most I see is three-fourths of this assembly going on the aircraft available.*

Then, too . . . hmmm . . . the 532s won't range all the way to Balboa. Note to Fernandez: have the boss consider attacking them at wherever their forward staging base will be.

Oh, and now that I think about it, they could move everything forward to Cienfuegos or Santa Josefina so that the second echelon comes in hard on the heels of the first. Eh . . . that's really not my job or expertise. Let the people whose job this is to analyze do their jobs, Khalid, and you do what you can from here.

The Tunnel, *Cerro Mina*, Balboa, Terra Nova

Wallenstein had practically had to drag McQueeg-Gordon—tall, slender, and unintelligent looking—to the Tunnel by his earlobe, like a naughty child. The general didn't seem to understand even that there *was* a secure operational headquarters, less still that circumstances were changing so quickly that he'd better get his ass into it.

De Villepin, still chief of intelligence, had met them at the Tunnel's entrance, duly checked out Esmeralda's allegedly eighty-seven-year-old body, given Marguerite a dirty look for inflicting the Anglian fool on them, then led them all into the bowels of the hill.

Fortunately, procedures and drills instituted by the Gaul, Janier, were still largely remembered among the staff. By the time Wallenstein deposited a sputtering McQueeg-Gordon in Janier's old office, the other important players from Building 59 had already moved into the Tunnel.

The command still had a Gallic intelligence chief, de Villepin, a Gallic operations chief, Bessières, and a Gallic chief of staff, Moncey. What chance had a simple Anglian, whose mother wasn't entirely sure of his paternity, when faced with such a solid consensus to ignore him?

Ah, thought Marguerite, *now I understand. The Gauls are still running the show, and have no intention of letting their Anglian pseudo commander have anything much to do with it. Such are the benefits of coalition warfare, I suppose.*

Though few recognized her, her initial admission by de Villepin, plus the security badge he pinned on her granting her unlimited access, saw her able to traverse the Tunnel, all its side corridors, and their offices without let or hindrance. And what she saw was impressive.

"Anglian pathfinder team, Aserri airport... all okay for reception..." and someone would duly check a block on a small monitor, which check would be reflected on one or more of the large screens. "420th Dragoons report vehicles loaded..." and another check would appear. "37th Commando reports assault position for Fort Williams occupied..."

Then came the frightening announcement, the one that set hearts to racing: "Balboan television and radio are reporting that the reserve echelon is called to duty. Repeat, the enemy reserves are called to duty."

"What aboot their fookin' militia?" asked someone aloud. Marguerite thought she recognized the voice of the delightful Anglian captain she'd met briefly on a previous trip.

"I report what they tell me, Captain Campbell," answered a Gallic accent. Even as the Gaul spoke, the message flashed back to the Tauran Union, stilling yet another few tongues among those who might have had their doubts about the coming attack.

Finally satisfied that a) McQueeg-Gordon was a useless ninny, but that b) Janier's old staff had the situation well in hand, Marguerite had rounded up Esmeralda, turned in her badge, and left for Brookings, Atlantis Base, space, and the *Spirit of Peace.*

CHAPTER THIRTY-SIX

Nous entrerons dans la carrière
Quand nos aînés n'y seront plus,
Nous y trouverons leur poussière
Et la trace de leurs vertus (bis)
Bien moins jaloux de leur survivre
Que de partager leur cercueil,
Nous aurons le sublime orgueil
De les venger ou de les suivre

[We shall enter the (military) career
When our elders are no longer there,
There we shall find their dust
And the trace of their virtues (repeat)
Much less keen to survive them
Than to share their coffins,
We shall have the sublime pride
Of avenging or following them]

—Claude Joseph Rouget de Lisle,
  "La Marseillaise, Couplet des enfants"

Pedregal Military Academy, Balboa, Terra Nova

Twelve boys aged fifteen to seventeen stood at attention in their squad room in one of the academy's barracks. Each wore civilian clothes and carried one of the unmarked black overnight bags that the six military schools issued to cadets. In the bags were a pair of boots, two sets of battle dress, a change of socks and underwear, plus the cadets' individual load-bearing equipment.

A middle-aged Volgan tribune, dark haired with bright blue eyes and not a trace of a gut, looked them over carefully, gauging willingness to fight from their boyish faces. The Volgan, Tribune Depreradovich, was one of the mercenaries hired by the legion in the mists of the past, who had elected to ship over and take up Balboan citizenship.

"At ease," ordered the Volgan, satisfied of the boys' attitudes. "Are you sure you can find the address, Salazar?" he asked the seventeen-year-old cadet sergeant.

"*Si, señor*. No problem." If the cadet was remotely fearful, it was hard to tell. Mostly, to Depreradovich, the boy seemed quite eager.

"All right, then. Take your squad and start walking. Remember to chat and look casual. I'll see you, I hope, sometime late tomorrow near the airport."

There was nothing especially unusual about mufti-clad senior cadets sauntering out the main gate of the academy when their training day was done. A few girls made moon eyes, which the boys returned. The boys then continued on their way to a house with a vault overlooking Herrera Airport.

On the airstrip, itself, large and apparently heavy concrete-filled drums were being placed just off of the runways, where they could be rolled into position to prevent an assault landing.

Meanwhile, back at the school, as most of the older boys filtered out, a few, along with some adult cadre, were left behind in charge of the thirteen- and fourteen-year-olds. These were employed in being run through approximately twice as much as the normal amount of formation attending, mess hall line standing, physical training, and just plain choreographed walking about, to simulate the full complement of cadets.

San Miguelito Military Academy, Balboa, Terra Nova

Across town, the eldest half of the San Miguelito Military Academy were doing the same thing as at Pedregal, but in the opposite direction. Instead of forming up in a defensive position around the main airport, the San Miguelitos moved in dribs and drabs toward some warehouses a few miles from Fort Muddville and

Brookings Air Force Station. As with all the other schools, the remaining half of the cadets, mostly the younger half, would be left behind to simulate, through well-scripted formations, marches, and other formal and informal assemblies, that the full eighteen hundred and twenty-seven cadets were present for instruction.

Carrera's great fear was still that the academies would look *too* normal to prying eyes. For this reason some semi-public anti-Tauran protests by the remaining cadets, complete with banners, drums, and pipes, were scheduled for different times over the next few days.

Penonome Military Academy, Balboa, Terra Nova

The Penonome Military Academy was built in the form of a large quadrangle. In honor of what the boys felt were their spiritual antecedents the school had been nicknamed by its denizens as the "Kurt Meyer School for Bad Little Boys" (*La Escuela por Chicillos Malos, Kurt Meyer*), Kurt Meyer having been the former commander of the 12th SS Panzer Division—*Hitler Jugend*—on Old Earth.

It had been in existence long enough that no one anymore gave a lot of thought to the nuances of its construction. Still, during the construction culverts, tunnels, and covered walkways had been built—even then generating little suspicion amidst all the other innocent construction—to connect the barracks, classrooms, and headquarters. A tunnel also led from the cadet mess hall to a large covered shed. Beginning the night before, the school's cooks had set up in the shed a rest stop for trucks; trucks that were carrying loads of ammunition in semis from *Lago Sombrero*'s Ammunition Supply Point to the Sixty-first Artillery Tercio at Santiago. The loads of all but the first six trucks were considerably less than either the full capacity of the trucks or the amount of time they had spent at *Lago Sombrero* loading ammunition would indicate.

Still, to an overworked imagery analyst aboard the *Spirit of Harmony*, in orbit over Balboa, having seen, via ship's camera and the one skimmer sent down, the growing piles of ammunition in the artillery park in Santiago, not having been alerted by anything that would suggest other than a movement of artillery ammunition to a distant post, nothing seemed amiss. She *had* checked the first few trucks with the full spectrum of capabilities of the satellites and computers at her command. Heat and magnetic signatures had been consistent with loads of ammunition. Radar, she hadn't tried, since that was useless against the metal-walled trailers. And visual, to include IR, had been badly degraded by the rain at times. The stopover near what her maps said was a school for young boys did not alert her. It was SOP, standard operating procedure, around the planet to provide such rest stops for vehicle convoys, using whatever assets were available.

By the time the later trucks—each carrying forty-five to fifty cadets, aged fourteen or fifteen to, in a few cases, eighteen, along with some of their more adult leadership—had turned back from Santiago to *Lago Sombrero* ASP for a second load the analyst had turned her attention elsewhere.

Isla Picaron, Balboa Transitway Area, Balboa, Terra Nova

The "Isla" wasn't actually an island, though it could become one if the water levels of the lake happened to rise. In the current downpour, Pililak wondered if they wouldn't. No matter, a little water wasn't going to stop her where snakes and bugs, *antaniae*, caimen, black palm, and one altogether too inquisitive and now thoroughly dead juvenile smilodon could not.

Unfortunately, she was starting to run a little low on food. This had the benefit of lightening her pack, but carried the downside of possible starvation in the not too distant future. She'd been sure she'd brought enough, yet every leg of her journey had taken two or three times longer than she'd expected. Getting lost once hadn't helped a bit. And having to crawl for four hours on her belly to avoid the thin line of soldiers who were out in the jungle looking for her had been a little rough, too. She'd known they were there for her because they'd called out her name in both languages.

"To hell with that," she muttered, wading ankle deep through the mud to the "island" that sat closest to her next point.

Realizing that she really didn't have the food to continue with her original plan, Ant had modified it. She was going to cut across the narrow part of the Transitway, taking her chances with the passing ships. That way, she'd be certain to find the railroad that nearly touched the water there. With the rail line to guide her there'd be no question of getting lost, no question of having to slash her way through secondary growth, and best of all, "No more fucking black palm."

By the time she'd struggled across the mud to the barely less muddy "island," then gotten her air mattress blown up, it was pouring down in a deluge, the rain hard and cool enough to make her shiver.

Visibility dropped to maybe twenty feet, if that. That was a serious danger. She'd counted on crossing to the rail line at night, when no one would be likely to see her but she would be able to see the running lights of the ships. She could wait, of course, for night but there was no guarantee that the rain would stop. She'd seen it rain for as much as seventeen days straight without the slightest let up since she'd come to Balboa from her native, and rather dry, Pashtia. She'd heard it was worse in towards the center of the country, where she was.

"No," she insisted to herself. "I'm going. Nothing will keep me from my lord, Iskandr."

Lumière, Gaul, Terra Nova

After being up and down, then up and down again, on the subject of invading Balboa, Janier found that this time it was easier, with most of his doubts dispelled. Partly, this was because he was being told to do it rather than plotting to make it so he would be told to do it. Partly it was the steady report of increased Balboan preparations, that made it seem inevitable anyway. But the real factor was that, in the current emotional overload, he was being given everything he asked for.

And when has that ever happened?

Still, it wasn't all sweetness. There were questionable spots, driven in good part by areas of uncertainty. For example, given the sheer intensity of the threat represented by the Balboans First Corps (Mechanized), it was understandable that Janier, back in Taurus, was not content with either intelligence reports from the Tauran Union Intelligence and Security Agency, nor the reports filtered down to him by High Admiral Wallenstein's flagship.

"Everything they send," he'd fumed, starting about an hour after the commencement of the present crisis, "*everything,* gets analyzed for deeper meaning and then sanitized to follow whatever party line is important to the TUISA leadership, today. Just as was that report from that charmingly female Anglian captain, back in Balboa.

"Well, fuck it. *This* is why military organizations insist on keeping their own intelligence gathering ability, no matter what notional benefits there may be in consolidation." Janier then called his aide, Malcoeur, and said, "Get me through to de Villepin, in Balboa, on the secure line."

And why not? Admittedly, no one has ever authorized me to send reconnaissance parties into Balboa, but no one has ever denied me the authority either. And we'd planned on it, back in the day. Let's see if de Villepin has been able to preserve that part of the plan from that butterfingered oaf, McQueeg-Gordon.

And, if not? Then we simply tell him to put it back in, since the limey reports to me.

Lago Sombrero, Balboa, Terra Nova

It had seemed natural, too, to de Villepin to put eyes on the ground to see and report on the legion's First Corps. Moreover, there was still an MC-61 available at Brookings to insert them. That was the relatively stealthy version of the old standby transport, the C-61. Moreover, it was flown by the best pilots in the Gallic Air Force. Knowing that, knowing the plane was available, de Villepin hadn't waited for authorization the dithering Anglian probably wouldn't have given. Instead, he'd sent the plane, with an eighteen-man commando section, on a flight toward Santa Josefina, with a brief fly-by of an area not too far from *Lago Sombrero.*

The aircraft had lifted off with its doors and ramps sealed. Not long after, it had dropped pressure and lowered the ramp. This set the commandos to using the bottled oxygen that came with their kit.

An amusing feature of their equipment, for certain constrained values of "amusing," was that the complete set for a high altitude-high opening jump was possibly the only one the manual for which mentioned, not less than a dozen times, that failure to do X (1 through 12) would cause Y (1 through 12), "resulting in the DEATH of the parachutist."

At a normal, nonsuspicious flying height for this distance from Brookings, which was fourteen thousand two hundred feet, the eighteen commandos had jumped. The jumpmaster had calculated in a dispersal of four hundred and fifty meters between when the first jumper exited the aircraft and when the eighteenth did. He'd also factored in a three-hundred-meter early release to account for forward throw, which is to say retained velocity from the aircraft. The eighteen commandos had come spilling out, then opened their canopies almost immediately. The meticulously packed steerable, gliding parachutes had opened heroically. Then, by night vision goggle-enhanced sight, with a single, not too visible, infrared chemlight on the central jumper, they'd assembled into a loose staggered trail formation. They'd then used their highly glidable parachutes to navigate to a lonesome farmer's field, about fifteen kilometers from *Lago Sombrero*.

The aircraft had continued on its innocent way to Aserri.

The Gallic commandos were genuine professionals, well trained, well led, well equipped, and highly experienced. Among their equipment was included one Balboan F-26 rifle. The Gauls had managed to purchase two of those, from disgruntled legionaries, but the other one had been sent back to Taurus for testing and evaluation. Most of them were accoutered in the pixelated tiger-striped camouflage of the legion, plus a close copy of the legion's standard helmet. The team had two relatively dark-skinned Span-ish speakers. One of those carried the F-26, on point, while the other in the rear, more mufti, in case it was useful to appear to be a local civilian to gather their intelligence. All were highly briefed on Balboan military culture, acronyms, ranks, slang, etc.

After dumping their parachutists' equipment in a hastily exca-vated hole, they'd immediately taken up a standard formation and begun the move to the general vicinity of *Lago Sombrero*.

The commandos moved fast, as one would expect of pros. Arriving before dawn, they'd set up an observation post without incident. They saw three maniples report in at about the same time. Had they looked at the ASP it was just barely possible they might have seen the cadets; there was enough moonlight, if barely, for that, at least if looking from a point nearer the ASP. But their mission was to look at the base, not a bunch of ammunition bunkers. The cadets falling in on their equipment in the bowels of the earth remained undetected.

In an earlier time the Taurans might have been safe enough once they had found a reasonably secure position. Piña's old Balboan

Defense Force had not been so very well trained. The tercios of Carrera's legion, however, had in years earlier and recent been humiliated often enough, badly enough, at the training center at *Fuerte* Cameron—often by closely placed and undetected recon parties—that counter-reconnaissance had become something of an automatic action, if not even a fetish.

Three mobilized maniples of regular and reservists began to sweep the exterior of the base for infiltrators and spies some time around midnight. While most of the mobilized legions and cohorts units had very restrictive rules of engagement, the First Corps, and a few others who were in position to safeguard the secret of the hidden cadets, were under orders to shoot on sight.

The commando—arguably over-officered in comparison to most Gallic units—had a lieutenant in charge, assisted by an *adjudant* as his second in command. They carried their own radio, occasionally trading off. Each of the four teams, of four men each, consisted of a sergeant, a *caporal*, and two privates, except for one of the teams which was led by a *sergent-chef*, a senior sergeant.

Since they expected to be here for a while, three days at a minimum, before extraction, the troops split up their duties, watch on, watch off. Thus, it was the second in command, *Adjudant* Tréville, who was watching when the first Balboans were glimpsed through the jungle trees.

"Lieutenant," whispered the *adjudant,* "we've got people behind us and I'm sure they're not ours." When that didn't work Tréville placed a hand over his officer's mouth, shook him slightly, and repeated the warning.

The lieutenant's eyes came open. He nodded for the sergeant to remove his hand, and asked, "Where?"

Wordlessly, Tréville pointed to the barely silhouetted figures of men—the shadows told of rifles in their hands—less than one hundred and fifty meters away, to the northeast.

"Get the rest of the men up," said the lieutenant. "It's time to get out of here."

"Sir."

"Did you hear that?" asked a Balboan sergeant in a low whisper.

"Hear what, Sarge?" answered his corporal.

"I don't know what it was. A rustle of grass maybe. Then

again"—the Balboan sergeant shook his head—"then again, maybe not." The sergeant motioned for his squad to halt while he listened with more care and attention.

"Shit. I think they've spotted us." Tréville moved a thumb slowly and silently took his rifle off of safe.

The lieutenant gave the hand and arm signal for his section to take up hasty ambush positions. There was some unavoidable sound from that, rifles being propped up, knees scraping the ground, the little creaks of stiffened joints.

"I heard *that*," quietly agreed the Balboan corporal. "An animal, maybe?"

The squad leader shook his head. Placing his radio's microphone to his lips, he reported a possible contact and asked for assistance. "Wait," was the reply. "We'll mount a platoon and have them there in about ten minutes. Out."

"Oh, shit. They've called for help," announced Tréville, still in hushed tones. He had heard, faintly, the sound of the Balboan radio breaking "squelch."

The Gallic lieutenant immediately called for evacuation at a precoordinated point some twelve hundred meters away. To Tréville he said, "We've got to break contact and get out of here. Get ready to take out these guys and move like hell to the PZ." The "PZ" was the pickup zone where they would be met by the recovering helicopter. "But . . . no helicopter's going to be here in less than an hour. I think we have to fight."

Tréville crawled from man to man, giving the order to prepare to fight or to run, at command.

The Balboan sergeant cursed the slowness of the reinforcing platoon. Impatiently, he lifted his head, keeping as close as possible to a tree trunk, for a better view and, more importantly, a better listen.

Just raise your head a little more, old son, thought Tréville as he took careful aim through his rifle's starlight scope. In the grainy, greenish light of the scope's viewing lens he saw the Balboan sweep his helmeted head from side to side, obviously looking for something. Tréville began to squeeze the trigger.

✧   ✧   ✧

"I can't see or hear shit," said the Balboan sergeant to the corporal, still keeping his voice in a whisper. "If there's . . ."

A single shot rang out, followed by a fusillade from the Taurans. The sergeant heard none of it, however, as the first bullet had entered his right temple, blowing his brains out the left rear of his skull.

Initially paralyzed, the Balboans were slow to return fire, trying desperately to find some cover from the storm of copper-covered lead that assailed them. The corporal was the first to gather his wits, which was the more surprising in that the late sergeant's brains had fallen across the corporal's face and body. Other rifles, and a few moments later a machine gun, joined in as their bearers found discipline and duty a greater factor than fear. Within a minute, both sides were thoroughly pinned by each other's wild fire.

Not that the Balboans were hitting anything. Only their machine gunner had a night vision scope, and he was not in position to see much with it. The other Balboans couldn't see anything but muzzle flashes, which were notoriously difficult points of aim at night. Instead, they just sprayed the general area to their front, counting on chance to at least hold the Taurans until help arrived. Once the rest of his men had joined the fight, the corporal patted the ground for the microphone. His first call was not to the reinforcing platoon, but to the on call mortar section. As he spoke to the mortars, the corporal became aware of anguished cries from his own side.

A few miles away, in the 1st Mechanized Tercio motor pool, a complete mechanized platoon looked up almost as a single man. Suddenly a flood of tracers arced through the sky. The reports of heavy automatic fire followed. A lackadaisical preparation quickly became frenzied. The platoon's four Ocelots, and forty odd soldiers, were heading for the post gate in less than two minutes. On the post parade field, a mortar section began to fall in on their guns.

Fifty miles away from the desperate little battle, three helicopters, two gunships and one troop carrier made their tortuous way across and above the jungle. The helicopters dipped into little valleys—had the crews not been inured to the constant roller-coastering they might well have thrown up—and barely scraped over the treetops.

The crews of all three helicopters heard frantic cries for help from the commandos they were racing to rescue. They were treated, if that's the right word, to a blow-by-blow description of the unequal fight.

"Romeo Five-three, this is Charlie Two-seven. You've got to help us now."

"Five-three, Two-seven. There's no way we can make it to the PZ—" The call cut off temporarily as a nearby mortar explosion forced the radio operator's head down. "... we're taking heavy fire; mortar fire. We are stuck. Come in soonest with full firepower."

"Five-three, Two-seven. The lieutenant is down ... crap, he's dead. Took one right through the head. Shit! Five-three, you've got to get us out now!"

A new voice spoke. It was still Tauran. "This is Two-seven! I say again, Charlie Two-seven. We're taking heavy direct fire from at least four armored vehicles! They're chewing us ... the *adjudant*'s down ..."

That was the last transmission heard from Charlie Two-seven by Romeo Five-three.

CHAPTER THIRTY-SEVEN

> Just because something isn't a lie does not mean that
> it isn't deceptive. A liar knows that he is a liar, but
> one who speaks mere portions of truth in order to
> deceive is a craftsman of destruction.
>
> —Criss Jami

La Chorrera Military Academy, Balboa, Terra Nova

Although using teenagers as soldiers has its disadvantages, there
are equally weighty advantages. For one thing, they are extremely
easily led. For another, they are so naturally far below adults on
the social scale that they don't ask too many questions of their
adult leaders; they obey. For a third, they tend to be somewhat
unrealistically enthusiastic and idealistic.

That idealism counts for much. Though it is an element of
received wisdom that causes count for nothing, and that soldiers
fight only for their comrades, this is, at best, a half-truth and, like
other half-truths, is wholly misleading. For the cost of battle is
blood: wounded, crippled, and dead friends. Those costs weigh.
Eventually they can weigh so heavily that the soldiers stop fighting altogether. Why fight, after all, when it involves such loss and
pain? Why fight for your comrades when you can knock them
over the heads and hide them from friend and enemy?

This is where causes and ideals come in. They justify, at least
in part, that pain and those losses. They are usually not infinite
in their strength and reach, but they need not be. They need
only last, or to cause those who adhere to them to last, just a

few days, a few hours, sometimes just a few minutes, longer than their adversaries.

Only Suarez and a few of his key staff knew the real reason the Corps was out maneuvering through the godforsaken jungle.

Approximately nine hundred young, idealistic, and enthusiastic cadets, with their adult instructors, sat waiting for parts of Second and Fifth Legions, plus Thirteenth Brigade, Twenty-second Combat Support Legion—in other words the bulk of Second Corps' regular and reserve echelons—to sweep by on their maneuvers toward, but not into, the Transitway Area. The adults supervising the cadets put on a good show, whatever their fears. The young boys sat essentially without fear.

Places would be left by Second Corps, several large holes on the ground with neither troops nor heavy equipment. Into this space the cadet cohort would fit. Indeed, it would fit and be lost to outside observers among the thirteen thousand other mobilized troops of Second Corps.

The Corps would sweep forward, also picking up the cadets from the Arraijan Military Academy on the way—a different set of spaces was to be left for them—until it reached the old Transitway borders. At the same time, it was expected, if there were Taurans on the ground looking, that the mass of Second Corps would probably drive them out of eyeshot until the cadets had hidden.

Until they disappeared into underground hides, warehouses, housing developments, and whatever else had been prepared for them—which included at least one sewer—the cadets and their instructors, perhaps twenty-one hundred officers, warrants, non-coms, and boys, from both schools combined, would blend well with—indeed they would be indistinguishable from—the mobilized soldiers of the Second Corps.

Then, once the boys and their cadres were well hidden, and the Taurans in an absolute panic over the suddenly materialized threat, the men of Second Corps would go home on trucks and on foot, leaving the Tauran Union Security Force-Balboa none the wiser and feeling much more secure.

Aleksandr Sitnikov, one time officer in His Marxist Majesty's Fifth Guards Motorized Rifle Regiment, had joined Suarez's party early, along with the former's small staff, then marched along with them for the duration. Well over fifty, now, Sitnikov still didn't look a lot older, nor much different, than he had when he'd first come to the legion as a contract instructor on armored fighting vehicles and armored warfare. Balding then, he was almost totally bald now. Other than that, though, he could still pass for a man of about forty or even a bit less. His fierce regimen of physical fitness training probably accounted for some of that. More was to be found in his boyish, good-natured smile.

At a construction site not far from the border, Sitnikov and Suarez shook hands. "We're counting on you, you Volgan bastard," said the latter.

"The boys won't let you down," Sitnikov assured the Balboan.

"I'm sure they won't," Suarez agreed, "and I shall offer a special prayer that fate doesn't let them down."

Military Academy *Sergento* Juan Malvegui, *Puerto Lindo,* Balboa, Terra Nova

Cristobal was the touchiest province to move the cadets around in. Road nets were few, land very constricted by the Shimmering Sea and the lake that formed such a large chunk of the Transitway. Moreover, a substantial number of cadets had to be infiltrated to Clay Dairy Farm—right into the middle of territory that was jointly controlled. Only the density of the jungle and the secondary importance of the area stood on Balboa's side.

Carrera had been almost ready to change the plans for the *Puerto Lindo* cadets, to let them fight with their own small arms and the heavier equipment that had been stashed in the nearby Sabanita Maintenance Facility, even though it was not in an ideal position for their mission.

In the end, it was the possibility that he was ready to change his plans to save his boy that forced him to force himself to leave them alone, except for asking Muñoz-Infantes, at Fort William, to change his plans and dispositions, to put on a more aggressive display with his battalion of Castilians than Carrera had originally asked for.

Ham and the other eighteen hundred cadets were awakened—at least the few who had been able to find some sleep had been awakened; Hamilcar Carrera was not among them—at "Zero

Dark Hundred" by the cadre who had already been up for an hour by then, barring only the few who had been able to snatch an hour or two's sleep. An hour later, an hour before sunrise, the entire *Puerto Lindo* corps of cadets, with their leaders, over twenty-one hundred strong, assembled on the glacis of the old fort. The cadres, a mix of Volgans and Balboans, carried pistols only. The cadets carried a mix of baseball bats, bunk adapters, unfolded entrenching tools, ace handles, and a hefty number of homemade clubs, courtesy of the trees near the academy. Each cadet maniple, further, provided a four-man team bearing signs like "*Balboa es Soberana en la Area del Transitway,*" "Taurans out of our Country," or something in the same general spirit.

After receiving the report, Chapayev, commandant of the school, ordered, "Right...face. Forward...MARCH!" and the entire twenty-one-hundred-strong corps, uniformed and carrying their normal field packs, marched out the main gate of the school, past the memorial to the heroic sergeant who was, uniquely, their namesake, around the beautiful bay, through the ramshackle town, past the neater ship yard, and down the road to Cristobal, about twenty miles away.

Pipes and drums from the school's band alternated their positions in the column to give every maniple a fair ration of resounding bang-bang-bang and cats-locked-in-a-death-struggle. When the band rested, the boys picked up on their own with a medley of patriotic songs.

The latest census said that on the order of sixty thousand people lived on or near the roadway between *Puerto Lindo* and Cristobal. At least eighteen thousand of those joined the cadets. Schools emptied out. Businesses closed. A group of Santandern hookers from a brothel in *Sagrada Incarnación* left work early, and without anybody even having to pay the Balboan bartender to let them go.

At the same time, Jimenez had sent two tercios, which was to say, at this mobilization level about two cohorts, uniformed and fully armed, to march, one of them, on Fort Melia, and the other to begin blowing up rubber boats on the eastern face of Cristobal, the one facing the Tauran-held Fort Tecumseh, across the bay.

Jimenez, sitting in his Fourth Corps headquarters in Cristobal, just imagined the panic in the Tunnel, the existence of which was by no means secret, as a dozen or more battalions, at both ends of the Transitway, converged on their mandate borders before pulling back. In the case of the Castilians, under Muñoz-Infantes, there was no pulling back beyond borders; they were already inside, and in a de facto state of mutiny, *within* the Transitway borders.

Contemplating the Taurans' panic, Jimenez thought, *And they're likely to notice a thousand kids disappearing in all that? I really don't think so.*

Ham, now a second in command of a platoon of cadets, was footsore and tired by the time the column reached the fifty-seven buses parked in half a dozen spread-out splotches just before the split in the roadway that led, one way to Cristobal, the other past the town of Magdalena, then toward Forts Williams and Melia. Between cadets, legionaries, civilians, and, of course, the couple of dozen Santandern hookers, there were probably forty thousand people milling about. In that crowd, Ham took the half of the platoon that was his responsibility, ducked into a bus, changed clothing rapidly—a tough thing while lying flat on one's back on the narrow, dirty rubber mats of the bus's floor—and emerged into the crowd into which the boys now blended much, much better.

By this time, Ham's half of the platoon included all five of the Pashtian boys that had been sent to school with him. Carrera wanted the boy to learn, yes, and wasn't going to shelter him from the risks he needed to run if he were to lead others. But he wasn't a fool either and fully intended that his son, heir, and—with luck—replacement would have every possible chance to survive, even if it cost a few Pashtian boys.

"Where to now, Sergeant?" one of the younger cadets asked Ham, as a half a load of still younger and still uniformed cadets piled onto the vacated bus.

"It's a place they used to call 'Clay Dairy Farm.' No cows there anymore, only some houses and some small warehouses...that sort of thing. Just follow me. And don't march; mill." He led them back in the direction from which they'd come along *Avenida* Scott, then north along a side road that led to a small housing development on one side, and to a temporary storage yard on the other. The yard was guarded by a uniformed civilian, bearing only a shotgun. There was a Volgan warrant officer there, though, named Ustinov, to convince the guard to let the boys into the wired-in compound. Ustinov was designated as maniple commander for the coming battle.

Ham didn't know, but he was pretty sure that Ustinov's next mission would be to disarm the guard and disappear him for a while. As it turned out, he was wrong. The guard position was another one of those veteran-only jobs. The guard would stay there, guarding the boys now more than other people's property, until the fighting began.

The other part of Ham's platoon, under his seventeen-year-old boss, Cadet Signifer Delgado, arrived an hour and a half later, Delgado's group having instructions to mill around a bit more indirectly. By the time they arrived, Ham, his boys, and Ustinov had the partitions between certain theoretically rentable compartments opened, several dozen F-26 rifles out, ammunition for those and two rocket grenade launchers broken down and ready for issue, along with hand grenades, signal grenades, smoke grenades, radios, night vision, batteries, first aid and other medical equipment, and whatever else a platoon of infantry might need.

And then they turned on the radio and waited for the code phrase. They had to turn the radio's volume up very high, since the daily rain, once it commenced to pound the tin roof, made hearing normal sounds all but impossible.

Among the other organizations at the academy were several clubs that catered to the cadets' aspirations for branch assignments, when they enlisted. The legion paid serious attention to those clubs and aspirations, too. After all, why pay to train some man to do X who has already been trained as a boy to do Y? The clubs included, among others, the Cazador club, which was nowhere near as difficult as *Escuela de Cazadores,* a close cognate of Federated States Army Ranger School. Mostly the Cazador Club taught techniques and engaged in some very limited character-building and toughening exercises. Then there was the Artillery Club, a number of the members of which were currently falling in on half a dozen containerized 85mm guns with all the accouterments and ammunition. The Medical Club had mostly split up to provide platoon medics, though a dozen or so stayed with the school's two doctors, in a couple of hotel rooms not far from the presumptive scene of the action.

Then there were clubs for air defense artillery, combat engineers, and armor, light and heavy. All of those went to the Sabanita Maintenance Facility, where ammunition and equipment awaited them. This included fourteen Ocelots in their configuration as assault guns. So who was to notice that a facility dedicating to fixing, among other things, Ocelots, happened to have some extra Ocelots that only looked like they needed fixing?

Isla Darien, Balboa Transitway Area, Balboa, Terra Nova

Pililak sat under a tree, rain pouring on her, even so, arms wrapped around her folded knees. She rocked back and forth, weeping. Sometimes she looked up with eyes full of fright like a rabbit on a fox's menu. Her face was swollen almost beyond recognition. This wasn't from the tears, but from the hordes of vicious mosquitoes who had acquired and then endlessly satisfied a new found love of Pashtian cuisine. And where was her mosquito net? Somewhere at the bottom of the lake, she supposed.

Her back was in shreds, she knew from touch. She didn't want to even think about what it looked like.

The thought, *My lord will never want me now, not with the ruin I've become,* gave birth to a renewed bout of heartbroken weeping.

She had nothing of her own anymore; all she'd been able to save was her lord's rifle, and that needed a cleaning she no longer had the equipment for. Saving the rifle had very nearly cost her her life, but she'd far rather have died than lost Iskandr's arms.

And how had she lost her carefully pilfered equipment and almost lost her lord's rifle and her own life?

She'd stepped off of the muddy bank, into the murky water, with trepidation more than matched by determination. *Courage, Pililak,* she'd thought. *Be like your namesake, small, perhaps, but strong and fearless.* Her air mattress she'd placed partly in the water, with one end resting lightly on the bank to hold it in place for a moment. It had been little problem to put her now much lighter pack on the air mattress, nor to get herself and Ham's rifle aboard as well. She'd pushed off from the bank, then paddled—that the water was still helped here, enormously—to turn around and place her head toward the opposite bank, or where her compass told her the opposite bank must be.

Then, using arms alone, she'd paddled for all she was worth. She couldn't see a damned thing but falling rain and her compass, nor hear a damned thing but the rain.

She was almost exactly halfway across when the merchant

ship, suddenly, with no warning, loomed out of the rain, towering impossibly high and moving faster than she could hope to paddle out of its way. Even though she couldn't, still she tried. The ship struck her, spinning her air mattress so that both compass and pack flipped off to disappear into the light brown water. Barnacles scrapped it and her, ripping both open. A long spasm of pure agony shot up her back and down her legs as the wandering crustaceans shredded her flesh. She barely managed to hang on to the rifle, and that took both hands, with her feet kicking desperately to keep her nose above water.

It was actually the barnacles that saved her life for the nonce. Entangled in her clothing and digging deeply into her skin, they, along with her kicking, and the forward drag of the ship, held her aloft for perhaps twenty or thirty life-saving seconds. This enabled her to get the rifle's sling over one shoulder and across her chest, freeing her hands in the process.

At the time, she understood none of this. In a panic, whatever positives she did were matters of automatic response coupled with sheer luck.

The resistance of the water tore her away from the barnacles, leaving bits of flesh behind, as well as a red train from the hull to her back. Still in full flight mode, she began to swim frantically to get away from the ship. Its passage, though, caused drag, that pulled her backwards, cancelling out her frenzied paddling. Indeed, more than once the drag and the induced current in the water spun her around so that she found herself swimming *toward* the dark and menacing bulk passing by.

The worst moment, though, came when the ship had just about passed her. That was when the inward-running trace of the stern caused the water to pull her strongly into the center line...the center line where the propellers churned the water and would have readily churned the girl.

Screaming aloud, "*My Lord, Iskandr! Give me strength!*" she found strength. Though Hamilcar, called "Iskandr," by some, didn't give it to her; her faith did. Still, it was close, and before she broke free of the tug of the ship, she felt the wash of the propellers, massaging her legs and beckoning.

She saw the ship go, after that, and, knowing the way it had come from gauged her proper direction from that. She might have guessed, but didn't, that the ship had dragged her well to the east. Almost exhausted, swimming slowly to conserve what little strength remained to her, she came to the shore of Darien Island. There she pulled herself out of the water, then lay like one dead, except for the soft sound of a young girl's weeping.

It was light now, but would be dark soon. Then the homicidal mosquitoes would come out, to feast on her, even further reducing her already low levels of blood.

But I don't know where I am anymore. I don't have a map. I don't have a compass. I can't see the stars...

She was about to shriek with her frustration and her sense of complete failure. And then she heard it, loud enough that even the rain couldn't drown it out. It was the train, said to be the "fastest transcontinental train on the planet," since it took only two hours to cross two continents.

She remembered the lay of her lost map. *There is only one train here. It is only on one side. When I reach it, I need only face to the left and follow it, and it will bring me closer to my lord.*

Tears forgotten, Pililak—"Ant" the small, yes, but also the strong, the determined, and the very brave—stood, grabbed Hamilcar's rifle, and began the not-so-very-long walk, some of which would be through water and mud, to the train tracks that ran toward the Shimmering Sea, *Puerto Lindo,* and the boy she believed was her god. With the passing train's rumbling and whistle growing ever louder and more distinct, Ant looked heavenwards at the unseen stars, thanking her lord's true father for his aid at a time she desperately needed divine aid.

CHAPTER THIRTY-EIGHT

Simplicity, patience, compassion.
These three are your greatest treasures.
Simple in actions and thoughts,
you return to the source of being.
Patient with both friends and enemies,
you accord with the way things are.
Compassionate toward yourself,
you reconcile all beings in the world.

—Lao Tzu,
Tao Teh Ching

UEPF *Spirit of Peace,* in orbit over Terra Nova

A single large ship with half a dozen much smaller escorts crawled across the screen in Marguerite's conference room. Telling her ship's computer, "Get me Khan, male," she asked the latter just whose little flotilla that was.

"New Middle Kingdom," Khan answered. "But as to whether they intend to join in the attack on Balboa, something I am inclined to doubt, or have some other reason—"

Khan female piped in, "Give you odds, husband, that they're going to try to evacuate their civilians and nothing else."

"Civilians?" asked Wallenstein.

"Yes, High Admiral. Nobody officially made much of it, though I understand the Balboans were seething inside, but the Taurans hired a large number, eight or nine thousand, Zhong to run the Transitway. They came cheap, I understand, and the revenues from the Transitway went a long way toward paying for the defense of the Transitway. Perhaps, even, a bit more."

"All right," Wallenstein said. "But what kind of ship is that?"

"Wait a sec, please, High Admiral," Khan, male, requested. Wallenstein heard keys being tapped. In a few minutes he came back with, "She's either the *Luyang*, or the *Anshan*, but not the *Jiangwei*," Khan answered. "Those are all midsized aircraft carriers, though the latter pushes that definition. The *Luyang* and *Anshan* are real aircraft carriers, not just amphibs. Even so, they're better configured for helicopter and antisubmarine operations than surface actions.

"They're just not that big."

"Could they engage the Balboan Navy with success?" she asked.

She couldn't see him, but she could almost hear wheels turning in Khan's head. When he answered, it was to say, "Not really my area of expertise, High Admiral, nor anyone in the Peace Fleet's. That said, the Balboan carrier, the *Dos Lindas*, carries precisely no high performance aircraft, while the Zhong ship can carry about fifteen or eighteen, depending on how many helicopters they're carrying. I should think, then, that the Zhong could take them out. At least at sea, some distance from Balboan land-based air, I think they could.

"On the other hand..."

"Yes?" Wallenstein prompted.

"On the other hand," Khan continued, "if the Zhong intended something like that, they'd have sent all three. If they'd had four, they'd have sent all four."

"So what the hell do they want?" she asked.

"I haven't the first clue, personally," Khan admitted, "though my wife's instincts for such things are generally sound."

Mar Furioso, Anshan Battle Group, Imperial New Middle Kingdom Navy, Terra Nova

Eight bows plowed furrows in the waves, rising and falling in the way of ships moving at speed. In the center, the largest two bows rocked perhaps a bit less than their half-dozen escorts, all of which kept in a fairly tight ring around the mother ship, the carrier *Anshan,* and the large fleet replenishment ship which was indispensable for getting the task force to where it was and wanted to be.

Vice Admiral Yee Ten Li, commanding the Northern Fleet Expeditionary Force, had sailed with three dozen sets of sealed and coded contingency orders locked in a safe in his own staff's area of the *Anshan*. Heavens forbid he should return to home port with a set unsealed that he had not been authorized to open and read. Ordinarily, given modern communications ability, carrying sealed orders would seem silly. Realistically, given the ability to break communications on the part of some of *Xing Zhong Guo's* adversaries, carrying contingency orders which could be activated was much more secure, where those could be made appropriate.

The battle group had been engaged in antisubmarine training in the rough middle of the ocean, against the Federated States Navy. With that group the Zhong were, for the last twenty or so years, on very friendly terms. It had not gone especially well, even though Admiral Yee had the sense that the round eyes were going easy on his crews.

But you'll get that when you're using out-of-date ships, with out-of-date sonar, and out-of-date computers, and crews basically new to their jobs, thought the Admiral. *We have reason to be concerned, yes, but no reason to be ashamed. My men did well, given their disadvantages, especially in going up against the class of the planet, the FSN.*

Even so, he *had* been embarrassed for his country and his service. Thus, it had come as something of a relief when he'd received coded instructions to open a particular sealed envelope, a thick, yellow thing, which had directed him to proceed to the northern shore of the Republic of Balboa, take no part in any hostilities beyond self-defense if attacked, but to begin evacuation of imperial subjects upon the outbreak of hostilities, or upon their imminence, should that be obvious enough to judge.

The orders were about as clear as he could have expected. The problem was that the staff weenie who had written them up, anywhere from six months to six years...or sixteen years... prior, hadn't really thought about the likely situation on the ground. Yes, there were about nine thousand imperial subjects in Balboa, working on the Transitway. There were *also* an additional twenty-two thousand family members the staff weenie seemed to have forgotten about. To make it worse, about half of those were in easy range of the sea the Balboans called the *Mar Furioso*. A quarter were midway across the isthmus of Balboa, which was hard to get at, while the last quarter were all the way on the other side, by the Shimmering Sea, which Yee thought would be impossible to get helicopters to, and impossible for the civilians to evacuate from should fighting break out across the country. There was after all, only a single road and a single railroad, both of which were sure to be cut within minutes of the first fusillade.

The prospect frightened Admiral Yee. In political and military circles in Taurus, the Federated States, Volga, Yamato, and some other spots that mattered, the Zhong were reputed to care little for human life, even their own. This was base calumny. The Zhong cared *deeply* about Zhong lives. They were just realistic: They lived in an imperfect world, surrounded by adversaries real and potential. They were not rich, while some of those adversaries were filthy rich. Thus, sometimes, when it was necessary or so advantageous as to be nearly necessary, or when it was a case of lose one to save ten, the Zhong could be quite ruthless. This did not, however, mean that they didn't value the lives lost, nor weep for the suffering of those killed and those left behind, bereft.

Still, thought Yee, *the simple fact is that my orders are impossible. I cannot evacuate thirty-one thousand civilians, some of whom will be two hundred kilometers away, with the miserable thirty helicopters at my disposal, even tossing in the utterly unsuitable four on the escorts, and the two on the replenishment ship. I couldn't do it if I moved right up to the coast. The best I can hope for might be to get the half that are on the* Mar Furioso *side. The very best. And then only if I move in very close.*

Which—sigh—I suppose I'm going to have to do. Glad I stood down all the helicopters for the last week or so, so they'll be ready when the time comes, if it does.

SSK *Megalodon, Mar Furioso, Bahia de Balboa,* eighty kiloyards north of the *Isla Real,* Terra Nova

The fleet, such as could move, was gone from their normal moorings in the port of Balboa or the hook of the *Isla Real.* Where they were going, none but the legion's naval commander, Roderigo Fosa, knew. Everyone knew, though, that nothing Balboa could field on the surface of the sea was a match for much of anyone with a real navy.

Still, not every vessel in Balboa's little fleet had scampered off.

The SSKs, the coastal defense subs, remained on local waters, as did a number of patrol boats and corvettes.

"Skipper," said the sonar man for the original of the SSKs, the *Megalodon*, Antonio Auletti. "I've got something...something big, I think."

Conrad Chu, Warrant Officer Chu, captain of the *Meg*, had been dozing, as had most of his crew. No real need, after all, to keep everything continuously manned when all you're doing is resting on a sandy bottom, mostly surrounded by seaweed. Still, some things did require continuous monitoring, sonar, life support, some aspects of engineering. That still left most of the crew unoccupied and either bored to death or, in preference—and in anticipation of possible lengthy periods of time without rest—dead asleep.

Chu hit the lever on the side of his chair, itself sitting on a low dais, and leaned upward as the chair's back moved with the quietest of hisses. Once upright, he rubbed sleep from his eyes, then asked, "Identification?"

"Nothing I've heard in these waters before," Auletti replied. "It sounds a little like the St. Nicholasburg class the Volgans trained me on, but...mmm...smoother. Plus a big support ship; that one's noisy. And some numbers of escorts but I can't make out their number or types."

"St. Nicholasburg...hmmm...any sounds of air ops?" Chu asked.

"None, Skipper...ah...ah...wait." Auletti held up a finger, then clasped his left hand around his headphone. "There it is. I make it as a jet takeoff."

"Attack carrier then," Chu decided. "Weapons?"

"Yes, Skipper."

"Make that 'target one.' I want a continuous firing solution kept for it."

"Aye, aye, Skipper."

Mar Furioso, Anshan Battle Group, Imperial New Middle Kingdom Navy, Terra Nova

Yee had tried getting in touch with the Balboan government through his country's embassy. "Sorry, Admiral," the embassy reported, "but the Balboan government seems to be a little out of touch...yes, that means we can't reach them for anything, lately."

He'd tried calling directly. No luck. He sent a message through some chums in the Federated States Navy. They reported that the FSC's ambassador, Thomas Wallis, also was out of communication with the Balboan government. He'd asked permission to take a helicopter ashore but that his government had refused.

"Perfumed princes floating on high on their ancestors' achievements," he'd judged it. "But what can I do? Orders are orders."

Guano Island, Hurricane Straits, north of Caimanera, Cienfuegos, Shimmering Sea, Terra Nova

The house could have been magnificent. Once it just might have been. About sixty feet on a side, originally double floored, with tall and elegant windows, sadly *sans* glass, the thing, reconstructed and reroofed, would have done for a wealthy misanthrope's mansion, or a monastery, in fine fashion. It even had a highly desirable interior courtyard.

As it was, a husband and wife couple squatted in a tent among the ruins. They were originally from the nearby island of Manteca. The husband had joined the legion a decade or so prior. Now they drew a standard salary for him, with a not-insubstantial hardship allowance for them both, for keeping a look out. They interspersed that with fishing as a cover.

Carrera didn't have recon satellites and, though a compromised television screen aboard the Earthers' flagship sometimes got him some important intelligence from the Yamatans who had provided the TV, it was always a bit iffy and always subject to what the Yamatans thought. They defined his "need to know" as whatever would be good for them, if he knew. Otherwise, they could be extremely reticent. They'd never even admitted to the TV.

So, as with most things, he and his legion made do. They had the Condors, which were fine for long-range recon, though too secret for the nonce to be lightly risked. They had spies, especially in Taurus. And then there were the "island people," which was how Fernandez referred to them. These were sometimes Balboans, sometimes sympathetic and trustworthy local hirelings, living out on the islands of the Shimmering Sea, traveling around by boat, often making their living by boat, and reporting in.

Just this once, though, for that husband and wife team squatting in the ruins of the old Federated States light keeper's house, sheer awe interposed itself between the thing to be reported on—things, rather, thirty-six of them—and the report itself.

From a window a quarter of the way up the lighthouse came, "Holy Fucking Shit." That was Sergeant Miller, in his native language, a kind of English.

"What's that?" asked Mrs. Miller, from about forty feet below.

"*Unu ron*, woman," said the sergeant. "You bring me deh pen un deh pad."

His tone said, *Hurry; it's really important.* Not questioning his judgment on such things, she ran up the spiraling concrete stairs. When she looked out the window she, too much the lady, didn't say anything. She thought, however, *Holy fucking shit.*

In the Spanish they'd both learned, while living in Balboa, Miller said, "Get the radio up. Make contact with headquarters. They need to know about this."

Hurricane Straits, north of Caimanera, Cienfuegos, Shimmering Sea, Terra Nova

First in order of sail came His Anglian Majesty's Ship *Furious*, followed at a distance of about four nautical miles by HAMS *Indomitable*. Behind *Indomitable*, at a slightly greater distance, about eight kilometers, came *Charlemagne*, no stranger to these waters, and *Charles Martel*. Those were just the carriers, all four of the same class though with minor national differences. Between them, they loaded two hundred twelve first-rate combat aircraft. They and the task force moved as quickly as practical consistent with maintaining their antisubmarine screen. This ranged around twenty knots, and not the much more economical fourteen or so they'd have done in a normal passage or in peacetime maneuvers. The reason for their caution was that a Balboan SSK had once taken out a Gallic nuclear sub and a frigate.

The formation was somewhat more dispersed than sound doctrine would have called for. This was because both the Royal Anglican Navy and the Navy of the Republic of Gaul totally and thoroughly detested and distrusted each other. Neither wanted to give the other an excuse for an "accident."

Around the carriers, in a complex defensive formation, were some twenty-six visible escorts, destroyers, frigates, and four cruisers. Between the Anglian contingent, and the Gallic, in two columns, sailed the seven fuelers, reefers, ammunition haulers, and grand parts bins for the rest. Unseen, but presumptively below and far out to the fore and flanks, were four nuclear powered submarines, keeping their own distance from the TU's task force and its noise. The other reason to keep the subs out was that, with the credible Balboan submarine threat, the area closer in to what amounted to the core of the Gallic and Anglian navies was a free fire zone.

Also unseen, in the seventeen-hundred-meter depths of the sea bottom around Guano Island, rested another of Balboa's thick-walled, deep-diving, virtually coastal defense submarines. The *Orca II*, named for a submarine lost in action against the Gauls some years before, was, like *Meg*, under orders to fire only if fired upon or on unambiguous evidence that war had broken out. And then, it was expressly not to go after warships, if it could be avoided, but to close the straits by threatening and sinking freighters and support ships that might move through them to resupply the combatants. Other passages were covered by other subs. Their rules of engagement were driven only in part by the strategic value of targets and more by concerns that the limited experience of Balboan sub crews was not up to going after major surface combatants without a massive element of surprise in their favor.

The captain, Warrant Officer Ibarra, formerly Chu's exec aboard *Megalodon,* didn't need sonar to tell him anything. He could *hear* the passage, even through the layers of thirty-seven surface vessels, especially with their supply ships straining at maximum speed just to barely keep up. The constant pinging in the audible frequencies of twenty-six medium frequency sonars in the escorts gave Ibarra no little discomfort, despite the stealthy characteristings of his boat's hull. After all, enough Gauls, pinging constantly, had done his command's namesake to death. The lower frequency pings of the Variable Depth sonars added a measure of poignancy, where that was defined as terror-induced sweat.

These were mostly known signatures. As sonar identified them and gave them classifications and target names on the big screen, forward, Ibarra whistled softly. *We're quiet, as quiet as anything on or under the sea. And our target strength for active sonar is minuscule. Even so, I wouldn't want to try to break through that screen, less still to try to break away after launching on one of the carriers while their helicopters track us like bloodhounds.*

Military Police Cohort Guard House, First Corps, *Lago Sombrero,* Balboa, Terra Nova

The base, itself, was built around the intersection of a substantial, north-south running airfield, and the InterColombian Highway. It had once been a small Federated States base of about a dozen significant buildings, hosting air, infantry, and light coastal artillery assets. Later it had been turned over to the then Balboa Defense Force. Stormed by the Federated States during its invasion of Balboa, its ruins had lain abandoned for over a decade, until Carrera had begun the creation of the *Legion del Cid.*

Since then the place had expanded enormously. It wasn't really capable of comfortably housing the entire First Corps, but it could provide headquarters down to maniple level, billeting for all the officers, warrants, centurions, and noncoms, space for all necessary medical facilities, plus motor pools for the bulk of the Corps' vehicles, five or six thousand of them. The other facilities were adequate to the regular cadre of about two thousand, plus a thousand new troops going through their assimilation tour, but not more than that.

Medics had been called to the barred cells to dress the Tauran captives' wounds. For two of those the medics asked, "Why bother? Outside of a major hospital they're going to die anyway," but did what they could even so. The other four, who were conscious, were likewise treated, though given no pain medication. Whether this was a violation of any convention against torture was a case, in Balboan terms, of, "Who gives a shit?"

The other dozen men of the Gallic recon team were, oh, very dead indeed. They lay under tarps, outside of the guard house, pending a team from Graves Registration showing up to deal with them. Since "Graves Reg" was a very low priority call up, the bodies were likely to begin rotting and stinking long before anything was done.

The intelligence officer, or 1c, First Corps glanced over the four surviving Tauran—he assumed they were Tauran—soldiers as they were being treated for their wounds. He noted that two were in civilian dress while two others wore unmarked uniforms that could easily be mistaken for legionary battle dress in a dim light. He'd also seen geuine legionary battle dress on a couple of corpses, outside.

"So what happens to us now?" asked Tréville, in Spanish. The *adjudant*'s voice was strained with pain from his wounds.

The 1c answered in fairly colloquial French. To speak some French had become almost *de rigeur* to be assigned as an intelligence officer in the legion, though English was more common. In any case, the 1c spoke better French than most.

"Kind of depends. A court-martial for spying, of course. Punishment? If there's no attack by the Tauran Union, I imagine you might get off with something relatively minor. Or perhaps Carrera will exchange you for something. Who knows? Not my style of prophecy. On the other hand, if your boys attack...and don't win...well, I expect you'll be shot...for spying. Our Articles of War are pretty traditional. That is the specified penalty for spying."

"But we were just doing a recon, keeping an eye on you!" exclaimed Tréville. "That's nothing to shoot a man for!"

The 1c smiled, coldly. "In civilian clothes? Or not wearing your own country's uniforms but ours? With our type weapons? Shooting up our soldiers? Near a vital military center? C'mon. You'll only be shot because the crime doesn't call for hanging."

Suddenly, as if it were a new thought, the intel officer looked upward. "Although we could hang you, I suppose; for murder. Four of our men are dead...and we are *not* at war. On the other hand, the penalty for murder is crucifixion." He shuddered, adding, "And let me tell you, that is one shitty way to go. I've seen it." The 1c left a pregnant pause in the conversation, then continued. "Of course, you could always turn state's evidence, so to speak."

Tréville said nothing. Seeing that he wouldn't, the 1c said, "Your funeral," and left.

The 1c immediately went to an office off the block of cells to listen to whatever the microphone planted in the cell might pick up.

"Are they serious, *Adjudant*?" asked *Caporal* Moreau, one of those in Balboan battle dress. The corporal was still in serious pain, a searing agony in his shoulder from a gunshot wound, so was perhaps not thinking clearly. "*Shoot* us? For what? *Crucify us?!* What kind of maniacs are these people?"

"Relax," answered Tréville, not so badly hurt and thinking more clearly. "And stop talking before you say something you should not."

In the office, eavesdropping, the 1c told the MP in charge

of the desk, "I want six men with rifles, one with a pistol, and several shovels. Take them out and have them start digging, the ones that can. Start to go through the motions of shooting them, but assume I'll come and stop you before it's too late. Do NOT shoot them."

The Tunnel, *Cerro Mina*, Balboa Transitway Area, Balboa, Terra Nova

As it had been almost since the disappearance of Patricia Britain and her women, the Taurans' headquarters was a flurry of activity, most of it with a point. Staff officers consulted over maps while drawing operational overlays with alcohol pens. Messengers hurried frantically from one officer's desk to another. A team of wiremen checked connections between the field telephones strung between staff sections.

Walking calmly from place to place, McQueeg-Gordon's chief of staff, Moncey, who was for all practical purposes still Janier's chief of staff, inspected maps and charts to ensure integration and coordination between the various sections and subordinate commands. Given the sheer number of languages, it was a toughie.

Moncey stopped for a conversation with the C-2, de Villepin. Before speaking, he looked over the Intelligence overlay on the map on de Villepin's wall. Even as he watched the famously large-breasted Anglian captain used an alcohol wipe to erase something from the area of the map labeled, "*Lago Sombrero.*"

That, he had heard already, was the disappeared reconnaissance team.

In other places on the map, arrows pointed to the Transitway Area, and then away. They described a maneuver, rather, a series of them, that the operational graphics didn't quite cover. Whoever had done them, though, appeared to have decided that the lunges were mere feints.

"De Villepin," asked the chief, "just what the hell are the Balboans doing?"

As he searched the top of his desk for the pointer he knew had been there just a few minutes ago, de Villepin said, "Trying to keep us off balance, I think, while they try to find the men who murdered those women. I don't think they realize that that doesn't matter anymore. The planes and airships are in the air, with the former very close. The carriers start launching shortly. We couldn't call this off if we wanted to . . . Aha, there you are." He held up the pointer, triumphantly, extended it, then walked to the map.

The end of the pointer touched on a twisted arrow drawn on the map between the nearby towns of Las Mesas and San Juan Bautista, homes of two regiments of legionary infantry, and the *Isla Real*.

"Nothing surprising in this," said the C-2, "and it works to our advantage. These two tercios, in battalion strength only, are moving by hovercraft and helicopter, some small boats too, to the big island and these two smaller ones." The pointed end touched briefly on a couple of the larger islands around the *Isla Real*, then returned to the big island. "The trainees here—most of them—on the island are also taking up defensive positions. They've no effect on our plans and can be expected to surrender after the country falls."

De Villepin's pointer tapped lightly on a dozen spots on the island, as he explained, "And we've seen, by air and satellite, a literal shitload of trucks moving troops and equipment from place to place."

"What kind of equipment?" asked the chief.

"About what you'd expect, sir. Artillery, mortars, some armor—mostly light armor—and general supplies."

"Numbers of troops?"

"Hard to say, sir. There are maybe ten thousand trainees and students on the island, plus a couple thousand instructors. Between what we've seen moving to the island, what's still waiting at the casernes, and what's on the road to Las Mesas and San Juan Bautista, I estimate another fourteen or fifteen soldiers beyond that. Which is all to the good. They may as well put up 'prisoner of war camp' signs, because they'll be surrendering after their state goes down.

"Note, though, that the islands are . . . well, to say 'heavily fortified' would be a considerable understatement. National assets"—spy satellites and spy planes, also, though they were not "national assets," info fed to them by the UEPF—"have identified over thirty-thousand bunkers and other positions, something over one hundred per square kilometer. There is probably nearly as much concrete on that island as there was in the entire Maginot Line, back on Old Earth. I'm pretty sure many of them, maybe most, are fakes. But the Intelligence and Security Agency can't tell us yet which is which. They are *very* good fakes."

"What about the Second and Fourth Corps?" the chief asked.

"They've stopped moving towards the Transitway and appear to be dispersing or retreating. Frightened of us or our reaction? As I said before, Chief, I think they're trying to disconcert us to buy time."

"Artillery?"

"The mobilized units have brought theirs out with them. Tenth Artillery Legion's guns are still in their parking spots."

The chief wiped a sweaty hand across a sweatier brow; the tunnel was an oven in Balboa's heat, even at night, even with the air conditioning going. There were just too many people in too small a space for it to be otherwise.

He asked, "Do you believe all of it, de Villepin? Do you believe everything they're showing us?"

"No, sir." The C-2 shook his head. "No, I don't. I think we're being painted a picture . . . or maybe a kaleidoscope is a better way to put it. They've got so many troops on the ground right now that they could be hiding anything, doing anything, without our knowing about it."

"So what *are* they doing . . . or hiding?"

De Villepin turned to his map again. "Sir, I just don't know. And that worries me."

"You think the Balboans are going to attack?" The chief's voice was strained with the immediate worry.

"No . . . not exactly. But I do think that these maneuvers are a ballet, something to keep our minds occupied with while something else is planned."

The chief considered. "Can you articulate your suspicions to Janier?" Neither Gaul really cared about the opinions of McQueeg-Gordon.

"Sir, I can tell him what I suspect. I probably can't make him believe me since I can't produce any hard data to back it up. He's the type who really needs hard, understandable, manageable data."

"Call him and try. Do the best you can. Now tell me what happened with that SF recon team."

"Sir, all I know is what the chopper pilots reported. The team was compromised and tried to fight their way out. They were shot up pretty badly. Some may have been captured."

"Have the Balboans said anything?"

"Not a word. Which is kind of strange, if you think about it."

PART VI

CHAPTER THIRTY-NINE

Never interrupt your enemy when he is making a mistake.

—Napoleon

Fort Nelson, Balboa Transitway Area, Balboa, Terra Nova

The alleged phenomenon of decision cycling had perhaps never really worked as it had been billed in the history of warfare on two planets. That said, sometimes one could present one's enemy with so many decisions at one time that he either fell into paralysis or, in attempting to meet them all, fell victim to micromanagement and violation of span of control.

To some extent Carrera had already done this to the Tauran Union forces in Balboa. Taking advantage of their penchant for micromanagement anyway, he had presented them with so many targets, so widely dispersed, that the Tunnel had taken command of platoons, bypassing brigades and battalions in the process.

For example, the Gallic Thirty-fifth Commandos' combat elements consisted of three companies of commandos, each of three platoons, plus small mortar and antitank elements, and a headquarters which had scout, medium mortar, and antitank platoons, plus the "ash and trash" usually found in a headquarters.

The Thirty-fifth, however, hadn't been given a battalion mission, nor even three company missions close enough in space for battalion to exercise command and control. Oh, no, because of the target array presented by Carrera, one company, Company B, was assigned to helicopter to Fort Guerrero to attack the headquarters of Second Tercio and Second Legion. Another rifle company, Alpha, had three separate platoon missions, none of them within easy supporting distance of any other. The last rifle company, Charlie, was more fragmented still, having one mission for a platoon, one for a platoon minus one squad, and four for individual squads.

Command- and control-wise, these arrangements had one imagined virtue to the man theoretically at the top, McQueeg-Gordon. Being an artilleryman himself, dedicated to the maxim that guided virtually all artillery thinking—"maximum feasible centralized control"—to him this form of mission tasking ensured that all the real control, all the real decision making power, remained with his headquarters.

The Thirty-fifth had one more difficulty to contend with. When the better part of the equivalent of a Tauran infantry division had begun bearing down on Arnold Air Force Base and its own Fort Nelson, the commandos had to abandon planning and rehearsing for its offensive missions in order to dig in like madmen in case they had to defend their own turf.

Forts Melia and Tecumseh, Balboa Transitway Area, Balboa, Terra Nova

Much the same story held true for the Fourteenth Infantry and Thirty-seventh Commando on Fort Melia, as well as the Two Hundred and Seventeenth Infantry currently enduring the jungle school at Fort Tecumseh. When those had been threatened by the maneuvers of Jimenez's corps, covering for the cadets, with the added possibility of civilian rioting to contain, both battalions had had to suspend offensive preparations and begin to dig in with most companies, while rehearsing riot control with at least one each. This would all change once the Taurans moved and seized the initiative, of course. It was only a temporary matter, and unimportant, that they were currently reacting to Balboan moves.

Fort Muddville, Balboa Transitway Area, Balboa, Terra Nova

The dragoon battalion, the 420th, plus the Sachsen Panzer Battalion, the Fifteenth, were also pinned, even though no one was obviously threatening the Fort Muddville-Brookings area. With units of the Balboan Third searching *Ciudad* Balboa City house by house for traces of the murderers, so many small units that they proved impossible to keep track of, the two heavy battalions had had to stay put, organized into two heavy task forces, one Gallic dominated, one Sachsen, with their recon elements well to the south to watch the approaches into their area. Any other choice would leave both the key installations, Muddville and Brookings, at the mercy of a Balboan surprise attack. Possibly even the Florida Locks could have been endangered.

Pedregal, Balboa, Terra Nova

An assistant helped Fernandez move his wheelchair onto the specially made lift on the right side of his staff van. The lift descended to the asphalt parking lot that abutted the warehouse. A signifer of the Eleventh Tercio by the name of Boyd reported to him.

"Sir, this looks like the place."

"Show me," Fernandez ordered.

The signifer saluted and turned to lead the way. As he walked he looked over his shoulder to explain what he had seen. "There is a lot of dried blood and shit on the floor. I'm not a policeman so I can't say who or what the blood is from. But the place has never been used for a slaughterhouse, the realtor tells me. There are also some things that I don't think police use much. Blowtorches. Vise grips. A rope run over a pipe. Big pile of shit under that one."

"Where is the owner?" Fernandez demanded.

"Actually the realtor, sir, and he waiting for you, sir. Inside. He also says he can give a description of the man who rented the place."

From his wheelchair Fernandez turned his head as far as he was able and ordered an underling, "Get us some composite sketch people here immediately. I want a video team and a forensics team as well." The underling began to dial on his cellular phone.

The signifer continued, "Sir, inside there's also a van painted in NDI colors and some police uniforms."

Fernandez's wheelchair reached the open garage door and looked inside. "Oh, yes. This is the place all right. Boyd, you and your men have done well. Please deploy them around the site to secure it."

Looking around the foul smelling room, Fernandez contemplated a problem. *Should I even tell Carrera we've made a serious leap in solving the case? He's ready to fight now; or will be within a few hours at the latest. He might change his mind if he thinks peace is possible.*

Fernandez was one of the very few people who knew essentially all the details of the national-size ambush Carrera planned to spring on the Taurans. He closed his eyes to shut out distractions so that he could concentrate. *But this was a once in a millennium chance. If we let those boys come out of their hides and go back home the secret will never be kept. Carrera knows that as well as I do. And . . . I think that he's decided war with the Tauran Union is inevitable. Damned likely anyway.*

It was my job, once upon a time, to provide the spark that would ignite an Tauran invasion. I wonder if Carrera knows that one of the plans I considered was to have an Tauran woman, a soldier or a soldier's wife preferably, grabbed off the street by some thugs and beaten, raped and killed in front of a video camera?

Ah, well. I'd better tell him and let him decide what to do.

A few hours later, when the composite artists had produced a picture of the man who had rented the warehouse, Fernandez swore at length and with eloquence. "Arias!" He knew exactly where to find a photo of the culprit. And he knew that the folder with the picture would have an address.

"Boyd, give me one squad," demanded Fernandez.

Paitilla, *Ciudad* Balboa, Balboa, Terra Nova

Quickly and quietly the squad from Boyd's platoon fanned out to surround the house. No sirens alerted the occupants; it wasn't that kind of a squad. When the squad was in position Fernandez gave a signal. Doors were smashed down, to the alarm of the neighbors. In a few moments the soldiers emerged, dragging a woman and four children aged six to thirteen. Fernandez said not a word as two soldiers unloaded scrap wood onto a pile and set it alight. Once the flames were roaring he turned to the woman.

"Where is your husband?" demanded Fernandez. The woman said nothing.

Turning to the squad leader Fernandez commanded "Throw one of her brats on the fire . . ." He pointed to the youngest and said "That one!"

The woman shrieked, sank to her knees and began to beg for the life of her child.

"Madam," said Fernandez, and his voice was colder than any ice, "you have a choice. Tell me what I want to know or see your children burn alive. For their sakes, I hope you know where your husband is."

The woman gibbered until the soldiers reluctantly picked up her baby and made ready to throw it into the flames. Sobbing, then, she murmured an address.

Lumière, Gaul, Terra Nova

An aide ducked a head into Janier's office, announcing that Carrera wished to speak with him.

"Janier."

"We have a photo, now, of one of them. We expect to have more within a few days."

"Do you have them in custody?" Janier demanded.

"I don't recall that a picture leads to instantaneous capture in the Tauran Union," Carrera retorted. "Can you give me an example?"

Janier ignored the jibe, answering, "The Tauran Union isn't facing what you are if those men are not captured."

"Good point," Carrera admitted. "On the other hand, we're maybe a little tougher to take on than some others, as well. It might be that the Cosmopolitan Progressive Neo-Aristocracy that runs your Union has forgotten that." Carrera's tone was not conciliatory.

Yes, it might be, Janier silently agreed. Even so, he said, "But whatever they have remembered or forgotten is irrelevant. Before it's too late, you had best remember you can't win, not against the full might of the Tauran Union. Find those bastards, quickly. And, by the way, whatever happened to the men we sent to *Lago Sombrero* to ensure that you were abiding by your word?"

"They're being held." *Those still alive.*

"Good. Nothing had better happen to them. Janier, out!"

Imperial Base Camp, Imperial Range Complex, Balboa, Terra Nova

Since the beginning of the crisis, the Balboans had, for a change, pulled all their people out of the base camp, leaving it free for the TU. Into that slightly superior facility the helicopter-borne troops of the Gallic First Airmobile Brigade had moved, not a bit sorry to leave behind their inadequate tents.

There were only a few powers in the world willing to pay the expense of maintaining a completely airmobile division. The Federated States did. The late Volgan Empire had. And the Gauls had. Now that division was reduced down to about the size of a brigade. Of that brigade, two full combat battalions, plus all the helicopters needed to lift one of them simultaneously, waited expectantly for the word to move. The full brigade headquarters was there, along with artillery and engineer detachments. There would not be enough lift for those last two until the infantry had been shuttled out.

In the wooden-walled and tin-roofed square shack that served as the command post, the commander of the brigade, a lantern-jawed colonel, listened while his company, troop, and battery commanders, one after the other, back briefed their parts in the next day's operations.

The brigade was initially assigned to eliminate the Balboan Tenth Artillery Legion at and around Alcalde Flores. The Tenth was scattered in eight different casernes around the area. Accordingly, the brigade had assigned its three artillery batteries and two scout platoons to insure that two of the casernes were under sufficient observed fire that mobilization would be impossible. The artillery batteries were, of course, available to fire in support of other units.

An infantry battalion's three rifle companies had the same mission for another six casernes. The remaining battalion's job was to tackle and quickly destroy one of the casernes and the leaders expected to be found on it. They would then be helicoptered to another, until it was neutralized. This would free up another company, so that the four maneuverable companies could fly to and link up with two reduced companies that were still static, and overrun yet two more casernes until those were taken. The two reduced companies that were freed up by that would close on their still engaged sister companies. It would take several iterations, but there was nothing in principle wrong with the concept. That said, even though it was not a bad plan, it did, perhaps, depend too much on things going well from the start.

Casa Linda, Highway *InterColombiana*, Balboa, Terra Nova

Carrera stopped by the house on his way to *Lago Sombrero,* the place he judged, more than any other, to be the center of gravity for the battle to come.

"It's time to go, *miel,*" he told Lourdes.

"But, Patricio, this is only our home. Why should they bomb us here? Surely they wouldn't. After all, you'll be gone. It will only be myself and the children and our 'helpers' here."

"They don't know that. I've actually gone to some trouble to make sure they don't know where I am. And I don't know that they will bomb or they won't. I *do* know that they might...to get me."

Bowing to the inevitable, Lourdes nodded sadly. Tears in her eyes, she began to direct the servants, the guards, Alena, the children, and Ham's wives, to save what they could of the most important of her and her husband's treasures, things more sentimental than valuable. Carrera, once he had seen that there would be no further argument, gave her what might be a last hug, kissing her lips and neck, and left for *Lago Sombrero* in his unescorted and nondescript sedan.

Aserri Airport, Santa Josefina, Terra Nova

Calderón probably never really understood the full implications of bringing Tauran troops into his country. Raised to accept the artificial fantasy of neutrality based on impotence, he hadn't even considered that, once he brought foreign troops in, he had already given up his country's neutrality. Indeed, he'd given it up so thoroughly that the Taurans didn't even bother to consult with Santa Josefina as they took over airfield and port in the course of building up for the coming invasion.

Part of that build-up included the Anglian Parachute Brigade. One of its battalion commanders, a Lieutenant Colonel Marshall McIntire, climbed the short ramp leading into the aircraft with more seeming calm than he felt. Behind, ahead, and around him about two thousand parachute infantry likewise clambered up narrow steps and through cramped doors toward the uncomfortable troop seats. They were their nation's best, fittest, and bravest. Few of them felt McIntire's qualms. They had the best training, the best arms and equipment, the best men in the world. And they were going to attack *Balboa,* for Christ's sake! What reason had they to worry?

Hotel *Santo Hijo*, Santiago, Balboa, Terra Nova

Outside the fairly modern motel were parked four light trucks of the Sixth Mechanized Tercio. Inside, and under cover safe from prying satellites, some forty-two reservists watched television, ate the motel's excellent sandwiches, or simply slept on the floor of the open-air restaurant under the tin roof. The platoon leader waited by a telephone.

Herrera Airport, *Ciudad* Balboa, Balboa, Terra Nova

Balboa had relatively few combat aircraft, none of them truly modern. Two of those they did have sat unmoving but well attended on the tarmac strip. Another two were being readied for flight in one of the airport's many hangars. Another two were already aloft.

Two Volgan-born pilots, both of them independently wondering what had ever possessed them to emigrate to Balboa, sat in the confining space of their Mosaic Ds. Having flown much more modern aircraft, the ex-Volgans knew beyond a shadow of a doubt that they were absolutely outclassed by even second-rate Tauran equipment. Why they chose to stick it out with Balboa neither could have said.

Shimmering Sea, sixty miles west of Cienfuegos, Terra Nova

Flying low to avoid radar, twenty-three Tauran aircraft—an attack package complete with all the specialized equipment needed for a modern aerial assault—closed on Herrera Airport. The pilots knew there would be jets on the other side. They were also certain that those enemy jets had less than an ice cube's chance in hell of surviving to see the next sunset.

More than a hundred more planes were aimed at each of the wretched little airstrips to which Balboa had dispersed its air force. The Balboan aircraft themselves were not cost effective targets. But the airfields could be temporarily shut down. The Tauran Union Air Force had armed these planes for that mission, for runway cutting.

Cristobal, Balboa, Terra Nova

In a warehouse abutting the bay that faced Fort Tecumseh, over two dozen legionaries worked frantically in the dark to fill small rubber boats with air. As each boat was finished, four men moved it away from the air compressor and stacked it atop its brethren.

There were enough boats stockpiled to move slightly over a battalion in one lift.

A Balboan cursed as it became apparent that one boat would not fill. "The son of a bitch has a hole, sure as shit," he exclaimed.

"Can we patch it?" asked his centurion.

"In this light? I don't think so. It just means that some squad will cross over on a later lift." The legionary quoted something Carrera had once written. "'No kingdom has ever *really* fallen for lack of a horseshoe nail.'"

East Slope, *Cerro Gaital,* east of *Ciudad* Balboa, Balboa, Terra Nova

Global Locating Systems satellites send a time signal to ground receivers. By comparing the time signal from different satellites, the receiver can know its location to a considerable degree of certainty. The receiver merely notes the time differences between the signals received from however many satellites are available to receive from, then calculates its position based on the differences in the time sent by each satellite.

Anyone can receive these signals. They will give a location to within ten to fifty meters. There was, however, a special encrypted signal sent by the satellites and useable only by military GLS. This signal gave a far more precise location. Modern high-tech weapons depended on this more accurate military signal to a great degree for their effectiveness.

Others can receive the military signal, in theory, but cannot make use of it because of the encryption.

The legion had no real capability to decode the encrypted military signal. But, they could receive the signals that were sent. They could record them. They could delay them. They could amplify and direct them. And they could retransmit those signals. By doing so they could spoof any GLS that was capable of receiving the military signal.

Electronic warfare sergeant Valdez stood over two of his subordinates as they carefully aligned a satellite dish with a known GLS satellite. It took a few minutes for them to adjust the dish to gain the strongest possible signal. As soon as they had that signal acquired, the team began to adjust the next of its eight dishes to another satellite.

Satisfied, Valdez walked away from the reception team of his section over to where another team was setting up a directional antenna, a half rhomboid. Valdez checked the set up; *especially* did he check that the direction was perfectly in line with the Tauran firebase at Imperial Base Camp, just east of the Transitway. With a grunt of approval, Valdez walked on to the amplification team.

The amplification team had the simplest job. All they had to do was insure that the system was wired to take the signals from the dishes, amplify them, then send them on the antennas that would direct them in a fairly narrow arc toward the Taurans.

The rest of Valdez's platoon were deployed in other places, including the *Isla Real*, the Continental Divide, and a substantial hill north of the academy at *Puerto Lindo*. There were also some part of his cohort and tercio doing related and similar missions both on land and at sea, off of Balboa's coasts.

Lumière, Gaul, Terra Nova

With just over two hours remaining until the invasion kicked off, the analysts of the Tauran Union Intelligence and Security Agency were even more frantic than the legionaries in that Cristobal warehouse. Every thirty seconds, it seemed, some minor functionary reporting to some member of the Tauran Union Security Council or one of the national authorities called with some new request for information.

What could the TUISA report? Balboa was to all appearances sleeping. The were no unusual heat signatures, no remarkable new traffic. From high above, the Union's most sophisticated spy satellites found absolutely nothing out of the ordinary.

The Tunnel, *Cerro Mina*, Transitway Area, Balboa, Terra Nova

While the Council was the primary user of the intelligence gathered and analyzed by the TUISA, the Tauran Union Security Force-Balboa headquarters had been a close second for the past few days. But the TUISA had had little to offer in the way of hard intelligence. They could, and did, report that "X" amount of equipment of "Y" type was present—or sometimes not—at "Z" location. The TUISA could, and did, mark the locations of Carrera's miserable little fleet and air force, such as was known to exist.

Yet, even without useful input from the Agency, Janier's staff assembled a remarkably complete—and remarkably wrong—picture of Balboa's defensive posture. Literally hundreds of staff members marked maps, made inputs into computers, gave briefings, and filed reports. Several dozens, just in the headquarters alone, manned radios and field telephones.

The Taurans were not merely interested in the status of the legion however. The Tauran Union was engaged in a major military operation. Well over half of the staff's efforts went to keeping track of every little squad and platoon engaged in the mission. From over in Gaul, Janier, himself, pestered the local staff mercilessly for information, as they in turn pestered him to grant dispensations and make the "hard" decisions.

Fully fifteen enlisted men in the headquarters had no other function than to ensure that tea and coffee were always ready in case a senior officer should show up demanding to be briefed.

CHAPTER FORTY

*Il nous faut de l'audace, et encore de l'audace,
et toujours de l'audace.* [We need audacity, and
yet more audacity, and always audacity.]

—Georges Jacques Danton

Ammunition Supply Point, Legionary Base *Lago Sombrero*, Balboa, Terra Nova

In comparison to the staff of the Tunnel and Building 59, to say nothing of Janier's headquarters in Gaul, and less still of the TUISA, Carrera's command post was simplicity itself. It consisted of Carrera, Soult, Siegel, and a mixed crew of nine, mostly operating radios and telephones. There were no huge map displays, no grandiose charts and graphs. Even Carrera's coffee came from a thermos filled by Lourdes before she had had to abandon the *Casa* Linda.

Inside the bunker, Siegel received a message from a runner and checked a block on his clipboard. "The dragoons and Panzers at Fort Muddville are rolling out of Fort Muddville," he announced softly. "With their past performance, that means they hit us at zero one hundred hours."

He walked outside, gave the same word to Carrera, then returned to the bunker.

Carrera stole a quick glance at his watch. *Fifty-five minutes until midnight.* Impatiently he paced the small area defined by the door, the berm of concrete-revetted earth that was designed

432

to protect the contents of the bunker from either an accidental explosion or a near miss from a deliberate attack, and the two angled projections from the door to the access road. In this little trapezoid, hands clenched behind his back, Carrera paced out his frustrations and anxieties.

All three moons were up, Bellona, Hecate, and Eris. They bathed the world beneath them in a bright and, because of their spacing, virtually shadowless light.

Under those moons, just outside the door of bunker number twenty-three, a huge meter-thick assemblage of old and very, very strong concrete, *Duque* Patricio Carrera gazed up into the night sky. Though trees blocked his view of the ground to the south, he knew he could see the airstrip if he wanted by just climbing to the earthen, treed roof of the bunker. He didn't bother; he already knew exactly what it looked like.

A set of night vision goggles hung by their straps from Carrera's neck. The goggles rested high on his chest, itself covered with the peculiar custom-made, slant-pocketed, pixilated tiger-striped camouflage that the *duque* had selected for his legion's jungle wear. Between the two was the legion's silk and liquid metal *lorica*.

Above goggles, *lorica*, uniform, and chest was a salt-and-pepper haired, deeply tanned face, with striking eyes, a narrow, aquiline nose, and more wrinkles than Carrera's years should have accounted for.

The sky was clear, unusually for Balboa's wet season. Mosquitoes droned in Carrera's ears. From farther off the nighttime cries of the *antaniae*, Terra Nova's winged, septic-mouthed reptiles, came softly, muffled by the surrounding jungle. *Mnnbt...mnnbt...mnnbt.* As with the mosquitoes, Carrera likewise ignored the moonbats. Besides, they were fairly harmless except to children, the physically disabled, and the feebleminded. Cowardly creatures, they were.

Carrera stole another quick glance at his watch. *Forty past midnight.* He remained inside the trapezoid defined by the bunker's door.

"*Duque?*"

Carrera turned to his driver, just emerging from the shelter of the bunker. Without another word Warrant Officer Jamey Soult handed his commander a cup of coffee, black and bitter. It was an old routine. "Sir, how do you *know* they're coming?" Soult asked.

Soult, tall, slender, and rather large-nosed, had been with Carrera in two armies, over as many decades. He was more a son or a younger brother than a subordinate. Even so, the term that best described the relationship was probably "friend."

The corners of Carrera's mouth twitched in something that vaguely resembled a smile. "Jamey, I know they're coming," he said, "even if I don't know which units or in what precise strength, because they think they've no choice. I *made* them think they have no choice."

In point of fact, Carrera actually did have a pretty good idea of who was coming, the units and the strength. After all, his enemies in the Tauran Union only *had* so many airborne units of the requisite quality.

Anglian Paras or Gallic, he thought. *Sachsen, just possibly. But I don't think so. Probably Gauls.*

Around the airfield proper, four Volgan-built self-propelled air defense guns stood; one at each end of the strip and two to the sides where the InterColombian Highway bisected the strip. Sandbagged in on three sides, the guns were unmanned. Still their radar was turned on. Other, simpler, air defense guns stood manned by solitary Balboan soldiers. These were in the open; they had to be manned to be credible. More bait.

Within a radius of fifty or sixty miles of the base more than twelve thousand reservists and militia of the First Legion (Mechanized) waited in their homes or clubs with pounding hearts and with their issue rifles at hand for the call to report to their units at *Lago Sombrero.* Some of the legion's wheeled vehicles had already been dispersed to pick-up points to bring the reservists in a hurry when called. Still others had their private vehicles and pickup rosters. Some would go to pre-planned pickup zones to await helicopters, assuming any survived the initial Tauran onslaught. Buses from what Carrera liked to think of, and hoped was the case, as the "hidden reserve" would take still more.

All this was known to both the Taurans and the UEPF. Indeed, it was knowable, in broad terms, to anyone who cared to study. Without the threat of those reservists, and hundreds of thousands more like them, waiting for the trumpet's call, the Taurans would probably never have jumped.

Not everything was known though. Carrera would have bet—in fact *was* betting—that six secrets had been kept. Inside the ammunition bunkers was one of those six real secrets. Hidden away, as they had been for the last three days, roughly eleven hundred young Balboan troops waited, unknown to anyone outside of a very small circle. They were little more than boys, most of them; the average age was just under sixteen.

The boys had been painstakingly smuggled in from their military academy just after the most recent outbreak of tension between the Tauran Union and Balboa. They had found in the bunkers a complete set of all the equipment needed for them to form a mechanized cohort, a very *big* cohort.

"But it's as perfect as I can make it." Carrera turned and left his post outside the bunker, going inside to speak with the commander of the hidden force.

Once out of possible observation, Carrera lit a cigarette. The smoke drifted up and hovered about the ceiling of the bunker. "Rogachev, are you ready?"

Unseen by the light-blinded Carrera, former Volgan Army major, and current legionary tribune III, Constantine Rogachev nodded in the affirmative. Rogachev was a typical, even a stereotypical Volgan: a short, stocky, hairy bear. Above his round head and light blue eyes was a thatch of blond hair bright enough to gleam in the flash from Carrera's lighter.

"We're as ready as we're going to be, sir," the Volgan answered. "All of the vehicles that are going to start are topped off with full fuel tanks. The ammo is loaded. My cadre knows its mission . . . well, the mission is simple enough. Let the Taurans land. Pop out of these shitty bunkers. Get in formation. Drive off their close air support, and crush them with armor.

"The only thing that has me worried is the traffic jam we'll have trying to get out of this place and into formation." Rogachev shrugged ruefully. "Couldn't really rehearse *that*. If the Taurans notice us, or the UEPF does, and a couple of thousand tons of steel moving is very noticeable, sir, they could destroy us before we're properly deployed."

"I know the risk, Tribune. There is nothing to be done about it, except get your air defense systems out first, before anyone really notices."

Rogachev nodded briskly. "Yes, sir. We know that's the plan." He chuckled, apparently at himself. "Maybe I'm nervous about it because that's all that could go wrong. A soldier has to worry about something after all."

Carrera laughed a little. "Indeed we do. Fine. I'm going back out. I suggest you get your boys into their tracks now. It can't be too much longer." Carrera threw his cigarette to the ground and stepped on the glowing ash.

Outside again in Balboa's thick, even stifling, air, Carrera did climb to the top of the earth-covered bunker. He lifted his night vision goggles to his face before turning them on, lest their green glow betray him to a possible sniper. He then scanned the sky through the grainy, green image.

Was that a flash? he wondered, looking toward the west. *Maybe.*

From this position he could even see part of the airstrip itself, one spot where an air defense gun's radar dish spun on its axis. Even if its radar picked up something, there was no one on board to see and report it.

Carrera's question of a moment before was answered. He saw the first impact of a homing missile—*Radar homing? Contrast imaging? Terminally guided? Who knows?*—as the SP air defense gun disappeared in a great flash. The echoes of other explosions told of similar bombs hitting elsewhere around the field. Each concussive blast was felt in the form of rippling internal organs at least as far away as the bunker.

Carrera hated that feeling. Even so, he looked up and smiled. *If you were planning a long war,* he mused, *these bunkers would be the better target. But you're not; you're planning for a very short one. Amazing how often such plans fail to quite work out.*

Overhead the screech and sonic crack of the jets was nearly loud enough to drown out rational thought. In Carrera's view, one of the barracks expanded and crumpled from a direct hit by an aerially delivered bomb. Vainly, a lone and very brave Balboan gunner fired his air defense gun into the sky. Carrera could see his tracers rising in the black night and then more as another gun joined him. He made a mental note to check the boys' names for later—Carrera assumed they would be posthumous—awards.

The Balboans' tracers didn't rise for long. What Carrera had almost seen a few moments before was the shadow of a Federated States of Columbia-built aerial side-firing gunship. This now poured down a stream of fire.

Like something from a science fiction movie, thought Carrera. The defenders' guns went silent, both of them. *And gunships. Hmmm. So it'll be the Anglian Paras, not the Gauls'. They're the only ones outside of the FSC that have gunships. That's a pity,* he thought, and meant it. *I'd hoped they'd stay out of this.*

The air shook as more fighter-bombers raked over the legionary base. Down came regular unguided—dumb—bombs, 20mm cannon shells, rockets, cluster bombs. Had there been any serious opposition on the ground around the airstrip these might well have broken it, even though well dug-in troops were not terribly vulnerable to air attack.

Joining the air armada now came a flight of half a dozen helicopter gunships, presumably flying out of the Tauran-held Transitway Area, or perhaps even from something at sea.

Hmmm . . . more proof of Anglians.

The helicopter gunships didn't carry anything like the airplanes' firepower. They made up for that lack, however, in the attention to detail they could apply to a mission. By the glow of the burning buildings, Carrera could make out the gunships' track as they shot down legionaries attempting to flee from them.

Holding a fist in front of his chest, Carrera spoke out loud to himself. "Now," he commanded to no one who could hear. "Now! Report that the area is clear enough to jump."

Carrera's order, or prayer, or wish, was quickly rewarded. Under the bright moonlight, he saw the outlines of the first of twenty-four medium and fourteen large cargo transports and troop carriers, approaching the *Lago Sombrero* airfield. Coming in low, Carrera thought maybe just over one hundred and twenty meters, these planes began disgorging their loads—over fifteen hundred Paras of the Royal Anglian Airborne Regiment. At that altitude the Paras didn't even bother with reserve chutes. If their main parachutes failed there wouldn't be time to open the reserves anyway.

I wonder what friends I have up there, jumping to their deaths.

The first of the medium transports made its pass over the airfield and surrounding cleared area in about forty seconds. Then, duty discharged, it turned to head for home. Others, in a long double trail behind it, were still dropping troops. Hundreds of these were already on the ground struggling to free themselves from their parachutes and harnesses. When Carrera was sure that enough had landed to guarantee the others would also land despite any danger, he shouted down to Soult, "Jamey, radio silence off. Get on the horn to fire the caltrops. Tell Rogachev to roll."

Outside, on both sides of the airfield, plastic drums began blowing up. The explosions were mostly low, though linear shaped demolition charges to cut the tops off the drums were high explosive. The tops being cut off, the lower explosive charges lifted the drums' cargo, tens and hundreds of thousands of stiff plastic antipersonnel caltrops, up and out, scattering them across the open area. It was confidently expected that the *average* landing paratrooper would be stabbed at least twice, about two inches deep, in the course of landing.

The boys must have felt the shuddering bombs and rumble from the caltrop projectors, even deep down in their concrete hides. If it frightened them, there was little evidence of it. Carrera heard song, boyish voices supplemented by older ones, coming from the now opening vault doors:

> "A young tribe stands up, ready to fight.
> Raise the eagles higher, *mis compadres*.
> We feel inside the time is right,
> *La época de los soldados jóvenes*.
> High, from His Heaven, the God of battles calls us.
> Ahead, in ranks, march the ghosts of our slain.
> And in our hearts no fear of falling.
> *Legion, Patria*, through the steel rain!"

Carrera looked skyward, past the incoming transports, and whispered, "Enjoy the show, Marguerite."

CHAPTER FORTY-ONE

Strike 'til the last armed foe expires.
Strike for your altars and your spires.
Strike for the green graves of your sires,
God, and your native land.

> —Fitz-Green Halleck, "Marco Bozzaris"

Alfaro's Tomb Gates (back gates), Brookings Air Force Station/ Fort Muddville, Balboa Transitway Area, Balboa, Terra Nova

NDI had only taken over security for the site where the Tauran women had been tortured and killed scant hours before. Even then, it had been a couple more hours before authorization was granted to release the troops that had been guarding it.

Exhausted from searching and guarding, as well as from the perennial worrying that was a signifer's lot, young Boyd let the *thrum* of the bus's engine and the steady droning of the wheel lull him to sleep on the drive back from the warehouse. The driver's instructions were to take the men to a point in *Ciudad* Balboa from which the troops could easily walk to their homes.

For all that he was bone weary, the signifer slept uneasily in the front seat of the bus. His mind, asleep though he was, noted his body being pushed to the right, and automatically adjusted for it, as the bus made a sharp left-hand turn to avoid going through either of the checkpoints the Taurans had at the rear of the two installations. Boyd came half-awake when he heard a shout, in French-accented Spanish, for the bus to halt.

Looking out the front window, Boyd saw a machine-gun-armed

439

vehicle—a Sochaux S4—blocking the road. The driver pulled a lever to open the door as the signifer arose to his feet. Then Boyd went for the door, intending to go outside and explain. Surely the Tauran would appreciate that this was the unit that had found so much evidence concerning the murder of the Tauran women. As he descended to the ground, Boyd heard, though did not so much understand, a shout of alarm from the half-dozen Tauran soldiers he could see. Surprised, he gripped his submachine gun more tightly and turned toward the shout. It was with greater surprise that Boyd saw bright yellow blossoms blooming from the muzzle of the Tauran machine gun. His surprise was short lived, however, since the gun was pointing directly at him.

From the west side of the bus a platoon's worth of rifles and machine guns, hidden in the jungle that bordered the road, began to riddle it from one end to the other. Balboans caught dozing died with spasmodic jerks without ever understanding what was happening to them. A few—brave souls or determined—tried to shoot back. They were quickly silenced.

Finally, a burst of fire with at least one tracer punctured the gasoline tank. Flames began rising through the floor. Even unwounded Balboans began to scream as the flames found them.

Still the Tauran fire continued. In action already and with a deadlier action fast approaching, the Taurans were far too keyed up to cease fire, except to change magazines. Finally, with flames from the bus beginning to rise dangerously, the Taurans withdrew a short distance to a safe position. The footsteps were followed for several minutes by a lone Balboan's screaming. The cries didn't stop until the bus blew up.

The Tunnel, *Cerro Mina,* Balboa Transitway Area, Balboa Terra Nova

De Villepin swore as the report of the "fight" at Brooking's back gate came in over the radio. Then, thinking how little good a mere fifteen minutes' warning was likely to do the legion, he relaxed, shrugging the incident off as a mere matter of timing.

In the Operations Room, in an even deeper part of the Tunnel under the hill, the chief of staff paced nervously from wall to wall. While he paced, staff officers and noncoms posted the latest reports of the troop movements that were expected to catch the legion largely unmobilized and unprepared for the invasion. Radios crackled with reports of helicopter lifts taking off, flights of medium and heavy cargo aircraft reaching checkpoints in the air or landing at Tauran Union controlled air fields, armored vehicle convoys reaching their release points and lines of departure. At this point in the Tauran Union's invasion of Balboa the chief had little to do but fret. The intricate planning had been done months and years before. Every known legionary mobilization point and headquarters had been assigned a force adequate to either overrun it or, at least, keep it from mobilizing before an adequate force could descend to take it out. The chief of staff, Moncey, stopped pacing from time to time to look over the chart that tracked the movement of troops to their assault positions. Of the ninety-seven legionary targets listed for action by Tauran forces at H Hour, each a distinct operation in the plan, virtually all were moving on schedule. None were off schedule by more than a few minutes.

The chief strode to the main operations map and asked to be briefed.

"Sir," said the watch officer, a rather bored seeming Sachsen *Oberst*, "the friendly situation is as follows: the fighters are about two minutes out from their main targets at *Lago Sombrero* and Herrera Airport. Those are eight sorties each of fighter-attack aircraft plus the usual support. Other, smaller, packages are aimed at the following legionary dispersal sites." The *Oberst*'s pointer tapped a number of locations about the large, horizontally laid, map.

"The Anglian Paras are in the air less than eighty kilometers miles from *Lago Sombrero,* south of it. The Gallic Parachute brigade is closing on Herrera, also from the south. The Sachsen Panzer Battalion is moving up the InterColumbian highway toward *Nuevo Arraijan.* They should reach the town in about twelve or fourteen minutes. They'll cross the border in two. The highway into Cristobal has already been cut. The Four Hundred Tenth Infantry and Four Hundred Seventeenth are in their positions to take out the Castilian Battalion plus the legionary tercios at Fort Melia and Lone Palm. The jungle school is guarding the locks and dam on the Shimmering Sea side already. The Four Twentieth Dragoon, plus one company of Sachsen Panzers, are in their assembly areas ready to roll down on the legion's Second Corps headquarters.

The Thirty-fifth Commandos are already seventy percent on the ground around Fort Guerrero and their other jump-off points..."

The Sachsen continued for some time in that vein. Eventually, the chief was satisfied. From the operations room, he strode to the C-1/C-4 sections—Combined Admin and Combined Logistics. From the latter's charts, all supply categories looked adequate.

The J-1's wall charts held the chief's eyes for some time, especially the anticipated casualty chart. To the chief, four hundred and seventy-five to five hundred and fifty dead—most of whom were going to be Gauls—seemed a very high price to pay.

Balboa Railroad, *Isla Repressa*, Balboa, Terra Nova

Railroads, Pililak discovered, *have their crossbeams set the distance apart they are not for any reasons of strength, or economy, or anything remotely like that. Oh, no; they're set the distance apart they are because that distance is shrewdly calculated to make it as painful as possible for a human being to walk on them. Bastards. No good rotten motherfuckers. Stinking shits. Why, why, WHY did you old-time railroad builders have to make the things just that far apart? They make everything hurt. You didn't even know me; why did you hate me already?*

The rain that had been beating down on the girl let up momentarily. She didn't expect the respite to last, of course. In the last few days since crossing the water and nearly being killed she'd seen more rain that she had in her entire *life* back home in Pashtia.

How do the people here stand it? she wondered. *That and the heat...always the heat...always the rain...they must be very fierce. But of course they are or my lord would not have chosen one of them to be his mother.*

And what's more...

The girl stopped her wretchedly uncomfortable walking on the hateful tracks. There was something, a motor sound, off to her left, in the water, where it ought not be. And it was more than one. She concentrated hard to separate out the motor sounds and finally decided, *Four of them. Big. Powerful. But not straining hard...at least as far as I can tell.*

She was almost at the point where the train tracks left the edge of the island. She didn't know if the boats—*They must be boats*—could pass under the tracks. If not, they were going to land on her island and probably capture her. *That wicked, evil tyrant whom my lord calls "Father." Even here he sends his hounds to pursue me and keep me from my duty. I must hide. Maybe they'll miss me.*

Trawler *Pericles*, *Puerto de* Balboa, Terra Nova

TUSF-B made a habit of changing the frequency hopping codes of its radios precisely at midnight. Being an orderly people, much given to routine, this day was to be no different. In truth, the Taurans had much reason on their side. Every change to radio frequencies or codes meant a period of confusion and delay while every station—and TUSF-B as a whole had literally thousands of stations—reestablished contact with its higher headquarters and supporting units. Had it not been for a persistent nagging feeling that the legion just *might* have some electronic warfare capability, the Taurans would probably have made the change much earlier than the usual midnight switch.

Still, the trawler *Pericles*—not at sea but gaining the protection of being in port, one among dozens—was not one's average, everyday catcher of fish. Despite appearances, the *Pericles* was an electronic warfare vessel. Its job, and that of its mixed Balboan and Volgan crew, was to capture the codes used by TUSF-B's radios, then interfere with that radio traffic. It was equipped with the best radio intercept and decoding capability available from Volgan arsenals.

Long before midnight, the *Pericles* had acquired a complete frequency hopping code for the TUSF-B. That old code became obsolete exactly at midnight when every unit in TUSF-B changed to the new.

Of course older transmissions were not worthless. The *Pericles* had a whole library of voice tapes from almost every important sender in TUSF-B, as well as simple radio operators.

None of that would be of any use until today's code was broken.

Fortunately, in the rush to reestablish communications after the daily changeover, TUSF-B was providing a great rush of data for the *Pericles'* decoders.

Fire Base Eagle, Imperial Base Camp, Balboa, Terra Nova

There was none of the normal semi-confused hustle and bustle around the guns. The firing platoons and batteries were already and long-since laid on their primary targets. Fuses were set; charges cut. Each gun was loaded with the first of some hundreds of preplanned shells it would soon begin firing at Carrera's legions.

That there was no "hustle and bustle" did not mean that the crews were bored; far from it. Each gunner was, understandably enough, scared silly. They were confident, of course, that their side would prevail. Their confidence in personal survival was rather less absolute.

The gun positions were well dug in for towed artillery pieces. A thick berm—a wall of earth—surrounded each gun, the berm being substantially cut only for the entrance to the position. Also well dug in, better, in fact, was a headquarters to which each battery of guns reported. At those headquarters, which were also the fire direction centers, noncoms and officers scanned their watches as the minutes and seconds ticked down. The crews around the guns likewise kept track, and also fidgeted continuously with bad cases of nerves. The gun chiefs kept field telephones glued to their ears, waiting...waiting...waiting...

"Fire!"

Herrera International Airport, *Ciudad* Balboa, Balboa, Terra Nova

A frantic warning sounded in the ears of the Mosaic-D pilots waiting on the airstrip. Radar had picked up incoming hostile aircraft. The pilots quickly engaged their engines to taxi down the runway. They made it less than a quarter of the distance before one of the two planes blossomed into a fireball in the night. The other pilot scarcely had time to utter a short prayer before he too was blown into the next kingdom.

Two Tauran fighters then spent several minutes bombing likely targets. They couldn't cut the runway, because the plans required capturing the runway intact to facilitate further reinforcement. With flames and smoke rising behind them, weapons exhausted, the Tauran planes turned toward home. The pilots' radios chattered with reports of other missions successfully completed all over the country, many of which did include cutting airfields. Balboa's tiny air force was out of the picture for the time being.

Fort Melia, Republic of Balboa, Terra Nova

The Shimmering Sea side of the Transitway Area, the part near Cristobal, Balboa, was just a side show to the main effort taking place on the *Mar Furioso* side. While thousands of paratroopers descended upon the presumably sleeping Balboans and hundreds of aircraft and helicopters ferried and dropped other troops, while scores of combat aircraft from four huge nuclear carriers and scores more from bases in the Tauran Union and Santa Josefina bombed and strafed legion installations, the job of taking out the cadres of the tercios of Jimenez's Fourth Corps, or most of it, fell upon the men of the Fourteenth Anglian and Four Hundred and Seventeenth Gallic Infantries, Thirty-seventh Gallic Commando, the Nine-forty-fifth Tuscan Military Police, a battalion of Tuscan light guns based at Fort Tecumseh, the cadres of Tecumseh's jungle school, and a company of Sachsen engineers flown in the day before. Little helicopter, and no air support, were made available to this purely secondary operation. Only one company of landing craft, the Nine-seventy-first Medium Boat, from Cimbria, some trucks, and a couple of dozen helicopters had been allocated to Task Force Shimmering Sea for the upcoming attack.

The units on the Shimmering Sea side, for all they were treated as bastard stepchildren, still had one huge, and not unrelated advantage. While everyone on the *Mar Furioso* side had had to rehearse every move under the watchful eyes of the TUSF-B staff, Task Force Shimmering Sea had been able to rehearse one approach, while planning something completely different.

Thus, while this battalion had repeatedly demonstrated before that it would come over land, most of the battalion was actually currently loading landing craft. The rest were boarding helicopters. This was, in fact, the only area of general surprise anyone on the Tauran Union Security Force-Balboa had managed to spring on the Balboans. This was also probably not the first time in human history that a military organization had gained a distinct advantage because of its distance from headquarters. Moreover, the one battalion due to fly in from the *Mar Furioso* side had never at all rehearsed its assault, in conjunction with the Fourteenth Anglian, on Muñoz-Infantes Castilian battalion on Fort Williams, so surprise there could be expected to be fairly complete as well.

The Fourteenth Anglian left one company, "Mad Dog" Alpha, on the Fort Melia Pickup Zone, or PZ, to move by helicopter to assault the Fourth Corps headquarters in Cristobal. The better part of the battalion headquarters company was left to guard the fort. The remainder, two rifle companies, the battalion tactical operations center, or TOC, and the scout, mortar, and antitank platoons had moved, well before H Hour, by foot and truck to the western edge of post, to where the water touched, right behind the dental clinic. There, the landing craft were waiting, which took those companies and platoons to the back side of Fort Williams. Rain, not unexpectedly, began to drive down into the open topped boats once they were out in the lake.

The boats dropped off the troops in waist-deep water about a mile from the main trapezoidal barracks for the post. Fifty-caliber machine gunners on the boats trained their guns on the shore, just visible through the driving rain. This was the tensest moment. If the Castilians were waiting for them there would be a terrible massacre.

Each man who could see breathed a sigh of relief as the point man from each of the four boats reached shore without incident. The Castilians, like the legion, seemed to have bought the previous month's demonstrations. Quickly the rest of the men were landed ashore, soaking and bug eaten but otherwise fresh and unbloodied. The Scout Platoon raced along the open area between the locks that faced the Shimmering Sea and the jungle. Behind them, the rest of the battalion, minus Mad Dog, assumed a widely spaced tactical column and began the march to the trapezoid to the south.

A thousand meters in, the jungle fell off, opening up to the post golf course, a relic of days when the FSC had owned this ground. Here the column turned south by southwest, even as Company B turned further out, pushing the pace harder, as well, to bring the two rifle companies' points on line. Both companies used the railroad tracks they'd just passed over as reference points.

The post seemed nearly deserted. It was, in any case, as quiet as a cemetery. Without opposition, the soldiers of the Fourteenth Infantry glided noiselessly through the tree-darkened and night-shaded streets and alleys, between the bungalows of the family housing area on the edge of the golf course, and right up to the long building that marked the northern limit of the quadrangle. If they made a noise it was covered by the heavy rain pelting them and everything around them.

To the south, on the sharp-sided hill overlooking the fort, lights shone from the Castilian battalion's headquarters. That was the scout platoon's target, theirs and the antitank platoon's. Those two passed west of the post's octagonal theater, heading almost due south.

There was yet one more way in which the Anglians benefitted from lack of close supervision from higher. Because Castile was part of the Tauran Union, even if their battalion in Balboa was in a state of mutiny, the roles of engagement said that Muñoz-Infantes' men were to be given the chance to surrender before they could be engaged. The Anglian commander had read those orders, smiled, and said, "Fuck that shit."

Only two minutes after H hour a green star cluster, the signal to begin the attack, streaked overhead. The clouds glowed green above as red tracers lanced out, smashing windows and walls, and bowling over such Castilians as began pouring out of their barracks.

Clay Dairy Farm, Southwest of Fort Melia, Balboa, Terra Nova

The boys in the warehouses around Clay Farm and at other points on the Shimmering Sea side didn't, really couldn't, know if the ruse had been successful. They could only know that they were still alive, and draw what limited conclusions could be inferred from that. So they waited, not knowing if the next few minutes or hours would bring a rain of Tauran bombs to send them to eternity.

One entire maniple, of seven organized by the Academy at *Puerto Lindo,* was situated in a largish warehouse south of *Avenida* Scott. Inside that warehouse was a small office set aside for the commander of the Academy, Legate Chapayev. The phone in that warehouse rang, causing every cadet in the warehouse to tense at the sound. No one would call such a place at this hour unless it was to call them to action or send them back to school. However much they may have hoped, none believed they would be returned to their academy soon. The maniple commanders and academy staff, regular Balboan and Volgan officers, stood up as Chapayev's door opened.

"We have firm word. The Taurans are on the move all over the country. Many more are flying in from the Tauran Union. Based on flight times they are expected to hit within fifteen to twenty minutes. The plan is unchanged. While they are hitting Fourth Corps, we march to Melia and Lone Palm and kick them in the ass. Only then, when they're reeling from the loss of their base, do we march to relieve Fourth Corps in Cristobal and its subordinate units. Fourth Maniple—"

Chapayev stopped speaking as the phone rang again. Not having bothered to close his office door, his voice reverberated off of the walls of the warehouse—"What? Fuck! By boat? Shit... All right... we'll handle it. Yes, *Suegro,* I won't let you down or Maria wouldn't give me a moment's peace for the rest of my life. Just hang on, it's a longer march. But we'll be there as soon as possible."

However he'd sounded in semiprivate, when he stepped out of the office Chapayev looked the very soul of calm. His eyes hunted for his Fourth Maniple commander. Seeing him, Chapayev said, "Koniev?"

"Yes, sir."

"The Taurans are hitting the Castilians at Fort Williams. It's odd, since they didn't rehearse that. No matter. The tanks and Ocelots are yours and your maniple's. Load up and fight your way to Williams, relieve the Castilians under attack there. Once they are relieved put yourself under the command of Colonel Muñoz-Infantes. He will have further orders by then. I hope.

"Everybody, ready to march within ten minutes. Mortar and rocket launcher batteries can unmask now. Air defense can unmask now, weapons free, engage anything that flies and is in range. Tanks and Ocelots can start engines now. Recon maniple move out as soon as you're ready. You had better already *be* ready. Report when your tail is out of the buildings. Now, all of you, go!"

At Chapayev's command his officers left to carry out their instructions. Within minutes the sound of tank engines overpowered the pelting of the rain of the warehouse's tin roof.

Some miles away shouting cadets, mostly the younger ones, rushed out of the makeshift barracks to break open conexes containing their 81mm and 120mm mortars, and Grad rocket launchers. Manhandling—rather, boy handling—the tubes into position went fairly quickly. Then the cadets returned to cart the heavy boxes of ammunition to the firing positions. An instructor or older cadet went forward of each firing position to lay the guns and launchers in with an aiming circle. The guns were soon up and had enough ammunition on hand for immediate needs.

By the time the indirect fire weapons were ready at Sabanita, the Recon troops had moved out from Clay Farms. Chapayev had the rifle maniples to follow in two long, snaking columns. Between them, on *Avenida* Scott, Koniev's tanks and Ocelots, the drivers and commanders using night vision goggles, took the asphalt road in between the two lines of foot troops. The armor quickly outpaced the infantry cadets.

Fifty meters to either side of the last tank, teams of cadets carried and laid communication wire from the battalion to the TOC and fire support coordinator at the warehouse.

As soon as Koniev crested the hill at Magdalena, he saw the sky in front of him lit up with the flashing fires of the Tauran Fourteenth Infantry, the return fire of the Castilians, and the glow of at least one burning building.

"Faster, boy," Koniev said into the microphone of his vehicle crewman's helmet. "Faster or there won't be much left to save."

CHAPTER FORTY-TWO

In one of his handwritten memos to himself entitled "Things Worth Remembering" the methodical Arthur Currie had included as Item 3: "Thorough preparations must lead to success. Neglect Nothing" and as Item 19: "Training, Discipline, Preparation and Determination to conquer is everything."

—Pierre Burton, *Vimy*

Santisima Trinidad II, Bahia de Balboa, Mar Furioso,
Terra Nova

She was at least the eighth vessel to bear the name. Moreover, in all honesty, the name was not a particularly lucky one. Of the preceding seven, three had been captured, of which one had sunk in a storm, taking its prisoner crew to the bottom. Another, the most recent predecessor, had had to ram itself into another ship, a terrorist suicide ship, to save the ship it was escorting at the time, the aircraft carrier *Dos Lindas*.

Glorious and admirable that might have been. Lucky it was not.

Now the ship, a small corvette—about nine hundred tons displacement—formerly of the Volgan Navy, patrolled around the legion's major training base on the *Isla Real*.

The crew was on alert, there having been reports—confused and fragmentary to be sure—of fighting on the mainland. Still, "alert" didn't mean much to a ship with twenty rather short-ranged surface-to-air missiles, a 76mm gun, a twin mount with 57mm guns, a number of elderly antisubmarine weapons, including a rather massive array of antisubmarine rocket lauchers forward of the bridge, and radar that was, charitably, not of the best and latest.

In any case, alert or not, the corvette was not particularly stealthy, while the carrier launched aircraft that popped up over the *cordillera central* and acquired it was quite stealthy. A more modern radar would not have helped.

That aircraft, a P-53 off of the carrier HAMS *Furious*, launched a single Dark Cloud antishipping missile. In this case, the half-ton warhead of the Dark Cloud was probably overkill.

The missile, rather stealthy itself, followed the lay of the land until reaching Balboa's northern shore, then sped out just above the waves at about a thousand kilometers an hour for the last sighted position of its target. It neither knew nor cared the nature of the target.

Twelve minutes after launch, give or take a bit, the missile went high, reacquired the *Santisima Trinidad*, then kicked in rockets to go high supersonic. It struck the corvette about four-tenths of the way back from the bow, right below the superstructure, where the radar return signal was greatest. The half-ton warhead was bad enough, but the hit was also terribly close to the anti-submarine rocket launchers just forward of the bridge. Worse, on a small ship like this one, the ammunition magazine had to be automated and placed near to the weapons they served. And armor was, of course, right out. The ship didn't so much blow in two as disintegrate by phases.

Most of the crew of the *Santisima Trinidad* never knew or saw what hit them. Those of the sixty who survived the shock of the initial hit did so with multiple broken bones, flash burns on their exposed skin, ruptured organs, and even a few inhalation burns. If any lingered in agony after surviving that, they probably found it a blessing when the propellant and warheads of the ninety-six antisubmarine rockets ahead of the bridge went up. Even exclusive of the propellant, the warheads massed two and a half tons of high explosive.

SSK *Megalodon, Mar Furioso, Bahia de Balboa,* eighty kiloyards north of the *Isla Real,* Terra Nova

Auletti ripped the headphones off his head in agony, as if someone had set off a large firecracker in each ear. "Son of a *BITCH!*" he exclaimed. Then, after shaking his head to clear it, he told Chu, "Skipper, that was an explosion. A big, and very brissant, explosion."

"War then," said Chu, softly and sadly. He was sad for the commencement of the war, not for anyone in particular who'd been lost in it already. He'd been there before, seen it before, and learned that, while he could do it, it wasn't anything to cheer over.

"Start warming the tanks."

The Meg class had an odd—really a unique—method of flooding and evacuating its ballast tanks. Like the pressure hull, these were cylindrical. Basically, the boat took advantage of the very low boiling temperature of ammonia. The ammonia was kept inside of flexible tubing made of fluorocarbon elastomer with a seven-hundred-fifty-angstrom-thick layer of sputtered aluminum, followed by a five-hundred-angstrom layer of silicon monoxide with an aerogel insulation layer. Heating elements inside the tubes—called "rubbers" by the sailors and designers, both—heated the ammonia into a gas, which expanded the "rubbers" and forced out the water. To dive, the ammonia was allowed to chill to a liquid rather than be heated to a gas. Chilling was really only a factor when quite near the surface, and then only if the water was unusually warm.

"Bring us up to fifty meters. I want to try to lift a radio buoy to see if we can get some information as to where we can apply ourselves best."

Fuerte Guerrero, Balboa, Terra Nova

Sergeant Major Cruz had been under artillery and mortar fire before, in Yezidistan, Sumer, Pashtia and Kashmir. He'd also had a taste of it in training. Those had, in many ways, been worse than what he experienced now. True, the Tauran shells were far more accurate. And their sizzling shards drove Cruz's head down again and again. But the intensity of fire was not so great as the Sumeris had thrown, nor was there the surprise the enemy in Pashtia frequently had counted on. Moreover, Cruz's concrete shelter was rather better than a scrape hole in the sand.

Give the Devil his due, though, thought Cruz, as a nearby barracks wall was shattered by a direct hit, *these fuckers are good.*

The real bitch here was that the incoming artillery, for all that it wasn't killing many legionaries, was still almost completely effective in keeping their heads down, or ruining the aim of those ballsy enough to put their heads up. This allowed lift after lift of helicopter-borne infantry—Cruz thought he saw a couple of field pieces, too—to descend to the parade field, golf course, park, causeway . . . pretty much anywhere they wanted to, form up at their leisure, and move to assault positions.

Now let's hope Cara listened and did not pick up a rifle to try to help.

Cruz hadn't heard from the commander of the cohort, still less from Legate Chin. He was, he believed, the senior man at least in this barracks building. *Decision's mine, I guess*, he thought. *When the time comes, there won't be a lot of time to give orders. So . . .*

"Fix bayonets!" He shouted, loudly enough to be heard throughout the building, even over the incoming artillery. Other people picked up the cry and passed it on: "Fix bayonets!" . . . "Fix bayonets!"

And, mused the sergeant major, *that's as much about letting each other know we're determined to stick it out to the bitter end as it is about actually sticking it to someone else.*

Carrera's Command Post, *Lago Sombrero* ASP, Balboa, Terra Nova

Tracers drew bright lines in the sky to the south. Carrera watched them calmly, no movement or expression betraying his nervousness. Around him the RTOs of his command post called off the morning's disasters. Carrera closed his eyes and simply listened to the reports of invasion.

"For Christ's sake, sir, order the cadets into action. They're murdering us!" exclaimed Siegel. In fact, Carrera had ordered one and permitted another of the six cadet cohorts to attack. It was around the Tauran main effort that he was holding them back.

"Not yet, Sig," he answered. "Not yet."

"What are you waiting for?"

"I want them to feel like they're doing well," answered Carrera.

At Siegel's low-voiced curse Carrera explained further. "Sig, I want them to be fully committed before we make our move. I want every body they can commit to action committed and tied down. Up to a point, the longer I can wait, the more committed they will be."

"Then why permit us to act here and around Cristobal?"

Carrera sighed. Not everyone had quite his grasp of timing, and human possibilities. *No shame in that, though.* "Here," he answered, "we're too far away for them to react. For Cristobal, it's almost as far away and they don't have the mindset that the Shimmering Sea side much matters."

"Okay, sir," Siegel conceded. "That's fine for us, but there's a moral factor in there. What about those poor bastards taking it up the ass? They need us to move now."

"Sig...they're buying me...buying Balboa...time with their lives. There are worse ways to go, I think."

Carrera continued to listen to the reports without obvious emotion. One could hardly have told, from anything he did or said, that he was bleeding inside. Finally there came a report that the Gallic parachute brigade had reached the defensive perimeter of Herrera Airport. The cadets were fighting a desperate holding action. There, though, Carrera needed to give no orders. Third Corps was already mobilizing as quickly as one could hope for. Let the cadets hold on for as much as ninety minutes and the Gallic Paras would be facing eighty-*thousand* Balboans with vengeance in their hearts.

Carrera looked south to where fighting raged at the *Lago Sombrero* garrison area. He turned to Siegel slowly. "Let the big dog hunt," he said simply. With a shout of triumph Siegel ordered the cadets' commander, Sitnikov, to emerge and attack.

The Anglian Paras' command post was nothing more than a half-dozen radios and their operators clustered around the brigade commander. Two of the radio operators were wounded from some strange four-pointed jacks they had rolled on in landing. Allegedly several hundred more men, maybe as many as a thousand, had also been perforated by the caltrops, and wounded worse when they pulled the barbed monstrosities out. Still, they were Paras and Paras didn't stop for little wounds. The men in the line battalions continued the attack even as agonized radiomen stuck to their commander despite the pain and dripping blood.

The area around the command post was lit by the flames of burning legionary self-propelled antiaircraft guns. By the flickering firelight the brigade commander, Brigadier Porter, read his map and received reports of his battalion's consolidation and movement to action.

The flames of the burning ADA pieces were some comfort to Porter. Had the Royal Anglian Air Force failed to take them out initially his brigade would have been dog's meat on the drop zone. Now they had a decent chance to accomplish their mission without heavy loss.

One thing bugged Porter. Though his men had driven the Balboans back to the general vicinity of their barracks, there were reports—as in the report of a cannon's muzzle—coming from the south-southeast. And he had limited contact with the battalion down that way.

Tracers arced over Porter's head as he issued orders into the radio. The legion troops were apparently still in the fight. To suppress this, or destroy it, from time to time the aerial gunships lashed down at the legionaries in the barracks and bunkers to the north, west, and east with a stream of fire: 20mm Gatlings, interspersed with 40mm cannon, highlighted with blasts from the gunships' 105s. Wherever their streams of death touched, resistance ceased—at least temporarily.

Had Porter been one for reflection he might have paused at how unfair the discrepancy in firepower was. Neither Porter's character nor his mission allowed for much reflection at this point. Tough enough to take out the cadre of a mechanized corps from the air, in the dark. Any advantage he had seemed no more than fair.

One of the RTOs handed Porter a microphone. It was the commander of his second battalion, and that commander had a complaint.

At almost the first sign of the Tauran assault *Lago Sombrero*'s defenders had fired off their caltrop projectors, over a hundred otherwise innocuous looking plastic drums. Nearly a million of the sharpened four-prong jacks now littered the field. The caltrops were slowing down the brigade's assault on the legionary positions.

Over and over again, Porter's battalion commanders called to say they were being delayed by the nasty little obstacles more than by the legionary fire that covered them.

"A quarter of my men have been wounded by those caltrops, Porter," said the second battalion commander, inferior in rank but in the peculiarities of Anglian military culture a complete social equal.

"Yes...yes...we're still moving to the north to continue the attack. But a company slows down when its men do, and a man slows down when every rush might land him on four or five spear points, or every step might mean five centimeters of sharp, barbed plastic through the foot."

That was worrisome, of course, and added to Porter's natural anxiety. Even so, that anxiety began to lessen as the first battalion commander reported that the Balboans in one of the barracks had been silenced—dead or driven out—and his troops were clearing the building.

Porter's satisfaction was short-lived. So far his regiment had landed and consolidated with relatively little opposition. Then, from overhead, he heard the freight train sound of incoming artillery, a lot of it, coming from the southeast. Porter called for a gunship to suppress those legionary. That got him a, "Wilco," followed shortly by the sound of powerful aircraft engines and a very satisfying stream of tracer fire to the southeast.

The commander of the Anglian Paras felt only a momentary satisfaction. In contrast to the sheets of tracers descending to the ground, three streams of green tracers arose and intersected on the gunship, causing it to fireball in the tropic night.

Carrera still stood atop the ammunition bunker that served as the Cadet Cohort's command post, as well as his own. From where he stood he could see the red and green tracers arcing up over the barracks to the north.

A good sign, he thought. *If they're still fighting now they should hold out strong until the cadets can stick it up the Paras' asses.*

The cadets' recon maniple was already in contact. That, however, was only thin-skinned stuff, armored cars and the like. The cadets had made contact, then pulled back to observe and report.

From underneath and around Carrera the "ammunition" bunkers continued to disgorge their seventy-odd armored vehicles and nine-hundred-plus cadets and cadre. The first vehicles out had been the air defense guns carrying their own crews but with the light missile gunners hitchhiking on top. These raced to their preplanned firing positions while the second group of tracks, the mortar carriers, began to emerge to head a few hundred meters north to their own posts. Then came the infantry carriers, Ocelots with reasonably modern night vision equipment. The Ocelots were followed by the cadets' maniple of motorized infantry in wheeled armored personnel carriers. These raced ahead to sweep down the trail west of the airstrip. Last out, emerging from a dozen bunkers, came the tanks.

From the maintenance facility to the east, the artillery began to fire in support of the First Corps cadre, cadet forward observers calling in the fire from observation posts atop the bunkers even before the combat vehicles were lined up in formation. Mortars likewise fired from the north.

Like a magnet, the mortars drew the attention of the Tauran air. Helicopter and fixed-wing gunships turned from suppressing and silencing the legionary defenders to the south to engage and destroy the new threat. But two aerial gunships and nine attack helicopters were at a grave disadvantage when faced with an unexpected eight four-barreled, radar-guided, self-propelled antiaircraft guns, and twice that many shoulder-fired-missile teams. Add to that the fires of almost a thousand rifles and machine guns. It was going to be ugly . . . at least from the Tauran point of view.

Carrera saw the first gunship explode as three streams of tracers from the mobile air defense guns ripped it apart. More cannon, machine gun, and rifle fire sought out the other aircraft of the invading Tauran force. Light IR guiding antiaircraft missiles, not so good a weapon as the Taurans had but not so bad, either, added to the toll of Tauran aircraft. In minutes, the badly shot-up survivors were seen limping from the area, some trailing smoke and flames. The night sky was lit by the burning remnants of others, not so lucky. As the cadets gained security from the air, the artillery and mortars continued their pounding of the Paras on the ground.

From his position in the center of the cohort, Tribune Rogachev chivvied his troops into position. Nothing fancy was envisioned. A simple on line attack was all that would be needed. The cadets formed up, east to west. The infantry dismounted from their tracks and lined up close behind them. At Rogachev's command the entire formation faced toward the Taurans and began a stately procession to the sea. Up front, the tanks' 125mm guns lanced out regularly and frequently with high explosive and canister, munitions against which the unquestioned bravery of the Anglian Paras would be of little avail.

Once he heard the cannons beginning to belch, Carrera lifted a microphone to his lips and ear. He spoke into it to a small to a small fishing vessel sitting at dock at the Port of Balboa. The ship—the *Pericles*—answered "Roger, out." When finished contacting the ship, Carrera made hurried further calls to his scattered units.

TUSF-B Headquarters, The Tunnel, *Cerro Mina*, Balboa Transitway Area, Balboa, Terra Nova

McQueeg-Gordon stayed in his office and hid. It was just too humiliating the way the Gauls who ran the operation patronized and then ignored him.

Conversely, now that the action had begun Moncey had more to do than pace. Both the Anglian and Gallic Para brigades had reported that they were on the ground meeting serious but sur-mountable resistance. The chief also had cause for satisfaction; better than when the Federated States had invaded, decades before, *his* attacks had jumped off on time.

As gratified as the chief was at the excellence of the timing, his C-3 (Air) was positively jubilant. Report after report flooded his work cell area of targets successfully engaged and destroyed by the air armada sent to fire the first shots in the action. As each report was received the C-3's staff, under his direction, ordered the attack aircraft on to their secondary targets or, somewhat more commonly, released them to fly home as the airplanes reported low fuel or ordnance.

When the chief asked his C-3 (Air) how he knew the targets were genuinely destroyed, the answer was basically that the pilots had said so. Had he been a little more careful he might have asked about the extent to which armored vehicles attacked had shown signs of secondary explosions, fuel and ammunition blowing up, after the attacks. The chief, a tanker by background, knew that overestimation of the damage done to a target was an unavoidable vice of all pilots, in all countries, at all times. Still he didn't worry overmuch. Things really did seem to be going like clockwork.

There came a spate of calls from headquarters attempting to establish radio contact. This would not have been unusual except that those headquarters had *already* established contact. More than a few RTOs answered with a slightly surly tone.

In a few minutes the calls to establish contact ceased. Their place was taken by reports of action and requests for orders or information. These, too, lasted only briefly before an NCO manning a radio sat straight up and shouted, "That was my voice, Goddamit. We're being spoofed!"

TUSF-B began to work through the jamming, then to change codes. The code changes, especially in light of the jamming, were time-consuming, incomplete, and—for the men in action—unutterably confusing.

Initially, the *Pericles* almost kept up with the changes. Eventually, it caught up.

The chief returned to his pacing, though now it was quite nervous, when a strange and eerie piece of music began to blare from the loud speakers connected to the radios. More jamming. The general couldn't quite place it until one of the headquarters radio operators, a Castilian-born enlistee into the Gallic army announced what it was.

"*Deguello*," the citizen of Gaul said with wonder. "Who the fuck is playing *Deguello?*"

The private had no more than spoken the words when a major rushed into the Operations Center. Looking around quickly, the major spotted the chief and hurried over. Speaking in hushed but excited tones the major told of what he had seen from the top of the hill. "Sir, Arnold and Brookings are both under attack. Rockets I'm sure of; I could see them. Maybe mortars or artillery too. Heavy fire sir, I counted over fifty rounds a minute landing in both places."

Heart sinking, telling his staff he was going topside, the chief rushed out of the Operations Center to see for himself. When he'd climbed to the very topmost crest of the great hollowed out hill, his heart leapt to his mouth. It was worse than the major had said. Fire—rockets, artillery, mortars, and God knew what else—wasn't just coming from one or a few places. It seemed to be coming from *everywhere*.

My God, thought the chief, as a fireball blossomed over Arnold AFB, *how will we ever keep the troop flow going?*

CHAPTER FORTY-THREE

Now that was the story my grandfather told,
As he sat by the fire all withered and old.
"Remember," said he, "that the Irish fight well,
But the Russian artillery's hotter than Hell."

—"The Kerry Recruit," Traditional

Santa Cruz, east of Arnold Air Force Base, Balboa, Terra Nova

Tribune Ilya Kruptkin, XO for the cadet cohort, was thankful beyond words at finally getting out of the hot, stuffy, and miserable little warehouse in which he and more than two hundred cadets had been hiding for three days. As he emerged he heard the cohort's artillery "club"—rocket launchers, 85mm guns, 81mm and 120mm mortars—pounding on the enemy to his west without mercy. A suddenly bright glow, the source hidden by the sharp ridge overlooking the air base, suggested the fire was particularly effective where aircraft were parked.

To the south, more artillery and mortar fire, 120s and 81s, added their voices to the rising din. Another fierce glow from the same direction suggested to Kruptkin that the indirect fires had found at least one more of the Tauran aircraft on the ground.

No building could have caught fire so quickly. Burn, you bastards.

As the executive officer, Kruptkin was responsible for initially overseeing the deployment of the fielded cohort of the Seventeenth Cadet Tercio's air defense and other heavy combat assets. Those were "clubs," too.

A roar from massed engines came from behind, then crept

forward. At the head of the crawling column a wheeled armored personnel carrier came to a stop. From it emerged one of the adult cadre, a Balboan tribune, in this case.

Kruptkin didn't have time to chat. He gave the commander of the motorized rifle company with its attached tank platoon the go-ahead to move across Santa Cruz Drop Zone, then promptly forgot about it as he turned and walked the short distance to give a little personal attention to getting the towed air defense guns and shoulder launched SAMs into action. Not nearly so effective as the self-propelled, four-barreled jobs, still the dual 23mm guns were dangerous enough to low flying enemy aircraft to ensure that they would be the first priority target once they made their existence known. Hopefully, they would last long enough to allow the cadet rifle companies to close with the defenders of the base.

Brought up on tales of young men, even boys, being asked to give their lives for their country in the Great Global War, Kruptkin only regretted the need, not the decision, to use Balboan boys for a similar reason.

All around Kruptkin, often not visible but still audible, the cadets of the Seventeenth formed up in the streets of Santa Cruz and began their march down the slopes toward Arnold Air Force Base. No Tauran air had interfered so far. Kruptkin knew that probably wouldn't last. The sound of a heavy cannon firing told him that the tanks he had previously sent forward had engaged the outer defenders of the base. Seeing that the junior tribune in direct charge of the air defense needed no further help from him, Kruptkin mounted his personal vehicle, put on his night vision goggles, and then rushed westwards. He passed the cadet formations that were deploying on either side of him as he moved forward.

At the easternmost edge of Santa Cruz Drop Zone, Kruptkin saw the twenty-odd vehicles, tanks and wheeled armored personnel carriers, moving forward toward the base. Occasionally one of the tanks would stop to fire at one or another of the defender's positions. The APCs' heavy machine guns kept up a constant chatter. As the APCs and tanks reached to within three hundred meters of the wood line the infantry began to dismount from the side access doors. Through his goggles Kruptkin saw the boys struggling to fix their folding bayonets and then forming skirmish lines. A detached professional voice told the Volgan that the whole show seemed less than snappy. The experienced veteran's voice answered back that it wasn't bad, the boys being under fire for the first time and all.

Although he was too far away to hear it, especially over the thunder of the guns, Kruptkin knew that the commander of the unit ahead had given the order to conduct the assault. The cadets started marching forward, firing from the hip. The light given off by thousands of tracers threatened to burn out his goggles. Even over the sound of firing Kruptkin did hear the wild shrieks of over a hundred voices as the boys suddenly started their charge. He couldn't be sure, but he thought that he saw some of the defenders running away.

Kruptkin called his boss on the radio and told him that the initial defense of the base was broken. "For God's sake hurry up. We can take this place in an hour."

Kruptkin was worried that the rear echelon motherfuckers in the Second Corps' headquarters might give up before they could be rescued. Time was critical.

Second Corps Headquarters, the old *Comandancia, Ciudad Balboa, Balboa,* Terra Nova

Sergeant Frederico Perez, of the Tenth Infantry Tercio was, in peacetime, a full-time supply sergeant for one of the infantry maniples. He would have been very happy if he could have remained so until his retirement. Now, however, he was stuck in a fighting position just inside the *Comandancia's* thick concrete walls. He couldn't see through the walls but that didn't matter. His job for now was to watch over the open space of the interior for any Tauran helicopters that might try to land. Other people of the three headquarters stationed at the *Comandancia* were responsible for the exterior. This was almost perfectly fine with Sergeant Perez. It would have been better, of course, if he had been somewhere far, far from any fighting. As it was, if someone had to actually fight, Perez was quite content for it to be someone else.

Without warning the interior of the courtyard blew up. Only partially stunned by the blast, Perez could see that one of the *Comandancia's* buses was burning side by side with a jeep. Almost simultaneously a loudspeaker began to announce a demand for surrender. Through partially deafened ears Perez could still make out the insistent demand. He began to crawl over the concrete wall that separated the *Comandancia* from the outside.

With his torso and right leg on top of the wall Perez tried to move his left over as well. It wouldn't budge. Perez looked down to see a strong hand holding his trouser leg tightly. A few feet from the hands stood Junior Tribune Torres, just twenty-one and as fanatical as could be imagined. Perez's eyes opened wide to see that Torres had a pistol in his hand, the muzzle pointed at Perez's head.

Thus it was that the first official legionary response to the Tauran demand for surrender of the *Comandancia* was a shot that didn't go very far past its walls.

Fort Guerrero, Balboa, Terra Nova

Major Christophe Pittard, Executive Officer of the Thirty-fifth Commandos, like all the other members of his paratrooper unit, had hoped that the headquarters of the Balboans' Second Infantry would give up without too much of a struggle. That did not appear likely, now. Although there had been a fair degree of surprise— the bodies of Balboans cut down as they tried to get from their barracks to their defensive positions attested to that—the Second was resisting ferociously from its barracks and the few outside positions that were manned. Even the fire from the helicopter gunships didn't seem to do more than temporarily suppress the return fire coming at the Tauran Union forces.

From a partially covered position in the housing area to Pittard's rear a 105mm howitzer fired directly at the northernmost legionary barracks. Great chunks of wood, plaster, tile, and concrete flew into the street and the golf course opposite with each high explosive round. After fifteen rounds of HE, the gun crew switched to white phosphorus. The building, what there was of it, began to burn.

Pittard couldn't see them, but he knew a platoon of Third Company was using the cover between the flat ground of Fort Guerrero and the shore of the Bay of Balboa to approach that barracks. The rest of Number Three Company followed.

On the point of that company's approach, Sergeant Thomas Gilbert led his squad forward. Occasional tracers flying overhead gave proof that the company's route was in defilade from the legionary positions. Even an observer in the top windows of the barracks couldn't see a man moving at a crouch.

As he shuffled forward, Gilbert heard the impact of something explosive on Arnold Air Force Base a few kilometers to the west. He wasn't overly concerned. While his company was based on Fort Nelson, an annex of Arnold, his wife had long since flown back to their little home in Gaul. Just about everybody else in the world he cared about was in file behind him. Arnold and Nelson were someone else's responsibility. Gilbert and his comrades only had to clear their chunk of Fort Guerrero.

Gilbert didn't need a pace count to tell him when he had reached his destination; the gut-rippling explosions of the 105 shells told him exactly where he was in relation to the first objective. He stopped his squad, then crawled up the embankment to steal a peek at the building.

Gilbert's commander, Captain Bernoulli, slithered up beside the vantage point Gilbert had chosen. Bernoulli was accompanied by Lieutenant Garonne, the first platoon leader. The three had worked and practiced together for long enough that no words were needed. A few hand and arm signals directed the troops to their assault and support positions. A quick look around told Bernoulli that everyone was ready. He took a green star cluster from a side cargo pocket and fired the signal that would shift the artillery support and send his cutthroats into the assault.

The 105 firing in direct lay on the barracks shifted to the next one over. Machine guns kicked in to keep down any legionaries that were still in a mood to resist. At the signal from Bernoulli, Gilbert and his squad, followed by the rest of the first platoon, rushed forward screaming like banshees.

Ciudad Antigua, Ciudad Balboa, Balboa, Terra Nova

In this old and quaint area of Balboa—the place where, centuries prior, Belisario Carrera had attacked, captured, and burned the headquarters of Old Earth's United Nations in Balboa—the mobilization of the Tenth Infantry Tercio went on fairly unhindered. While it was unavoidable that the artillerymen of the gun battery should have to actually enter the armory to get the keys to unchain their guns, most of the troops assembled in nearby houses. The gunners took serious losses from the Tauran aircraft overhead as they tried to get their guns into action, but the foot soldiers managed to assemble mainly unscathed.

Under the Taurans' plan, the Tenth Tercio was supposed to be engaged and held in place by airpower and some minor number of infantry as they became available. With the natural friction of the operation the Tauran infantry had not yet arrived. It remained to be seen whether they could arrive or would instead be diverted to some other mission.

When the broad spectrum jamming began and cut both Tauran and Balboan radio communications, the tercio had been somewhat stymied in a way they really hadn't remotely expected. Carrera—the thoughtless son of a bitch—had kept the Volgan built "trawler" a very deep secret. This lasted until the commo chief realized that he could probably get phone communications with either his legions or Second Corps headquarters in the *Comandancia*. When the *Comandancia* answered on the first ring, he passed the phone to the tercio commander.

The Tenth's CO, Umberto Pizzaro, could hear the *crump* of Tauran artillery through the phone as well as through the air. He asked for the Corps commander, but was informed that Legate Suarez was having a wound treated.

"Serious?" Pizzaro asked.

"I'm always serious, sir," the man at the other end of the line answered.

"No, you dipshit, I mean is the wound serious?"

"Oh, sorry, sir. We are told the legate will live."

"Fine, give me the corps exec."

"Here he is, sir."

"'Berto, this is Dario. The old man's down, 'Berto. I don't think he'll die; the medics say 'no.' Hell, the medics say he'll be back on his feet inside of two hours. But come quick with your troops, friend, or we're all going to die. The ever-so-peace-loving Taurans are using everything they've got on us, jets, gunships, artillery, tanks. They've gotten over the wall twice already, but we kicked their asses out again. We can't keep it up forever. Come running or we're dead. Keep someone on this line 'til you get here."

Pizarro sent runners to bring his company commanders. Then he ducked into a hallway, pulled out flashlight and map, and began planning how he was going to relieve the headquarters.

Lago Sombrero, Balboa, Terra Nova

Carrera left his CP, guarded only by Soult. He and Jamey walked in the path the cadets had trod.

The cadets had attacked on line and at a pace little faster than a walk. With the tanks leading them, firing their machine guns and canister rounds from their 125s, the Ocelots fired high explosive and machine guns. Behind the Ocelots marched the cadet infantry, firing off to the sides.

Though the attack proceeded at a fast walk, it was still faster than the Paras could react to, since they, under all that fire, could only move with any chance of survival at a belly crawl They had barely stood a chance. The bodies—some crushed and leaking—littered the runway where Carrera walked. These showed that, even fucked by fate, they had still tried.

They were trying still. Up ahead, Carrera could see a group of them trying desperately to break down a bundle that might contain enough antitank weapons to let them defend themselves. Carrera watched them keep trying while machine guns closed on them. He watched without expression as the same guns tore them to bits.

Not that the cadets hadn't taken losses, too. Almost a half-dozen armored vehicles flickered and smoked in the breeze. Nor were all the bodies Tauran, although most of them were. To the southwest, where the trail was free of caltrops and the wheeled APCs had gone, more firelight showed where the Paras had made a more costly, although still futile, stand.

Behind the lines as he was, Carrera was in only incidental danger from the Paras' rifles and machine guns. They had enough to do without bothering with a lone man far from the action. Thus when two navy jets off of HAMS *Indomitable* came in to investigate the scene at *Lago Sombrero* and discovered the disaster that had overtaken the Paras there, Carrera was nowhere nearby. When the two pilots decided to try to do something to help out on their own initiative, Carrera was also nowhere near the impact points for the bombs and twenty millimeter cannon. He added another half-dozen tracks and perhaps fifty cadets to the loss column. It was a small satisfaction that one of the jets was taken out by the Balboans, spinning down to a flaming landing by the coast, while the other flew off.

By radio Carrera spoke to Rogachev. The jamming didn't interfere much with radios so far from *Pericles* and so close to each
other. His orders were simple—finish off the Paras, stay until at
least two of the reserve mechanized tercios were fifty percent
mobilized, then move east toward the city. He, Carrera, would
meet them on the road near Arnold Air Force Base. Carrera also
made a call to the First Corps commander, telling him to move
when he was ninety percent mobilized. Carrera then had himself
driven to the east, toward the City.

The Tunnel, TUSF-B Headquarters, *Cerro Mina,* Balboa Transitway Area, Balboa, Terra Nova

The three principles of the effort—Moncey, de Villepin, and
Bessières—couldn't know for certain that their plans were collapsing. Even so, the latter put two and two together and came
up with the mathematically perfect answer: "We're fucked."

And that was relying only information given and information
missing down in the concrete lined bowels of the hill. Conversely,
from his vantage point atop *Cerro Mina,* Moncey could hear the
impact of explosives on both Arnold Air Force Base and Fort
Nelson, to his southwest, and Brookings Air Force Station to his
northeast. Nothing was hitting Dahlgren as of yet.

But that's mostly because Dahlgren hardly matters, he thought.
At this range he couldn't distinguish the tank gun fire from the
other explosions. He could, however, see green tracers where
none should be. The legion was attacking where it should not
have been possible for them to attack. The amount of firing told
him that these attacks were in strength. *Where could they have
gotten such strength?*

Mind racing, the general rushed back to the stuffy ops center
below. It was well that he did, since just before his entering the
Tunnel, the wave of fire from *somewhere* swept over the hill's
topographical crest, precisely where he'd been standing. Crossing
himself at the narrow escape, Moncey entered the Tunnel and
practically ran to de Villepin's intel office.

There it was in black and white on the intelligence chart. All of
the legion's maneuver tercios were unmobilized except for those
of the Third Corps, which were scattered about the City looking
for the murderers of Tauran female supremacists, and a couple

at *Fuerte* Cameron, far from the center of action. Satellite, air, and such ground recon as had been possible all confirmed that. None of the training battalions on the *Isla Real* had moved back to the mainland by sea. The tercios at *Fuerte* Cameron, the Fifth Mountain, undergoing annual training at Mobilization Level II, and Twenty-second Airborne (Volgan . . . though it was at least forty percent Balboan by this time), were scattered all over creation.

But in at least two places he knew of, the legion was attacking, while in two others, there were troops defending that ought not have been there.

This Moncey thought impossible until a sudden thought occurred to him: *Oh, shit. The cadets.* And if there were two groups of cadets on the attack, there had to be at least six. Maybe more. *Bastards, using children.*

Moncey looked to the main operations map. The military schools were posted on it as "no fire areas," places where the Tauran forces couldn't fire without permission from the commander of TUSF-B himself. If the legion had moved them into attack positions not too far from their schools there would most likely be one at *Lago Sombrero*, one or, more likely, two for the east bank of the Transitway, opposite *Cerro Mina*, one more that was probably attacking Brookings, one for the Shimmering Sea side, and the last one . . . that would be at Herrera International, which explained why the Gallic Para brigade was stuck.

"Two, Three, Air, get over here!"

Once they arrived, Moncey began to lay out what he suspected was happening to their operation and roughly what he wanted done to fix it. In a flurry of activity the TUSF-B staff began to try to formulate a reaction that would—or at least might—save them all from disaster. Radio communications were out, the jamming was broad spectrum—even the frequency hoppers couldn't get through reliably. The phone lines, on the other hand, worked perfectly. Orders began to crackle out over those. That orders went out to the subordinate brigades made little difference, however, since those brigades had no telephonic commo with the battalions.

One very notable exception was the Thirty-fifth Commando. From his TOC at Fort Guerrero, the commander of that unit did receive his orders. So it came about that, just as Number Three Company of the Thirty-fifth was getting ready to rush another of the legion's barracks, the order came to cease the attack, get control of the artillery, and move to the Bridge of the Colombias.

The Balboan defenders of the Second Cohort, Second Tercio didn't know why the assault they were expecting to continue suddenly stopped. Most figured it could only be a good sign.

Can't be a bad sign, anyway, thought Sergeant Major Cruz, turning his back to the wall and sliding down the bare concrete to the floor. He wasn't wounded, just exhausted.

Fort Melia, Balboa, Terra Nova

On the other side of the Transitway, at Fort Melia, near the Shimmering Sea, there was no communication between the TOC, located on the hill overlooking the post, and the companies currently clearing Fort Williams and the barracks at Lone Palm. From Fort Melia a Sochaux S4 set out carrying a message for the forward companies. The Sochaux raced at breakneck pace up the jungle bordered road until a well-laid ambush near the old Transitway Area dairy farm between Forts William and Melia opened up on the vehicle, killing both driver and messenger.

Headquarters, One Hundred and First Air Defense Tercio, *Ciudad* Balboa, Balboa Terra Nova

With the clouds having cleared for the nonce, and all three moons glowing above, the rooftop was bathed in light. There were few shadows on the ground either. The last of the troops-carrying helicopters that had brought Captain Guillaume Le Blanc's commando company to the roof of the caserne's armory had long since departed to complete other missions. Le Blanc, CO of Number Two Company, Thirty-seventh Commando, didn't mind in the slightest. The "truck drivers" were a nuisance anyway.

Beneath le Blanc, who was crouched on the roof of the armory, the commandos were methodically clearing the building, top to bottom. From around the meter-high wall that surrounded the roof others were keeping a watchful eye on the low buildings in the vicinity. The men were especially careful to cover the legion's heavy surface-to-air missile launchers that were parked on line in the motor pool area.

The leader of one of le Blanc's platoons popped up through the access way, then scampered across the roof to report. "Sir, the building's just about clear. No friendly casualties. Two Balboan dead. No civilians."

"What about POWs?" asked le Blanc.

"None, sir. That was it, those two guys at the front desk. They went for their guns. The boys had to take them out."

"Fine. Report it to headquarters. I wonder where the hell everyone was."

CHAPTER FORTY-FOUR

Everybody has a plan until they get punched in the face.

—Mike Tyson

UEPF *Spirit of Peace*, in orbit over Terra Nova

Alone in the main conference room, watching events unfold on the big Yamatan screen, Marguerite wanted to scream. She had seen it as soon as the armored vehicles had begun to debouch from their thick-roofed, concrete bunker at *Lago Sombrero*. As soon as she'd seen those, and realized where they had to have come from, who they had to have been, she'd immediately seen also that the Tauran plan was going to unfold in disaster. And there was no one useful she could tell. Janier in Gaul had a communicator, and she'd advised him through it. But she'd advised him about the time that communications between Taurus and Balboa had been cut.

And she could see where the communications had been cut. On her screen, set to detect electromagnetic radiation at high power, all indicators pointed to the largish trawler pulled up to a dock. And she couldn't tell anyone in a position to do anything.

She could have served as a first rate—or a better than first rate—artillery spotter, too. She could see every Balboan firing position, down to the glowing tubes of what Kahn, male, told her were 81 or 82mm mortars.

And there's no one, NO ONE, *I can tell about it in a position to do anything.*

I could just weep.

471

Oh, well; there's this much solace. Obviously Carrera planned this from the beginning. And the Taurans are using the same basic plan they intended to when I was pushing them to war. But I didn't push them to this war; this one they did on their own, albeit because somebody—Elder Gods You know it wasn't me—butchered some Tauran women.

I wonder who did that. If I ever find out, I'll give that information, at least, to Carrera and he can make them scream for a while.

TUSF-B Headquarters, The Tunnel, *Cerro Mina*, Balboa Transitway Area, Balboa, Terra Nova

Moncey wanted to scream. He couldn't raise Arnold AFB on the phone. Brookings had stopped answering as well. The glow reflecting off whatever clouds hovered over the buildings suggested why.

Though originally scheduled to attack into Balboa, with an objective of the area around the Arraijan Ordnance Works, the Haarlem Marines had shifted to covering Dahlgren Naval Station as soon as they saw strong indicators that things were beginning to unravel. They were now, their commander reported, under attack, but holding on well. They offered to break a company loose to investigate what was happening to Arnold. The general told them not to, to hang on to Dahlgren and secure the Bridge of the Columbias until it could be reinforced. He was quite sure there was little they could do to help Arnold Air Force Base, Fort Nelson, or the naval station that was an annex to Arnold. Observers on top of *Cerro Mina* had reported that it appeared many buildings and aircraft were burning. They had also seen that the Balboan rocket and mortar fire had shifted off the base and onto Fort Nelson.

Moncey was having a little more luck at getting a coherent defense of the west bank of the Transitway set up. The Thirty-fifth had broken off from Guerrero and was sending two commando companies to keep anyone from crossing the bridge. Unfortunately, the bulk of Tauran combat forces were out of touch with their own headquarters which had, in any case, little to do since the Tunnel was exercising command and control down to platoon level. Those Moncey hadn't been able to pull back were slugging it out with whatever defenders the legions had on hand, seemingly oblivious to the disasters around them.

An aide de camp came over to the chief of staff's side. "Sir," whispered the aide, "the SF reported over SATCOM that the local Balboan Air Defense Battalion headquarters has been neutralized. They also report that almost no one was there. Fortunately, all the launchers are there that were supposed to be.

"Another thing, sir; it looks like things are going badly for the Mech down by the *Comandancia*. I had *Hauptmann* Lang take a few MPs down to investigate but they haven't come back yet. That's not a good sign either."

Moncey nodded. Initiative in an aide de camp was a wonderful thing. He asked, "Do we have a fix yet on where the jamming's coming from?"

"No, sir. The RF people have only pinpointed it to one of the ships docked at Balboa. They're all docked close together."

"Any ID of the flag of those ships?"

"No, sir. We could sink 'em all, but what happens later when we've sunk a half-dozen neutrals? I called about getting a patrol boat to investigate but they're all supporting something else and are all just as much out of communication as the rest of us. They wouldn't do any good anyway. They don't carry the manpower to search a bunch of ships."

"Here's what I want you to do. Get the grids on the likely culprits. Have the C-3 call the First Airmobile Brigade. I want them to hold the first fourteen troop carriers they can get their hands on. Then I want them to airlift troops—cooks and truck drivers will do if that's all they have—onto the decks of those ships. I want my units to be able to talk again!"

Three hundred meters southeast of Second Corps Headquarters, at the *Comandancia*, *Ciudad* Balboa, Balboa, Terra Nova

A Roland tank rested in the street with its turret ajar. It wasn't burning yet, though the thin smell of smoke around it might have meant it was about to. On the opposite side of the street lay the Balboan who had destroyed it by wedging a satchel charge under the turret. Behind him, in a ragged line leading to the alley from which he and his squad had charged, lay a half-dozen of his comrades, also dead, shot while trying to get at the tank.

A Tauran soldier who had helped shoot them shook his head in wonder. *Gutsy bastards, weren't you. You might be the enemy, but you were still gutsy as all hell. I hope to fuck they're not all like you. And good luck to you all, wherever you are.*

At his squad leader's order, the Tauran soldier rushed with a friend to the other side of the street to make sure no more Balboans were waiting. Lying on shards of shattered glass next to a store front, he heard voices coming from inside the store. Reaching for a grenade, he signaled his squad mate to do the same. "On three. One. Two. Three."

After the grenades blew what little glass remained out into the street the two rushed in through the storefront window. Three Balboans lay on the floor, two of them very dead indeed. The two Taurans began to move toward the back room of the store when they were met by a heavy fire. Both were hit instantly.

Crawling to where his friend lay, the less badly wounded of the pair returned fire at the Balboan muzzle flashes. Using his last grenade to drive back the legionaries, he grabbed hold of his unconscious buddy's harness and began to drag him back out of the store. Badly wounded as he was, he could not move quickly enough. A rifle bolt slammed home. He threw his friend out onto the street and turned to fire at the sound. A half-dozen bullets found his body before his finger could tighten on the trigger.

Moving up to the side of the window opening, a sergeant of the Tenth Infantry Tercio looked around at the dead and wounded Balboans and Taurans. *Buen' viaje, compadres. You fought well.* "Gomez, set the M-26 up here. And get a medic to check out the wounded. While you're at it, have him check the Taurans. Maybe one of them's still alive."

Fifteenth Cadet Tercio Command Post, *Lago Sombrero,* Balboa, Terra Nova

Cadet Sergeant Miguel Cordoba stole a quick peek from the smashed window that looked over the last few buildings in which the Paras had rallied. What few street lights remained working cast an uneven glow over the main cantonment area at *Lago Sombrero.* Tracers leapt back and forth between what was left of the Anglian Paras Infantry and the cadets surrounding them. Often enough, when the Paras fired their rifles at the Balboans, the return fire was high explosive from a tank or Ocelot. Few antitank weapons seemed to remain in Para hands. At least they were being very frugal with whatever they had.

Cordoba's vision was aided by an Ocelot that burned brightly near one of the buildings held by the Taurans. He didn't see any good reason to assume the Taurans were out of effective antitank munitions. Four of the cadets that had not been killed outright when their track was hit had been shot down near it. Cordoba was looking forward to getting even for them.

Behind Cordoba, in the same room as the rest of his squad. They had not lost anybody yet. As part of the tercio's Combat Engineer Club, reformed as the Combat Engineer Platoon, they had been held out of action until now. At the call from the commander of the company they supported, they had rushed up in their armored personnel carrier, checked their weapons and moved to an assault position. Now they waited for Cordoba to lead them into the assault. Cordoba himself was waiting for the order to move from the commander. The plan, as he understood it, was for one of the rifle platoons to fire to keep the Paras' heads down, while the engineer squad moved up to flamethrower range and roasted the Taurans out.

Consulting his watch, Cordoba thought, *Ought be right about—*

Although he knew what was coming, Cordoba still jumped at the sudden and vicious volume of fire that poured over onto the Tauran-held building. Tribune Rogachev shouted through the door for the engineers to move out.

Screaming "Follow me!" Cordoba leapt out of the window and rushed for the building opposite. One by one, the squad followed. The last boy out had no luck, however, as a random shot from a Para spun him around and left him spread-eagled on the ground.

On reaching the building wall, a cadet engineer pulled the igniter on a ten kilogram satchel charge. He waited for the fuse to burn nearly to the blasting cap. Then, using the charge's strap for leverage, the cadet hurled it through a window. Shouting and the sound of people scrambling to get through a narrow passage followed. The explosion blew debris from the window.

A two-second burst of jellied gasoline from a flamethrower, followed by another, set the interior of the room on fire. A man screamed heartrendingly from inside.

The engineer squad moved on to the next window. Taking a chance that whoever might be occupying that room was stunned by the satchel charge's blast, Cordoba tossed a grenade through the window. His boys carried few satchel charges. Flame followed the grenade. The cadet engineers moved on.

Before the cadets reached the next window, a hand grenade fell on the ground to their front. Most of the boys hit the ground. Cordoba fell only to one knee and bent his head over to shield it with his helmet. The explosion sent serrated wire through his thigh and shin. He gasped with the tearing pain.

Even as he gasped, Cordoba popped back up in bare time to fire a full magazine at the shadow of a man—a Para who tried to follow up the grenade with rifle fire. Blood from a roughly torn leg dripped to the ground at Cordoba's feet. *Damn, they catch on quick,* he thought through the red agony.

Grabbing one of his three flamethrower men by his combat harness, Cordoba pulled him into position and ordered, "Bounce it off the inside of the window into the room. Give 'em three seconds of it." The bright tongue lanced out, drawing agonized screams from inside the building. The screams went on and on. Arm thrown over the shoulder of one of his men, Cordoba shouted the others into further action as he was carried to the rear.

A kilometer to Cordoba's north, the first truck and car loads of reservists were arriving at *Lago Sombrero.*

Third Corps Headquarters, near Herrera Airport, Balboa, Terra Nova

In the Operations Center, located in the basement of the head-quarters building, telephone operators received reports of the assembly and mobilization status of the Corps' two infantry legions, one infantry brigade, one combat support legion, and one service support brigade.

Though in theory the corps should have had eight maneuver tercios, in fact there were five, plus one of First Corps' mecha-nized tercios, the Fourth, that was based in the City and under the operational control of Third Corps until First should make it across the Bridge of the Columbias.

There was a substantial artillery park, consisting of Seventy-third and Seventy-sixth Artillery Tercios, with full manpower if all were called up but only about three-eighths a full level of guns and rocket launchers, at fifty-four of the former and eighteen of the latter. There were also tercios of engineers, the Ninety-third, and Air Defense, the One Hundred-third. Their reports were posted on a status chart that hung on the wall next to the operations map.

Legate Hannibal Padilla read the status of his units while himself being briefed via telephone by the Eighteenth Cadet Tercio, the defenders of the airport. From what he could gather, the Gallic paratroopers were still contained, albeit not easily, inside the airport's environs. The cadets were also paying a terrible price to hold that outside perimeter. Inside the airhead, in and around the airport terminal, the cadets defending were just barely hanging on. From that spot, however, they were in position to call in devastating indirect fires on any assembly of the Tauran troops that was large enough to have a chance of breaking out.

An orderly made a change to the chart in grease pencil. The chart on the wall now told Padilla that his Third and Eleventh Infantry Tercios were almost fully assembled and ready to move. The Fourth Mechanized, on the other hand, was under more or less continuous air attack. They were effectively pinned for now. Padilla handed the phone he had been using and took another from one of the staff. This one was tied to the Third Infantry Tercio.

"Rodriguez? Padilla here. Look, the Fourth Mech's being shot up pretty badly and the Eleventh won't get here for a couple of hours. They've got too far to move. I'd rather wait until they did get here and have you attack together but I don't think the cadets can hold that long. What's your assembly level now? . . . Eighty-four percent . . . Good, that's enough. Move out now and hit the southern tip of the airport, then strike north. You're the main effort. Everything I can scrape together will go to you. Good luck. Oh, and Rodriguez, we can win this. But you must move fast." Padilla gave over the phone.

"Get me the Seventy-third and Seventy-sixth Artillery on the line. Now!"

Fort Muddville, on the boundary with Brookings Air Force Station, Balboa, Terra Nova

The rockets and mortars hitting Brookings had stopped firing an hour ago or more. Lieutenant Allison Peters of the Anglian Army didn't know if that was good or bad. She had been ordered, along with her platoon of military police, to stop their movement on the old dog kennel area behind Brookings and take up a position to guard the boundary. When the order had come her platoon had already stopped moving while she tried to figure out what to do about the fighting she could hear ahead. Her questions about the reasons for the change, as well as about what was going on at Brookings, were cut off. She thought her company commander didn't tell because he, himself, didn't know.

The MP platoon had moved back to the Fort Muddville NCO Club, then north as far as the road would take them. They had then dismounted and moved on foot to their current position. The MPs had been waiting there since before the heavy firing at Brookings had stopped. Already the troops were slackening. To her right she could see a cigarette being lit. Like many second lieutenants, Peters was none too sure of herself. That she was a woman in what was still, unofficially, a man's world didn't help her when it came to imposing her will on someone. So she hesitated to order the cigarette put out.

A hundred meters or so from Peters' position, a light machine gunner of the Nineteenth Cadet Tercio tracked the cigarette in his Volgan-made starlight scope. The cadet hadn't been able to properly zero his M-26 light machine gun while he had waited in a warehouse by Alfaro's Tomb, pending the order to attack. A mechanical zero, just putting the sight on a certain setting by manipulating its knobs, had had to do. Still, it had worked well enough so far. When the cadet had fired up the Tauran MP gate at Fort Muddville's back door in the first part of the attack on Brookings, his tracers, bright in the scope, had showed he was close enough.

The MP gate had fallen quickly, of course. With it out of the way the tercio had smashed right through the Air Force Security Police gate at the back entrance to Brookings. Then it had been a running fight through and around the buildings of the Air Force Base. The gunner hadn't had to fight on Brookings, there really hadn't been all that much resistance. In a mental fog, that was how little he remembered of the attack, he and his platoon had moved northwest until they had come to a high chain link fence. The platoon leader, normally a first classman at the school, had held them up and set up a hasty defense while he tried to get orders for his next mission. The cadets had known in advance about the jamming that would be aimed at the Taurans and hadn't really been able to come up with a good way to make themselves immune. Without radios it had taken hours for the cohort to pull itself together enough to accomplish the rest of its mission.

When order had been partly restored the cadets had begun moving toward Fort Muddville. They were as silent as possible. Still, it seemed to the gunner, the Taurans had to have heard them coming. Thus it came as a great surprise to him to discover that the platoon had gotten within range without being detected. To either side of the gunner the cadets of his platoon crept on line to attack.

Lieutenant Allison Peters had just decided to put her foot down to make the irresponsible trooper put out his cigarette when she heard a rifle or machine gun bolt slam home. She stopped and turned toward the sound. As she turned, she realized that it had not come from her platoon's position. Before her mouth could open to shout a warning to her soldiers a long burst of fire cut through the jungle to her right. Before that burst was half completed it was joined by fire from a line stretching out to either side. Four bullets, beginning at her right thigh and ending at her left shoulder spun Peters around before depositing her, face first, on the ground. She felt no pain at first. Then the pain came, worse than she had ever imagined possible. No return fire came from her platoon. *They couldn't all be dead,* she thought. She tried to rise and found she couldn't. Neither could she make a sound to give an order. She could still hear well enough to realize when the firing stopped and also to hear someone shouting for bayonets. Then came the screaming of dozens of men—*no . . . not men . . . voices too high . . . just boys . . .* —and the breaking of trees and bushes. Peters heard more screaming, this from her own people as they were bayoneted. Peters began to cry, without sound. She cried only briefly before a long, narrow bayonet entered her back. Then she died.

The sixteen-year-old bayoneter never realized that he had killed a woman.

Fort Williams, Balboa Transitway Area, Balboa, Terra Nova

In two hours of action the Fourteenth Anglian Foot had succeeded in driving the Castilians out of most of their buildings to either take shelter in the few structures remaining in their hands or to melt into the surrounding jungle. Many, being dead or too badly wounded to move, could do neither. The long support building had fallen, as had five of the barracks. The remnants of the cadre still in the fight were mainly holed up in one half of one of the long, two company, billets, and in the three buildings up on the hill overlooking the post.

A number of buildings could be held by neither side; they'd either been burnt or were still burning. This was no mean feat in the rainy season on the Shimmering Sea side.

That it was the rainy season had other implications. Koniev's maniple of heavies had started off making good progress toward Williams. Unfortunately, the roads were narrow, the jungle thick, and the ground watery. Just a mile or so past the town of Magdalena, they'd run into a—*Company? Battalion? I don't fucking know, sir. All I know is they toasted one tank and two Ocelots, totally blocking the road from drainage ditch to drainage ditch. What's that, sir? You're shitting me. Didn't you ever look at how fucking wide and deep the drainage ditches are on this side?*—something Koniev wasn't willing to pay a higher price to find out what.

Faced with a nasty case of reality, Chapayev had ordered the armor to leave one platoon to guard the road and then go relieve the legionaries still holding out at Lone Palm. Then he'd ordered his foot cadets to make a quick job of trashing the Tauran rear at Fort Melia and strike out for Williams as soon as they'd finished it. One of the maniple commanders—it was Ham's commander, Ustinov—suggested instead taking their time with Melia, but cutting one maniple loose to drive on to Williams.

"Do it," Chapayev ordered.

The cadets of the Academy Sergeant Juan Malvegui navigated toward Williams by the light cast by the burning barracks. As far as could be told their movement had not been discovered yet. Guiding on a trail they'd reconnoitered months before, the cadets marched with a long snaking column of infantry on either side of it.

There were, besides the tanks and Ocelots of Koniev's maniple, a half dozen in the assault gun platoon of the combat support maniple. Three of these went with Ustinov, though getting the ten-and-a-half-foot-wide vehicles through the narrow gaps between trees was difficult, time consuming, and highly frustrating.

Behind the command section, wire laid by the communications section led back to the tercio's start point around Clay Farm.

The cadets were not precisely quiet in their movement, the light tanks still less so, but over the sound of the small arms fire mixed with the pounding rain, no one fighting at Williams could hear them.

Ham was up ahead with the point squad. They were separated from the maniple's main body by about a quarter of a mile. When they broke out into the open Ham spent a few minutes looking, then told the squad leader to sit tight and wait for the rest of the company. Ham then raced back to report to Ustinov. He had to shout to make himself heard over a suddenly redoubled downpour.

The maniple commander, Ustinov, paused only a moment to consider before he started issuing orders. He held up the Ocelots and the two columns of infantry, then ordered to point of each column to take a ninety-degree turn to form a single straight line perpendicular to the trail. While this movement was being executed, a matter of about twenty minutes, he spoke over the telephone line to his fire support officer, or FSO, back at Clay Farms to confirm that the mortars and rocket launchers were ready to fire on command. He told the FSO to cancel any targets he had preplanned for the approach march, to prepare to put everything onto the fort. He also told the FSO to try to contact the Castilians' headquarters to do the initial adjusting of fire. Lastly he asked for an updated report from the Muñoz-Infantes.

By the time Ustinov knew everything that could be known about the situation ahead, the cadets were on line. The Volgan then passed the word down the line to begin to move forward when the artillery fired. After a suitable interval to allow the order to be passed, he ordered the FSO to commence firing.

From Sabinita Maintenance Facility and Clay Farms a half-dozen 122mm multibarreled rocket launchers, along with eight 120mm and twelve 81mm mortars began to throw tons of high explosive at Fort Williams. In just under thirty seconds the first shells landed. Within the next half minute, three hundred ninety-eighty high-explosive shells had rained down upon the fort. This rate of fire continued, with pauses to reload the rocket launchers, for the fifteen minutes it took the cadets to almost reach the open areas of the post. In all, three hundred eighty-four 122mm rockets, a like number of 120s, and hundreds and hundreds of 81mm shells pounded the Fourteenth Anglian Foot and the Castilians alike. The difference was that, while all of the Castilians were under some degree of shelter, the Taurans were, many of them, caught out in the open. The attack on the buildings still in Castilian hands halted abruptly as men sought shelter from the steel splinters shredding air, wood, and flesh. Fires lifted and shifted onto other targets as the FSO judged an area sufficiently prepared or when the Muñoz-Infantes requested over the telephone that the fires be shifted.

The first cadet unit to break out of the jungle was the assault gun platoon's two Ocelots. These moved slowly then, turrets traversing and machine guns chattering as they swept over any Taurans caught in the open.

More than a few of the Anglians so engaged had been caught by the barrage fired from Clay Farms. These lay on the ground, some dead and some wounded, rapidly being hurled into death by the cadets' light armor. Taught in the armor club to make full use of terror, the Ocelots ground over dead and wounded with equal impartiality. Other Tauran soldiers, unhurt or, at least, still able to fight, shot at the tanks with whatever they had available. Machine guns from the tanks shot these down almost as quickly as they showed themselves. Cadets emerging from the jungle joined their fires to those of the tanks. The area around the hill below headquarters was soon cleared.

At first the regular Castilian troops defending from the lower floor of the headquarters didn't realize that someone had come to rescue them. When they did realize that they had been saved they began to cheer. Cadets sweeping forward to finish off the remaining Taurans were heartened by the cheer, though it came from only a dozen throats.

CHAPTER FORTY-FIVE

If we seek merely swollen, slothful ease and ignoble peace,
if we shrink from the hard contests where men must win
at the hazard of their lives and at the risk of all they hold
dear, then bolder and stronger peoples will pass us by, and
will win for themselves the domination of the world.

> —Theodore Roosevelt,
> President of the United States

Dahlgren Naval Station, Balboa, Terra Nova

Unlike the bulk of the TU forces engaged in invading Balboa that
morning, the Haarlem Marines defending Dahlgren had never
entirely lost communications with their higher headquarters.
Radio was right out, of course, but they had their barracks and
their barracks had telephones.

Warned by the fires descending upon Arnold Air Force Base,
the Marine commander had, on his own initiative, canceled the
planned move on the town of *Nuevo* Arraijan, pulled his unit back
to a hasty defense of the Naval Station and the Arnold AFB tank
farm, and then requested further orders via telephone. Told by
TUSF-B to split his unit to defend both Dahlgren and the Bridge
of the Columbias, the marine lieutenant colonel had complied. So
far it looked like the decision to pull back had been a sound one.
Scattered probing of his defensive line indicated that the Balboans
had little or no idea where the Marines had fallen back to. No
indirect fires, except for a few random harassment rounds, had
fallen anywhere near the Marine positions.

Now the Marine battalion straddled the highway, with its right flank anchored deep in the jungle and its left hanging out in the thin, mostly open, air of the Arnold Tank Farm, which was a very large fuel storage facility. The battalion reserve guarded the Bridge of the Columbias. Despite TUSF-B's instructions not to send aid to the air force under attack at Arnold, the Marines had sent a single squad-sized patrol to find out what had happened to the left. Moving up a well-beaten trail that paralleled the road the squad had discovered the debacle overtaking the base. Upon their return they reported that the army troops stationed on Fort Nelson were still fighting back, though they couldn't offer an opinion on how long that resistance could last.

Fort Nelson, Balboa Transitway Area, Balboa, Terra Nova

Sergeant Guilbeault, an infantryman crippled in a training accident months before, had been left behind when the rest of his company had airlifted over to Fort Guerrero on the other side of the bay. Standing there by the ground floor door of Fort Nelson's Building 804, while the rest of the company moved to the helicopter pick-up zone to be lifted to Guerrero, had been a gut wrenching experience for Guilbeault. He didn't want to go to war, exactly, but neither did he want to be left behind when his friends moved off to war. He felt cut off, left out, and angry. Worse, there was no one really to be angry at except himself for getting hurt in a stupid training accident.

The men going on the attack had felt a sympathy for Guilbeault's being left behind as great as Guilbeault's anger at not going along. When the first sounds of firing at Guerrero announced the beginning of the assault, Guilbeault had felt as low and useless as a man can. That was how it came to pass that, when the rockets and mortars started pummeling Arnold Air Force Base, Guilbeault was sitting on the curb outside the barracks, smoking a cigarette dejectedly. He stared a few moments at the fireworks display before understanding had him running inside the barracks to gather up whatever force he could. This turned out to be three soldiers; all, like Guilbeault, too badly hurt to go along with the rest of the company.

Guilbeault told the senior of the three, a *caporal* from the antiarmor section, to take one of the privates down to the edge of the big drainage ditch that divided the battalion street in two along its length. He told another of the privates to call, in order, battalion, brigade, and TUSF-B headquarters until he reached someone he could report to. Then Guilbeault ran to the mess hall to round up any of the cooks who might be on hand.

By the time Guilbeault had gone through the mess hall, each of the battalion's company barracks, plus the engineer barracks, he had found a total of twenty-three soldiers. When he arrived at the west end of the drainage ditch with the last of them in tow, he discovered that a few others had joined from the artillery unit whose building was just north of the ditch's opposite end. In all, Sergeant Guilbeault then had thirty-two soldiers, including himself. He set about organizing his little command.

"Until someone comes along to tell us what to do, our mission is to defend Fort Nelson. Eventually, probably sooner rather than later, those air force pukes are going to bug out. Then, whoever is attacking them is probably going to turn on us. We can't let them have the post. Number Two Company?"

"Here, Sergeant," answered a young, frightened looking man with unlaced boots. "I'm Superior Private Seton. I'm senior. Three men with me."

"Seton...good. Take your guys and set up to defend Building 801." Guilbeault pointed to the building just north of where the soldiers stood. "Orient your fires north and south along the main drag to Arnold and toward Fort Nelson Beach. Don't let the bad guys get a foothold on the artillery barracks. What's your ammo?"

"We ain't got shit, Sergeant. Twenty-eight rounds per man."

"Right. Figures." The sergeant turned to one of the cooks. Pointing into building 804, he said, "Jennette, there's a case of rifle ammunition and about half a dozen antitank rockets first platoon left behind in their CP. Go get 'em and anything else you can find.

"Take off now, Seton. I'll get you topped off for rounds as soon as I can. Artillery?"

The soldier in charge of the remnants of the artillery spoke up. "Here Sergeant. *Caporal* Maillard, with four gunners."

"Maillard, take your men and go back to your own barracks. Orient your fire northeast across the road toward Radar Hill..."

Guilbeault continued on, assigning small teams of men to defensive positions, layering his deployment to have at least a little depth, with the troops in one building covering the approach to others. As he spoke, the sound of firing from Arnold rose to a crescendo and then dropped off. Before he finished issuing instructions to the last of his men he heard the sound of feet hitting pavement. Others, too, heard the sounds. Bolts of rifles slammed home as rounds were stripped from the magazines and chambered.

"Don't shoot! Don't shoot!" The troopers clustered around Guilbeault held their fire until seven aviation maintenance personnel stood in front of them, bent over with exertion and fear. They were weaponless, unhelmeted, and unkempt, as broken men often are.

"Who are you?" asked Guilbeault.

"Maintenance Squadron…" answered one, breathlessly. "We were on the base perimeter when the locals attacked. They had tanks, man. No shit, tanks! We hightailed it. Where did they get tanks?" The wrench turner sounded almost offended by the injustice of it.

Guilbeault's lip curled with distaste. "Get in the ditch."

"No way, man. We can't fight tanks."

Guilbeault flicked off the safety of his rifle and repeated himself. "I said, 'get in the fucking ditch.'" The SPs hesitated a moment until they saw that Guilbeault's rifle was pointed at them, backed up by the rifles of several more. Then they climbed down.

No sooner had they climbed into the ditch than a tank gun fired from vicinity of the airfield, about a third of a mile to the east. A shell screamed over Guilbeault's head to impact on a wall behind him. Then another shell, from a different tank, followed. Machine gun fire tore at the grass that grew thick around the sides of the ditch. Risking having the top of his head blown off, Guilbeault peered through the grass at the pair of tanks. They were moving forward slowly. Behind the tanks Balboan infantry walked. Soon their fire was joining that of the tanks. The east-facing walls of buildings 801 and 802 were splattered with lead.

Guilbeault had never before heard the cloth-ripping sound of standard Balboan rifles and light machine guns. It was… *a little frightening.*

Despite the splattering, shots from the defenders answered back. Guilbeault saw several Balboans fall. Still they kept coming.

"Sarge, I'm coming with the ammo!" Guilbeault looked to see Private Jennette, antitank rockets slung across his back, with a box of rifle ammunition in each hand, running from Building

804 toward the ditch. He had almost made it when something, a bullet no doubt, sent him flying. The ammunition he had been carrying hit the ground along with Jennette's body.

Davout, a boy from Guilbeault's own company, ran back to where Jennette lay. He took the cartridge boxes from the lifeless hands and threw them to the floor of the ditch. Then he pulled Jennette's body in as well and stripped it of the antitank weapons. These were one-shot, disposable rocket launchers, the basic design of which had become ubiquitous across Terra Nova. Gathering up all of the ammunition, Davout ran to where Guilbeault lay against the edge of the ditch.

Guilbeault took the ammunition boxes from Davout, opened them both, and pulled out two-thirds of the ammunition from each, eight bandoleers or eleven hundred and twenty rounds. Handing one back to Davout he said, "Take this over to 801 and give it to Number Two Company's people. Drop off four of the antitank rockets. Crawl over. Crawl *low*." He detailed another troop to carry the other box, and two antitank weapons, to the men in Building 802.

By this time the Balboan tanks and infantry were only 150 meters away, still advancing at a walk, as their large Volgan instructors had trained them to. Risking the bullets that lashed the area, Guilbeault extended one of the antitank rocket launchers, took aim and fired at one of the tanks.

"Fuck, I missed!" he exclaimed as he ducked back down into the ditch. The return fire from the tanks plastered the area around him as the tanks concentrated on the greatest apparent threat.

While the tanks, and their accompanying infantry, concentrated on Guilbeault's position, Davout reached the east side of Building 801, crawled through a window, and ran toward the rooms from which he could hear gunfire.

"Here, take this," he said as he threw a rocket to Seton. Davout tossed the box of ammunition to another of A Company's stay behinds. Then he joined Seton in extending the launchers.

There wasn't time to take the ammunition and load it into magazines immediately. Still, knowing that they had more was reassuring enough to cause the men in the building to increase their rate of fire greatly. This fire was joined, moments later, by fire from the artillerymen in Building 802 on the other side of the ditch. A rocket lanced out from the Tauran positions. It missed but was followed by another that hit. One Balboan tank stopped dead and began to burn. Faced with this sudden reversal of fortunes, the Balboan cadets, and their remaining tank, elected to pull back out of range of the LAWs until they could hit again with overwhelming force. They retreated, bounding back by squads, and still firing.

Breathing a sigh of relief, Guilbeault had the remaining ammunition distributed to the other positions on Fort Nelson. He noticed, for the first time, that the seven Air Force wrenches were no longer in the area. *Good riddance,* he thought. *But I'd still like to shoot the bastards...personally.*

A soldier clapped Guilbeault on the back, then asked if they could hold the Balboans again.

"Sure we can," Guilbeault answered, while thinking: *For a while. Then we're dead.*

Alcalde Flores Township, Headquarters, Tenth Artillery Legion, Balboa, Terra Nova

Of all the reserve units in the legion, only one had been given major command permission to mobilize above Mobilization Level Two (excepting the Third Legion which had been fully mobilized to hunt for the killers of the Tauran women but was also scattered because of that hunt). That unit was the Tenth Artillery Legion. Consisting of eight tercios, two each of eighteen 180mm cannon, one of eighteen super heavy multibarreled rocket launchers, three of thirty-six each 122mm multiple rocket launchers, one of super heavy mortars, and one of antishipping missile crews without missiles; the Tenth Artillery was at about forty percent manning, its six percent regular cadre, an additional eighteen percent reservists called up and another sixteen or so percent of the militia. Thus, of the Artillery Legion's full mobilization strength of over eleven thousand, fully four thousand were waiting for the Gallic Airmobile Brigade when it arrived.

A few days before, when doing the final planning and coordination of the semi-mobilization and demobilization that would, with other factors, cause the Tauran Union to invade at the desired time, in the desired way, with the right force, the Tenth Legion's commander had questioned Carrera on the limitation of forty percent. It did not seem prudent to do less than mobilize fully.

"Legate," Carrera had answered, "you can't even let them so much as *suspect* I'm letting you go to forty percent. If they thought you had mobilized completely, the first news you would get of an invasion is when they carpet bombed your ass from miles up and to hell with civilian casualties in the town.

"The idea is to make a threat they think they can deal with using less force than bombing you to obliteration, but still be strong enough to hold out for several hours until you can be relieved. Twenty percent is my best estimate of what that force is, but I'm going to let you o forty, anyway. Live with it."

The mobilization had indeed drawn TUSF-B's attention, enough so that, when it became known that the artillery brigade was already so heavily manned, the Airmobile Brigade of infantry was assigned to the attack. The brigade's attached aviation battalion, direct support battalion of 105mm guns, and all of their air force support were also committed to the effort. This was a measure of how seriously the TUSF-B chief of staff took the threat posed by the Tenth Artillery Legion. The entire Tauran Union's operation and presence in Balboa would be jeopardized if the guns, mortars, and rocket launchers of the Tenth were freed to support their brother defenders.

Although there had been no real surprise in the fact that so many Taurans would assault the Tenth, the legion had been shocked at the timing of the attack. More shocking still was the aggressiveness and élan brought to the action by the Gauls, who retained the spirit of their Para ancestors. They had also been deployed away from the Tauran Union, and out from under the malign influence of the late Marine Mors du Char, long enough to become real soldiers again.

In the first minutes after H Hour, dozens of troop-carrying helicopters had deposited troops at every major legion facility in and around the township of Alcalde Flores. Fighting had erupted instantaneously and brutally over virtually the entire area. Still, few were the legion casernes in which the Taurans did not gain at least a foothold. A steady stream of helicopters brought more men to the scene. Where the fighting was particularly fierce, Tauran helicopter gunships and artillery intervened. Although some of the Balboan gunners tried to man their pieces to help hold out against the attack, radar-directed counterbattery fires from the 105s across the canal quickly put them out of action with appalling and grotesque losses. From there the fight had degenerated into a slug fest, with rifle and grenade predominating. House by house, room by room the Balboans were driven back, killed, or forced to surrender. By four AM perhaps two-thirds of those men of the Tenth Artillery Legion already mobilized were still in the fight.

Cerro Mina, overlooking the fight around Second Corps Headquarters, Balboa, Terra Nova

From where he stood looking down onto the fight around the *Comandancia,* Moncey could not make out how his men below were doing. Tracers, red and green, crisscrossed through the night. The occasional major explosion told little. Was it an Tauran tank firing? A legionary antitank weapon or satchel charge? A civilian automobile blowing up? No one not on the scene could have said.

Many of that area's older, woodbuilt structures had burned in the Federated States' invasion. They'd been rebuilt in brick and concrete. No fires could be seen in those areas. Other areas, spared during the earlier attack, were burning now. The Gallic chief of staff said a brief prayer that the civilians would have more luck getting away now than they had had then. He doubted they would, though. The fighting this time was more intense. Any civilian who took to the streets was risking being shot as he ran.

Moncey gave an involuntary shudder. *Better to be shot than burned.* Like most people, he had a great fear of being burned to death, great enough he would prefer never to see even an enemy burn.

The chief's field of view shifted a bit, to where he could observe a helicopter gunship firing down at something, or rather someone, on the ground. The possibility of casualties from friendly fire wasn't high on the Gaul's list of concerns in the II Corps area. All of the Tauran troopers had patches of infrared reflecting tape sewn to the tops of their helmet covers, which the legionaries did not. Nor did the tercio from the *Ciudad Antigua* area have any armored vehicles in immediate support to confuse the helicopter gunners.

Moncey was startled as a streak of light and smoke tore up toward the gunship. The helicopter began to smoke after the rocket exploded beneath it, sending a continuous rod of steel flying up.

The helicopter started to twist and turn violently. Then it dropped below the line of buildings. A bright flash, followed by a sound like distant thunder, indicated to the chief what at least one of the explosions he heard was. "Shit," was all he could say at the death of the helicopter and, most likely, its crew.

The general still stared at where the gunship had gone down when his aide found him on the side of the hill. "Sir, the Airmobile Brigade has lifted off a platoon of cooks to take out whatever's been jamming us. They should be touching down on the docks right about now."

Nodding, still saddened at the fate of the helicopter, the general walked to the entrance to the Ops bunker.

Haarlem Marine lines, a few hundred meters east of Dahlgren Naval Station, Balboa Transitway Area, Balboa, Terra Nova

Little had gone quite right for the Sixteenth Cadet Tercio so far this morning. First they had had trouble getting into position to ambush the Haarlem Marines that were expected to come up the road toward the Arraijan Ordnance Works. Then, after the Marines had passed the forward observation post and were almost in the kill zone east of the town, the Seventeenth Cadet Tercio had begun its attack on Arnold to the south. Sure as hell the Marines had sensed something was wrong greater than a mere barrage on the airbase and turned around. Then the jamming had started, cutting communications, so that the commander of the cadets, Legate Olveira, couldn't get his boys reoriented quickly. It had taken over an hour to get them up and moving, south of and parallel to the InterColombiana, to go after Dahlgren. Even so Olveira had no idea of what was happening with his tank platoon and motorized rifle company. They hadn't been put into the ambush position, but had been left behind to move up into the attack on Dahlgren after the ambush had gone off.

It's bad enough that no plan survives contact with the enemy, Olveira fumed. *Ours hasn't even survived without contacting the enemy.*

Ahead of Olveira grew the sound of a rapidly developing firefight. Red tracers whipped through the leaves overhead. This was somewhat disconcerting to the legate. All of his life, in training and in combat against the Sumeris and Pashtians, the enemy tracers had always been green and his own red. Now it was reversed and the red streaks struck him as somehow more malevolent.

On the Balboan firing line, mere meters from where the Haarlemers were sending tracers toward Olveira, a terrible fight was in progress. Eighteen- and nineteen-year-old Tauran kids traded shots, grenades, and sometimes bayonet thrusts with sixteen- and seventeen-year-old Balboan kids. Screams of pain, fear, and anger resounded in the dense jungle. Under the pressure of nearly three-to-one odds the Haarlemers were being driven back.

Olveira advanced with his small group of staff and currently useless radio operators. By the light of the moon filtering through the trees Olveira saw terrible scenes the fight had left behind. Here a Balboan cadet, sixteen but looking younger still, clutched at his belly and moaned. A closer look showed that he was trying to hold his intestines in where a bullet or fragment had ripped open his abdomen. There a somewhat older Haarlemer lay dead, bayonet in the gut and his hands still gripping the knife he had shoved into the boy whose bayonet had pierced him. Olveira almost tripped over a helmet that lay on the ground, then again over the boy—Tauran or Balboan, he couldn't tell—whose smashed skull the helmet had failed to protect . . . brains in the helmet, brains on the ground.

Still the cadets, and Olveira, advanced. The Marines contested every foot gained bitterly. In places one side or the other ran low on ammunition. There the fight became very intimate.

Olveira heard a sound behind him and to his right. *About time,* he thought. The tanks and BTRs were coming up the road from *Nuevo* Arraijan. *Now we can get moving.*

Trawler *Pericles, Puerto de* Balboa, Terra Nova

"Captain," announced a lookout, quite unnecessarily, "we've got Tauran helicopters coming in on the dock!"

The Volgan-born captain nodded, then directed his boat to cease jamming, to reverse engines, and to back out into the waters of the Bay of Balboa.

No way those people can land on top of us, what with all the cranes and such sticking up. We'll find another position and see if the Balboans want us to keep jamming or not.

CHAPTER FORTY-SIX

For the old Roman Valor is not dead...

—Machiavelli, *The Prince*

Carrera's Command Post, Arraijan Ordnance Works, Balboa, Terra Nova

Carrera had a sneaking suspicion that the Ordnance Works—once it had been a mere rifle factory but there had been quite a bit of expansion—was on the Tauran Union's "Do Not Destroy" list. For one thing, it made one of the finest and most advanced infantry rifles on the planet. For another, they didn't want to be saddled with the cost of rebuilding Balboa after the war, while the works could be modified to producing civilian goods, keeping people employed, and cutting down on the amount of future revolutionary activity thereby.

The CP, itself, was in an alcove that had been built into the works for no other reason than to be a command post at some future date.

Carrera wasn't in the CP at the moment, though, he was on foot up by the main highway, accompanied by Soult carrying a radio. That was where he flagged down the Armored Cavalry Troop—which is to say the "Armored Cavalry Club"—of the Fifteenth Cadet Tercio. The troops were now halted along the road where Carrera flagged them down, the vehicles spaced out in a herringbone pattern and hidden under trees. The Fifteenth was a little unusual among the cadet formations in having, in its clubs, the nuclei for two heavy units. Their "clubs" likewise provided for two batteries of 122mm self-propelled guns rather than the single one even the legions' mechanized tercios were given.

The head of the cavalry troop, an ex-officer of the Jagelonian Army, jumped down from his Ocelot to stand beside Carrera. Saluting, the Jagelonian announced that he was the lead element of the Fifteenth, that the rest of the tercio was strung out over about the next twenty kilometers back. He also told Carrera that they had been attacked by Tauran aircraft on the way, with some losses to themselves and none, so far as they knew, to the Tauran Union.

"We might have gotten one, maybe more, if this goddamned jamming hadn't kept us from spreading the word that the aircraft were around."

Carrera nodded. "I know. It's part of the price to pay to beat the Taurans. Did you think it would be cheap? We've lost some men from it, even a few opportunities and some time. But they've lost control of themselves and of the battle. It's a better than fair trade. Besides, Tribune, it won't last much longer now.

"Now here's the situation. The Seventeenth Cadets took Arnold and are taking Nelson and the navy annex. The Sixteenth Cadet Tercio is out of communications but we know they're attacking Dahlgren. I don't have any idea about how that one's going. You, go now, as fast as you can drive, and get me the Bridge. I'll tell your boss what you're doing when he gets here."

At that moment, Carrera's radio crackled back to life. He picked up the microphone and called his Military Intelligence Tercio.

Cerro Gaital, Balboa, Terra Nova

Sergeant Valdez took the message and issued a simple command to his men. A few switches were thrown, a few buttons pushed.

High, high overhead, eight satellites in geosynchronous orbit sent a continuous stream of encrypted data. The data, however, said little more than "at the tone, the time will be..." Valdez's men could not read the data.

It didn't matter. They knew what the data had to say: "at the tone, the time will be..." The eight satellite dishes around Valdez took that interpretable data—and the unencrypted time data—delayed them ever so slightly, then fed them to an amplifier. The amplifier, in turn, sent all eight streams to several directional antennas.

The antennas sent fairly narrow—and immensely powerful—radio signals in the directions of the fire base at Imperial Range Base Camp, Herrera Airport, Balboa City, and Cristobal.

Taken collectively, each directional antenna's retransmission said "at the tone, the time will have been..." Any Global Locating System that did not use the encrypted signal and was within the arc of that powerful directed signal containing the stream of eight satellite messages would interpret them perfectly. By comparing the minor—fractions of nanoseconds—variances in the time from the eight satellite signals, the GPS could calculate nearly exactly the receiver's position. Unfortunately, without the delay in the signals the position the GPS would calculate would be the position of the PDF receivers on *Cerro Gaital*, not its own. The delay not only ruined the data, it made it very difficult and maybe impossible for a GLS operator to destroy the jammers by calling in artillery or air power to attack the grid on his receiver.

For the more sophisticated GLS, the stream of data would be ignored because it did not, could not, mesh with the data being received from the other satellites. That is, it would be ignored until the other sections of the Anti-Navigation Company overpowered the true signals of the other satellites with their own overpowering jamming.

Electronic barrage being fired, Valdez cleared his men away from the hill. He took with him a remote switch to start and stop the electronic barrage as his future orders might dictate.

Fort Guerrero, Balboa, Terra Nova

The Commander of the Second Tercio, Legate Chin, was surprised to hear his radios come to life after so much static, music, and false traffic. Unlike some of the other places the Taurans had attacked, at Guerrero they'd seen to cutting the telephone lines beforehand. Therefore, the Second's headquarters had been out of touch with anyone since a few minutes prior to the attack.

"Chin, Chin. This is Carrera. Do you read me? Over. Chin, this is Carrera..."

Headquarters above cohort level, and some at cohort level, had been given Volgan-made encryption capability for their radios. As a general rule, the devices were as good as anything made in the Federated States or Taurus, *for encryption purposes*. What they were not, however, was small and light. This, more than factors of cost, was what restricted them to high level units.

Almost ready to jump for sheer joy, Legate Chin answered back, "Patricio, this is Hector. What the fuck is going on? Over."

"Couldn't be better, Hector. *Lago Sombrero* held out and the Anglian Paras are history. The rest of First Corps is barreling down the highway. The Fifteenth Tercio will reach your area a lot sooner than that, though."

"Fifteenth Tercio? Who...what is the Fifteenth Tercio?... Oh, you ruthless bastard; you used the cadets?"

"Yep," answered Carrera cheerfully. Considering that he had not word one from the *Puerto Lindo* School, hence no clue as to his only boy's survival, he answered a lot more cheerfully than he felt. "The kids, Hector. The cadets. We had all six academies fit out full battalions out of their oldest cadets and their Volgan and Balboan cadres. I couldn't tell you before. Sorry."

"Like I said, 'you're a bastard,' Patricio. Is that what I've been seeing at Arnold and Nelson?"

"You're right, Hector, I am a bastard. And yes, Arnold, Nelson, Brookings, Muddville, *Lago Sombrero*, Melia, and Dahlgren. Because we had the force they didn't know about, maybe couldn't have believed in if I'd given them the plans—just too, too distressing and distasteful for words, doncha know—we are going to win. Big. Don't doubt it for a minute. Got to go now. You keep hanging on. Mobilize as you can and help the Tenth Tercio relieve the *Comandancia*. I'll be in touch. Carrera, out."

"Help the Tenth?" queried Chin. "Those assholes? Well...if you insist."

Gallic Airmobile Artillery Battalion, Imperial Range Base Camp, Balboa, Terra Nova

"What the hell is this crap?" The chief of the fire direction section took one look at the firing data that had just been sent to the guns, another at the last mission that had been fired, then shrieked into the field telephone, "Cease Fire! Cease Fire!"

"What's the problem?" asked a fresh-faced computer operator.

"The GLS is fucked up. I'm going to try to fix it. In the interim, I want you to manually input the call for fire data. Use the grid coordinates that we've been using."

Vicinity of the *Comandancia*, Balboa, Terra Nova

Like flypaper, getting into a battle in a city is a lot easier than getting away from one, once it's begun. The Four Hundred and Twentieth Gallic Dragoons were discovering this the hard way.

Through the mostly ruined buildings around the Second Corps Headquarters, the Tenth Infantry Tercio's troopers swarmed like so many angry ants. Being a poor place, this one had more than its share of residents who were members of the reserve and militia. Reinforced by reservists and militiamen of the Second Tercio's recruiting district who voluntarily attached themselves to the Tenth Tercio—"Okay, maybe they're assholes but they're our assholes!"—the Tenth was growing stronger, not weaker. The Gallic Dragoons had gone from attacker to defender almost seamlessly, as the force ratios inverted. Moving through the area's maze of alleys and back streets, the Balboans concentrated on blocking a street the Taurans had taken, preferably by taking out one of the rearmost armored vehicles, then forcing the Tauran infantry to take to the buildings to try to protect the vehicles. Since the dragoons only had maybe two hundred real infantrymen to start with, and something over half that in combat vehicle crewmen, the legion's Tenth Infantry, heavily reinforced by individuals from the Second, had about a twenty to one advantage in foot soldiers. This advantage was continually growing as more and more reservists and militia rejoined the colors. It didn't hurt the Tenth any, either, that they also knew the area much better.

For the Taurans it was no longer a question of taking the *Comandancia* but of holding on long enough to be rescued. If there was anyone who could rescue them.

Command Post, Twentieth Gallic Parachute Brigade, Herrera Airport, Balboa, Terra Nova

"Goddamit, it just isn't possible!" exclaimed the brigade fire support NCO. "This fucking GLS is telling me that we're damned near fifty fucking miles from where I fucking *know* we are."

The fire support officer, or FSO, looked at the display. "No shit," he said. "Cut the bitch out of the system. Go to voice and map operations."

"Sir, this is going to seriously slow down our response times."

Tauran Attack Helicopter Yankee Five Five, over Cristobal Province, Balboa, Terra Nova

"I hate this shit," cursed the pilot as he strained to see *anything* with his night vision goggles. The rains of Cristobal Province, falling in a torrent now, defeated his best efforts. There were power lines and towers around somewhere, he knew. Hitting them could prove fatal.

"Don't sweat it, Bob," answered the copilot. He patted a machine which displayed glowing numbers. "I know *exactly* where we are— Huh?"

The pilot asked "'Huh,' what?"

"This contraption suddenly changed its coordinates." The copilot slapped his GLS, hard. No change.

"You mean you *don't* know where we are!"

"No! Pull our asses up and out of here!" the copilot shouted.

His shout came too late as, out of the black, a steel tower loomed. The pilot veered to avoid the tower but, in doing so, went straight into a set of power lines.

There were no survivors.

Tauran News Network, Headline News Studios, Lumière, Gaul, Terra Nova

None of the troops fighting on the ground in Balboa would have, nor even could have, understood the cheerful tone in the announcer's voice. Did they have *no* emotional connection to the people fighting at their behest? It had been, after all, the newsies who had drummed up a fever for war, not the soldiery.

Cheerfully detached, though, the voice was. "Good morning ladies and gentlemen and welcome to TNN Headline News, English Desk. Our top story this morning: War. We turn now to our Tauran Defense Agency correspondent, Brad Lupus. Brad?"

The screens of thirty million televisions in the Tauran Union alone changed to show a crowded and busy briefing room that, from years of watching, viewers knew was located somewhere inside the former Gallic Defense Ministry that had been given over to the Union.

"Good morning, Drew. I'm here at the TDA where the Combined Chiefs of Staff are about to issue an initial official statement on this, the Tauran Union's most recent military operation in Balboa. As you know, Drew, there has been a lot of ill feeling between the Tauran Union and Balboa's military government in the last several years; ever since the Balboan military overthrew its legitimate civilian government. These have apparently come to a head since five Tauran women were kidnapped and brutally murdered, apparently by members of Balboa's military or internal security apparatus. Early this morning Tauran Union forces invaded, it is said to preempt a Balboan attack on the Tauran forces guarding the Transitway Area. Knowledgeable TDA insiders report that the fighting is said to be heavy and bitter, with many casualties on both sides."

Without shifting scenes back to TNN, the voice of TNN's resident English-speaking talking head asked a series of questions.

"Brad, how much of this story of preempting the Balboans from attacking our forces can we believe? After all, didn't the incident with the women from NOUMCWW alone give the Tauran Union sufficient reason to attack?"

"That's a hard question to answer, Drew. Certainly the murders of those five Tauran women, one of them a high ranking minister, raised the possibility of war, but whether their deaths were really the cause...we can't say at this point. The TDA's unofficial position seems to be that the *Legion del Cid*, the mercenary organization that has taken power in Balboa, was about to attack our forces in and around the Balboa Transitway precisely because they feared a Tauran invasion; which caused the Tauran Union to have to go over to the offensive to protect our service men and women."

The "head" asked, "Was that a real possibility, Brad? What kind of fighting force could Balboa have used against us?"

"Drew, the Balboan legion was a large, reasonably modern and well-trained force prior to this morning's events. They could have thrown as many as four or five divisions' worth of soldiers against our forces in the Transitway area with anywhere from hours' to days' warning, but probably no more than hours."

"You said, Brad, that the legion was...moderately well trained. What should that mean to our viewers?"

"They were predominantly a militia army, Drew, something like Helvetia's or Zion's. It might be incorrect to put them in the same category as our reserve forces, though, since a lot more attention was paid to the reserves in Balboa than is true in the Tauran

Union. A retired Sachsen Army general I spoke to earlier this morning said they were a force to be reckoned with."

"Do we have any idea yet, Brad, of how long it's expected to take before the fighting is wrapped up?"

Before Lupus could answer pandemonium broke out in the briefing room. Lupus's attention moved quickly away from the camera to a man who was trying to speak on the center stage. Lupus listened for a few moments before turning his attention back to the camera. "Drew, it looks like things have gone badly wrong for the Tauran Union in Balboa."

TUSF-B Headquarters, The Tunnel, *Cerro Mina,* Balboa Transitway Area, Balboa, Terra Nova

From a large television screen overlooking the main briefing room, General Janier glared down at the assembled senior staff officers still in the Tunnel. "What the fuck is going on?" he demanded. "What the *fuck* is going on?"

That last was nearly shrieked. Around the central briefing area a multitude of staff officers busily tried to gain some understanding of the extent of the disaster. They were distracted in this by the steady crump of artillery, soft because cushioned by the thick concrete, rock, and earth of the Tunnel. A few were more distracted still by the knowledge that there was a strong likelihood that Carrera's legion would come knocking before the day was out. The C-3, or combined operations officer, in particular, was taking things badly, if it can be said that withdrawing to a corner and whimpering was a sign of some personal discomposure.

Campbell and Hendryksen remained calm, rocks of sorts arising from amidst the swirling maelstrom of confusion. De Villepin, to no one's surprise greater than theirs, was also standing firm.

Disgusted with the rest, Moncey gravitated to that area, as much from aversion to the disorder reigning elsewhere as because it was de Villepin's job to determine what the legion was up to. He tactfully didn't mention that de Villepin had failed—*badly* failed—to anticipate the nationwide ambush laid by Carrera. Just as tactfully, de Villepin didn't bring up the fact that neither Janier nor Moncey had been willing to listen to any doubts.

Without waiting for Moncey to repeat his question, de Villepin pointed to a map that hung on the wall. "I can't give you any hard data," he began. "There isn't any that's all that important by itself. I can make an educated guess at what's happening." The intel chief cocked an eyebrow to see if Moncey would shut him out because of the lack of mechanically sound data. The chief of staff simply motioned him to go ahead.

With a nod, de Villepin said, "Okay, sir. The son of a bitch suckered us. We know that already. Here's how I think he did it.

"There were six military academies...junior military academies. One was at Penonome. They were apparently trained as mechanized infantry. I think the bastard smuggled them in to *Lago Sombrero*. I don't know where he kept the equipment for them, not for sure. We've received a couple of satellite photos from just before the Paras stopped talking. Based on those my guess is that it was in the ASP there..."

Moncey shook his head with disbelief. "Not bloody likely. We've been watching the legion for years. We'd have seen that kind of stockpiling—"

Ignoring rank, de Villepin cut Moncey off. "Yes, sir. They began *before* we started watching closely, years before. Carrera has been planning and preparing for this for, I would guess, ten *years* as a minimum. In any event, it was the same with the other five. The equipment must have been sitting there, unused, for a very long time. As for the placement, well, we weren't very hard to predict..."

That came very close to being a personal insult. Moncey began to bridle.

Campbell interjected, "Sir, how did you pick our targets for this invasion?" She went ahead and answered her own question. "You did it based on known legion deployments and installations. Do you think Carrera's knowledge of his own organization was inferior to ours? I'll go a step farther. I think he set up his military bases specifically to be targets...then placed the academies where their cadets could be most easily moved to defend those installations without being noticed until used."

Moncey looked positively sick. "But that would mean..." His voice trailed off.

"Just so, sir," said de Villepin. "We thought we would have the initiative because we were to be the ones acting. We forgot that initiative is a subtler concept. Carrera dictated where we would attack by his dispositions, then prepared the right response. He's had the initiative all along or . . . at least once the decision to invade was made."

"Well, what the hell are they doing now?"

De Villepin shrugged, "Again, I can't say for sure. He started with just the cadets and whatever—and it couldn't have been much—of the legions he had alerted to defend, though maybe delay is a better word. They've had limited success: The Anglian Paras are gone, that seems certain, along with Fourteenth Anglian Foot, and the Four Hundred and Seventeenth on the Shimmering Sea side. Our Para Brigade is pinned inside a perimeter at Herrera. The Marine battalion is decisively engaged east of Dahlgren. Arnold, Nelson, Brookings, all overrun. Muddville's under attack. I think that takes care of the six military schools. One's at Nelson with no place to go quickly, although we'll see them again if the legion takes the Bridge of the Columbias. One is pinned around Herrera and, probably a part of it, Paitilla. The one on the Shimmering Sea side must be pretty much fought out by now, having taken on parts of two infantry battalions. One is decisively engaged with the Haarlem Marines. Another is still fighting for Muddville and cleaning up Brookings. Only the cadets who ambushed the Paras at *Lago Sombrero* seem free . . . and they should take some time getting here, say two to four hours for the main body."

"On our part, the dragoons are fighting for their lives in and around the Second Corps Headquarters area. They've been screaming for help for hours. We don't have any to give. I think they're engaged by the legion's Tenth Infantry. How they mobilized so quickly? I would guess that it was simply easier because they were based in such a population dense area.

"The three mountain battalions are engaged in little pissant fights all over the City.

"That's the bad news. Not all the news is bad. The airmobile brigade can still be pulled back, although if we do that we're looking at some serious Balboan artillery a few hours later. I would say it will still be some hours before the rest of the legion comes on line. The two tercios at their training center at Fort Cameron, which are their Volgan Tercio, the Twenty-second Airborne, and the Fifth Mountain Tercio, probably won't be in action until sometime tonight. They're scattered over four hundred square miles of jungle. I wouldn't expect to see their mechanized brigade come down from *Lago Sombrero* before noon today, at the earliest—"

"Expect them sooner," Moncey corrected. "One of the things we knew was that Carrera was scattering some of his wheeled vehicles so we couldn't take them out easily. I'd be willing to bet that he scattered them to assembly areas so they could bring his mechanized corps troopers to fall in on their equipment on the double."

De Villepin shot a glance to where the C-3, Bessières, gibbered in a corner. Whether the C-3 had lost it over the fear of imminent death, or because he knew his career was in ruins, the intel chief couldn't have said.

"He's a waste," de Villepin said. "You need to relieve him and put up his second."

He continued with advice that should have come from the C-3, "I think we have to write off the Marines east of Dahlgren. We might as well consider the Shimmering Sea side to be lost. The dragoons, the Sachsen Panzers and the mountain battalions will go under fairly soon, certainly within a day or two. Once the Third Corps and the Fourth Mech Tercio mobilize we can assume the paratroops at Herrera won't last very long. They'll be a bare three infantry battalions—not dug in—facing seven infantry battalions, the equivalent of two mechanized battalions, or maybe three, a tank battalion, and God knows how much artillery.

"But we *can* hold onto something, maybe enough to let us be withdrawn under truce...with our dependents. I don't think Carrera wanted this fight...not this time. He might settle for just being rid of us."

"*Withdrawn under truce,*" Moncey repeated in his mind. *God, how I hate the idea of that. Truce? I wonder if Carrera would accept a truce now? No. Not if he doesn't have to. I wouldn't. But if we can drive up the price in blood? Maybe, just maybe.*

"All right. How long until the Tenth Artillery Legion can mobilize?"

"Hard to say," de Villepin answered. "I don't doubt that we've hurt their leadership. Maybe badly. Say four or five hours. Maybe as much as twelve if we're incredibly lucky."

Moncey contemplated what could be done in four or five hours. Decided, he said, "Take over the C-3 slot, de Villepin. Pull the Airmobile Brigade out of Alcalde Flores, except for some stay behinds to delay the Balboans' mobilization. Put them into an attack to retake Muddville and Brookings. Get whatever escaped of the Thirty-fifth Commandos and the rest of the original Infantry Brigade to guard the Bridge of the Columbias and our southern boundary with the City. We'll drop the Sachsen *Fallschirmjaeger* Brigade and the last battalion of our Para brigade in behind the airmobiles. Then I want you to establish a perimeter from south of Muddville, through Brookings, then to the northern base of this hill, and then on to the Transitway. We need to evacuate the Haarlem Marines to this side of the Transitway, too."

Moncey gestured with contempt at his former C-3, "And get that miserable piece of shit out of here."

CHAPTER FORTY-SEVEN

And you know, sonny, there's no bad shots
at five yards' range.

—Sinn Fein aphorism,
Traditional

Iglesia de Nuestra Señora, Via Hispanica, Ciudad Balboa, Balboa, Terra Nova

Among the many missions given to the ad hoc brigade of mountain battalions, which is to say, sometimes down to platoons and squads of mountain troopers, directly, an important one was to block major transportation arteries running through *Ciudad* Balboa. One, or rather two, of these crossed each other in front of the beautiful white church that fronted *Via Hispanica*. A mountain infantry company had air assaulted—come in by helicopter—early in the operation, the helicopters touching down near the fountain of a nearby hotel.

Two platoons of the company moved out from the intersection to block other roads, one moving up past the University of Balboa, one toward the sea. The company headquarters and mortar section stayed in the vicinity of the church, along with the remaining infantry platoon. Within minutes of the landing all of the vantage points overlooking the intersection had been occupied by at least a couple of soldiers each.

The troops at and around the intersection passed the first four hours with no more excitement than that provided by the original helicopter insertion. Their commander was not surprised

by this. The local reservists and militia were from a battalion of
the legion's transportation tercio; they were not combat troops.
Certainly, he thought, the same kind of unit in the Tauran Union
armed forces would not be expected to put up much of a fight.
Less was expected from *part time* support troops.

However, unlike some other armies, the legion did not believe in
a line separation between support and combat echelons. Moreover,
every officer and centurion was a graduate of Cazador School,
hence guaranteed to be tough and to have a belligerent mindset.
Lastly, even though the transportation tercio had a primary mission
of moving troops and supplies it retained an official secondary
mission of *fighting as infantry*. True, it was only trained to about
one-third the standard of an infantry tercio, but that was not a
contemptibly low standard. The drivers were trained to attack
successfully with a ten to one advantage in numbers, to defend
against even odds.

Moreover, unlike the combat tercios, where the leadership had
to be offered up as bait to the Tauran Union, the truck drivers'
leaders were mostly at their homes in the city. So, while it had
taken some considerable time for the platoons and companies to
assemble, well before sunrise a battalion of truck drivers was in
a position to attack the nearest Tauran soldiers.

The first news the Taurans had of this was when a leading
squad of truck drivers stumbled upon a small team of mountain
infantry on the roof above a ladies' clothing store. Within half an
hour, the southern side of the intersection was cleared of Tauran
soldiers. Caught in the open, the company mortar section was
driven—with heavy losses—away from their tubes.

Finding no opposition to the east and west, the transportation
battalion had crossed the broad street, turned inward, and rolled
up both Tauran flanks. Three dozen or so Taurans took refuge in
the church. Repeated, desperate legionary assaults failed to dislodge
them. Ultimately, the transportation battalion commander called
off the attacks, though not before several dozen of his men had
been hit. Their bodies were scattered all along the open spaces
surrounding the church. Then, with the radios finally cleared, the
Taurans used their artillery to good effect in keeping the truck
drivers from massing nearby for an assault.

Sniping at the defenders continued.

Command Post, Gallic Twentieth Parachute Brigade, Herrera Airport, Balboa, Terra Nova

The colonel ducked instinctively as the air was once again torn by the blasts of Balboan artillery. "Can't we get any goddamned air on those bastards?" he demanded. "They can't be all that hard to find."

The Brigade S-3 (Air) shook his head in negation. "There isn't any to be had, boss. We're on our own for now."

The Operations Officer, the S-3, gave a triumphant shout. "Sir, Second Battalion reports they've finally gotten through the people who've been holding us up. We've got a route to the Third Corps Headquarters. It's a damned narrow way, though."

"That's more like it," said the colonel. "Put everything we've got into supporting Second Battalion."

For the next several moments the TOC seemed more like normal. The brigade had broken through and everything was going to work out. Then came the message, "Sir, Third Battalion reports they've got tanks and infantry carriers moving up on them from the south. They are taking casualties."

Four hundred meters east of the One Hundred and First Air Defense Artillery Caserne, *Ciudad* Balboa, Balboa Terra Nova

Though the caserne had been given up with no more than a token sacrificial fight, the officers, centurions, and men of the ADA had themselves by no means given up. From their humble houses to their neighborhood rally points they had gathered. Now, by platoons and companies, with no more than their government-issued but personally kept small arms, they moved forward to take back what was theirs—their guns and missile launchers—and then to fight for the skies over their country.

They moved raggedly. Though each man had gone through infantry training, close combat was not their primary duty. But there were nearly three thousand of them on hand.

Eighty-first Artillery Tercio Caserne, Alcalde Flores, Balboa, Terra Nova

The artillery was, if anything, even more ragged than the air defense when it came time to assemble an attack to regain the use of their guns. For one thing, more of their leadership had been trapped defending their buildings and artillery parks. For another, they had put in a hasty attack too early, while the Taurans were still in full strength and good form. This had been beaten back with considerable loss.

So they had waited for hours, gathering up their reservists and militia. The commander of the Tenth Artillery Legion now had nearly eight thousand men under his control. They were poised to retake four of the eight casernes that dotted the east side of the township. Still, the commander hesitated.

Then, a half hour or so ago, he had heard the flutter of dozens of helicopters. *Mierde,* he had thought. *The bastard Taurans have been reinforced.*

This had made him put his counterattack on hold. Little by little, though, he had come to suspect that the Taurans were not reinforcing but rather withdrawing. Finally, the commander had made his decision. He would attack.

Fire Base Eagle, Imperial Range Base Camp, Balboa, Terra Nova

Janier's forces initially had but a single battery of cannon larger than 105mm, the standard light gun used to support light infantry. This battery consisted of six 155mm lightweight pieces attached to the airmobile brigade. Dug into a pentagonal-shaped fire base, surrounded by fighting positions and barbed wire, this battery had provided general support to invasion forces.

Some hundreds of miles away yet, the ad hoc division of Marines under Anglian command had three batteries aboard their transports. Likewise, two more full battalions were to be flown into Balboa later in the plan, about thirty hours hence. For now, however, one single battery was *it* for medium artillery.

Unlike the 105s, the 155s were able to fire scatterable mines. Unfortunately, the mines were strictly antiarmor, as the Tauran Union had sworn off using politically incorrect antipersonnel mines. Even had it not, however, there had been no reason, prior to the turn of fortunes in the invasion, to anticipate their need. Worse, while there had been artillery ammunition containing antiarmor mines available, it had not been convenient to locate and move to the battery.

Finally, however, the mine ammunition had been found, moved, broken down from its containers and made ready to fire. Unfortunately, since each round of ammunition contained but nine mines, the placement of a mine field west of the Bridge of the Columbias in support of the Haarlem Marines would take considerable time.

Around the single battery of 155s, another six batteries—the 105mm artillery of Gallic airmobile brigade, plus three much shorter-ranged guns from the mountain battalions, fired more or less continually in support of their own and other units. They were slower to respond to a situation that could have been described as chaotic than Tauran artillery was wont to be. Their GLS still insisted that the artillery was located somewhere other than where the artillerymen knew they actually were.

SSK *Megalodon, Mar Furioso, Bahia de Balboa,* eighty kiloyards north of the *Isla Real,* Terra Nova

Captain Chu bit at his upper lip. Nerves, doubt—maybe too—regret, assailed him. "Sonar, have you nothing else?"

"No, Captain. Not since that one explosion," answered Auletti, the sonar man. "The one that went off near where the *Santisima Trinidad* was supposed to be on patrol. The other sounds might—or might not—have been helicopters."

"What of the carrier ship that passed by?"

"She's still out there, noisy as hell, about eighty kiloyards away. She's moving in a sort of box...back and forth, side to side."

His orders had been to stay submerged and undetected until and unless fighting broke out between the Tauran Union and the Republic of Balboa and then to use his initiative to defend the territorial waters as he thought fit. Although the explosion could have been the signal to that outbreak, he did not think that it, alone, was enough. And there had been some kind of jamming that made civil radio reception impossible. Chu thought that, too, to be a signal for war, but was loath to start the war all on his own if he were wrong.

Suddenly signals looked up brightly. "Skipper, I've got reception. *Estereo Bahia* came through for me!"

"Skipper?" said Signals. "It's the mobilization call...And there's someone reporting live on heavy fighting in the City...people are fleeing their homes. A good chunk of the place is in flames.... But we're holding our own, it seems."

Chu's face grew angry, then determined. "Auletti, any change of the location of that fucking Tauran ship. No? Helm plot a course. Take us as near as possible but first go down under the thermal. Speed six and a half knots. We're going in quiet. Weapons, make a last check on your babies. That ship's going under if I have to use all of them."

One Hundred and First Air Defense Artillery Caserne, *Ciudad* Balboa, Balboa, Terra Nova

A few dozen commandos really hadn't been sufficient to hold the caserne against the legion's counterattack. Superb though the commandos might have been as light infantry, and relatively poorly trained though Balboa's ADA people had been, as noninfantry, odds of nearly a hundred to one gave the Balboans a quality all their own. Sprawled and bleeding Gallic and Balboan bodies littered the grounds and rooms of the caserne. A few wounded prisoners, le Blanc among them, were being given first aid under guard.

The commandos had had just sufficient time to damage a few of the launchers and gun systems. Most were still quite serviceable. The commander of the tercio, with his maintenance chief, was just now in the motor pool sorting out the good from the bad and sending the good to their firing positions as quickly as their crews could be assembled.

Their munitions were not kept on board the heavy launchers. Balboa's climate was far too wet for that. So the vehicles had to be taken to the bunkers and loaded. This was time consuming. Still, the ADA tercio, like most heavily equipped BDF units, had only forty or so percent of its equipment, enough to equip it to level II mobilization. The rest of the bodies, the militia, could and did speed the work of getting what they did have into action.

For the moment, Balboa had nothing but tactical air defense, the batteries and battalions assigned to the tercios and legions. Within a half an hour, possibly less, that would change. It was changing with every passing minute.

UEPF *Spirit of Peace*, in orbit over Terra Nova

Her recent experiences in acting stood Esmeralda well for the moment. As the display being continuously updated by Khan's crew showed the disaster unfolding on the Taurans, she was able to keep from cheering her distant cousins, the Balboans.

Inside, though, she still thought, *Die, you swine, die. I know where your society leads and death is still too good for you.*

The high admiral was past tears. She had to laugh at the scope of the disaster torrentially expanding below. She laughed again as one of Khan's analysts exclaimed, "Shit, there goes another one."

That was a Anglian Navy aircraft, the fifth so far, fireballing in the skies over Herrera. The analyst couldn't tell if the pilot had been able to bail out or not; the skimmer they'd sent down had only so much discrimination. And it was hard to sort an ejecting pilot quickly from the other debris that filled the skies.

"Can you get locations on the launchers?" asked Wallenstein, pretty sure she already knew the answer.

"Sure, High Admiral," Khan replied, "for all the fucking good it's going to do. They're moving after each firing... moving them faster than we can report if not see. And we can't always see, either. The skimmer is low in the sky. The Balboans are using the buildings and trees of the city and jungle to get out of sight when they move. This shit was never meant to see through buildings, you know."

"Are we feeding Janier what intel we can?" she asked.

"Yes," Khan said, "but he's not been able to make any real use of it."

"Would it help if we broke in to the local telephone or radio net and began giving it directly to the Taurans at *Cerro Mina?*"

"Oh, don't do that, High Admiral," said Khan, wife. "We don't want our fingerprints on any part of this disaster."

"I think my wife's right, High Admiral," said the other Khan. "Besides, things are so far gone that nothing we can do short of dropping nukes—"

"Don't even joke about that," said Wallenstein.

"Yes, High Admiral. Sorry, High Admiral. But there's still precisely nothing we can do."

Southern Perimeter, Herrera International Airport, Balboa, Terra Nova

The commander of the airborne brigade entered the shack that served as his command post. The bodies had been moved but the bloodstains on the floors remained. He ignored them.

He had been out trying to get a better feel for the battle than the radio would provide. Artillery fire was coming in steadily now, far heavier than it had been even a half hour ago. If the colonel had to make a guess he would have said that he thought it was coming from around Alcalde Flores. The colonel shuddered as another aircraft overhead made the dot to the exclamation point of a Balboan missile.

"Well...at least the bastards are trying," said the colonel to no one in particular. He turned to his operations officer. "What's the word north and south?"

"Not good, sir. The Second Battalion is meeting increasing resistance...if they're still advancing it's at a crawl. And Third Battalion in the south is only barely holding on against increasing pressure."

"All right...all right. Tell Second to hold on to what they've got. See what you can scrape up to help out Third Batt. If you can get a hold of the Navy or TUSF-B, put their air on helping Third." The colonel swore, not for the first time that morning. "Goddammit, I wish we had some kind of armor, even a couple of shitty light tanks. Anything. Damn."

"There's one piece of good news, sir. The Balboans that were holed up in the terminal have been taken out. No survivors, sir."

"Well, that's something."

"Yes, sir...but sir, the First Battalion commander reports that they were mostly kids, not more than seventeen years old, with two adults. Most looked younger still."

Along the northern perimeter of the airhead established by the paratroopers the pressure was increasing rapidly. The Eleventh Infantry Tercio was finally making its appearance, fully self-mobile troops and whatever could be stuffed onto a truck or jeep coming first. The tercio's light armor, Ocelots, and medium and heavy mortars were already driving the Gallic Paras into whatever cover they could find. There was little return fire from the paratroopers to interfere with the Balboans. Under cover of their supporting weapons they moved, mostly by squads and platoons, to assault positions close to the paratroopers.

When the Eleventh's commander decided he had enough combat power forward, he would order the assault...with bayonets fixed.

Adjudant-Chef Jung knew this almost as if he were privy to the Balboans' orders group. He had been trained as a soldier in his younger days, not a peacekeeper. This was not so true for most of the men of his company. They had initially been trained as soldiers, true. But years of worrying more about international peacekeeping than real fighting had dulled them. Still the Paras had been given less of this to distract them than other types of organizations had. They were not so dulled that Jung's boot couldn't send them back up to engage the Balboans. But he could only influence the men immediately around him. It would have taken many months of training for battle to have made them all risk their lives on their own.

Meanwhile, the Eleventh Tercio grew stronger with each passing minute.

East of Dahlgren Naval Station, Balboa, Terra Nova

The remaining Haarlem Marines, wounded and unwounded alike, heard the ominous sound of diesel engines through the fog and smoke. For better than an hour they had been listening to the faint puffs of overhead mine shells dispensing their cargoes. Few had bothered to count the number of incoming shells. They were too exhausted with the morning's fight.

When the mines had first begun landing a fairly senior officer, a major, had walked the ragged line, informing the men what was happening. He told them to dig in as best they could. This they had done, shallow scrapings on the surface of the earth.

Through the smoke a forward Marine, on Observation Post, faintly glimpsed the outline of an armored vehicle, a Balboan Ocelot. The vehicle eased forward cautiously. Even more faintly seen were several more behind it.

Although Carrera had ordered the Jagelonian cavalry officer to move forward aggressively, his little command had been so subjected to attack by Tauran aircraft, and slowed by them as it took to side trails, that it had actually been caught up with by the bulk of the Fifteenth Cadets.

Suddenly there came a great explosion. The Ocelot lurched to a stop, smoke billowing from its open hatches. As the cadet crew began to disembark, those still alive, the Marines opened up, killing several. This may have been unwise as Balboan artillery was soon pounding the Marines' line. Within a short space of time the Haarlemers were the unwilling recipients of a pounding steady and heavy enough to drive them down into their holes. They therefore could no longer see the mine field as cadet combat engineers began to clear paths through it. There were none of the aesthetically unappealing, multiculturally insensitive antipersonnel mines to slow the cadets' work. These, influential elements in the Tauran Union had helped to outlaw internationally.

Soon, through breaches made in the mine field, Balboan light armor was in and among the defending Haarlem Marines. Completely unaffected by the minefield that had no antipersonnel mines, the infantry of two cadet tercios simply stood up and, firing from the hip to upset the Marines' aim, walked, then jogged, forward into the assault. The boys' bayonets were fixed.

The Balboan artillery lifted at the last possible instant. For some of the boys short-falling rounds made the lifting a lifetime too late. For most, it was salvation.

The Haarlem Marines did not run but rather, outnumbered and outgunned, they died on their line. To some it seemed unfair somehow that their much vaunted long-range marksmanship did them so little good when the range had closed to under fifty meters.

CHAPTER FORTY-EIGHT

When given the German command, [Varus] went out with the quaint preconception that here was a subhuman people which would somehow prove responsive to Roman law even where it had not responded to the Roman sword. He therefore breezed in—right into the heart of Germany—as if on a picnic, wasting a summer lording it on the magistrate's bench, where he insisted on the punctilious observance of every legal nicety.

—Marcus Velleius Paterculus

Tauran Defense Agency, Lumière, Gaul, Terra Nova

Monsieur Gaymard, president once again of the Tauran Union under rotating presidency, was announced to Janier and the chiefs of land, air and naval forces, as, "The President of the Tauran Union," just as if that office were real and meaningful, rather than an honorific passed among the true executives, the Cosmopolitan Progressives, or Kosmos, of the Tauran Union Security Council. The other chief members of the executive council—Anglia, Sachsen, Tuscany, and Castile—followed Gaymard into Janier's private conference room.

Janier was surprised at the presence of the Castilian. *Perhaps he doesn't know we did our best to destroy the Castilian battalion in mutiny in Balboa. Or perhaps he cares more for the rejuvenation being offered by the high admiral. Yes, I am sure that is it.*

"General," began Gaymard, "what the hell is going on in Balboa and what can we do about it?"

Janier sighed. This was a painful duty. After steeling himself for the inevitable, he said, "Right now, Mr. President, it looks something like equilibrium. That would be a false view, however. We began this invasion with six battalions of parachutists, two of commandos, one of dragoons and one of Sachsen Panzers. There were also three mountain battalions, six infantry battalions, plus a fourth that was, so to speak, visiting. We also had in place a fine battalion of Haarlem Marines.

"Of those twenty-one battalions, some of which we call 'regiments' but are battalions all the same, at this point, and to our certain knowledge, we have lost three Paras, two infantry, the dragoons, and one mountain, and one commando. Most of the rest are badly attrited, as well. Also, most of the rest are fully pinned, unable to extricate themselves and with our forces in Balboa unable to help them in the slightest.

"We further anticipate the destruction of the Haarlem Marines, the three Gallic Paras, two more infantry, and God knows what else. Lest you misunderstand, gentlemen, short of using nuclear weapons, those units' destruction is inevitable. As is the loss of all of the troops we have in Balboa."

Gaymard chuckled mirthlessly. "Nuclear weapons? In the same hemisphere as the Federated States? Let us try to find some less radioactive way to commit suicide, shall we, General?"

"Could not agree more, *monsieur*," said Janier. "Further, the Balboans have managed to put up their air defense...navy is quite definite on that, they've taken appalling losses in aircraft.

"Maybe worse...the Balboans started with maybe the equivalent of ten or eleven ground combat battalions, six of which we never suspected and not all of which were in a position to fight. The intelligence people have now identified maybe twenty-four battalions, which they call 'cohorts,' in or very near the combat area. Another six are moving from the Balboan training center at Cimarron and will be in action before nightfall. A further six or eight are moving down the highway from *Lago Sombrero* toward the Transitway. And they have managed to mobilize something like twenty battalions of artillery that are in range with even more on the way.

"At those odds...we simply cannot win."

"I...see." Gaymard's face was ashen. He'd expected the news to be bad but *this*? This was beyond bad. "Is there any possibility of stopping the Balboans diplomatically?"

Janier laughed. "Monsieur, at their current state of political, social, and philosophical development, the Balboans are centuries behind us. Centuries ago, was there a single state in Taurus that, attacked without warning in the dead of night, their soldiers killed and their citizens sent scurrying like rats for shelter, would then have said, 'Oh, well, sure you can go home, no hard feelings.'"

The general laughed again, this time bitterly. "No matter, in any case. A couple of days ago I had communications with their government. They have since become...ah...unavailable."

The general then added, "Mr. President...they're going for the kill. They won't be happy with anything less than our complete humiliation and expulsion from their country."

"Can we reinforce them, General Janier?"

Janier looked over at the Chief of Staff of the Air Forces. That officer answered, "My planes have another brigade of parachutists, the Sachsen Brigade of *Fallschirmjaegers,* en route. But I believe we should call them back. If the Balboans have a credible air defense...?"

Navy answered, "It's credible all right. We've taken up to twenty percent hits—though losses were less than that, thank God—on some missions. We just haven't had the *time* to analyze their defense and put together the right packages to suppress it. Another thing... some of our smart weapons don't seem to be acting all that smartly."

Air Force resumed speaking to explain. "The tight security and short notice we were operating under meant that we couldn't alert more than a tiny fraction of our air power. And we expected to be able to reuse what we had alerted by refitting them at Arnold... which is lost now.

"That's starting to be corrected, but it will still be another two hours—at a minimum—before we can flood Balboan air space with power. The Sachsens are going to have to go in before that, or we'll have to refuel them in flight. But, if we refuel them in flight, we'll either have to reduce the bomb load being carried by the attack aircraft that are almost ready to take off or delay long enough for the tankers to land and top off again."

Gaymard said to the Air Force Chief of Staff, "I don't understand this. It's what?...a six-hour flight to Balboa, less from Santa Josefina. What have we been paying for, if you can't get there with overwhelming force in a few hours?"

Air Force suppressed a sigh. "Mr. President. You and the security council gave us the order to attack with minimal notice. We had a choice. We could invade Balboa when they were fully mobilized and ready...and take unacceptable losses. Or we could use surprise. Surprise has its costs. Not every unit could be notified without word getting out. And if word had gotten out, you can be sure that Balboa would have gotten that word and would have been fully mobilized. That would have meant higher casualty figures.

"But even if we had managed to keep surprise while getting all of our units ready...the Balboans are a militia army. Most of the time there's nothing to attack except maybe their bedrooms and workplaces.

"What we intended, and expected, was that we would be able to take out their leadership with minimal destruction and maximum surprise, bringing combat packages on line in a neat orderly fashion after the fighting had started and delivering firepower as and when needed.

"And again, even if we had put everything in the air in a few hours, and if we'd been able to keep surprise, it would have been anywhere from hours to days before those aircraft could return to action, hours to days in which our forces would have had little or *no* air support.

"Mr. President, have you any idea how hard it is to change an air tasking order less than three days out?"

Ignoring the implicit criticism, President Gaymard asked Janier, "Will dropping that brigade make any difference to the final outcome?"

Janier replied, "We don't think so, sir. We're talking about changing the odds from seven or eight to one, against us, to at best six to one. The most we could hope for is to delay the inevitable...slightly. And drive up our own casualty lists...which are going to be impressive enough in any case."

Air Force spoke up again. "Mr. President, I can probably inflict more delay from the air than that one brigade can inflict on the ground, but only if we don't hesitate any further...if delay is what you want."

"Delay? Yes. Until we can get the Balboans to let our people go." Wearily, and with a genuinely aching heart—he was no so much a bad man as a very, very weak one—Gaymard said, "Recall the paratroopers. Please tell General McQueeg-Gordon for me."

Why? wondered Janier. *You've already told the general who matters.*

The Tunnel, Tauran Union Security Force-Balboa, *Cerro Mina*, Balboa Transitway Area, Balboa, Terra Nova

The news from Janier was a death knell for the defenders. They had little enough chance with the Sachsen paratroopers. Without them there was none.

Moncey, long Janier's underling and supporter, took it particularly badly. Pounding his desk repeatedly, he exclaimed, "That cowardly son of a bitch! Get me de Villepin!"

When de Villepin arrived, a matter of less than a minute, Moncey explained what he wanted done. "Everybody holds on until we can get the wounded and civilians out." He spit out his next words. "Then I'll try to surrender to Carrera...if he'll accept a surrender."

"But where the hell do we evacuate the civilians and the wounded to?" de Villepin asked. Surrender was too uncomfortable to talk about, even when imminent.

"The Navy. That's the only safe place there is."

"I suppose," de Villepin agreed. "The Zhong have been evacuating their civilians for hours now."

SSK *Megalodon, Mar Furioso, Bahia de Balboa,* eighty kiloyards north of the *Isla Real,* Terra Nova

The *Meg* had not even managed to close half the range to the Tauran ship it stalked. The zigzag pattern made it seem unlikely to Chu they would ever get much closer.

"Sonar? What's the range?"

It was there on the display screen but, what the hell, Auletti figured the skipper was nervous and wanted a human sound. "Sir, thirty-eight thousand yards. It's extreme if you want to fire now."

The XO piped in, "Sir, we'll never hit them at this range; if they keep on this course the wire will run out before we hit while, with their unpredictable behavior the torpedo will not hit without guidance."

Sonar raised a hand for silence. The whole bridge waited expectantly. After some minutes of listening with great care the sonar man announced, "They've changed course, sir. They're heading almost exactly toward us. I make their speed to be...call it sixteen knots. The escorts are tagging along."

"All stop," ordered Chu. "Fine. They can come to us."

Southern Perimeter, Herrera International Airport, Balboa, Terra Nova

Every Balboan tercio had a small band of pipes and drums. Most Tauran soldiers didn't know this. Nor had the morning's festivities done much to inform them, since most of the pipers and drummers had dropped instruments and picked up rifles as they received news of the invasion. It came, then, as something of a surprise when, through the twisting smoke, was heard the sound of a dozen and a half pipers playing "*el Pato*," a brisk Scots' tune, perhaps drearier than most but giving a profound sense of impending violence. They also couldn't know that "The Duck" was used in the legion to signal precisely that: "Make your hearts ready for the fight." But then, that was pretty much the story with all bagpipe tunes, not least the wedding march.

Adjudant-Chef Jung sensed the meaning of the message before most of his company. "Goddammit! Get ready! They'll be here soon!"

No counterbattery radar could hope to acquire bagpipes. No sophisticated satellite would notice them. The most subtle propaganda had no effect on them. A precision guided bomb had no more likelihood of hitting a piper than of hitting anyone in particular. It was not for nothing that England had forbidden them to the Scots as a "weapon of war."

Radio waves carried complex messages, with detail and—sometimes, at least—clarity. Friendly pipes sent a simpler message: "You are not alone. You will not have to fight alone." To the enemy on the receiving end, the message was different: "We're coming to kill you. You can't stop us. All you can do is surrender...or die. And, by the way, we're not all *that* interested in prisoners."

"Incoming!" shouted Jung, along with a dozen or so of his men. Suddenly, the wailing of the Balboan pipes was drowned out by the shrieks of dozens of incoming shells. Soldiers of the Para Brigade hugged earth as best they were able. Even so, some were flung into the air, torn apart by hot flying shards of steel and iron. Amidst the explosions, they never heard the revving of engines as legionary Ocelots raced forward.

A near-landing shell tore Jung's left foot away. He fainted with pain and loss of blood. "The *Adjudant-Chef's* down!" cried a nearby Tauran soldier. Another shouted "Tanks! Tanks!"

Balboan rifle and machine gun fire picked up to a furious crescendo. Bullets cracked and spat against walls and streets. It was death to put one's head into the air, or so it seemed. It would have taken better training, and been more expensive in money and blood than the country was willing to pay, to have convinced the soldiers otherwise. It was, in any event, far too late for that.

The artillery lifted. A soldier took one look at a nearby Ocelot and raised his hands in surrender. The tank shot him down; no time for prisoners.

A breach made, the Eleventh Tercio poured in to the center of the Airborne's perimeter. Rout became general. First one, then another, of the Tauran artillery batteries were overrun. Not dug in, with no armor to protect them, the gunners died by their guns. The wounded were abandoned.

To the north the Third Tercio, painstakingly reassembled, renewed its attack. An hour later the commander of the Gallic Para Brigade died by his command post, fighting to the end and cursing politics and politicians to the last.

Later in the day, as the survivors of the Airborne brigade were herded away, a lone soldier was seen to take his wallet from his back pocket. He removed a card from the wallet. On the card were instructions telling those who had given him his initial training some years before that they were to stop harassing and intimidating the soldier should he produce the card. With a remorseful look back toward the place where his brigade had been destroyed, the soldier proceeded to rip the card into very tiny pieces. Then, prodded by a rifle butt, he began his journey into captivity.

Alfaro's Tomb, *Ciudad* Balboa, Balboa, Terra Nova

"Take them!" Fernandez ordered. Though as a cripple he'd ordinarily have had more sense than to go near the fighting, in this case, the importance of the capture and the fact that the Taurans were on the run made him be at the site.

Grenade launchers coughed out rounds of tear gas. Then a half dozen of Fernandez's own men hurled themselves against the doors and windows of the little house. Fanning out through the rooms, they used rifles as clubs to subdue the occupants.

A few minutes later Fernandez entered. The prisoners were already bound and gagged. "Your wife sends her regards," he said to the leader, Arias. "Now you and I are going to have a little *chat*."

Alcalde Flores, Balboa, Terra Nova

The Tenth Artillery Legion had had a fight of it taking back their casernes and guns. The defenders on the ground were badly outnumbered, true. But they had had the support of a full battalion of good guns, even if the guns were slower than usual. The Tenth Artillery had paid in cash for every building and gun retaken.

The legate of the Tenth had been torn between offering his batteries in support as soon as the casernes had been recaptured or waiting until he could assemble a sizable, even decisive, number of guns, mortars and rocket launchers. In the end he had listened to the pleading of Third Corps' commander and assigned two batteries of heavy guns to help that brigade crush the Taurans at Herrera International. The rest were held quiet for the nonce, except for those that smoldered, wrecked, where a Tauran aircraft had penetrated the legion's air defenses umbrella.

There had also been the problem of getting the guns away from their artillery parks. Many a brave, and rather unlucky, Balboan boy had given his life trying to move the pieces away to safer firing positions while 105mm harassing and interdiction fire fell around him.

Only the Tenth Artillery Legion had a substantial counterbattery radar capability, radar that could trace incoming enemy shells back to their point of origin. The artillery tercios in the ground combat brigades had less of it, and far less sophisticated models. This was a cost saving measure on Carrera's part, one that he later came to regret.

The Tenth's legate, however, didn't really need his counterbattery radar just yet. Certainly he didn't want to use it while the Tauran artillery could trace it back and knock it out. Besides, he knew with a fair degree of surety the four square kilometers around Imperial Base from which the Tauran guns were supporting their ground troops.

"Four klicks square, four klicks square?" he mused. "Tell me, XO, do we have enough to crush four square kilometers?"

The XO of the Tenth Legion did a few quick and rough calculations in his head. "Our first minute of firing on Empire we can throw ... mmm ... four thousand rounds of 122mm rocket, about one hundred and twenty rounds of 180mm ... oh ... maybe three hundred, at least two-fifty, rounds of 300mm. Call it ... ah ... two hundred and fifty tons. The first minute." He continued, "The last intel update we had before they hit us the Taurans weren't all *that* well dug in there."

"Fine," said the legate. "Except for what we're giving Third Corps, have the batteries hold their fire until the last of them is in position or in ten minutes, whichever is sooner. Then give those motherfuckers twenty good minutes of everything we can throw. Then we'll light up the counterbattery radar to catch whatever we may have missed."

The exec nodded agreement, then asked, "They'll have a lot of ammunition around their guns, sir. Vehicles with full fuel tanks too, I'd imagine. Shake and Bake?" That meant throw mixed high explosive and white phosphorus.

"Yes, by all means, Shake and Bake the sons of bitches. Let's see how they like being on the receiving end for a change."

The XO ran into the Brigade Fire Direction Center to give the necessary orders.

Fire Base Eagle, Imperial Range Base Camp, Balboa, Terra Nova

Reality often, even usually, frustrates theory. The apparent exception to this, academia, isn't really an exception as reality is rarely allowed to penetrate to frustrate academic theories. In any case, there had really not been time for the Tenth Artillery Legion to do the calculations that would have made the first volleys fall on time, simultaneously. Thus the first rounds—they were thirty-two 180mm shells—landed rather raggedly over the entire area. Few men were hurt by them, although there were a few cries for medics immediately thereafter. A rather larger number had more brown stains on their uniforms than red.

In a way, the early shots helped the Taurans rather than hurt them. Given the warning, most men—all who could—scrambled for the safety of bunkers and firing positions. The firing of the big guns stopped as legionary gun crews went through the laborious process of reloading the heavy shells.

Few if any of the Tauran gunners had ever heard of the *Birkenhead Drill*. No more did they know of the spirit behind it. Their civilian lives had trained them to think their individual lives to be rather more important than perhaps would be true under all foreseeable circumstances. Their military experience had not perhaps done all that was possible to change that.

Even though the Balboan fire stopped, the Taurans remained in their shelters rather than manning their guns to return fire.

Then came the flood. They heard it first from a distance, a muffled continuous... *fooshing*. This was followed by a sort of a moaning wail. Then over four thousand rockets, each with a hundred-pound warhead, slammed down on them at a rate of just over twenty per second.

The rockets had no particular accuracy. They didn't need it. They landed everywhere. No place above ground was safe. Few were safe below it, if a rocket fell near enough.

Men cowering behind the earth walls of their guns' firing positions were stunned, sometimes killed, by concussion alone. Others, those unfortunate enough to have a white phosphorus rocket land nearby, were driven mad by the pain of chunks of the awful stuff burning into their flesh. These ran screaming until cut down by a later falling round.

Near one battery a fuel tanker was first ruptured by high explosive then set afire by the white phosphorus. Burning fuel leaked along the ground to where it touched upon some of the charges that launched the Taurans' shells. These began to burn, then exploded. A nearby store of ammunition soon joined the conflagration. A soldier who survived later reported seeing a big 155mm gun sailing end over end though the air from the blast.

Other fuel tankers were burst. In places the raging fuel leaked into bunkers, driving their occupants out into the steel-shredded air. Not everyone had the choice of burning or shredding. In places the flames made exit impossible. Those men died very badly indeed.

Still, making sure, the legionary fire continued to fall until the full twenty minutes were up. Then, ignorant and uncaring—should they have cared?—of the human damage done, the legion's guns and launchers shifted fire to other, still living, targets.

They left seven wrecked batteries behind them.

CHAPTER FORTY-NINE

He will meet no suave discussion,
but the instant, white-hot, wild,
Wakened female of the species
    warring as for spouse and child.

> —Kipling,
> "The Female of the Species"

Perish any man who suspects that these men
either did or suffered anything unseemly.

> —Plutarch, *Pelopidas*

Between the old *Comandancia* and *Cerro Mina, Ciudad* Balboa, Balboa, Terra Nova

Legate Suarez took his binoculars from his eyes. He held them in his left hand, his right arm and shoulder being tightly bandaged to his chest. He could not see much anyway, what with the shell smoke still hugging *Cerro Mina*. His eyes were also blurred, perhaps from the smoke of the fires razing the neighborhood, perhaps from having seen some of his wounded.

Suarez had been in the briefest of radio contacts with Carrera, still directing the First Corps and Sitnikov's half-brigade of cadets, east of the Transitway.

"I'm up to my eyebrows, Suarez," Carrera had said. "I want you to take *Cerro Mina* at any and all costs, as soon as possible... except quicker than that."

"Take it with what?" he asked himself, for the dozenth time.

"Second Tercio won't be near mobilized for another hour and a half. Tenth Infantry's fought out for now. Fifth Legion's over with Carrera and he damn well knows it, too. All I can do is pound the bastards with artillery until I get more force."

Suarez's Ia, his operations officer, walked near his chief and coughed slightly.

"What is it, DeSantis?"

"Sir...I've got a tribune...name of Avila, outside. He says he has two fully mobilized infantry maniples for you."

"Avila? Avila? Where have I heard that name?"

"*Tercio Gorgidas,* sir."

"The queers?" Suarez's eyes rolled. "What the hell do I need with *them.*"

DeSantis framed his answer with some care. "Sir, we may not like them. We may not want them mixed in our units. And we're probably right in that. But by themselves? Why not? Besides, they may just take the fucking hill."

Well, I have no better ideas, thought Suarez. "Okay, fine, bring the cocksucker up."

"Sir."

A few minutes later a tribune reported to Suarez, with his executive officer, who was also his partner, at his side. They had a female tribune in tow.

Adorable little thing, thought Suarez. *What a fucking waste what I'm going to use her for.*

Suarez tried had to keep the contempt from his voice. Mostly, he succeeded. "I'm told you have two infantry maniples, Tribune."

"Yes, sir. One from my own tercio and one of the Amazon maniples."

"So...what brings you here?"

"It seemed obvious, sir. You need to take that hill. We're here to do it."

"Yeah, well...with all respect, Tribune, I don't think you can."

"Perhaps more important, sir...we *do.*"

Suarez looked at the legionary in front of him. *Who knows? Maybe they can. Certainly they've at least got more of a chance of taking it soon than my boys do...because we can't yet.*

"All right, Avila. We'll see what your queers and your cunts can do. Come over by the map."

Avenida de la Victoria, Ciudad Balboa, Balboa, Terra Nova

It was appropriate to use the old name, *Avenida de la Victoria,* the name Belisario Carrera had given it in centuries long past. Whether the talismanic use would grant the victory remained to be seen.

Not far from where the Second Tercio had fought the Gallic Dragoons a few years past, Number One Maniple of the *Tercio Amazona* waited with heaving breasts and wide eyes. To their east, but out of sight, was Avila's maniple. No bullets cracked around them. Perhaps the Taurans on the hill were short on ammunition. The maniple was clustered so close together that they had to hope it was true.

The Amazon tribune—she was the maniple commander—listened intently into the radio. Avila had been given all the support Suarez could muster. The female tribune overheard him controlling and correcting artillery fire.

Sergeant Maria Fuentes, she whose daughter had once given Carrera flowers near where an Tauran helicopter had been shot down, lay on the ground nearby. She was simply scared to death. Lying down let her control her shaking a bit better. She didn't want the others to see.

On the hill ahead of Maria the tempo of artillery fire picked up noticeably. *Cerro Mina* seemed to shake with the impact of hundreds of high explosive rounds falling in rapid succession. *Please kill them or make them run away,* she thought. *I don't want to fight anybody.*

"Fix...bayonets!" the Amazon tribune commanded. Down the line the word was passed. "Fix bayonets...fix bayonets." Maria's shaking hands reached toward her belt, unsnapping the large-handled knife and fixing it at the end of her rifle. A steady click-click-click told her the rest of her company was doing the same.

Other sounds assailed her ears: magazines being inserted into rifles, bolts being drawn back and released to slam home. One woman of her squad was praying on her knees, there on the hard pavement. Maria heard her include the Taurans in her prayers.

Another girl was crying; Maria didn't know what or who for.

On the hill above, the artillery seemed to redouble its fury. Maria noticed that her internal organs rippled with the blasts. It was a sickening sensation. She felt like throwing up.

The tribune handed the microphone back to her radio operator, who held it to her own ear, listening. She looked at her F-26 rifle, then shook her head and slung it across her back. The tribune then took the maniple's eagle from its bearer, crossing herself as she did so. She had discussed what she was going to do with Avila. He had agreed and decided to emulate her.

She cast her voice wide, "On your feet, *Amazonas!*" The tribune waited for her girls to rise. "Now ... for your old parents and grandparents back in the City; for the children you have or hope to have; for our country ... for OURSELVES! The Future is at the top of that hill! Follow me, you cunts!"

Holding the eagle high, the tribune raced out into the street. She had almost made it halfway across before three things happened: the artillery stopped falling on *Cerro Mina,* the rest of her women realized what she had done, and two Tauran machine gunners on the slope simply shot her to pieces.

The tribune was dead, very dead, even before her body hit the ground. Broken staffed, the eagle fell to the pavement. The rest of the Amazons—those who were in a position to see—looked on, speechless, for a moment. Their reactions told the others what had happened.

It took some moments for it all to register, for their anger to build. Then with hate-filled cries they swarmed en masse across the street.

Maria ran with the others. More machine guns joined those that had killed their leader. A long sweeping burst cut down the woman—more of a girl really, she was no more than eighteen— beside Maria and three more Amazons past her. They fell to the pavement with cries and screams.

Maria continued on. Half of those who had begun the charge fell before the other side of the street was reached. The rest reached the wooded slope and, firing from the hip, began the slow ascent. They reached a line of triple concertina and went to ground or one knee until it could be cleared, available cover depending. Some girls detached their bayonets to use with the scabbards to cut their way through. The enemy concentrated their fire on those trying to cut through. They were hit, wounded or dead.

The assault broke down, and not for anything the Amazons did or failed to do. A few pockets of women tried to move forward or even back. The Taurans were having none of it. Still those survivors might have been safe enough but that some of the wounded raised their rifles to their shoulders to fire—at a Tauran or perhaps merely where one might be. They couldn't know if they had hit anything.

Half a kilometer to the east the company from *Tercio Gorgidas* had, ultimately, found no greater success. Avila—bearing the eagle—succeeded in reaching the far side of the street unscathed. Still, the avenue was liberally littered with bodies.

Looking around him, Avila saw something unexpected. Where neither man in a pairing was hit they behaved as normally as one could hope for under the circumstances. But where one member was hit...or killed...the survivor tended to act in one of two ways. Either he stopped completely, broken-hearted, or he charged mindlessly to attack those who had shattered his life.

Avila saw one such soldier actually succeed in reaching a Tauran position. The soldier had there gone into a frenzy of killing and mutilation, slashing with his rifle and baronet until it was broken, then pulling an entrenching tool from his harness to continue the mayhem. He was still standing, defiant, over three or four butchered Taurans when he, in turn, was cut down.

Thought Avila, *Carrera made a mistake with us. We should not have been formed as infantry. We should have been grouped as pairs of pairs in tanks, where we could live or die together.*

The maniple XO took one knee beside Avila and reported, "The Amazons are fucked. It's up to us if this hill is going to fall now."

"What happened to them?" Avila asked. "The Amazons, I mean."

"Just shitty fucking luck," said the exec. "I never saw anything braver in my life."

Avila affectionately patted his partner's helmet and said, "Then let's get a move on, Juan. We've still got most of a maniple." He adjusted his grip on the eagle and began to move forward, shouting encouragement to his men. His shouts were cut short as a 40mm grenade exploded beside him. Sections of serrated wire ripped his lungs and a number of important blood vessels. Avila fell.

Juan, his XO, rushed to Avila's side, calling for a medic. When the medic arrived, the XO grabbed the eagle's staff and began his own charge. It didn't last long.

Northern Slope, *Ciudad* Balboa, Balboa, Terra Nova

Captain Bernoulli looked out over the scene, what he could see of it, with some satisfaction. After being left hanging out to dry at Guerrero, he and his men had escaped through Balboa, held in position for a while, then moved again to this slope. There they were told to occupy the defensive positions...fast. His men had done well. A full assault, in nearly battalion strength, had been broken.

Bernoulli looked at one of the Balboan bodies. It hung on the barbed wire to his front. The corpse—no it wasn't a corpse, was it—twisted to try to free himself—no, no...the long hair said it was a woman. She cried to herself, softly and piteously, sobbing at times. She did succeed in freeing an arm briefly before it was caught again on the wire. In the brief time it had been free she had tried to gather her intestines from the ground to put them back into her torn belly.

Sergeant Tom Gilbert came up behind his commander. His wife was Balboan. "Let me go to her, sir. Please?"

There was still some wildly inaccurate Balboan fire coming in. With great sadness Bernoulli said, "No, Tom. I'll do it."

Crouching, Bernoulli stepped toward the dying girl. A shot rang out, from where exactly, none but the firer could tell. The bullet passed through Bernoulli's nose, out the back of his skull, bounced from the inside of his helmet, then lodged in his already destroyed brain. He fell without a sound.

Gilbert was by Bernoulli's side in an instant. Not bothering to check for wounds or cover himself, he dragged the corpse back to the company's line. A medic pronounced the captain dead.

"Where did the shot come from? Where did the fucking shot come from?" Gilbert demanded.

No one knew. Some soldier ventured, "Down there somewhere. One of the ones we hit, maybe."

Roughly, Gilbert pushed a machine gunner aside. "They want to play that fucking game, do they? Well...we'll see how they like the payback." Then, slowly and methodically, Gilbert proceeded to put a burst of fire into each body, dead and wounded alike, in his field of view. The first one he shot was the girl hanging on the barbed wire, though that was done as much in mercy as in anger. As word spread down the company line that their beloved CO was dead, and how he had been killed, the other men of the company joined in. A few, like Gilbert, knew they were shooting women and didn't care anymore. Most didn't know.

Perhaps a hundred meters down slope from where Bernoulli had died, Maria Fuentes—bullet hole through her abdomen—hid in a small shell crater. She wasn't in much pain. That, she supposed, would come soon enough.

Several others had joined her there in the muddy pit. All but one were hurt. For some reason, the gringos were still firing like mad. Maria didn't know why until she heard a friend call for help, that the Taurans were killing the wounded. A short burst of firing and her friend made no more sound. Maria began to cry too. Then the pain began in earnest. She soon lost consciousness.

There hadn't been any more intel to gather, nor much point in trying to gather any. This fight was as good as over, Jan Campbell knew. So she and Hendryksen had gone topside, ducking the incoming shells as best they could, until they found an empty fighting position they could occupy.

They'd had their part, too, in defeating the charge of the Amazons. They hadn't known it at the time. Then Hendryksen had crawled out to try to succor one of the Balboan wounded. She'd died about the time the Cimbrian had discovered the he was a she. He crawled back to Campbell, then lifted her bodily from the hole.

"We've got to get out of here," he said. "Those weren't men we killed. Those were women."

"So?" Campbell asked. She didn't see what possible difference that could make.

Hendryksen, being a man, did understand. "We killed their women," he said. "When they take this hill—and they will—they're not going to leave anyone alive. This place is a massacre just waiting to happen. And we need to get away from it."

Just north of *Avenida de la Victoria, Ciudad* Balboa, Balboa, Terra Nova

Suarez went to one knee beside the stretcher bearing Captain Avila. With a raised eyebrow he looked up to the medic attending. The medic shook his head "No." Suarez nodded and turned his attention back to the tribune.

"Your men did great, son," he said. "Just great."

"Son . . . my father would never call me son after . . . you know."

"I imagine. Well . . . he should be proud of you today."

"My boys?"

"Casualties were pretty bad. But,"—Suarez lied—"they've just about gotten to the top of the hill."

"Juan, my . . . XO? I thought I saw him fall."

"Maybe he tripped. Anyway, he's fine. A few minutes ago he reported that he'd be pulling down the Tauran flag momentarily." Another lie. There had been no report of late from anyone in the two shattered maniples.

"Good . . . good. Tell him not to miss me too much, to take over the company and find someone worthy to take his place."

"I'll do that, son."

"I think I need to sleep now, sir."

"You do that. The medics will take care of you." Suarez patted the dying man's shoulder and stood up. He walked out of the makeshift aid station. Outside DeSantis, his operations officer told him, "Second and part of Tenth Infantry Tercios are ready to go in now."

De Villepin threw down the microphone in frustration. "Fucking cowards."

Hearing, Moncey asked what the problem was.

"It's the goddamned aviators. They're saying its getting too hot around the hill to come in to the hospital any more. How the hell are we supposed to get the wounded out without helicopters?"

"Give me the microphone." When he did Moncey keyed it and spoke in the clear.

"Who is this?" Moncey demanded. "No . . . I mean your name and rank . . . Good. Let me make this clear as a bell, Colonel, as completely unopen to interpretation as anything in this world. This is General Moncey. You *will* come in and continue to pick up the wounded until they are *all* evacuated or you and your men are *dead*. I'm already sending lists of commendation to Taurus. I'll be happy to add a list—a short one—with recommendations for trial by court-martial. Not that I'll let you live long enough for that . . . Yes, I'm *sure* you were only thinking about the safety of the wounded, Colonel. Let me worry about that. Moncey, out."

The chief shook his head, then said, "He'll go in. How's the evac of the civvies going?"

"Better, sir. Their pick-up zones are not under fire yet. I shudder to think about what will happen when they are."

"The pressies?"

"Refuse to leave, sir. Insist we cut loose some troops to guard them."

"Right. Fuck 'em. Can the Navies take all we have to send them?"

"They're not complaining yet."

"Imperial Base?"

"They've been off line for a little while now. I think they've had it."

"Yes . . . I suppose so."

CHAPTER FIFTY

Will you yield, and this avoid,
Or guilty, in defense, be thus destroyed?

—William Shakespeare, *Henry V*

Front Street, Cristobal, outside 4th Corps Command Post, Balboa, Terra Nova

Jimenez stood next to the wave-lapped bay. Opposite him, Fort Tecumseh's huge barracks stood, clearly silhouetted in the light of morning. To the north, Eighth Tercio was even now battling for possession of the Shimmering Sea Locks. The cadre of the Taurans' Jungle School were putting up a strong resistance.

Along the piazza-covered walkways of Front Street the First Cohort of the Ninth Tercio clustered by squads around the pitiful rubber boats that were to carry them across the bay. Men from Jimenez's transportation company stood by each boat. They would carry the infantry across and return for the next load.

The other two infantry cohorts of the tercio were marching and trucking toward Cristobal as fast as possible. This was not all that fast. They had taken losses and were very tired as well.

In the long narrow park toward the eastern side of the city Jimenez's six heavy mortar batteries and two rocket batteries stood manned and ready, fifty-four mortars and eighteen 122mm launchers. They were recruited from Cristobal itself and had assembled with little trouble.

The First Cohort's heavy and light mortars had found other little open areas from which to support their infantry. The other battalions' mortars were with their own battalions and would be along sometime.

Jimenez barked a command. Word was passed. The small boats were dragged from behind him to the water. Squads of legionaries carried, pulled, and dragged them into the salt water, then clambered aboard themselves. Coxswains pulled the starter ropes on the small engines mounted to the back of each boat. Some started reluctantly, a few refused to start at all. For these the coxswains passed out short wooden paddles on the theory of better late than never.

The line of boats, it was nearly two kilometers long from north to south, put-putted for the far shore.

Jimenez waited until the boats had almost reached the halfway mark before ordering the Ocelots to follow. They moved through the water at nearly twice the speed the boats were capable of.

He didn't give the order for the heavy mortars to fire until the boats were fifteen hundred meters from Fort Tecumseh. Before the first lance of defensive fire could lash out, the far shore was wreathed in smoke and fire.

Fort Williams, Balboa, Terra Nova

Ham was the platoon leader now. Delgado had died after being hit but while being evacuated. He hadn't quite turned eighteen yet. Sitting in the ruins of the post, looking around at dinosaur-chewed walls, crumpled roofs, fire, and smoke, Ham thought, maybe inanely, *Dad is going to be pissed. He loved this post.*

The cadets had suffered badly. They'd never really had the numbers on this side, and surprise only carried them so far. Indeed, it had been touch and go until Ninth Tercio had intervened.

Give the fuckers their due, thought Hamilcar, *the Anglians are tough.*

The Anglians, such as remained, were gathered under guard in the middle of the post's trapezoidal parade field. By eye, Ham estimated no more than two hundred prisoners. He didn't know how many might be back at Fort Melia. He also didn't know how many wounded were being treated. Certainly a number of the less seriously wounded were still out on the parade field under guard.

One of the Anglians began to sing. The song had elements of faith to it, of course, but also a degree of defiance. The Anglian sang:

"Abide with me; fast falls the eventide"

Twenty or so more joined in:

> "*The darkness deepens; Lord with me abide*"

Fifty more added their voices:

> "*When other helpers fail and comforts flee*"

All of them sang now:

> "*Help of the helpless, O, abide with me.*"

And then Ham and a couple of others stood. They knew this song from services back at the academy:

> "*La luz del día aquí conmigo está*
> *Desaparece ya la oscuridad*
> *Tu das la fuerza y la libertad*
> *Siempre contigo vivire verdad*"

And in two tongues one song filled up that sky.

Fort Muddville, Balboa Transitway Area, Terra Nova

It was a nightmare: screaming women, civilian men, children, without order and control, all desperately trying to get aboard any helicopter as it touched down. From every side, at a distance but growing almost imperceptibly closer, came the sound of rifle and machine gun fire. Windows rattled as the big tank cannon fired. Whimpers were heard whenever an artillery strike landed.

To the east, the last holdouts of the dragoons' headquarters troops—cooks and mechanics—were buying time, dying gallantly on and around Florida Locks and the swing bridge that would let hundreds, or perhaps thousands, of Balboan troops take Muddville in flank.

The tattered remnants of crushed military police units attempted to maintain some kind of order in the unplanned evacuation. Whenever a Navy or Marine helicopter touched down to pick up a new load, the MPs were forced to use their sticks to prevent the helicopters from being swamped by a horde of terrified refugees.

Anshan Battle Group, Imperial New Middle Kingdom Navy, *Bahia de Balboa*, Terra Nova

The Zhong evacuation was going better. For one thing, they had more naval helicopters of greater carrying capacity than all four Tauran carriers combined. For another, they'd started sooner, having put out word through their own channels for their people ashore to muster at certain key points. For a third, they weren't part of this war; their people had no reason to expect being punished for the actions of their government. Lastly, not being part of the war, the *Anshan* and her consorts had come in closer to shore, thus cutting flight times drastically. Finally, they were simply better disciplined than the hedonistic, individualistic Taurans.

Even so, a crowd of weeping women and screaming children, many more than the helicopter should have been carrying, were driven off into the welcoming arms of a reception committee made up of sailors and Imperial Marines. They joined there some thousands of others who had already been lifted from the mainland. A few had been injured, artillery being no respecter of persons or neutrality. These were carried below as they were triaged. Most were expected to live—the others, the *expectant* ones; expected to die—had been left ashore to die in peace.

The *Anshan*'s escorts hovered around her and her replenishment ship like guard dogs, the more so with her new cargo.

SSK *Meg*, one hundred meters below the surface, *Bahia de Balboa*, Terra Nova

The submarine had moved a bit to keep ahead of the incoming carrier, then slowed to a crawl in order to be sure of approaching the target ships so closely that the carrier would have no chance to make its escape once engaged. It had not broken the surface in any way since Chu had decided his duty lay in attack. Even this far down, the sub's sonar man could, faintly, make out what he swore were helicopters, many of them, transiting from ship to shore. The crew was tense, without even the privilege of drumming their fingers for relief.

"So the attack is still on, is it," Chu said softly. "Well, Taurans, your part of it ends in about half an hour. I hope you've all had a nice filling lunch."

Chu couldn't know, but might have wondered, why the ship had taken from moving in a large box at considerable speed to almost keeping station in a much smaller area at much less speed. Probably the answer he'd have come up with would have been, *So we lost ashore, did we? Well, some of you won't be around to celebrate.*

The *Meg* continued to close.

Northern Slope, *Cerro Mina,* Balboa Transitway Area, Terra Nova

"C'mon, *Segundo a Nadie!*" Cruz shouted to his men. "Let's show the Taurans just what us little brown fuckers can do!"

With the lesson of the fate of the *Gorgidas* and *Amazonas* maniples literally before them, Second Tercio attacked with much more care. Its own normally attached artillery battery, 85mm guns, and its own mortars kept Tauran heads down until it had passed the broad avenue with its scores of Amazon and Gorgidas bodies. Machine guns stationed on the friendly side of the street added a steady rattle. Even fired at random, they helped.

Cruz walked forward in the customary position of the cohort sergeant major, behind the mass of the unit. He seemed rather nonchalant as he sauntered confidently across the street and up the slope, stick under one arm except when he used it to point the way to a befuddled trooper. He looked to his right and saw a legionary's face assume a vicious expression as he stepped over a uniformed woman's shattered body.

Oh, oh. I don't like this. A wide-ranging glance told him the rest of the cohort was equally enraged at the slaughter of the women. The men picked up a chant—perhaps from one who had described what happened to the Amazons. They chanted, "Massacre! Massacre!" Up ahead, a rapid fire began to build. The lead elements of the cohort were in contact.

The came an explosion to Cruz's right front, then another to the left. The tercio's engineers were blowing lanes in the wire. The volume of fire increased, enough so that Cruz was forced to the ground. He heard a shout; then a dozen more. There was a clash of metal on metal as though a fight with cold steel had broken out, as indeed it had. The firing from Cruz's immediate front ceased. It was replaced by screams and what Cruz thought might have been pleas for mercy.

Cruz was distracted from the fight ahead by the sound of diesels, hundreds of them, moving along *Avenida de la Victoria* to his rear. *About time,* he thought, *that First Corps showed up.* He couldn't know, and didn't much care, that the bulk of the mechanized troops had been mercilessly attacked by the Tauran air forces.

Casualties had been high enough. Time, however, had been the greatest cost. The rumble of diesels and treads continued past, the Corps was on its way to attack the Taurans still fighting at Muddville and Brookings.

Cruz reached the line the Thirty-fifth Commandos had once defended. He didn't know any of them, of course. On the other hand, he wouldn't have recognized any even if known, because the leading troops of his battalion had bayoneted them, gutted them, smashed their faces to red pulp. Two or three—it was hard to tell—had no obvious heads attached. Cruz walked on, not shouting encouragement any longer.

He reached an open area and saw a small female Tauran fleeing. *A soldier,* Cruz thought, though she was actually a Navy clerk attached to TUSF-B. Her helmet was off and blond braids streamed behind her. As she ran the girl kept turning around to see the Balboan who pursued. At length he reached her and, swinging his rifle butt against her head knocked her to the ground. She landed on her back. The butt-stroke had not been hard enough to kill.

The girl was screaming as the bayonet pinned her to the earth. Another Balboan soldier joined the first. He too, stabbed down at the writhing and shrieking girl. Together they shifted their grips on their rifles, picked her up on the ends of their bayonets, lifted her, still crying, screaming, and pleading, tossed her up in the air and caught her again on the points. They tossed her again. On the third toss, the girl made no motion, her formerly frantically waving arms and legs still. The two dropped the corpse and went looking for other Taurans to kill.

Cruz's eye caught sight of a video camera lying on the ground. He noticed abstractly that the camera said TNN. A face-down body clothed in fatigues lay beside it. A Balboan straddled the body, beating down, again and again, with the butt of his rifle. Two others, also in Tauran battle dress but without insignia, raised their hands in surrender. They were simply shot where they stood. They were shot again where they lay.

All over the top of *Cerro Mina,* Balboan troops were avenging themselves on the people who had killed "their" women.

Not entirely incongruously, pipers played a stirring tune amidst the massacre. Janier's old house was soon in flames. Someone— Cruz never knew who—ran to the flagpole and cut the lanyard holding the Tauran flag. It fluttered to the ground.

A petite and very pretty woman, also in fatigues without insignia—but a military contract civilian rather than a reporter— lay on her back and spread her legs before she could be killed by the unusually large legionary sergeant who stood before her. The invitation was plain. The sergeant began to unbuckle his trousers. Cruz shot him because, while massacre was an occasional and unavoidable fact of war, rape was indiscipline. Then, because Centurion School had taught him to expect this sort of thing to happen from time to time, and because he had been trained to ensure that, when it did, there were to be no unfriendly witnesses left alive, Cruz—reluctantly—took aim to shoot the woman. Well... she *was* in uniform, after all, and had not surrendered to him.

Cruz's finger began to exert pressure on the trigger. Seeing that he was aiming for her, the petite woman grew wide-eyed and screamed for her life, her hands moving frantically to undo her belt and pull down her fatigue trousers. Cruz's finger stopped squeezing for a moment, began again and again stopped.

Crap. I can't just shoot her while she's looking at me. He walked to where the woman struggled with the confining clothing.

"Keep your clothes on, girl," he said. "I didn't shoot that son of a bitch to have you myself." Cruz reached a hand down for her. "Here, stand up. You'll be safe now."

It will be easier for her if it's a surprise. "Now put your hands up and start walking slowly to the base of the hill," he commanded.

The woman began to comply. Once she looked back at Cruz, half expecting him to shoot anyway. He gave her a friendly wave. When she was about twenty-five meters away, Cruz raised his F-26 to fire. He had an idea that caused him to lower it.

"Come back here, girl."

Reluctantly, and very nervously, she did.

"I don't think there will be many survivors on top of this hill. I also think there's going to be a court-martial or board of inquiry over this," Cruz announced to her. "At the very least over the swine I had to shoot. What did you see?"

Truthfully, the woman answered that she hadn't seen much; just some hand-to-hand fighting and the large oaf to whom she had offered herself.

"All right, that may be useful. What's your name?"

"Lydia. Lydia Frank."

Cruz looked around him until he spotted a soldier who looked fairly calm. "Corporal Leon! Post!"

A legionary junior noncom ran up and stood at attention in front of Cruz. "*Si, Sargento-Major.*"

"Take this woman—her name is Miss Frank—down to the tercio POW area. Make sure she sees all the dead *Amazonas* on the way. Special tag her as a possible witness to what happened up here. If anything happens to her, Corporal Leon, your balls will be my kids' dog's breakfast. Do you understand?"

"*Si, Sargento-Major!*" Leon had no doubts whatsoever that Cruz meant it.

As the woman was led away, she thanked Cruz for the first time for saving her life.

The officers were all forward. Cruz waited for the slaughter to burn itself out before taking control of currently uncontrollable men. *Never give an order you can't enforce.*

Only at the great steel doors that barred the way to the Tunnel did the slaughter atop the hill stop. Except for Cruz's female POW, none of those caught above ground were taken prisoner. None escaped that hadn't made their escape long before Second Tercio showed up.

Even as he watched, engineers began affixing four shaped charges to the great steel doors, intending to make holes in them for the gasoline some others were unloading from a light truck sent up from below. They ran det cord from one shaped charge to the next until all were linked.

Another squad was about to take axes to the huge air conditioning unit before their centurion stopped them, shouting, "No, you stupid shits. We *want* to feed them all the air they can take. Can't make a fire without oxygen, after all."

It's gonna be a hot time in the old town tonight, thought Cruz.

Private Brickley and *Gefreiter* Czauderna had taken one look at the building massacre, then ducked into the Tunnel and slammed the doors shut. There was some beating on the door, very faintly heard, for a while, but that had given way to a series of sharper raps which had then given way to silence.

Their commander, *Hauptmann* David Lang, stood by, wondering, *How do I let the Balboans know we'd like to surrender? Do I even have authority to surrender? Do I need any authority? After all, my men really can't resist anymore.*

"Wait here," he told the two enlisted men. "I'm going to go . . ."

KaaawhoomFFF!

None of the three really knew what hit them. All that the privates knew was that they felt as if every square inch of their bodies had suddenly and simultaneously been struck by baseball bats. Lang didn't know that much. He'd had the misfortune of standing precisely were a hot jet from the shaped charge burned through. It burned off his face and eyes at the same time, setting his screams to reverberating down the long, concrete-lined tunnel.

And then they smelled the gasoline. It poured along the down-sloping floors. The privates set off running for below. They didn't see it when a burning flare was pushed through one of the shaped charge-created holes, soon to be followed by a completely unneeded other.

At that point it became a race between fast-flowing, burning gasoline and stunned, staggering, bouncing-off-the-walls-while-trying-to-outrace-it privates.

The gasoline won the race. It was never really a contest since blast doors farther on had activated automatically once the shaped charges went off.

Herrera International Airport, *Ciudad* Balboa, Balboa, Terra Nova

The Gallic Para Brigade was no more, barring only prisoners of war and a few die-hards being flushed out like rats. Split from north to south, artillery overrun, under pressure from all sides, the men of the brigade had—mostly on their own—surrendered.

When the men of the Eleventh Tercio retook the airport terminal, they spread the word that all of the cadet defenders appeared to have been killed. It was only the timely intervention of the tercio commander—and his fully sincere threats of summary execution—that kept his soldiers from lining up their hundreds, rather thousands, of prisoners and shooting them.

So reluctantly, the paratroopers were spared. In a short time they had been separated into eight groups. The seven groups of the hale were marched west to temporary captivity. At the Balboan legate's command, the wounded Taurans—and there were many of these—were treated equally with his own by his scanty medical resources.

Unfortunately, it was at the time when the POWs were at their greatest density, formed in a long, thick and winding column, that a Gallic Air Force relief mission flew overhead.

Unknown Hurricane Fighter-bomber, over Herrera International Airport, Balboa, Terra Nova

The new pilot—a senior lieutenant fresh out of flight school—was frankly terrified. Pulled from his warm bed and warmer Cienfuegan bedmate, filled to the brim with coffee, scarcely briefed on his mission and superficially briefed on the threat, he had been nervous since well before takeoff. Even the in-flight refueling he had done over the Shimmering Sea had been sloppy.

Scared or not, the kid intended to go in. His mission commander's chatter kept him informed as the threat materialized below. *Christ! Training was never like this!* the kid thought as flak began to blossom around his plane. He forced down bile and pushed his stick slightly forward.

There they were, *the bastards.* The kid saw a column of soldiers. At least he assumed they were soldiers, though he couldn't possibly have seen any weapons. He bore in.

Shit! Shit! His warning buzzer had sounded. Some SOB had a radar lock on him. *Where are the fuckin' EW folks when you want them?* he asked of no one. He continued on.

"Missiles!" came over his radio. A sixth sense told that one, maybe more, were meant for him. But he was brave. In the last fraction of a second of life remaining to him he made a final minor correction to his aircraft and released his bombs . . . all of them.

His instructors would have found no fault with his aim.

The Eleventh Tercio commander promptly threw up when he was driven to the scene. More than two hundred and fifty Tauran

POWs, and nearly thirty of his own men, were shredded beyond recognition. They were shredded beyond recognition as human beings let alone as individuals. In a tree hung an impaled corpse. Balboan? Tauran? Who could say? The uniform had been ripped off by the blast along with all four limbs and the head. The remnants were darkened by bruising and smoke.

Still, nearly half of those in the impact area had survived, even though this had been a perfect saturation attack on perfectly exposed troops. But the survivors were in no fit state to help the wounded.

CHAPTER FIFTY-ONE

But blood for blood without remorse
I've taken at Oulart Hollow
And laid my true love's clay-cold corpse
Where I full soon may follow
As 'round her grave I wander drear
Noon, night and morning early
With breaking heart when e'er I hear

—Robert Dwyer Joyce,
"The Wind That Shakes the Barley"

SSK *Megalodon, Mar Furioso, Bahia de Balboa,* eighty kiloyards north of the *Isla Real,* Terra Nova

The submarine moved ahead slowly but steadily. Twice in the last half hour, the Tauran ship had changed course slightly. Now, again, they were heading back toward the *Meg.* In ten minutes, ten at the most, she would pass directly overhead.

At his XO's expectant look, Chu nodded gravely. *Maybe,* he thought, *I should come up to periscope depth but ... no, the Earth-pigs are possibly aiding the Taurans and who knows how far down into the water they can see?*

"The carrier's a big whore," said the skipper. "It's going to take two solid hits to be sure of sinking her. A cynic, or someone used to Volgan quality control, might say three. The replenishment ship, though, is dead meat with just one. I've only got two control units. So ...

"Weapons, set up attacks on the carrier and the replenishment ship. Fish One to WCU One for the carrier. Fish Two to WCU Two for the replenishment ship. Set torpedo speed for slow. Passive search mode. Set up Fish Three and Four for high-speed and active-passive search. Assign them to the WCUs as soon as the latter are free."

"Targets for Three and Four, Skipper?" asked the exec.

"I want the follow-ons for a quick attack on the carrier," replied Chu. "Report when ready."

"Ready one . . . ready two, Skipper."

Chu and the XO stepped up behind the weapons console operators, then shared each a sideways glance. The glances as much as said, *Oh, my God this shit is real. We're firing. We're going to kill people . . . a lot of people. Oh, shit.*

Came the commands, crisp and clear, "Fire One! Fire Two!" Chu watched the weapons operators, each steering his torpedo into the sonar signature of his target. Chu put his hand on the shoulder of the operator on the second console. "Son," he said, "be ready to set up on the carrier as soon as you have acquisition with your fish." The operator nodded. "Yessir."

CIC, *Hengshui*, Imperial New Middle Kingdom Navy, *Bahia de Balboa, Mar Furioso*, Terra Nova

Onboard the escort ship *Hengshui* a sonar operator puzzled and concentrated on his screen. "Damn pistol shrimp!" he cursed. Weary from constant false-alarms by the torpedo alert function of the sonar system, the copy of a stolen Gaul design, he touched a button and used his track-ball to mark an area on the screen.

SSK *Megalodon, Mar Furioso, Bahia de Balboa*, eighty kiloyards north of the *Isla Real*, Terra Nova

"Aquisition on two!" reported the operator. "Hand off two, cut wire on two, set up number four on the carrier!"

Chu looked expectantly at the operator on console one. "Aquisition on one! . . . Hand off, cut wire, set up three! . . . Ready four! . . . Ready three!"

CIC, *Hengshui,* Imperial New Middle Kingdom Navy, *Bahia de Balboa, Mar Furioso,* Terra Nova

The sonar operator on the *Hengshui* put his hands on his earphones. His face rapidly lost all color. "Chief! I've got a torpedo on bearing 172!"

"*Nĭ de lăo mŭ,*" muttered the senior chief. It was a Mandarin expression ripe with meaning. In this case, though, while "Your old mother" was a literal translation, "What the fuck?" would have been a fairly good idiomatic translation. The antisubmarine warfare chief looked at the principal warfare officer. Both were also wearied by how the torpedo alert algorithm reacted to the noise signature of the Bay of Balboa's pistol shrimp colonies. He inserted the plug of his earphones into the supervisor slot on the sonar console. When the PWO saw him abruptly straighten in obvious shock he frantically pushed the talk buttons on both the ship and the task force circuits. "Torpedo! Torpedo! Torpedo! Torpedo on bearing Tango Three Uniform 165!

"Sir, I hear two torpedoes! I have got to get the urgent attack out!"

An "urgent attack" was a counterattack designed and intended to disrupt an incoming attack. At the very least, it's hoped to force an attacking sub to cut its guidance wires.

The PWO with one hand hurriedly turned a dial on the lightweight torpedo weapon console while placing an icon on his screen display using the other and his trackball. He pushed a button, announcing, "Viper away. Dogbox established. Dogbox expires minute four."

SSK *Megalodon, Mar Furioso, Bahia de Balboa,* eighty kiloyards north of the *Isla Real,* Terra Nova

"Fire three! Fire four! Hand off and cut wire as soon as the fishes have left the safety zone!... Three cut! Four Cut!"

"Nav, dive. Let the ammonia chill and flood tanks. Do not release noisemaker. Increase speed to nine knots with glide. Cut jet pump speed when we have enough forward movement to glide. We'll glide to the side; drop under the layer, turn, rise, and engage again, if necessary."

Anshan, Imperial New Middle Kingdom Navy, *Bahia de Balboa, Mar Furioso,* Terra Nova

"Torpedo! Torpedo! Torpedo! Torpedo in bearing Tango Tango 165!"

Also saying, "What the fuck?" the CIC watch officer nevertheless reflexively pushed the ship's circuit's talk button. "Step aside port! Launch torpedo countermeasures!"

Admiral Yee had been on deck, greeting new arrivals, when the announcement came and the deck began to tilt as the carrier sped up with the rudder hard over. "What the fuck?" he asked of the universe, as he began to trot across the flight deck, heading for the CIC. "What the fuck?" Yee repeated, as he entered CIC after hurrying through his ship as it heeled over sharply into a tight turn. The CIC watch officer however was listening to the *Hengshui*'s PWO's latest announcement on the task force circuit and picked up the microphone for the 1MC. "All hands! All hands! Brace for torpedo impact. I repeat..."

The *Anshan* lurched as nearly seven hundred pounds of high explosive went off under her keel.

"What the fuck?" Yee repeated, rising unsteadily to his feet from the deck where the blast had thrown him. He repeated, as he entered CIC. "What the fuck? We weren't attacking anybody? Why this?"

CIC, *Hengshui,* Imperial New Middle Kingdom Navy, *Bahia de Balboa, Mar Furioso,* Terra Nova

"The second torpedo is homing on Sierra Five Romeo!... Shit, that bucket of an oiler won't survive a hit! We have no helicopter in readiness for ASW. I have to form a ship search attack unit."

"Loud torpedo noise in bearing 169!"

"Damn! They are going for the kill on the *Anshan*! So much for the urgent attack."

Hengshui's captain announced, "I am forming Golf Romeo Two and Uniform Echo One into a SAU with us for a line of bearing search. Handing the rest over to Delta Six Echo; he needs to take over On Scene Command for the rescue operations."

SSK *Megalodon, Mar Furioso, Bahia de Balboa,* eighty kiloyards north of the *Isla Real,* Terra Nova

"Sir, I've got a lightweight torpedo sonar on intercept. It's weak. Probably above the layer and off bearing."

"Keep below the layer and on course," ordered Chu. "We need to further separate from our attack bearing!"

CIC, *Anshan,* Imperial New Middle Kingdom Navy, *Bahia de Balboa, Mar Furioso,* Terra Nova

The *Anshan* had taken damage, leaking damage, to one side. To compensate for what the pumps couldn't handle, a minimal amount of counterflooding had been ordered. This kept the ship aright. There was even minimal propulsion power available on number three shaft.

The pattern of jammers ejected by the *Anshan* shortly before the first hit transmitted broadband noise and random active sonar pulses in the presumed torpedo frequency. *Meg*'s torpedo four, however, passed right between two of the jammers—just damned bad luck, really—then acquired solid lock on the *Anshan.* It exploded in almost the same spot under the ship's keel as had its predecessor.

"Damage report!" The ship's XO called in. "Captain, I can't tell you what's holding her together. But I'm looking at her keel and she's never going to make port on her own. One more hit, sir—two at most—and we're going down. And, sir, power will be out in a few minutes. There's a damaged cable and water..."

Torpedo three had been confused by the jammers and passed the *Anshan* on her starboard side. Its electronic brain noticed that its original impact time had passed and switched to reattack mode, turning sharply.

CIC, *Hengshui,* Imperial New Middle Kingdom Navy, *Bahia de Balboa, Mar Furioso,* Terra Nova

The *Hengshui* and her two co-escorts had shaken down into a line-abreast formation and continued searching down the initially reported torpedo bearing while the rest of the ships tried to rapidly close with the stricken *Anshan* and the oil slick under a towering column of smoke that was all that remained visible of the replenishment ship.

SSK *Megalodon, Mar Furioso, Bahia de Balboa,* eighty kiloyards north of the *Isla Real,* Terra Nova

With the time for the fourth explosion having passed and still eager to sink the carrier Chu ordered a tight turn—forty degrees—and neutralization of buoyancy. The sub slowed as it lost the ability to glide on its outsized fore and aft diving planes. In effect, it stalled.

Chu let the sub continue under its engine power for a mile and a half, ordering the ballast tanks to be slowly and silently warmed. With the ammonia in its condoms beginning to boil, the *Meg* rose slowly.

"Come to periscope depth."

The XO looked doubtfully at Chu. "What about the Earthpigs?" he asked.

"Fuck 'em," answered Chu. "I want that carrier. And the sonar picture is too confused. Set up five and six for snapshot on wake-homer!"

"But..."

"Look, Exec, the Earthpigs were dangerous when the task force had the carrier to hunt us, if they'd told the carrier about us. They can tell all they want now, that whore's not launching anything anytime soon. So they can see us if they want.

"Now do it!"

"Aye, aye, sir."

CIC, *Hengshui,* Imperial New Middle Kingdom Navy, *Bahia de Balboa, Mar Furioso,* Terra Nova

Chu's periscope had been picked up by radar.

"Riser! Riser on bearing zero-eight-six, eight kiloyards!" The PWO cried out in frustration. *"Damn, we've passed him by and he is out of our lightweight torpedo range. Golf Romeo Two! Attack Riser with ASROC!"*

SSK *Megalodon, Mar Furioso, Bahia de Balboa,* eighty kiloyards north of the *Isla Real,* Terra Nova

Chu took a quick look with the periscope. If the target had been less enveloped in smoke, he might have seen some indicator that it was a neutral ship. All he saw in his quick glance was the top of the superstructure and a fragment of flight deck.

"There is the carrier! Bearing Three-One-Three! Mark! Snapshot five down Three-One-Three!" He swiveled on to the left. "Damn! There are three escorts searching for us! Bearing Two-Six-Six! Mark! Snapshot six down Two-Six-Six!"

Chu saw the smoke column of a vertically launched antisubmarine rocket rising above one of the escorts. "Nav! Emergency dive, hard starboard rudder come to course Zero-Two-Five! Launch type two noisemaker now!" Chu bit his lips and quietly damned his own eagerness.

CIC, *Anshan,* Imperial New Middle Kingdom Navy, *Bahia de Balboa, Mar Furioso,* Terra Nova

"Close the goddamned seacocks, for Heaven's sake!" screamed the captain into the intercom.

The answer came back. "Too late, Captain. We can't get at the 'cocks."

I have to abandon ship, Yee thought. *With the seacocks jammed open we will go down in a few hours. It will be a nightmare but we should at least get the majority of the civilians onto the escorts or into lifeboats and life rafts.*

Torpedo three's wake detector detected a faint trace of a ship's wake above it. The torpedo corrected its course to starboard...

A young Zhong wife shivered almost uncontrollably on the stern end of the flight deck. It wasn't the temperature; the woman was terrified for herself and her children. She had a baby clutched in her arms and a young son holding onto a sash at her waist. Her two other children—a boy, nine, and a girl, seven—sat on the deck nearby. The woman was simply a wreck. Between the fighting, the dimly sensed disaster, worst of all no word from her husband, and all this something her own government had had nothing to do with...

Then the hurried evacuation to this passing strange environment. She shivered.

"Mommy, what's that?" asked the boy, too young to see this as more than a really great ride.

The woman looked to where her son pointed. A faint trace of bubbles, though not so faint as the carrier's weak wake, were coming straight for her and her children.

SSK *Megalodon, Mar Furioso, Bahia de Balboa,* eighty kiloyards north of the *Isla Real,* Terra Nova

Chu's sonar operator turned white as he turned his eyes toward the skipper. "Captain Chu, we have a splash within half a kiloyard of our position. It is a lightweight . . . It's spooling up . . . It's pinging, it has turned on us. Captain! Skipper, it's homing!"

The *Hengshui's*—also known as Golf Romeo Two's—missile-launched torpedo turned immediately on the noise and bubbles of the noisemaker. What might not fool a ship-borne sonar could still fool the much less sophisticated and capable guidance package of a missile-launched torpedo.

Or it might not; once the torpedo passed the noisemaker by, its small electronic brain began the search anew.

Chu sat strapped in his command chair. His fists were clenched and his eyes were closed. He tried to visualize the positions of all the targets and dangers around him. The sub was nose down in a straight dive, moving far faster than her own power would allow. Sonar continued to report that the Tauran's torpedo was following.

The captain thought, *Damn, we should have gone with that expensive Zion "poison" decoy. That Volgan shit didn't work!*

"Level up over the sea bottom," Chu ordered. "Ahead at flank speed."

The Zhong torpedo sensed a faint shadow of a sonar reflection. The self-guiding torpedo began to ping rapidly. She nosed over and dove for what her tiny brain thought might be a target. Even a stopped clock is right twice a day.

"Captain," Auletti announced, "that whore of a torpedo is on our tail."

Chu decided to try something desperate. "Chill the rear tanks, superheat the nose tanks. Release another noisemaker! Pull out of the dive. Ahead full!" His guts, and those of his crew, lurched as the *Meg's* stern continued to fall while her bow stopped and turned upward.

"She's still on us," screamed Auletti, followed by a softer. "Hail Mary, full of grace..."

"Brace for explosion," screamed the XO.

One hundred thirteen meters below the surface, the lightweight torpedo punched through a cloud of bubbles, then, with a solid return signal from the ocean floor, she sped on ahead, impacted on the sea bottom, and blew up.

"We're fuckin' lucky to be alive," said Auletti.

"No, Chief, you're wrong," Chu countered. "They are. And their luck is out."

Auletti nodded, then reported, "Captain, huge explosion on bearing Three-Zero-Five! Bigger than anything I have heard today, That cannot be anything but the carrier!"

The XO sharply looked at Chu. "You are a prophet!"

Chu shook his head and answered, "Must have been fish number three, five has still too much time on its clock."

CIC, *Hengshui,* Imperial New Middle Kingdom Navy, *Bahia de Balboa, Mar Furioso,* Terra Nova

"Underwater explosion on Zero-Eight-Two..." The short report barely cut into the grief felt by the PWO on the destruction of *Anshan.* Nevertheless, "Release the SAU, we need to support Delta Six Echo in the Rescue operations."

The PWO didn't dream that the horrors for the day were not yet over.

"Sir, a wake-homing torpedo has just overrun our towed array!"

"That is eight hundred yards back! Flank speed ahead"

The PWO knew that at this stage evasive action was futile and he had less than eighty seconds to live. He, unknowingly, echoed his admiral's earlier sentiment. *Why? We were on a mission of mercy. Why?*

The petty officer working the surface picture had trained the electro-optical sensor platform on the gigantic smoke column rising above the *Anshan's* position since the last torpedo hit had turned it ablaze in burning fuel and secondary explosions. This allowed the PWO to view this transient monument to his failure. Then the waterjet of *Meg*'s torpedo six explosion tore through *Hengshui*'s CIC, killing the ops crew instantly

CIC, *Siping*, Imperial New Middle Kingdom Navy, *Bahia de Balboa, Mar Furioso*, Terra Nova

"Bore in, goddammit! There may be survivors." The captain nearly wept.

The crew, some of them, did as well. Three and a half sea miles away the *Anshan,* with over a thousand sailors and an uncounted—now probably uncountable—number of noncombatants aboard burned like an oil well gone out of control. Thick smoke billowed up into the sky. At the smoke's base, there was an inferno of flame.

When the third torpedo had hit *Anshan,* the aviation gasoline had been set off; then the stored munitions. These made a hash of sonar, sound waves thrumming the water.

"Captain...there are no survivors we can help. But she is burning fiercely and the main air ordnance magazine might blow any second," said *Siping*'s XO.

"But we've got to try," answered the captain.

SSK *Megalodon, Mar Furioso, Bahia de Balboa,* eighty kiloyards north of the *Isla Real,* Terra Nova

"Head for base," an exhausted Chu ordered. "We've stopped their carrier, the Tauran shits. That's enough for one day." *And I don't want to fight anyone else. I feel like my luck is all used up.*

Twelve sea miles from the *Meg* its torpedo number five exhausted its fuel after finding no target on its bearing and slowly sank to the bottom of the Bay of Balboa.

Via Hispanica, Ciudad Balboa, Balboa, Terra Nova

Pipes playing "The Men of the West," Fifth Mountain Tercio moved into and through the city. The Twenty-second, the Volgans, were already engaged against elements of the ad hoc Tauran Mountain Brigade. Intelligence reports were fragmentary, at best, but local citizens braved the random fire to update the tercios. The two tercios' orders were clear: "Find and destroy or capture any and all Tauran forces in the City."

The Mountain Brigade would last until sometime after midnight, but no longer.

The Tunnel, *Cerro Mina*, Balboa Transitway Area, Balboa, Terra Nova

Moncey sat unmoving by his desk. For the first time in his life a disaster had left him stunned. Then, too, it was the first disaster of his life. All communications with the outside had long since been lost. De Villepin brought Moncey a cup of coffee and sat down beside him.

"It's all over," the chief of staff said, then repeated, "It's all over."

"Yes, sir. We tried though. What should we do now?"

Moncey answered distantly, "Surrender the men. See if you can get contact with the legion and offer surrender."

"Yes, sir," said de Villepin, "I'll see to it now."

As de Villepin turned the corner a few paces from Moncey's office he heard a single pistol shot. It echoed from the concrete walls. De Villepin shook his head sadly but did not bother going to investigate.

Fort Williams, Balboa, Terra Nova

Pililak stumbled into the quadrangle at Fort Williams. She still had a rifle clasped in one of her hands but, so swollen were her eyes and face from the hordes of ravenous mosquitoes that had assailed her, she had not a hope of seeing a target. Even to stagger this far had required that she use the fingers of one hand to pry an eye open.

Semi-delirious, she asked the first legionary she met, "Has anyone seen my lord, Iskandr?"

The fuzzy image of a man she spoke to was just a boy, aged sixteen. He had no clue who or what "Iskandr" was. "Sorry, *chica*," he answered, waving at his nose against the incredible stink of the girl. "I have no idea what you're looking for."

"Oh," she replied, softly. "Sorry. I'll look elsewhere."

She was staggering toward a large group when someone came

to stop her. "Sorry, honey," that boy said, "but you can't bring a rifle to the prisoners."

Frustrated, half out of her mind, the girl simply sat down on the grass where she was. Tears began to flow. Finally, in her psychic agony, she screamed out at the top of her lungs, "ISKANDR!"

Ham was conferring with his commander, Ustinov, when he heard the name he hadn't been called in years, "Iskandr." Even the five Pashtians, two of whom were now dead, who had followed him to the academy had been forbidden to use it. And yet he heard it.

"Sir," he asked of Ustinov, "may I be excused?"

Hamilcar walked at first, heading in the direction from which he heard his other name. Then, when he saw the thin ragged bundle, rocking and weeping on the grass of the parade field, he began to run.

He reached the girl and went to one knee. *Poor little thing; what's she been through to be so dirty?* He looked carefully for a few moments...this...creature looked familiar but...*No, the Pililak I knew was always fastidious. And not so well chested, either. Still...*

Ham bent his head closer and whispered, "Ant?"

The filthy creature looked up and, after prying the swollen lids of one eye apart, shouted, "My lord! My lord! My Iskandr!" before launching herself at Ham and more or less wrapping herself around him. Her tears flew freely again, as she informed him, "I brought you your rifle, my lord."

Epilogue

The Curia was subdued. There were at least a dozen spots that were vacant now, senators the Taurans had tried to arrest in their homes and who decided not to go gently, or others who, ignoring their years, had grabbed a rifle or machine gun and gone to find the regiments that had elevated them. Carrera wasn't back yet. He was somewhere in the Transitway Area, more specifically at Fort Muddville, watching a cohort burn out the last Tauran defenders of Building 59.

That didn't matter; he and Parilla were long agreed that the war could not be permitted to turn into one of those interminable Zion-Arab things that just went on and on. No, this would be fought to a finish, either the destruction of the Revolution in Balboa, and the legion that had brought it about, or the discrediting, humiliation, and casting off of the new hereditary aristocracy of the Tauran Union...and with it, United Earth.

A screen on the wall of the Curia showed a long tongue of flame lick out to splash against the brick wall before finding its way through a blasted window. Smoke began to pour from all the other windows at that end of the building. The hundred and eleven senators so far assembled watched the scene with grim satisfaction.

The senators stood in front of Parilla's dais and curule chair, rather than in their wonted marble benches. They'd had to vacate the space; those benches were now full of people in formal dress, mostly, though a few wore the battle dress of the legion. Farther down, towards the great bronze doors, still others in similar clothing held musical instruments.

Parilla stood at a podium that had been wheeled in for the occasion. He was flanked by the statues of *Balboa* and *Victoria*. The latter had been ready for some months, but Parilla had thought it better to wait for the victory that gave the statue her name.

"So I'm superstitious," he'd told the Senate. "So sue me. We wait until we *have* the victory before we proclaim it."

A cameraman at the far end, on the aisle by the doors, gave Parilla a high sign.

He began to speak:

"This morning the Republic of Balboa was suddenly and deliberately attacked by ground, air and naval forces of the Tauran Union. The *excuse* given for that attack were certain crimes allegedly perpetrated by members of Balboa's armed forces upon Tauran citizens. The real reason for the attack was to force upon Balboa a traitorous clique of puppets who would do the will of the Tauran Union even against their own country and people."

Parilla stopped speaking to take a short drink of water.

"In any event," he continued, carefully placing his glass back on the podium, "the criminals who caused this war—those, at least, who are in our hands—have been punished. Some few remain at large in the Tauran Union. They, however—being elected officials or unelected but well-connected bureaucrats—appear to have a certain immunity to criminal action at law. Still, do not be fooled. The war the Tauran Union began is not yet over.

"We currently hold some eighteen thousand Tauran prisoners of war. Many of them are wounded. We also have some thousands of Tauran civilians, former workers in the Transitway Zone. We are not nearly done with counting the dead and wounded, ours and theirs. So many were lost at sea that we may never have an accurate count.

"In the interests of possible peace we will, in three days, begin transferring prisoners of war, at the rate of one hundred per day, back to the Tauran Union. First we shall return the wounded, in accord with the severity of their wounds. Then we'll return the civilians. Then, if there are no further hostile acts, the Tauran Union will be given back her military personnel. This is contingent upon several factors.

"First: the conditions of permanent peace. We insist upon absolute renunciation by the Tauran Union of any interest in and over the Balboa Transitway and the Republic of Balboa. After all, the

Tauran Union can hardly claim any longer that Balboa is incapable of self-defense, can they? We also demand the repatriation of any and all Balboans held by the Tauran Union. Lastly, we demand reparations for the damages we have sustained, to recompense our wounded, to pay for property damage, and to care for the orphans and widows this artificially provoked invasion has left without a provider. We think a million drachma for each prisoner we hold should be sufficient for *that*.

"Further, Balboa demands that all hostile actions on the part of the Tauran Union government, to include the unwarranted 'drachma embargo' and all other interferences with Balboa's trade, cease.

"Return of prisoners and detainees will be through the port of Cristobal, by ship. We will march and truck them there. It is up to the Tauran Union to have transport waiting.

"And now, a final word from *la Republica de Balboa* to the people and bureaucrats of the Tauran Union."

Parilla smiled broadly and pointed at a formally dressed man holding a little stick, the conductor of the Balboa City Philharmonic. The stick tapped a few times, then pointed. A male singer, in battle dress, his head wrapped in a bandage, sang out. His voice was a deep base baritone: "O Tauran Union, den of iniquity."

A hundred voices raised themselves: "INIQUITY!"

The lone baritone continued: "Odiferous fief of a corrupt and unelected bureaucracy."

"BUREAUCRACY!"

Almost instantly, the hall was filled with music, more specifically the Old Earth composer Beethoven's "Ode to Joy." The words had been changed a bit, though. Balboa's granite Senate house rang with the lyrics:

> "Fuck the filthy Tauran Union!
> Fuck their courts and MTPs!
> Fuck their rules and regulations;
> Their whole vile bureaucracy!
>
> Asshats, Bastards, Cowards, Dimwits,
> Excrement-feeding Gallows-bait.
> Hang the swine Higher than Haman,
> Ignorant Jackasses, Knaves!

Watch them purge the bent banana.
See your taxes rise and rise.
See your nations fall to ruin.
Watch as every freedom dies.

Lick-ass Morons, Nincompoops, Oh,
Pity the Quagmire these Reds made.
Sycophants and Thieves, the whole crew,
Underworked and overpaid.

Friday mornings they will sign in
To ensure their holidays
Are paid for by lesser people.
Free men call those people, 'Slaves.'

Green on the outside, red on the
Inside, Watermelons, black of soul,
Xerox copies of each other,
Yahoos, Zeroes, one and all.

To the lampposts, Tauran People.
Tie the knots and toss the ropes.
Fit the nooses. Haul the free ends.
Stand back; watch your masters choke."

With a complex wave of the stick, the singing and music ceased. Every man and woman in the Balboa Philharmonic was smiling, perhaps smugly. Smiling more smugly still, the maestro turned to the cameras and bowed.

"And that pretty much sums up our feelings about *you*," Parilla said, also smiling. The smile disappeared. He raised his arms above his head and shouted for the cameras, "*Viva* Balboa! *Viva* Anglia *Libre*! *Viva* Sachsen *Libre*! *Viva* Gaul *Libre*! *Viva* Castile *Libre*! *Viva* Jagelonia *Libre*! *Viva* Tuscany *Libre*! *Viva* Lusitania *Libre*!

"Death to the Tauran Union!"

II

All the prisoners, and they were many, who could speak English were gathered in one camp. Likewise for those who spoke Spanish, or French, or Italian, or any other major Tauran language. Several hundred of the English-speaking prisoners were now under guard at Fort Williams' old, octagonal theater, one of the few places to be spared damage in the fighting.

Marqueli Mendoza spoke English. Thus, she inherited the task of being chief instructor for the many thousands of English-speaking prisoners. It was no small job.

Still, thought Marqueli, vanishingly petite, perfectly formed, beautiful, and wonderfully fragrant, *a journey of a thousand miles and all.* She began to mount to the stage.

One of the Anglians began to hoot. This lasted until his sergeant belted him, knocking him completely out of his theater chair. "Shut up, boy," said the sergeant. "Can't you tell a lady when you see one?"

If Marqueli saw or overheard the exchange, she gave no sign. She went to the central rostrum and directed that the assistants begin passing out books.

"I apologize," she said, "for the books we're giving you. They're translations and...well...maybe not the best translations that were possible. That's one reason I'm here, to guide you over the bad translations.

"But first, a couple of rules and a little explanation. The books are to help you understand what's gone wrong with your countries. You don't have to read them. You don't have to pay attention to anything I say or even to me." A born actress, she gave a little stretch then, illustrating perfectly why *every* male there ought be paying attention at least to her.

"If you'll look at the covers of the books," she said, "you'll see the title, *History and Moral Philosophy.* The names of the authors are my husband's and mine."

The assembled Anglians gave off a subdued groan. *Damn, she's married. Well, there goes that reason to defect.*

If Marqueli caught the reason for the groan she effected to ignore it. "This is the founding document, really, for why you ended up here as prisoners. It's also the refutation of the philosophy, and the people, who sent you here to become prisoners.

You know, the Kosmos? The cosmopolitan progressives to whom your lives mean nothing?

"Let's start by talking a little about cosmopolitan progressivism, shall we, boys?"

III

Estado Mayor, Ciudad Balboa, Balboa, Terra Nova

In four separate cells the four expatriates who had provoked war between Balboa and the Tauran Union waited. All had been interrogated, though without torture. When people were as lost and hopeless as these were, Fernandez usually found pain unnecessary.

"So what happens to me ... to my men?"

"Public crucifixion," Fernandez said simply. "Along with your families; though theirs will be semi-private."

The former policeman shuddered, his face growing pale in the bright cell light.

"Isn't there any other way?"

"No."

"What if I confess? I mean make a *really* good confession."

"I have discretion to spare your wife and children. The rest of you go to the cross."

"But it's not right," said the killer. "It's not right for Rocaberti to die easier than we do. It was all his fault."

"Well ..." said Fernandez. "Make your confession. If it's good enough ... maybe we'll just hang you. That's fifteen minutes of degradation against three days. My last offer ..."

IV

Palacio de las Trixies, *Ciudad* Balboa, Balboa, Terra Nova

"Last week," said Parilla, into the cameras, "on a day of shame, the Republic of Balboa was suddenly, and deliberately, attacked by ground, air and naval forces of the Tauran Union. The ostensible reason for this attack was certain crimes allegedly perpetrated by members of Balboa's armed forces upon Tauran citizens. The real reason for the attack was to force upon Balboa a traitorous clique of puppets who would do the will of the Tauran Union even against their own country and people. The man who ordered the crimes that were to be the Tauran Union's excuse for this unwarranted invasion was also the Tauran Union's chosen puppet... their intended ruler of Balboa." Parilla stopped speaking to take a short drink of water.

"Watch," he said, as choice excerpts from Arias's confession, and those of the others, were rolled for the cameras. This took all of ten minutes. It must be said that the confessions were not entirely truthful.

"Complete copies of these confessions have been made available to the world's major news services.

"It was natural enough that the Tauran Union government should have, through the agency of its puppets, arranged for an incident that would galvanize their people for war." Parilla paused for dramatic effect. "If those had been our women, we'd have gone to war too... even against the Tauran Union... or the whole world combined." He gave a nod to an unseen underling. "Now watch this..."

The camera changed scenes to the courtyard of the main jail. Four men stood upon a thick beam. The camera closed to show the faces of all four in detail. They were the same men who had just been shown on the videotaped confessions. Lengths of rough hemp graced their necks.

The beam was pulled out and the four men dropped a few inches each. Four guards cut the ropes that bound the men's hands behind them. Viewers all over the world had the chance to see them struggle with their hands with the constricting nooses. Cameras caught the ground under the four as they voided their bowels and bladders. Urine and feces stained the concrete.

After an interminable time, struggles ceased. The criminals were dead.

Parilla reappeared on screen. "I wonder," he mused. "I wonder what the Tauran Union will claim they were going to do to them that was worse than *that*.

"In any event, the criminals who caused this war, those—at least—who are in our hands, have been punished. Some few remain at large in the Tauran Union. They, however, being elected officials, appear to have a certain immunity to criminal action at law. Still, do not be fooled. The war the Tauran Union began is not over."

Glossary

AdC	Aide de Camp, an assistant to a senior officer.
Ala	Plural: Alae. Latin: Wing, as in wing of cavalry. Air Wing in the legion. Similar to Tercio, qv.
Amid	Arabic: Brigadier General.
Antania	Plural: Antaniae, septic-mouthed winged reptilians, possibly genengineered by the Noahs; also known as Moonbats.
ARE-12P	A Gallic Infantry Fighting Vehicle.
Artem-Mikhail-23-465 Gaur	An obsolescent jet fighter, though much updated.
Artem-Mikhail 82	Also known as "Mosaic D," an obsolete jet fighter, product improved in Balboan hands to be merely obsolescent.
BdL	Barco de la legion, Ship of the legion.
Bellona	Moon of Terra Nova.
Bolshiberry	A fruit-bearing vine, believed to have been genengineered by the Noahs. The fruit is intensely poisonous to intelligent life.
Caltrop	A four-pointed jack with sharp, barbed ends. Thirty-eight per meter of front give defensive capability roughly equivalent to triple standard concertina.
Caltrop Projector	A drum filled with caltrops, a linear shaped charge, and low explosive booster, to scatter caltrops over a wide area on command.

Cazador Spanish: Hunter. Similar to Chasseur, Jaeger and Ranger. Light Infantry, especially selected and trained. Also a combat leader selection course within the *Legion del Cid*.

Chorley A grain of Terra Nova, apparently not native to Old Earth.

Classis Latin: Fleet or Naval Squadron.

Cohort Battalion, though in the legion these are large battalions.

Conex Metal shipping container, generally 8' × 8' × 20' or 40'.

Consensus When capitalized, the governing council of Old Earth, formerly the United Nations Security Council.

Corona Civilis Latin: Civic Crown. One of approximately thirty-seven awards available in the legion for specific and noteworthy events. The Civic Crown is given for saving the life of a soldier on the battlefield at risk of one's own.

Cricket A very short takeoff and landing aircraft used by the legion, for some purposes, in place of more expensive helicopters.

Diana A small magnet or flat metal plate intended to hide partially metal antipersonnel landmines by making everything give back the signature of a metal antipersonnel landmine.

Dustoff Medical evacuation, typically by air.

Eris Moon of Terra Nova.

Escopeta Spanish: Shotgun.

Estado Mayor Spanish: General Staff and, by extension, the building which houses it.

F-26 The legion's standard assault rifle, in 6.5mm.

FSD Federated States Drachma. Unit of money equivalent in value to 4.2 grams of silver.

GPR Ground Penetrating Radar.

Hecate Moon of Terra Nova.

Hieros	Shrine or temple.
Huánuco	A plant of Terra Nova from which an alkaloid substance is refined.
I	Roman number one. Chief Operations Officer, his office, and his staff section.
Ia	Operations officer dealing mostly with fire and maneuver, his office and his section, S- or G-3.
Ib	Logistics Officer, his office and his section, S- or G-4.
Ic	Intelligence Officer, his office and his section, S- or G-2.
II	Adjutant, Personnel Officer, his office and his section, S- or G-1.
IM-71	A medium lift cargo and troop carrying helicopter.
Ikhwan	Arabic: Brotherhood.
Jaguar	Volgan built tank in legionary service.
Jaguar II	Improved Jaguar.
Jizyah	Special tax levied against non-Moslems living in Moslem lands.
Karez	Underground aqueduct system.
Keffiyah	Folded cloth Arab headdress.
Klick	Kilometer. Note: Democracy ends where the metric system begins.
Kosmo	Cosmopolitan Progressive. Similar to Tranzi on Old Earth.
Liwa	Arabic: Major General.
Lorica	Lightweight silk and liquid metal torso armor used by the legion.
LZ	Landing Zone, a place where helicopters drop off troops and equipment.
Maniple	Company.
Makkah al Jedidah	Arabic: New Mecca.

Mañana sera major	Spanish, Balboan politico-military song: Tomorrow will be better.
MRL	Multiple Rocket Launcher.
Mujahadin	Arabic: Holy Warriors (singular: mujahad).
Mukhabarat	Arabic: Secret Police.
Mullah	Holy man, sometimes holy, sometimes not.
Na'ib 'Dabit	Arabic: Sergeant Major.
Naik	Corporal.
Naquib	Arabic: Captain.
NGO	Nongovernmental Organization.
Noahs	Aliens that seeded Terra Nova with life, some from Old Earth, some possibly from other planets, some possibly genetically engineered, in the dim mists of prehistory. No definitive trace has ever been found of them.
Ocelot	Volgan-built light armored vehicle mounting a 100mm gun and capable of carrying a squad of infantry in the back.
Meg	Coastal Defense Submarine employed by the legion, also the shark, Carcharodon Megalodon, from which the submarine class draws its name.
M-26	A heavy barreled version of the F-26, serving as the legion's standard light machine gun.
PMC	Precious metal certificate. High denomination legionary investment vehicle.
Progressivine	A fruit-bearing vine found on Terra Nova. Believed to have been genengineered by the Noahs. The fruit is intensely poisonous to intelligent life.
Puma	A much improved Balboan tank, built in Volga and modified in Zion and Balboa.
Push	As in "tactical push." Radio frequency or frequency hopping sequence, so called from the action of pushing the button that activates the transmitter.

PZ	Pickup Zone. A place where helicopters pick up troops, equipment, and supplies to move them somewhere else.
RGL	Rocket Grenade Launcher.
Rolanda	Gallic main battle tank, or MBT.
RTO	Radio-Telephone Operator.
Satan Triumphant	A hot pepper of Terra Nova, generally unfit for human consumption, though sometimes used in food preservation and refinable into a blister agent for chemical warfare.
Sayidi	Arabic form of respectful address, "Sir."
SHEBSA	*Servicio Helicoptores Balboenses,* S.A. Balboan Helicopter Service, part of the hidden reserve.
Sochaux S4	A Gallic four-wheel-drive light truck.
SPATHA	Self-Propelled Anti-Tank Heavy Armor. A legionary tank destroyer, under development.
SPLAD	Self-Propelled Laser Air Defense. A developed legionary antiaircraft system.
Subadar	In ordinary use a Major or Tribune III equivalent.
Surah	A chapter in the Koran, of which there are 114.
Tercio	Spanish: Regiment.
Tranzitree	A fruit-bearing tree, believed to have been genengineered by the Noahs. The fruit is intensely poisonous to intelligent life.
Trixie	A species of archaeopteryx brought to Terra Nova by the Noahs.
TUSF-B	Tauran Union Security Force-Balboa.
UEPF	United Earth Peace Fleet, the military arm of the Concensus in space.
Volcano	A very large thermobaric bomb, set up by a seismic fuse.
Yakamov	A type of helicopter produced in Volga. It has no tail rotor.

Legionary Rank Equivalents

Dux, Duque: indefinite rank, depending on position it can indicate anything from a Major General to a Field Marshall. *Duque* usually indicates the senior commander on the field.

Legate III: Brigadier General or Major General. Per the contract between the *Legion del Cid* and the Federated States of Columbia, a Legate III, when his unit is in service to the Federated States, is entitled to the standing and courtesies of a Lieutenant General. Typically commands a deployed legion, when a separate legion is deployed, the air *ala* or the naval *classis*, or serves as an executive for a deployed corps.

Legate II: Colonel, typically commands a tercio in the rear or serves on staff if deployed.

Legate I: Lieutenant Colonel, typically commands a cohort or serves on staff.

Tribune III: Major, serves on staff or sometimes, if permitted to continue in command, commands a maniple.

Tribune II: Captain, typically commands a maniple.

Tribune I: First Lieutenant, typically serves as second in command of a maniple, commands a specialty platoon within the cohort's combat support maniple, or serves on staff.

Signifer: Second Lieutenant or Ensign, leads a platoon. Signifer is a temporary rank, and signifers are not considered part of the officer corps of the legions except as a matter of courtesy.

Sergeant Major: Sergeant Major with no necessary indication of level.

First Centurion: Senior noncommissioned officer of a maniple.

Senior Centurion: Master Sergeant but almost always the senior man within a platoon.

Centurion, J.G.: Sergeant First Class, sometimes commands a platoon but is usually the second in command.

Optio: Staff Sergeant, typically the second in command of a platoon.

Sergeant: Sergeant, typically leads a squad.

Corporal: Corporal, typically leads a team or crew or serves as second in command of a squad.

Legionario, or Legionary, or Legionnaire: Private through specialist.

Note that, in addition, under legion regulations adopted in the Anno Condita 471, a soldier may elect to take what is called "Triarius Status." This locks the soldier into whatever rank he may be, but allows pay raises for longevity to continue. It is one way the legion has used to flatten the rank pyramid in the interests of reducing careerism. Thus, one may sometimes hear or read of a "Triarius Tribune III," typically a major-equivalent who has decided, with legion accord, that his highest and best use is in a particular staff slot or commanding a particular maniple. Given that the legion—with fewer than three percent officers, including signifers—has the smallest officer corps of any significant military formation on Terra Nova, and a very flat promotion pyramid, the Triarius system seems, perhaps, overkill. Since adoption, regulations permit but do not require Triarius status legionaries to be promoted one rank upon retirement.

ACKNOWLEDGMENTS

in no particular order:

Yoli and Toni who, in their different ways put up with me, TBR (the *Kriegsmarine* contingent of the bar), John Biltz, Chris Nuttall, Brian Carbin, Joseph Capdepon II, Nigel the Kiwi, Mike Watson, Seamus Curran, Arun Prabhu, Alex Shishkin, Jon LaForce, Michal Swierczek, Harry Russell, James Gemind, Mike May, Chris Bagnall, Guy Wheelock, Ori Pomerantz, Krenn, Paul Arnold, Steve Saintonge, Jasper Paulsen, Andrew Stocker, Nomad the Turk, Mark Bjertnes, Paul 11, Matt Pethybridge, Conrad Chu, Geoff Withnell, Joe Bond, Rod Graves, John Becker, Sam Swindell, Bill Crenshaw, Andy and LTC Fehrenbach at old Cambrai-Fritsch Kaserne, Mike Sayer, Jeff Wilkes, Bob Allaband, Henrik Kiertzner, John Jordan, Keith Wilds, Greg Dougherty, Andy and Fehrenbach from the 233rd BSB, Wade Harlow.

If I've forgotten anyone, chalk it up to premature senility.